Real readers love E**gas:**

'I was **hooked** fr

'Got me reading **till the wee hours of the morning**'

'I love books based on the lives and communities in WW2 and **this book had it all . . . Cannot wait for the next one**'

'So many **fantastic characters, and twists and turns galore**. Couldn't put the book down'

'An emotional rollercoaster of a read. **I loved** it'

'A **fantastic** read with lots of surprises and moments that **make the hairs on the back of your neck stand on end**. Can't wait to read the next book from this talented author'

'Twists, surprises, sadness and happiness all intermingled in a **riveting** story'

'Emma Hornby's books **just keep getting better and better**. Honest, gritty, lovely characters'

'Emma is a **wonderful storyteller** and I can't wait for the next one!'

'Similar to Rosie Goodwin and Dilly Court, Emma Hornby **tells a brilliant story** that will keep you guessing with twists and turns. **Pure talent**'

www.penguin.co.uk

By Emma Hornby

A SHILLING FOR A WIFE
MANCHESTER MOLL
THE ORPHANS OF ARDWICK
A MOTHER'S DILEMMA
A DAUGHTER'S PRICE
THE MAID'S DISGRACE
A MOTHER'S BETRAYAL
THE CHIMNEY SWEEP'S SISTER

Worktown Girls at War
HER WARTIME SECRET
A DAUGHTER'S WAR
A SISTER'S FIGHT

A SHILLING FOR A WIFE
and
A MOTHER'S DILEMMA

Emma Hornby

PENGUIN BOOKS

TRANSWORLD PUBLISHERS

UK | USA | Canada | Ireland | Australia
India | New Zealand | South Africa

Transworld is part of the Penguin Random House group of companies
whose addresses can be found at global.penguinrandomhouse.com.

Penguin Random House UK, One Embassy Gardens,
8 Viaduct Gardens, London SW11 7BW

penguin.co.uk

A Shilling for A Wife was first published in Great Britain in 2016 by Bantam Press
an imprint of Transworld Publishers
Corgi edition published 2017
Copyright © Emma Hornby 2016

A Mother's Dilemma was first published in Great Britain in 2019 by Bantam Press
an imprint of Transworld Publishers
Corgi edition published 2019
Copyright © Emma Hornby 2019

This Penguin paperback omnibus edition published 2026

001

Copyright © Emma Hornby 2026

The moral right of the author has been asserted

This book is a work of fiction and, except in the case of historical fact,
any resemblance to actual persons, living or dead, is purely coincidental.

Every effort has been made to obtain the necessary permissions with
reference to copyright material, both illustrative and quoted. We apologize
for any omissions in this respect and will be pleased to make the
appropriate acknowledgements in any future edition.

No part of this book may be used or reproduced in any manner for the
purpose of training artificial intelligence technologies or systems. In accordance
with Article 4(3) of the DSM Directive 2019/790, Penguin Random House
expressly reserves this work from the text and data mining exception.

A Shilling for A Wife was typeset in 11/13.25pt New Baskerville by
Thomson Digital Pvt Ltd, Noida, Delhi.
A Mother's Dilemma was typeset in ITC New Baskerville by Jouve (UK), Milton Keynes.
Printed and bound in Great Britain by Clays Ltd, Elcograf S.p.A.

The authorized representative in the EEA is Penguin Random House Ireland,
Morrison Chambers, 32 Nassau Street, Dublin D02 YH68.

A CIP catalogue record for this book is available from the British Library

ISBN:
9781804999837

Penguin Random House is committed to a
sustainable future for our business, our readers
and our planet. This book is made from Forest
Stewardship Council® certified paper.

A SHILLING FOR A WIFE

For those whose belief in me never waned, especially Mark and Mum, thank you. Without your support and encouragement, this book would not have seen the light of day. And my ABC, always x

I think people really marry far too much; it is such a lottery after all, and for a poor woman a very doubtful happiness.

Queen Victoria

Chapter 1
Mid-October 1853

THE AIR IN the dank kitchen was thick with desperation.

'Please, I have no idea what you're talking about!'

'Liar! I know you're lying, you whore. Tell me the truth or by God, I'll beat it from thee!' As he roared the threat into Sally's face, Joseph Goden drew back his huge arm, fist more than ready to strike.

'Joseph, please. I need help.' Her voice a strangled whisper, she screwed up her face in dreaded anticipation of the blow. She knew only too well the world would explode into sharp bursts of light and blinding pain.

Yet despite her terror and the agony tearing through her back and stomach, determination not to crack burned fiercer. She wouldn't tell him. She wouldn't!

Her eyes flickered to the sofa; if she hadn't been in the latter stages of labour, she'd have bolted behind it. Not that it made a difference. Her instinct to hide when he lifted his fists offered no protection. He'd laugh in grim satisfaction as she cowered and, more often than not, wet herself with fear waiting for his next move.

Sometimes, he'd simply grow bored with torturing her and bellow, 'Clean up your filth, whore!' He'd then resume his terrorisation as, cheeks flaming with humiliation, she scrubbed the floor, kicking out at her and sending her sprawling across the wet flags.

Otherwise, he'd reach behind the sofa, grab her hair and lift her clean over the top. Then he'd beat her so badly, she'd be unconscious for hours. Or, dear God, he'd drag her to bed, which was like visiting hell itself . . .

Even if she'd been physically able, the thought of running into the row and screaming for help didn't enter her mind. She'd find no sanctuary there. He'd seen to that.

Upon their arrival at Spring Row to begin wedded life, he'd gripped her by the throat and whispered into her face, 'Now you listen to me, my girl, for I'll only say this once. You ever blab your mouth off to anyone outside of this here cottage and I'll snap your scrawny neck. D'you understand?'

Five years of abominable marriage later, she understood, all right. She didn't disbelieve his threat for a second.

He'll do it this time. Oh, how could I have been so foolish? she thought now, trembling on all fours, awaiting the torrent of blows that always came when he'd had a bellyful of porter.

His drinking had worsened considerably of late, his weekly visits to Ma Thompson's for a jug of her strong, home-brewed ale now a nightly occurrence. Little went into Sally's hand for the housekeeping. Though she'd had to be frugal since the beginning with what he allowed her from his wages, lately it was a constant battle putting a meal of sorts on the table and making the impossible amount of coal she could afford last.

Of course, Joseph fared better at mealtimes. She survived on almost nothing, to prevent his wrath if his meals were insufficient. No amount of imploring would see him tip up another farthing. He blamed her for not being careful with what he gave her.

'I'll give thee summat in a minute, all right, but it'll not be brass,' he'd snarl, raising his hand, if she dared beg for more.

So far, somehow, she'd managed. Now, it seemed all her hard work and careful planning were for nothing.

Hearing him lumber from their bed several hours ago, still half-drunk from last night, she'd stuffed the ball of cheap wool and knitting needles into the dresser drawer and hurried to the fire to heat the kettle. Even with her back to the staircase, she'd sensed his foul mood as he stomped down to the kitchen. Minutes passed in silence as she brewed tea and cut the loaf, while he sat nursing his aching head in his hands. Then, placing his breakfast before him, her world had crumbled around her.

Grabbing her wrist, he'd stared at her hard, head cocked, and asked, 'What's that?'

Ignoring the pain caused by his dirty nails, she'd frowned. 'Bread and drip—' He'd cut her off with a backhanded slap to her mouth.

'Not the grub. That.'

Nursing stinging lips, she'd followed his gaze to a length of pale wool dangling from the drawer. She'd felt blood drain from her face.

'Please, Joseph, I cannot manage on what you give me. It's not enough to make ends meet,' he'd whined mockingly, grip tightening. 'Yet you can manage to buy wool, you lying bitch, yer. No one steals from me! What else has tha bought without me knowing about, eh? What else has tha been frittering my brass on?'

'It's for the infant. It will need clothing when it's here. The wool only cost—' To her horror, searing pains ripped across her middle before she could finish. They, and Joseph's threats, had only intensified with the hours.

Now, her work-reddened hands flew protectively to her stomach. Relentless beatings had snuffed out all previous life to grow in her womb. She'd fight to the last breath to protect this one. This child was a fighter. The risks she'd secretly, patiently, carried out for years were for this: the child to survive its father's abuse.

On cue, Joseph's fist struck out. It flew by her head, missing her by inches. Gasping, she forced herself to look at her husband.

Dark eyes glinting, he released a bark of laughter. 'Fricken you, then, did I? That were a warning but next 'un won't be if you don't tell me the truth, you sneaky, thieving young slut.'

She didn't know how much more she could bear on top of the waves of pain threatening to split her in two. Asking him to fetch help was pointless. Being Sunday, the row's residents would be at the Meadow Lane Chapel and besides, her husband wouldn't want anyone seeing the rainbow of colours covering her face from his last attack.

Another contraction ripped through her, making her scream out. 'Joseph, p–please. The child is coming. It's coming now!' The last word ended on a torturous wail and in desperation she fumbled for the hand squeezing her upper arm. To her astonishment, his grip loosened.

Her eyes widened as he smoothed her drenched hair from her brow with the coal-dust-ingrained hand poised to strike moments before. 'Oh, Joseph, help me,' she whispered on a sob, taking advantage of this tenderness she'd never known from him. 'It hurts so much. Please . . . I don't know what to do.'

He ground out his reply. 'Are you going to tell me what you've been up to?'

She closed her eyes, heart sinking. She'd have to confess. Any chance of receiving help rested on it. *But if I do, it will all have been for nothing. Dear Lord, what do I do?* she agonised.

Mind consumed with hopeless options, she didn't notice that the hand stroking her hair had slid, until it clamped her breast. Her eyes sprang open and her heart banged at his leering grin.

Mother of God, surely not! The thought exploded through her brain. 'Joseph . . . ? What are you *doing*?'

'Tell me the truth or I'll force it from thee the hard way.'

Her dress had ridden to her hips with her writhing; her heaving breasts, glistening with perspiration, spilled over the top. Eyes raking over her, his breathing quickened.

She stared around wildly. Surely to God he wouldn't – couldn't – take her as she was about to give birth? How could he contemplate something so disgusting? She knew from experience he was capable of anything, but not *that*, surely? He was bluffing. He had to be!

'You wouldn't,' she forced herself to whisper.

His grin deepened. 'Oh believe me, my girl, I would.'

Panting through another contraction, she glared up in complete disgust, fear giving way to uncontrollable anger at his expression of enjoyment. 'You've gone too far this time. Mary, Mother of God, how could you think to do that while I'm in agony bearing your child? That is sick beyond belief, even for you.'

'The truth, then!' he bellowed, but she saw him waver and, to her sheer relief, he grunted, gave her breast a last, hard squeeze then released it.

As she stared in repulsion at the face she loathed, twisted with evil, words dripping with long-suppressed hatred poured from her. 'Lord above, I detest you. I wish you were dead, do you hear, *dead*. You make me sick to my stomach, you despicable bastard.'

After a moment of stunned silence, his eyes bulged and with a roar he threw back his arm. 'You midden-mouthed whore, I'll murder thee!'

His arm swung and she whimpered, her bravado vanishing at the sight of the fist heading for her face. 'Please, no!'

A furious voice from the cottage door pierced the air, reverberating like a gunshot:

'Don't you fret, my lass. He wouldn't dare!'

As the congregation spilled from the recently built, sandstone edifice of the Wesleyan Chapel, Arthur Morgan shielded his eyes and squinted at the chattering worshippers making their way homeward. The brisk breeze soothed his bewhiskered face after the muggy chapel and he breathed it in gratefully. Humming along to the faint strains of the organ at his back, he scanned the women's bobbing heads for his wife's fawn-coloured bonnet, but couldn't see it.

Where the heck has she got to? he wondered in bemusement before strolling down the stone steps and on for Meadow Lane towards home.

Earlier, seeing the preacher bringing out the collection tin, Ivy had hissed in his ear, 'Eeh, I've forgot my bleedin' purse!'

He'd left his precious coppers at home. Each Saturday, he ungrudgingly handed Ivy his full wage and she'd then give back several coins for him to do with as he pleased. It wasn't much, enough for a few pots of ale and a twist of tobacco, but it suited him. She had a hard task making ends meet but was a thrifty housewife; she had a knack of stretching a farthing to tuppence.

Kicking a stone across the lane, he smiled, recalling the disapproving frowns at the colourful words she'd dared speak in the Lord's house. A chuckle gurgled in his throat remembering her response.

'Youse lot mind your own, for I've a fair few words what would shock you more than that.' At her growled warning, the listeners, aware of her fierce temper, had looked away. However, the braver ones turned again when she muttered, 'I'll have to go home and fetch the bugger.' But at her hard look as she slipped from the pew, their heads had soon snapped back to the front.

By, she's a rum 'un, he thought fondly, turning into Spring Row.

Some ten years old, the cluster of cottages nestled in a fold between the Wesleyan Chapel – or the Meadow Lane Chapel, as locals referred to it – and the Coach and Horses public house. Though idyllic-sounding, Spring Row was deceptive in its name, as pleasing to the eye it wasn't.

The two-up, two-downs, with back bedrooms open to the staircase, were damp and alive with vermin, the shared privy middens in the back lane foul and stinking. Despite most residents' dogged attempts to keep them tolerable, the sight and smell were sickening, especially in fine weather.

However, the rent was manageable and with the cottages facing south towards Bury Road, the occupants were compensated by rich fields stretching for miles behind, Breightmet Bleach Works at Red Bridge the only blot spoiling the beautiful view.

Aye, but it's not so bad, he mused. There were worse places. His and Ivy's last dwelling, one of a mound of hovels by aptly named Rough Close, near the Old Hare and Hounds public house, sprang to mind. He shuddered at the memories. Yet as his home came into view, all thought melted at the unbelievable sight that met him.

Joseph Goden was hammering at Arthur's door with both fists, bellowing, like a crazed bull, threats and insults to Ivy within.

White-hot fury surged through Arthur. When he reached his wicket gate, grim-faced neighbours stepped aside but his fellow miner didn't notice until he gripped his shoulders and spun him around. Joseph grunted angrily but the normally placid Arthur's rage-filled state visibly threw him.

'What in the name of God d'you think you're doing, Goden?' he roared incredulously. Though older and not as powerfully built, he was none the less solid-muscled, more than capable of standing up to him.

'Your interfering bloody wife's got my Sally in there,' Joseph blustered, thrusting a thumb. 'Come barging into my bloody home without being invited, she did. She wants putting in her place. By God, she does!'

Arthur's advancing fist paused as Martha Smith from two doors down shouted, 'Aye, what, like your wife, you mean? The lass has started with the babby and yon Ivy's took her into yours to aid her, like,' she added to Arthur. 'Covered in bruises her poor face were, an' all.' Swinging her ample frame forward, she spat to Joseph in disgust, 'You want stringing up treating that lass as you do, you bully yer.'

A red hue crept up his neck and she laughed derisively. 'D'you think I don't know how tha treats that young wife of yourn? You can tell a mile you lead her a dog's life. Flits to the privy and to and from Percy's shop like a frightened rabbit, she does, and them's the only times we see her leave yon cottage. She don't speak a word to nobody. You make sure of that, don't you?'

The silence was deafening; then followed other bystanders' murmurs of agreement.

Arthur shook his head. 'You snidy, evil . . . You hid your colours, all right, didn't you? Well, the game's up, now, Goden. In nowt but seconds, I could round up half a dozen fellas with a click of my fingers to give you the going over you deserve; aye, happen I should.' He nodded and the neighbours jeered their support.

Joseph's Adam's apple bobbed as he glanced around. He licked his lips. Then puffing out his chest, he lifted his chin. 'And what of it, anyroad? A fella's entitled to discipline his wife if need be. Pity others don't follow my example,' he added, looking pointedly at him.

'You bullying swine, yer!' Arthur swung his fist but Joseph swerved and hurried down the rutted path. A chorus of angry voices, thick with threat, mingled with the sound of his clogs as he ran down the lane.

'You should've given the divil what for, speaking ill of yon Ivy like that,' Martha muttered disappointedly when he disappeared from view.

'Ay, don't fret, wench. I'll have my day with him.'

Arthur spoke quietly but the steely edge pacified her enough for her to say, 'Aye, tha will that.' As her words died away, a piercing scream from his cottage filled the air.

Sally's baby was born.

Chapter 2

OPENING A BLEARY eye, Ivy frowned as the wispy mew sounded again. It took a moment for her tired brain to register it and she smiled as recognition dawned. She heaved her thin body from the straw mattress, still spiky and itchy despite the two blankets, and lifted her shawl from the foot of the bed.

She tried in vain to stem a shiver. The early morning breeze still found a way through the draughty window, despite the rags stuffed around the edges, and it seeped through the threadbare shirt of Arthur's she wore for bed.

By, I bet the babby's freezing, she fretted, wrapping the matted shawl around her shoulders.

She slipped out of bed, careful not to wake her husband who would have to be up soon enough for the pithead at Breightmet Colliery; its two pits provided employment for many locals. After padding to the makeshift cot – the bottom drawer from the kitchen dresser which, lined with a ragged blanket, had served all eight of hers – she lifted the scrap of life, swaddled in old clothing, and headed for the door.

It was still pitch black behind the lengths of worn sacking that served as curtains. Cradling the baby in the crook of one arm, she held out the other as a guide. She could have lit the stub of candle on the chipped saucer by the bed, but was loath to. Brass was tight with but two children at home and Arthur's meagre wages.

Granted, they were better off than some and she counted her blessings daily for what they had but still, life was a constant struggle. After rent, food and coal, little remained for luxuries.

Jonathan whimpered and she shushed him quietly. 'All right, my little lad, all right. Let's get you a drop of milk afore you waken the men. Oh, did he waken thee?' she added guiltily as Arthur stirred. He'd allowed her since the start to have the child in with them so she could care for him during the night to let Sally rest.

'Nay, wench, it's all right,' he answered on a yawn. 'What's the hour?'

'I'll go and see. Stop in bed while I light the fire and make breakfast.' She lifted her bottle-green weekday dress from a chair and descended the stairs.

Gasping as her bare feet met the kitchen's cold flagged floor, she hurried to the fire and laid the baby upon the colourful rag rug before it. Squatting beside him, she raked out the dead ashes then built a small pyramid of twigs and dried moss on the faintly glowing cinders.

When it crackled and smoked, she added lumps of coal from a pail and watched in satisfaction as they turned crimson, bathing the room in a cosy glow. She then filled an iron kettle from another pail, hooked it on the bar and swung it over the fire.

She chuckled as the baby stared up at her intently, quieter now warmth radiated through the bars. Noticing his napkin was sopping, she poured the warmed water into a tin dish, stripped him, cleaned him with a scrap of cloth and dressed him in a woollen vest from a string line above the fire, cooing and smiling as she worked.

She removed her shawl, wrapped him in it and returned him to the rug. She then washed herself with the remainder of the water in the dish and slipped into her dress.

Her mouth curved in a smile as she glanced at the clock ticking quietly on the mantel. Her husband and sons still had half an hour's luxury of staying in bed before another day's grafting on the coalface began. The perilous work was gruelling; they needed all the sleep they could snatch.

She brushed a kiss across the child's fuzzy hair. 'Come on, my little love, let's get your belly filled.' Opening the door to the front room of the cottage, she allowed her eyes to become accustomed to the gloom before making for the narrow, iron-framed bed.

Sally lay on her back, covers pulled to her chin. Even sleep couldn't lift her troubled expression, Ivy noticed sadly. The bruises were now myriad faint yellows and blues and the near fortnight in her care had put some much-needed flesh on the young bones. But body and mind were exhausted.

When she roused from the slumbers that consumed her each day, Sally's tearful apologies at being such a burden brought a lump to Ivy's throat. She'd assured the pathetically grateful woman that she and her child were welcome for as long as needs be.

Anger bubbled inside her at the thought of Joseph. 'What's he done to thee?' she whispered to the broken girl. Sighing, she shook her gently. 'Lass, Jonathan wants feeding again.'

Sally struggled into a sitting position. 'What time is it?'

'It's early yet. Latch him on and go back to sleep. I'll keep an eye to him.'

The young woman slipped her shift from her shoulders. Her son, blue eyes wide, nudged at her open-mouthed, and laughing softly, she guided him to her. 'He's perfect, isn't he, Mrs Morgan?'

Emotion rose in Ivy at the sight of mother and child. 'Aye, he is that. Now, are you for kipping or stopping up? If it's the latter, you fill his belly and I'll fetch summat to fill yours.'

The smile slipped from Sally's face. 'Wait a moment until he's had his fill and I'll help you. It's not right you waiting on me; let me mash the tea at least.'

Halfway to the door, Ivy turned. Despite the offer, her eyelids were drooping. 'It's all right, lass. You rest with your babby.'

Sighing, Sally snuggled against him. 'Thank you, Mrs Morgan. Thank you.'

When the door clicked shut, Sally smiled softly with gratitude. The sounds of suckling and faint clinking of crockery from the kitchen were comforting, safe; blissful feelings she'd thought she'd never again encounter.

She still couldn't quite believe she was here. It had taken days to comprehend that, after all these years, she'd finally escaped. It seemed like a lovely dream, and that any moment she'd wake to find herself back in the nightmare she'd suffered so very long. She ran a hand through her hair and sighed. What was she to do? She couldn't stay here for ever, however much she'd like.

That these strangers had taken in her and her child without hesitation, showing nothing but kindness and understanding, still amazed her. She wished she'd told of the abuse years ago and Ivy had scolded her gently, saying the same.

Why didn't I knock when he was at the inn or pit and beg Ivy's help? she asked herself again. The answer was always the same. It was easy in hindsight to berate herself but quite another thing when in the thick of it, with seemingly no way out.

All those wasted years. All those beatings and poor babies born too soon. But this miracle child, thanks to Ivy, survived. He was her gift, her reason to fight. She could never repay this family. They had given not only her child but herself a chance at life.

Within days of her marriage, she'd begun planning her escape. Yet though she hated to admit it, even to herself, she wasn't sure she'd have ever found the strength. His hold had been so extreme that, but for Ivy, she'd probably still be next door.

She peered down at the baby. *Born from a monster's seed.* The thought flitted often, but this child wouldn't grow to be like *him*. *He* may have created this life with her but that was all he could lay claim to. Shaking her head to dispel the painful thoughts, she lifted the baby's tiny hand and kissed it. Her son, *her* son, would be a decent man and a good husband, she'd make sure of it. She had to stop thinking of the past and concentrate on the future, however uncertain.

She'd been terrified of Joseph turning up but knew now that as long as she was here, she was safe; Ivy had told of his running away when Arthur challenged him. A smile touched her lips. For once, he'd have known how it was to be scared. No, he wouldn't return. For now, she and her child were free from harm.

Movement from the floor above pulled her from her thoughts and she smiled again. She'd become used to the cottage's routine, knew that it was Arthur rising for work. His sons would be down shortly and the family would have breakfast.

She liked this time of day most. Each morning, she'd lie here listening to these people in wonder. The easy chatter, the banter, the elder son's deep, infectious laugh ... The cottage exuded warmth and happiness and she drew strength from it, soaking it up like a thirsty flower in a downpour. This was how a home should be.

A surge of anger towards Joseph and the home he'd created caused her chest to constrict and she closed her eyes, revelling in it. She'd become so used to being afraid for so long, she'd almost forgotten how it was to feel anything else. Pride flowed through her as she remembered venting her fury that day and the astonishment on his face. She was glad she'd spoken her mind. And she'd meant every word. She did detest him and did wish he were dead.

She'd also managed, despite everything, to hold fast about the money.

Maybe the old Sally *was* inside somewhere, she thought with a smile, slipping back into a peaceful sleep.

Pushing and shoving one another down the well-scrubbed stairs, the Morgan sons halted, their laughter dying, as Ivy hissed, ''Ere, youse two, the lass and babby are akip in there.' Hands on hips, she scowled. 'By, you're a pair of noisy swines.'

Shaun raked a hand through his mop of light-brown curls. 'Sorry, Mam. I didn't think.'

'Aye, sorry, Mam. Not used to having a babby in t' house. Nor a bonny lass, eh, Shaun?' Tommy winked slowly then laughed as he dodged a swipe from his red-faced brother.

'Aye, you can stop that sort of talk right now, my lad.'

'I'm only jesting, Mam. Our Shaunie boy's hardly noticed her. Have you?' Draping an arm across his brother's shoulders, Tommy gave another exaggerated wink and Shaun shrugged it off and stalked to the table. 'Ay, come on, Shaunie boy. I'm only jesting with thee.' Grinning, he chucked him under the chin.

Taking another swipe, and missing again, Shaun glowered. 'Well, it's not funny. And stop calling me Shaunie boy.'

'Right, youse two, give over,' Ivy said over Tommy's laughter. 'You're not too big forra clout and you'll not dodge mine as fast, Tommy lad.'

'Aye, and hers will hurt a damn sight more.' Arthur crossed the small space and joined his sons at the table, smiling fondly at her. 'Gorra reet belting left hook, has your mam.'

'Don't talk daft, Arth— Oi, you, mucky hands!' Placing a smoke-blackened pan on the table, she clicked her tongue when Tommy scooped out a dollop of porridge. She rapped his knuckles with a wooden ladle and he grinned then popped his finger into his mouth. And despite her best efforts, she couldn't help smiling back.

Nineteen-year-old Tommy was strikingly handsome and the apple of her eye. Though she'd have never admitted to having a favourite, he was hers. With floppy hair as black as the coal he'd mined for nigh on ten years and sweeping eyelashes any woman would be proud of, framing grey-blue eyes that crinkled at the corners when he smiled, and a strong, square jaw – not to mention his muscular physique – he cut a fine figure.

It's not his looks, mind, she mused as she spooned porridge into three bowls and sprinkled on the last of the sugar. *It's his way with folk.*

The joker of the family, nothing got him down; not even working the pit, which Shaun hated with a passion. There was nothing to dislike about Tommy and she was proud to call him her son. Her surviving children were precious, all five, but he brought her that little more joy. Ashamed as she was of this, she couldn't change her feelings.

With a small shake of her head, she pushed away the guilty thoughts, reached for the cream, pockmarked teapot and poured weak tea into four handleless cups. After passing them around, she lifted her own and took a hesitant sip.

I'll have to see if Percy will let me have a few more bits on tick, later, she thought, grimacing at the unsweetened brew and noticing Arthur and the lads doing likewise.

The old man, who had converted the front room of his cottage into a shop, allowed Spring Row's women to make purchases 'on the slate', clearing their debts on Saturdays when their menfolk were paid.

As she was busy mentally listing what she needed, a loud bark made Ivy jump. She cursed as tea sploshed from her cup, settling in the grooves of the table.

'I'll throttle that scraggy pest. I'm bleedin' sick of it.' She craned her neck to the window for a glimpse of the black dog that had hung around the lane for months. 'Some bugger must be feeding it; just wait till I find out who.

'Now come on, you three, afore you're late,' she added, mopping at the table with her coarse apron. 'The hooter will be sounding if you're not careful. You know they'll tolerate no excuses for bad time-keeping; you'll finish up having your wages docked. Or losing your places.' She shuddered. No family could risk that.

Shaun, as usual, dragged his feet as he made for the door with his father and brother.

''Ere, lad.' Her tone softened as she handed him his bait tin containing a hunk of the bread baked last night, smeared thinly with pork dripping, for his midday meal. Arthur's and Tommy's contained the same, though her husband's was marginally thicker.

Shaun took the battered box and immediately checked inside for the stub of candle he insisted on carrying, 'just in case'. His logic behind this, she neither knew nor asked. If the grubby block of wax brought the lad comfort, made his working life more bearable, it was fine by her.

His young face relaxed a little to see it, which pierced her heart, but as all pit wives and mothers must, she hardened herself to it. She had to; what choice was there? For men of their class, uneducated and unskilled in everything but lifting a pickaxe, it was the pit or starve. It was that simple.

She'd have given her right arm – both legs, too – for the lads to have the chance of bettering themselves, as their father hadn't. But her determination that they would avoid the inevitable direction of the pit came to nothing. Hopes and dreams she'd fiercely held while lovingly cradling her children had been just that: pointless hopes and shattered dreams.

Reality had proved very different. Their daughters, married with children of their own, made counterpanes in a cotton factory, as did many of Breightmet Fold's residents; their husbands worked at the bleach works. Their eldest son, who toiled alongside his father and brothers, lived with his new wife in a tiny, wood-built house on Red Lane, a short distance from Spring Row.

The township of Breightmet, where she'd dwelled her whole life, lay on the east side of the Parish of Bolton, in Lancashire, between Bradshaw Brook to the west and Blackshaw Brook to the east. Harwood straddled its northern boundary. Its name literally meant 'Bright Meadow'; views from its upper ridge revealed a landscape dominated by hills.

The jumble of scattered homesteads housed a relatively small population. Though most were pitifully poor, the sprawling greenness, dotted with springs and babbling brooks, seemed to hold them in a hypnotic trap; leaving was, to many, incomprehensible. However, three of her and Arthur's younger children had left. And dear God, how they missed them.

An outbreak of cholera had raged throughout the town in '48 and stolen them, ravaging their little bodies until she, their own mother, prayed for their deaths and an end to their suffering. Thankful as she was that it spared her others, memories haunted her day and night.

Now, seeing Shaun, her baby, his freckled face etched in misery no fourteen-year-old should know, soul-corroding grief and cruel injustice bubbled like a cauldron set to explode.

On impulse, she drew him to her flat bosom. Silence filled the kitchen. Though not a cold wife or mother, open shows of affection were not in her nature.

Arthur touched her shoulder. 'Me and our Tommy and James allus keep an eye to the lad. He's gorra get used to it, as do we all, and should've by now,' he said gruffly.

She sniffed, nodded and gently pushed Shaun from her. *But he's not like most lads*, she wanted to protest. *He's sensitive, unhappy, scared.* Yet she didn't. What was the point? It wouldn't make a scrap of difference. Instead, she wiped tears from his flushed cheeks and cleared her throat. 'Aye, they'll keep an eye to thee.'

'Aye.' Tommy flashed a smile that didn't reach his eyes. 'We'll allus have your back, Shaunie b— Shaun.'

The amendment didn't go unnoticed. Shaun smiled ruefully. 'Don't be telling all the fellas I've been bawling on Mam's shoulder, our Tommy. I just hate it down there.'

For once, Tommy made no joke or quip, nor laughed his hearty laugh. He didn't even smile. 'No fear, lad.'

Back to her brusque self, she shooed them through the door into the row, where a slight drizzle fell from a slate-grey sky. The men pulled their jacket collars around their chins and, heads lowered, trudged down the path.

Standing in the doorway, she wrapped her arms in the folds of her apron against the cold and, when Arthur turned, called, 'Aye, I'll not forget.'

Satisfied, he swung through the gate and fell into step between his sons, merging with others on their way to work, the nails in their pit boots ringing in the misty dawn.

Reaching on tiptoe then stooping, she bolted the door. No one had seen nor heard a word of Joseph Goden, but he'd be back. They knew that for sure.

As she cleared the table, her brow creased. He was an evil swine capable of anything, as that Sunday proved. His rage-filled face, as he'd towered over his wife, had shocked her to the core.

When she'd heard Sally's cries when passing their cottage to retrieve her purse, her first thought was she'd gone into labour and was having a difficult birth. Knocking several times and getting no reply, she'd opened her neighbours' door, the offer of assistance on her lips. The sight that met her had rendered her speechless.

After pouring hot water into a ceramic basin, she now put in the breakfast dishes and attacked them with a cloth as the memories ran on. He'd been about to beat his defenceless wife. That in itself was bad enough but by God, the lass was in labour. What make of man would do such a thing? *That's just it*, she thought, nodding grimly. *He's not a bleedin' man. He's a dirty great coward.*

Despite her anger, she couldn't suppress a smile as she recalled striding forward and delivering an ear-splitting slap to his cheek, sending him stumbling into the wall. He'd stood slack-mouthed for a good half a minute as astonishment, slowly followed by rage, passed over his face. In that time, she'd managed to half carry, half drag Sally out.

They were barely in the safety of her cottage when, his shock seemingly having worn off, Joseph's barrage of abuse began outside her door. She was just thankful Arthur arrived when he did.

She plucked a huckaback cloth from a rope line beneath the window and, muttering to herself, dried the assortment of dishes and placed them on the rack. From the old bruising and what little she'd gleaned from Sally, that wasn't the first time he'd raised his fists. Yet in all the years living next door, she'd seen no indication he was leading Sally a dog's life; not a sound penetrated the stone separating them.

Aye, he's a snidy one, all right. He'd have known he could fair do as he liked without anyone hearing, she thought angrily. And whenever she'd glimpsed Sally in the row, she had her shawl drawn low, obscuring her face. No doubt to hide her many bruises.

Easing into a chair, Ivy shook her greying head and poured herself the stewed dregs from the pot. He wasn't the friendliest of neighbours, granted, but discovering he treated the lass as he did came as a huge shock. The rage Sally's escape evoked must have chased all caution of revealing his true self. Others had voiced their suspicions but – she felt ashamed admitting it, now – she'd thought it nothing but idle gossip. She'd even gone as far as defending Joseph, when Martha Smith questioned her in Percy's one afternoon.

'Surely you must know, Ivy, dwelling next door, like. You heard owt untoward?'

Folding her arms, she'd stared back fixedly. If there was one thing she couldn't abide, it was gossip. 'You want to be careful flinging mud like that about, Martha, for some might stick. I've neither seen nor heard owt amiss from yon Godens' cottage and unless you have, you ought to keep your opinions to yourself.'

'Well, there's summat queer about that fella, if you ask me. And that young wife of his is like a frightened rabbit. Never given no one the time of day, they've not, since moving here.'

'Aye, well. You just mind your own and let others mind theirs,' she'd retorted, convinced that Martha's problem was there were people in the row she knew nothing about; Martha made it her business to know everyone else's.

Ivy and the Godens had never spoken except for a cursory 'hello'. Some folk were like that, preferred keeping themselves to themselves; she hadn't given it a second thought. She should have listened to Martha's concerns. If she'd pressed for an explanation, could they have avoided this?

Tongues will be wagging now, all right. Gossip must be rife, she thought with a sigh. She crossed the room and lifted her outdoor shawl from a nail in the wall. Imagining Martha's gloating face when their paths next crossed, she heaved another sigh. She wasn't relishing the 'I told you so' speech Martha had undoubtedly rehearsed.

A stab of unease pricked as she dragged the bars across. Arthur wouldn't like it if he knew she'd left the door unbolted but she had to get the evening meal in, not to mention sugar for a decent brew. Sally usually locked it behind her but she was reluctant to disturb her. The poor girl needed all the rest she could get.

Percy's was only five doors down and being early, it shouldn't be busy. She'd be no longer than a minute or two, she reasoned. She drew the shawl across her shoulders, knotted the ends beneath her breasts and picked up her basket.

Thankful the rain had stopped, she stepped into the weak sunshine. But glancing left to Sally's cottage, apprehension ran down her spine.

Frowning, she dithered a moment longer. Then pulling the door shut, she hurried down the path.

'And how's the lass fettling?' Lifting Ivy's requests from various shelves, Percy Flint smiled over his shoulder.

'She's bearing up, Percy.'

She heard sadness cloud her voice and knew the old man had, too; he tactfully changed the subject. A weeping woman in his shop was the last thing he'd want. Though he knew she wasn't the soft sort, clearly he wasn't taking any chances.

'Right, Ivy love. Milk, sugar, ham shank, tatties and a screw of tea. Owt else, lass?' Squinting through rheumy eyes, he grinned across the dust-speckled counter, revealing shiny pink gums beyond his sunken mouth.

Remembering all the bread had gone into the men's bait tins, she nodded. 'Can I have a stone of flour and a quarter of yeast, please, Percy? I'll clear up with you the morrow when Arthur and the lads get home.'

'I know you will, lass, you allus does. Not like some I could mention.' Despite her being the only customer present, he lowered his voice. 'It's rich they must think I am. They gets stuff on t' tick then come up with all the excuses under the sun come payday. But for folk like your good self, my belly would be meeting my backbone by now.'

Placing her purchases into her basket, she chuckled. 'Now you know Nancy wouldn't see that happen. Thinks the world of thee, that lass does.'

His only child called twice daily with his midday and evening meal. Her mother had succumbed to pneumonia the year before and Ivy knew he relied on the visits and hearty meals more than he'd admit. His wife's passing broke his heart but, fiercely independent, he'd declined Nancy's offer of her and her brood joining his lonely but comfortable abode.

Despite his grumbles of customers' shortcomings, his convenient little shop, which sold all manner of foodstuff and more, was, Ivy suspected, a lucrative business. And shrewd Nancy likely knew it, too.

Running a gnarled hand through his shock of white hair, Percy smiled impishly. 'Aye, she keeps me in grub, don't see me clemmed, but it's not out of the goodness of her heart, let me tell you. She's got her sights set on this place when I've kicked the bucket; that's all what's dragging her arse here!'

'She's a long wait if them's her intentions, eh? Fit as a new fiddle, you are. You'll outlive us all.'

'Well, we'll see about that, Ivy, for it wouldn't surprise me if she were adding summat to them dinners she fetches,' he mused, stroking his whiskery chin.

She hooted with laughter. 'Don't talk so bleedin' daft!' Lifting her laden basket and resting the handle in the crook of her arm, she headed for the door. 'I'll be seeing thee, Percy love, and thanks.'

Having written her purchases in a leather-bound ledger, he returned it to a shelf beneath the counter. 'Aye, lass, I'll be seeing thee. I'll be seeing our Nancy shortly, an' all.' Licking his lips, he winked. 'Mmm, arsenic stew. I can't wait!'

She was still smiling as she walked the short distance home. He was a canny sod. The sharp-tongued Nancy might be a grabbing article but looked after him well enough.

Turning through her gate, her breath caught in her chest, thoughts of Percy vanishing, when she saw the half-open door. A deep voice from within spilled into the row and she marched up the path and shoved the door, sending it crashing against the wall. The scene sent fury through her veins.

The man towering over Sally turned sharply. Dropping her basket, she met his equally hostile stare. 'What the divil's going on here?'

Chapter 3

FROM A FLAWLESS teapot garlanded with pale-blue forget-me-nots, Ivy poured tea into three delicate cups and placed a matching plate on the lace-edged cloth. 'Barley cake, sir?' she proffered stiffly.

Oliver Bailey ran a finger beneath his stiff collar. 'Thank you, Mrs Morgan.'

Sipping their tea, she and Sally watched him warily as he took large bites of the generous slice.

He popped the last piece into his mouth, swallowed and cleared his throat. 'Well, now. Isn't it pleasant to sit, have tea and discuss matters amiably?'

Ivy stared back blankly.

Unperturbed, he continued. 'Firstly, allow me to make one thing quite clear. I did not come here to in any way *bully* Mrs Goden, as you so slanderously put it, into anything whatsoever. Neither, madam, will I be spoken to in such a disrespectful fashion. Do we understand one another?'

Hostility thickened the air. She placed her cup in its saucer and folded her arms. The local preacher was a formidable man, widely feared by his parishioners, which, she suspected, he knew and relished only too well. He put the fear of God, literally, into most but she – all seven stones of her – was afraid of no one.

'For what reason are you here? You were shouting at the lass summat shocking just now and I for one didn't like the tone of your voice.'

'Madam! I—'

'Please, both of you, enough.'

Ivy and the preacher turned in surprise.

'He wants me to return home to my husband.' Sally lifted a hand as Ivy made to respond. 'Please, Mrs Morgan, let me finish.'

Ivy stared in open-mouthed admiration at her sudden change.

Steely-eyed, Sally addressed the preacher. 'Sir, I will never, *never* again dwell with my husband. I don't intend burdening Mrs Morgan much longer – though I'll be eternally grateful to you and your family for treating my child and me as you have. You've been wonderful,' she added to Ivy, squeezing her hand.

'Mrs Goden, may I remind you that you are a married woman and that your rightful place is by your husband's hearth—'

'No, sir! No more! That man has beat me since the day we wed. He's done things to me, terrible things, treated me in ways I cannot bring myself to mention; things you wouldn't believe. He stripped away everything I was and for years, I sat back and allowed him. Well, no more.' She swiped away angry tears with the back of her hand. 'I will never return. It's finished, sir, finished. Nothing and no one on God's green earth will ever change my mind.'

Sitting back, he brushed an imaginary crumb from his black garb and Ivy stifled a grin. She could almost hear his cogs of thought turning – this wasn't going as he'd obviously planned!

'Our good Lord weeps at such talk,' the preacher cried passionately, piercing eyes gleaming with religious zeal. 'He wept to see I had to browbeat you and your husband to attend chapel when you moved here. He weeps still that He does not see you as regularly as He should. An ocean of holy tears! You, madam, are under my jurisdiction. Trouble amongst my parishioners, I will not tolerate.'

'Nothing and no one will change my mind,' Sally repeated.

A slight smile touched his mouth. 'Nothing, Mrs Goden?' he asked slowly, almost deliberately. 'Not even your child?'

Ivy's eyes narrowed. ''Ere, hang on—'

'My . . . child?'

He blinked, his face a picture of innocence. 'Surely you are aware that a man has full claim to his children, even over the mother? Your husband would be well within his rights to walk in here at this very moment if he so wished and take his child from you. That is not what you want, is it? I'm sure matters are not nearly as bad as they seem. All marriages have their difficulties but they can be resolved. Now, your husband—'

'He's sent you here to threaten me, hasn't he? Hasn't he? He has, hasn't he!'

'Madam, control yourself! Your husband is residing with his sister – a Mrs Russell, I believe – on Deansgate and indeed, he has asked me to visit to remind you of your wifely duties. He feels coming himself would not be wise owing to Mr Morgan's threatening behaviour—'

Ivy's angry gasp interrupted him but he continued before she could protest.

'He wants you home, madam, and rightly so. The poor man has not even seen his child. Now, as your confinement is over, I suggest you collect your belongings at once and I will escort you home.' Seemingly blind to their horrified expressions, he drained his cup. 'Have you given thought to the baptism? I shall be free tomorrow evening if you and your husband would care to discuss the matter.'

Smiling, he rose. 'Thank you for your hospitality, Mrs Morgan,' he drawled with barely suppressed sarcasm, 'and for taking such good care of Mrs Goden and the child.' To Sally, he added firmly, 'Come along. Let's get you home where you belong.'

Ivy was speechless. The snidy, slippery old... However, Sally stunned her further by rising from the table. 'You've never let him talk you into returning to that lunatic?'

'Mrs Morgan, I have warned you already. You will respect my authority.'

'Oh, authority tripe! I'm not frickened of you, you bullying owd tyrant, yer.'

'How dare you!'

'It's all right, Mrs Morgan.'

Their furious exchange ended abruptly when Sally opened the door.

The preacher smiled smugly and strode forward. 'Ah, sensible girl! Fetch the child, come alon—' The last word rattled in his throat as Sally gripped his collar and shook him hard.

Yanking him close until his startled face was inches from hers, she murmured, 'Tell my husband he will never set eyes on *my* son so long as I breathe. And,' she added, pulling him closer, 'if you know what's good for you, *you* will stay away from us, too.' She flung him through the door and slammed it shut. Sagging against it, she closed her eyes, her breathing ragged.

'Oh, love. That were . . . That were bleedin' brilliant!'

A dazed Sally dropped into a chair. Beside her, pressing her apron to her mouth, Ivy bent double with mirth.

For several minutes, the cottage rang with their stunned laughter.

'Oh, Mrs Morgan, what on earth possessed me? I threw a clergyman through the door and spoke to him like muck. He simply enraged me speaking of Joseph as though he were the victim. As for threatening me with my son, I wasn't standing for that. I . . . snapped. He won't let this slide; as if I need further enemies.'

'Love, it'll be all right. Owd Bailey won't do owt. He'd not dare; not after that, anyroad!' Chuckling when Sally moaned and covered her face with her hands, Ivy put her arm around her shoulders. 'Look, I can fair understand why you did what you did, and if you hadn't of thrown that owd sod out on his ear, I would've.

'He pushed you to it and no one round here will blame you; they'll bleedin' well shake your hand, lass. It's my fault, anyroad. I should never have gone out without telling thee. Leaving the door open like that, what were I thinking?'

'You weren't to know. I heard knocking and was not about to open the door, naturally, but he walked in, bold as you like. I got the shock of my life, I can tell you. For a moment, I thought it was Joseph.' Sally shuddered. 'At least it was the preacher and not *him*.'

'He just come marching in? Well, of all the . . . He's a bullying owd swine if ever there were one. Now come on,' she added with a smile as tears welled in Sally's eyes, 'dry up, lass, and see to the babby. There's no use upsetting yourself, for what's done is done.' Nodding, Sally made to leave but Ivy clasped her hand. 'I don't think you've owt to fret about with him, love, but I promise, whatever happens – with him or Joseph – I'm here for thee. Just you remember that.'

Avoiding Sally's face, she cleared her throat, embarrassed at revealing the extent of her feelings. She felt protective of this lass as if she were one of her own.

Tears spilling, Sally sank to her knees and rested her head in Ivy's lap. Choking back tears herself, Ivy stroked her thick, chestnut-coloured hair.

'You've been so good to me. I'm sorry I was such a nuisance lying in bed all day while you waited on me hand and foot. I'll make it up to you, I promise. Please, Mrs Morgan, you *have* been good to me, all of you,' Sally insisted when Ivy clicked her tongue. 'All you've done . . . for Jonathan also – you and Mr Morgan must be exhausted with the broken sleep. Even your sons made sacrifices, giving up a bed for me and having to share.

'You've rescued me, given me back my life. No one could be as good a friend as you. In fact, you've been more like a mother. Thank you, so very much.'

Looking into blue eyes brimming with tears of gratitude, bright and brilliant in her heart-shaped face, it struck Ivy how attractive Sally was. She frowned curiously. 'What age are you, love?'

Sally smiled, revealing pearl-like teeth framed by full lips, transforming her face into one of even more beauty. 'Twenty-one.' Slowly, her eyebrows drew together. 'Twenty-one . . . I feel much older, Mrs Morgan.'

'I knew you were young, but . . . By God, what age did you wed that husband of yourn?'

'Sixteen, just.'

'How did you meet, lass? It's just you don't sound like you're from these parts; talk reet nice, you do.'

Sally's smile returned. 'I had a very dear friend who spoke ever so nicely. We were fascinated by each other's accents, would roll around laughing for hours asking one another to say certain words.' Her eyes filled with longing. 'I began speaking as she did. I worshipped her, wanted to be just like her, and she loved teaching me.

'She was my complete opposite – soft and gentle, whereas I was loud and quick-tempered.' She laughed when Ivy's eyebrows rose. 'Oh, believe me, I wasn't always a pushover. I miss Dicksy so very much.'

Recalling the incident with Oliver Bailey, Ivy nodded. 'Aye, thinking on it, I can fair believe that. You're a dark horse beneath. And Dicksy? There's a queer name if ever I heard one.'

'Isobella Dickinson,' she murmured. 'We never addressed one another by our given names.' She smiled softly. 'To me she was Dicksy and I was Silly Sally.'

'And Joseph?'

Sally released a long sigh. Eyes vacant, she stared into the depths of the fire. 'He bought me, Mrs Morgan. He bought me.'

After a moment of stunned silence, her gasp pierced the air. 'He *what*?'

As though lost in the hypnotic flames, Sally continued in an emotionless tone. 'I grew up in the workhouse. I knew he was evil the second I laid eyes on him, I just knew, but didn't believe anything could be worse than living in that place, not after Dicksy left.' A hollow laugh caught in her throat. 'How wrong I was.'

'Mother of God. What's the world coming to?'

'Girls were usually sent into service upon reaching fourteen. I believe that's what happened with Dicksy. The master summoned her to his office one day and I never saw her again. What she was doing in that place, I have no idea. It was clear she was of good breeding. She cried a great deal in the beginning but never spoke of her family, and I didn't ask. I hated speaking of my own, it hurt too much, and understood she felt the same.

'The parting broke my heart. I thought I'd be stuck in that hellhole the remainder of my days. The master said no employer would want me, that I was too pretty. He said ladies insist upon having unattractive girls working for them so their husbands and sons are less inclined to try something they shouldn't.

'He sold me to Joseph, instead. It happened often. If the price was right, of course,' Sally finished bitterly. She rose and crossed to the window. She folded her arms, and her tearful gaze swept the hills. 'How much do you think he paid, Mrs Morgan?'

'Lass, you don't have to—'

'A shilling. He bought me for the princely sum of one shilling.'

Ivy cringed with pity.

'I was sold like cattle at the market for a single shilling. And my God, he never let me forget it.'

'Ay, lass.' As she made to rise, Sally gave a soft smile.

'Oh, it's all right, really. That part of my life is finished, as is my marriage. All he wanted the day he came searching for a wife was a servant he didn't have to pay. Someone to keep his home clean and bed warm. Someone like me. A workhouse rat with no one to care where I was or how I fared. For years, he enjoyed that power, but he won't any more. It was the final nail in the coffin, what he threatened before you walked in—' She clamped her mouth shut.

Seeing revulsion ripple through her, Ivy shook her head. 'Dear Lord, he never did . . .'

'But it's all right, now, it will be all right,' Sally continued passionately. 'I have my son and never will I let anything happen to him. I'm not giving Joseph the opportunity to hurt me again. He'll take my child from me given the chance, believe me, he will. But he shall have to find us first. Monday, we'll go to Manchester.'

'Manchester?'

'My mother's sister dwells there – Ancoats. I've dreamed of finding her for years. The preacher's words made up my mind; I must try. I remember visiting as a child, before my father passed away. Afterwards, my mother couldn't make ends meet. She tried. My God, how she tried. But she was weak, in mind and body. It was either throw herself and her daughter upon the workhouse's mercy or starve.

'She died the following month, though no one bothered to inform me until I kicked up hell and refused to leave her the day Joseph parted with his coin. They separated families upon admission, you see, parted husbands from wives, took children from parents. According to the official policy, infants under seven could remain with their mothers in the women's quarter but, as in our case, they often overlooked this. Ten years, Mrs Morgan. Ten whole years my mother had been rotting in some paupers' pit and I had no idea.'

Wrapping her arms around the sobbing woman, Ivy rocked her. 'Oh, love. Shhh, shhh.'

A gusty cry sounded from the next room as they drew apart.

Glancing down at her earth-coloured dress and the wet patches over each breast, Sally blushed. 'I think he's hungry.'

Ivy smiled, but her mind spun from the shocking revelations. 'See to him, lass,' she murmured. 'I'll brew us some sweet tea.'

*

Later that day, the baby was asleep in his drawer. Sally had placed it beside the fire while she helped Ivy prepare the evening meal and as they worked, they discussed the upcoming departure.

'We shall be away Monday at first light. The sooner I put some distance between us and Joseph, the safer we'll be.' Glancing at her son, she felt the strongest urge to pluck him from his bed, hold his little body close and never let go.

Never will that monster get his hands on you. I'll kill him first. I'll protect you with my life, my darling, I promise. As she made the silent vow, he smiled in his sleep, as though sensing her devotion, and overwhelming love coursed through her. Blinking back tears, she returned her attention to the bread dough.

'That ham shank's smelling good.' Ivy sniffed appreciatively at the mouth-watering aroma pervading the stuffy kitchen. Reaching for a black-bottomed pan hanging by the fire, she sighed as she too glanced at the child. 'Eeh, I'll miss you and the babby, aye. But I support your decision.' She threw in potatoes, added hot water and a little salt then placed the pot by a pan of cabbage to cook. 'Set that dough to baking, lass, and we'll have a sup afore the men get home. Unless you'd rather lie down?'

'No,' Sally answered determinedly. 'It's time I pushed through this lethargy.'

'Summat's nagging me,' said Ivy as they drank their tea. 'What if your mam's sister don't dwell there any more?'

Sighing, she placed her off-white mug on the clothless table.

Ivy had returned the attractive tea service and snow-white cloth to the dresser upon the preacher's departure. She'd revealed they were wedding gifts and her pride and joy, used only on high days and holidays or when a visitor called. Whether she liked the caller or not, she'd have never poured them tea from a pockmarked teapot into chipped, handleless mugs!

'I don't mean to put a damper on things but if your aunt's upped and moved, you and the babby will be stranded. And by God, that's one place you'd not want to be alone. I've heard it ain't half grim. There's folk up there what would sell their own granny forra shill—' Ivy slapped a hand to her mouth. 'Bleedin' hell, sorry, lass. Eeh, I could chew this tongue off at times. I'm a brainless, daft owd—'

Sally laughed softly. 'It's all right, Mrs Morgan. And I share your concerns, but I have no one else to turn to. There's also the risk of passing Deansgate . . . But I must try.' Her mouth curved with fondness. 'She's a kind soul, Aunt Grace, from what I remember; happy, always smiling. She wouldn't recognise me, now. And whether I'll be welcome is another worry.' She forced a reassuring smile when Ivy frowned. 'I'm sure it will be fine. It's just that she and my mother quarrelled shortly after my father died and never spoke again.'

Ivy's frown deepened. 'The falling out must've been a bad 'un if your mam chose to knock on t' workhouse door over her own sister's.'

'I agree, but this is my only option. Besides, there is an advantage: Joseph doesn't know she exists.'

The bubbling vegetables and crackling fire were the only sounds as the woman fell silent, immersed, Sally was certain, in the same thoughts. Had Grace moved? And if not, would she be prepared to help her desperate niece?

Chapter 4

HAROLD RUSSELL RAISED tired eyes to where his wife banged dollops of mashed potato on to a row of mismatched plates – clanging and clattering that had dragged him from his sleep. She glanced back and her scowl turned into a contemptuous snarl.

He heaved himself from his fireside chair with a grunt and crossing to sit at the table, smiled faintly at his children, huddled on a filthy pallet.

With a flick of her wrist, Alice threw the lumpy mess on to another plate. 'Well? Were you taken on anywhere?'

He met her icy glare with a sigh. 'Not now, woman.'

The crash, as she slammed the pan down, made him jump several inches from his seat. The smaller children whimpered, covered their ears with grubby hands and pressed against their older siblings.

As he peered into her ugly face – the only way to describe the filthy, scab-dotted skin framed by straggly hair stiff with grease – a flush of fury rose up his neck to meet a muscle pulsating in his jaw. With a roar that surprised himself, he grabbed the steaming pan and hurled it at the wall with such force that it chipped the brickwork then clattered across the room, splattering the cowering children with its grey-coloured contents.

In heavy silence, he and his wife glared at each other across the table. And this was the scene his brother-in-law met with as he stumbled through the back door.

Joseph kicked the door shut, dragged an arm from his coarse jacket and, with one eye, took in the adults' stiff faces, the children frantically licking potato from their arms and hands, then the pan sitting on the flagstones as though it belonged there. He hiccuped twice and grinned. 'All right?'

Neither Alice nor Harold responded.

Still grinning, he yanked his other arm from his jacket. This sent him staggering and he made a grab for the table's edge, almost knocking off a plate. 'All right?' he slurred again in Alice's face.

She grimaced. 'Skenning drunk again? Though why I bother asking, I don't know. Anyone with half a nostril can tell you've spent the day with yours at the bottom of a tankard.' He hiccuped again and she shook her head in disdain. 'Sit down, you drunken fool, afore you fall down.'

Holding out both arms, he dropped on to a stool. Alice stomped across the room and snatched up the pan, and he nodded. 'Let's have it, then. I'm fair clemmed.'

'Oh!' Scraping out the dregs, her lips stretched against the blackened stumps remaining in her otherwise empty mouth. 'And why didn't you get a meal at Nellie's? I take it that's where you've been all day again?' She shook the spoon under his nose. 'Nay, but you'll not, will you? Too busy wasting brass you've not got on ale to buy grub, ain't you? Well, I'm warning you, brother or no, you'd best start getting your hand fast in that pocket of yourn or you'll be out on your ear.'

Pushing a plate towards him then slamming another in front of her husband, her voice dripped with scorn.

'There you are. Must feed the hard-working men, mustn't we?' She slapped her forehead. 'Eeh, I forget. Youse *don't* bloody work, do you!'

Harold's head snapped back. 'There's nowt about, woman. I've tramped the length and breadth of Bolton forra day's graft, from dawn till dusk, for nigh on a month. Folk won't take me on at my age, not when they can employ someone younger – or Irish – for less wages.' He looked at his plate with a hollow laugh. 'Them Irish should spend a night beneath this roof; they'd soon know the real meaning of famine.'

She ignored him and turned back to Joseph. 'And *you'll* not find work sitting on your arse in that inn. You leave a steady job and don't bother looking for another. Then there's that cottage of yourn lying empty. And as for that workhouse whore you call a wife—' She stepped back as he thumped the tabletop, sending the plates rattling in protest.

'I told thee, she'll come begging me to take her back once the preacher's put her straight. You'll see, I'll be back at Spring Row come the new week. And by God will she pay for forcing me from my own home.'

'You've likely lost that cottage by now, you bleedin' fool.'

'Nay. Them there cottages have nowt to do with the mine. De Mathers don't own them so losing my job don't mean I've lost my home,' he told her, referring to the owner of several Bolton pits who resided at Breightmet Hall, a centuries-old mansion with sprawling grounds and gardens situated on a peak of land overlooking the town. Lord de Mathers provided dwellings for his miners but the dilapidated hovels were a last resort if no alternative was available.

'Regardless, you've not kept the rent up.'

Folding his arms, he grinned. 'That's being taken care of.'

Alice jerked her head to the children. When the bundles of rags scuttled back to the mattress with their plates, she cupped her chin and frowned. 'What d'you mean, the rent's taken care of? Who's paying it, then?' She shook her head when his smile broadened. 'By God. That gullible whore's dafter than I thought.'

'You don't know the half of it.'

Alice and even Harold, his curiosity roused, stared at him in confusion. Laughing, he lumbered to his jacket and rummaged in a pocket. The children, cheeks bulging with potato, gawped as, like a conjuror at a magic show, he pulled out a string of fat sausages with both hands. He whipped out the remainder with a flourish. 'Ta-dah!'

Alice rose slowly, eyes like saucers. 'Eeh, Joseph . . . Meat? We've not had meat in bleedin' weeks.' She snatched it from him, held it to her nose and sniffed. 'Fresh, an' all!' she marvelled.

'That's not all.' He extracted a paper-wrapped parcel from another pocket which revealed, when Alice tore it open, a large pork chop.

Harold shook his head in wonder. 'She give you them?'

'Aye.'

'And she's paying your cottage's rent while you're here?'

'Aye.'

'Well.' He blew through puckered lips. 'You're a rum bugger, Joseph, you are. That wench must be besotted, poor cow.'

As Alice bustled around the fire with the frying pan, he eased into Harold's chair with a sly smile. He could still feel the fleshy folds of the woman he'd fondled in Nellie's, and her smell lingered on his hands.

She'd simpered over him, as she always did, and handed over the stolen meat with a seductive wink. She'd also paid for his ale all day and, in the dim recess where they always sat, willingly lifted her long skirts, letting his fingers probe roughly. He'd exposed breasts that glistened in the golden glow of the open fire, could still hear in his mind her groans of pleasure and pain as he sucked and bit her ruby-red nipples.

Nellie had ambled by at one point collecting empty tankards, murky eyes the colour of dirty dishwater lingering on them as she passed. He'd caught her eye and a smirk touched her lips. As she was often heard saying, her customers could do as they pleased so long as they lined her pockets in the process.

Establishments like hers, where hardened criminals and drunkards spent the majority of their waking hours, were the environments where he felt most comfortable. Home was merely somewhere to lay your head, have a meal and have your wife at your beck and call – in the bedroom as much as anywhere. *Or at least it had been,* he thought, jaw tightening.

He'd go to Bailey on Monday, see how his threat went down concerning the brat; the preacher put the wind up most people. Pity for him he couldn't spot a good liar when he saw one, Joseph reflected, his grin returning.

He'd been at the end of his tether, wondering how he could return to Spring Row without getting his skull kicked in, when by sheer luck, he'd spotted the preacher in Bolton town the day before. He'd laid it on by the shovel-load and the old man swallowed every word. Sally would have got it both barrels. She'd come crawling through that door before too long.

He didn't care a fig for the child, but *she* was his. He owned her. And when the time came and he tired of her, he'd sell her on. She'd fetch more than a shilling in the right places. He'd only got her at such a bargain price because the devil who ran the workhouse owed him. He could make a tidy profit on her in the future, even rent her out for a while first . . .

His smug smile turned to pure evil at the thought of the Morgans. 'Youse will pay, an' all, humiliating me and harbouring that whore,' he hissed. 'Aye, by God, you'll pay.'

Chapter 5

'DEAR GOD, HELP me!'

The fast-approaching footsteps grew louder. Sally hitched up the baby, her boots slapping the uneven cobbles as she pushed on through the foul-smelling alley, her every nerve and sinew urging her on. Joseph was drawing closer. Closer . . .

Pain scorched as he made a grab for her hair and wrenched her backwards, almost tearing it from her scalp.

'Please, no!' Her tortured plea rebounded off the damp bricks and his laughter swallowed it.

A blow to her temple forced her to her knees, but the pain in her heart seared far more when he snatched the baby from her. Skidding to her feet, she clawed at his jacket. A howl ripped from her throat as he bolted, Jonathan's screams ringing in her ears as they disappeared into the frosty night . . .

Sally sat bolt upright in bed with a loud gasp. Her chest throbbed from her heart's heavy beating, the wind whistling through the eaves icy as it met her sweat-slicked skin. Bile rose as the hellish nightmare flooded back. With a trembling hand, she felt for the drawer, almost not daring to check. Her fingers brushed her son's velvety cheek and she sagged.

Though now wide awake and aware they were in the safety of the Morgans', her thoughts remained tumultuous. Would that dream become reality? Was it a premonition? Could they really escape in a few short hours, start a new life in Manchester? Slowly, her every muscle tautened with determination and a love only a mother could understand streamed through her veins like new lifeblood.

Sudden visions from her childhood assaulted her mind. She used to be tough; her abominable upbringing in the workhouse had forced her to be. Any chance of surviving such a place required a quick mind and a hard heart. Constant hunger, beatings, complete lack of love and utter hopelessness, for years on end, could break the strongest person. For a girl of six, it was soul-destroying.

To enter the workhouse was to surrender your prior existence, freedom, relationships; many would sooner die in the gutter than knock at the poorhouse door.

Life before her father's death was far from idyllic. She'd regularly gone to bed with an empty stomach if he was out of work which, not from want of trying, he often was. But at least she'd felt safe, loved, *alive*. In the workhouse, you were not a person but an inmate. You ceased being human the moment you stepped over the threshold of that grey world.

Slipping an arm out of the covers, she fingered the crescent-shaped scar at the base of her temple. The overwhelming workload had taken its toll one particularly arduous day and she'd fallen asleep during her duties scrubbing the laundry-room floor. The matron's unforgiving hand, wielding a hot flat-iron, remedied that. The force of the blow had lifted her bare feet clean off the ground.

And that was the day the change in herself took root, she realised now. Something inside died and her heart hardened. The expression of shock – and slight admiration – on the matron's face, when she'd staggered to her feet and resumed her work without a word or tear, had jolted her from her coma-like existence. She'd felt alive – which she hadn't in a long time.

That new-found strength, that hardness, was her crutch throughout the years before Dicksy's arrival, when she'd ached for the warmth of a hug, a kind word, a smile. The only physical contact they were sure of receiving were beatings. And for some poor individuals, the horror of the master's flabby, sour-smelling body invading their innocent flesh at night. She'd sworn that day that no one would break her, as so many had been broken.

Yet *he* had.

Her nails dug into her palms as her fists tightened. He'd bent her, slowly, slowly, until eventually – she couldn't even recall when Joseph began winning his battle over her – she submitted to his will. Well, no more. The nightmare of him taking her baby had awakened what she'd believed long dead but had in fact been slumbering deep within: strength and a fierce determination to survive.

The realisation was like a rebirth. From this day onward, she'd never be the same. This was where her life changed for the better.

'You won't win, Joseph,' she whispered into the darkness. 'I'll stick a knife between your ribs if I must but I swear to God, so long as I have breath in my lungs, you won't win.'

Today was the beginning of the rest of her life. Soon, she must leave Spring Row and forge a new existence for herself and her son. Thoughts of returning to her birth town of Manchester evoked both longing and sadness.

Despite the hardships, the old weaver's cottage she was born in held comforting memories, still vivid in her mind. But her loving parents were no longer there. Her father, overworked and undernourished, had gone years before. And her poor, gentle mother . . . But Aunt Grace was there. *Dear God, please let Aunt Grace be there.* That her hope and saviour might no longer be where she remembered was a thought she forced away before panic could swamp her.

She caressed her son's hand. 'It's just you and me.' This conjured up a range of emotions. She'd soon have to leave these people for whom she'd come to care a great deal.

She felt humbled by how fortunate she'd been. Ivy's kindness had known no bounds; she'd even sat through several nights and knitted Jonathan an assortment of clothing from an unpicked jumper of Arthur's. Sally wished there was a way, however small, to repay them. And her mouth curved as an idea, a way to help Ivy this morning at least, formed.

The wind had eased and rain drummed steadily against the window as she slipped out of bed. Tensing her jaw to stop her teeth chattering, she hurried to a side table where her clothes lay neatly folded and tugged them on with hands already stiffening with cold. Journeying in weather this bitter, with a newborn in tow, wasn't something she was relishing. *But needs must when the Devil drives.*

She padded to the door.

She felt refreshed, despite the hour, and knew it was early as no movement sounded behind the door or from above. No Ivy lighting the fire in the kitchen and preparing breakfast, no Arthur dressing for work. Last night, for the first time, she'd had the baby in with her. Despite Ivy's assurance that it had been no hardship, she knew the older woman would have been glad of the uninterrupted sleep.

She'll have an easy morning, too, Sally thought, smiling, as she entered the kitchen.

She dropped to her knees before the near-dead fire and in no time it was crackling nicely. Reaching for a pan beside the hearth, she brightened further at the prospect of Ivy coming down to a warm kitchen and porridge bubbling away. Yet as she turned from the fire, her breath caught and the room swayed.

'Joseph . . .'

The name froze on her lips. Her legs buckled and she fell to the floor in a dead faint when, from the gloom, a figure rose from the table.

The tender hold was comforting. Sally snuggled into the broad chest, lips parting when they brushed his neck. A voice murmured her name, told her everything would be all right and in her half-conscious state, she felt completely at ease. It was as though she was supposed to be in these arms, as though she'd been away for a long time and was back where she belonged. Like she'd come home.

'There, now, that's it. Open your eyes.' A coarse, though not unpleasant, hand stroking her hair accompanied the soothing words. He laid her down gently.

She instantly missed his touch, was about to reach out in search of it when the world came into focus.

The figure stood motionless by the table. He'd lit a candle and the flickering flame illuminated his silhouette. She eased herself into a sitting position. The dim room swayed and, groaning, she flopped back against the chair.

Tommy was at Sally's side in seconds. Without a word, he carried her to the front room. She curled into him and the swell of her breasts pressed against his chest. His heart jerked beneath the soft mounds and it took him aback when a flame ignited in the pit of his stomach. His surprise mounted at the overwhelming urge to take the globes in his hands.

Frowning, he laid her on the bed and knelt before her. A sliver of moonlight fell across her face and he waited, watching, the only sound the rain pattering against the panes.

This was the first time he'd looked at his neighbour properly. He'd seen her occasionally over the years in the row as she scurried by, head down, and at several mealtimes since she'd been here, when she felt up to it. They had shared the odd smile and word, it was true. However, he'd not *seen* her, not really. Not like this . . . Until now.

The Sunday she came began like any other. His mother and father had gone to chapel, Shaun was out with friends and he himself was meeting Dolly Jenkins for their weekly stroll by the river.

Not particularly religious, his parents attended chapel most weeks more through habit than anything; it allowed them to catch up with friends and broke their monotonous routine for a few hours. They didn't mind that he and Shaun rarely attended service. They understood their need for fresh air and sunshine on their precious day off after working underground all week.

He'd been shocked, therefore, upon his return, his cheery whistle dying mid-tune, to discover Sally asleep in the front room, having just given birth to the squawking bundle in his mother's arms.

He knew the gist of why she was here. His mother had disclosed enough to quell her sons' curiosity, gain their understanding that Sally needed peace and plenty of rest, and warn of Joseph's likely return.

That madman wants his head testing, he thought now, drinking in her delicate features. Again, that flare sparked low within him. His eyes travelled down and he glimpsed old bruises streaking the creamy skin of her neck. His hands bunched into fists. He wished that swine was next door. He'd do more than bruise *his* neck; he'd snap the thing.

Suddenly, Dolly's smiling face flitted through his mind but he pushed it away, realising with a jolt that for the first time, it wasn't a welcome image. What was wrong with him? The bewildering thought was forgotten when Sally stirred.

He watched intently as she licked her full lips. She opened her eyes and he smiled. 'Easy, now. Feeling better?'

Sally nodded. Her mind was clearing and a memory, a feeling . . . She glanced at Tommy's arms, chest, neck . . . the neck she'd pressed her lips to. She looked away quickly, confused, feeling redness creep over her face.

'I am sorry. I saw you come into the kitchen and go to the fire, but you had your back to me and I didn't want to startle you. I know you've had a hard time of it lately.' He looked away and cleared his throat. 'I'll fetch thee some tea.'

When his footsteps faded, she released a breath she hadn't realised she held. She covered her hot face with her hands. What happened? She remembered leaving this room, entering the kitchen, lighting the fire... *Joseph.* She'd turned to the table... Dear God, Joseph had risen from the gloom! The huge figure, its outline a hazy red from the glow of the fire, loomed and the floor had hurtled towards her.

Her fuddled brain screamed at her to run: *Joseph's here! He'll take the child! Run! Run!* Her body jerked involuntarily and she leapt from the bed. She absently scraped back a lock of hair – and her hand froze. Tommy... Tommy had stroked her hair, murmured softly, held her close. Strong arms, his smell, his heart beating against hers...

Bewildered, she shook her head recalling the emotions his touch evoked. To know these... from a man? How, in God's name, after everything...? She brushed her lips with her fingertips. The warm skin of his throat still lingered. Joseph wasn't here. He didn't rise from the table, Tommy did. Tommy had held her in his arms, and she'd... A knot of shame twisted her stomach. What on earth was she thinking? What must *he* think of *her*?

Her brow furrowed in disappointment as her thoughts switched back to Joseph. She'd broken her vow. She'd believed she was growing stronger, was putting her fear of him behind her. Clearly, she'd been mistaken.

The clinking of crockery drifted through and with a jolt she remembered that Tommy was making tea. Heat returned to her face. He'd be back any moment. Here, in this room. With her.

She reached the door in a heartbeat.

He paused when her footsteps sounded, but didn't turn. He placed the teapot on the table. 'Are you well enough to be up, Mrs Goden?'

She flinched that he'd addressed her by that monster's name and before she could stop herself, said too sharply, 'My name is Sally. Goden is *his* name, not mine.'

Tommy blinked, nodded, then inclined his head to a steaming mug.

Ivy spoke of him highly and often; Sally felt she knew this man already, it was true. None the less, it struck her that she was alone with him and she felt a little afraid. She hesitated and his eyes creased in a look akin to pity.

'That babby of yourn's a real beauty, Sally. Reet bonny, he is.'

She sensed something behind the murmured words. Not in the statement itself, but the way he said it seemed to hold almost a whisper of reassurance, that she needn't fear his presence. That not all men were like Joseph Goden. Whether she imagined it, she didn't know, but it put her at ease. Smiling, she slipped into a chair.

'Thank you. Yes, he is.'

She stole a glance at Tommy's bowed head as she sipped her tea. Catching sight of his hands, which dwarfed the mug they held, her skin tingled at the memory of his touch. The ensuing silence was stifling. In desperation, she stammered, 'Couldn't you sleep? It's rather early to be up when you've a day's work to get through.'

He rubbed tired-looking eyes. 'I've matters on my mind. Our Shaun.' He motioned to the ceiling. 'He's miserable. It's fair cutting me apart inside – Mam, an' all – seeing the lad like that. I've got to do summat. I just don't know what.'

The depth of feeling in his tone touched her. 'If you don't mind my asking, what's wrong with him?'

He rose, crossed to the dresser and opened a drawer. She tilted her head but his broad back blocked her view. Eventually, he turned, arms piled with wooden objects. He placed them on the table and sat.

She gazed at the items as he arranged them in a line. Finely carved animals and people stared back. The intricate detailing took her breath away. She reached out to touch a rearing horse then drew back for fear of breaking the delicate structure.

'It's all right. Here.' Smiling, he pushed it towards her.

The mane curved along the horse's head and down its back in swirling lines. Sally ran a finger over it, shaking her head in wonder at the facial features. The body was accurate in every way, from the muscular shoulders and perfectly shaped legs and hooves to the flowing tail; it was exceptionally crafted.

She shook her head again at the others: a cow with calf alongside; a shorn sheep mid-bleat; a bird balanced on one leg, exquisitely detailed wings outstretched as though preparing for flight – the list seemed endless.

'Did you . . . ?'

'Our Shaun.'

Her eyebrows arched in surprise. He was little more than a boy – an extremely talented boy at that. She fingered a figure of Ivy, complete with flowing apron and shawl. It was an exact replica, down to the fine lines around her eyes and mouth. 'Tommy, these are unbelievably good. I've never seen anything like it.'

His handsome face shone with brotherly pride. 'This is what he were born to do. He can turn a lump of wood into a work of art in the blink of an eye. That lad shouldn't be down the mine. He's not cut out for it. I can see the light in his eyes dying and one day it'll go out altogether unless summat's done.'

'Couldn't he try for a place involving woodwork? Any carpenter in the land would give his right arm to apprentice someone with this level of talent, surely?'

'I've been thinking the same. D'you know, he's carved these with all sorts of odds and ends: an owd knife, a few rusty nails, even bits of sharpened stone. Think on what he could do with the right tools and a master carpenter to guide him. The only problem would be the loss of his wages, for as an apprentice, he'd get nowhere near what he earns now.

'We'd all feel the pinch but I'm willing to do all the overtime I can; I'll even get work on one of the farms at the weekend. I'm not sure what a master would ask where tools are concerned and the premium for taking him on. It's a crying shame, seeing him the way he is. I'm going to try my damnedest to do this for him.'

Excitement stirred. Sally had wanted a way to repay Ivy and her family. Maybe this could be it. Joseph's face flashed across her thoughts and she gulped at the memory of their last afternoon. She'd begged and pleaded – had lied through her teeth. He'd suspected her of stealing his money and he'd been right.

'I awoke early to surprise your mother. I was planning to prepare breakfast, save her the job for one morning. It was all I could think of to repay her—'

'And I spoiled it by scaring thee senseless. Sorry for that.'

'It's not your fault. My nerves are in ribbons at the moment. What I wanted to tell you, to ask you, is whether, well, whether you and your parents would let *me* help. With Shaun. With the money.'

'You? But Joseph doesn't . . . well . . .'

'Seem the type to allow his wife her own money? You're right, he isn't. But I found a way.'

'You mean you put brass aside forra rainy day, so to speak?' he asked with a wink.

'I'm not proud of myself. Stealing is stealing, whichever way you look at it, but I did it for my child. I buried a little away when I could and Joseph was none the wiser. However, I had to buy wool to clothe the baby and he discovered it. He was furious and wouldn't let up until I told him the truth. But I didn't. And shortly, I'll be able to get away, as I've planned for such a long time. I shall be free of him. We both will.' Now-familiar panic rose, forcing her to stop. *Let all go well, please . . .*

Tommy lowered his gaze. 'I'm sorry. I meant nowt by that, Mrs— Sally. And by no means are you a thief, by God, you're not. That swine no doubt owes thee a damn sight more than what you've took. But there's no way we'll take your money.'

She frowned in puzzlement. Had she insulted him, bruised his pride? She heard the tinge of hurt in her own voice. 'But why?'

'If you've worked as hard as you say for that brass, we'd not accept a farthing. Besides, you'll need it for you and the babby. Mam would never agree.'

Her face relaxed in a smile. She'd planned to do this on her way to the coaching house but now was as good a time as any. 'Would you keep an ear to Jonathan? I shan't be long.'

'Aye.'

She glanced to the clock, nodded, then made for the door.

'Where you going?'

'Next door.' She wasn't surprised her response wasn't 'home'. That place had never been one. It had been a prison and she thanked heaven her sentence was over.

'But you can't! Joseph . . . The babby will be all right. I'll come with you.'

Her stomach flipped at the concern in his eyes.

'He might be lying in wait, could have returned in t' dead of night any time during the last weeks. I . . . can't see you go alone.'

After some deliberation, she nodded and they stepped into the darkness of the row.

Squinting left and right through the drizzle, she slipped through the gate. Tommy was right behind. At her own, she studied the dark windows for signs of life. His nod spurred her on and she hurried down the path.

When they reached the door, she turned and headed for the side of the cottage.

'Where are you—?'

'You'll see,' she whispered.

She halted at the rear and peered up at the low roof. Then she stood on an upturned pail, lifted a loose chunk of moss-choked slate and felt beneath.

'I should've guessed. You couldn't have hidden it inside the cottage; Joseph would've stumbled upon it eventually.'

She felt a warm glow at the admiration in his voice but seconds later icy dread replaced it. 'No . . . The money's gone. It's *gone*!'

Before Tommy could respond, a snapping twig punctured the stillness. He whirled around, fists poised. A huge dog leapt at him, knocking the air from his lungs. Standing on its hind legs, it rested its front paws on his chest and licked his face frantically.

'Get down, you daft divil, yer!' he hissed.

A moment later, Sally's desperate fingers brushed damp cloth. She heaved a sigh then clicked her tongue. The dog jumped down instantly, trotted over and lay at her feet. She scratched its ear with one hand. With the other, she dangled a bulging pouch between thumb and forefinger and grinned.

Tommy returned the smile then scowled at the dog, its legs in the air and tongue lolling on the stubbly grass. 'That thing's a menace. Barking in t' lane at all hours, and now this. My heart fair left my chest, there. And that breath – smells like week-old cabbage water. Near floored me, that did.'

She stifled a giggle. 'I feel sorry for him. I've been giving him titbits over the months whenever I've seen him skulking around.'

She didn't mention they were leftovers from Joseph's plate, which she'd sneaked for herself. Despite her hunger, she'd shared whatever scraps she obtained with the dog, understanding the all-consuming need when your guts gnawed from lack of sustenance. However, she'd never been tempted to dip into her hoard. She'd have sooner starved. The hunger for freedom had been far more intense.

'Oh, Lord,' he said on a chuckle.

She smiled. 'What's wrong?'

'Nothing, nothing. I were just thinking on summat Mam said about the dog the other day.'

At the mention of Ivy, she nodded determinedly. 'Speaking of your mother . . . Come, let's get back inside. I need you to do something for me before she wakes.'

Chapter 6

'LASS, ARE YOU ready?' Ivy rubbed her eyes with her shawl. There was a break in her voice as she added, 'Eeh, I must be getting a cold.'

Sally didn't attempt to hide her tears; they ran freely. Her gaze swept the kitchen, drinking in the image, knowing she might never see it again. She wiped her face and nodded.

The rain had ceased and the dew-drenched meadows winked in the weak sunshine like a sea of crystals. A fresh but biting breeze from across the hills whistled through the row as, head lowered against it, Ivy ushered them down the path.

Sally didn't look at her cottage and hoped she never would again. She hadn't been over the threshold since Ivy helped her across the day she gave birth, and she had no intention of ever doing so.

Other than the money, she'd retrieved nothing before leaving because the sad truth was, not a thing belonged to her besides the ragged shawl she'd left behind. An ancient one of Ivy's which, much to Sally's gratitude, Ivy insisted she have, lay across her shoulders. It was thin and matted but warmer than nothing.

Her patched dress and boots, issued to her the day she left the workhouse, were all she possessed. Joseph hadn't spent a farthing on her throughout their marriage.

No, she'd *never* go back. Lifting her chin, she walked on.

As they passed through the row, she glanced at the tatty canvas bag in her hand and smiled tearfully. It held the baby's clothes and a paper-wrapped parcel. This contained two cold sausages, a slice of bread and dripping and a hunk of currant cake to, in Ivy's words, keep her going on her travels to 'That Manchester'. This consisted of the upcoming cart ride, the train, then the trek from the station in Manchester to Grace's district – a journey of some two hours, she surmised. And inside the bag there was another item she couldn't quite believe was there.

Earlier, when the men were leaving for work, she'd shaken their hands and thanked them for their kindness. Arthur wished her well, as did Tommy – though she'd imagined he held her hand a little longer than his father. Before leaving, Shaun had rummaged in the dresser drawer and thrust something into her hand.

She'd blinked at his bowed head then looked down. It was the beautifully carved horse Tommy had showed her hours before. She'd gasped and tried to return it, insisting she couldn't accept, but he'd stepped away mumbling, 'Take it, for the babby.'

She'd never known such kindness, felt humbled to her very soul.

The coaching house came into view and she breathed deeply. This was it. Would she depart from Bolton undetected? Would she remember how to locate Grace's home once in Manchester? Would she find her larger-than-life aunt there if she did?

Ivy's voice broke her thoughts. 'Oh, that's all we need.'

Following her gaze, Sally groaned inwardly.

'Good morning, Mrs Morgan, Mrs Goden.' The stiff greeting belied the smile accompanying it.

'Sir,' they mumbled.

Noticing Ivy's lips twitch, nervous laughter bubbled inside her. Clearing her throat, Sally met his steely glare. 'Sir, allow me to apologise for my behaviour Friday. I acted disgracefully, throwing . . . throwing you . . .' She paused as another wave of giggles threatened to escape. 'I had no right evicting you from Mrs Morgan's cottage. I hope I . . . didn't hurt you when I threw you down the path.'

Ivy turned her snort into a cough. 'Excuse me, sir. I've started with a shocking cowd this morning.'

The preacher's nostrils flared and one eye twitched rapidly. 'The Almighty has, I am certain, an appropriate punishment prepared for you come Judgement Day. However,' he added grimly, '*I'm* prepared to forget the incident if you heed my advice and return to your husband today.'

She stiffened in outrage but before she could deliver a retort, Ivy flashed him a disarming smile.

'We've spoken on that and realise you're right. Sally sees she's been hasty, that she should try and make her marriage work. She loves the bones of yon Joseph, despite their disagreements, and is on her way to catch the carrier's cart to Bolton town. Going to his sister's, she is, to beg his forgiveness. Aye, rest assured, she'll do her best to smooth out matters. Won't you, lass?' she added with the briefest of winks.

'Oh. Oh, yes. Indeed. It was wicked of me to tell such lies about him. I love my Joseph dearly.'

He looked at them in turn through narrowed eyes. After what seemed an age, he nodded. 'I knew you would see sense. Your husband will be most pleased, though as I am sure you know, you have a great deal of apologising to do, madam. However, Mr Goden is a just man. He shall forgive you eventually. You should count your blessings to be married to one such as him.'

'Yes, sir.'

'Excellent. Well, I shan't keep you.' With a half-bow, he bade them farewell and strode down the lane.

When he was a fair distance away, they broke into laughter.

'Come on,' Ivy spluttered, 'we'd best get on. You don't want to keep that saint of a husband waiting, d'you?'

'Thank you, Mrs Morgan, for your quick thinking. But what about you? He'll be furious when he discovers we lied.'

'Humph! Don't you fret over me, lass. I'm not frickened of him. He can rant and ask as many questions as he likes. All he'll get from me is a clog up his arse.'

Dissolving into laughter again, they hurried to the waiting cart which, according to the sign in the coaching house window, departed for Bolton each day bar Wednesdays and Sundays.

'Hello, Ivy! Lovely morning, in't it?'

Ivy frowned at the murky sky but smiled none the less. 'Aye, lovely morning, George.'

The carter, a thickset man with mutton-chop whiskers and a weathered face, grinned then turned his bleary gaze to Sally and tipped his cap. 'Morning, lass.'

She smiled warily. This man was clearly drunk. She'd seen enough with Joseph to know. Hugging the baby closer, she whispered, 'Mrs Morgan, I . . . believe he's . . .'

Ivy nodded and strode forward. 'George Turner, are you sozzled again? You're a danger to your passengers, you are, driving that cart of yourn in that bloody state. Yon Sally here wants a ride into town and she's gorra young 'un with her. You best mind how you go, or you'll have me to answer to. Bloody shocking, it is.' Hands on hips, she shook her head but a smile played at her mouth.

The waiting passengers chuckled when he threw back his head and roared with laughter.

'Now, wench, you rest easy. Never had no accident yet, I've not. I allus have a nip of summat to warm my owd bones but these here hosses do the work.' Brown eyes dancing, he gave the mares' necks an affectionate pat. 'Know the way closed-eyed, they would.'

Stretching to her full height, which barely reached his chest, Ivy wagged a finger under his nose. 'Aye, well. You've been warned.'

Sally watched the exchange in astonishment. Men turned nasty with ale, didn't they? They threatened you, hurt you in ways no one should be. Yet this one wasn't angry, wasn't snarling at anyone or threatening to thump them. He was smiling broadly and her lips stretched into one, too.

He swayed to the cart and hauled himself into his seat behind the horses' rumps. Ivy chuckled. 'Have no fear, lass, he's harmless. He knows Bolton like the back of his hand. You'll come to no harm with owd George.'

Sally tried to smile but her lips wobbled and with a sob she threw an arm around Ivy. 'Oh, Mrs Morgan, I'll miss you more than you'll ever know. Take care of yourself. And please, don't ever change.'

Ivy sniffed, coughed, sniffed again. 'No fear of that, love. I'd not change for no bugger, prince nor pauper.'

'Ready, lass?' asked the carter softly, and she nodded.

While she climbed aboard, Ivy held the baby. She gazed at him for a long moment then kissed his brow tenderly. 'Goodbye, fella. Look after your mam, there's a good lad.' Eyes bright, she laid him in Sally's arms. 'Take care, lass. And just you remember, I'm here if you need me. Always.'

With a 'Whey up, there!' from George, the cart jolted forward.

Sally laughed through her tears and the passengers grinned when Ivy called, 'Think on what I said, George. I'll flay thee alive if harm comes to that lass or her babby. Just you mind where you're going, you bugger.'

With a nod and a wink, he touched his cap. 'Goodbye, wench!'

Standing at her father's door, Nancy Skinner nodded a greeting to Ivy passing through the row. She received a watery smile in return and frowned curiously. That the older woman was upset about something was clear to see.

Turning back inside the shop, a thought occurred and her cheeks burned with excitement. Hiding her smile, she entered the back room and reached for a plate from the dresser.

She was right, she just knew it. She'd been awaiting this day for months and now, *finally*, things would go her way.

As she dished out leek-and-potato pie for her father's dinner later, her heart danced. 'Please, Lord, let it be true,' she murmured, her smile spreading into a grin of pure delight.

Sally sat mesmerised as they rolled through Breightmet. After living as a virtual prisoner, as a workhouse inmate and then as Joseph's wife, she couldn't tear her gaze away. The last time she'd passed through was en route to Spring Row shortly after her wedding but, consumed with fear and dread, she hadn't noticed her surroundings.

Gurgling streams meandered alongside fields snuggled by farmers' cottages, surrounded with thick trees and snow-white sheep, grazing peacefully. Closing her eyes, she drew in scented air. Despite everything, she'd miss this little community.

She'd prayed for years in the dead of night, as Joseph lay snoring beside her, to make her escape but knew it wasn't Spring Row she'd craved to leave. She consoled herself with hopes that, one day, she and her child might again live amongst these hills, happily.

'Eeh, he's a bonny young thing. Your first?'

The innocent question, from a woman in her middle years seated beside Sally, stabbed her heart. She'd never forget the poor souls born to her too soon, nor cease to wonder whom they might have grown to become, but in a way, this child *was* her first. The first to survive the Devil's evil.

'I'm not prying, lass, just making conversation. Passes the journey quicker, is all.'

The soft words snapped her from her reverie. 'I'm sorry. Yes, he's my first. And he's so good, hardly ever cries.'

The woman chuckled. 'Aye, well, enjoy it. Others will follow soon enough and peace will be nowt but a memory.'

She forced a smile. *If only you knew*, she thought bitterly, glancing to her left hand.

Ivy had stopped her wrenching the thin band from her finger this morning with the sage advice, 'Whatever that there ring represents, it'll bring thee respectability.

And when times are lean, it'll fetch a few bob at the pawnshop.'

Though the sight of it turned her stomach, she'd left it where it was for now.

As they neared the centre of town, fields petered away. Rich green turned to grey as they weaved through crooked streets flanked by houses, shops and inns. Huge chimneys, almost shrouded from view beneath an overhanging pall, dotted the skyline, belching out dense smoke, and her chest tightened.

From what she knew, Bolton, situated in a natural valley on a vast sweep of moorland, developed on the banks of the River Croal. The upsurge in textile manufacture saw it gradually spread out as more and more people arrived, seeking jobs in the cotton trade. Sally remembered the noxious smell of the factories from her childhood; Manchester, some ten miles south-east, was also a thriving manufacturing town, on an even larger scale.

'They're an eyesore, ain't they, lass?' murmured the woman. 'Mill Town, folk are calling us, and no wonder. Everywhere you look a fresh 'un's sprung; nigh on seventy, now, so says my husband. We'll not see our hands afore our faces in a few years, I'm sure.'

Nodding agreement, Sally covered her nose and mouth. Despite the rapid growth throughout many towns, Breightmet remained relatively untouched, and the clogged air wrapped around lungs now unaccustomed to it.

Her heartbeat quickened as they approached one of Bolton's oldest roads, where she and Joseph lodged before and shortly after their wedding: Deansgate. Dark and miserable, riddled with ruinous, one- and two-storey homes and shops leaning shoulder to shoulder with as many alehouses, the grinding poverty was tangible.

Beneath Alice's roof, she'd had the role of slave forced upon her immediately. She'd rebelled, yet quickly realised her error. The punishments Alice doled out for her insolence had known no bounds. Without mercy, she'd lash out with fists, feet, even teeth, while Joseph looked on in amusement.

Yet despite her loathing for Sally, Alice had told her brother in no uncertain terms to get a band on her finger. Whatever her faults – and they were plenty – she wouldn't condone the mortal act of living in sin, thus shackling them for life. For that alone, Sally reciprocated Alice's ill feelings tenfold.

The preacher said Joseph was dwelling here. What if he saw her and snatched the baby? Surprise brought a smile when her inner voice growled, 'Let him try it.'

Her emotions were up and down. One minute, she was drowning in rage and the next – proven this morning – a quivering wreck at the thought of seeing him. It was a terrifying notion but she was determined to leave the fear behind. Her old hardness was increasing steadily and she was glad of it. Nevertheless, when the cart passed her sister-in-law's street, she sighed in relief.

Hope and excitement stirred. Not long, now, and she'd be free of him.

'Whoa there, my bonny girls!' At the carter's command, the horses slowed to a walk.

The woman smiled as they rattled to a stop. 'Here we are, lass. Want a hand down with the babby?'

Sally couldn't speak. Since escaping, she'd revelled in new experiences: speaking and laughing with others; eating more than she ever had; being free of the beatings that were part and parcel of daily life – all a wonder. However, the sights, sounds and smells before her now were like nothing she'd encountered.

She gazed in awe towards New Market Place, which Ivy had spoken of once or twice. Situated on an area of land to the south side of Deansgate, it claimed to be the finest uncovered market in the country.

Shops bordered all sides, taking advantage of the customers who flocked each week: cloggers, grocers, butchers, beer-sellers and bakers huddled alongside pawnbrokers, drapers, haberdashers and hatters, all jostling for business around the bustling square.

Accepting the woman's help, she stepped from the cart. She barely heard her warm goodbye, returning it just in time. Alone, she looked about and smiled. All around stood carts and stalls piled high with produce mostly locally grown and made. Meat and poultry, bred on the surrounding homesteads; fruit and vegetables; confectionery; grain; seeds; hay; straw – the variety seemed endless.

She was wandering through the swell of people when a hand on her shoulder stopped her in her tracks. Spinning around, she almost cried out in relief to see George's beaming face.

'Eeh, sorry if I frightened thee, but you've left summat behind.'

She stared at the carter in puzzlement. The sleeping baby lay in her arm and she was clutching the canvas bag. She possessed nothing else. 'You must be mistaken, Mr Turner. I have everything I set out with.'

'Nay, lass. You're wrong there.'

She followed his gaze. What she saw at his feet astonished her. Panting heavily, tongue hanging from the side of its mouth, was the dog from Spring Row.

George chuckled and patted its back. 'This fella's followed us from Breightmet. Watched him all the way, I did, running alongside the cart. And d'you know summat, lass? He never once took his eyes off thee.'

'But he's not mine, Mr Turner! I have seen him around, but—'

'Well, I'd say you'll have a job getting shot. Took a shine to thee, he has. He's a bonny chap; bit on t' thin side, mind.' Eyeing an inn behind a stall, he licked his lips. 'Anyroad, I'm off forra jar afore I wither with thirst. Think on with that there dog. He's a big 'un if ever I saw one.' His eyes softened. 'He'd be sound protection for them as needs it.'

She smiled gently. 'Thank you.'

'Take care, lass. I'll be sure to tell Ivy you survived the journey!'

When he'd gone, she looked down. 'How about it, Dog? Do you fancy a trip to Manchester?' It answered with a shake of its tail. 'Come along, then. We need to take the train.' Following Ivy's directions, she turned for Trinity Street Station.

Stallholders' and customers' chatter, peppered with laughter as they haggled and indulged in banter, enveloped her as she passed, the dog close on her heels. Men predominated but bonneted women in long aprons also sold their wares and their shrill voices, as they urged the townsfolk to buy, carried further:

'Fresh produce, here, lovies. No better in t' whole of Bolton. Golden butter! Delicious cheese! Eggs not long left my hens' backsides, still warm!' one rang out, followed by another at the next stall, and the next.

'Three and six for three pounds of butter? A prime swindle, that is! Throw in a few of them eggs and you've gorra sale. And none of them shit-smeared 'uns, neither,' a customer cackled.

The stallholder roared with laughter but, hurrying on, Sally missed her reply. Alice's home was too close for comfort; she couldn't hang around.

Minutes later, however, she had to stop; Jonathan seemed to grow heavier by the second. She moved him into her other arm and flexed the aching one he'd vacated.

The man whose stall she'd halted by smiled sympathetically. 'Little things, babbies, but they're dead weights after a while, ain't they?'

'Indeed they are!'

'Strap a saddle on that big beggar and let the babby ride on its back.' He nodded to the dog and laughed. 'Travelling far today, lass?'

Her smile froze. No one could know where she was heading. For all she knew, this kindly looking man might know Joseph or Alice. 'Some distance, yes,' she answered cautiously.

'Aye, I thought as much. You don't talk like folk round here; speak reet nice, you do.' He rummaged around his stall, shoved aside boots, kitchenware and medicine bottles containing colourful liquids. 'Not like the nobs what sound like they've a hot poker up their backsides but still, you speak nice. Proper, like.' He moved other mismatched items then, grinning, held up a basket. 'Lay a blanket in here and the babby will be lovely and snug.' He produced one and placed it inside. 'Will that do thee?'

'Oh, yes. Thank you.' From Jonathan's coverings, she extracted the bundle of coins from the eaves. 'How much, please?'

His eyes widened. 'Oh, call it a crown, eh, lass? Good quality that there blanket is,' he stated, fingering the coarse material, 'and the basket's in sound health, an' all.'

She glanced at the numerous holes where the wicker had snapped through age and use, but nodded none the less and counted money into his hand. She didn't like to question the price, not when he'd been so kind and thoughtful and, besides, he was the trader, not she. He obviously knew best.

Suddenly, a child no older than five years appeared from nowhere. Her bare feet were filthy, as was her ragged dress, which was several sizes too small for her scrawny frame. Sally's eyes softened with pity but the stallholder's hardened.

Holding his gaze through long tendrils of hair the colour of rats' tails, the girl addressed him boldly. 'At it again, Bob?' She pulled a face at Sally's purchases. 'You're a robbing owd goat. Falling to bits, them are, and you're asking a crown? You've a cheek asking tuppence, you swindler, yer.'

His face turned puce. 'Bugger off, you young imp, afore I ram my boot up that raggedy arse of yourn.'

'Your crusty owd legs wouldn't catch me. Give the lady a fair deal. You're trying to swindle her and you know it.'

Sally turned to him, hurt, and he flushed further. He looked at the coins in his hand. Then he poured the majority into hers without a word.

The girl grinned, snatched up the basket and steered her to the edge of the market.

They halted by an ornate drinking fountain and after laying Jonathan inside the basket, Sally smiled wryly. This child, who clearly knew the ways of the world better than she, had saved her a fair amount of money and she was grateful, if not a little embarrassed. Her naivety would be her undoing unless she wised up, and fast. 'What's your name?'

The girl wiped an arm across her dripping nose. 'Folk call me all manner of things, missis, but my proper name's Lily.' A grin spread across her face when Sally laughed.

'Well, Lily, I think you deserve this for your help back there.'

'Bloomin' hell. Ta, missis!'

Her stomach knotted as she handed over a silver shilling. She hated those coins with a passion. 'You're very welcome.'

Watching her replace her purse beneath the baby's covers, Lily frowned. 'You want to watch that bag of brass, missis. Hide it under your skirt on a bit of string. It'll be safer there.'

'Do you know, you may be right? You are a clever little thing, aren't you?'

The child smiled in delight. 'Ta, missis. You're nice, you are. You don't half talk queer, mind. Where you from?'

'You don't miss a trick, do you?' Talking about Dicksy had brought back painful memories. Unwilling to relive them again, especially with a child, she said, 'I'm from Manchester. Have you heard of it?'

Lily snorted. 'Have I! Went with Father, I did, last year. My sister skivvied in a big house up there but let the nob's son get her in t' family way, silly cow. Slat her out, they did, and Father went and thumped the son, right on t' nose. My father made *his* father give our Lizzie some money and we fetched her home.'

'What happened then?' Sally asked, agog.

'She gorra belting off Mam for her loose ways and losing a steady wage, and ran off in t' night. We've not seen her since.' She wiped her nose again. 'Don't matter. There's too many children at home. Didn't want another there, anyroad.'

Sally bit her lip. Despite the indifferent tone, tears pooled in Lily's eyes. She extracted the parcel of food from the canvas bag and the young face brightened instantly as delicious aromas wafted from within. 'Are you hungry?'

The child smiled at what she clearly deemed a daft question. 'Do fishes have a fondness for water?'

Chuckling, Sally handed her a sausage and the hunk of currant cake. She gave the salivating dog the other sausage, re-wrapped the bread and dripping and returned it to the bag. She watched with pity as the girl devoured the food ravenously. 'Better?'

Lily ceased licking crumbs from her grubby fingers to pat her stomach. 'Aye. Ta, missis.'

'Well, I have a train to catch so I'm afraid I must be going. Look after yourself and thank you again for your help. Goodbye.' She made to turn but Lily gripped her shawl.

'Will you take me with you? Please? Mam won't mither. Let me come home with you, missis, *please*.'

The sheer desperation in her eyes brought a lump to Sally's throat. 'You cannot come with me. What about your family?'

'They'll not mind, honest. And Mam's an 'orrible pig; *she'd* be glad to see the back of me.'

'Oh, lass. I cannot just take you with me, much as I like you. I'm sorry.'

Fat tears rolled down Lily's cheeks but she nodded miserably.

Sally took the remainder of the food from her bag. 'Here, take it. Goodbye, Lily.'

She hurried for the station without looking back. Guilt and the memory of Lily's sad blue eyes followed her all the way.

The sooner she was out of Bolton, the better.

Chapter 7

LILY RUBBED AN arm across her face and turned reluctantly for home. She normally hung around the market all day; there was more chance of filling her belly there. Distracted stallholders didn't usually miss a swiped piece of fruit or bun but if they did, and her forced tears didn't work, her thin legs could outrun any of them. Today, though, she wasn't in the mood.

She hugged herself as the final day of October's harsh wind whipped her mottled skin but didn't quicken her pace. The longer she could avoid home, the better. The odd stone bit into her as she dragged her feet but as she'd never worn shoes, the skin was so coarse she barely noticed.

She paused at the entrance of Chapel Alley, debating whether to return to the market, but decided against it after glancing at the sky. She didn't like the rain. Due to the lice she couldn't recall not having, her head itched ferociously when wet and open sores on her scalp burned when she scratched.

Despite her foreboding as she neared her door, a smile stirred. She'd wolfed down the bread and dripping and was wonderfully full for once. That grub had been the best she'd ever tasted. She wished the lady had taken her with her. She'd been kind, had smiled and spoken to her softly. Not like her mam, who screeched at her and slapped her face for nothing.

She glanced around then unclenched her fist and grinned. A whole shilling! She smoothed a thumb over a young Victoria, feeling even richer than the pretty monarch. Saliva filled her mouth with thoughts of the food she could buy with the precious piece. Sighing happily, she slipped inside.

The stench of stale cooking and unwashed bodies enveloped her. Her mother was by the fire and after shooting a glance at her stiff back, Lily hurried to the corner. Damp from the rotten pallet seeped through her dress and she winced when straw poking through the thin fabric scratched her leg. Pressing against the wall, she wrapped her arms around her knees.

'And where have *you* been?'

Lily hugged her knees tighter. 'Market.'

Her mother stabbed the fire savagely with the poker. 'Well, don't get too comfy. That useless father of yourn won't have found work, you can bet your life on that, so you best get your arse back down that market later and see what you can scavenge. Bone idle, that's his trouble, the good-for-nowt wastrel.'

Lily's nails bit into her palms as the scathing voice rattled on. She didn't like it when she spoke of Father that way. He wasn't idle or useless, he was nice and kind. Nicer than *her*, anyroad. She hated being alone with *her*. Thankfully, her siblings would soon be home from work. Her father would follow, tired and miserable after another day tramping the streets in vain.

Her brow creased at the thought of her twin brothers. It was anyone's guess when they would be home; they were hardly ever in. At six years old, they were not yet in work but their pockets always held pennies or food. She didn't know where they found their spoils but *did* know their mother wasn't aware of it. She smiled inwardly. They were clever and she must be, too, if she was to hold on to her shilling.

She squeezed her hand, imagining the endless possibilities it afforded. She could buy a whole bag of fruit, apples, aye, or juicy plums, and stuff her face with the sticky treats; maybe a few cakes, too. Or later, she could sneak to the alehouse for a potato pie. She could buy two, even three—

'What the bugger have you to grin about?' her mother snapped, dragging her from her daydream. 'I'm sure you're a bit simple, you. 'Ere, make yourself useful forra change.'

Lily crossed the room and took the steaming mug held out to her.

'Take that in to your Uncle Joseph, and mind you don't spill it. It's about time he were from that pit of his. Go on, then, hurry up.'

Sticking out her tongue in concentration, Lily headed for the door. Watching the pale-brown liquid swishing back and forth with every step, she remembered the uneven flagstone too late. Her toe stubbed the jutting corner and she stared in horror as the mug and shilling flew from her hands.

The mug landed with a smash but she didn't react when hot tea splashed her bare legs. All her attention was on the coin. She watched, transfixed, as it spun in a circle then rattled to a stop.

'You silly bitch, yer! I told thee to be careful, you gormless young—' The outburst died at the sight of the shilling.

Lily whimpered but a slap silenced her.

Her mother snatched up the coin and waved it under her nose. 'You snidy, sly little bitch. Where the bugger did you get this?' She shook her shoulder hard. 'Shurrup bawling and answer me. Where did you get it?'

'A l–l–lady gave it m–me.' Lily's stuttered explanation earned her another slap.

'What lady, you bleedin' liar?'

'I'm not l–lying, honest!'

'What the hell's afoot, here?'

They turned to see Joseph standing in the doorway.

Running a hand through his hair, he scratched his bare chest and yawned. 'What's all the caterwauling? You can't get a wink of kip in this dump.'

Her mother shot Lily a contemptuous look. 'We've been sat here without a scrap of grub in t' house and this little bitch had a shilling and didn't say nowt. Said a lady give it her, lying cow.'

Joseph stepped over the shattered mug and lowered himself into the fireside chair. 'All that wailing for that? Bloody hell.'

'Listen 'ere, we can't live on fresh air, you know, and I don't see you handing over no brass. This lying swine should've give me this straight away but nay, were planning spending it on herself, no doubt. Selfish through and through, she is, just like her rotten father.'

Bunching her fists, Lily glared at her. 'I'm *norra* liar! A lady *did* give it me. She were from Manchester. I helped her buy a basket to carry her babby in, for the stallholder were trying to swindle her. She were going on a train and she said I were clever. Reet nice to me, she were.'

Her mother laughed scathingly. 'Clever? Thee? Huh!'

Joseph's dark eyes narrowed. He silenced his sister with a flap of his hand. 'Did she tell you her name?'

Lily shook her head. 'I never asked.'

'Take no notice, you fool, she's lying. I bet she's robbed it from somewhere, the little—'

'Alice, will you shurrup a minute, for God's sake?' Before his sister could respond, he turned back to Lily. 'What did she look like, this lady?'

Lily cocked her head in thought. 'She wore a brown dress and her hair were brown, an' all. And she spoke queer.' She reached up to touch her temple. 'Had a scar like a half-moon, she did, just here.'

He paled. 'And she had a babby with her?'

'Aye. Tiny, it were.'

With a roar, he leapt up and rushed from the room. He returned fully dressed, face now purple with rage. 'I'll kill her. I'll bloody well *kill* her!'

'You don't reckon it were Sally?' asked her mother.

'Course it bloody were, the scheming whore. I *knew* she'd been thieving off me; where else would she of got brass to throw about? Catching a bloody train, were she? Well, she'll not get far. By God, she'll not!' He snatched the shilling and bolted from the cottage.

Staring at the open door, Lily's mind whirled. She'd heard them talk about someone called Sally before but from what they had said, she sounded horrible. The lady at the market wasn't; she was lovely. It couldn't be her!

Eyes swimming with tears, she sloped to the corner and curled into a ball upon the mattress.

Jostled at every step, Sally, hugging the basket close, made her way across the crowded platform. Smartly dressed gentlemen, and ladies in beautiful dresses and hats, breezed towards the first-class carriage of the waiting train, porters scurrying behind with trunks and boxes. At other compartments, beshawled women, children, and men in rough clothing and caps dominated the entrances.

She looked around uncertainly. The bustling market had been noisy but the atmosphere jovial, relaxed. This was something else. Footsteps pounded the platform. Children's cries and laughter mingled with the hum of conversation. Porters' shouts rang, unintelligible amidst the throb of noise. Yet it was the train that was turning her legs to jelly.

Upon leaving the workhouse, she and Joseph had travelled to Bolton on an open cart. Never had she been on one of these huge, hissing beasts; the prospect filled her with panic.

She continued hesitantly when passengers in front began entering the carriages. However, as she reached the entrance, her resolve wavered and she turned, ready to bolt from the station. But she knew she had no choice – she *must* get on. Inwardly cursing Joseph to the bowels of hell, she turned back.

The dog had already leapt aboard and stood, head cocked, as though urging her on. With a deep breath, she stepped forward. She'd barely entered when a hand gripped her shoulder and hauled her back on to the platform.

'What d'you think *you're* playing at?'

Her legs almost buckled. Twisting around, she found herself facing a broad chest. Slowly, her eyes travelled up, not wanting to see the face she knew it was. She'd almost done it. By sheer misfortune,

Joseph had found her. Dear God, he'd kill her for sure, he'd—

'I asked thee a question. What d'you think you're playing at?'

She tried yanking free but he held on tight. 'Let me go! I won't go back with you, I won't! I'll scream this station to the ground if you don't *let me go*!' Her last words were indeed a scream and she shoved him hard in the stomach.

His grip loosened and, gasping, she made to jump aboard but the dog knocked her aside and leapt from the carriage. It landed on the man and passengers stared open-mouthed as he hit the platform.

The animal planted its huge paws on his chest and pressed its face close to his, snarling menacingly. She suspected it was only her cry of horror on realising he wasn't Joseph after all that stopped it sinking its teeth into the man's neck. It looked up, awaiting her instruction.

'What the . . . ? What the . . . ?' The stationmaster craned his neck slowly so as not to provoke the dog further. 'What's its name? Call it off, God damn it, call it off!'

'He hasn't got a name. I haven't given him one, yet.'

'Well, think of one and quick. It's crushing my bleedin' ribs, here!'

The dog watched her calmly as she approached. She laid a hand on its head. 'Off, Dog. It's all right, I'm all right. Off.'

The stationmaster gasped in relief when it obeyed. He staggered to his feet, eyes blazing, and pointed a quivering finger in her face. 'You . . . you swine, yer. I'll have you and that thing strung up! I only asked what you were playing at fetching that fiend on t' train. Animals ain't permitted in here.'

Sally lowered her eyes in mortification. 'I'm sorry, I am, really. You startled me. I thought you were someone else.'

'Sorry, is it? Tha bloody will be when—' A man stepped from the crowd, silencing him.

'You're the one who'll be sorry if you don't leave this lass alone. 'Tis a disgrace how you dragged her from the train; and her with a babe in arms, too. The dog acted admirably and *I'll* be the one knocking ye back down, so I will, if you don't back off.'

Sally gazed at him then touched the stationmaster's sleeve. 'Let the dog on the train. I've said sorry and I'll pay extra. Please?' He glared from her to the stranger uncertainly and she turned to the young Irishman who had defended her. 'Please, I'm quite all right. You're making matters worse.'

His green eyes danced in amusement and a slow smile spread across his handsome face. 'As you wish, acushla, as you wish.'

A shrill whistle rang out and she turned back to the stationmaster, face creasing in desperation. 'Please. I *must* catch this train.' She fumbled in the basket, drew out a handful of coins and held them up.

Catching the eye of the Irishman, who nodded, he flapped a hand. 'Oh, give me your fare. I've had a bloody bellyful. Go on, get gone.'

Sally almost cried out in relief. She handed over the money and she and the dog hurried aboard. Taking a seat on the wooden form, she heaved a sigh.

'I suppose the carter was right, Dog. You did well protecting me, there!'

It lay at her feet and rested its head on its paws. Patting the dog, she peered across the platform. She caught sight of the stationmaster and pulled back quickly, covering her mouth as laughter bubbled. Peeping back, she scanned the faces and frowned. The Irishman had gone.

She sat back and shrugged. It was no concern of hers. Besides, he'd had no right interfering. Nevertheless, as the train pulled away, she again glanced out but great clouds of steam obscured her view.

Sally shrugged once more, placed the basket next to her and closed her eyes. Her stomach fluttered with a range of emotions. She could scarcely believe she was leaving Bolton after all these years. And what would she face in Manchester? Her heart lurched, already aching for Ivy and her safe little cottage.

A tall, muscular man with floppy, coal-black hair and grey-blue eyes assaulted her mind's eye. Allowing herself to study him, she recalled the time they spent together in his cosy kitchen. She remembered how his shoulder muscles rippled through his shirt when he scraped back his hair, heard his smooth, deep laugh . . . She hugged herself, a smile caressing her lips.

As the train rattled along the tracks to her birthplace, she slipped into a light sleep.

The train was spluttering to a halt when a growl woke Sally. She was startled to see the dog staring beyond her shoulder and turned slowly.

'Lily?' As soon as she uttered the name, she knew she was mistaken. The child, though plainly dressed, was neat and clean and whilst her hair was the exact colour of the other girl's, it wasn't falling across her face in greasy tendrils but lay in tidy plaits.

'Begging your pardon, lass, but I heard you telling the stationmaster you were Manchester bound.'

She hadn't noticed a man standing behind the girl and jumped in surprise.

'You were out for the count and I didn't know whether to waken thee in case that big beggar took a chunk from me.' Flashing a wary glance at the dog, he laid a protective hand on the child's shoulder.

She smiled sheepishly. 'Are we in Manchester?'

'We are, lass.' He touched his cap then hastily guided the girl from the carriage.

Sally looked down and sighed. 'You're going to get me into trouble. I don't need shielding from everyone.' She nodded thoughtfully. 'That is an ideal name; I cannot continue calling you Dog. How about it? Shall we name you Shield?' He woofed softly and she smiled. 'Shield it is, then.'

She lifted the basket but looking inside her smile slipped. Jonathan was wide awake and sucking his bunched fist. 'Come, Shield, this fellow needs feeding.'

The long, single-storey building of Manchester Victoria Station milled with people. She made for an empty bench, lifted the grizzling child and after positioning her shawl around them, opened a few buttons on her dress.

Shield sat by her feet, scrutinising all who passed. Women glanced in their direction, smiled understandingly and looked away. But the lingering stares of some men had his hackles rising and she softened towards him further.

He clearly held a deep distrust of men; they had an affinity in that sense. Then the memory of him jumping up excitedly at Tommy swam across her mind and she smiled. Well, not all men. That was another connection they shared – they recognised a good one when they saw one.

The suckling ceased and after repositioning her clothing, she laid the baby in the basket and rose.

She'd done it. She'd escaped and Joseph was none the wiser. God willing, she'd soon be seeing her aunt. Her heart beat furiously with terror and excitement.

She took deep breaths. Then squaring her shoulders, she walked from the station.

Chapter 8

THE FIRST THING Sally noticed when she stepped from the station was the all-encompassing smell. Wrinkling her nose, she stared around and above. Soot-blackened buildings, their chimneys spewing thick smoke, greeted her mournfully.

The factory-building boom had transformed the Manchester she knew; it had expanded at an astonishing rate. The area she stood in looked densely populated and was much busier than she remembered. She'd have guessed there were well over three times the residents encased amidst these grimy surroundings than in those she'd just left.

She glanced right to the run-down tavern where Joseph had taken her upon leaving the workhouse and grimaced, remembering his leering face as he scrutinised her young body from top to toe. He'd drunk jar after jar of ale while she huddled in the corner, scared witless and aching with grief for her mother. They left for Bolton that night and she hadn't set foot in this town since.

She fought to keep her eyes from straying in the opposite direction. Yet she knew she had to see it, one last time. Maybe then, she could lay the past to rest. Slowly, she turned to the place of her nightmares.

Behind high walls, New Bridge Street Workhouse stood tall and intimidating on the hilltop, its black chimneys rising against the dull sky. Rectangular windows dotted the exterior, staring at a world most wretched inmates beyond the panes wouldn't again know.

She reeled back as though slapped by an invisible hand. Her mother's and Dicksy's faces assaulted her mind and she tore her gaze away with a sob.

Sensing her distress, Shield whined and pawed her leg. Swallowing her pain, she patted him. 'I'm all right, Shield.'

'You've given the fellow a name, then? Ah, Shield's grand. It suits him, to be sure.'

Whipping around, Sally raised her eyebrows then drew them together in a frown. 'What are *you* doing here?'

The Irishman grinned. However, it slipped from his face when her eyelids fluttered. She swayed drunkenly and he grabbed the basket's handle and caught her around the waist.

Her vision cleared; blinking in bewilderment, she pulled away. 'I'm sorry, I don't know what came over me. I'm quite well, now, thank you.'

Handing back the basket, he glanced to the workhouse and frowned. 'Are you sure? 'Tis mighty pale, your face, so it is.'

She nodded then breathed deeply when nausea swept through her.

'No, you're not, acushla. Come with me.' Taking her elbow, he guided her across the busy road.

She allowed him to lead her but when he halted at the familiar tavern, drew back sharply.

''Tis all right in here. You need a hot meal inside you, put some colour back into that pretty face of yours.' He took her arm again but she snatched it back.

'Thank you, but I'm quite well. I must go.'

'If you're sure . . . ?'

'Quite. Goodbye.'

'Wait, let me pay for a cab. You could have another turn and there may not be a handsome man around to catch you next time.'

At the teasing twinkle in his eyes, her lips twitched. 'You ought to save your money and buy yourself a larger cap.'

He laughed heartily. 'Come now, acushla. You don't believe you're the first to fall at my feet, do you?'

Rolling her eyes, she smiled lopsidedly. 'Very well, Mr . . . ?'

'Con Malloy, ma'am, at your service.'

'Very well, Con Malloy, I'll take a hansom. But I'm paying.'

She realised that, albeit a shocking extravagance, it was sensible. Many years had passed; she'd likely never locate Grace's home otherwise. She only remembered the street because it was her aunt's married name; Grace had often teased that she and her husband owned the road.

Con made to protest but when she raised an eyebrow, laughed in defeat. He whistled to a waiting cab, which was at their side in seconds, and swept an arm theatrically. 'Your carriage awaits, acushla.'

Hiding a smile, she stepped aboard.

'Well, Mrs . . . ?'

'Sally Swann. And it's Miss.' She'd decided this morning to revert to her maiden name and relished the familiarity on her tongue.

He glanced at Jonathan then to the band on her finger, but didn't comment. 'Well, *Miss* Swann, perhaps our paths will cross again. Goodbye.'

She frowned as a thought struck. 'You never answered my question. What *are* you doing here?'

'And why wouldn't I be?' He spread his arms wide. ''Tis my home, so it is.'

'But I looked— What I mean is, I didn't see you on the train.' Heat scorched her cheeks when he smiled slowly. 'Well, goodbye.' She inclined her head then tapped the cab. 'Boslam Street, please.'

Con watched her go, his smile deepening. Miss Sally Swann . . . Their paths would indeed cross again. Of that, he was certain.

As the hansom rattled through the streets, Shield running alongside, Sally's stomach churned. She'd assumed her dizzy spell to be exhaustion but now recalled hardly touching her porridge this morning, worry over the departure having chased away her appetite. And she hadn't eaten a scrap from Ivy's parcel. Maybe she did need a hot meal.

She frowned at the thought of the man she'd just left by the roadside. Who was he and why did he seem to appear when she needed help? His knowing smile, when she'd let slip about searching the platform, brought fire back to her cheeks. What must he think of her?

She told herself it didn't matter. She wouldn't see him again; not a third time, surely?

They turned down another cobblestoned road and the tumbling in her stomach intensified. They couldn't be far from Boslam Street, now.

Please, *please* let Aunt Grace be there, she prayed. And yet, what welcome would she receive? As Ivy pointed out, the reason behind the sisters' estrangement must be serious for her mother to have taken the desperate step of entering the workhouse. But Grace was her only relative. Whatever the outcome, she had to try.

Continuing through the maze of narrow streets of back-to-back houses, made more miserable by the drizzly weather, she breathed a sad sigh. Since leaving Victoria Station, she'd barely seen a speck of green.

Mills and multi-storey factories abounded as well as foundries, engineering factories, glassworks and more. Clearly, such high need of manual labour had brought droves of people to the district but she'd seen no parks, grounds or recreational facilities for this large population. It seemed every available space had been used for industry and housing.

Hastily built dwellings, to accommodate the influx, were painfully apparent; their quality and condition were dire. The majority of streets she'd passed were undrained and ran with human waste from the privies and ash pits at the rear of houses. The stink was overwhelming. She dreaded to imagine how poor souls living in unventilated cellars fared – they must swim during heavy downpours.

Watching young and old scuttling by or lounging in courts and streets, Sally ached for the rolling hills she'd taken for granted. The thought of raising her child in these dark surroundings filled her with horror. We *will* return to Breightmet some day, she vowed.

The cab finally halted and she alighted, nauseous and aching everywhere. Shield bounded around her. Stroking his damp fur, she peered about.

The rain had abated but the dull sun barely pierced the pewter clouds. Wind whipped her skirt and shawl, making her shiver. Glancing up and down, she tried to remember which house was her aunt's but it was useless: each was exactly like its neighbour. The basket rocked and as she looked inside, desperate tears pricked her eyes when Jonathan screwed up his face and wailed.

'All right, lass?'

Sally turned to see an elderly woman, craggy face creased in smile. 'I'm looking for my aunt's house.' She raised her eyebrows expectantly, adding, 'Grace Boslam?'

'Grace? Aye, I know her. But you'll not find her here. Not any more, anyroad.'

Her stomach lurched but the woman chuckled.

'No need to look so worried, lass, for she's not moved far.' She jabbed a finger to an entry between two houses. 'Go through the ginnel, there, and turn right. Grace's is the second-to-last house on t' end.'

'Oh, thank you. Thank you so much.'

She smiled and ambled away, soggy black skirts trailing in the filth behind her.

Sally made for the narrow passage. It gave entry to a row of terraced houses and she crossed the cobbles quickly, eyes fixed on one in particular. Halting before it, she sent up a prayer. In a moment, she'd know what the future held for her and her child.

Heart hammering, she knocked on the door.

Chapter 9

'AYE?'

Sally stared at the young man who had answered her knock. Did she have the wrong house? She stepped back, glanced left and right. No, this was it.

'Can I help you?'

'Yes, I'm sorry, I . . . A woman said my aunt dwells here. Grace Boslam?' She frowned when his face paled. He blinked and opened his mouth but uttered nothing. 'I'm sorry, are you all right? You see, she directed me here. She said that Grace's was the second-to-last—' His crushing hug smothered her speech.

Shield growled but the lad didn't seem to notice. He held her at arm's length. 'Sally Swann? Is it really thee?'

Before a stunned Sally could respond, a weary voice sounded within the house: 'Stan, who is it, lad? Don't leave them standing on t' step, it's perishing out there.'

Air erupted from Sally's lungs. She pushed past Stan into the house.

A cry escaped her. The ash-blonde hair, though bound as usual at the nape, was lank and flecked with grey, and she seemed smaller than Sally remembered. Rosy cheeks, which used to dimple when she smiled, were pasty, the lines around her eyes unfamiliar. But it was her aunt, all right!

'Aunt Grace? Oh, Aunt Grace, I cannot believe . . . After all these years!'

Grace rose slowly. Stan came to stand beside her and she gripped his arm. 'Is it . . . ? Really . . . ? Oh!' She threw herself at Sally and flung her arms around her neck.

Sally smiled at the faint scent of lavender she remembered so well. Burying her face in her aunt's shoulder, she heaved a long sigh.

A cry broke through their tearful laughter. Peering inside the basket, Grace covered her mouth.

'Our little Sally a mother? I don't believe it.' She stroked the baby's cheek then her niece's. 'Oh, where have you been all these years, lass?' She glanced to the door, as though searching for someone else, and her smile faded. 'How's your mam? How's our Rose?'

Fresh tears welled in Sally's eyes at the longing in her aunt's. How could she tell her?

'It's all right, I understand. She'll never forgive me, will she? I don't blame her, honest I don't, but I miss her . . . so very much. Norra day's passed that I've not thought of you both, you know. Norra single day.'

'Oh, Aunt Grace . . .'

'Tell me, lass, please; is she all right, our Rose? Is she well?'

Sally clung to her, heart breaking at what she must say. 'My mother's dead.'

Time seemed to stand still. Then the heavy silence was shattered when, bending double, Grace howled like an injured beast.

'Mam, come and sit down.' Stan led her, sobbing and shaking, to a fireside chair. 'I'll brew some tea.'

Sitting opposite, Sally clasped her hand. 'I'm so sorry, Aunt Grace, so very sorry.'

'I . . . can't . . . My lovely Rosie. And you. Oh, you poor girl.'

She lowered her head, Grace's devastation too painful to witness. She hadn't meant it to be like this. For years, she'd planned this meeting, intended to break the news gently, not blurt it out.

'What happened, lass? When did . . . ? Where have you *been* all these years? Did she ever talk about me? Did she ever forgive me? Did she—?'

'Easy, Mam.' Stan abandoned the teapot to wrap his arms around her, and she crumpled.

'She's been gone these fifteen years,' Sally choked. 'They didn't tell me, Aunt Grace. I had no idea and it near killed me when I heard. I don't even know what happened. It haunts me day and night imagining . . . I'd give anything to feel her arms around me again, anything.'

'Fif . . . fifteen years? How did you not know? What in God's name happened?'

A faint voice drifted from the gloom: 'Mam, where are you? It hurts. It . . . hurts, Mam.'

Grace jumped up and hurried to a narrow bed in the corner. Sally gazed across in surprise; she hadn't noticed anyone else present. Stan beckoned and she followed him outside. Shield was right behind her. He lay on the cobbles by the door, eyes never leaving her.

Stan closed the door to and sat on the step. 'Our Peggy took ill last week. The neighbours have been kindness itself, 'specially Mrs Knox next door. She fetches round a meal of sorts when she can, but her offers of relieving Mam of her bedside vigil are allus refused. Nowt will shift her from Peggy's side.'

'Oh, I am sorry.' Sally lowered herself beside him. 'I had no idea I had cousins. Your mother hadn't been married long when I saw her last. I remember attending the wedding.' She smiled at the memory. 'How is Uncle Ed?'

'He's all right.'

'He's a good man, your father.'

A look passed over Stan's face but was gone before she could determine its meaning. He smiled faintly and looked away.

'I remember him vividly. He would sit me on his shoulders and run up and down the street pretending to be a horse.'

This time, her cousin's smile was as warm as hers. 'He did that with Peggy when she were younger.'

'Is it just the two of you? How old are you both?'

'Aye, just us. I'll be sixteen next month, and Peggy . . .' His face darkened. He kicked the step with his heel. 'It's not fair. It's not *bloody* fair. Eleven year old . . . She's nowt but a babby.'

'Stan? What's wrong?'

His answer was barely above a whisper. 'She's dying. There's nowt can be done for her any more.'

'Oh my . . . ! I didn't realise—'

'You weren't to know. It's just not fair. It's killing Mam.'

'Is there really nothing that can be done?'

He stared at the sky through dull eyes, ran a hand through his dark-blond hair. 'Nay, not now. It's the consumption, but Mam won't believe it. She's convinced she'll get better. She used to get ill then rally but the last time, she coughed up blood.

'That's a sure sign, that is. I've seen it enough round here to know. There's nowt for you once that gets a grip of you.' He looked at Sally for a long moment. 'I'm glad to finally meet thee. I don't know what went on betwixt our mams, for she's never said, but she's allus spoke of you and Aunt Rose. She's missed youse summat awful. I don't know how she'll get over your mam, what with everything else . . .'

She squeezed his arm. 'I'll help whichever way I can. I'm here to stay if you'll have me. I'm so glad I've found your parents – and you and Peggy.'

He covered her hand with his. 'Aye. I'm glad, an' all. It's queer but d'you know, I feel as though I've known thee all my life.'

Sally smiled curiously. 'Do you know, I feel the same with you?'

She was so thankful Grace hadn't turned her away, as she'd often feared she might. Whatever had happened between the sisters, Grace clearly didn't hold it against her. It felt so good to be amongst family. Ivy and Arthur were wonderful but there was no real substitute for blood. For the first time in many, many years, Sally felt like she belonged.

At the thought of the Morgans, Tommy flashed through her mind but she pushed him away. It was time to nip those foolish imaginings in the bud; he'd been being kind, nothing more. She must put the past behind her, for she had a new future here, now. Her family needed her.

This brought a rush of happiness. She curled her fingers through Stan's. 'Let's get back inside and see if your mother's all right. We have a lot of talking to do. I cannot say I'm looking forward to it but she has a right to know.'

'I'll find a scrap of summat for the dog and dish up some broth for you and Father. He'll be home shortly.'

Her stomach rumbled at the mention of food and she smiled gratefully. She didn't want to swoon again, needed a clear head for the painful yet unavoidable conversation to come.

When they reached the kitchen door, Stan paused. A teasing smile played across his mouth. 'This talking what must be done, will it shed light on why you speak like the bloomin' gentry?'

She pushed him playfully. They were going to get along well, she just knew it. He already felt like the brother she'd never had.

The lamplighter's whistle broke through the quiet room. Sally wandered to the window and lifted the faded curtain's edge. Absently, she watched him extend his long pole, bring the gas lamp to life then continue on his rounds, leaving a misty pool of yellow-gold in his wake.

Leaning her forehead against the cold glass, she closed tired eyes. It had been a long day, and the dreaded conversation had been as painful as she'd anticipated. She and Grace held each other for hours and, slowly, the flowing words had eased Sally's shoulders of their long and heavy burden. From entering one hell to escaping the second, and everything between, she left out nothing.

Between sobs, Grace had repeated one question: 'Why didn't my Rosie come to me instead of the workhouse?' Unable to answer, Sally could only hold the broken woman. Grace had, however, managed a smile for the Morgans and blessed them for helping her escape 'that divilish bastard', as she venomously referred to Joseph.

Now, returning to her seat, Sally smiled softly at her aunt, who was asleep in the chair opposite. To have someone, be part of a family again – for Jonathan as much as herself – left a warm glow deep within. She bent to stroke Shield, stretched before the fire. She didn't know what life he'd led but suspected this would be his first home in a long time, too.

It had been a day of highs and lows. She smiled to herself, imagining Ivy's reaction when Tommy revealed her gift for Shaun. His handsome face swam in her mind but again she forced it away. Yes, quite an eventful day, she mused once more. Sorrow at leaving the Morgans, pleasure at gaining Shield, helplessness over little Lily, the stationmaster gazing up from the platform . . .

Her lips curved then bunched in rumination with thoughts of Con Malloy. Who was he? He'd appeared from nowhere in Bolton, then again in Manchester. She had to admit he seemed nice enough. He'd helped her both times without wanting anything in return.

The workhouse, she immediately banished. That building and all it stood for was in the past, she told herself firmly. She'd dwell upon it no more. Her mind switched instead to the reunion with her aunt and the surprising discovery of cousins. Their open-armed welcome was more wonderful than she ever could have envisaged.

She peered inside the basket at her slumbering son and stroked his cheek. 'We did it, little one. We got away.' This brought a surge of quiet jubilation. 'You lost, Joseph,' she murmured. 'You lost.'

Peggy's harsh cough pulled her from her thoughts. Admiration for her aunt filled her when, despite the deep sleep she appeared to be in, she instantly awoke and hurried to her daughter. A mother's love was a powerful thing.

Stan, dozing beside Peggy, stirred when his mother approached. He raised himself on an elbow. 'Is he home?'

Grace felt Peggy's forehead, crossed to a shelf and lifted a bottle of laudanum. 'Nay. He shouldn't be long, now.'

'Not long enough for me.'

She sighed. 'Not now, son.'

Sally frowned. What did Stan mean by that? And where *was* Uncle Ed? He must have finished work hours ago.

Peggy coughed again. Murmuring soothingly, Stan smoothed hair from her forehead. Grace watched with a soft smile then measured medicine from a dark bottle and added it to drops of laudanum in a cup. Stirring the mixture, she glanced across the room. Sally smiled.

'Oh, I thought you were sleeping, lass. Come say hello to your cousin while she's up, for she'll be asleep again soon. She'll be that pleased to see thee.'

'She can hear you,' Stan told Sally as she neared. 'Say summat, tell her who you are.'

Purple eyelids flickered when she covered a small hand with hers. 'Hello, Peggy. I'm Sally, your cousin. It's lovely to meet you.'

Soft brown pools rested on her face. The girl gave a half-smile and said laboriously, 'Ah . . . in't she . . . bonny, Mam?'

Grace and Stan nodded, eyes misty, and tears pricked Sally's.

'Not as pretty as you, Peggy, not by a mile,' she whispered.

Peggy managed another smile and closed her eyes. She nodded when Grace asked was she in pain then squinted up again. 'Nice to . . . meet thee, Sally.'

Too choked to speak, she kissed Peggy's hand then moved aside while her aunt administered the medicine. Stan put his arm around her shoulders and led her away and they had just sat down by the fire when the sound of the front door opening rattled through the house. Moments later, Ed entered.

Grace made no mention of his absence. 'Look who's here, Ed. Our Sally's come home.' She smiled when her husband gasped and embraced Sally warmly.

'Eeh, I don't believe it! Where have you been hiding, lass?'

Sally knew instantly where *he'd* been; the smell of porter was unmistakable. Yet as with George Turner the carter, she now realised not all men were violent brutes she must avoid at all costs when they had taken a sup.

'Oh, Uncle Ed, it's lovely to see you.'

He hugged her again then eased into a chair, almost stepping on Shield's tail. 'Is this big divil yours?' When she laughed and nodded, he cocked his head, eyes thoughtful. 'By, you're the image of your mam, lass, you are that.' Shooting a glance at his wife, his smile vanished. 'Is she here, your mam?'

Sally shook her head.

'Nay, don't suppose she would be, and who could blame her?'

'Ed, please, you don't understand,' whispered Grace. 'Rose . . . My Rosie's dead.'

He blinked at her bowed head then turned to Sally. 'I'm sorry to hear that, lass, I am really. I thought . . . She were a sound wench, your mam, a sound wench.'

Sally suppressed a frown. What was behind her aunt and mother's falling out? From the little she'd gleaned, Grace seemed to be in the wrong. She determined to ask her aunt, but not yet. They had shed enough tears this night. Right now, she wanted to enjoy her family.

'There's someone I'd like you to meet, Uncle Ed.' Stooping by his chair, she lifted the basket. 'My son,

Jonathan. The moment I held him, I knew what to name him. And if he turns out to be half the man my father was, I'll be the proudest mother on earth.'

He stared at the infant for a long moment, smiled faintly and looked away.

'Stan, is that tea ready, lad?' Grace asked, cutting through the silence. 'And warm the rest of that mutton broth for your father.'

'Aye, hurry up. And when you've done that, you can run to the Blue Bell and fetch us all a penny pie. Our Sally's back and what better way to celebrate than with one of Betty's meat and tatties?'

Stan's back stiffened at Ed's tone, but his eyes remained fixed on the table. He poured tea into a large mug and passed it across.

'And the grub?'

'It's warming.'

'Aye, well, take yourself to the inn while you're waiting, boy.'

Stan's jaw tensed as he took coppers from Ed. When the front door slammed, Sally caught Grace's eye and the older woman lowered her gaze.

Ed stared at the door and breathed deeply. Then he rose and crossed to the bed. He gazed at his daughter. 'How's she been?' he asked. The edge to his voice when he'd spoken to Stan had gone.

'No better, no worse. She managed a drop of broth earlier.' Grace smoothed dark hair from Peggy's brow. 'My poor lass.'

He stared down at her bowed head. When he lifted a hand to her shoulder, Sally made to look away from the private moment between husband and wife. She was confused, however, when he flexed his fingers inches from her aunt then let his arm fall to his side.

She bit her lip. Something was wrong with her family; she could have reached out and touched the strained atmosphere. She wondered whether it was simply the stress of Peggy's condition, but discarded this. The child's illness was obviously distressing for everyone but something else was afoot here that she couldn't put her finger on.

Lost in thought, she jumped when the front door clattered. Stan entered and, smiling, she took the steaming parcel from him. 'Allow me. You warm yourself by the fire.'

He thanked her and held his hands to the leaping flames. 'It's beyond cowd out there. I reckon we'll have snow afore the night's out.'

Returning to his chair, Ed nudged him aside. 'Don't talk daft. It's not *that* bloody cowd.'

Stan didn't respond and as she unwrapped pies and dished out broth for her uncle, Sally kept her head lowered. These exchanges were uncomfortable to witness. Doubt snaked down her spine. Had she done the right thing coming here? It seemed her family had enough troubles without her adding to them.

Ed rubbed his hands as she approached with a delicious-smelling pie, hunk of bread and bowl of broth. 'Eeh, that smells good.'

After passing Stan a pie, she turned to her aunt. 'Aunt Grace, will you eat this now?'

'Nay, I'm not hungry.'

'Come and get some grub down you, wench, while it's hot,' Ed murmured without looking up. 'It'll do you good.'

The whisper of a smile lifted the corners of Grace's mouth. 'Aye. Aye, all right.'

When his wife sat, he began to eat. He didn't see the eyebrow Stan raised at him – or the curling of his lip – but Sally did.

Lowering her head again to hide her frown, she nibbled her pie without tasting it. Tomorrow, she'd have that word with her aunt. Something wasn't right here and she was determined to find out what.

Dodging a pile of manure, Nancy Skinner hurried across the frosty cobbles. Her heart fluttered in anticipation of the meeting to come and she smiled, glad she'd made the extra effort.

She'd donned her best dress, a revealing item in deep maroon, which clung to her curves and accentuated her large breasts. Her hair she'd brushed until it crackled and the soft tresses fell across her shoulders like burnished copper.

Along the length of the street, laughter and bawdy singing poured from alehouses when doors opened to admit or eject a customer. Before they could swing shut, sickly streaks of light from within sliced across the cobbles, revealing the silhouettes of rats scuttling by. Watching her step, she lowered her shawl and turned left.

Across the street, a group of rough-looking men peered at her as she passed and she tossed her hair, knowing the gas lamp would highlight the amber-flecked locks she was so proud of.

'How much, love?' Leering laughter followed and the speaker grinned at his friends.

Eyes narrowing, she looked him up and down. 'Trust me, fella, you couldn't afford it. And I'm fair certain you'd not know what to do with *that*.' She inclined her head to his crotch and smirked when his friends roared with laughter.

His face darkened. 'Trust *me*, whore, after I'd finished with you, you'd not be able to sit forra week. Come over here if you want proof; though you might find this here wall a bit rough on your face, for I could only stomach doing thee from behind.' His friends snorted and patted his back, and now he wore a smug expression. Yet it slipped from his face when she crossed the road.

Halting, her barely covered chest almost touching his, she gazed up from beneath her lashes. 'That right, lad? You saying I've gorra face like the back end of a horse?'

The group fell silent, mouths dropping open when she cocked an eyebrow at their friend then eased down the neck of her dress. Each emitted a whistle – including the man before her. She cupped his quickly swelling crotch, smiling inwardly when he groaned low in his throat.

'Still prefer doing me from behind, would you?' She drew his eager hands to her breasts. 'You'd not like to press your face into these, then, nay?'

Seemingly oblivious of his grinning friends, he squeezed and tweaked her nipples, his breathing heavy. 'Nay, lass, I didn't mean what I said. You're a fine figure of a woman. By God, you are that.'

She smiled in satisfaction at his simpering tone. Men were such fools. They didn't understand the power women had over them, didn't know when they were being played once their pricks took over. She rubbed his solid member, smile deepening at his gruff moan. Then in one sharp movement, she closed her hand and squeezed hard. The man yelped, eyes widening in pain and confusion.

'For your information, I'm norra streetwalker, you shovel of shit. Give me one good reason why I shouldn't rip this sorry excuse forra prick off.'

The stunned group loomed, faces twisting in anger, but when she tightened her grip and the man whimpered to them to back off, they stepped away.

'Now, then, lovey, what d'you say? One little word and tha might still be able to use it. Otherwise . . .' She squeezed again and grinned when he squealed.

'Sorry! I'm bleedin' sorry! Leave go!'

She released him and he fell to his knees. As his friends crowded around him, she readjusted her dress and walked away. Within seconds, she'd dissolved into the misty night. She smiled as the men's heavy footsteps, shouts and curses filled the air. The maze of dark alleys and passageways swallowed a body in the blink of an eye; they wouldn't get to exact revenge for their friend.

Her lip curled in distaste. No one disrespected her and got away with it. No one. That sorry excuse she'd left snivelling in the gutter, and many she'd encountered over the years, didn't have a clue. They didn't know how to treat a woman, nor satisfy one. Not like the man she was meeting. Now *he* knew how to show a lass a good time. Her skin tingled in anticipation. No man would ever match up to him.

Turning into Deansgate, she quickened her step. She patted the package beneath the folds of her skirts and smiled, knowing he'd be pleased. It was getting harder to sneak away the gifts but she'd continue to. Keeping her man happy was all that mattered. For him, she'd do anything.

Upon reaching the familiar meeting place, she smoothed her hair with shaking hands. Then, taking a deep breath, she slipped inside Nellie's inn.

Her gaze immediately went to the dim recess and at the sight of the slumped figure, her heart leapt. She sat on the hard bench with a giggle. 'By, I've missed thee summat rotten.'

Nursing a tankard, eyebrows knotted in a black frown, Joseph ignored the hand she tried to place in his and downed the rest of his ale. He slammed the tankard on to the plain-topped table and she jumped to her feet.

'I'll fetch you another.'

As she reached for the empty jar, he grabbed her wrist. 'Leave that and sit down.'

'But I want one meself. I'll not be—'

'I said leave the bugger!'

Flinching, she lowered herself beside him. 'What's wrong? Is it summat I've done? Did I keep thee waiting? Sorry if I did, lad. It were that daft daughter of my neighbour's again. Seven sharp, I told her to come round to keep an eye on t' children but she—'

'You don't half bore the liver out of me at times. No wonder that husband of yourn snuffed it years ago; you probably bored the bugger to death. Shut tha mouth for one minute and listen. There's summat I want you to do.'

Swallowing the pain his words brought, she produced the package, desperate to please him. 'I've fetched you this, love, and I paid your rent.' She placed the meat on the table then ran a hand up his chest. 'Now, what d'you want my help with? Just say the word, lad. I'll do owt you want, you know that.'

'Shift your hand, for Christ's sake. You're like a bitch on heat.'

The sharp slap brought tears to her eyes. She held up her hands. 'All right, I'm sorry.'

'Don't try me, girl, for I'm not in no mood for it. I've had a bellyful today. Just sit there and shut your trap.'

She lowered her eyes to the earth-packed floor.

'How long have we been meeting, now?'

His question surprised her. 'Three or four months, in't it, love? Aye, 'bout that, yeah.' She nodded slowly, as though contemplating her answer, but knew exactly how long, down to the day. Their meetings were precious. As far as she was concerned, life held little meaning before them.

She'd first caught his eye at Ma Thompson's when fetching a jug of ale for her father; she'd seen him once or twice in the row but they hadn't spoken until that night. He'd remarked on her hair's lovely colour and she'd blushed in delight, instantly drawn to the rugged miner.

Ten minutes later, she'd been on her hands and knees in a field with her skirts over her head. When Joseph, trousers around his ankles, collapsed across her back, she'd known he was the man for her. She'd never felt so wanted, fulfilled.

Their meetings continued at Nellie's following the trouble at Spring Row, but she didn't mind the tramp to Deansgate. She'd walk to earth's ends to be with him.

'Aye. Suppose it is a few months.' He shot her a sidelong glance. 'You said you'd do owt I wanted just now, didn't you?' At her eager nod, he added, 'I've had a right day of it. Our Alice's lass spotted Sally this morning in t' market.'

Her stomach lurched. She knew it! Ivy's face, earlier, had said it all; she *knew* she'd been right! She also knew, however, that Joseph couldn't know. If he discovered she'd suspected Sally of leaving hours ago and did nothing, he'd ... Well, Lord knew. She wasn't taking any chances.

'That right, lad?'

'Well, the lass fair described her exactly but . . . Oh, I don't know.' His tankard rattled as he banged the tabletop. 'Either that gormless cow's mistaken or Sally's cleverer than I thought.'

'Why, were it not her, then?'

'I don't know, do I? That's what I'm trying to tell you,' he snapped. 'I pelted down to the train station and questioned the master, and he said he'd had a run-in with someone what sounded like her, but—'

'Station? I thought the young 'un saw her in t' market?' Her words melted when he turned slowly to face her. 'I'm sorry, I didn't mean to interrupt. Ignore me, love.'

Nostrils flared, he ground out, 'He said it sounded like her but that she'd had a ruddy great dog with her; attacked him, it did, by all accounts. We've never had no mutt.

'I were all for forgetting the whole thing till I spoke to Bailey, earlier. Said he'd seen her not long since with that owd bitch from next door to us, on her way to catch the carrier's cart. She told him some cock and bull tale of how she were going to our Alice's to beg my forgiveness.'

Nancy's excitement mounted but she kept her voice even. 'Did you ask him if it were right? George Turner, I mean.'

'Well, of course I did. The varmint looked me straight in t' eye and swore blind he'd not seen hide nor hair of her.' He rubbed his stubbled chin. 'I don't know what's afoot, if she's still at Spring Row or no, but believe me, I'll find out.'

When he lapsed into silence, she stared into the depths of the open fire beside them. If Sally *had* gone – *and pray God she has,* she inwardly pleaded – Joseph would be hers. She didn't know his wife but from what he'd said, she sounded like a right uppity little bitch. He clearly didn't care a fig for her – he'd proven that by asking Nancy back to his cottage on their first meeting, even though his wife was home, she recalled with amusement.

Though tempted, she'd suggested the nearest farmer's field. Her father's cottage had been too close for comfort. The old man might get on her nerves at times but when all was said and done, she loved the bugger and wouldn't do anything to bring shame upon him if she could help it.

Nancy picked her words carefully. 'Would it matter if she has scarpered, for you said yourself she means nowt to thee? Lord, the bitch had been thieving off you, hadn't she? Aye, from what you've told me, you're well shot of her.'

Why he'd even married the girl was a mystery. She'd questioned him months ago but he'd become angry and told her to keep her snout out.

It didn't matter, now, she thought happily. *With her out of the picture, he'll finally be mine for the taking.*

When he didn't respond, she ran tentative fingers along his strong jaw and down his neck. Emboldened when he didn't slap her away, she slipped her hand inside his shirt and stroked his thick chest hair.

'So long as you have me, you'll never need another woman,' she purred. She leaned in, pressed her breasts against him and circled his earlobe with her tongue. Her heart swelled when her skirts lifted. He squeezed the inside of her thigh and she moaned.

'I'll kill her when I get my hands on her. *They'll* get what's coming to them, an' all. Harbouring that whore's going to cost them,' he growled against her lips.

'Who, the Morgans?'

'Aye.' Wrenching down her dress, he buried his face in her breasts. He drew an erect nipple into his mouth then rolled and flicked his tongue over the glistening peak. When he raised his head, his next words were thick with menace: 'And you're going to help me.'

Chapter 10

IT WASN'T UNTIL the following Monday that Sally managed to get Grace to herself. She'd tried to find a moment to have a private word with her but there was never the right time. Due to inclement weather, Ed and Stan had hardly moved from home. When on occasion they did, Grace was either catching up on much-needed sleep or attending to Peggy.

The strained atmosphere between father and son hadn't intensified over the week but neither had it abated. There had been a particularly uncomfortable incident when, despite the temperature, only wind and rainfall accompanied it; Ed's prediction that it wouldn't snow proved correct.

He'd seemed to revel in mocking Stan, and she'd ached for her cousin as Ed's scathing remarks rang all morning. Stan's silence paid off; eventually, Ed had stopped, much to her relief. The misery in her cousin's eyes was painful to witness and she'd been on the brink of telling her uncle to leave him alone.

Throughout, Grace sighed several times but, to Sally's bewilderment, said nothing. When Ed left the room, the look Stan threw – first at the door then at his mother – scared her. It held what she could only describe as utter contempt.

Now, sitting with Grace at the table and Shield, as usual, sprawled by her feet, she knew this was her chance. The men had left for work and Peggy was sleeping. Monday was washday and Grace would soon be too busy; she'd asked if Sally would help with washing Peggy's sheets a moment ago.

Having just fed the baby, she rubbed his back and breathed deeply. She'd rehearsed what to ask yet now the time had come, didn't know where to begin. To her surprise, Grace did it for her.

'So, how you liking it back in Manchester, love?'

'It's still rather strange but I'm very happy. Since being a child, I always prayed I'd see you again one day.'

'Ah, lass.'

She smiled when Grace leaned across and patted her knee, then continued hesitantly, 'Aunt Grace, may I ask you something?'

Nodding, her aunt reached for the teapot. Refilling their cups, she glanced up. 'Go on, lass. What's on your mind?'

'I wondered whether, well, whether I'm in the way. I don't want you to feel you must have me here because I'm your niece.' When Grace made to protest, she added, 'Perhaps you all have enough worries without the burden of a runaway wife and newborn adding to them.'

'You've noticed, then?' She sighed when Sally lowered her gaze. 'Aye, course you have. You'd have to be blind not.'

'Aunt Grace, I—'

'Don't be embarrassed, lass, it's not your fault. Ed and Stan . . .' Raising dull eyes to the damp-patched ceiling, she shook her head. 'Eeh, where do I start?'

'What's wrong, Aunt Grace? Why are they so . . . cold towards one another?'

'Our Stan, poor lad. He don't bother no more, not like when he were younger, and who could blame him? All his life he's strived for Ed's love. I think he accepted . . . well, that it weren't to be. But it's not Ed's fault, it's not, lass. It's hard for him, an' all. He tried in t' beginning but . . .'

She fell silent and foreboding filled Sally. Something unpleasant was coming, she could feel it. Moments later, Grace proved her right.

'You see, I'm the cause, what I did . . . And Ed, he loved me so vowed to try and forget. Course, he couldn't. It were a constant reminder when I began to show.'

Sally reached for her hand. 'Are you saying Uncle Ed isn't Stan's father? Is that what you're trying to say?'

'I . . . I were expecting afore we married.' Her words were barely audible and Sally had to lean in. 'He's a good man, your uncle, a good man. I don't deserve him. My actions ruined him – ruined our marriage afore it began.

'You could've knocked me down with a feather last week when he invited me to join him in that pie supper. The way he spoke . . . it's the nicest I've heard forra long, long time. Whether it were because you were there, or because he felt sorry for me after hearing of Rose, I don't know. Either way, it were lovely.'

Sally laid the baby in the basket and knelt beside Grace. 'Oh, please don't cry.' As she wrapped her arms around her aunt, her mind spun.

Whatever she'd expected, this certainly wasn't it; although it made everything clear. What on earth she was to do, she didn't know. She'd sworn to herself that whatever the problem, she'd do her best to help. How in the world could she, with something as deeply rooted as this?

'I'm sorry, love, I shouldn't have told thee. What must you think of me?'

'Please, don't think that. You don't have to explain yourself to me. I'd never judge you, never. You're my aunt and I love you. I love all of you.'

'He don't know, lass. Our Stan don't know. He's asked me time and again why Ed's the way he is with him, but I can't tell him. He can't know the truth, he can't. Please, don't say owt to him. He'd hate me.'

'I'd never say anything if you didn't want me to. It's not my place.' She frowned as a thought occurred. 'Did this cause your rift with my mother? Was she . . . ashamed of you?'

Grace answered with a moan, and Sally sighed. She *knew* the cause must have been serious.

She'd longed to know the truth, yet now felt nothing but heavy sadness. All those wasted years! All she and her mother suffered in that awful place because of one woman's mistake and another's inability to forgive.

Her aunt, too, had suffered, that was clear. She also understood her uncle's pain. Then there was poor, sweet Stan. Through no fault of his, what had he gone through all his life? What an utter waste. It was all so sad.

'I'm sorry, for both you and my mother, that you were unable to be reconciled. She must have felt very strongly about your actions. However, I don't. Your past doesn't change my feelings for you. You're the nearest thing I have to a mother, now, and I promise, if there is anything I can do to help, I will.'

Grace's shoulders heaved with sobs. 'Oh, lass, you don't understand. What I did . . . It were wicked, *wicked*!'

'I do. I understand you made a mistake. No one is perfect; we all do things we later regret. Don't torture yourself any longer. It's the future that matters. I don't want to lose you a second time. We have the rest of our lives to get to know each other again, to be there for one another. Please, wipe your tears. I hate seeing you upset.'

For an age, Grace stared back through pain-filled eyes, then nodded. 'I don't deserve your kindness, nor deserve you for a niece. By, I don't that.' She caressed her cheek. 'Eeh, I do love you, lass.'

Sally kissed her brow. 'And I you. Now, let's have that tea.' After passing Grace her cup, she took a sip from her own. 'Aye, we'll have a sup then get on with that washing,' she informed her in perfect imitation of her strong Lancashire accent. 'Them sheets won't wash their rotten selfs.'

Her aunt spluttered on her tea, chuckling, and Sally smiled, relieved that the tension had passed. She'd do her best to help heal her lovely family. How, she had no idea, but she had plenty of time to try. She wasn't going anywhere. These were her only relations in the world. She wanted a different childhood for her son, filled with people who loved him. She'd sooner die than have him suffer a second of what she had as a child.

Her mother's smile swam across her mind. *Why, Mam?* she pondered. *Was it impossible to forgive the sister you adored one mistake? Was the shame of an illegitimate child really too much to bear?* She pushed the upsetting thoughts away. As she'd told Grace, there was no point dwelling on the past. The future mattered and she was determined to make it a happy one.

Peering at the band on her finger, she was thankful Ivy had persuaded her to keep it. The money from the eaves wouldn't last for ever. She'd given a fair chunk towards Shaun's carpentry and had enough to pay her keep for several weeks, but what then? She couldn't live here on charity; her family were barely scraping by as it was.

To remain and help them, as she desperately wanted, there was but one solution. She'd have to find employment.

Several hours later, the washing was billowing in the wind in the tiny backyard. Having brewed fresh tea, Grace placed a plate of bread on the table. A pot of jam, which Sally treated her to yesterday, stood alongside. Backs and arms aching, they sat gratefully.

'Aunt Grace, where could I secure a position? My money won't last for ever.'

Grace popped bread in her mouth and licked raspberry stickiness from her fingers. Since the revelation, her whole demeanour had changed. Her eyes were less haunted, face smoother, as though the worry lines had melted. It seemed the sheets were not all Sally had helped wash; she'd cleansed Grace's tortured mind of bad memories, too.

'Depends, lass. What were you thinking of?'

Sally thought for a moment. Along with the workhouse girls, she'd learned female duties such as sewing but not much else. She'd have to take whatever was available.

'I'll do anything, scrub floors if I must. I'm not proud.'

'I dare say you'll find summat if you're that willing. Course, there's the mills. I'll bet they're allus looking for spinners and such. Jonathan will be all right. I'll gladly watch him if you get taken on.' She smiled at him. 'He's good as gold and I'm in all day with our Peggy, anyroad.

All you'd need do is call in your dinner break and give him his feed.'

Sally brightened. 'Yes, that would work. Are you certain you wouldn't be taking too much on, what with caring for Peggy?'

'Nay, love, it'll give me summat to do. The lass sleeps a lot. I'm only rattling round fretting about her all day. The babby would take my mind off it.'

'Well, if you're sure, I'll look around. I must admit, I'm nervous. I've never had a job. What if I find I'm not good at anything?'

'What, a clever lass like thee? Whatever you find, you'll take to it like a fish to water. Now, finish your tea and go look. Flash one of them bonny smiles of yourn, be polite, and they'll snap you up. You'd best leave the dog here, mind. He might put folk off.'

Filled with hope at Grace's encouragement, she donned her shawl and set off.

The streets were quiet; those lucky to be in employment were toiling in the many factories. Mainly, she encountered beshawled housewives buying in the evening meal, and sullen-faced men on street corners, another morning's search for work having proved futile.

Other men squatted on pavements tossing coppers, their angry curses when their gambling didn't go in their favour ringing through the frosty November air. Occasionally, a policeman appeared up ahead and the groups would scoop coins into flat caps and quickly disperse, only to re-form in the next street.

Her small smile never wavered as she passed along. Since arriving, her fears had diminished considerably. No one knew of her whereabouts besides Ivy, and she knew hell would freeze before her friend revealed them. Feeling worry-free, sure that Joseph wouldn't suddenly appear as she'd often feared since escaping, was wonderful.

An enormous, seven-storey cotton mill came into view as she turned into Bradford Road. Glancing skyward at the columns of smoke streaming from its tall chimneys, she shuddered. Confinement within those sweltering death traps filled her with dread, but she needed money. Thousands upon thousands endured it to feed their families and keep a roof over their heads. She must try.

Approaching the gates, she read the sign and nodded determinedly. Brunswick Mill. With luck, she'd be an employee before the day was through.

'Get off me, you swine! Get *off* me!'

Sally heard the furious voice before seeing the speaker. Squinting towards the mill, she frowned when two figures emerged. One held the other by the scruff of the neck and as they drew nearer, she gasped to see that the shorter was a young woman. The man towering above dragged her, kicking and cursing, to the gates.

'You sod, yer! Make you feel big, does it, bullying lasses?'

His face twisted in a snarl and Sally stepped hastily aside when he hauled open the gates. With an almighty shove, he sent the woman flying into the gutter by Sally's feet and slammed the gates shut.

'Now bugger off, you idle bitch. There's wenches aplenty what will fill your place – hard-working wenches at that.'

The woman's eyes blazed. 'Idle? *Idle?* I'm one of the best spinners in that place and you know it. You've lied through your rotten teeth to get me out 'cause I told you where to go when you tried it on, you dirty swine, yer. Can't keep your filthy hands to yourself, can you?

Aye, well, you can shove your job where the sun don't reach! I'd sooner starve in t' gutter than you touch me.'

Sally, already horrified by the brutal treatment, could hold back no longer. She shook her head at the smirking man in disgust. 'Is this true? You've dismissed this woman for *that*?'

With a curl of his lip, he looked her up and down. 'And what the bugger's it to do with thee? Go on, clear off the pair of you, afore I fetch a constable.' He threw the last words over his shoulder and strode away.

She watched his retreating back in disbelief then turned to the woman, a pretty thing with dark hair and an elfin face, sitting on the flagstones. 'Disgraceful! He cannot get away with that, surely?'

Chuckling, she allowed Sally to assist her up. 'By gum, lass, you don't know the way of things reet well, d'you? Course he'll get a-bloody-way with it. Anyroad, I'm not mithered. I'm glad to be free of that place; least I'll not have that sod's roving hands to fight off any more.'

Sally helped her brush dirt from her skirt and shawl, thankful she'd witnessed the incident before enquiring for a position. She certainly didn't want to work in environments like that, with people like him.

'I came seeking employment. I'm glad I didn't get the chance, now. Are you all right?' she asked when the woman winced and rubbed the arm that had taken the brunt of the fall.

'Aye, tough as owd leather, me. Ta for speaking out for me. What's your name?'

'Sally Swann. You?'

The woman shook the proffered hand warmly. 'Maggie Benson. Nice to meet thee, lass.'

A sigh chased away Sally's smile. 'I don't know what I'm to do. I'd pinned my hopes on finding work there.'

She frowned, realising Maggie was now in the same position. 'What about you? Will you find alternative employment?'

Maggie bit her lip. 'I hope so. I'm a widow with two young 'uns to feed. Mam helps out but we'll not manage with no wage coming in.' She glanced up and down the street. 'I'd best get looking. Take care, Sally, and good luck to you, lass. I hope you find summat. 'Ere, if you're ever passing, I live at Davies Street, number thirty-two. You'd be welcome any time.'

'Thank you, Maggie, that's very kind. Good luck.'

She watched her hurry down the road and hoped fervently that Maggie would find something soon. She didn't deserve dismissal because that awful man couldn't keep his hands to himself. Life was so unfair.

She turned and retraced her steps. She'd walked no further than a hundred yards when snow began to fall. Her first thought was Stan. He'd been right, after all – albeit a few days out. Drawing her threadbare shawl over her head, Sally trudged on.

She glanced in every shop window for the small cards placed when staff were needed, but each proved empty. Halting at the end of the street, she shivered and peered about uncertainly. People rushed in all directions, heads lowered against the flakes spiralling from the yellow-tinged sky, footsteps muffled as flags and cobbles disappeared beneath a blanket of white.

Maybe she should call it a day, she thought reluctantly, heart heavy with disappointment. She couldn't stay out in this much longer. Her face was stinging, fingers and toes numb. She'd have to try tomorrow. And the day after, and the day after that if necessary. No matter what, she *would* find work.

The promise of hot tea and a hearty fire urging her, she turned for Grace's. As she crossed the road, a girl by a string of shops caught her eye. Drawing level, Sally watched curiously as she continued to peer through a pawnbroker's window. However, she wasn't admiring the array of goods on sale but staring at a white card.

Her stomach lurched. They must have a position, yet she'd spotted it too late. This girl, no older than fifteen, would surely leap at the chance of shop-work rather than a mill.

The girl squinted at the scrawled words a moment longer. Then to Sally's surprise, she snorted, muttered, 'Aye, not bloomin' likely!' and walked away.

Frowning, she hurried to the sign. Her workhouse education was limited, to say the least, but she could read a little. She traced a finger across the cold glass:

Seeking companion for elderly lady
Must have lots of patience
Apply within to Miss Sharp

Sally read it again. After the third attempt, she still hadn't deciphered what she must have 'lots of'. Dicksy had taught her many big words, whose spoken meaning she understood. Reading them was another matter.

She read the tricky word out loud, prodding each letter: 'P–a–t–i–e–n–c–e.' Still none the wiser, she shrugged, excitement stirring. Miss Sharp would surely tell her what she required.

She lifted her face to the snow-filled sky. 'Please, Lord, let me get this position,' she whispered. Pushing the girl's words from her mind, she turned the brass knob.

A bell tinkled as she entered and a willowy figure, mousy-brown hair bound in a neat bun, emerged through a door behind the counter. Her disarming smile immediately put Sally at ease. Lowering her damp shawl, she stepped forward.

'May I help you, dear?'

Sally fought the urge to raise an eyebrow. The articulate tone contrasted sharply with how the majority of Manchester's inhabitants spoke. 'Are you Miss Sharp?'

'I'm Pru Sharp, yes.'

'The card in the window said apply within. Is the position still vacant?'

Pru's eyes widened. 'Indeed. Do you wish to apply?'

What was it Aunt Grace said? she thought quickly. *Flash a smile and be polite, that was it.*

'I'd be most grateful to be considered for the position, Miss Sharp, and believe that, given the opportunity, I would be a worthy employee. I would not cut corners or shirk my responsibilities. My full attention would be on the job in hand at all times. You'd receive complete dedication from me, I assure you. You have my word and my honour.'

Pru's lips twitched. 'Well. That was a mighty fine speech, Mrs . . . ?'

Sally flushed. Had she ruined her chances? Her tongue had run away with itself in her desperation to make a good impression. 'Swann. Sally Swann.'

'Well, Sally, you certainly have a way with words. You're not from around here, I presume?'

'I was born here. I have recently returned and am residing with my aunt—'

'And in order to pay your way, you're seeking employment?'

'Yes.'

'Agnes, my mother, requires constant care. However, the shop needs running and I cannot be in two places at once. She is bed-bound and hasn't left her room in many years.' Brow furrowing, Pru looked Sally up and down. 'The position would require lifting, to bathe and dress her and suchlike. Do you believe you are up to it? She's small but can be somewhat difficult when she chooses. You would need a lot of patience.'

Patience! *That* was what she'd need lots of. Her shoulders relaxed. Putting up with Joseph all those years was proof she had the patience of a saint. 'I'm very patient, Miss Sharp, and stronger than I look.'

'The position has been open for some time. That was how I knew you were not from these parts. You would not have enquired if you were.'

The girl in the street's scathing comment came back to Sally. She frowned curiously. 'I don't understand.'

Pru glanced to the ceiling. 'I'll be honest with you, Sally. My mother can be rather . . . fractious. Another young woman used to care for her. There was . . . an incident, shall we say, and afterwards . . . Well, I can see why people are reluctant to take the position.'

'Incident? What kind of incident?'

Dull banging sounded. They looked up in unison.

'What incident, Miss Sharp?' she repeated.

'Prudence? Prudence!'

At the gravelly voice from above, desperation flickered in Pru's eyes. 'I must see what she wants. So, dear? Are you up for the job?'

After a brief hesitation, Sally nodded. What choice had she? She needed the money. Besides, how bad could the old woman be?

'Good! That is good! I will see you tomorrow morning, nine o'clock sharp.' Hurrying out from behind the counter, Pru ushered her to the door. 'Goodbye, dear.'

'Wait, what about payment? What of my hours?'

'Prudence Sharp! Do you hear me?'

Her smile slipping as she glanced to the ceiling, Pru flapped a hand. 'Oh, we shall discuss the necessary details tomorrow. Now, I really must go.' She turned on her heel and disappeared inside the shop.

Sally stared in bewilderment at the closed door then turned for home. Her emotions were conflicting. On the one hand, she was elated to find work so quickly, yet a worm of doubt was growing. What had occurred between the elderly lady and her previous employee? She'd ask Grace. Miss Sharp said most knew of the 'incident'; surely her aunt had heard?

By the time she reached the entry, she'd all but dismissed her misgivings. Whatever had happened, she wouldn't let it put her off. She was just thankful she'd soon be bringing in a wage. Besides, at least she wouldn't be working in the factories, fighting off the advances of men like him at Brunswick Mill.

She said a private prayer that Maggie Benson would manage to find another position. She'd ask Grace for directions to Davies Street and visit her on her first day off. Perhaps they could become friends.

Feeling brighter about the future than she had in a long time, Sally hurried across the snow-covered cobbles with a happy sigh.

She couldn't wait to tell her aunt the good news.

Ivy Morgan flopped into a chair and wiped her brow with the back of her hand. Peering at the wooden rack above the fire festooned with sheets and clothes, she pulled a face and reached for the teapot. She hated

Mondays with a passion. The scrubbing, wringing and heavy lifting played havoc with her ageing bones.

She glanced at the clock, swore under her breath and gulped down her tea. The men would be home shortly and here she was sitting on her backside, with the tin bath to fill and evening meal to prepare.

After filling at the well and boiling on the fire pan after pan of water for the bath, she dragged herself to a cupboard, selected vegetables and returned to the table, collecting a knife on the way. Deft hands peeled and chopped and in no time the veg was bubbling away, adding to the steam from the drying clothes and bath.

The stuffy room became too much. She refilled her cup, opened the cottage door and, leaning against the frame, let the breeze soothe her flushed cheeks.

Snow had at last ceased and the pure white landscape was breathtaking. Bright domes of hills looked magical, like summer clouds that had fallen from the sky. It had even transformed the row from grubby to beautiful.

'Bugger it! God-awful snow.'

Ivy glanced to her left and watched Martha Smith, slipping and sliding, in amusement. ''Ere, Martha. Watch your bleedin' step, wench. Don't you go falling and showing the row your dimples.'

Martha's head shot up, making her wobble dangerously. Round face beetroot-red, she stretched out her arms to steady herself then shook a beefy fist. 'You swine, yer! Nearly went arse over elbow, then.'

Ivy burst out laughing and Martha, grinning, shuffled on her way.

Ivy had been dreading seeing her but Martha had been surprisingly understanding yesterday. She'd tried making eye contact several times at chapel but Ivy had looked away. When service was over, she'd made a beeline for her outside but Ivy quickly struck up conversation with another neighbour, and Martha hadn't approached. However, Ivy had arrived home to find her waiting at the gate.

Martha's expression, soft with friendliness, had thrown her, and when she invited Ivy to her cottage for a sup of tea, she had been unable to refuse.

She was glad she hadn't. The hour spent in Martha's spotless kitchen was pleasant. Over tea, they had a good natter. Conversation had eventually swung to the Godens and though Ivy didn't disclose anything Sally told her in confidence, she did admit guilt at not noticing what was going on – even after Martha voiced her concerns.

Martha had told her not to be daft. 'You don't expect it on your own doorstep, wench. Least she's out of it, now, thanks to thee. You gave her the means and strength to leave the divil.'

Curious, Ivy had asked how she'd guessed the poor woman's plight when she herself had had no idea. Martha confided that she had suffered like Sally during her first marriage.

'My Reg's my second husband,' she'd revealed of the local mole catcher. 'Wed thirty-odd year we've been and I couldn't be happier, but me first 'un . . . He were an evil blighter like yon Joseph,' she'd murmured. 'I noticed the signs, for I'd been in t' same boat meself.'

It's queer how folk look in a different light, Ivy mused now, returning to the kitchen. Since their chat, they were like old friends.

The door opening pulled her from her thoughts and she smiled at Arthur, Tommy and Shaun. Weary faces smiled back, coal-blackened skin glistening in the firelight.

'Get washed while I see to the grub,' she instructed.

Behind a length of curtain, the bath stood waiting. Arthur trooped off first to scrub his tired body and she dished out the meal. Her hand stilled, however, when she glimpsed Tommy's drawn face as he headed for the stairs.

Her son wasn't himself. Usually he lit up a room. Even after a full shift he'd return with a cheery smile, would chase her around the kitchen for a kiss while she shouted at him to 'Bugger off covered in that muck!' But for days he'd been subdued, as though the worries of the world were on his mind.

Midway through the meal, she tackled him. 'You all right, Tommy lad?'

'Aye, Mam.'

'You've been morose these past days. You crossed swords with Dolly, or summat?'

Frowning, he lowered his gaze. 'Nay, why?'

'Well, when you meet her of a Sunday, you're usually out all day but you were gone no more than an hour yesterday. Frightened the bloody life from me, tha did, when I returned from Martha's and found you sat here.'

'Dolly were snuffly. We cut our walk short so her cowd didn't worsen.'

He speared a potato with his fork and resumed his meal and she let the matter drop. Maybe she was reading into things that were not there. She'd had a niggling suspicion what – or more to the point, who – had caused this sudden change in him and had tried dismissing it, hoping to God she was wrong.

Her mind drifted to the morning Sally left. After waking, she'd headed for the kitchen but halfway down the stairs was taken aback to see Sally and Tommy at the table.

He'd smiled like he did as a child when caught doing something he shouldn't. Ivy asked why he was up so early and he'd said he couldn't sleep. Sally explained she'd wanted to repay Ivy's kindness, had motioned to the pan of porridge, and their explanations placated her. However, her unease returned when she'd mentioned Sally's upcoming departure.

Tommy's head had shot up. 'You're leaving today?' At Sally's nod, his smile quickly returned.

Ivy had watched the exchange through narrowed eyes. She knew her son too well, especially when he smiled like that. Forced. *What went on before I wakened?* she'd wondered. She'd sensed something between them, some . . . spark. And if she was honest, she didn't like it.

She did feel a lot for Sally, and the cottage seemed empty without her and the child. Nevertheless, Sally was a married woman. She didn't want her Tommy mixed up in something like that; particularly when the other man was as unstable as Joseph Goden.

Absently pushing food around her plate, she felt, for the first time, relief that Sally had left. But it was tinged with guilt and she offered up yet another silent prayer that she was safe and well. The lass deserved happiness, by God she did. She just hoped that aunt of hers was looking after them.

Sighing, Ivy pushed the youngsters from her mind. Sally was gone. It was pointless fretting over what might be her imagination.

After mopping up gravy with a hunk of crust then popping it into his mouth, Arthur pushed away his plate and burped appreciatively. 'Eeh. Lovely, that were.'

She reached for the teapot. 'Bugger these pots, I'll wash them later. You want another sup?'

'Aye.' He moved to his fireside chair and reached for his clay pipe on the mantel. After pressing paper-thin slices from a stick of tobacco into the bowl, he held the slender stem between his lips, took a spill from a pot by the hearth and lit it. As he puffed, he glanced at her. Despite her smile, his brow furrowed. 'You still fretting over that lass?'

She passed him his cup. 'Aye, summat like that.'

'Wench, she's shot of Goden. He's never showed his face again at Spring Row and you said yourself, he don't know she even has an aunt, so she's no worries there. And she promised to return if she had no joy in Ancoats, didn't she, so stop fretting.

'Anyroad, anyone what can stand up to the preacher as you said she did can more than take care of theirself! I bet the owd swine got the shock of his life.'

Shaun joined in his laughter. 'Aye, good on her! I dread crossing his path. He's allus saying I'm destined for hell for not attending chapel.'

Ivy flashed him a crooked smile then glanced at Tommy. He looked away, and unease gnawed again. Whenever anyone mentioned Sally, he reacted the same way. She *knew* she'd been right; it was written all over his face. Well, this needed nipping in the bud. 'Tommy, why don't you call on Dolly the morrow after work, ask her to come for her dinner on Saturday?'

Every face showed surprise. All knew she wasn't keen when Tommy began walking out with the dairymaid last year. She'd voiced often that the lass was too flighty for her liking; she smiled too much; her laugh set Ivy's teeth on edge . . .

Ivy and her son stared at each other. After a long moment, he nodded. Then he rose and left the room.

Tommy threw himself on to his bed. His father's bemused voice, asking Ivy what was wrong with their son, drifted up and when she answered that he was probably just tired, heat crept over Tommy's face.

She knew exactly what ailed him. He'd seen it in her eyes – that same knowing look when she found him and Sally alone. Any grain of hope she *didn't* suspect, she'd shattered when suggesting he ask Dolly to dinner. She'd never encouraged their courtship, had certainly not invited her round before.

He squeezed his eyes shut. His father's question was a good one – what *was* wrong with him? He didn't know himself. It was like a ten-ton weight bearing down on his chest, the ache inside like an itch he couldn't scratch. A yearning for . . . something . . . wouldn't leave him but he couldn't grasp what it was or how to make it better or go away.

He peered at his calloused palms and, as he'd done a hundred times, thought back to when they held Sally. The ache intensified; he could almost feel her softness. He scrambled from the bed. He needed to get out of this stifling cottage before he went raving mad.

When he bounded downstairs, everyone looked up in surprise. Averting his eyes, he snatched up his jacket and threw it on.

'Where's tha going at this time, and in this weather? It's bleedin' perishing out there.'

'Out. I need some air.' Before his mother could question him further, he swung the door shut behind him.

Stars peppered the blue-black sky and the row held a stillness that soothed his jumbled mind. Golden fire and candlelight from cottage windows slowly faded as he walked on through the deserted night.

A low stone wall stood out against the darkness. He brushed off snow with his sleeve and sat down. Silence enveloped him and digging his hands into his trouser pockets, he closed his eyes. Sharp air burned with each breath but he relished it; it was a welcome relief to the pain in his heart.

What had come over him? What switch had been triggered in his brain to turn him from the happy-go-lucky chap into this snappy, distracted one who could think of nothing but the married woman no longer here? At the thought of her, his stomach bounced and he sighed in frustration. This wasn't like him. No woman had ever had this effect upon him – not even Dolly, he admitted.

An open face framed by corn-coloured hair floated across his mind. He smiled sadly. A fine-looking, lovable woman, was his Dolly. Creamy skin with its dusting of freckles lent her an almost childlike appearance. But her plump body, from what he'd felt, was definitely that of a woman.

He allowed his thoughts to wander. Her soft buttocks, which she sometimes let him squeeze when they were alone by the river, and her hips, which swayed when she walked, made his hands itch for her. Then there was her generous bust, like overripe melons awaiting discovery, which pressed against him when they kissed. And yet . . .

He heaved a sigh. Despite his carnal desire, despite her cheery disposition and saucy laughter, he'd never felt that . . . *something*, that special spark. The spark that hit him like a thunderbolt the other night when gazing upon Sally in the moonlight.

He hadn't realised something was missing until he felt it with Sally. Never had his heart jolted so violently. Never had his loins burned with a desire that engulfed him. Never had anyone so completely, hopelessly, consumed him.

He wasn't a vain man but was aware what impact he had on the opposite sex. He'd had his pick of

Breightmet's lasses but Dolly's sunny personality and cheeky ways hooked him. She was full of life, a breath of fresh air to be around after being holed in the ground's inky confines with sweaty men all week.

His mind drifted to the day before and their usual weekly stroll by the river. *The first afternoon with her he'd had to drag himself to.* He hadn't lied to his mother; Dolly *had* been snuffly. But she'd insisted she was fine, that nothing would keep her from seeing him. He'd used her slight cold, however, as a means of cutting the meeting short.

Picturing her blue eyes deep with hurt at his words, he cringed. Hardly able to keep the edge from his voice, he'd told her she'd be better off going home, had almost sighed in relief when she eventually agreed. Conversation was stilted on the walk back, and when they reached her door his lips barely touched her cheek before he strode away.

Shaking his head to dispel the guilty thoughts, he rose and paced up and down, unseeing. He was a simple fellow, always had been. As long as he had a meal in his belly and clothes on his back, he was happy. All he wanted in life was for he and his loved ones to be content and one day to raise a healthy family of his own. He'd had his future mapped out but now, his whole world had turned on its head.

What was he to do? How could he visit Dolly tomorrow, sit with her at dinner on Saturday, make small talk, act like all was well? How could he pretend nothing had changed, that one day, as they both thought inevitable, they would wed? How could he sign away his life to someone who stood beside him in the flesh yet came second to the one in his heart?

He couldn't do it. Marriage was for ever and he wouldn't live a lie. He didn't deserve to spend the rest of his days unhappy and, more importantly, neither did Dolly.

That he was considering this! Dolly, his Dolly . . . He'd never imagined his feelings could so rapidly change because of another woman – one he'd spent just a few hours alone with, at that. And what of Sally? She was miles away, bound for life to a husband a few cows short of a herd. And for all he knew, she might have already forgotten him.

Chest constricting at the possibility, he slapped the wall. She'd shown no indication she felt anything for him, except for pressing against him when she fainted. She'd clung to him, reached out when he laid her in the chair. But that was the workings of her fuddled mind, he realised with a jolt.

Say he did call it off with Dolly; what then? Track Sally down and declare his love? She'd either laugh in his face or ask when he was due back at the asylum.

He sat down and covered his face with his hands. How in God's name could he imagine she might feel the same?

Tightness in his chest returned at the prospect of never seeing her again, but with great effort he ignored it. For days, he'd pined for someone he could never have. He'd been so damn *foolish*. Relentless thoughts of her were even affecting work; he'd been yelled at down the pit today for not paying attention. He knew hardly anything about her, yet couldn't rid his mind of her.

She was like no one he'd ever met. He was constantly going over every word she'd uttered in that well-spoken voice, every little smile, how she'd looked up at him from beneath her lashes . . .

He rose and turned for home. This had to stop. He was acting like a lunatic. She'd flitted in and out of his life without knowing the impact she'd left on him and she never would. He *must* forget her.

Nearing Spring Row, his thoughts switched to the money beneath his mattress. He'd been flattered when she asked his help, had hidden it before the house stirred. It had felt like their little secret, something they shared that was just theirs, and he hadn't wanted anyone taking that away. Well, this fantasy ended now. Tomorrow, he'd inform his family of the generous gift.

Despite his inner turmoil, his mouth curved, picturing Shaun's face when he discovered he could finally shake off the pit's shackles. The lad had been born with a talent few people were lucky to have. He had no doubts he'd make a fine carpenter.

His heart swelled with brotherly pride. He might jest with Shaun but, deep down, loved him dearly. Recalling teasing him over taking a fancy to Sally, he smiled ruefully. He'd known the lad hadn't, was simply of an age where the mere mention of a lass had him blushing to the roots of his hair. The irony was almost laughable.

'Tommy Morgan? That you, lad?'

Peering through the darkness, he saw Ma Thompson at her cottage door. 'Aye, it's me. Everything all right?'

'Eeh, lad, am I glad to see thee. I thought I'd be stuck with him the night. Will you lend a favour to an owd woman and help him home? He come forra jug of ale, supped it in one then fell asleep and for the life of me, I can't waken the swine!'

'Who is it?'

'George Turner, lad. It's not the first time he's done this, nay it's not, but I were worried sending him on his way in this snow. With the state he's in, he'll finish up breaking his skull. He were fair skenning when he arrived. I'm buggered if I know how he managed to get here at all.'

In the kitchen, the inebriated customer sat sprawled across the tabletop, snoring loudly.

'George Turner, wake up, you bugger,' she called in his ear.

The carter moved not a muscle and Tommy smiled when the old woman turned red and shook the shoulder harder.

'I know tha hears me. Come on, gerrup. I want my bed.' She jumped when, suddenly, George sat bolt upright.

'Eeh, wench, that's the best offer I've had all year,' he slurred, snaking an arm around her waist.

Tommy burst out laughing and George grinned across at him.

'Get out of it, you bleeder, yer!' she shouted, swatting his hand. 'You might be sloshed but I'm not. Come on, out!'

'Come on, Mr Turner, I'll see you home.'

Chuckling, George lumbered to his feet and blew Ma Thompson a kiss. 'Goodnight, God bless, my lovely.'

'Oh, go on with you.' Clicking her tongue, she shooed him from the cottage. 'You will see him right inside, won't you, lad?' she asked Tommy as he took the carter's elbow and led him down the path.

'Aye. Goodnight.'

With a grateful smile, she bade him goodnight, rolled her eyes at George and closed the door.

Tommy steered him into the row. 'You had a lucky escape, there, Mr Turner. I thought she'd go at thee with the poker.'

'She's a feisty one. Just my kind of wench, lad, just my kind of wench. D'you know, I'd marry her the morrow if she'd let me. She'd make a fine wife.'

Tommy hid a smile, suspecting her greatest asset to the carter was her ale-brewing abilities.

After zigzagging to George's home, he helped him inside and lowered him into his fireside chair. 'Will you be all right, now, Mr Turner?'

'Aye, lad, aye. Eeh, you're a good 'un, Tommy.'

'It were no bother. Goodnight.'

'Goodnight, God bless. 'Ere, give a message to your mam, tell her I got the young Goden lass to Bolton in one piece, will you?' He peered up through one eye. 'Said she'd have my guts for garters if I didn't look after her. By, she's a fine woman, your mam, she is that.'

At the mention of Sally, Tommy swallowed hard. 'I'll tell her.'

'Aye, the lass will be all right with that big bugger she's took on. No one will try owt with him by her side.'

Halfway over the threshold, he turned. 'What's that?'

'Ruddy great mutt followed us on t' cart; took a shine to her, it had. She took it with her for protection, like.'

'Big black 'un?'

'Aye.'

He smiled. 'I don't believe it. Well, I'm glad to hear that. It did seem fond of her.'

'Aye, lad. And I hope that if it ever gets a grip of that divil, Goden, it rips his rotten throat out. Gorra grip of *me* Monday night last, he did, snarling like a rabid dog, wanting to know if I'd given the lass a lift. Aye, well, he went off with a flea in his ear, for I told him I'd not seen hide nor hair of her. Bloody fuming, he were. But he got nowt from me, he didn't that.'

As the grinning carter closed his eye, Tommy gripped the door frame. 'Joseph? He's been back to Spring Row?'

'I were on my way home from the Old Hare and Hounds – been forra jar to warm my bones – and he cornered me in t' lane.'

'But he can't ... How did he find out so soon?' Without waiting for a reply, he mumbled goodbye and left the cottage.

Sprinting through the snow towards home, his mind raced. How in hell had that madman found out so quickly? What if he discovered where she'd gone? It didn't bear thinking about. Was Sally aware he was on the prowl? Tommy very much doubted it; she probably felt safe, now. But if what George Turner said was right, she was anything but. She needed warning.

He couldn't just forget her. He couldn't switch off his feelings, had been foolish to think it. She'd possessed his very soul. He'd do anything to protect her.

No one would harm her again. Not if he could prevent it.

Chapter 11

PEERING THROUGH A speckled sliver of mirror propped on the mantel, Sally smoothed her hands over her hair. Deep-blue eyes stared back, her apprehension visible.

Soon, she would meet the old woman she was to care for. The old woman whose company she'd be in for most of each day. *The old woman who had struck her previous employee around the head with the poker, sending her hurtling into the open fire . . .*

She squared her shoulders. She wouldn't allow anyone to bully her, not again. Whatever the old woman tried, she'd put her in her place right away. No one would treat her as muck beneath their boot, man or woman. Those days were over.

'Eeh, I don't know whether you're brave or barmy. You'd not get me within ten feet of that vicious owd swine. You should take the dog; he could savage the blighter if she tried owt.'

Sally looked to Shield, stretched beside Peggy's bed. As though sensing it, he lifted his head and peered at her with one eye, and she smiled. 'He's taken a shine to Peggy, hasn't he?'

'Aye. He did nowt but whine when you went searching for work yesterday; nowt I said would shut him up. But our Peggy began coughing and no word of a lie, he stopped like that,' Grace marvelled, clicking her fingers. 'He lay by her bed and went to sleep. I couldn't believe it.'

'He's a good dog. I'm so glad I brought him along.'

Grace's smile mirrored hers, but it soon vanished. 'Are you sure you'll be all right, lass?'

'I'll be fine. I'll not deny that what you told me hasn't shocked me, and I can understand why no one applied for the position, but I need this job, Aunt Grace. Miss Sharp seemed amiable; she'll be there should I require assistance. I simply cannot believe a lady of that age could be so . . . well, so—'

'Ruddy wicked? Well do. That owd 'un might be knocking ninety but she ain't nobody's fool. Her legs are useless but her mind's as sharp as her tongue from what I've heard. And that's nowt on t' slaps she's not shy of dishing out. Aye, her legs are neither use nor ornament but there's nowt wrong with her arms. The lass what worked there last would vouch for that, I'm sure.'

'What do you think became of her?'

'Lord alone knows. As I said last night, after what that nasty swine did that day, the lass apparently flew from that shop like hell's hounds were at her heels. If you are sure about this, you be careful. Keep your eyes on her. If she does try owt, you get out of there, and fast.'

Sally heaved a sigh. She'd been so pleased to find work but upon relaying the news to Grace, her happiness had rapidly diminished. All evening, Grace had tried talking her out of it. Even Ed and Stan, when informed, frowned disapprovingly. But she was determined and told them so. Whatever this job entailed, she'd stick at it. If she could endure what she had at Joseph's hands, she could cope with anything.

At the thought of her uncle and Stan, hope stirred. Ed had rushed in from work the previous evening yelling, 'Rotten snow, I'm frozzen!' A smile touched Stan's lips and, catching his eye, Ed had looked away. Yet as he hurried to the fire, she'd spotted, much to her delight, the hint of a wry smile as he glanced once more at Stan.

It was a good sign, surely? she mused again. He hadn't conceded but neither did he berate the lad about his 'I told you so' smile.

'Now, you sure you're sure about this?'

She couldn't help chuckling. 'Yes, Aunt Grace, I'm sure.' She looked from the baby to the deathly pale girl in the bed. 'Are you sure *you'll* be all right managing with Peggy *and* Jonathan?'

'Course, lass. And this little lad will be sound; the feed he's just had will see him through to dinnertime. Anyroad, never mind fretting over us. Just you look after yourself today.'

It was lovely knowing people held concern for her welfare. She'd worried that her aunt's confession might cause awkwardness, but instead it had strengthened their bond. A woman's love and guidance were what she'd missed and she was so thankful to have found it in not only Ivy, but her aunt.

Grace and Ivy were much alike. They shared those motherly qualities; one felt cosseted by them. In other ways, they were oceans apart. Her aunt was soft, mild-mannered – the opposite of direct and self-assured Ivy. Yet Sally loved both wholeheartedly, knowing that she couldn't have chosen two kinder women to look to.

Her mother's and now Ivy's absence was gut-wrenching, but bearable thanks to Grace. On impulse, she kissed her cheek.

'Ay, lass, what were that in aid of?'

'For being you. I miss my mother and Mrs Morgan terribly but having you makes up for it. Thank you.'

'Our Rosie . . .' Grace had shed enough tears over the weekend to fill the River Irwell. Still, her bottom lip trembled. 'Eeh, you'll have me blubbing like a babby in a minute. Now go on, you'd best get going. See you at dinner, lass.'

Sally kissed her fingertips and brushed them down Jonathan's cheek. Eyes the exact colour as hers stared back from the haven of Grace's arms and she felt a pang at leaving him. Her touch lingered, then, bidding her aunt goodbye, she set off.

Pru's welcoming smile was a mixture of astonishment and relief.

'Sally, how lovely to see you! Come, sit down, dear. Would you like a cup of tea?'

'Good morning, Miss Sharp. Yes, thank you.' She removed her shawl and when Pru patted the stool beside hers, joined her behind the counter. 'How is your mother today?'

'Fine, dear, fine. I must admit, I didn't think I would see you today. You have surely heard by now . . . ?' Pru raised her eyes to the ceiling.

'Yes, but I need the money,' she answered honestly. 'I do so want to get along with your mother. I hope we can become friends.'

'I feel wretched for her previous employee. And despite what people believe, so does my mother. You are probably wondering what happened. The truth is, I really don't know. My mother said she suspected the woman of stealing, admitted lashing out but insisted the fall was not caused by her hand, that the poor woman tripped on the rug by the fire. I had no chance to ask or even help; she left in such a hurry and I have neither seen nor heard from her since.

'My mother gets angry, you see, stuck in her room day and night. She . . . loses her temper sometimes. However, I'm not defending her actions. No, no, I'm not. What happened was terrible, simply terrible.' Pru massaged her temples with her fingertips. 'You may have wondered why the position advertised was not for assistance in the shop; after all, why should one residing with their daughter require a companion?

'The truth is . . . It's difficult, Sally. I'm the only soul she has in the world. She's my mother and I love her, yet sometimes . . . sometimes, I cannot stand the sight of her.' Her eyes widened with guilt. 'Does that make me wicked?'

'No, no.'

'Thank you, truly. It is nice having someone to talk to. I get so very lonely at times. Look, after what you have heard . . . if you've changed your mind, I will understand and—' A thud from above cut short her speech.

Sally placed her cup on the counter. 'May I meet her now, Miss Sharp?'

'Yes, yes, of course. Thank you. You have no idea how grateful I am, dear.'

She followed Pru up the narrow stairs, heart thumping. Should she have bolted when she had the chance? What on earth was she walking into?

Pru paused at a closed door, whispering, 'You'll be fine.'

Following, Sally entered the musty-smelling room. Dust motes swirled in splinters of sunlight filtering through partially closed curtains. She glanced through the gloom to the unlit fire then looked away quickly. Yet at the sight of the poker propped by the bedside, her stomach turned. Mrs Sharp must use that to summon her daughter. *And as a handy weapon when the mood takes her* . . .

'Well, well, well. What have we here, Prudence?'

Sally froze, and saw Pru's back stiffen.

'Mother, this is Sally. She is here to—'

'I know why she is here. Oh, yes. I know why she is here, all right.'

'Mother, Sally is extremely nice. I'm sure once you get to know her—'

'I will be the judge of that. Go, get downstairs,' ordered the old woman with a jerk of her head. 'The shop will not run itself.'

Pru lowered her gaze. 'I shall leave you to it, Sally. Bang on the floor if you require anything.'

Sally had to fight the urge to grab her arm, beg her not to leave her with this acid-tongued woman. When the door clicked shut and Pru's footsteps faded, she raised her head.

Swamped in a tawny-coloured nightgown buttoned to the throat, Agnes Sharp sat propped against a mound of pillows. Despite the half-dozen thick blankets, Sally could see she was painfully thin; her small frame barely made an impression beneath. Tufts of snowy hair sprang in all directions and a crimson birthmark stained one side of her forehead, finishing below her temple.

Yet it was the piercing, almond-shaped eyes she couldn't tear her gaze from. They were the deepest, most vibrant green; so out of place in her face. Her sunken mouth, long thin nose and withered skin seemed to have dried up and died years ago, but those eyes . . . They burned with vitality.

'Are you a mute, girl?'

The question threw her. 'Am I . . . ? No, Mrs Sharp.'

'Are you dim-witted? A touch simple-minded?'

'I am not,' she answered indignantly. 'Are you?' The last words were out before she could stop them. 'Oh! I'm sorry, Mrs Sharp, I don't know why I said that!'

Agnes's mouth curled at the corners. 'Witty, very witty. Tell me, do you make a habit of being an insolent little bitch?'

Her mouth dropped open, anger flooding through her. She'd suffered enough intimidation in the past. She wouldn't stand for it again. Lifting her chin, she looked the old woman in the eye. 'No, Mrs Sharp, not always. Only when spoken to the same way, by people who ought to have been around long enough to have learned some manners.'

Agnes arched an eyebrow, mouth curving once more.

After a full minute of silence, Sally's fight drained away. Grace, and even Pru, had warned her; they'd told her what this horrible woman was like, yet she'd ruined everything by stooping to her level. She'd have to try the mills. She'd learned her lesson today, would keep her mouth closed if fortunate enough to find another position.

Meeting Agnes's cold stare, she asked flatly, 'Shall I just go?'

'Yes, yes, I think you *should* just go.'

She inclined her head and walked away. At the door, Agnes's voice stopped her.

'Go and make me a cup of tea, that is. Make haste, girl. No dawdling.'

Turning in surprise, she swallowed a sigh of relief. 'Yes, Mrs Sharp.'

Pru appeared before she was halfway downstairs. 'You're not leaving already? What has she said? What did she—'

'Miss Sharp, I'm not leaving. Your mother wants tea.'

'Oh, thank goodness. Come through, dear.'

'I'd better hurry. She said no dawdling and I don't want to annoy her further. We've had . . . words already.'

Pru spun around, teapot in hand. 'So soon? What has she said?'

'To be perfectly honest, it's more what I said. I'm afraid I lost my temper and . . . said some things I shouldn't have. I'm sorry, Miss Sharp. It won't happen again.'

'I don't believe . . . What did you say?' Pru breathed, hand fluttering to her throat.

'Well, first I implied she was dim-witted then I accused her of lacking manners.'

'Good Lord. And she still wants you here? I really don't . . . What happened?'

Sally glanced towards the stairs. 'Could we talk later, Miss Sharp? I'm hanging on by the skin of my teeth. I must get back.'

'Yes, yes, you're right. Here's the tea, you run along. We will have a cup later and you can tell me all about it.' Her eyes shone with admiration. 'I'm glad you're here, Sally. I have a feeling you are going to cope just fine.'

After flashing Pru a less-than-confident smile, she mounted the stairs. Pausing at the old woman's door, she resolved to treat this entrance as a fresh start. She'd be polite, wouldn't under any circumstances rise to the bait. She nodded determinedly and entered.

'You took your time.'

Lowering her gaze, she placed the tea on the bedside table. 'Do you require anything else, Mrs Sharp?'

'Yes.'

She waited but when Agnes remained silent, glanced up. She was staring at her intently and Sally had to fight the urge to look away. Those eyes . . . It was as though they were looking into her soul, as though they could see exactly what she was thinking, feeling.

'Can you read, girl?'

Heat crept over her face when Agnes fumbled beneath her pillows and produced a small black book. 'Not very well,' she admitted. 'Did you want me to read to you? I'll try but as I said—'

'No matter, you'll learn.'

Sally took the book and crossed to a chair by the window. The weak sun peeping through the thick curtains offered little light. She squinted at the title. 'May I open the curtains, Mrs Sharp? I cannot see the words properly.'

'No. Sunlight annoys me. Light the candle if you must.'

For over an hour, she stumbled and stuttered over the hardly visible, strange new words. She was on the brink of screaming in frustration and hurling the book through the window when Agnes held up a hand.

'That will do. Extinguish that flame, it is giving me a headache.'

She closed the book and blew out the candle. 'Do you require anything else? Another cup of tea?'

Agnes shifted beneath the mountain of covers. 'You can bathe me, now. I'm sticky and this nightgown is starting to smell.'

The rest of the morning passed in a blur, with Sally performing her duties in silence. As she'd resolved, she'd kept her head down and only opened her mouth when spoken to. And with a tangible air of irritation, Agnes was tolerating her presence.

She'd bathed and clothed her employer. Then Agnes ordered her to brush her hair. She'd stroked the heavy brush over the rough tufts until her arms ached. Finally, eyes drooping, the old woman had indicated with a flap of her bony hand that she could stop. Those tasks were all she'd asked of her.

Long periods, she'd spent on the hard chair, awaiting the next demand, and her mind filled the inactivity with worrying thoughts of Jonathan and whether Grace was coping.

None the less, before she knew it, Pru's voice drifted up, informing her she could take her dinner. Hurrying downstairs, Sally smiled proudly. She'd survived the morning at least. What the afternoon held, however, remained to be seen.

Entering the shop, she saw through the window snow falling in earnest. 'Oh, I didn't know it had started again. The curtains upstairs are almost drawn.'

'Yes, I'm afraid so.' Pru bade a customer goodbye then asked eagerly, 'How are you getting on, dear?'

'All right, I think. I'm sorry, Miss Sharp, but I must go. My aunt is minding my child and I promised to call in to give him his feed.'

'Of course, dear, of course. We shall talk later when work is through.'

Thoughts of Jonathan screaming for her milk and the burning need to see him propelled her through the streets and in no time, she was at Grace's door.

'I've found you at last. I knew I would eventually.'

Sally whipped around to see a tall figure, almost shrouded from view in the fast-falling snow. She blinked flakes from her lashes and squinted harder, heart hammering.

He stepped closer and she shook her head in astonishment. 'What are *you* doing here?'

Chapter 12

GRACE SMILED AT the man seated at the table. 'More tea?'

'You're an angel from heaven, to be sure. Isn't she an angel?' he asked Sally.

She glared at him then cast her aunt a tight smile.

'Oh, go on with you.' Grace laughed, flapping a hand. 'You Irish. Charm the birds from the trees, you would.'

''Tis both a blessing and a curse, Mrs Boslam.'

Grace laughed again and Sally rolled her eyes. For fifteen minutes, she'd had to force smiles and make small talk with this man. What he was doing here, she didn't know. He had no right turning up like this.

Initially, the accent didn't register and she'd been petrified, believing Joseph had tracked her down. Before she could ask what in the world he was doing here and how he'd found her, her aunt appeared at the door. Grace had taken an instant shine to Con Malloy; his easy smile and charming ways made it difficult not to. When he explained that he and her niece were friends, she'd invited him inside for a sup to 'thaw him out', much to Sally's exasperation.

Grace had been anxious to hear how her morning had gone but, unwilling to discuss her business in front of a near stranger, she'd said they would talk later. While Grace brewed tea, she'd taken the baby into the next room to feed him but not before throwing Con an angry look. He, however, had merely smiled.

Her annoyance grew when his deep brogue drifted through, telling her aunt of their previous meetings. Grace's responses showed she was suitably impressed and by the time Sally rejoined them, the smooth-talking Irishman had well and truly won her over.

Now, as Grace made to refill his cup again, she'd had enough.

'Aunt Grace, I think it's time Con was leaving. I must get back to work.' To him, she added stiffly, 'I'm sure you have business to be getting on with. Please, don't let us keep you.'

His slow smile appeared. Taking Grace's hand, he kissed it soundly. ''Twas a pleasure meeting such a grand woman as yourself, Mrs Boslam.'

'And you, lad. You're welcome any time. A friend of my Sally's is a friend of mine.'

Sally dropped a kiss on to Jonathan's head and passed him to Grace. Then taking Con's elbow, she steered him to the door.

'Your aunt's a sound woman, so she is. Was the colleen in the bed your cousin? I didn't like to say inside but she looked mighty poorly.'

She remained silent until they reached the entry, where she halted and glared up at him.

'What the hell do you think you're playing at? What are you doing here? How did you find me?' He answered with his slow smile and her anger rose. 'What is it you find amusing? That you twisted my aunt around your finger? That you managed to track down a woman, for God alone knows what reason, whom you barely know? Look, I'm grateful for your assistance last week but—'

'You're even more beautiful when you're angry, acushla.'

'I am not your acushla! I don't know what your intentions are but I can assure you—' He wrapped his arms around her and kissed her hard, smothering her rant. She was so shocked, she couldn't move. However, he drew her closer and her senses returned like a thunderbolt. She sprang back as though he'd scorched her. 'How *dare* you!'

He ran a hand through his hair, his breathing heavy. 'I shouldn't have done that. Forgive me. I just . . . I don't know what it is about you. From the moment I saw you standing on the platform in Bolton, looking so lost, so vulnerable, I felt something in here.' He tapped his chest. 'I always did have a soft spot for a damsel in distress.'

His smile stirred but when her face remained stony, it died. 'I remembered you telling the cab driver to take you to Boslam Street. I asked around but no one had heard of you. I was about to give up when I caught sight of ye rushing through this here entry. I wanted to get to know you, find out more about you. I hoped that seeing me again, you'd—'

'I'd what? What did you expect I'd do, Con? Throw myself at your feet? I certainly wasn't wrong when suggesting you need a bigger cap.'

'No, Sally, I—'

'We spoke no more than several words last week. I never expected to see you again. Then today, I find you lurking in the shadows. It's all a little . . . odd. I don't know a thing about you.'

He reached out tentatively and took her hand. 'Give me a chance. Get to know me, as I want to get to know you. I'm nothing special, Sally, 'tis true, but . . . Please, can't we at least be friends?'

She sighed. Hope creased his eyes and Sally found herself softening. Despite her experience of men, she felt no fear with this one, feeling comfortable in his presence from the moment they met. 'Well, maybe we *could* be friends . . .' she heard herself say.

His face spread in a grin. 'I'd like that, Sally. I'd like that very much.'

'Let's forget today and start afresh, shall we? If you're free, you may call again on Sunday. Now, I really must get to work. I only started this morning; it won't look good if I'm late back. Oh, and Con?' she added over her shoulder.

'Aye?'

'Don't ever creep up on me again. I don't like it.'

Still smiling, he nodded, and she set off.

Hurrying through the streets, uncertainty tugged at her. She touched her lips. Would agreeing to be friends give him the wrong idea? He was nice, and there was no denying he was handsome, but after Joseph . . . She could never feel *that* way for any male. He'd warped her perception of men for ever.

One with floppy black hair and grey-blue eyes flashed in her mind and she realised that this wasn't entirely true. She *had* felt something, with him.

She still did.

Three pairs of eyes gazed from Tommy to the table.

'Eeh, the silly girl. The silly, *silly* girl. Why the bloody hell didn't she keep it for herself and the babby?'

'She insisted, Mam.'

'But how did she get away with taking all this? How did Joseph not notice?'

'She didn't tell me the ins and outs, just said she buried coppers away over the years.'

His father ran a hand over the mound of coins. 'I can't fathom it. If she worked so hard saving this up, why leave it here, with thee?'

Tommy pulled out a chair and sat down. Excitement flowed through him when Shaun traced a finger over a shiny penny. God willing, this would change his life. 'This here brass is for you,' he murmured. 'Every penny, every copper coin, it's all for you.'

'Aye, very funny, our Tommy.'

Grinning, he turned to his mother. 'You remember the morning Sally left, when you came down and we were already up?' Her lips tightened into a thin line and he continued quickly, 'I said, didn't I, that I couldn't sleep? It were because I had matters on my mind.'

'What matters?'

'Our Shaun. It's no secret he loathes the pit, Mam. I were sitting here racking me brains forra way to help him. Sally came in and . . . well, we got talking. She wanted to repay thee for taking her in. When I told her of our Shaun's talent, that I were going to try and secure him an apprenticeship, she offered to help. As tha knows, they might require a premium, then there's his tools—'

'You wanted to do that?' Shaun cut in, brown eyes shining. 'You *both* wanted to do that? For me?'

'Aye.'

Ivy covered her mouth, her own eyes bright. 'That lass. What an angel. She got one over on that divil, all right. Eeh, the clever girl.' She shook her head. 'All that morning . . . over breakfast, on our way to catch the carrier's cart, she never said a word.

'Mind, now I think back . . . Assuming she were potless, I gave her a few coins for her fare and there were a definite twinkle in her eye as she took them. Why the bugger didn't she say owt?'

'She knew you'd not accept. We planned how she'd let you pay the cart so you'd not suspect,' Tommy admitted, winking. 'She said to tell thee to take the fare, and whatever it's cost for her stay, out of this.'

'Eeh, you pair of sneaky swines. Well, nowt needs taking for her stay. She hardly cost us a thing; she had the appetite of a swallow.' Her face was suddenly serious. ''Ere, she kept some aside for herself, didn't she? This ain't all the money she had, is it?'

'Nay. Don't fret, Mam.'

As she squeezed his hand, her voice was tender. 'You're a good lad, son.'

His smile came with deep guilt. This had quelled her suspicions regarding him and Sally, he could see it in her eyes. How wrong she was. He wanted her more than ever.

'Can you believe this, Shaun? God willing, we'll get thee apprenticed somewhere, eh?'

Face set like stone, Shaun pulled from her embrace.

'Lad?'

'This is a dream, in't it? I'll waken in a minute and it'll be morning, time for work down that bloody pit. Things like this don't happen, not to folk like me.'

'Oh, lad.' She took his face in her hands. 'Now you listen to me. Thanks to that lovely lass, you're getting out of that pit and you're going to make summat of yourself, d'you hear? It's real, lad. It's *real*.'

Shaun laughed brokenly. Then he jumped up and punched the air.

As the trio chattered excitedly about the future, Tommy smiled. It warmed his heart something lovely to see them happy. And it was all down to Sally. *Sweet, beautiful Sally.* George Turner's words returned to haunt him. He glanced at his mother, debating whether to tell her, but decided against it. This was Shaun's moment and he wanted him to enjoy it. He wouldn't wipe the joy from their faces.

Dolly assaulted his mind but he hastily pushed her out. He couldn't think of her; the guilt was unbearable. Earlier, he'd lingered by her cottage for an age but couldn't bring himself to knock at her door. When he returned home, his mother had asked if she'd agreed to come to dinner and though he'd felt terrible lying to her, the tale concocted on the way back slipped easily from his tongue.

He'd told her Dolly couldn't come, she was needed at the dairy. To his relief and shame, Ivy believed him.

It would have been torture; he'd have been unable to pretend all was well. Yet there was another reason he hadn't invited Dolly – he wouldn't be here. When he finished work on Saturday, he was going to Manchester.

He didn't have a clue where in Ancoats Sally's aunt lived, but he'd find out. He'd have gone this very second, walked if he must, but it was impossible. He couldn't miss work. His family's reliance upon his wage was too great.

What excuse he'd use, he didn't know, but he was going. He had to warn Sally. He *had* to see her. Nothing, no one, would stop him.

Chapter 13

WEDNESDAY AND THURSDAY passed similarly to Sally's first day. Routine remained the same and Agnes had seemingly resigned herself to the fact she wasn't going anywhere. There had been no further altercations and Sally was certain if she continued speaking only when spoken to and kept her head down, things would be fine.

Today was Friday and as Agnes handed her the tattered book, her heart sank. The daily torture was taking its toll. It was ridiculous straining to see when opening the curtains a touch more would solve it. How did sunlight annoy one, anyway? She had to say something. What use would a blind mother be to her son?

'Mrs Sharp, I know we've spoken about this but could I open the curtains just a little more? The light in here is incredibly weak. I'm worried that my eyesight—'

'You have the candle, do you not?'

'Well yes, but—'

'Then cease your whining and read the damn book, girl.'

She breathed deeply. 'Mrs Sharp, the candle is insufficient. My eyes have become painful since working here. Opening the curtains would help enormously and would make such a difference in here, too.'

Pru's long hours in the shop, and reluctance to spend time with her cantankerous mother, had resulted in a dreadfully neglected room. Dirt and dust covered every surface. Ancient cobwebs drooped from the ceiling and a musty smell pervaded the air, adding to the morose feel. A good clean and sunlight would cheer it up no end. Maybe the old woman would be happier in less dismal surroundings.

Agnes's eyes narrowed. 'Difference?'

'Well,' she began hesitantly, 'perhaps I could do some cleaning. The dust cannot be good for you, surely. It wouldn't take long. Then there's the light. Opening the curtains would brighten everything and I could open the window and . . .' Her speech died, her enthusiasm with it, as Agnes shook her head. However, when the old woman spoke, she pleasantly surprised her.

'You're persistent, girl, I'll give you that. I suppose you will drone on and on if I refuse?' Annoyance tinged her guttural voice but a hint of amusement glimmered behind her eyes.

Sally's lips twitched. 'I simply believe the change would be most beneficial, as much to you as to me.' She clasped her hands to her chest. 'Do I have your permission, Mrs Sharp?'

'All right, girl. I'm willing to humour your silly whim. But I warn you, if I do not like the changes you decide upon, you will put back everything exactly as it was, however hard you've worked. Do I make myself clear?'

Sally had a sneaking suspicion she'd decide this just to be difficult, but had to try. 'Yes, Mrs Sharp. Do you require anything before I begin?'

A whisper of a smile played across her shrivelled mouth. 'No, no. You go ahead.'

Beaming, Sally headed straight for the window.

Besides rushing home to feed Jonathan and fulfilling Agnes's occasional request, she worked nonstop. By late afternoon, her body screamed for rest and she was terribly grubby, but it had been worth it. Hands on hips, she blew her hair from her face and gazed around.

Every piece of furniture she'd pulled out and cleaned thoroughly. She'd swept and scrubbed the floor and skirting boards, and stripped the walls and ceilings of the many cobwebs. Most importantly, the curtains, which she'd taken down, shaken well then rehung, were open wide, as was the gleaming window.

The difference was unbelievable. Sunlight uncovered things the gloom had disguised. Wallpaper, though faded, revealed swirling sprigs of pale-green flowers. The large rug, after she'd shaken out years of muck, showed traces of the vibrant colours it once held. Paintings that had hung limply – from cavalry charging across a battlefield to a countryside complete with rushing stream – were now vivid depictions.

She glanced to the old woman, who was snoring softly. All day, she'd been aware of Agnes watching her. It was unnerving having her every move silently scrutinised and she'd sighed in relief when she'd fallen asleep. Now, however, Sally pondered whether to waken her. The bed was the only thing she hadn't touched; she itched to give behind it a good clean.

Taking another look around, she smiled proudly. Everywhere sparkled; the smell was gone. Surely Mrs Sharp would like it?

After closing the window and drawing the curtains, she knelt before the cleaned and blackleaded fireplace. Within minutes, flames danced up the chimney. As she rose, the door opened and a smiling Pru appeared.

'I've brought you both a cup— Oh! What an absolutely wonderful job you've done!' She placed the tea tray on the bedside table then traced her fingers over the walls and furniture. 'I'd forgotten how this room once looked. I cannot believe the difference you have made, dear.'

Sally smiled in delight. Pru had ventured up several times to see how it was progressing but she'd been told she couldn't see until it was completed. Chuckling, Pru had sidled back downstairs. Sally was glad she'd made her wait; her reaction was proof she'd done well.

'Has she seen it?'

'Not yet. I do hope she likes it, Miss Sharp.'

'I think she just may. I still cannot believe she gave permission. You must think me a dreadful slattern. I . . . couldn't . . . Life is much easier if I keep my distance. She finds my very presence irksome. I don't know what it is about you but she has accepted you as she never has anyone else.'

'I believe an unspoken truce was made when I stood up to her.'

Pru's gaze flicked to the poker propped against the wall. 'Just remain watchful, dear. Don't let your guard down for a moment. Promise me, Sally. Promise me you'll be careful.'

She sensed more behind the whispered warning. 'This isn't only about her last employee, is it, Miss Sharp? Has your mother used that blasted poker on you, too?'

'Of course, dear. Many times. But I don't want anyone else getting hurt, not again.'

As the shocking admission hung in the air, anger gripped Sally's chest. How could anyone treat their own child like that – particularly one so sweet and kind? She glared at Agnes in disgust. Why did some people behave this way? What pleasure did they derive from causing others misery?

'Miss Sharp, I suffered a bully's hand for years. He beat me into submission for no other reason than that he could. A dear friend helped put a stop to my torment.' She marched forward and snatched up the poker. 'Now it's my turn to help another.'

'What are you doing?' hissed Pru.

'Something which should have been done a long time ago.' She wrenched the curtain aside, opened the window and threw the poker out. It struck the cobbles with a loud clang and she nodded in grim satisfaction.

'You're still here? What time is it?'

Whipping around, Sally found Agnes staring at her, green eyes mere slits. Sally was about to give her a piece of her mind when Pru's pleading gaze caught her eye.

'I think you *are* a mute, girl, after all. I asked you a question. What's the wretched time?' Suddenly, peering around, Agnes's lips twisted in a smirk. 'Well, well, well. I see you've been busy.'

'Isn't it wonderful, Mother?' Ashen-faced, Pru wrung her hands. 'I brought tea. It is on the table, there.'

Agnes ignored her and turned back to Sally. 'We had an agreement, did we not? I stated quite clearly that if I did not like it, I wanted it putting back exactly as you found it.'

'Let me guess. You don't.'

'Actually, it is rather pleasant. You've done well, girl.'

Sally and Pru glanced at each other in shared surprise and distrust.

'There is just one question I would like you to answer,' Agnes murmured, bony fingers gripping the bedclothes. 'What do you propose we now use for the fire?'

Under the intense stare, Sally felt colour stain her cheeks. But glancing to a terrified-looking Pru, anger lifted her chin. 'That poker hasn't been used for what it was intended for, for a long time, Mrs Sharp, and you know it.'

A range of emotions flitted across the lined face. When a scratchy laugh leaked from her mouth, her expression told it was as much a shock to her ears as theirs.

'You are without doubt the most insolent, hard-faced little bitch I have ever encountered,' she spluttered. She threw her head back and laughed harder at Sally's outraged frown. 'Oh, put your face straight, girl. I mean that as a compliment. If only this useless chit had an ounce of your gumption. She's brought me nothing but disappointment. What he saw in her, I will never know—'

Pru's harsh gasp sliced through her words. 'Don't you *dare* talk about that. I have warned you before; never, ever talk about that! I made a mistake, Mother. One mistake. Am I to suffer it the rest of my days?' A solitary tear slipped down her cheek. 'Haven't I suffered enough?'

Sally looked on in confusion. Her perplexity grew when Agnes's eyes deepened with what she could only interpret as guilt. Pru's ragged breaths were the only sound until, softer than she'd ever heard, Agnes spoke.

'Pull yourself together and fetch the poker before some scoundrel pilfers it.' She nodded once. 'Go on, Prudence.'

Pru left the room. Moments later, without a word, she returned the poker to its home by the bedside.

'As for you . . .' murmured Agnes to Sally. 'Ever behave in such a foolhardy manner again and you will be dismissed faster than you can blink. I like spirit but I will break yours if you attempt to push me too far.

Remember your place, girl. Now, go on home. Your child will be wanting your milk.'

Too bewildered to argue, she stole a last look at Pru and headed for the door.

'Girl?'

Her hand stilled on the knob.

'Thank you.'

Sally glanced around the space she'd worked so hard on then slipped from the room.

Chapter 14

SATURDAY DAWNED BRIGHT and clear. The snow had finally exhausted itself and Sally's walk to work was through a sea of grey-black slush. Carts crawled along the patchwork of icy cobbles; the horses' safety was paramount. A slip of a hoof could, she knew, claim not only the beast's life but a driver's family when no work meant no food and coal.

In biting temperatures, with dwellings often as cold as the streets, inhabitants clung to life grimly, praying for spring. Many, particularly the young, old and infirm, wouldn't see this spell through.

'Spare a penny, missis?'

This, delivered through a beggar boy's chattering teeth, no longer shocked her as it had when she first arrived in this town.

Children fortunate to own clogs had enjoyed the white blanket that encompassed their world; the lanes had rung with screeching laughter. Others, who worked the streets trading everything from their bodies to kindling – and those like this bundle of bones shivering beneath old newspaper in a doorway, bare feet probably plagued by burning chilblains – no doubt hadn't shared the fascination.

'Ha'penny, then?'

Yesterday's performance with the Sharps had wrapped around her a veil of dejection. She'd lain awake all night, dreading returning. Why was nothing ever simple? Why had she always suffered so? Why were a select few born into a life of privilege and ease while others were clawing for survival upon leaving the womb?

The morose thoughts had swamped her yet now, looking at these people around her, skin blue, eyes utterly void of hope in sallow faces, Sally felt ashamed.

'Missis, please. My guts ain't known grub since Thursday.'

Lord, what had she to gripe about? Her clothes and boots, though thin and patched, dulled the edge of the cold. She'd suffered the workhouse then as Joseph's wife, but was free of both. Countless children were lost but she had Jonathan. Evil drove her from Spring Row but she now had a safe home. Her parents had passed away but she had Aunt Grace, Uncle Ed, cousins. Dicksy had gone but she had solid friends in Ivy and her family, and potential ones in Con and Maggie Benson.

And she had her job. Though it wasn't the most enjoyable, nor safest, many would give their eye teeth to be earning an honest crust. No, things were never as bad as they seemed.

She pressed a coin into the beggar's hand and continued on her way.

Tomorrow, her day off, she was determined to make the most of. She'd visit Maggie. She couldn't wait to see her and hoped she'd found another position. She'd take Jonathan. Spending time with him would be lovely and Grace deserved a break.

Also, Con was calling. She was rather looking forward to that, was glad she'd decided to try his friendship. There were things she didn't know about him but then, there were things he didn't know about her. However, he was a decent man who deserved a chance.

Entering the shop, she found Pru busy behind the counter. When she closed the door and Pru didn't turn, she bit her lip. She usually greeted Sally warmly; was she cross about last night? She should never have slung the poker through the window or spoken to the old woman as she did. From where had that spark of courage come? It seemed the old Sally, that feisty, defiant girl who, mindless of the consequences, thought nothing of standing up to the workhouse matron – master, too – with bunched fists and eyes, and tongue spitting venom, was slowly but surely resurfacing, whether she liked it or not.

Nevertheless, what went on with mother and daughter was between them. From now on, unless Pru asked for her help, she'd keep out of their affairs.

'Miss Sharp, my conduct last night . . . I'm so very sorry. I simply loathe one suffering at another's hand, for I know how it feels. It will never happen again.'

Still, Pru didn't turn.

Sally lowered her head. Would she dismiss her?

'Don't apologise, dear. You have nothing to be sorry for.'

Her head jerked up. She sighed in relief. 'I'm truly sorry, Miss Sharp, I— Oh!' The word ripped from her throat as Pru turned.

'I'm quite all right. It looks worse than it is,' Pru murmured, hands fluttering to her face.

Sally covered her mouth in horror. Pru's face was badly swollen. Her gentle eyes peeped through puffy slits and dark bruises streaked the skin in livid patches.

'Can I get you a cup of tea, dear?'

'A cup . . . ? Miss Sharp, what on earth has *happened* to you?' She shook her head slowly. 'That wicked old woman did this, didn't she? What is *wrong* with her? She could have killed you!'

Pru's split lips parted but whatever she'd been about to say remained unspoken.

Glaring at the ceiling, Sally was consumed with fury. Moments later, she was sprinting upstairs. She burst into Agnes's room, strode to the bed and stared in disgust at the sleeping form.

'Sally, please.'

Glancing to the doorway, her face softened. Pru was wringing her hands furiously, eyes wide in desperation.

'If you question her, you'll make matters worse for me. Please, dear.'

She shot Agnes a last look then followed Pru downstairs. 'I'm sorry, Miss Sharp,' she said when they reached the shop. 'Of course I don't want to make things more difficult for you. It's just . . . She cannot get away with treating people like this!'

Pru patted the stool beside hers. 'Come, sit down. We shouldn't be disturbed. No one will be in to redeem possessions until they receive their wages, later.'

'Is this about last night? Did she take it out on you because of my actions?'

'No, no, dear. Don't blame yourself. It's entirely my fault. I foolishly continued the argument after you left. You would think I'd have learned by now, wouldn't you?'

Recalling their exchange, she frowned. 'Miss Sharp, I couldn't fail to hear what your mother said regarding . . . a man? It's none of my business but if you ever want to talk . . .'

'Thank you, dear. She hasn't mentioned . . . that, in a while. She brings it up now and then to hurt me. And Lord, her words *do* hurt. Far more than the feel of that poker. She believes it a necessary measure; spare the rod, spoil the child, so to speak.' A small sigh escaped. 'I'm able to ignore most of what she says, but not that.

'It's the one thing she knows will garner a reaction. And I fall for it every time.' She patted Sally's hand. 'You're a lovely person. I appreciate your concern, truly. One day, I may take up your kind offer and release my demons. But not yet. The memories are very raw, dear.'

Sally covered her hand with hers. 'I understand, Miss Sharp.'

'Mother will shortly be awake. Go on up and I shall bring you both some tea. And Sally, please don't mention this, will you?' Pru entreated, pointing to her face.

Sally sighed inwardly. How was she to bear that woman's company? She'd love nothing more than to shake her awake, give her a piece of her mind, leave and never return. But she couldn't. She needed this job, and Pru needed her.

'I won't, you have my word. But Miss Sharp, what will you do?' she couldn't help asking. 'You cannot continue living in fear of her beating you whenever the mood strikes. I lived that way for a long time and it near killed me.'

'It shan't happen again, dear. If she ever mentions . . . I'm determined not to rise to it. I have no choice. She has no one in the world but me. I must simply grit my teeth and get on with it.'

Heart heavy with pity, Sally reluctantly headed upstairs.

The level of poverty in Manchester was like nothing Tommy had encountered. Since he'd stepped from the train and met the abjectness of Sally's new home, an ache had taken root in his chest. Settling back in the hansom hailed outside the station, he prayed Ancoats wasn't as bad as the parts he'd already seen.

He didn't have a clue how he'd find her. Unsure where to begin, he'd simply instructed the driver to drop him 'somewhere in Ancoats'. The man had scratched his head and stared at him as if he were mad. But when Tommy raised an eyebrow and jingled coins in his pocket, he'd shrugged and told him to hop aboard.

Rattling through the streets, Tommy kept his eyes peeled. It was a long shot but he might just spot her; she could be anywhere, after all. His breathing quickened at the prospect. The urge to see her was like coiled rope in his stomach, tightening, tightening. He felt like a man possessed. Nothing would stop him until he found her.

His mother's smile returned to haunt him and he gripped the seat. He'd lied to her again; only this time, he'd gone further – he'd used Dolly as an alibi.

Unable to think up an excuse, he'd informed her he was off to see the dairymaid. Then, remembering his previous lie, that she couldn't come to dinner because she was needed at the dairy, he amended his words, adding he'd wait at Dolly's until she returned from work. His mother hadn't suspected a thing. How he'd kept his tone even, his fixed smile in place, he didn't know.

What he *did* know was that he hated himself for it. Lately, the lies flowed and it worried him. Being deceitful wasn't in his nature. Yet where Sally was concerned, he couldn't help himself.

They turned into a road teeming with carts and people. Reasoning the busier the place, the better the chance of someone having heard of her, he tapped the cab, alighted and stared about.

The sheer magnitude of his task slammed home. He hadn't thought this through at all. After working a half-day then travelling here, the day was almost through. If he had no joy, he'd seek a lodging house and try tomorrow, he resolved.

As for his overnight absence, he'd tell his parents that after leaving Dolly, he'd met a pit lad at a tavern and, after too many jars, was unable to make it home and had bedded down at his cottage. His mother wouldn't be best pleased but he'd face her tongue when the time came. Right now, all he could think of was finding Sally.

Questions tumbled over themselves in his mind, each more worrying than the last. Was she even here? Perhaps, unable to locate her aunt, she'd moved on.

As he turned from the roadside, a hand brushed his buttocks and hot breath fanned his neck. Jerking around, he saw a woman of indeterminate age, gaudily painted face fixed in a seductive smile.

'By gum, lad, you're easy on t' eye. You looking for some fun?'

He peeled her arms from his waist, his colour rising. That she was a streetwalker didn't surprise or embarrass him; he'd seen plenty in Bolton in his time. It was being propositioned in broad daylight that rendered him speechless. Prostitutes usually loitered in back lanes, attainable yet concealed. And this clearly wasn't a random act; people passing barely batted an eyelid.

'I know somewhere warm and dry we could go.' Her simpering tone held the desperation in her eyes when he'd removed her hands. 'I'll do owt you've a fancy for, lad.'

Taking stock of her, he sighed. She wasn't a woman at all. Behind the painted eyes, lips and cheeks, her pinched face was that of someone no older than fourteen or fifteen.

He extracted coppers from his pocket, took her icy hand and pressed them into her palm. Then he put his lips to her ear. 'Go home, lass.'

Tears filled eyes old long before their time. Standing on tiptoe, she kissed his cheek and walked away.

Watching her scuttle through the throng of bodies, his guts lurched. What if Sally was in the same desperate situation . . . ? No. He wouldn't, *couldn't*, think that. She was safe, well. She had to be.

A deep voice cut through his thoughts. Across the road, he saw a tall, good-looking man catch a beshawled woman around the waist. Smiling down, he guided her inside a pie shop, and Tommy swallowed a pang of envy. Would he one day be that happy? Would he ever hold Sally again?

As he peered around, a lump formed in his throat at the hopelessness of it all. He was never going to find her.

'You see, 'tis to be there when you need rescuing I was put on this earth, acushla.'

Meeting the Irishman's laughing eyes, Sally couldn't help smiling. 'Con, this is serious. I don't think I can return. How I held my tongue today, I do not know.'

'Hush, now, and start from the beginning. Sure, 'twas a stroke of luck I spotted ye leaving.'

She took a sip of her tea. 'I'm glad you did. I couldn't have allowed Aunt Grace to see me like this. She didn't want me taking the position in the first place. Whenever she asks how I'm faring, I say all is fine. She'd only fret if she knew the truth.' She placed her cup on the table and closed her eyes. 'Oh Con, she is wicked, *wicked*. Miss Sharp's face . . .

'My anger as I ran up those stairs . . . *I* could have taken the poker to *her*.' A man at the next table glanced over and she lowered her voice. 'She believes it's for her daughter's good, that if she didn't remind her of the feel of the poker, it would only be a matter of time before she sinned again. Can you believe that?'

'What sin has she committed before?'

'I don't know. Miss Sharp seems the last person to do anything immoral; a more decent and generous soul you couldn't wish to meet. However, Mrs Sharp said something about a man, that she didn't know what he'd seen in her daughter.'

Con leaned forward, his slow smile surfacing. 'It sounds like your Miss Sharp is a touch *too* generous.'

'Whatever her past, it doesn't excuse her mother's actions. Nothing can justify what she's done to her poor face – has done many times.'

'What will ye do?'

She stared absently through the window. 'I honestly do not know. I need this job but am not sure I can be around such evil. The way she was today . . . she must have known I'd seen her daughter's injuries, yet she showed not a flicker of shame.

'Do you know something else? Yesterday, I broke my back cleaning her room. I thought she'd announce she didn't like it, to be awkward, but surprisingly, she said I'd done well.'

'That's grand, isn't it?'

'No, Con, I don't think it is. I believe she intended to dislike the room before I even began but, when she noticed Miss Sharp there, saw it as a perfect opportunity to belittle her. She merely sang my praises to hurt her. How could she derive enjoyment from her child's misery?'

He took her hand, the pleasure in his eyes when she didn't shy away, clear. 'When are you next in?'

'Monday.'

'And will ye go? Can you brave this out or will you look for something else?'

'If I do stay, it will be for Miss Sharp. I doubt she'd find anyone to fill my position and the duty would fall to her. She'd be at that monstrous woman's mercy completely.'

Stroking her fingers, he smiled. 'You're a grand woman. You're gentle and caring, yet you've a feistiness I find irresistible. You intrigue me.'

His hand strayed up her arm and she pulled back, cheeks flushing.

'Sally, I'm sorry, I—'

'I'm sorry, too, Con. I don't feel for you as you do for me.' She glanced at him and sighed. 'You're handsome, you make me laugh, I feel safe in your company . . . but we cannot be more than friends.'

'Because of this?' He tapped her wedding band. 'Whatever the reason your marriage broke down, who and where your husband is, it doesn't bother me. I don't care about your past. I just want to be part of your future. 'Twas fate, us meeting as we did. And whenever you're in need, I always seem to be close by, to help and look after you. 'Tis like it's meant to be, acushla.'

His heartfelt words touched her and when she spoke, there was a catch in her voice. 'Aunt Grace was right about you Irish. You *could* charm the birds from the trees with your blarney.'

He flashed a weak smile. 'But . . . ?'

'There's no future for us, not like that.'

'Is your heart already claimed by another?' he asked suddenly. 'Was your wistful smile on the train for him?'

Her cheeks burned but she tossed her head. 'Con Malloy, I don't know what you're talking about. I harbour feelings for no man.'

He grinned. 'I don't believe you.'

'Believe what you will,' she said mildly. 'Furthermore, there are several questions *I* would like to ask *you*.'

'Such as?'

Her lips twitched when his infectious smile grew. 'Why were you in Bolton that day? What do you do for a living? Where and with whom do you reside?'

'We have a lot to discuss, to be sure. And you know what that means?' He winked, his grin returning. 'I get to spend more time with ye.'

Rolling her eyes, she laughed. 'You're incorrigible. Now, I'm afraid I must go as Jonathan will be needing me. You're welcome to walk with me if you're going my way.'

'Feeling better?' he asked when they exited the pie shop.

Sally linked her arm in his. 'How could I not with a friend like you to cheer me up?'

He nudged her playfully and, laughing, she hurried him along the street.

Chapter 15

JOSEPH SQUINTED THROUGH the gloom. His mouth was parchment dry, his head thumping.

'Bloody thick heads grow worse as I get owder,' he muttered, hauling himself up in the lumpy bed.

A leg wrapped around his, making him jump. Wrenching back the covers, he frowned, trying to cast his mind back to the night before, but the pounding in his skull pushed out all thought.

Nancy lay on her side, arms entwined above her head, hair streaming across the pillow. He shoved her hard.

''Ere, what—?'

'What the hell's tha doing here?' he cut in harshly. 'Get up, get dressed and get gone afore our Alice wakens.'

Stretching like a lazy cat in the sun, she smiled sleepily. 'You asked me back last night, you daft beggar. We had a nice fumble in Nellie's as usual, but when we went into the back lane like normally at kicking-out time, I said I were sick of lifting my skirt for thee outside and you fetched me here.' She dropped kisses on to his chest. 'You not remember?'

'Nay, I bloody well don't.' He dragged a hand through his hair. 'I must've had a reet skinful.'

She pouted. 'Oh, ta very much.'

'Listen, you daft sow, if our Alice finds out I've had thee here, I'll be out quicker than that,' he growled, clicking his fingers. 'Reet funny, she is, 'bout things like that. Get moving.'

Arching in another stretch, she laughed when his glare flicked to her bare breasts, which had risen invitingly. 'We've a few minutes, ain't we? It's early yet. Look.' She motioned to the window. 'It's only just gone light.'

Irritation sparked but he didn't object.

'Good lad. You lie back and enjoy.'

His eyes narrowed with desire as she straddled him. 'You're a bitch. My head's splitting.'

Hips moving rhythmically, Nancy smiled. 'And that's what you like about me, in't it?'

Ivy couldn't keep the smile from her face. Her husband and sons donned jackets and caps and her stomach fluttered in excitement.

'Wish us luck, Mam.' Shaun bent and kissed her cheek. Making for the door, he checked the cloth bag's contents for the dozenth time.

'Good luck, son. You got the money?'

Tommy patted his pocket. 'I've got it, Mam.'

'You got them carvings?'

Shaun held up the bag. 'Aye.'

She nodded, then frowned at Arthur. 'You got that package I made up for your dinners?'

'Aye, wench, stop your fussing.' He rolled his eyes at his grinning sons. 'Let's get moving afore the day's gone.'

She watched them pass down the lane. When they reached the end of the row, Tommy lifted an arm in farewell and she smiled. She returned to the kitchen and, reaching for the teapot, clicked her tongue at her trembling hands.

'Be calm, Ivy,' she told herself. 'What will be, will be.'

They had barely slept last night – indeed, no one had much since Tommy had poured the money on to the table. Anticipation had stroked the cottage; she couldn't believe the day was here. It seemed they had waited weeks for Sunday to crawl around.

Naturally, Shaun felt it more. Dragging himself to the pit was difficult before – having to do so with that money sitting here had been unbearable. She just prayed to God he was taken on today.

She smiled as her musings switched to Tommy. Whatever had ailed him wasn't a sickening for Sally, she was now certain. He'd simply been fretting over Shaun's future and she felt terrible about her suspicions. She was even thankful that Sally had left, she remembered shamefully. Why had she harboured such foolish notions? Sally was a lovely lass, her Tommy a good lad smitten with the Jenkins one.

At the thought of Dolly, she sighed. She'd shot herself in the foot, there; her daft imaginings even saw her encouraging the courtship. She didn't know what it was about the dairymaid, couldn't put her finger on it. There was something about her she couldn't take to.

That there *wasn't* anything wrong with Dolly, that merely, in her eyes, no one was good enough for her Tommy, niggled, and she sighed again. She just loved the lad, wanted him to be happy, that was all.

With a yawn and a stretch, she settled into Arthur's chair. Closing tired eyes, her mind remained on Tommy. If that Jenkins lass was who he wanted, she'd have to accept it. He wasn't getting any younger. It was time he thought about settling down.

A sudden thought struck and her eyes sprang open. 'I wonder . . . ?' she murmured to the empty room.

He only met Dolly on Sundays yet yesterday, Saturday, he visited her cottage. He was gone all day and, now Ivy thought about it, preoccupied on his return. Had her inviting Dolly to dinner spurred him into taking things further? Would her apparent support bolster him to propose? With effort, she told herself that, whatever occurred, she'd keep her opinions private. It was his life, his decision.

Nights of shattered sleep, coupled with the fire, took effect. Before Ivy drifted to sleep, a young woman appeared in her mind. However, it wasn't Dolly, but Sally. And she realised, if circumstances were different, there was no one she'd want more for a daughter-in-law.

His lust spent, Joseph pushed Nancy off and climbed from the bed.

''Ere, I weren't finished. What's the rush? Tha getting bored of me, or summat?'

He turned sharply and grabbed her by the throat. His grip tightened and he forced himself to stop. He could happily beat her to a pulp; her whining was really getting to him, lately. But it would raise questions. That father of hers would surely notice and want to know what had happened.

She held up her hands. 'I'm sorry. I'm a grumpy cow of a morning. Leave go, eh, lad? I'll get dressed quick and be out of your hair.'

With a curl of his lip, he slung her away, sending her sprawling across the bed. He watched with increasing anger as she scrambled up, rubbing her neck.

He'd have to get shot of her. She was a convenient tool to sate his carnal needs, and the stuff she thieved from her father's shop placated Alice, but the urge to hurt her – and the struggle not to – mounted with each meeting.

That's where he'd been clever with Sally. He'd had plenty of flings before her but none lasted. When they got on his nerves and he'd used his fist to shut their gobs, they scarpered. But not Sally. She couldn't, with no one and nowhere to run to.

As he pulled on his trousers, admiration filled him for the workhouse master. He was on to something, there, all right. He knew plenty of men would pay well for women who did as they told them. Women with no ties, to use however you wanted without fear of their fathers or brothers giving you a good hiding. He'd had it until that interfering old bitch next door stuck her nose in. And by God, he'd have it again.

Snarling at Nancy's smile, he flung on shirt and jacket. Aye, this whore had to go soon, before he lost his rag. It was coming, there was no doubt about it. He wasn't prepared to dangle at the end of a rope for her, however tempting. Once he'd used her to find Sally and get back at the Morgans, he'd get rid of her.

Amusement bubbled. She was still paying his rent, probably hoping he'd move her in. Silly bitch. He couldn't return, with them next door, not without getting a round of clogs to his head. Even if he did, this dried-up sow certainly wouldn't be in tow. Sally would.

His jaw tightened in fury. Had she left Bolton? He'd told Nancy to keep her ears open for shop gossip but so far, customers hadn't mentioned her. *Was* it her who Alice's girl and the stationmaster had met? If so, why would she return to Manchester? She had nothing there, no roots to lay claim to besides the workhouse.

His hand stilled on the button he was fastening. Had she somehow discovered . . . ? No, she couldn't have. The master assured him she never would.

'Did you hear me, love?'

At Nancy's sickly-sweet tone, he longed to knock her teeth down her throat. 'What you on about now?'

'I were saying, my kiddies will be all right with my neighbour a while longer; d'you want to get summat to eat and drink afore I make for Breightmet? I could murder a sup. Nellie will find us some grub so long as we've the brass; I've a few coppers, here. You want to, love?' she finished, soft-eyed with expectancy.

He shrugged. He might as well. He wouldn't get anything here, that was for sure. They hadn't had a scrap in for days. Dragging on his cap, he headed for the door.

As they slipped to the kitchen, he was grateful it was early. Alice would have a fit if she knew he'd had a woman back. He couldn't risk her slinging him out. It might be a hovel but it kept the chill from his bones and rain off his head.

Glancing at the sleeping children in the corner, he smirked in satisfaction then pushed Nancy into the muck-strewn alley.

'Shaun, mind out!' Tommy hauled him from a cart's path. 'Christ, wake up, will thee? An inch closer and you'd have been under their hooves.'

Shaun's smile, a fixture since waking, didn't waver. He scanned the length of Deansgate. 'Are there any round here?'

Their father scratched his chin. 'Aye, I've seen one up this end afore, I'm sure.'

As they continued in search of a carpenter, Tommy fell behind. He smiled when Arthur pulled the distracted Shaun from a pile of horse manure, glad he'd accompanied them. It not only offered an excuse not to meet Dolly but a much-needed diversion. Dear God, what he'd witnessed yesterday . . .

A low moan escaped when the vision returned to torture him. He didn't believe his eyes when she emerged from that pie shop, had laughed aloud, convinced he was the luckiest devil on the face of the earth. His sweet Sally had appeared, right there in front of him. *As had the good-looking man she'd clung to.*

He winced at the image now forever burned in his memory. Why was he foolish enough to hope she felt something, too? Rancour for the man she'd smiled up at, face alight with – was it love? – scorched his veins. Who the hell was he? Where and when did they meet? She'd left Spring Row not a fortnight ago!

If she'd rebuffed his declaration, of course, she'd have devastated him. But another man? That was too much; his heart had wilted. Staggering back to Victoria Station, he'd been thankful for the emptiness inside, considering the pain he knew would come once the shock wore off.

Throughout that day, she'd consumed his thoughts yet, surprisingly, sleep claimed him when his head met his pillow. But his dreams tormented him more than consciousness ever could.

He shook his head to dispel the cruel trick his mind played last night. He dreamed he and Sally were married. They were in bed, entwined in each other's arms. He stroked the dawn rays playing across her bare shoulders and she smiled. Yet when he made to kiss her, she turned away. And the man from the pie shop had entered, swept her up and carried her off . . .

Tommy quickened his pace to catch up with his father and brother. He was safe with others, felt forced to suppress his anguish. He wanted nothing more than to kneel by the roadside and howl his throat raw, but he couldn't. He *couldn't*. All he could do was try to forget her.

'All right, son?'

Wrenched back to the present, Tommy blinked back tears he hadn't realised had formed. 'Aye.'

His father frowned but before he could enquire further, Shaun spoke in his ear:

'Look. Over the road, there. It's Mr Goden.'

As they glanced around, the thickset man turned.

Then all hell broke loose.

Chapter 16

MONDAY ARRIVED SOONER than Sally would have liked. Yesterday, she'd spent a lovely afternoon with Maggie Benson, her mother and small twins. She'd taken along Jonathan and Shield. Flo and Harry had squealed in delight over the dog and played with him all day. The gentle beast would make Jonathan a fine friend when he was older.

Passing through the dreary streets to work, she smiled, recalling the warm welcome. Ellen had thanked her for defending her daughter, railed over the mill overlooker and his filthy ways and bemoaned that Maggie hadn't found further employment. Yet despite their problems, Maggie and Ellen were great company, had her in fits of laughter.

When leaving, Sally had promised to keep eyes and ears open for a position for her new friend. Along Davies Street, into Ridgeway Street, past St Philip's Church and on down Butler Street towards home, she'd racked her brains for a solution to the family's dilemma. And as she reached the corner of Bradford Street and Bradford Road, an idea had formed.

Now, hurrying on, she crossed her fingers that Pru would agree. There was no harm in asking – nothing gained, nothing lost.

Entering the shop, she gave her Pru best smile. 'Good morning, Miss Sharp.'

'Ah, Sally, good morning.' As had become habit, she patted the empty stool. 'You're in high spirits, dear.'

'I am, though I'm afraid you may deem the reason impudent.'

'Impudent? I'm intrigued.'

She took a deep breath. 'Miss Sharp, I have a friend in desperate need of work. Her name is Maggie Benson and until recently she was an employee of Brunswick Mill. Through no fault of hers, the overlooker dismissed her; she spurned his advances, nothing more. She's widowed with twins, and I, I wondered—'

'Whether I had a position for her?'

'She's trustworthy and hard-working. She'd prove most helpful in the shop. Just several hours a week would ease her financial woes.'

Pru frowned in contemplation. 'I must admit it is difficult managing this place alone. Naturally, some days are busier than others – Mondays and Saturdays are somewhat arduous. I don't suppose it would take long to train her . . .'

'Oh, it wouldn't,' Sally readily agreed. 'She's a lovely woman. You'll like her, Miss Sharp.'

Pru tapped a finger against her lips, eyes thoughtful. 'I don't doubt it, if you recommend her. I respect your judgement. It *would* be nice to have company in here . . . Very well. She may help out Mondays and Saturdays for the time being and if she proves satisfactory, I shall increase her hours. There will be a fortnight's trial period, you understand?'

Grinning, Sally nodded. 'Yes, Miss Sharp. Thank you.'

'Inform her that she starts on Saturday. We'll discuss wages and so forth then. Now, we'd better get to work.

The shop will be filling soon and Mother will be awake shortly.'

At the mention of Agnes, Sally's happiness dipped. 'How was she over the weekend? She wasn't ... hasn't ... ?'

'No, dear, no. She was no more difficult than usual.'

Sally couldn't contain a small sigh. 'I'm glad to hear that, Miss Sharp.'

Pru filled two cups. 'Here. Tea for you and Mother when she wakes.'

Another day with the pernicious old woman stretching before her, Sally squared her shoulders, needing all the resolve she could muster.

'Please don't mention Maggie to Mother. I shall tell her myself, soon.'

Smiling sadly in understanding, Sally climbed the stairs.

'The bastards! The rotten, stinking bastards!' Nancy fumed. She shifted the hot pie dish in her arms. 'You should've let me at them, lad. Cowards, that's what they are. Bleedin' cowards!'

Joseph stared ahead, mind clearly on the upcoming task.

'Who do they think they are, anyroad? And that young 'un what flew at thee, well, you can see he takes after his mam. She can be a vicious bitch at times, can Ivy. Then there's Arthur: why drag his son off you then thump you one hisself?'

'For the love of Christ, will you shut that gob of yourn? Tha knows why. That bitch must of told them a pack of lies about me.'

She shook her head in disgust. 'Well, after what they did to you yesterday, I'd happily swing for the lot of them.' As she gazed at his bruised face, her heart contracted. 'It were reet thoughtful of you to push me into Nellie's when you spotted them. They'd have shouted their mouths to my father about us seeing each other. I do love thee, you know that, but I can't bring shame upon him.

'Once you've dealt with Sally, we can be together proper, can't we? Then you'll not have to stop at that filthy cottage of your sister's; we can live together. Aye, not long now and I can shout my love for thee, to anyone who'll listen, from the bloody rooftops.'

She ignored the usual prickle of unease when wondering what he planned for Sally. All she knew was he wanted rid of her for good. And more than anything, so did she. With her out of the way, they could be together for ever. She just didn't like dwelling on how he'd achieve it.

Skirting a small stream, Joseph continued through the field. He began to laugh and she smiled.

''Ere, what's tickled you?'

'Is that what you thought I did, pushed you out of sight for your reputation's sake?' Her smile slipped and he laughed harder. 'You're a stupid bitch at times, you are really. Aye, I didn't want them knowing you've been messing with me, you're right there. But it weren't for you, you daft sow.

'I did it because if all that lot you've thieved from your father's shop comes out, I don't want my name dragged into it. Folk will know you swiped it for me. That's why I did it, you silly bitch.' Snorting with mirth, he quickened his pace. 'Now move it, for God's sake. I've been waiting for this. I'm going to get so much pleasure from wrapping my hands round that scraggy throat.'

Gulping heartache, Nancy hurried after him. Yet doubt, for the first time, tugged at her. Staring at his broad back as he scaled a wall and dropped behind Spring Row, she bit her lip until she tasted blood. *He does love me. He does. He doesn't mean to be cruel, it's just his way*, she told herself firmly. She rested the pie dish on the wall and hauled herself up.

Joseph hopped from foot to foot. 'Hurry up and jump afore someone spots us. 'Ere, give me your hand.'

His large one closed around hers and she melted. 'Ta, love.'

When she stood beside him in the deserted back lane, he placed his hands on her shoulders and grinned. 'By God, I'm going to enjoy this.'

She pressed her lips to his. He pushed her against the wall and her body relaxed. She knew she'd been right; he did love her. Feeling him harden, she smiled inwardly. The thrill of danger turned him on something rotten and she knew just how to stoke the flames.

Crushing Nancy closer, Joseph sucked and bit her neck. But, returning his lips to hers, he gasped and stumbled back. For a split second the face before him had been Sally's.

'Love?'

He shook his head. What in hell had just happened?

'You all right? You've gone a shocking colour.'

'Eh? Aye. Get that dish and get moving.'

Rage made his blood boil. That bitch was sending him mad. She was constantly on his mind. He had to find her. And when he did, she'd suffer more than she could imagine.

'I'll be away, then.'

He nodded. 'You sure you know what to do?'

'Aye. Serve Father his meal then keep an eye out from the shop door.'

'And?'

'And if I see anyone making for Ivy's, sing as loud as I can to get your attention.'

'Are you certain that father of yourn won't think it queer you squalling all of a sudden?'

'Nay, I'm allus bursting into song. Love singing, I do. It sends him barmy, mind.' She smiled at the admission. 'I'll not let you down, love.'

'You'd better not. Mess this up and you'll regret it, girl.' Glancing to the cottage, his spine tingled. 'The owd bitch won't be so brave this time.'

'Scare the liver from her, lad. She'll soon talk. And don't fret, I'll be ready if I see anyone coming.'

When she'd rounded the corner, he looked left and right then sprinted to the Morgans'.

Pressing against the stone wall, he craned his neck to steal a glance through the kitchen window. He grinned to see that Ivy had her back to him, peeling vegetables by the fire. Silently, he eased open the door.

His fists tightened in hatred. She'd suffer for her meddling, his humiliation, for slapping his face. She'd suffer for harbouring Sally. And she'd suffer for her husband's and son's blows.

Baring his teeth, he crept across the flagged floor.

Midday seemed to take an age to arrive and Sally sent up a thank-you when Pru's voice drifted upstairs. She was home in no time and after feeding Jonathan, cuddled him tenderly. She treasured these snatched minutes before she had to leave him again.

Grace pushed a cup across and motioned to a plate of bread and butter. 'Eat up, lass.'

As she ate, Sally told her of Pru's decision. 'I cannot wait to tell Maggie the good news. I'm so glad Miss Sharp agreed.'

A mischievous smile played at Grace's mouth. 'So Con was right. He said no one could deny you, didn't he?'

She laughed softly. 'You can look at me like that all you like. I'm sure he'll make some woman very happy but—'

'It'll not be thee. Aye, you've said. Eeh, you want your bumps feeling, lass. He's a good 'un, he is, and thinks the world of thee; you can see it a mile off. Ed and Stan got on with him yesterday evening, didn't they? And you know I approve. Just don't rule him out altogether. I know you're still married but you don't know what the future holds. Tha might be a free woman one day—'

'And I'll remain one,' she murmured, all trace of laughter gone. 'I couldn't be with any man . . . like that . . . again.'

The memory of Con's kiss brought back a small smile. It was a good thing Grace didn't know of that; she'd plan to have the banns read!

'You still fret over that divilish bastard, don't you?' Sally lowered her gaze and Grace sighed. 'You're rid of him, love. He'll not hurt thee again. You've your family, here, now. You're not his to do with as he pleases, with no one to question him, not any more.

'Anyroad, you said yourself he don't know you're here. And if your Mrs Morgan don't tell him, he ain't likely to find out. It's time to start living, lass, to lay the demons to rest and look to the future – for that babby's sake as well as yours.'

Tears pricked her eyes. Sally wanted desperately to agree but couldn't. The horrors he'd put her through haunted her. Him finding her, snatching Jonathan – even killing her – were very real possibilities.

'Aunt Grace, I'm in heaven, now. Life before was hardly worth fighting for.' She stroked Jonathan's cheek. 'It is, now, and I've this one to thank. However, I cannot deny I'm terrified that fiend will find me. He'll be trying, you can be sure of that. I pray daily, until I run out of words, he doesn't succeed.'

Grace's eyes flashed with protective love. 'I half hope he does turn up, for he'd get his comeuppance, have no fear of that. Your uncle would thump his warped head in. Raging, Ed were, when I told him how that swine treated thee over the years. I'll say that for him, in all the years of our marriage, he's never once lifted a finger to me. Though by God, I've give him cause to many a time.' She chuckled. 'Aye, he's been a fair husband.

'I only wish things were better betwixt him and our Stan, but you can't have it all, can you, lass? Maybe in t' future . . . ? What I'm getting at is I want that for thee, to know the love of a good man. And as far as I'm concerned, you'll not find it with no one nicer than Con Malloy.'

Peggy's hacking cough saved Sally from responding. As Grace murmured over the skeletal figure, Sally pondered over Con. Could she take a chance on love? As Grace pointed out, she might indeed be a free woman one day. Would she rue it if she let him slip through her fingers?

The more she saw of him, the more she found to like, it was true. He'd revealed he ran a clothing stall at nearby Smithfield Market. The day they met, he'd been visiting Bolton market as he was considering opening a stall there, too, which his cousin would run. She knew if this cousin was anything like Con, it would be a roaring success.

Con had a way with both women and men; he'd had Ed and Stan in his palm last night. Grace's opinion of him also strengthened when he'd sat by Peggy's bedside and, with real tenderness, told her what a big brave colleen she was and promised to buy her a pretty ribbon for her hair.

And yet . . . She sighed. *Was* it her experience with Joseph or for an altogether different reason that she'd rebuffed his attentions?

'Oh! Sally, help me, lass!'

Thoughts of Tommy melted. She placed Jonathan in his basket and hurried to the bed. Peggy's mouth, nightdress and sheet were stained crimson. She grabbed a rag and dabbed at blood still trickling between the grey lips, while Grace rushed for a clean nightdress.

When the flow ceased, she lifted a small hand and kissed it. 'Rest, now, good girl. Shall I fetch Thunder?'

At Peggy's weak nod, she lifted Shaun's carving from the shelf. Though too frail for play, the girl found comfort in the wooden beast she'd lovingly named, would tuck it in beside her.

Sally watched the chest rise and fall laboriously. To see her withering away pained her dearly. She and Stan sat by her bedside each night, talking to her, holding her hand. Sally just wished she'd met her sooner, that she had memories of her before this hideous disease.

When Peggy was sleeping, she went in search of her aunt. As she passed Shield he looked up dolefully, as though sensing the child's plight, and she stroked his ear. She found Grace in the backyard, slumped against the mangle, Peggy's nightdress pressed to her mouth. Her muffled sobs tore at Sally. She wrapped her arms around her aunt with a sigh of despair, wishing she could take away her pain.

'She's dying, i'nt she? There's no use denying it any longer. My little girl's dying.'

There was nothing she could say. She held Grace tighter, her own heart breaking.

After throwing carrots into a pan by her feet, Ivy reached for the cabbage. Her back muscles twinged and she sighed, knowing she had a pile of clothes and sheets in steep to see to once she finished here.

When she felt the searing pain around her neck, her reaction was to scream but the pressure restricted it. She tried twisting around; the grip tightened and light spurted behind her eyes. She clawed the hands choking her but the world was fading . . .

Suddenly, they released her. Rearing back, she took an almighty breath and whirled around, but her streaming eyes blurred the room. When the voice cut through her splutters she didn't need to see to know to whom it belonged.

'That's just for starters, Poison Ivy.'

Bending double, she fetched up a stream of bile. She spotted the dropped cabbage and knife beneath her chair but moments later, his large hand snatched up the latter.

She drew a trembling hand across her mouth. 'How . . . I thought I'd locked . . . ?'

Sitting down at the table, Joseph smiled. He ran the blade's tip under his nail and wiped the dirt on his trousers. 'Tha needn't fret on that. It's what I'm to do now I'm in what's important.'

'You demented bastard, yer. I ain't scared of thee.' Glancing at the knife, Ivy's mouth ran dry but she lifted her chin. 'I'm warning you, Joseph. Get from my cottage and Spring Row on your two feet or I swear on all that's holy, you'll leave in a box.'

He threw his head back and laughed. 'I've gorra better idea. Tell me where that slut of mine is and I might let *you* live to see the morrow. I could've snapped your worthless neck just now and believe me, I'll not stop squeezing next time if you don't start talking. Where is she?'

'Out of your evil reach, that's where.' Despite her fear, she stepped closer. 'You'll not harm her again. Threaten me all you want. I'd sooner you gut me like a fish than tell you where she is.'

With a roar, he leapt up, grabbed the front of her dress and lifted her off her feet. 'Tell me!'

'Never! You don't frighten me, you bastard,' she bluffed. 'I ain't no slip of a lass and I don't bully easy. Go on, do your worst. You'll not get far. My Arthur and the lads will be home any minute.' She ran her gaze over his bruises. 'Did a right number on you, didn't they? They'll finish the job, mind, when they find you here.'

Grinning, he tossed her to the floor. 'Did you really think I'd swallow that, you stupid owd bitch? They're at the pit, will be for hours.' She looked away and he laughed. 'You see, I've been racking my brains forra way to get youse back. I were thinking on burning yon cottage to the ground while you slept, kill four birds with one stone, but that's not my style.

'You'll suffer, all right, but I want to see the terror on your faces while I do it. I'll pick you off one by one, torture the lot of you till you're begging me to put you out of your misery. I were going to bide my time but your husband and son, jumping me yesterday like the cowards they are, put paid to that. The time for waiting's over.'

Her blood ran cold at the eerily soft words but the threat to her family sparked fresh bravado. Lunging, she landed a punch to his mouth. He staggered back and she leapt forward and snatched the abandoned knife from the table.

Panting with pure fury, he charged. She jabbed the blade at his face. Lightning fast, he grabbed her wrist and twisted. She fought like a raging bull but the pain of the bone close to snapping was too intense. To her horror, the knife clattered to the floor.

Joseph threw his hands around Ivy's neck, bent her over the table and squeezed with all his might.

'You're first to go but don't fret,' he hissed, pressing his face to hers, 'your family will be joining you shortly. I'll find Sally without your help. And when I do, I'll watch the life drain from *her* worthless body, an' all.'

As her flailing limbs stilled, singing rang out from the row.

His mouth fell open. He flung Ivy's inert body aside and bolted. Knocking at the front door sounded as he reached the back one. He scrambled through into the lane.

Sprinting away, he smiled jubilantly as the scream of Ivy's visitor filled the air.

Chapter 17

AGNES WAS IN a foul mood. For two hours, she'd lain silently, facing the wall. She'd refused a bathing, rejected breakfast, and the tea Sally brought up upon her arrival sat untouched by the bedside.

Itching with boredom, Sally shifted on the hard chair. Though tempted to ask what ailed Agnes, her expression deterred her.

She'd wondered whether she'd annoyed her by returning late yesterday, Peggy's incident having prolonged her break, but dismissed this. Agnes wasn't one to hold back; she'd have made her feelings known immediately. That perhaps she knew about Maggie, she also rejected; Pru hadn't mentioned anything earlier, was her quietly cheerful self.

Glancing for the hundredth time at the clock, she sighed inwardly. Lunchtime was a while away and this inactivity would only prolong the delay until its arrival. Her eyes flicked to the bed. Agnes wasn't talkative at the best of times but this brooding silence was unnerving. In desperation, she tried again.

'Would you like some fresh tea, Mrs Sharp?'

Agnes grunted refusal.

'I could read to you, if you'd like?' Sally persisted. 'Or perhaps fetch you a bite—?'

'How much does your child mean to you, girl?'

The unexpected question, and its nature, took Sally by surprise. 'Why, he means the world to me, Mrs Sharp. He's my entire reason for living.'

'When you are parted, do you pine for him?'

'Indeed. I know he's well cared for, but still—'

'You're bereft in his absence?'

'Yes, yes, I am.' She waited. Silence. Curiosity got the better of her. She crossed to the bed. 'Is something wrong, Mrs Sharp? You seem somewhat—'

'She was such a tiny baby. Such a delicate scrap of life. I didn't think she'd survive the night but she proved me wrong.' Agnes turned and her eyes were unusually soft. 'Did you have a difficult time bearing your child?'

A smile touched Sally's lips. 'I did. But I had the most wonderful help at hand that anyone could wish.'

'I shall remember it until my dying breath. The weather was atrocious; it fitted the occasion perfectly. Never in my life had I prayed as fervently as that night. Never had I begged the Almighty's help, nor needed it as much. I waited, waited, watching that chest rise and fall. And as the new day dawned, I knew He would not claim her. My pleading had come to nothing.' Sighing deeply, the old woman closed her eyes.

She gazed at her, aghast. 'Why, Mrs Sharp? Why would you wish such a wicked thing?'

The answer was like a whisper on the breeze. 'It matters not. None of it matters, now.' Suddenly, her features returned to normal, the maudlin look leaving her eyes. From beneath the bedclothes, she extracted an envelope sealed with a black wax stamp. 'Would you deliver this when you leave at lunchtime? The address is not far: number forty, Great Ancoats Street.'

'Yes, Mrs Sharp.'

Agnes handed it over with a curt nod. 'Now, I think I shall have that tea. Make haste, girl. No dawdling.'

On the walk home, Sally still reeled from the confession. She'd heard and seen enough the past week to gauge her employer – today's behaviour was out of character.

To spare Pru's feelings, she didn't mention the conversation and had carried out her mother's request with barely a word. When she'd returned to the room, Agnes's expression held no trace of remembrance, and Sally's bewilderment grew. The rest of the morning passed as usual, and now she half wondered whether she'd imagined the incident.

Then there was the letter. As instructed, she'd delivered it before heading home. A maid had received it without a word. What it contained, who the recipient was, she didn't know; the envelope lacked an addressee. The oddness of it all made her head ache.

Grace and her close friend and neighbour, Winnie Knox, greeted her warmly. After feeding Jonathan, she joined them at the table. She inclined her head to Peggy's bed. 'How is she, Aunt Grace?'

Grace raised her hands in a helpless motion. 'Like I've just been telling Winnie, no better, no worse. She's peaceful, and for that I'm grateful.'

Sally smiled at the rotund woman beside her. 'It's nice to see you, Mrs Knox.'

'Aye, lass, and thee.' Leaning in, Winnie added in a loud whisper, 'How's things going with owd Sharp? She not tried clouting you one, yet?'

'Winnie!' spluttered Grace.

'What? I'm only asking.' She folded her arms beneath her mountainous bust. 'Queer pair, them two. I don't know how tha stomachs it. I'd be frightened to death alone with them all day.'

Pushing the morning's event from her mind, Sally smiled. She liked Winnie a great deal. She'd been a pillar of support to the family since Peggy became ill.

'It's going well, Mrs Knox. My friend starts work in the shop on Saturday, too.' She smiled again, recalling Maggie's delight yesterday upon hearing the news. 'Mrs Sharp doesn't seem so bad.' The blatant lie tasted bitter, but she had no choice. Troubles aplenty plagued her aunt as it was.

Winnie's chins wobbled as she nodded. 'Aye, well, just mind her, lass. If she does try owt, thump the bugger and run straight home.'

Grace hooted with laughter. 'Run straight . . . ? She's norra babby, Winnie. Eeh, I don't know, the things you come out with. *You're* bloomin' barmy, never mind them two.'

'Well, you know what I mean. Anyroad, she'd do well to, regardless, with that madman on t' loose.'

They fell silent, expressions sober, and Sally's smile died. 'Madman?'

'It's awful, lass, awful. I don't know what this world's coming to. It's a good job you left when you did.' Grace turned to Winnie, who nodded gravely. 'I said to you when you told me, didn't I, said it's a good job our Sally came here? It don't bear thinking in, does it?'

'It don't, Grace.'

Sally's face creased in bemusement. 'I'm sorry, has something happened in Bolton?'

'Eeh, it's terrible, lass. A wench were strangled yesterday – in her own kitchen, by all accounts, while her family were out at work. What if the swine what's done it makes his way up here? I hope they catch whoever's responsible, quick, and make him swing. Shocking, it is.'

'Goodness, that's terrible!'

'Our Fanny's husband were saying when he arrived home this morning,' Winnie continued. 'His mam dwells in Bolton and he were visiting her forra few days, for she's not long for this world, poor wench. He said the attack's on everyone's lips; no news travels faster than bad.

'He don't know the ins and outs, like, but whatever's gone on, it's shocking.' Frowning, she drummed the table with podgy fingers. 'Where did I say it occurred, Grace? Summer . . . summat or other?'

'Nay, not Summer, Spring. Spring Row.'

'*No* . . .' Sally reared back, mouth stretched in a silent scream.

Grace and Winnie's confused cries rang in her ears, then blackness consumed her.

'Now what d'you think you're about?' Brows knitted, Martha jerked her head to the fireside. 'Get your arse in that chair, Ivy Morgan, and stay put. I told thee last night, I said don't be doing nowt, that I'd do whatever were needed this afternoon.'

Ivy suppressed a sigh. Though aware that her friend was trying to help, Martha was beginning to get on her nerves. If not so weary, she'd have told her – nicely but firmly – to bugger off home. She couldn't stand this idleness, however much everyone insisted.

Martha raised Ivy's chin and peered at the angry welts. 'I'll give them another bathe in a minute. They still sore?'

'Aye,' she admitted, 'but don't tell Arthur or the lads I said. They fret as it is.'

Sitting at the table, Martha took over peeling the vegetables. 'D'you know, the day all this began, yon Arthur flew at that bugger, Goden, outside this here cottage. The coward scarpered but he swore to me, Arthur did, he'd have his day with him. Now, I know you're worried, wench, but it's been coming, has this.'

'He'll not let this go; it's gone too far for that. He blames hisself, you know, said if him and our Tommy hadn't thumped Joseph Sunday, this mightn't have happened. I don't believe that. It'd been brewing since Sally came. I knew he'd be back. He's not someone to walk away. He wanted revenge and got it.'

'Aye, and Arthur will get his the night. Tommy still set on going with him?'

'Oh, is he. I've never seen the lad as he were last night. Well, you saw yourself. I thought he'd explode with rage.'

Reaching for another potato, Martha nodded. 'I were bubbling, an' all, wench. The state that Jenkins lass were in, I thought he'd done for thee. It's a bloody good job she called when she did. It don't bear thinking on what would've happened if she hadn't interrupted the swine.' At Ivy's frown, she clicked her tongue. 'I'm sorry. I don't mean to be maudlin.'

'Nay, you're right. I owe my life to that lass. And to think . . .' Colour touched her cheeks. 'I've allus believed she weren't good enough for my Tommy, foolish sod that I am.'

'Well, I'd say you're stuck with her, Ivy. Anyone with half an eye can see she's fair smitten. She don't seem a bad lass.'

They lapsed into companionable silence. Gazing across the hills through the window, Ivy's frown returned as she recalled Dolly's words yesterday. The lass said she'd had to come, was worried as she hadn't seen Tommy in a while. What was going on? He clearly hadn't invited her to dinner, nor met her Saturday. Why lie? Where on earth *had* he been?

Her hand drifted to her neck. That bastard. What would follow? He'd said he'd pick them off. Was Arthur next? Her sons? Meeting those hate-filled eyes yesterday, the world slipping, she really thought it was the end. She'd woken, in more pain than she'd ever known, to Martha and Dolly cradling her, faces awash with tears.

She smiled, couldn't deny Martha had been an angel. She'd refused to let them send for the doctor so, with gentle care, Martha tended Ivy herself. Her friend had also calmed down Dolly, tidied the room and prepared a meal for the men. She'd known food would be the last thing on their minds, but Martha had meant well. She was deeply grateful for her support.

'That's the veg done. Shall I brew some tea?'

Ivy nodded. As Martha bustled around the fire, her thoughts returned to last night. Pandemonium erupted upon her husband and sons' return. Their anguish and fury were a terrible sight. Arthur made back for the door, intent on finding Joseph and smashing his head to a pulp, but Martha had stopped him, pointing out that his wife needed him.

He'd relented but insisted no one inform the police. He'd dole out Joseph's punishment. And it would be harsher than what any court in the land could decree.

'I want to say again how grateful I am to thee for stopping Arthur,' Ivy murmured as Martha poured tea. 'There's no telling what would've happened with the rage he were in.'

'He'll still give him the beating of his life when he finds him, Ivy – yon Tommy, an' all. He near murdered his mam, wench. You can't blame him for wanting to go with Arthur.'

She heaved a sigh. 'I'm frightened to death of what will happen. Don't get me wrong, that bastard deserves all he gets; I'd have gutted him meself given the chance. But if they finish up doing for him . . . They'll not swing for him,' she ground out. 'I were glad upon hearing they'd given him a thumping, but this . . . this is different. The murder in their eyes last night . . . I'm frightened, Martha.'

'I know. Were it my Reg and our lads, I'd feel the same. But they need to do this, their way. As Arthur said, there's no use going to the police, for that swine will no doubt have an alibi. It'd be your word against his. When all's said and done, you were the only one to see him. You have to let your men do what they need to. You've no choice, not with this.'

'They'll be home from the pit, soon. Mother of God, I pray they don't go too far. Happiness filled this cottage when that carpenter took our Shaun on. Over the bloody moon, we were; I didn't think owt could dampen my mood. Goden's ruined that. He's put a black cloud over my family, and after this night it'll only darken.'

'Eeh, wench, now don't you cry,' Martha chided softly when tears welled in her eyes. 'This ain't the Ivy I know. Don't you let him crush that spirit of yourn, don't you dare. Once he's got his, later, it'll be over.

'You've much to be happy about, and not just with young Shaun. There'll be a wedding to look forward to soon, you mark my words; all what's occurred will no doubt bring Tommy and that Jenkins lass closer. This time next year, there might be the patter of little feet, just think on that. All this, it'll be long forgotten.'

With effort, Ivy smiled. There *was* much to look forward to. Shaun started his carpentry work shortly, and Tommy . . . Would he and Dolly wed? From what the dairymaid said, something was afoot. When this business with Joseph blew over, she'd sit him down for a good talk, she determined.

'I'll find Sally without your help. And when I do, I'll watch the life drain from her worthless body, an' all.'

The haunting threat continued to plague her. She just prayed Sally would stay in Manchester, where she was safe. If she ever returned and he discovered her . . .

The consequences didn't bear thinking about.

'Sally, this is madness! Ed, will you tell her it's madness?'

Her uncle reached for his pipe. 'I agree, but it's her decision.'

Grace clicked her tongue and turned back to Sally. 'Please, lass, don't go. It mightn't be Mrs Morgan or owt to do with that husband of yourn. Whoever she is, she survived, so there's no need for you to go. Tha can't just up and leave. What about work? The babby?'

Sally's chin lifted: her mind was made up. 'Aunt Grace, I'm going. I understand your fears but I must. Mrs Morgan saved my life. I *must* make sure it's not her. I have Miss Sharp's consent to take tomorrow off work and, as you know, Mrs Knox shall ask Fanny to wet-nurse Jonathan.' Glancing at Ed's and Stan's worried frowns, she sighed. 'I have to do this.'

Grace turned away in frustration. 'You'll be like a lamb to the slaughter, don't you see? If this is his revenge for them helping thee, who d'you think he'll be on t' prowl for now? Please, don't go. I'll not lose you again.'

Sally forced herself not to rush to comfort her; Grace would only up her pleas until she conceded. She couldn't risk that. She must return to Breightmet. If Ivy had almost lost her life for saving hers and Jonathan's . . . Dear God, she'd never forgive herself. That woman was her saviour. She'd never live in peace until she knew.

Quiet weeping filled the kitchen and her heart ached with contrition. She hated seeing Grace upset – more so, knowing she'd caused it. She'd inadvertently sparked another row, too. Unwilling to risk taking Jonathan, she'd been grateful for Winnie's suggestion that Fanny feed him, but Grace was appalled and had blasted her friend for encouraging the 'bloody senseless plan'.

Grace wiped her face with her apron, eyes suddenly bright. 'If you must go, take Con. He seems the handy sort if you do cross paths with that husband of yourn.'

She was aghast. 'I cannot do that!'

'He'd agree if you asked, I'm sure.'

'Aunt Grace, I cannot journey with Con unchaperoned. What on earth would people say?'

'Take Ed, then. He'd give the divil a good hiding if you did see him. Will you, Ed? Will you go with her? Please?'

Her uncle opened his mouth but Sally got in first. 'Uncle Ed has work in the morning. He couldn't possibly take time off and I wouldn't let him.' Sighing, she wrapped her arms around Grace. 'I know you're worried and I hate myself for putting you through this but please, please don't make this harder for me than it is already.

'I don't expect you to understand but for my peace of mind I must do this, and do it alone. This is my and Joseph's mess and I'm damned if anyone else will suffer for it.'

'But Sally—'

'I'll take Shield. He's all the protection I could need,' she cut in gently. 'You have my word, Aunt Grace. As soon as I see with my own two eyes that Mrs Morgan's well, I shall come straight back.' She turned to her uncle and cousin. 'Do either of you know anyone with a cart who would take me in the morning? The train scared the life from me last time; I couldn't bear it again. I've money to pay them.'

Stan shook his head but Ed, avoiding Grace's eye, nodded. 'Aye. I'll call on him when I've had some grub.' His gaze softened. 'You watch yourself the morrow, d'you hear? I'd accompany thee if I could, you know that, don't you? I can't shirk work, lass, not with our Peggy's medicine to buy on top of everything else.'

'Oh, of course, I understand. Thank you.'

Admitting defeat, Grace trudged to the fire to begin the evening meal.

Sally strove to calm her thumping heart. Would Joseph discover her? Pure loathing consumed her at the thought of him. Would Shield be adequate protection? Should she heed her aunt's advice, send Con a message?

Fear of inciting gossip *had* been good reason to reject the suggestion. But deep down, as much as she hated admitting it, she knew her reluctance to have the Irishman accompany her was due to Tommy. She didn't want him believing she and Con . . . Not that he'd care, but still . . .

Heat flooded her face. However hard she fought the memory of him, of her body's response to his touch, it crept to mind often, filling her with longing and shame.

Now, as well as the terror of Joseph discovering her, of Ivy having suffered at his hands, a different one took root – fear of being unable to conceal her feelings for the man she could never have.

It hadn't taken Tommy and his father long to discover where Alice Russell dwelled.

They received information at the first inn at which they enquired. Whether folk disliked Joseph as much in Deansgate as in Breightmet, or the shillings slackened the tongues, they neither knew nor cared. They had the address. That's what mattered.

Passing down the ruinous street to Chapel Alley, they garnered mixed reactions. Prostitutes and customers, preoccupied in doorways, paid them little attention. Some doorways appeared empty but as they neared, wan-faced women sidled out, touting for business.

Bands of savage-looking men peered from the shadows, likely deliberating whether these strangers' pockets contained anything worth stealing. But Tommy knew their murderous expressions – if his was anything like his father's – coupled with their thick muscles, would deter them from trying. Plenty of ale-soaked sots spilling from inns, later, would make easier targets.

Scouring the decrepit cottages for number thirteen, he clenched his fists. Lying awake last night, he'd thought long and hard what he'd do to Joseph. He'd make him pay for what he'd done. Fury like no other engulfed him – interwoven with crippling guilt. He could have prevented this. If he'd told his family what George Turner had revealed, they would have been prepared. Too wrapped up in Sally, he hadn't thought of their safety.

Because of him, his mother had almost died. And to top it all, he'd failed Sally, too. His own wants overshadowed the purpose of his trip to Manchester. Was she next? Would Joseph do to her as he'd done to his mother?

His step faltered. The need for her, to love her, protect her, burned just as brightly, until he truly suspected he was going mad.

When his father pointed to a door, Tommy cleared his mind. He must remain focused. Sunday proved Joseph to be the devil they knew he was. He was damned if he'd let him off as lightly this time. This beating would be for his mother, who had never harmed anyone in her life, who had nurtured and cared for him always. Who had nearly died at the hands of the bastard behind this door.

He wanted revenge for her. And he wanted it for Sally. Whatever happened this night, he'd gladly face the consequences.

'Right, lad, remember what I said. Give him the beating of his life but don't lose it. He's not worth dancing at the end of a rope.'

Nodding, Tommy made to thump the door but Arthur stopped him.

'I'm serious, here. You need to keep a level head. Last Sunday . . . I've never seen thee like that.' A curious frown appeared. 'The venom in your eyes when you looked upon him fair shocked me, it did.'

Tommy was unable to meet his gaze. Seeing the man legally bound to the woman *he* loved more than life, a ferocious mist had descended. His feet had taken on a life of their own and propelled him across the road.

He still remembered the feel of Joseph's face meeting his fist. He'd landed a blow to his cheekbone, another to his mouth. If his father hadn't dragged him off, he wouldn't have stopped until the cobbles ran red, so extreme was the swell of loathing.

'Look, I know you were angry, lad; I bloody were, an' all,' his father added. 'After dragging you off, I were willing to leave it, figured he'd got what he deserved.

But when he started spewing insults about your mam, well, that's why he gorra thump off me, an' all. It's a good job he scarpered when he did.

'What I'm saying is this: that bastard knows how to rile us. We must play it different the night. He'll suffer, all right, and tha can have the pleasure of delivering the first blow, but we must keep our calm. Understand?'

'Aye.'

Arthur continued staring at him. Slowly, his eyes widened with a mixture of surprise and horror. 'You're in love with that lass, ain't you?'

Tommy could only blink.

'Your reaction to Goden . . . I *knew* there were more to it than met the eye. That's where your mind's been at for weeks, in't it?'

'I . . .' Words failed him. It was pointless denying it.

'We'll talk about this later. Let's get on with what we came to do. Now, remember what I said. Keep your calm.'

Glaring at Alice's door through tears of shame and despair, Tommy lifted a fist and thumped hard.

The smell emitted when it creaked open brought grimaces to them both. They pushed past the slovenly-looking woman without a word.

''Ere, what the divil's your game? Who d'you think youse are, barging in here?'

Ignoring her, they peered about. With no fire in the grate and only the guttering light from a single candle on the table, it took them a moment to become accustomed to the gloom. A man rose from the fireside chair and Tommy lunged. Grabbing his throat, he slammed him against the wall.

'What the—!'

'Shut your *stinking* trap. Did you really think you'd get away with it? Did you?' he shouted, grip tightening.

The woman screeched and rushed forward but Arthur blocked her path. 'What's *he* done?' she squalled, trying to claw past.

'What's he done? I'll tell thee what he's—'

'It's not him.'

'Son?'

'It's not him.'

Squinting at the figure, Arthur swore under his breath. 'Where is he?'

'Who?'

'Don't try me, woman. Where's that bastard, Goden?' He turned to the coughing man, who was clutching his throat. 'We know he's dwelling here. Tell us where he is or by God, you'll have more than a sore neck.'

'Listen 'ere, youse two. I don't know what's afoot but if it's our Joseph you're after, you're out of luck. We've seen nowt of him for days. You ask my husband. We ain't seen him, have we, Harold?'

Harold glanced at them in turn then shook his head.

Disgust filled Tommy. He'd noticed the warning glint in the wife's eye. How could they protect the evil swine?

'Well? What you still doing here? Clear off afore you get the poker across your skulls. He ain't here so you'll have to try elsewhere, won't you?' She swung the door wide. 'Go on, bugger off.'

Tommy brought his palms down on the littered table. 'How can you harbour that bastard after what he's done?'

'Son . . . Christ's sake.'

He followed his father's gaze. On a pallet, shapes shifted. Candlelight danced across small faces, white with fear. A child rose, skittered across and wrapped her arms around Harold's legs.

"Ere, sit your arse back down, you.'

Ignoring her mother, she gazed up. 'My uncle ain't here, mister, honest. Please, don't hurt Father again.'

Tommy drew a hand across his mouth then turned to Arthur, who nodded.

'This ain't the place, lad. He'll get what's coming to him but not here, not like this.'

'That's it, go on, get from my home,' Joseph's sister jeered as they pushed past.

'You'd best start praying for that foulness you call a brother. Me and my lad, we'll find him.'

Her smirk slipped at the sheer venom in Arthur's tone. Then she slammed the door in their faces.

'What now?' Tommy ground out as they turned back into Deansgate. 'He can't get away with this!'

'And he won't. I swore weeks ago I'd have my day with him and have it I will. He can't hide for ever.'

'They gone?'

Alice let the scrap of curtain fall. 'Aye.'

'What the hell were that about?'

Reaching the bottom of the stairs, Joseph shrugged at his brother-in-law. He eased into his chair and rested his feet on the hearth. 'How should I know?'

'How . . . how should *you* know? They were here for thee; course you must bloody well know!'

'That bitch Sally's told them a pack of lies, ain't she?' He turned to the window and grinned. 'You told them good and proper, our Alice.'

It was her turn to shrug. 'You're my brother. Bastards, who do they think they are, barging in like that? I *would've* wrapped that poker round their brains, an' all.' Her eyes narrowed when Harold shook his head. 'What's wrong with thee?'

'What's wrong with me? *What's wrong with me?* I near had the liver kicked out of me because of him. I reckon they would've, an' all, but for our Lily. You want to wise up, you do. He's up to summat, he is. Folk don't come baying for your blood for nowt.'

Joseph laughed and it grew in pitch when Alice stormed to her husband.

'Look at the poor bugger's face. He's already black and blue.' She tapped her temple. 'That pair ain't full shillings. What did you want me to do, let him get another thumping for what his whore of a wife's been spouting? He's my brother—'

'And I'm your husband! I'm telling you, summat's afoot, here. And what in hell's there to laugh at, Joseph? Kin or no, I'll not have you fetching trouble to my door, d'you hear? Whatever you've done, you sort it – and quick.'

Joseph grinned at his sister. 'He's as barmy as that pair.'

'Aye. Happen I should've let them give him a pasting. It might've knocked some sense into him.'

Harold gazed at them, snatched up his jacket and cap and slammed from the cottage.

Joseph settled deeper in the lumpy seat. 'Ah, ignore him, he'll calm down. He's right about one thing, mind. The lass did well, there. I reckon they'd not have let it lie but for her.'

Alice lumbered to the chair opposite. 'First thing she's done right in her life, silly bitch.' She picked at a stump of black tooth, her eyes turning thoughtful. 'D'you think they'll be back?'

Fear lurked in his voice, belying his nonchalant shrug. 'They'll not find me.'

'I'm surprised Harold didn't put two and two together. Folk are talking, you know. It's spread from row to street to bloody village, by all accounts. You're certain the owd 'un's well?'

'Aye, Nancy said last night.'

'Right, well, keep your head low. Bide your time. You'll find the bitch, somehow.'

His knuckles turned white as he imagined slamming them into Sally's face. Where *was* she? Obviously, Ivy knew, but he'd get no joy from that quarter, now. He couldn't risk returning, not with Arthur and that son thirsty for his blood. Frustration burned in him. He closed his eyes.

Keep running, whore. Keep running, he inwardly seethed. *You'll slip up eventually and I'll find you.*

Alice frowned when his eyes sprang open. 'What's up?'

'I'm wondering if it'd be worth me going to Manchester. Happen the workhouse master . . . ?' His enthusiasm died with his words.

'What about him?'

Stroking week-old stubble, he sighed. 'It's unlikely . . . Maybe, just maybe, he's seen her. If yon lass did see her at the market, she'll not have returned to Manchester without good reason.'

'What, you reckon she's found out about—?'

'The master assured me she'd not, but . . . If she *has*, she'd have been back to Manchester like a shot.' Excitement stirred again. 'You think it's worth me going?'

'You'll lose nowt from trying. When will you leave?'

As her uncle discussed his scheme with her mother, Lily shoved her fingers in her ears to block out their cackles. She snuggled closer to the twins and, for the hundredth time, wished the lady on the market had taken her with her.

Chapter 18

TWO INCIDENTS WERE to scupper Sally's plans.

The first occurred during the early hours. The strained atmosphere the night before worsened after the evening meal when, true to his word, Ed secured a cart. Upon his return, the household fell into uneasy silence. The lamplighter had barely passed when, unable to bear it another moment, she'd feigned a headache and escaped to the next room.

She was still awake when sounds of the family retiring filtered through. Long afterwards, sleep was no nearer; the impending journey made it impossible.

When a whimper reached her, her exhausted brain hardly registered it. At the second, her senses awoke. She slipped from the horsehair sofa, padded to the kitchen and squinted about. All was still. Believing her sleep-deprived mind was playing tricks, she was about to turn when a black form shifted by Peggy's bed.

Thinking it was her aunt, she made to tiptoe back next door. She froze when the doleful moan, more insistent now, echoed again.

As Sally approached, another noise replaced it – rattling gasps she hadn't heard across the room.

Surprise halted her step and she saw the figure wasn't Grace, but Shield. He whined again and, shushing him, she peered at the bed. The jagged breaths were coming from her cousin.

She rushed to the chair and shook her aunt's shoulder. 'Aunt Grace, wake up. Peggy . . .'

Grace's eyes opened instantly. When she crossed to the bed and dropped to her knees, Shield sloped to the corner, soft brown eyes never leaving Peggy.

'I'm sorry, I didn't hear you, I— Oh my . . . Peggy, can you hear me? Where does it hurt? Speak to me, lass.' Her daughter answered with a racking cough and she clutched Sally's arm. 'Waken our Ed and Stan, tell them to come quick.' Sobs burst forth but she gulped them back. 'Go, Sally. Go now.'

Nodding blindly, Sally darted from the room.

Within seconds, four figures huddled around the bed. Ed and Stan's murmurs to Peggy mingled with the breaths bubbling in her tortured lungs, and Grace's crying.

Sally brought down Thunder and laid it beside her cousin. She swallowed hard, desperate to stem her own grief for her family's sake, but it was useless. She burst into tears.

Below purple-shadowed eyes, twin spots of colour burned high on Peggy's cheeks and despite her shivers, beads of perspiration glistened on her forehead. She grew weaker, each breath shallower than the last.

Ten minutes later, she died in her mother's arms.

After a moment of stunned silence, a cacophony of noise erupted. Anguished shrieks punctured the dawn, Shield adding to them as he howled at the ceiling.

Sally threw her arms around Grace's neck and hugged the screaming woman tightly. Stan bent double with sobs. Without hesitation, Ed pulled him into his arms.

The following hours were a fog of grief-hazed activity. Neighbours, alerted by the cries, flitted in to pay their respects, Sally brewed endless pots of tea, and the hum of subdued voices and quiet weeping permeated the house.

The sun was high above the grey rooftops when Winnie arrived. Sally saw her slip into the kitchen, red-rimmed eyes tinged with uncertainty – probably owing to Grace's tirade yesterday. Over her aunt's head, she beckoned her across.

Still clutching Peggy, Grace rocked back and forth, dry-eyed, staring at nothing.

Winnie touched her shoulder. 'Oh, wench . . . I'm so sorry.'

Grace frowned down. She traced a finger along her daughter's marble-white cheek. 'I want to die. Help me, Winnie. Make this pain go away.' She started to shake, then a torturous cry ripped from her.

Swallowing her own tears, Sally moved aside and Winnie took her place. As the friends hugged and wept, she peered around. As was customary, they had left the curtains drawn and though several candles flickered, it was difficult to see through the gloom.

She spotted Stan by the window, two neighbours comforting him. Her gaze swept the opposite side. Hunched against the door frame, her uncle stood alone, arms wrapped around himself. She could almost feel his devastation as he watched his wife. His eyes were deep with longing, as though he'd give anything to be the one holding her. They then rested on Stan and she sensed the same burning urge.

Before Sally could reach him, he took a last look at Stan and slipped from the room.

*

After pouring out her grief to Winnie, Grace rallied. She'd finally released her daughter and when the neighbours trickled home, she and Sally laid her out. Tears flowing, they washed her emaciated body and dressed her in a clean nightdress. Afterwards, Grace whispered she was in a better place, free from pain. This seemed to bring her some comfort.

Evening was drawing in. Sally cradled Jonathan by the dead fire, which they wouldn't light before laying Peggy to rest. She glanced at Shield by her feet. He seemed to feel her passing, too. It was as though he'd sensed the child's life ebbing. If not for his cries, she might have died alone.

Bending to scratch his ear, Sally sighed, mind and body exhausted.

'Would you throw a meal of sorts together, lass?' murmured Stan. 'None of us feel like eating but it'll be there if we do.'

'Of course.'

'I'll take Jonathan.' As he held him, Stan's eyes clouded. 'I'm scared,' he whispered. 'My family's disappearing around me. First our Peggy, and you'll be making other plans for Bolton. I've a feeling you'll not come back, that you'll send for Jonathan and we'll not see you again.

'Things ain't so bad since you came. Mam's been happier than I've seen her in a long time. I couldn't bear you leaving, now, never seeing you both again.'

'Oh, Stan.' Dropping into a chair, Sally rested her cheek against his. 'That will never happen. This is my home. Here, with my family.'

'You mean you're not going to Bolton?'

She chose her words carefully so as not to upset him. 'I still need to make a visit, but that's all it shall be. I know you all think I'm mad but I must. They were so good to me.' She glanced at Grace by the bed, stroking Peggy's hand. 'However, I cannot leave Aunt Grace, yet.'

Also watching, Stan dashed away a tear. 'I hate the thought of leaving her alone the morrow.'

Sally nodded. She'd harboured the same concern.

'My master understood when I called in t' baker's, earlier, gave me a stale loaf to fetch home and the day off but I've to be in the morrow. Father's won't allow him time, the sod. I'll not be surprised if he gets the push for not showing today. You due in the morrow, an' all?'

'Yes. There's Jonathan, too. I cannot burden Aunt Grace with him, now. Perhaps Mrs Knox would sit in—?'

'I'll be all right.'

They blushed at Grace overhearing them.

'You'll leave the babby with me, as you allus do, and I'll not hear another word.' She looked around and frowned. 'Where's Ed?'

'I saw him leave earlier, Aunt Grace. Maybe he needed to be alone a while.'

'Aye, mebbe.'

Sally crossed to a cupboard, took out a half-loaf and began on the meal. She was cutting it into thin slices when the front door rattled. She turned, but her gentle smile froze at the sight of her uncle.

Swaying in the doorway, he glared at them in turn and her stomach tightened. Something unpleasant was coming. After years of experience, her intuition was razor sharp; it hadn't proved wrong yet.

Ed ambled to the bed, dropped to his knees and covered his face with his hands. His sobs filled the kitchen and Grace rushed to him. She put her arms around him but he shrugged them off savagely.

'Leave me be, woman.'

'Ed—'

'Leave me be!'

Her face crumpled and Sally bit her lip. Stan passed Jonathan to her and rose. She caught his sleeve. 'No, Stan—'

'It's all right, Sally.'

She held her breath when he laid a hand on her uncle's shoulder. Ed's back stiffened and from the dread in Grace's eyes, it was clear she shared her concerns. He could barely contain his bitterness for Stan at the best of times – consumed with grief and drink, he was capable of doing, and saying, anything.

Suddenly, Ed leapt up, lip curled in a snarl, and Stan stepped back in surprise. 'Father?'

'Don't you call me that. *Never* call me that, not ever again, d'you hear? Only one child in this house had that right and she's laying cowd in that bed.'

Grace's gasp shattered the silence. She gripped the hair at her temples. 'Nay . . . What have you *done?*'

Stan whimpered, and anger burst through Sally. She placed Jonathan in the basket and ran to him. Devastation screamed from his eyes and her fury, which she'd always struggled to contain when witnessing injustice, erupted.

'I never had you down as a bad man, Uncle Ed, but that . . . How could you be so cruel?' she cried. 'My heart is breaking for your loss. To imagine what you're going through . . . However, people make mistakes. Aunt Grace shall suffer hers the rest of her days, but Stan? What sin has he committed? From the moment he was born, he was your son. He's *your* son, Uncle Ed, in every way that matters.'

'You . . . *you* knew?'

Breath caught in her throat. She turned slowly. 'Stan, I'm so sorry. I gave my word—'

'Nay!' Wild-eyed, he turned to Grace. 'Tell me they're lying. Please, Mam!'

The fight left Ed. Like Shield, earlier, he lifted his face and howled. 'Stan . . . Lord, what have I done?'

Her cousin's expression turned empty. Sally fumbled for his hand but he snatched it away.

'Everything makes sense. The way you've allus treated me . . . All my life, I've tried to make you proud, make you love me.'

'I do love thee! I loved thee the moment tha were born. But I can see him. I *allus* see *him* when I look at you. And you,' Ed added to Grace. 'I watched youse earlier, breaking your hearts in front of me, and I couldn't . . .' He ground his fist into his chest. 'It hurts too much in here. Our Peggy kept this family together. She gave me right to be here. What have I, now, eh?'

'Oh, Ed.' Grace reached out, gasping when Stan knocked away her hand. 'Stan—'

'Get away from him. This is your fault.' He embraced Ed, a small cry escaping him when Ed returned it. 'All these years . . . Who was it?'

'Stan, love, I never meant—'

'Tell me!'

Sally put her arm around Grace's shoulders. 'Stan, please—'

'As for you.' His features contorted in disgust. 'You're no longer family to me, d'you hear? I thought . . . we'd become friends. And all the time . . . I wish you'd never come.'

'No, Stan, we *are*, we—'

'You lied to me! You're as bad as her.'

'No, please.' She reached out to him but her aunt, face oddly calm, pulled her back.

'This ain't Sally's fault. I begged her not to tell. This has gone on long enough. I can't do it any more.' Grace paused. 'Sally's more involved than you think.'

Ed's head jerked up. 'Grace, you don't have to—'

'Aye, Ed, I do. It's time I paid for my wickedness. I should've told this long afore this night.'

'Aunt Grace? Aunt Grace, you're scaring me. What should you have told?'

'Think on this,' Ed pressed. 'There'll be no going back.'

Slowly, tentatively, Grace caressed her husband's cheek. He closed his eyes and she sighed. 'Stan, Sally. I love you more than you'll ever know. Whatever changes by the telling of this, please, allus remember that.'

'Aunt Grace?'

Grace squeezed her eyes shut. When she uttered what she'd clearly hoped she never would, her tone was flat.

'Jonathan Swann was father to you both. You're brother and sister.'

Chapter 19

'WILL YOUSE TWO leave that dog be and sit down? Mithered to death, he is, poor blighter.'

Sally heard Maggie's twins, Flo and Harry, cross the room, bare feet slapping the floorboards. It was the knocking of wood on wood, as they rocked on rickety chairs, which fully roused her.

Those initial seconds were blissfully memory-free. Too soon, recollection slammed home, bringing pain so acute that nausea rose. She'd have given anything to fall back to sleep, forget. She didn't want to feel, think, imagine . . . How, in the name of *God*, would she get through this?

'Granny, we've ate our porridge. Can we play with Shield, now?'

Ellen, her back to them at the fire, flapped a hand and they scooted across the kitchen. Gradually, their giggles grew and, despite her misery, Sally couldn't help smiling when their grandmother addressed them.

'Right, get your clogs on and take your games outside. You're giving me a thundering headache. Go on, afore I tan your backsides.'

Though they scrambled up, it was evident they had never felt her hand – they hooted with laughter. 'Can we take Shield?'

'Aye, go on. Just mind for carts and don't be bothering folk.'

As they skipped out, Shield bounding between, Sally closed her eyes. But memories trickled back and she knew she must get up. If sleep wouldn't release her, she'd have to hold them at bay by keeping busy. Allowing them free rein would send her stark, staring mad. For the first time, thoughts of work brought blessed relief.

'Morning, lass. Our Maggie's out; she'll not be long. There's a pot on t' table not long since brewed.'

Spying awkwardness in Ellen's eyes, she sighed inwardly. Who could blame her? 'Thank you for last night. I'm sorry for burdening you and Maggie. I didn't know where else to go.'

Relief passed over Ellen's face. She wiped her hands on her apron and sat opposite. 'Now, that's enough of that. You've been kindness itself to my Maggie; one good turn deserves another. Mind, I'm glad you mentioned it first, lass. I can't imagine how you're fettling this morning.'

'I understand. I just . . . Lord, what am I to do?'

'You'll have to talk it through with her sooner or later. Otherwise, it'll fester inside and drive thee ruddy mad. When all's said and done, she's still your aunt.'

Sally nodded. How she'd look Grace in the face again, however . . .

'You'd best waken the babby, give him his feed. And don't you be fretting. He'll have a lovely time.'

'I feel dreadful doing this to you. You have your hands full already—'

'And love every minute. I don't know what I'd do with meself all day if not for our Maggie's two.'

Sally smiled tearfully – she was fortunate to have such wonderful friends. What she'd have done last night without them, she didn't know.

'Go on, lass. Give him his breakfast and get yourself to work. Best thing you can do is keep busy.'

Lifting him from the basket, her stomach flipped. *Jonathan.* She couldn't bear that, now. She'd bestowed the name proudly, believing . . . lies. Everything she held dear, memories she cherished – all lies. Her mind had built up her father into some virtuous saint. For years, she'd mourned a man who didn't exist.

She watched the baby suckle, her thoughts in disarray. What heartbreak her father and aunt had made her poor mother suffer. They betrayed her in the worst possible way. It had affected *her* whole life, too. But for their actions, how might life have been? Would she have married a decent man instead of a monster? Would her mother be alive? The lost possibilities were difficult to dismiss.

Thoughts of Stan, however, quashed her growing resentment. The utterance of a few words had lost him not only the father he believed to be his, but respect and trust for his mother, and a sister he'd thought was his full sibling. Moreover, the cousin he'd longed to reunite with was now his half-sister. Her pain paled in comparison.

Sally squeezed her eyes shut at the memory of his devastation. Everyone he'd ever loved had concealed what he'd a right to know. Would he forgive her? Gaining a sibling was an almighty shock to *her*, yet was growing on her. Whether he'd warm to it, she didn't know.

Holding her now-fed son against her shoulder, she rubbed his back. She tried to focus on the twins' voices beyond the door, desperate for her thoughts not to switch to Grace, but it was useless. Despite the agony of betrayal, she ached for the woman she'd come to love as a mother, yearned for her comforting hug, her soft voice. Attempting to deny the hurt Grace undoubtedly felt was impossible.

Last night, she'd simply snatched up the basket and fled. Her friends insisted she must stay as long as she needed but she couldn't impose on them for long. Ellen was right. However painful, she must give Grace the chance to explain.

Sighing, she rose from the pallet. She couldn't be late today. Pru had already allowed her time off; it would seem she was taking advantage of her kind nature. Donning her shawl, she thanked Ellen and left.

The twins, sitting cross-legged on the flagstones stroking Shield, waved as she passed. She returned the waves, shook her head when the dog made to rise, and hurried on. Turning the corner, she collided with her friend.

'Mind where you're going, you clumsy— Oh, it's thee.' Maggie laughed then her eyes softened. 'I'm glad I caught you afore you left. How you fettling?'

'I'm unsure. Hurt, confused . . . It's such a mess.'

'Eeh, love. 'Ere, let me take these in to Mam and I'll walk with you.' Maggie motioned to the pot of dripping and bundle of kindling she held. 'She'll be wondering where I've got to; it took an age persuading him in t' shop for a bit more on the slate. It's a good thing you've done, finding me that position, lass. We'd be facing destitution but for it. Eeh, listen to me prattling on; I'll finish up making you late. I'll not be a moment.' Flashing a grin, she scurried off.

Sally smiled fondly. Maggie was a good woman. She was so glad Pru had agreed to her working in the shop; Saturday would be here soon enough.

That she'd helped this family yet was at a loss how to repair her own didn't go unnoticed, but she pushed it from her mind. To get through the day without breaking down, she couldn't dwell on it.

Maggie rejoined her. Sally linked her arm through hers and they set off. Arriving at the pawnshop, her friend peeped through the window.

'Eeh, a few more days – I can't wait! It'll be great after all the years in t' mills.'

Maggie's excitement warmed Sally's heart. 'Why don't I introduce you to Miss Sharp while you're here?'

'Won't she mind?'

'Of course not. She's lovely, Maggie.'

Pru glanced around at the tinkling bell but before Sally could beckon Maggie – and to her utter dismay – Pru lowered her head without so much as a smile. Heart sinking, she joined her friend outside.

'Actually, Maggie, Miss Sharp's rather busy. Introducing yourself on Saturday would be wiser.'

Unaware anything was other than it seemed, Maggie nodded. 'I don't want to set a bad impression by disturbing her work. Go on, you'd best get in. I'll see thee at dinnertime, lass.'

Guilt gnawing at her, Sally bid her goodbye. If her suspicions proved correct, should she have let Maggie see?

Knowing her friend would be curious about Pru's injuries, she'd casually remarked days earlier that Pru had taken a tumble on a patch of ice. She'd hated lying but didn't feel it was her place to reveal the Sharps' business. As did most, Maggie knew about Agnes's previous employee but wasn't concerned. As she pointed out, she'd be working in the shop, not upstairs.

Nevertheless, concealing goings-on beneath this roof much longer was hopeless; the evidence would be right under her nose. Whether customers believed

Pru's excuses, she didn't know, but Maggie deserved the truth.

As she re-entered the shop, unease twisted her stomach when Pru didn't look up. She crossed to the counter and squeezed her shoulder gently. 'She's done it again, hasn't she? Miss Sharp, let me see.'

Bruising from the previous attack had faded. But this split lip was clearly a more recent assault.

'*Why* does she *do* it?'

'It looks worse than it is. Would you like a cup of tea, dear?'

Sally heaved a sigh of frustration, pity, helplessness. 'You cannot continue like this. You cannot keep excusing her wretched behaviour and brushing this aside as if it doesn't matter. When will you realise that it isn't normal, Miss Sharp? You don't deserve to be treated this way, by anyone.'

The dull response was barely audible. 'What choice have I? I'm all she has. It's my duty.'

'Why has she done this again? You said last time—'

'And meant it. I was determined not to give her the reaction she so enjoys. I failed. She can be extremely hurtful, knows just what to say to . . . maintain my suffering. She goes on and on and I sometimes feel like . . .' Pru paused, cleared her throat. 'But she insists it's for my own good so I won't make the same mistake again.'

Sally resisted asking what mistake, why she must suffer, what in heaven was going on. When Pru deemed the time right, she'd be here. 'I don't know what to say that I haven't already said. It's your life, your mother, your business. Just please . . .' She sighed, wanting to say so much but knowing it wouldn't make a scrap of difference. 'Please. Be careful.'

Pru nodded then smiled brightly. 'Now, then. Let me get you that tea and you can tell me all about your trip to Bolton, before Mother wakes. I trust your friend is well?'

Sudden tears thickened her throat. 'As it turned out, I was unable to make the visit. My cousin passed away yesterday morning.'

'My dear! Oh, I'm so very sorry for your loss. Your poor aunt.'

'She is inconsolable. Peggy was just eleven years old.' Glancing up, she was taken aback. Tears streamed down Pru's cheeks. 'Oh, I'm sorry, I didn't mean to—'

'No, no, you have no reason to apologise,' Pru choked, wiping eyes raw with anguish. 'Please, do not be alarmed. I simply adore children. To hear of one's passing . . . It is the worst possible pain a mother could go through.'

A frown touched Sally's brow. 'Yes, I'm sure it must be.'

Hand fluttering to her throat, Pru's tortured stare intensified. 'Sally, I—' A thud from above cut her off.

She nodded encouragingly. 'Yes, Miss Sharp?'

'I . . . I . . .'

She held her breath but to her dismay Pru's shoulders sagged. It was clear by her next words that the moment had passed.

'I believe Mother wants her tea. You won't mention . . . will you, dear?'

Taking a last look at the swollen mouth, Sally shook her head. Concealing truths was all her life consisted of lately and she was heartily fed up with it.

Making her way upstairs, her footsteps followed the beat of the mocking mantra tormenting her mind: *Secrets and lies. Secrets and lies. Secrets and lies . . .*

*

As before, Agnes showed no sign in word or action of occurrences in Sally's absence. Neither did she mention Tuesday's disturbing mood and talk of unwanted babies. Her unpredictability was unnerving. How Pru bore her, Sally didn't know.

The day rolled along as usual and after bidding Pru goodbye, she left with a thankful sigh. Work *had* taken her mind off her family, but worry for Pru's had replaced it.

Weary workers trudged in all directions but she barely noticed. Her thoughts were on the old woman's deplorable ability to act as if nothing had happened. Agnes must know she'd seen Pru's injuries, and was possibly aware how they got there, yet didn't seem concerned in the slightest.

Whatever her past, poor Pru didn't deserve this treatment. She herself knew better than most how it was to live awaiting the next blow. Imprisoned by such poison, day in, day out, was unbearable. How long before Pru's patience burned out, as had hers? What the outcome when it did?

Deep in thought, it wasn't until reaching the entry that Sally realised her error. Her heart sank to her boots. She'd made for Grace's instead of Maggie's.

Turning for Davies Street, her tear-scorched eyes flicked to her aunt's. They fixed on a figure and she jolted to a halt. Pressing against the wall, she peered at him. *Her brother.*

He stood stock-still, cap low over his face. When he raised his head to look at the door, the pain in his eyes brought fresh tears to hers. He continued staring but instead of entering, thrust his hands into his pockets and rested his chin on his chest.

At the sorry sight of him, lost and alone in the darkening street, Sally's arms ached for him. She pushed herself from the wall but didn't go. Despite her breaking heart, her feet refused to budge and, moments later, Stan slipped inside.

She gazed at the door for an age. Then with a sob, she turned on her heel for Maggie's.

Chapter 20

'YOUR AUNT'S FRIEND came to see thee at work? What did she say, lass?'

'Mrs Knox was very understanding. She came to tell me . . .' Sally blinked as tears welled up. 'Peggy's funeral is on Sunday. She said my aunt's in a bad way. She's not eating or sleeping. She's dreading the funeral and . . . she's pining for me. She wants me home.'

'What will you do?' Maggie asked softly.

It was Friday night and peaceful in the small kitchen. The twins were in bed, Jonathan asleep in his basket. Shield lay by the fire and, for a long moment, his gentle snores were the only sound.

'I shall have to go and see her. Despite everything, I feel dreadful for leaving, what with Peggy . . . However difficult seeing my aunt and Stan will be, I cannot miss the funeral. I couldn't do that to Aunt Grace. It's too cruel.'

Ellen nodded. 'Mebbe after, you can talk through matters. It needs airing, lass. Summat needs to give.'

'What will I say? How can I look her in the face knowing she . . . they . . . ?'

No one had the answer. Sipping their tea, they jumped when a knock sounded.

'Who the divil's that at this time?'

Maggie went to see. When she revealed the visitor, Sally gasped.

'Con? What are you doing here?' His smile brought a lump to her throat. She crossed the room and fell into his arms.

'Easy now, acushla,' he murmured, holding her close.

Resting her head on his chest, Sally closed her eyes. 'Have you been to my aunt's? Did she tell you I was here?' Feeling him nod, she sighed. 'How is she?'

'You and your friend sit yourselfs down. I'll brew a fresh pot.'

Ellen's words brought heat to Sally's cheeks. She disentangled herself from him. 'I'm sorry, I don't know what came over me. This is Con, a dear friend.'

'You're upset, lass, no apologies needed. Come and sit down. And you, lad. You're more than welcome.'

Inwardly cringing, Sally resumed her seat. She hadn't thought twice about embracing him – she had missed him since their last meeting. Fleeing here the other night, she'd half expected to see him, having grown accustomed to him appearing when she was in trouble. Of course, he hadn't, but he was here now.

Though glad to see him, she couldn't help worrying what Maggie and Ellen thought. She'd told them a little about her marriage; would they believe her to be loose, a wedded woman throwing herself at another man?

Thankful when Ellen handed back her refilled cup with her usual smile, she stole a glance at Maggie. Her friend raised an eyebrow, twinkling eyes flicking to the Irishman, and Sally blinked. Maggie wasn't disapproving. She was smitten!

For the next hour, they talked quietly. Con expressed regret at Peggy's passing and each of them shed a tear when, from his jacket pocket, he produced a pale-green ribbon, purchased for her that morning.

Gradually, the mood lightened and Con, Maggie and Ellen chatted easily. Only half listening, Sally fingered the silky strip, which she'd promised to give Grace on Sunday. She smiled when Maggie laughed at something Con had said. Why couldn't others resist his charms yet she wanted only friendship? Why didn't her feelings run deeper? Was something wrong with her? Had Joseph's evil tainted any chance at love?

Tommy slipped into her mind and she quivered. She must visit Bolton, soon. She had to see that Ivy was well. And, however hard she tried denying it, she had to see Tommy, too.

Girlish giggles dragged her from her thoughts. Watching Con lean closer to Maggie, she sensed something between them; their laughter melted but their gazes lingered. Her chest swelled with pleasure. Then, to her disappointment, Con turned to *her* with his slow smile and the moment between him and Maggie was broken.

As Sally predicted, Pru and Maggie hit it off right away.

Throughout the day, laughter filtered upstairs and Agnes would cock an ear and frown. She was still unaware that Pru had employed her, and Sally would hold her breath, worried that she'd demand to be told what was going on, but she didn't. Whether Agnes took the extra voice to be a customer's, Sally didn't know. She was certain, however, that Pru couldn't conceal Maggie much longer.

It was minutes from finishing time. Preparing to leave, Sally sighed inwardly at the muffled laughter.

It had evoked mixed feelings all day. And the reason wasn't entirely due to Agnes.

Since Con's departure last night, she'd sensed a cooling in Maggie. Walking to work, she'd been giddy about her friend's first day and, though not snubbing her excited chatter, Maggie's short responses and tight smiles were out of character.

The journey to and from home at dinner wasn't much better. And whenever she'd ventured downstairs to fulfil Agnes's requests, Maggie would find a way to busy herself as an excuse not to talk. Something was wrong. She sounded her usual self with Pru.

Did Maggie suspect there was something between her and Con? she brooded, descending the stairs. Her friend had clearly taken to the handsome Irishman; was she perhaps jealous?

Bidding Pru goodnight, they drew their shawls tightly against the cutting wind and hurried home through the gloomy streets. Sally tried making conversation twice, and received short responses. After the third, she'd had enough. She forced her to a halt.

'Maggie, have I done something to upset you?'

Her friend's colour rose instantly. She lowered her eyes to the ground. 'Nay, course not.'

'Then what? I must have done something. You've been your cheery self all day with Miss Sharp.'

'I'm sorry. You're not to blame for, for what I . . . I made a fool of meself last night, didn't I?'

Sally sighed. She'd known this was about Con. Was Maggie embarrassed at showing a liking for him because she believed he and *she* . . . ? Linking her arm, she squeezed. 'There's nothing between Con and me. He's a good friend, nothing more.'

'Oh, lass, I know that! I never thought that forra second. Eeh, I'm sorry.' Maggie turned her gaze to the leaden sky. 'My late husband, my Danny, were the only man I ever had eyes for. His passing near killed me. Without a shadow of a doubt, if not for Mam and the little 'uns, I'd not be here. Last night, making cow eyes . . . I don't know what the divil came over me.'

Sally smothered a chuckle with her hand. 'I'm sorry. I'm simply relieved. I thought I'd upset you. Oh, Maggie, don't berate yourself for being human. You're a young woman with your life ahead of you. As for Con, my aunt swears he could charm the birds from the trees. Don't be embarrassed nor harbour guilt towards your husband's memory. Surely, he'd want you to be happy?'

'Aye. Eeh, I am sorry, Sally. I couldn't look thee in t' eye, I were that ashamed.'

Sally squeezed her arm again, a wicked smile spreading across her face. 'Lord, he *is* handsome, though, isn't he?'

Maggie clicked her tongue but soon she too was grinning. 'By, he is that!'

And as they hurried on, their giggles rang along the street.

As with her arrival in Manchester, the following morning Sally hesitated at her aunt's door. She breathed deeply. Was it only three weeks ago she'd stood here, as uncertain of the outcome? So much had happened that it was difficult to believe.

She glanced inside the basket. A posy of snowdrops purchased on Carruthers Street lay by Jonathan's feet. The flower seller, hearing what they were for, had added sprigs of baby's breath at no extra charge and

Sally sighed, wishing she were giving them in different circumstances.

Bringing a baby to a funeral wasn't ideal but not knowing what today held, she'd declined Maggie's offer of minding him. She'd need to be close by to feed him. And she knew Grace would be missing him.

Another deep breath did nothing to calm her as she knocked. In those seconds, the emotional storm, which had plagued her throughout the sleepless night, returned. How would she feel, seeing Grace? How would Stan react? She pushed her worries aside. Today was about Peggy. And whatever Grace had done, she needed her support. She'd soon have to bury her child. No woman deserved that.

Footsteps within sounded and the door creaked open.

'Hello, Uncle Ed.'

His weary gaze widened. He leaned across the step and embraced her.

When they parted, she glanced over his shoulder. 'Uncle Ed, I—'

'I know, lass,' he murmured. 'Ta for coming. It'll mean the world to your aunt.'

Grace's eyes tore Sally's heart. Agony had sucked her soul from their depths. As Sally crossed the kitchen, Grace lowered her head. Staring down at the slumped frame, her heart thumped but no anger arose. She felt nothing but heavy sadness.

She was relieved and dismayed that Stan wasn't there. Part of her dreaded seeing him, yet she longed to. Spying him Thursday evening haunted her. She just prayed that time apart had diminished his anger and sense of betrayal towards her.

When her gaze rested on the cheap coffin in the corner, loss and regret almost broke her heart. She'd barely got to know the girl lying cold within. Why was life so cruel? she raged inwardly, screwing her eyes to block the sight. And imagining this mother's pain, the last vestige of animosity faded. She stooped and put her arms around her.

Grace's shoulders heaved. Her arms flew around Sally's waist and she held on tightly, as though afraid if she let go, she'd take flight.

'I love you, Aunt Grace.'

The low cry was of sheer relief. 'Eeh, I'm that glad you're here. I'll get through this day a little easier with you by my side. Oh, I have missed you, love. I wanted to tell you . . . But I were frickened to death of losing you. My wickedness lost me my Rose. I couldn't lose thee, an' all. Not again. I couldn't, lass.'

Sally wiped Grace's tears. 'Let's not talk about that. I'll not make this day harder for you. I cannot begin to imagine what you're going through.'

'What's *she* doing here?'

They turned to find Stan in the doorway.

Ed rose from the table. 'Now then, lad—'

'You should've stopped away. In fact, you should've never returned to Manchester. We were all right till you turned up like a bad penny.'

The degree of resentment cut Sally to the quick. She moved towards him and frowned sadly when he stepped back. 'Don't hate me, Stan. I never meant to hurt you. It wasn't my place to tell you. Please try to understand.'

His eyes flared with pain. 'I thought we were friends.'

'Oh, Stan.' She took another hesitant step, heart fluttering with hope when he didn't move. 'What we've learned . . . To discover I have a brother – that *you* are my brother . . . I'm as shocked and confused as you. But let me tell you something: I will not allow this to come between us. The moment I arrived, I liked you. Since then, as with Peggy, I've grown to love you. I've lost her, Stan. I won't lose you, too.'

The room was still, all of them awaiting his response. When his lower lip trembled, she forced herself not to go to him. She must let him decide in his own time, his way.

A lone tear splashed to his cheek. He turned and left the room.

She stared at the door for a long moment then closed her eyes in despair.

Until this day, Sally wouldn't have believed it possible for a body to shed the tears her aunt had. Her level of grief was distressing to witness. When Peggy disappeared into the ground her mother's beast-like cries drew sobs from everyone.

They hadn't seen Stan again until leaving for Christ Church on Every Street. He'd slipped into the kitchen at the last moment without a word to anyone. Sally had felt his eyes from the doorway as, tears streaming, she laid Thunder beside her cousin. She'd then produced Con's ribbon and Grace tied it in Peggy's hair.

When Ed secured the lid and drove the nails through, shutting away their daughter for ever, Grace had wept herself hoarse. He'd held his wife tightly and Stan had screwed up his face in anguish. Sally made to comfort him but he turned away, and she'd had no choice but to leave him be.

Now, as Ed and Grace clung to each other by the graveside, Stan stood alone. Tears dripped from his chin on to the cap he clutched to his chest and Sally gripped the basket's handle, aching to go to him. However, he'd made his feelings clear. She must respect his decision.

The mourners drifted across the churchyard to allow the family private goodbyes. Sally said a silent prayer and dropped the delicate white flowers beside the small wreath atop the coffin.

'How you bearing up, lass?' asked Winnie when she came to stand beside her.

'My heart breaks for them. And Stan . . . I don't know what to do. He detests me.'

'The lad's just looking for someone to blame. He lost a sister and gained another in t' same day. He's hurt, confused, but he'll bear it, somehow. Give him time. He'll come round.'

Shortly afterwards, the small procession meandered back to Boslam Street. Sally walked in front with her aunt and uncle, Stan following with Winnie and the rest. Reaching the entry, she felt a tap on her shoulder. She thought it was Stan but, turning, had to swallow her disappointment.

Winnie drew her aside. 'Can you lend a hand with summat, lass?'

'Of course. What is it, Mrs Knox?'

Grace's friend explained how in the days following Peggy's death, she'd knocked at every house and, as the poor did in times of need, neighbours gave what coppers they could spare. After purchasing the wreath, she'd spent the remainder on the funeral tea, which she'd prepared at home last night.

Within minutes, they had carried the meagre spread to Grace's. As they placed the last dish on the table, gratitude and shame filled Sally. She fumbled inside the basket then pressed coins into Winnie's hand.

'What's this?'

'My belated contribution. With all that had happened, I . . . I feel dreadful. You're an angel to my family, Mrs Knox.'

'Now, don't be daft. What you've had to deal with, it's no wonder. Eeh, try and talk with Grace, won't you? You'll both feel better for it. She made a mistake but in my opinion, she's paid for it a hundred times over. Go on, lass. I'll mind the babby.'

Glancing across, Sally frowned. Could she bear it?

'The wench needs her family round her, now more than ever.'

She nodded. Brushing this under the mat wouldn't solve anything. Whatever the outcome, she must try, for all their sakes.

When she slipped into the chair opposite her aunt, she knew foreboding shone from her eyes – Grace's dimmed in response. A thousand questions whirred in her mind but her tongue stuck to the roof of her dry mouth.

'You ready to hear it, lass?'

Raw pain behind the words made Sally look away. 'I'm sorry, it can wait. I promised I wouldn't upset you with this today—'

'I want to. I've explained to Stan; I need you to understand, too. I know nowt can excuse what went on but if you hear it, you might just find it in your heart to forgive me. And your father. He weren't a bad man, love.'

Grace rose and motioned for her to follow.

Passing Ed, Sally was struck by the tender look he gave his wife. If nothing else, this sorry mess had united her aunt and uncle.

Grace led the way to the backyard. She leaned against the crumbling wall and folded her arms. 'I know this is selfish but I feel nowt but relief. My wickedness, it's been a black shadow, allus there, following me through the years wherever I went. It'll be a blessing to shift some of it.'

Sally went cold with dread but Grace clearly needed this release. 'I'll admit the thought of hearing this makes me shudder. However, if it will help you heal a little . . . I don't know how I'll feel afterwards but shall try my best to understand.'

'It's probably the owdest excuse in t' book but in our case, it really is true – we never planned it. At the time, I still dwelled with Father. Mam had cleared off years afore with the tripe dresser down the road. Did you know about that, lass?'

'I didn't. I don't remember my grandparents.'

'Aye, you'll not. Mam scarpered long afore you were born, and Father . . . Well, Rose didn't see much of him after she wed.'

'No?'

'Nay. She didn't know how lucky she were.'

Frowning, Sally waited for Grace to continue but she remained silent, as though lost in thought. 'Aunt Grace?'

'I knew what were to happen. It were the same every weekend. When I heard the door go, I shot upstairs but only got halfway. Father spotted me, ordered me back. My pleading usually worked; he'd leave me be and I'd escape to bed. That night, he were having none of it.'

Sally's frown deepened. 'I don't understand.'

'When Mam scarpered, it were left to me and Rose to look after him. I did the donkey's share to save her the burden; she were nowt but a babby. Father weren't mithered so long as the house were clean and a meal were on t' table of an evening.

'Anyroad, eventually, she met Jonathan. Father were dead set against them courting. He didn't want her marrying, same as he didn't me. He were frightened of being alone, you see, with no one to wash his clothes, clean his house and fill his belly. I begged him to give permission, promised him I'd never wed, would look after him all his days if he let her.

'She were smitten and I loved her more than owt in t' world. I'd have done anything for my Rose. Well, he agreed. I were that happy for her, lass, I can't tell thee. Eeh, but it were lonely in that house, after. Father's drinking were as bad as ever and she kept her distance. I can't say I blamed her. He'd never been a good 'un, really. His needs allus come afore owt else.'

'What happened, Aunt Grace?' she asked gently. 'What did your father do after ordering you downstairs?'

'He'd harp on summat shocking when at the drink. He'd shout and curse till the early hours, convinced I planned to run away with some fella or other. I'd promise I'd not leave, plead with him to stop, but nowt worked. I'd cry with relief when he finally passed out.' Grace's eyes burned with the pain of remembrance. 'I thought he'd go on as usual, thought I knew what were coming. Not that night.

'I could see in his eyes summat were different. I'd reached the bottom stair when the first blow came. Honest to God, lass, my head near left my shoulders. There weren't no pain at first; the shock, you know? His sniping I were used to but he'd never struck me afore. He dragged me across the room by my hair and like a man possessed, beat me black and blue.

'Someone had told him about Ed. We'd met the month afore. He'd started work at the tobacconist's where I went for Father's bacca. I knew he'd be furious but I fell for your uncle at first sight. I thought we'd been careful but some swine must've spotted us.'

Sally tore away her gaze. To think her grandfather . . . He'd been no better than Joseph. 'And *my* father?' she asked tentatively.

A red hue covered Grace's face. 'He were homeward bound from the tavern, been forra dram of brandy for Rose's toothache. Passing ours, he heard my screams. Next thing I knew, he were dragging Father off me. Well, they argued and Father staggered to bed threatening he'd never let me marry, would murder Ed if I saw him again.

'Jonathan sat me by the fire and, while he brewed tea, I prayed. I prayed Father wouldn't return to the kitchen. I prayed for strength. Most of all, I prayed for God's help to endure life without Ed. Anyroad, Jonathan adds some brandy to the tea for my nerves. Whether that . . . Nay, I'm making excuses.

'Brandy or no . . . He tried comforting me and I . . . Oh, Sally, I'm the wicked 'un. I threw meself at him, desperate forra bit of love. I thought I'd lost my Ed, were destined forra life of misery with Father. It's no excuse, I know. I don't know what I were thinking. I just, I just . . .' She burst into sobs. 'I begged him to stay awhile. I seduced him, lass. How could I do that to my Rosie?'

Hugging herself, Sally stared at nothing. 'What followed?'

'I disobeyed Father and continued courting Ed. When I realised I were with child, I went fair daft with fear but told Ed straight away. To my amazement, he vowed to stand by me. We told Father together and Ed made out the child were his. I were scared sick but besides shouting, then getting blind drunk, there weren't much Father could do. He'd not have wanted a bastard beneath his roof.

'We promised to dwell with him after we wed, save him being alone.' Grace's face contorted in pain. 'Rose were over the moon for me. I tried putting the betrayal to the back of my mind, but Jonathan were a wreck. He wanted to tell her but I pleaded with him. I knew it'd kill her, that she'd never forgive me. I were right on both counts.'

Sally closed her eyes. 'How did she discover the truth?'

'Jonathan, lass, confessed on his deathbed. As with me, it'd haunted him; he were never the same. He lived and breathed for Rose. That one act of weakness fair sucked the soul from him.' Glancing up, Grace winced. 'Your expression . . . It's like stepping back in time.

'Rose begged me to say it weren't true. And looking at her, widowhood but an hour old, I'd have given owt to. The lie were on my tongue – I were this close to uttering it.' She held thumb and forefinger an inch apart. 'But I couldn't. I looked down to our Stan, the result of my wickedness, near full-grown, and knew the time for honesty had come. She deserved the truth and I deserved to pay for my sin.

'My punishment were losing the best sister a body could wish. She swore she'd never forgive me, and she didn't. In the space of an hour, she lost not only her husband but her only sibling, for when them words left me, I were dead to her, an' all.'

Tears streamed down Sally's face. 'Was that the last time you saw her?'

'I plucked up courage and went round weeks later, but my knock went unanswered. Looking through the window, I wanted to die. Norra soul nor stick of furniture remained. You'd gone, taking my heart with youse.'

'Did she realise who fathered Stan?'

'I don't know, lass, and that's the truth. If she'd asked, I'd have had to tell her. She didn't. Whether she put two and two together, later, I can't say.' Through hooded eyes, Grace peered at her. 'There's nowt more to add but sorry. I'm so sorry, lass. Please tell me you forgive me, that things will be well betwixt us.'

Uneasy silence descended.

Part of Sally wanted to scream no, everything wouldn't be well. Her mother had been unable to forgive the sister she loved – would her doing so be betraying her? Would it make a mockery of all she'd suffered?

Yet anger and bitterness couldn't quell another emotion. She loved this woman. Grace had bent over backwards for her. She'd put a roof over their heads, food in their stomachs. She'd been a shoulder to cry on, her kindness knowing no bounds, despite her own burdens. Moreover, why must she carry the blame? Her father was as much at fault.

Could she cut from her life one of the precious few she had left, as had her mother? She couldn't deny the answer.

'I forgive you,' she heard herself say.

Slowly, Grace's expression melted into one of sheer serenity. As she heaved a long sigh, years of grief seemed to rise from her. She opened her arms.

Without hesitation, Sally walked into them.

Winnie was seeing out the last neighbour when Grace and Sally emerged from the backyard. Her eyebrows rose in trepidation. 'All well?'

Grace nodded. She turned to smile at Ed but catching Stan's eye, it slipped from her face. 'Don't look at me like that, son. Can't we put this behind us, start afresh?'

Sally looked away. Today had sucked all energy from her. She didn't have the strength to fight.

'Stan,' Ed prompted. 'Your mam's right. We shouldn't be tearing each other to bits. This day should be about those lost and those still here. We're a family, lad, and families stick together. For better or worse,' he finished to Grace, eyes gentle.

Stan rubbed the fine stubble on his chin. He ignored Winnie's encouraging smile and Ed's nod, also his mother's pleading stare. When his gaze rested on Sally, emotion flickered across his face then vanished as quickly. He shook his head.

Grace raised her eyes to the ceiling. '*Please*, son.'

'I can't. Can't . . . even *look* at her! It weren't meant to be like this. She were my cousin, not my . . .' He leapt to his feet. 'Peggy were my sister, not her. I don't want her as a sister. And I don't want her here. Either she leaves or I do.'

Grace and Ed made to protest but shaking her head, Sally stopped them. Returning Winnie's sad smile, she took the basket from her.

'Goodbye, Mrs Knox.' Stan's glare bore into her as she crossed the room. 'Goodbye, Aunt Grace, Uncle Ed.' Their looks of helplessness and despair cut her to the bone. As she opened the door, her step faltered. Unable to stop herself, she rushed to Stan and kissed his cheek. 'Goodbye, Stan. I love you – always remember that.' She turned and ran from the house, Grace's weeping ringing in her ears.

Blinded by tears, she passed through the maze of streets in a daze. Once again, she'd lost her family. Years of yearning, her efforts to find them, countless emotions she'd endured to maintain a relationship and for what? To have it all snatched away within weeks?

Was it worth it? Was her love for them enough for such upset, worry, pain of rejection? She didn't need to think about it – of course it was. What she carried in her breast for those people was beyond measure.

But what do I do? she asked herself.

Stan wouldn't come round, she realised that, now. He'd said he couldn't bear to so much as look at her. She dashed away fresh tears with the back of her hand. She understood, despite the pain it brought. His anger was a natural response, she accepted this. But as far as she could see, she'd had no choice. She'd promised Grace.

Should she have broken her vow? she agonised, walking on aimlessly. Deep down, she knew she'd made the right decision. However much she believed Stan deserved the truth, she couldn't have gone back on her word.

As she and Grace had resolved matters, her despondency diminished somewhat. They had eked one positive thing from this dreadful day at least.

Passing through Bradford Road, she glanced to the pawnshop and heaved a sigh. She seemed to roll on a continuum of worry and uncertainty. Complications followed her everywhere. Was a simple life too much to ask? Escaping, she'd craved calmness, security. The beatings were in the past but her future was as precarious as ever.

Drawing level, she looked up to Agnes's window. An unexpected sight chased away her troubles: Pru stood motionless, staring back.

She raised a hand and when Pru nodded slightly, then disappeared, she shrugged. Though surprised – Pru steered clear of Agnes whenever possible – at this moment, whatever the reason, Sally neither knew nor cared. She couldn't deal with further worries today.

None the less, heading for Maggie's, guilt spiked and she resolved to make it up to Pru tomorrow. Whatever was amiss, she'd bet her life Agnes was at the centre. She would set off early; they'd talk before work. She'd think up some reason to leave before Maggie. She just wished she didn't have to.

She couldn't continue lying. She'd learned a harsh lesson this week. Hiding truths had lost her Stan. She wouldn't lose Maggie, too.

Tommy flicked his wrist. The stone skimmed the water several times before sinking to the riverbed. Watching the ripples left behind, he heard footsteps approaching. He smiled as Dolly, curls poking from her bonnet and bouncing about her shoulders, rushed towards him.

'I didn't think you'd show,' she breathed, pink-faced with pleasure.

He pulled lightly on a curl. Released, it sprang back into shape and he smiled again. 'I promised, didn't I?'

She nodded and he kissed her plump cheek. She smelt of fresh butter and cream and when she slipped her hand in his, it was soft and warm. She was a lovely lass, too good for him. He'd treated her shockingly the past weeks. He didn't deserve her.

As though sensing his despair, she frowned. 'What's wrong, Tommy? Is it your mam? Has summat else occurred?'

He looked away, guilt rising. He wondered what would happen if he told her he was thinking of someone else entirely. Someone who, for the life of him, he couldn't forget. A woman who, if she returned tomorrow and declared *her* love for *him*, he'd drop Dolly for in a heartbeat.

He knew what. Dolly wasn't like other lasses. She wouldn't scream and curse or claw his face, much as he'd deserve it. She'd let him go without much fuss because she'd want him to be happy, even if that meant with someone else. She loved him, always had. Why couldn't he share that devotion? Why wasn't she enough any more?

He imagined the boot on the other foot – how would *he* feel if she admitted loving another man? The answer was like a blow to the stomach. He'd feel only relief.

'What is it? Has that divil been back?'

Letting her hand go, he ran his through his hair. 'He'd not dare. We searched for him Tuesday night but—' Her horrified gasp interrupted him. 'Nay, lass, don't fret. He's no match for us. Anyroad, we couldn't find him.' He didn't mention that he and his father wouldn't rest until they did, however long it took. 'And Mam's on t' mend. Tough as they come, she is.'

'Thank the Lord for that – and not just about Ivy. He's dangerous, he is.'

Tommy crossed to the knoll by the river. He patted the stubbly grass and when she sat beside him, asked, 'Dolly, are you happy?'

She cocked her head, considered this. 'Aye. Some folk are far worse off. I've a steady job, a good family and my health. And I have thee.' She smiled, slipping her hand in his. 'I'd say I've plenty to be happy about.'

'I want to say sorry.' She made to speak but he shook his head. 'Hear me out, lass. I've been cruel standing you up of a Sunday. I've had . . . matters on my mind, is all.' Sighing, he drew her towards him. She rested her head on his shoulder and he smiled sadly, gaze sweeping the meadows beyond. 'You're special to me. You know that, don't you?' He felt her nod. 'I never thanked you proper on Monday, were too angry to think straight. I am grateful, Dolly. But for you—'

'Don't dwell on that,' she cut in softly.

'Tha fair saved Mam's life. If I tried every day for the rest of mine, I couldn't thank you enough.' She curled into him. Her hand travelled up his chest, around his neck. Fingers played at his nape and he closed his eyes. 'Dolly, I, I must—'

'Shhh.' She tilted her head to gaze at him. 'Being with thee's all the thanks I could want.'

Shame so acute it brought bile to his throat, stabbed. He tore up a handful of grass. She loved him so much, yet he ... Chestnut hair tumbling around slender shoulders burned in his memory. He blinked furiously, longing and self-reproach giving way to resentment. He must stop this!

His arm tightened around Dolly. This was where his future lay; had all along. She wasn't to blame for his mind turning. She wouldn't suffer a second longer for his lapse in loyalty and common sense.

He didn't realise he'd squeezed his eyes shut until he felt pressure on his lips. Opening them, the expression he saw in Dolly's took him aback. They shone with love so true, it stole his breath. He read her thoughts in the liquid depths, knew she sensed something in him, that he was slipping from her. That she'd do anything to prevent it.

Here, entwined by the secluded river, innocent love he'd once held for her, unquestionably, stirred. The tip of her tongue tasted his lips hesitantly and his heartbeat quickened. Raised with high morals, they had always shown restraint; he'd never pushed his advances.

'You're happy, an' all, ain't you, Tommy?'

Fear tinged the gentle tone and all he desired was to reassure her, make her happy – free himself of the guilt consuming him from the inside out. He nodded.

There was an urgency to her kiss he'd never known. Fire low in his stomach smouldered and spread and when the swell of her breasts pushed against him, he could hold back no longer. He fumbled at the ribbon tied beneath her chin and tossed her bonnet to the grass. Burying his hands in her hair, he kissed her hungrily.

In that moment, he was powerless to resist. To feel wanted completely and loved so intensely was what his battered heart yearned for.

Chapter 21

'I DON'T MIND setting off early with thee. Mam will see to the children.'

Draping her shawl around her shoulders, Sally shook her head quickly. 'No, no. It's fine, Maggie.'

'If you're sure? Aye, as you say, a brisk walk will do the trick. I'll see you later.'

Wincing at her sympathetic smile, Sally mumbled goodbye and left. She *loathed* doing that. The deceit itself, that she needed to walk off a headache before work, was bad enough; Maggie's concern only added to her guilt.

She quickened her step. Pru at Agnes's window had stayed with her throughout the night. She just hoped there hadn't been further conflict over the weekend.

Sudden thoughts of her own family brought now-familiar pain and she forced her mind elsewhere. The issue with Stan was out of her hands. Her only option was to pray that one day, he'd forgive her.

Despite her inner turmoil, she couldn't help smiling as, repositioning her shawl, she glimpsed the garment beneath.

On returning to Maggie's yesterday, her friend told her Con had just left. He'd called to see how Sally was bearing up after the funeral, but her heart-to-heart with

Grace detained her longer than the time he could spare and she'd been saddened to have missed him by minutes. After the day she'd had, she'd have welcomed his company.

However, her dismay turned to curiosity at Maggie's soft eyes and pink cheeks – and the dove-grey blouse she held. Ellen had pointed to the twins, proudly sporting new cap and bonnet, and held up a cream-coloured blouse of her own in delight. She'd then motioned to a bundle on the table. They were gifts from Con from his market stall.

Though second-hand, everything was in sound condition and, holding the dark-blue blouse with black trim against herself, Sally had marvelled with the rest at the Irishman's generosity.

Like Maggie and her family, she'd never owned such a beautiful garment. The unfamiliar material felt strange against her skin but was a good fit, accentuating her curves to perfection.

Turning into Bradford Road, her smile deepened. He was calling again this evening. She couldn't wait to see him, to thank him. She was so fortunate to have him for a friend.

The pawnshop came into view and her smile melted as she saw a crowd huddled by the door. What on earth . . . ?

'It's locked, lass,' a perplexed customer announced. 'Been banging for ten minutes, I have. Summat's afoot. I've never known Miss Sharp be late opening.'

Sally glanced at each of them in turn. They held bundles containing Sunday-best clothes, which were pawned at the beginning of the week and redeemed on Saturday, for church the following day. It was the same week in, week out. The customer was right. For the shop to be closed at this hour, today of all days, something was indeed wrong.

Stepping into the road, she squinted at the upstairs windows. There was no sign of life this time. Curtains were drawn at each, including Agnes's. A customer banged on the door but still there was no movement beyond the panes.

'You work here, don't you? When did you last see the daughter?'

'I saw Miss Sharp at the window, there, yesterday afternoon.' As her answer hung in the air, dread crept through Sally, increasing when the customers' expressions showed they shared her concern.

At the back of the crowd, a stout woman turned to a girl beside her. 'Gertie, go and fetch the butcher, lass. This door needs kicking in. Wilf's a big beggar; he'll get it open.'

As the customers whispered amongst themselves, Sally watched the girl's spindly legs fly across the cobbles. *Please, Lord, let all be well*, she prayed. Yet deep down, she knew it wasn't. Her heartbeat quickened when Gertie emerged with Wilf. Crossing her fingers, she continued praying.

The butcher, bloodstained apron flapping in the breeze, nodded grimly at the woman's explanation. He stepped back, rolled his head side to side then ran and slammed his shoulder against the door. On the third attempt, there was the crack of splintering wood and after a final shove, it crashed open. Nodding to the subdued crowd, he motioned for them to remain outside.

Before he disappeared, Sally tugged his sleeve. 'Wait, I'm coming with you. I work here.'

He hesitated but at her determined look, nodded. 'All right, lass, but I'll lead. We could be walking into owt, here.'

A glance revealed the shop was empty. They hurried for the door behind the counter and mounted the stairs, calling Pru's name as they went, but silence greeted them.

On the landing, Wilf motioned to the closed doors. 'Which is the owd 'un's?'

Heart galloping, she pointed.

He pressed his ear to it then opened it slowly. 'Mother of God . . .' Staggering back, he hauled her away. 'Don't look, lass. Dear Lord, don't look upon that room!'

Sally heard herself scream. She pushed past and stumbled inside.

Agnes lay twisted at an odd angle in the blood-soaked bed. Emerald eyes, holding surprise, stared unseeing at the ceiling. Crimson splatters streaked her snow-white hair and beside her battered head lay her bloodied poker.

A noise like rushing water swam in Sally's ears. The room swayed and she gripped the door frame. Making to turn from the gruesome scene, she froze.

'Come away, there's nowt you can . . .' Wilf's words petered out as he followed her gaze to the window.

'I think it's Miss Sharp,' she whispered.

His voice was hesitant. 'Miss Sharp? Is that you?'

The kneeling figure lifted its head. A shaft of light from the slit in the curtains fell across the bruised face and, with a cry, Sally rushed forward. But the large knife in the woman's hand stopped her in her tracks.

Rocking slowly, a ghost of a smile touched Pru's mouth.

'Miss Sharp, it's me. Please . . . put the knife down.'

Pru stilled. A gentle frown accompanied her smile. 'Hello, dear.'

A sob caught in Sally's throat and she dropped to her knees. 'Oh, Miss Sharp, what—?'

'You must keep your voice down, dear.' Pru held a blood-smeared finger to her lips. 'Mother will be furious if we wake her.'

Wilf crouched beside Sally. 'Miss Sharp, let me have that knife, lass.'

He reached out and Sally held her breath.

Pru blinked. She gazed at the butcher, then at the knife. Then she began to laugh.

Time seemed to stand still and Sally could only watch as her friend raised her arm. Before Wilf could make a grab for it, Pru smiled softly and plunged the blade into her chest.

'Drink this. I've put in plenty of sugar for your nerves. Eeh, you poor girl. What an awful thing to witness. I can't believe it, I can't.'

'I don't understand. Miss Sharp . . . such a sweet, gentle soul . . .' Fresh tears burst from Sally. 'Her eyes . . . They were empty. Simply empty.'

Ellen sighed. 'She must've been in a dark place to do what she did but, harsh as it sounds, she's probably better off where she is now. She's at peace, lass, and she's free of her mother and all what went with it.'

'She was so thoughtful, so kind. Not once did she judge or question me regarding my marital affairs, though she must have thought it odd I never mentioned my husband. How has this happened? Perhaps I, I could have . . .'

Maggie knelt beside her. 'Sally, listen to me. Don't blame yourself for any of this. That troubled woman took her mam's life and her own. Her hands, not yours, brought about the deeds. There were nowt you could've done.'

'Drink your tea,' Ellen instructed softly. 'That constable said he'd need nowt more from you, didn't he, so when you've drunk that, you go and have a lie down. Rest is the best thing for shock.'

Minutes later, Maggie tucked Sally into her own bed. 'You'll not be disturbed. Try and get some sleep.'

'Please, stay with me awhile. Every time I close my eyes . . .'

'Eeh, course I will.' Her friend perched on the bed and shook her head. 'I should've come with thee this morning.'

'There's nothing you could have done. There's nothing anyone could have done.'

Maggie's eyes flashed with hurt. 'Why didn't you tell me sooner, Sally? I'd not have told no one. Honest, I wouldn't.'

Fear rolled through her stomach. She'd dreaded this. It was Stan all over again. Would lies and secrecy lose her her friend, too?

When she'd arrived home, leaning on the butcher for support, and revealed what had happened, their horrified cries rang through the house. They grew when she'd confessed all regarding the Sharps' relationship.

Though relieved to unburden herself of the terrible secret, she'd known their shock would dampen and she'd have some uncomfortable questions to answer. Now, trepidation overcame her. She sent up a silent prayer before attempting to explain.

'Maggie, I don't know where to begin. I strongly believed you deserved to know what went on behind those walls. Lying to you, making excuses . . . it's eaten away at me. I, I just—'

'I understand. Miss Sharp told you in confidence. It's fair wrong of me to say you should've told me. I'm just sorry I weren't there for thee, to give an ear to your worries. You must've felt wretched knowing what you did and having no one to talk to.'

Amazement slackened her mouth. 'You mean you're not angry with me? You understand my predicament? Oh, Maggie.' She threw her arms around her friend's neck. 'Thank you. Oh, thank you. I've been sick with worry at the thought of telling you. I thought you'd be furious, that you'd hate me, that you'd—'

'Eeh, course not,' Maggie soothed, rubbing her back as she would the twins'. 'I understand, lass, I do. I don't know what that there premicadent word were but think I can guess its meaning.'

Sally laughed through her tears. 'I thought you wouldn't want to see me again, like Stan. I'll never keep anything from you again. You have my word.'

Distraction tinged Maggie's smile.

'What's wrong?'

Maggie tapped her lips, eyes thoughtful. 'I've just remembered summat Miss Sharp said Saturday. I never thought nowt of it at the time . . . I were talking of the twins, how they can be imps at times, as children are. Well, she gorra bit teary. She said how she loved children, that if I ever needed a break, she'd gladly take them off my hands forra few hours. I thought it reet kind and told her so, but explained Mam helps out.'

'That was simply Miss Sharp's way. She mentioned after Peggy's passing how much she adored children.'

'Nay, that weren't all. She said how fortunate I were, that I had everything a woman could wish in life. She said to be a loving mother and *have* a loving mother were the greatest gifts a body could possess. I thought nowt of it, but . . . Eeh, lass, d'you think she were trying to tell me summat?'

Sally sighed. 'Almost every conversation we had, I felt she wanted to confide in me. But whenever I believed she was on the brink of doing so, she'd clam up. Their relationship was woven with long-held secrets and resentment. The atmosphere when they were together . . . well, it wasn't pleasant, put it that way.

'Miss Sharp admitted she couldn't bear to be in the same room as her. It's hardly surprising; I saw with my own eyes how her mother treated her. The feeling was clearly mutual. Mrs Sharp revealed she prayed for Miss Sharp's death after her birth.'

'That's wicked! How could anyone harbour such hatred for their flesh and blood?'

'I have no idea, Maggie. She once blurted she didn't know what some man or another saw in her daughter, but . . . Oh, I don't know. Whatever happened in the past seems irrelevant considering the enmity Mrs Sharp held for her before she even left the womb. There was such hatred, such a complete lack of love between them. It's so very sad.'

Maggie lowered her gaze. 'I know it's early on to mention this but, well, it needs thinking on sooner or later. We're out of a job, now, love. We need to think on what we're to do. Sorry as I am for what's occurred, I've the little 'uns and Mam to think of; as do you with the babby.'

'Do you know, I hadn't thought about that but you're right.' Sudden yearning for Breightmet, for Ivy and her family, the fields and meadows she missed so much, struck.

'We'll talk later. Try and snatch a few hours' sleep, it'll do you good.'

After Maggie left, Sally stared at the door for an age, thoughts tumbling. Recent events had taken centre stage in her mind and she felt wretched realising she'd almost forgotten about the attack at Bolton. She curled into a ball and squeezed her eyes shut. Peggy's death, discovering that Stan was her brother, the horrific incident today – all had consumed her thoughts, pushing aside the one person she owed her life to.

Shame stung and she hugged herself tighter, the urge for Spring Row rising. She didn't want to remain here any longer. The Manchester of her childhood was in a past she could never return to. There was nothing for her, here, now. Her relationship with her family was in tatters and, as Maggie pointed out, work no longer tied her.

Reliving the day's events yet again, tears burned. She could scarcely believe Pru and Agnes were gone. Pru's face at the window would haunt her for ever. What transpired over the weekend to tip her over the edge? Why, *why*, had she continued on her way yesterday when it was clear Pru needed her? Her presence was a cry for help – but selfishly, she'd walked away.

The constable had surmised that the murder occurred many hours before discovery. Had Pru already done the deed when she'd seen her?

For the remainder of her days, she'd never forget that haunted expression of someone beyond help. Agnes had provoked her, she *must* have, and after years of mental and physical torture, Pru snapped. There was no denying the old woman could be wicked beyond words.

Yet whatever Agnes's sins, she'd paid for them today and Sally hoped both were now at peace. It was just heartbreaking that it had to be in death; it clearly hadn't existed in life, for either.

These last days were the worst of her life. How much heartache could she bear?

Convulsing with sobs, she wept bitterly.

A loud rap woke Sally with a jolt. The slit of sky between the curtains was purple-black and gasping, she hauled herself up. Why had no one woken her? Feeding Jonathan her main concern, she hurried from the bedroom.

Tears she'd shed before falling into the fitful sleep had brought on a splitting headache. Reaching the kitchen, she shaded her eyes with her hand. 'It's as though my head has been trampled by a dozen horses. Why didn't you wake me?'

'There you are!'

Her head sprang up at the familiar voice and she saw Con in the doorway. Pain stabbed and she winced then shivered as the night breeze hit her.

Maggie rushed to her. 'Sit yourself by the fire, Sally. Con, come in and shut that door,' she added, then frowned to see he wasn't there. 'Where's he gone?' she asked her mother.

Ellen ceased pouring tea to look outside and almost dropped the pot when he suddenly reappeared. 'Mother of God, my heart!'

Con flashed her and Maggie a grin then winked at Sally. 'Close your eyes, acushla. I've a surprise for ye.' He returned to the street then sauntered back in, pushing a black perambulator. 'What do you think? 'Tis fit for a prince, to be sure.'

Sally gazed at the huge contraption. 'Is that for me?'

'Sure, you'd have a job squeezing in! 'Tis for your man, there.' He smiled at Jonathan. 'You didn't think I'd leave him out, did ye? I didn't bring it yesterday with the other items because I hadn't time to pick it up from my friend's stall. I collected it this afternoon. 'Tis clean,' he assured her. 'Sure, 'tis a little battered but it's solid and the wheels are sturdy. Aye, laid back in this, 'twill be grand he'll look, better than any toff.'

She forced a smile. 'You shouldn't have. Thank you; for the blouse, too. You're too kind.'

Studying her, his grin vanished. 'What's wrong?'

Maggie placed a protective arm around her shoulders. 'You've not heard?'

'Heard what, Maggie?' He sighed and rubbed his chin. 'The funeral. Jaysus, Sally, I'm sorry. Did something happen with the family? Weren't you able to be reconciled?'

Maggie bit her lip. 'It's not that. This morning . . . I don't know how you've not heard.'

'I've been out of Ancoats all day at your man's picking up this,' he said, nodding to the perambulator, 'then collecting stock for my stall. What should I have heard?' In two strides, he crossed the room and knelt before them. 'What's happened?'

'I tried telling you afore Sally came down. Con, summat terrible's happened. Miss Sharp . . . She's taken her mam's life and her own. Sally found them this morning.'

He shook his head in disbelief. Sally began to cry, Maggie's bottom lip trembled, and Con clasped them both in a hug.

Holding her friends close, deep sadness thudded through Sally's breast but she knew she must tell them. Longing for Spring Row and the Morgans was as acute as earlier. She'd made up her mind. Her friends needed to know.

She glanced at them in turn. 'I have to tell you something. I've decided to return to Bolton.' From what little she'd revealed, they were aware of her troubled marriage so she wasn't surprised when each of them protested, faces creased with concern. 'Please, I must. I'm aching to see the Morgans and . . . Well, the stark truth is, other than you all, there's nothing for me in Manchester. I barely have a relationship with my family, no position, very little money and no home.'

'You're welcome to stop here as long as you want, in't she, Mam?' Maggie cried. 'You see,' she added when Ellen nodded, 'you're a good friend, lass – the best. I don't want to lose thee.'

'Nor shall you,' she said with feeling. 'I don't know what will happen when I arrive or how long I'll be able to stay. And if I'm honest, at this moment, I don't know whether I'll return here afterwards. But I have to go. I have to, Maggie. I've left it far longer than I should. I must see Mrs Morgan is well. Whatever happens, wherever I am, I promise we'll always be friends.' Maggie lowered her head and she turned to Con. 'You'll look after her for me, won't you?'

His expression was unreadable. In answer, he squeezed Maggie's shoulder. 'When will ye go?'

'When Miss Sharp and her mother are laid to rest. I couldn't go without saying goodbye.'

He nodded curtly and strode to the door. He shot Maggie and Ellen a half-smile over his shoulder. 'I'll be away, so. Goodnight.' His gaze then flicked to her. 'Goodbye, acushla,' he murmured.

Sally hadn't time to respond. Within seconds, he'd gone, leaving her staring helplessly at the door.

Chapter 22

FOR THE SECOND time, a bounding Shield almost knocked Sally from her feet.

'Will you calm down, for goodness' sake?' she chided, steadying the basket. 'Be patient, boy.' Despite her firmness, she couldn't contain a sad smile. He'd missed Grace's as much as she.

Since leaving Maggie's, he'd seemed to sense where they headed and had leapt about like a puppy the length of the street. Wetness touched her hand and she glanced down. Tongue lolling, he stared back solemnly, as though apologising, and chuckling, she scratched his ear. However, when Boslam Street came into view, all laughter left her. As excited as Shield was, she felt nothing but anxiety. Yet visit she must. To return to Bolton, she needed her family's help.

As she opened the door, Grace's face contorted in shocked delight. 'Oh, love! Oh, come in, come in!'

Sally's arms ached to embrace her but she had to ask. 'Stan . . . ? Is he at work?'

There was a break in Grace's voice. 'Aye. Come in.'

She followed her inside. Her gaze went to the window and the empty space where Peggy's bed had been. The shelf was free of medicine bottles, the chair in which Grace had sat hunched over her dying daughter now against the wall. Averting her eyes, she placed the basket on the table.

Grace peered inside and smiled. She lifted a tiny hand and kissed it. Looking at Sally, her eyes were bright. 'I'm that glad to see you both. Aye, and you,' she added with a laugh when Shield nudged her arm. ''Ere, I heard about the owd 'un and her daughter. Shocking, in't it?'

'There was nothing we could do. The butcher made a grab for the knife but, well, it happened so fast. Oh, Aunt Grace, the blood . . . so much blood. He said in all his years as a butcher, he'd never seen so much before that day; it was like stepping into an abattoir . . . Never, for the rest of my days, will I forget that image.'

Grace slapped a hand to her mouth then grasped her niece's fingers. 'I didn't know you were there when . . . Oh, love. I wanted to come and see you at your friend's, knew you'd be upset. You'd grown close to the daughter, hadn't you? If I'd known you'd seen . . .' She looked away guiltily. 'I didn't, I mean I, I didn't know whether—'

'It's fine, Aunt Grace.' She could see helplessness etched in every line of her aunt's face. 'If Stan discovered you'd been to see me, it would have caused you no end of grief.'

'I don't know how you can be so understanding. My heart's breaking for thee day and night. I've tried talking to him . . . Me and Ed are at a loss what to do. You should be here, where you belong, with your family.'

Sally stared at their clasped hands. 'How are you coping, with . . . Peggy?' she asked, changing the subject. Grace was in an impossible situation and it didn't look as though circumstances would change soon. Raking over it was pointless.

'It's been hard, aye. But I know she's at peace and in no more pain. It helps to think on that.'

Sally nodded then said quietly, 'Aunt Grace, I wanted to ask if Uncle Ed would make arrangements for the cart. I've decided to return to Bolton once the Sharps are laid to rest.'

'Return? You mean visit?' Grace's eyes widened when Sally glanced away. 'Nay. Nay, tha can't leave for good. Tha can't, lass! He'll come round, our Stan. He will, I know it. He needs time, is all.'

'No, he won't. You know it as well as I.'

'Nay, he will! And what about that swine, Joseph? You'd not know peace with him on your doorstep. You'd allus be looking over your shoulder. Manchester's your home, lass.'

'No, Aunt Grace, it's not. Don't you see? Since the day I arrived, there's been nothing but trouble. Stan's right. I should never have come.' She shook her head as Grace made to protest. 'It's true. I've thought about this long and hard. Settling in Bolton is impossible, I realise that. I intend to visit the Morgans and afterwards . . . ?

'The only places I know, where I know *anyone*, are Bolton and here. I cannot stay in one and don't wish to stay in the other. Maybe I'll try somewhere new; Preston, perhaps, or Oldham. It will mean starting afresh, alone, but I truly believe a new beginning is what I need. I must leave. I need to see Mrs Morgan. I *need* to get away from *here*.'

Grace's eyes dulled. None the less, she nodded. 'I'll ask Ed when he gets in.'

'Thank you. I'll send word when I'm ready.'

'I'm so sorry for how things turned out. Your mam would be turning in her grave if she knew how I've let you down.'

'You haven't. Don't think that.'

As she'd done with Jonathan, Grace kissed her hand. 'Will you have a brew or must you be away?'

It was now Thursday and she planned to call at Christ Church on her return to Maggie's to enquire over the funerals. A ripple of horror had spread throughout the town; the sorry business had been on everyone's lips. She'd seen the looks whenever she ventured out, had heard the whispers. But she'd heard nothing about the burials.

Surely they would be soon? An investigation into the deaths wasn't necessary. There had been no mistaking the causes of death and no one besides the deceased was involved. She could see no reason for delay.

'I will, thank you. I have to call at Christ Church but there's no hurry.'

Busy at the fire, Grace glanced over her shoulder. 'The Roundhouse?' she asked, as locals knew it, due to its circular structure.

'I hoped to find out when the funerals will be.'

'Funerals? There will only be the one, lass.'

'One?'

'Sally love, Miss Sharp won't receive the same as the owd 'un. She committed murder and self-murder. She can't be buried in sacred ground, for the Church don't allow it.' Grace shook her head in disbelief. 'Didn't you know?'

'Mrs Sharp provoked her, she must have done! Surely the Church will understand? Surely they'll see she was as much to blame? What Miss Sharp did was dreadful, I'm not denying that, but surely . . . ?' Her words died when Grace shook her head again. 'But she doesn't deserve that! She was the kindest, gentlest person I've ever met. She deserves a decent burial. You agree, don't you, Aunt Grace?'

'It's not for me nor anyone else to say. Them's the rules. When all's said and done, she took a life. It's a mortal sin, lass, whichever way you look at it. In any case, she'd have been buried in unconsecrated ground, for if she'd lived, she'd have been hanged for murder and buried within the prison walls.'

Sally was lost for words. Maggie hadn't mentioned anything, must have assumed she'd know. How had she been so naive? Her ignorance of the world and its workings was bewildering. That's what growing up in the confines of the workhouse does, she realised. Your life is within those walls. You're blind to the outside and its conventions.

Grace pushed a cup across. 'Drink your tea, it'll calm your nerves.' She watched her, numb with shock, take tiny sips. 'You all right, love?'

'No, Aunt Grace, I'm not. This isn't right.'

'As far as the Church is concerned, she's not entitled to the comfort of religion. There's no way round it; it is how it is. Least they don't bury them at crossroads no more, like when I were a lass. Crowds would gather to watch, morbid beggars.' Grace shuddered at the memories. 'Miss Sharp will be buried in private. Be grateful for that.'

'So what will happen? Where *will* she be laid to rest?'

'In a plot away from the main churchyard.'

'She'll be tossed into the ground, just like that? No service, prayers? No mourners to utter a kind word or goodbye?'

'That's the top and bottom of it. Come on, eh, love? Don't dwell on what can't be changed.'

Despite the scorch of injustice and disgust, Sally nodded. She didn't want to spoil this meeting; she didn't know when she'd next see her aunt.

An hour later, she and Grace shared an emotional farewell on the step. Wiping her tears, she finally backed away.

'Goodbye, Aunt Grace. Please give my love to Uncle Ed. And Stan.'

Apron pressed to her mouth, Grace could only nod.

Sally tore her gaze from the crumpled face and walked away. Unlike Shield, who turned and whimpered, she didn't look back. She'd gain nothing besides more heartache. Of that, her mind and body could take no more.

Her heart screamed for Maggie and Ellen's comfort, but she didn't turn for Davies Street. Instead, she headed down Carruthers Street and on to Every Street. Passing through the gates, Grace's words echoed in her mind:

'*Them's the rules. There's no way round it; it is how it is. Don't dwell on what can't be changed.*'

She had no doubt Grace spoke truthfully. But was there *really* no way round it? Surely it was worth her trying? Covering her head with her shawl, she whispered to Shield to stay, and slipped inside the church.

The clergyman who had conducted Peggy's funeral smiled warmly. 'Good afternoon. Please, come in. I don't bite,' he added, eyes twinkling, when she hesitated.

Sally blinked in surprise. This one was certainly nothing like the preacher! Hope fluttering in her breast, she stepped forward. 'Good afternoon, Father Collins. I'd like a word, if I may?'

'Of course, my child. What is it you wish to discuss?'

A glance around showed the church was otherwise empty and she relaxed somewhat. 'It's rather a delicate issue. It's about Miss Prudence Sharp.'

His eyebrows rose, the smile vanishing. 'Oh?'

Her resolve waned at his change in demeanour but she swallowed her nerves. 'There's no easy way of asking so I may as well just say it. Miss Sharp committed a terrible sin but there were reasons, Father.

'She suffered appallingly at her mother's hands and I believe, from what I knew of her, she simply . . . snapped. A body can only bear so much. She wouldn't have planned what she did, I'd stake my life on it. Her mother beat her regularly. She treated her as no one should be treated, let alone by a parent.

'Miss Sharp's mental state at the time, well, she cannot have been of sound mind, for as God is my witness, I can truthfully say that woman would never have committed such a deed. She suffered enough in life. Please, don't make her suffer in death. Couldn't you allow her a proper burial? Couldn't you, Father? Please?'

He released his breath slowly. 'Come, Mrs . . . ?'

'Swann, Father.'

'Mrs Swann, sit down.' He motioned to a pew and sat beside her. 'I see you are grieving, my child. You cared a great deal for the late Miss Sharp?'

Tears stung. She nodded.

'You must have been a comfort to her. She often felt alone.'

'I didn't realise you knew her.'

'Oh, indeed. She used to attend mass regularly. Not to pray as such, as I recall. I believe it was sanctuary she sought. As her mother's health declined, she had less time to attend but when the opportunity arose, she would come.' His eyes softened. 'She was a troubled soul, Mrs Swann. I'm aware of the difficulties she faced with her mother, indeed I am—'

'However?' she cut in quietly. 'There is one coming, isn't there, Father?'

He gave a small sigh. 'Mrs Swann, what you are asking is quite impossible. I appreciate your feelings on the matter but, as saddened as I am by what has occurred, a conventional burial within the main churchyard is simply out of the question.'

She'd heard enough. Deep down, she'd known she was wasting her time. And to think she'd hoped he was different from that fiend, Bailey. They were all the same.

'This may bring God's wrath upon my head but to be perfectly honest, Father, I'm beyond caring. I say the Church is wrong. You're aware of Miss Sharp's suffering, you understand, and yet . . . ?' She nodded stiffly and rose. 'I'll trouble you no further and shall take my leave before I say something I may regret. Good day to you.'

'Please, sit down.'

Lifting the basket, she shook her head. 'I don't believe there's anything left to say, do you, Father? You've made your decision quite clear. Now, if you'll excuse me.'

Father Collins laid a hand on her wrist. Though he was clearly aware they were the only ones present, his eyes flicked around the church, then to the door.

'You didn't allow me to finish,' he murmured. 'A conventional burial within the main churchyard *is* out of the question. However . . . Sit down, Mrs Swann, and listen carefully.'

Tommy stared across the table. The scraping had gone on for hours and with each passing minute, his irritation mounted. Finally, he could stand it no longer.

'You don't have to do this.'

Absorbed in his creation, the tip of his tongue poking out in concentration, Shaun didn't look up. 'Eh?'

'I said you don't have to do this.' He struggled to keep an even tone. 'It's a reet nice thought, like, but . . .'

'Don't you like it, our Tommy?'

He glanced away, rubbing a hand across his eyes. 'Aye, lad, course I do. Ignore me. I'm tired, is all.'

Shaun's face spread in a smile. 'It'll look better, soon, and I want to do it, honest. This is my way of saying thanks. If it weren't for thee, I'd not have my apprenticeship. You expect your parents to want the best for you, but for your brother . . . Well, I'm grateful.'

'I did nowt. It weren't my brass made it happen.'

'Oh, aye, aye. I'm grateful to Mrs Goden, an' all.'

Tommy's jaw clenched to hear Sally's marital name but he forced a nod.

'You believed in me. You went out of your way to change my life. I'll not forget it.'

The noticeable change in his brother brought a genuine smile. The lad had grown up.

Shaun put down his knife, lifted the block of wood from the pile of shavings and studied it through narrowed eyes. He traced his fingers along two mounds, frowned as though dissatisfied and reached for the knife.

Tommy watched swift strokes add definition to a flat cap. When Shaun began scratching a bonnet's outline on the next mound, his tolerance burned out. He scraped back his chair.

Seated by the fire, his mother glanced up as he crossed to the window, then returned her attention to her darning. But his father continued watching him. Arthur's gaze strayed to Shaun then back to Tommy. He extinguished his pipe and rose.

Ivy looked up again when her husband extracted coins from his pocket and counted them. Arthur flashed her an easy smile.

'Now, wench, don't be looking at me like that.'

'Well, on a Thursday? You'll not get up in t' morning. It's murder trying to rouse you when you've had a sup the night afore.'

'I'll be up.' His father dropped the coins into his pocket and nodded to Tommy. 'Coming forra jar, lad?'

Ivy clicked her tongue. 'There better be no moaning from you, neither, the morrow. If you don't rise from your bed first time I shout, you'll get that pail of cowd water over your head,' she warned, pointing to where it stood beside the hearth. 'That goes for thee, an' all,' she told her husband.

Donning jackets and caps, they rolled their eyes at a grinning Shaun.

'Aye, I saw that! Oh go on, you pair of inebriates, afore it gets too late.'

Smiling, they left the cottage. They passed through the row in companionable silence and it wasn't until they were sitting with their tankards that they spoke.

'So what's this in aid of?' Tommy asked.

'Just fancied a jar.'

'At this hour, on a Thursday? Come on, I'm not daft.'

His father took a long draught of ale and wiped his mouth on his hand. 'I thought it were time we had that talk.'

'About what?'

'About you and that Goden lass.' He cocked an eyebrow in surprise when Tommy thumped the tabletop.

'Why won't folk stop calling her that? She's nowt to do with him any more. She's Sally. Just call her Sally.' Slowly, his face crumpled in horror. 'I'm sorry, I . . . I'm sorry.'

His father gazed at him. 'Lord above, you've got it worse than I thought. What's wrong with you, lad? You barely know her and besides owt else, she's a wedded woman!'

'D'you not think I've tried ridding her from my thoughts?'

'Try bloody harder! It's madness.'

'I went to Manchester to see her to . . . Well, I don't know. I didn't think on what I'd do when I arrived. I just . . . I had to go.'

Arthur raised his eyes to the ceiling. 'Christ's sake. And how did you plan on finding her? By tramping the lanes hoping to bump into her?'

A bitter smile touched his lips. 'Aye, as it happens. And believe it or not, I did.'

'Tha did what?'

'See her. Can you believe it, the size of that place, the amount of folk up there? What are the chances?'

His father's tankard paused midway to his mouth. 'Oh, lad. Please don't say you told her how you feel.'

'Nay, don't fret. As it turned out, she's met someone. Hanging off some fella's arm, she were. Reet ugly divil, an' all,' he lied, to soothe his ego.

'So what now?'

Averting his eyes, he took a gulp of ale. 'I'm going to ask Dolly to marry me.'

'Why?'

The question threw him. He cursed inwardly when heat crept up his neck.

'Son, I watched you with our Shaun. You couldn't bear to look at that carving of you and Dolly, could you?'

Shame and terror coursed through him. It must have shown, for Arthur frowned.

'Oh, what now? What have you done?'

Tommy crushed a fist to his mouth but couldn't contain the words. 'Sunday, by the river . . . May God forgive me, I lay with Dolly.'

'For the love of God, you bloody fool, yer!'

The innkeeper looked across and Tommy touched his father's sleeve. 'Please, calm down.'

'Calm down? *Calm bloody down?*' His voice dropped to a growl. 'You brainless young swine, d'you realise what you've done? What will her father say; not to mention your mam?' He closed his eyes. 'Lord, your mam. I'd not like to be in your boots when she hears.'

'What am I to do?'

The answer was firm. 'What tha said. Marry her.'

'But I don't love her. Well, I do, I think . . .' Tommy prodded his chest. 'It's not enough, in here. I thought it were but since Sally—'

'And what if she's with child?' A little of the anger had left his father's tone but his eyes were steely. 'You've no choice. You've deflowered the lass. No fella will want her, now. Get Sally from your mind. There's no getting out of this. You'll have to wed her.'

Emptiness filled him. 'I am fond of her. I'd not hurt her for owt.'

'You'll do the right thing?'

'Aye.'

'You know, don't you, if there were another way . . . if there were owt I could do, I would?'

A lump formed in Tommy's throat at the sincerity in the gruff words. 'Aye, I know. This is my mess and me alone must sort it. I'll not shirk my duty. I'll call on Dolly, Saturday, and if her father gives permission . . . I'll ask for her hand.'

When Arthur went to refill their tankards, Tommy covered his face with his hands. He wouldn't ruin her reputation, abandon her after having his way. He'd made his bed, he'd have to lie in it. *Beside Dolly, every night, for the rest of his life . . .*

'Sally,' he breathed. 'Dear God, what have I done?'

Chapter 23

A SUBDUED SALLY and Maggie passed through the streets. Christ Church came into view and Sally gave a half-smile of reassurance but her friend, after attempting to return it and failing, bit her lip.

'I appreciate your coming. Please, don't worry. Father Collins assured me all will run smoothly.'

Maggie nodded uncertainly. 'It's just, well, folk might wonder why we're going early. Mrs Sharp's service ain't till two; it's only just gone twelve,' she said out of the side of her mouth. 'Are you certain he's agreed to this? Happen you got it wrong.

'I've heard whispers of this sort of thing for babbies what die afore they can be baptised, but . . .' She glanced around. 'Not with folk who've committed murder or self-murder – and Miss Sharp committed both! I've not heard afore of any priest turning the other cheek to summat like this.'

'Well, now you have. He's a compassionate man. He understands the circumstances behind Miss Sharp's dreadful act.' As had Maggie, she glanced around before continuing. 'From what he hinted, it simply comes down to the humanity of individual clergymen. I'm thankful Father Collins is a sympathetic soul unafraid of defying convention.'

'He'd be in hot water if he were found out, though, wouldn't he? Mebbe us, an' all. And that'd be nowt compared with what would happen were folk to discover what we were about. A quick prayer and blessing of an innocent babby's grave is one thing; this is summat else altogether. I reckon many wouldn't approve.'

'I cannot speak for Father Collins. I don't know what the repercussions, if any, would be, but the decision was his. And I for one am grateful. I'm not concerned what people think. This is right, I'm certain.'

Re-tying string around a posy of roses, the flower seller, sensing their presence, smiled without looking up. 'Just a minute while I . . .' She made a knot and returned the bunch to her basket. 'There we are. Now, what would you like?' Recognition flickered in her eyes and her smile turned sympathetic. 'Hello, lass.'

Remembering her kindness with Peggy's flowers, Sally smiled warmly. 'Good afternoon. You were most helpful last week and regrettably, I need your advice again.'

The flower seller nodded understandingly. Many, many people, young and old alike, died daily around here. Attending more than one funeral in the same week, for some poor souls, wasn't uncommon.

'Who's being laid to rest?'

Seeing Sally hesitate, Maggie stepped forward. 'Two posies of white roses will do, ta. They're suitable for an owder lady, ain't they?'

'Aye, they are. It's important to pick summat right; flowers hold different meanings, you see. Aye, white roses – innocence, purity and reverence. A sound choice, lass.'

Sally paid with a mumbled thank-you. Once out of earshot, she glanced at her friend. 'Oh, if only she knew . . .'

Maggie sighed. 'Let's get this over with.'

Sally now knew that, away from the main churchyard, most parish churches held a marshy or overgrown plot for the interment of sinners beyond redemption.

In a remote corner beneath an ancient, bare-branched tree, Father Collins conducted a simple ceremony and, surrounded by countless unmarked graves, laid Pru Sharp to rest.

Murmuring a final goodbye, Sally placed a posy on the fresh earth then turned to the gravedigger. 'Thank you.'

The kindly faced man leaning on his spade touched his cap. He marked the sign of the cross over his chest and nodded to the priest.

Father Collins returned it. 'Thank you, Jackson.' He motioned to her and Maggie. 'Come, let us pray.'

They walked back to the church in silence.

Sally couldn't suppress a bitter smile as Father Collins' clear voice committed Agnes to the ground. No hushed tones, here. No glancing around before blessing the grave. No secrecy.

In her eyes, this woman had sinned far more than the one condemned to lie for eternity as far from the church as possible. Pru's resting place would remain unmarked by stone or cross; no inscription, no lasting reminder of someone more sinned against than sinner. Yet despite the years of misery she'd inflicted, Agnes would lie peacefully in the Lord's garden. It didn't make sense.

Father Collins closed his bible. 'I will leave you to say your final words.'

Alone with Maggie, Sally swallowed the pain of injustice and laid the second posy on the soil. She replaced the heartfelt apology whispered at Pru's graveside with one question: 'Why?'

Maggie reached for her hand. 'That's summat we'll never know. They've carried their secrets to their graves. Dwelling on it'll do you no good.'

Despite Agnes's entitlement to a conventional funeral, it was as lonely an affair as her daughter's, and as Maggie steered Sally away, sadness for both women overcame her. They'd had only each other. What-ifs haunted her but Maggie was right. Dwelling on what she couldn't change was useless.

Father Collins stood waiting by the church doors and she clasped his hand. 'I cannot express my gratitude for what you've done today. I'll never forget your kindness, Father.'

Eyes soft, he inclined his head. 'Have strength, my child. Remember, the Lord's house is always open.'

Maggie took her arm. 'Let's get you home.'

Those words were music to her. She yearned to sit in Maggie and Ellen's cosy kitchen and hold Jonathan close.

As they passed through the church gates, a gentleman collided with them. He struggled to keep hold of the sheaf of papers he carried and they rushed to assist him.

'Thank you, thank you, I'm most terribly sorry,' he mumbled, eyes flicking behind them to the church. 'May I ask, is Father Collins still present?'

Sally nodded. 'Yes, he's—'

'Thank goodness. Good day.'

'Clumsy beggar,' grumbled Maggie when he'd gone. 'He near knocked us flying, then.'

Looking back, Sally frowned. 'He was in quite a hurry. I wonder what was so important?'

'Lord knows. Come on, lass, I hear our teapot calling.'

A beshawled figure watched the women turn into Junction Street.

When they disappeared from view, she emerged from the shelter of the branches. Wary eyes darting, she hurried to a fresh grave. She dropped to her knees and ran her fingers over the earth. She mouthed words then dipped her chin to her chest, lips still. She straightened the roses, caressed the soil once more then rose. Quickly, noiselessly, she scurried back to the trees.

Reappearing at the opposite end of the churchyard, she drew her shawl lower over her face. She flitted between the gravestones, eyes fixed on another dark mound up ahead. Reaching this, she didn't kneel. No gentle fingering of soil or straightening of flowers. No whisper, no emotion. Glaring down, her every pore emitted pure loathing.

She spat on the ground and was gone.

Chapter 24

MAGGIE SCOWLED AT the elderly man atop the cart and despite her own heartache, Sally chuckled. She pulled her into a hug.

'Don't blame him, Maggie.'

'Well, I still reckon he's a blighter, taking you away from me.'

Sally kissed her cheek and held her at arm's length. 'Look after yourself and remember, this isn't for ever. I don't know when . . . but we will see each other again, you have my word. Goodbye. Thank you, for everything.'

Lowering her head, Maggie's tears dripped to the cobbles. 'Goodbye, love.'

Guilt thumping, she turned to Ellen, who was holding a solemn-looking twin under each arm. 'Goodbye. Thank you for all you've done for me. Goodbye, Harry, Flo. Be good for your mother and grandmother, won't you?'

The children broke free and ran to her, and Ellen covered her face with her apron, unable to watch the daughter and grandchildren she adored upset.

Small arms wrapped around Sally's waist. She stooped and kissed the bewildered faces. 'Shield shall miss you both very much. Would you like to give him a hug before we leave?'

They nodded and threw their arms around his neck. 'Bye, Shield,' they said in unison. He licked their faces, and giggling, they ran back to their grandmother.

Sally climbed aboard, Shield clambered beside her and she set the canvas bag and basket by her feet. Too large for the cart, the perambulator still stood beneath Maggie's kitchen window. She hoped leaving it behind wouldn't offend Con.

Thoughts of him brought an ache to her stomach. She'd seen nothing of him since revealing she was leaving. He'd been upset, it showed on his face, but still . . . Hurt stabbed again as she scanned the street. She'd hoped to see him, say goodbye, thank him for everything. She'd miss him greatly.

Swallowing disappointment when it became clear he wouldn't show, she held out a hand to Maggie, who gripped it. 'When you see Con, tell him . . . Tell him I'll be forever thankful for his friendship.' She squeezed her hand then glanced to Ed's friend. 'I'm ready, now, Mr Lynch.'

At his command, the large bay set off. She waved to her lovely friends, tears running down her face. Only when the cart turned and they were out of sight did she look away.

Drowning in conflicting emotions, she gazed around at the fetid homes and the tall chimneys invading the skyline.

'Goodbye, Manchester,' she whispered.

Maggie was certain afterwards that if the cart had departed a mere minute later, her friend would still be here.

As it happened, Sally didn't see Father Collins passing down Davies Street in the opposite direction. She didn't see him halt beside Maggie, or catch his words. Neither did she see Maggie's hand fly to her mouth, nor hear her hopeless cry of, 'Sally, wait! You'll never believe . . . Sally, come back!'

Ivy leaned towards the bubbling pot and sniffed appreciatively. After stirring the broth, she turned to the table. She'd already laid out the pretty crockery and she nodded, satisfied with her efforts. Today was important and she'd worked hard, cleaning and cooking since dawn. It looked queer seeing five places set again. Queer but nice, she admitted.

'All right, wench?'

She glanced up as Arthur entered the kitchen. 'I were just thinking, it's queer seeing the table set for one more again, in't it?'

Her fixed smile didn't fool him. He took her in his arms. 'Tha had to let go some time.'

'I had a feeling it were coming. Even Martha did, said all what's happened would bring them closer, but . . .'

'I know. It's a big deal forra mother, losing her son to another wench. I remember what you were like with our James's betrothal.' She smiled crookedly and he chuckled. 'Be happy for him, eh? I know you've a soft spot for the lad but he's a grown man. It's time to let him go.'

'Aye, I know. I just want him to be happy. I've only ever wanted all of them to be happy.'

'And they are. You've done a sound job, Ivy, better than any mother could've. Anyroad, you'll not lose him right away. It'll take them months to save for the wedding and afterwards, they'll be dwelling here till they find their own cottage.'

She pulled away when footsteps sounded on the stairs. Fixing on a smile, she turned to look at her sons.

Having scrubbed the half-day's work from their skin and hair, they stood stiffly in their best clothes. Tommy glanced from the table to her. He flashed a smile but didn't speak. Shaun, on the other hand, grumbled to himself, wriggling on the spot.

'Mam, must we wear this lot? This shirt's itching summat awful. Dolly won't mither if we're not in our best.'

Her temper rose to the fore. 'Give over grousing, Shaun. This here's an important day. I'll not have the lass here and us favouring a bunch of vagrants. She might think twice about accepting and run a mile at the thought of wedding into a family of ragbags. Stop your fidgeting and go and fill the pail at the well.' When he'd gone, she turned to Tommy. 'I were only pulling his leg. I've not worried thee, have I? Me and my big bloody mouth, saying things like that on a day like today.'

'Nay, Mam.'

'Good. Anyroad, the lass would need her head looking at, wouldn't she, Arthur? He's a good catch, our Tommy, in't he?' At his nod, she smiled proudly. 'Nay, she's fair smitten. Have no fear, lad.'

When his mother turned back to her cooking, Tommy shot his father a look. 'Nay, she'll not turn me down.'

Dull acceptance in his tone brought a sigh to Arthur. They stared at each other helplessly.

Unaware of the silent message passing between them, Ivy nodded to Shaun as he re-entered, lugging the heavy pail. 'Put it by the hearth, lad.'

'Wind's picking up out there. Oh, and I've just seen Dolly turn into the row.'

'What? And you didn't think to mention it as soon as you come in? You put the pail back and even remarked on t' bloody weather afore telling us! She's bleedin' early,' she muttered, patting her hair. 'And you remember what I said earlier, Shaun. Don't you go letting owt slip afore our Tommy's had chance to ask her. He got Nat Jenkins's permission yesterday but she knows nowt of it. Think on, d'you hear?'

'Aye, Mam.'

Arthur went to stand beside her and she squeezed his hand. 'You all right, Tommy?' she asked, glancing across.

'Mam, I . . .' His breaths came in short gasps. 'I don't think . . .'

She frowned. 'Son?'

Glimpsing the warning in his father's eyes, he swallowed hard, forcing a smile. 'I, I don't think there's a mam in t' whole of Bolton better than thee. Thank you. You've done me proud.'

'Eeh, Tommy.' Love thickened her voice but when her bottom lip wobbled, she quelled it with laughter. 'Ay, you soppy bugger, there's no need—' Knocking silenced her. She breathed deeply. 'Good luck, lad.'

The walk to the door was like stepping to the gallows.

Luck? A damn miracle couldn't save him.

The journey hadn't been a comfortable one. Hours of bumping through ditches and potholes, squashed by Shield's bulk, all the while struggling to placate the grizzling baby, had left Sally stiff and weary.

All the way, her emotions had swung dizzily. Excitement at meeting Ivy turned to dread with thoughts of her being the woman attacked. Throbbing anticipation at seeing Tommy, she'd forced away. Indulging in the memory of him was becoming impossible to suppress; it was almost an obsession.

Frequently, thoughts of Joseph had replaced them, bringing a churning sickness. Yet whilst her feelings for Tommy strengthened in her absence, anxiety over Joseph had blessedly diminished. The prospect of seeing him still sent fingers of fear up her spine – that would never leave her completely – but it wasn't the all-consuming, gut-wrenching terror she once knew.

She'd noticed the shift over the weeks. So much had happened since leaving. She felt a different woman. She was stronger, clearer of mind. She was in control. Never again would that monster hurt her.

Her shawl, lying loose across her shoulders, she involuntarily drew over her head when grey-brown Deansgate appeared. Eyes flicking around, her hand tightened on the basket. She released her breath when they passed and, after peeking back, just to be sure, lowered her shawl.

Eventually, the clogged air grew clear. Green strips winked on the horizon and her heartbeat quickened.

'Please, Lord, don't let Joseph discover my return,' she prayed. 'Please let Mrs Morgan be well.' Swallowed by the rumble of cart wheels and thudding hooves, her quiet pleas went unheard by the driver. 'And please, *please*, give me strength to act naturally upon seeing Tommy,' she added, flushing with shame.

At the turning of Spring Row, she signalled to the driver and with his assistance stepped from the cart. Shield sniffed the air and whined, as though sad to be back.

'It's all right, boy. You have me, now,' she told him.

From beneath Jonathan's covers, she lifted the pouch containing what little money she possessed. She'd given Maggie several shillings to see her through until she found work and had calculated that, after paying

Mr Lynch, she'd enough to keep herself for a few weeks. She just hoped she'd soon find employment, wherever she decided upon, following this visit.

'Thank you, Mr Lynch. I'm most grateful. I'll be fine from here.'

'Nay, lass, keep your brass. You owe me nowt.'

'But of course I do!'

'Nay, you don't, for your aunt and uncle paid me last night, said as how you're to keep your money for yourself and the babby. You've a sound family back there. Don't leave it too long, eh, for Grace's sake.'

She took the basket and canvas bag from him, eyes misty. 'I don't know what to say. Please thank them for me.'

He tapped his cap. 'Take care, lass.'

Heart overflowing with love, she sent up a prayer that, one day, her relationship with them – all of them – would be repaired. Shield trotting alongside, she entered the row.

She avoided looking at her cottage and fixed her gaze on the Morgans'. Nearing the gate, she saw their front door ajar and her heart leapt. Worry they might be absent had niggled at her throughout the journey. Not really knowing another soul, what to do would have stumped her.

Picking up scents of his former home, Shield wandered off. He turned when she halted and she flapped a hand.

'It's all right, Shield. Go and explore,' she told him, and off he went to visit his old haunts.

When she was midway up the path, a voice drifted from the cottage. Tommy. *Tommy*. Heady heat quivered through her. She forced herself forward, knocked then peeped around the door.

Gazing upon the scene, her smile froze. She barely noticed Ivy, Arthur and Shaun. It was the objects of their attention which struck her dumb and made her want to turn tail and flee.

Sitting with her back to the door was a woman. And on bended knee at her feet, holding a ring aloft, was Tommy.

Shock hit her like a slap to the face. In those seconds, streams of memories swamped her. His soothing voice, how he'd cradled her in his strong arms . . . Their time together after retrieving the money, his smile, his laughter, how he'd sweep back his hair . . . Hopes she'd harboured for weeks, countless nights she'd lain awake thinking of him . . .

She'd never felt as foolish, ashamed, confused. What had she been thinking? Had she really believed he felt anything for her? She was a married woman; nothing could have come of it . . . Such wild imaginings . . . What in God's name was wrong with her?

In the same moment that Ivy spotted her, the woman threw herself at Tommy, crying, 'Oh! Course I'll marry thee!'

'Sally? Is that you? I don't believe it!' Ivy's words surprised everybody. As one, they turned to the door.

The sight of the older woman dragged Sally to the present. She sagged with relief. Her dear friend was all right! It wasn't Ivy who had been attacked! She laughed brokenly. 'Hello, Mrs Morgan.'

'Oh, lass!' Ivy rushed forward and drew her into her arms. 'What the divil are you doing here?'

'I heard that a woman from Spring Row . . . Oh, Mrs Morgan, thank goodness you're well.'

Ivy half smiled and looked away, and Sally turned her attention to the others. Shaun was smiling, as was the woman. Though Arthur flashed a smile, he wore an expression she couldn't fathom. Yet she forgot everything when her eyes locked with Tommy's.

He rose slowly. At his intense stare, blood rushed to her cheeks. To her surprise, the woman stepped forward.

'Hello, Sally. It's nice to meet thee at last. I'm Dolly Jenkins, soon to be Morgan.' She gave a tinkling laugh. 'Eeh, it sounds lovely saying that!'

Hurt and envy crashed back. 'Please accept my apologies for interrupting.'

'It's all right, you weren't to know.' She looked adoringly at Tommy. 'Anyroad, nowt could've spoiled that.'

Sally glanced over Dolly's shoulder. 'Congratulations, Tommy.' His eyes creased but he didn't speak. To her horror, she felt tears prick.

''Ere, I've not congratulated youse yet, have I? Come here, lad.' Ivy caught him in a hug. 'And you, lass. Welcome to the family.'

As Dolly joined the embrace, Sally tore her gaze away. Catching Arthur's eye, she squeezed out a smile. 'Hello, Mr Morgan.'

It was a moment before he returned it. 'Sit yourself down, lass. Have you just come from Manchester? Did all go well with your aunt?'

'There's time aplenty for questions, Arthur. Why don't youse lot fetch a jug from Ma Thompson's to toast the happy occasion? Take your time,' Ivy added, shooting him a look. 'There's no rush back.'

'Aye. A walk will do us good after that feast.' Shaun and Dolly followed him to the door but Tommy remained motionless.

Sally gazed into the grey-blue pools. She sensed Arthur watching but couldn't tear her eyes away.

Tommy broke the spell. He sighed softly and followed them out.

She stared after him. The way he'd looked at her . . . It was as though he'd wanted to say something. Was he angry she'd interrupted his special moment? She'd have to apologise, later, however uncomfortable it would be.

'You shouldn't have come, lass. It ain't safe.'

The seriousness of Ivy's tone took her aback. 'It's quite all right, Mrs Morgan. I made sure to cover my head while passing Deansgate. I had to come, to see . . . Mrs Morgan? What is it?'

Ivy's hand strayed to her throat. 'You need to return to Manchester. You need to get far from here and never come back.'

'Mrs Morgan, you're scaring me. What . . . ?' She shook her head as realisation dawned. 'It *was* you, wasn't it? Joseph . . .'

'The bastard sneaked in when the men were at work. He wanted to know where you'd gone and did this when I'd not tell him.' Ivy lifted her chin, revealing angry welts, adding, at Sally's horrified whimper, 'It's all right, lass, he didn't do much damage. Dolly interrupted and he scarpered.

'Nay, you can't stay. As lovely as it is seeing thee, it don't bear thinking of if he got his hands on you. Please, for me, go back to Manchester. You're not safe.'

Sally dropped to her knees at Ivy's feet, her guilt akin to nothing she'd ever known. 'I've brought this on, all of it. Oh, Mrs Morgan, how can you ever forgive me?' She crumpled, gasping with sobs.

Tears glistened on Ivy's lashes but her voice was firm. 'Now you listen to me, this ain't your fault. You've nowt to be sorry for and I'll not hear another word like that, d'you understand?'

'I brought this trouble to your door. It's all my fault.'

'Nay, it's bloody well not. No one's to blame but him. Sally, look at me. Are you listening? It's not your fault, lass.'

As they clung to each other, her blood boiled with rage. 'I loathe him with every fibre of my being. Why won't he just *die*, Mrs Morgan?'

'He'll not get away with it, have no fear. Arthur and Tommy went looking for him at that sister's of his. He weren't there but wherever he's footed it, they'll sniff him out. He'll pay for what he did – to me and to thee. I just pray they'll not go too far, however much the bastard deserves it.'

Sally cringed, her shame overwhelming. That she'd dragged this lovely family into her mess . . . It was little wonder the men hadn't seemed themselves. They resented her bringing trouble to their door, and rightly so.

'I'm so very sorry, to all of you.'

A cry broke the silence and Ivy's face brightened. She lifted Jonathan from the basket. 'He's bloody huge, lass!'

Sally allowed herself a proud smile.

'Eeh, I have missed you,' Ivy cooed, brushing her nose against his. 'It were nice having a babby in t' house again. It weren't half quiet when you'd gone.'

Though it pained her, Sally kept an even tone. 'I dare say you'll be hearing the patter of tiny feet, shortly. I must apologise for interrupting. The door was ajar . . . I did knock.'

'Nay, don't be daft, you weren't to know. I left it open, for it were stuffy after cooking. Ay, I can't believe my Tommy's to wed. Her face were a picture when he asked her; fair brought a tear to my eye, it did, soppy bugger that I am.'

'You must be very happy.'

'Aye. But it's hard letting one of your own go. You'll see when this fella's owder.' Ivy's expression turned serious. 'Sally, I've thought of what I'd say if I saw you again but now the time's come, well, I don't know how to put into words . . .'

'Mrs Morgan?'

'Thank you,' she said simply. 'That brass for our Shaun – thank you, from the bottom of my heart. You've freed him from the pit, lass. He's gorra place with a carpenter. He's doing what he loves, what he were born to. What you did . . . You're an angel, that's what you are.'

'Oh, I am pleased! I so wanted to repay you a little for all you did for me.'

'Nay, it's more than a little. You've changed that lad's life. It'll not be forgotten, not by none of us.' Ivy cleared her throat of emotion. 'Anyroad, what's been happening with thee? Did all go well with your aunt? How you faring at that Manchester? 'Ere, I hope you've kept that carving safe; be worth some money, that will, when our Shaun's a world-known carpenter,' she teased.

At the mention of Thunder, tears sprang to Sally's eyes.

'Eeh, lass, what's wrong?'

'Oh, Mrs Morgan, it's been dreadful, simply dreadful. I cannot go back.'

She told her the whole, sorry lot. Afterwards, Ivy sat back, stunned.

'Word spread here of that murder but not forra second did I think it had owt to do with you. How could so much happen in a few short weeks? How the bleedin' hell haven't you turned stark, staring mad, lass?'

'I've come close. Do you see, I cannot go back? All of it . . . I've had enough.'

'What will you do? You know I'd have you back here in a heartbeat, but Joseph . . .'

'I know. As of yet, I've no idea. I'd fare better in one of the larger towns; there would be more chance of securing employment. I just have to decide which.'

'Well, you're stopping here the night, at least. You can think on what to do the morrow.'

Thoughts of spending all night beneath the same roof as Tommy had Sally shaking her head but before she could think up an excuse, the cottage door opened. Arthur, his sons and a giggling Dolly entered and her stomach dropped. But with Ivy waiting for her response, she had no choice but to accept.

One night, she told herself. *Smile, act naturally for one night, and tomorrow I can be on my way and it will all be over.*

She glanced at Tommy and her heart missed a beat to see him staring back. She dropped her gaze. Knowing he didn't share her feelings was painful enough. That he now hated her for Joseph's actions hurt far, far more.

It was going to be a long night.

Alice was ready to do battle when the knock came. The previous performance caught them off guard. Not this time.

She jerked her head to Joseph and when he disappeared upstairs, pointed a warning to the children. It wasn't necessary; she'd threatened what would happen if they slipped up. Still, it was best to remind them.

She wrenched open the door, all set to vent her fury, but before she knew what was happening, the visitor pushed her aside and rushed in.

'Oh no you don't, not again— Oh, it's you.' Her anger turned to surprise then swiftly back. 'What's tha doing here? I told our Joseph from the off, I'll not have whores in my home. Whatever he chooses to do is his business but I'll have no carryings-on under my roof. Go on, sling your hook and wait for him at Nellie's as you usually do, afore I scrag you out.'

Bent double, hands on her thighs, Nancy fought to catch her breath. 'Is my Joseph back from Manchester?'

Alice frowned at her wide-eyed desperation. 'Aye. He went yesterday morning but it were a waste of time. He found nowt out and were back by nightfall. Been in a right soddin' mood since, an' all. Why, what's afoot?'

'I saw her. She's back.' Nancy's eyes darted to the stairs as footsteps thundered down. 'Oh, love, you're there. Eeh, I ain't half missed you, lad.'

Joseph took the last few stairs slowly. 'Did I hear you say you've seen Sally?' At Nancy's nod, he ran a hand across his mouth. 'You better not be mistaken or I'll—'

'I'm not, love, honest. I saw her pass my father's an hour or so since and disappear inside the Morgans'. I came straight here; ran most of the way, I did.'

Alice shook her head at her brother. 'Well, I don't believe it. Fancy you traipsing there yesterday and she winds up coming back of her own accord. Mind, why would she?'

With a hoot of glee, he slapped his leg. 'Lord knows but I'll tell you summat, this time, she'll not be leaving. By God, she'll not.'

'You're a lucky beggar, you are, our Joseph. You were stumped what to do not half a minute since and now, she's fallen into your lap.'

He grabbed Nancy's arm. 'Come on.'

'But how will you get to her with Arthur and that son of his?'

'I'll figure that out when we arrive. Now for God's sake, get moving. I'll not let her get away this time. The things I'll do to that whore . . . She'll hurt in more ways than she can imagine.'

Alice grinned. 'Go on, lad. Go get the rotten bitch.'

As she hurried down the alley after Joseph, a sickly feeling rose in Nancy at the sheer venom in his voice.

She'd been numb with shock when discovering what he'd done to Ivy. She thought he'd meant to frighten the woman, not throttle her to within an inch of her life. Afterwards, she'd expressed her terror at what would have become of him. He'd laughed in her face, insisting if he had finished the old bitch off, he wouldn't have swung. Alice would have given him an alibi.

What he was capable of frightened her. She couldn't lose him. She'd sooner die than live without him.

Now, as he strode down Deansgate, she caught up and grabbed his sleeve. Peering into his jet-black eyes, she hesitated to ask the burning question tormenting her, petrified to think what his answer would be. But now was the time. If he gave the right one, whatever he planned this night, she'd support him all the way.

'Joseph, you do love me, don't you?'

Irritation flared in his eyes. He pushed her into a doorway, cupped her breasts and rubbed his palms over her nipples. She moaned and he smirked. Biting her lower lip, he stared deep into her eyes. 'I can't do this without you. You want the bitch gone, don't you?'

His smooth tone brought a flush of pleasure to her cheeks. 'Aye, course I do. It's just . . .'

'What?'

'Well, just . . . This *is* for us, in't it? You want us to be together, proper like, don't you? Once she's gone, we'll be free to wed, won't we?'

He nodded.

'Oh, love. Then whatever it takes, I'll understand. I don't want to know what you're planning but, well, whatever you must do . . . do it. Just be careful, eh, lad? Please, be careful. I can't lose thee.'

With a twisted smile, he squeezed her buttocks. 'Let's get the bitch. If I need your help, you be a good girl and do as I say, d'you hear?' At her nod, his smirk returned. His fondling intensified then he pulled away, leaving her panting against the wall. 'Come on.'

She sighed in adoration. Cocooned in her conviction that he did, as she'd believed, love her, she scuttled after him, heart singing.

The fact that he hadn't actually said the words, she ignored.

Chapter 25

BY THE LIGHT of the good fire, Dolly held up her hand and, for the dozenth time, admired her ring.

'I can't believe I'm wearing this. I knew Mam were keeping it for when I wed but still, it's a dream come true.' She stroked hair from Tommy's brow. 'Did Father mention whose it once were?'

He continued gazing into the fire.

'It were my granny's. D'you know, her and my grandfather were wed over fifty year? Let's pray ours lasts as long, eh? Tommy?'

'Sorry . . . What did you say?'

Rolling her eyes, Dolly chuckled, and Sally tried to imitate Ivy's smile but it was impossible.

'Is that jug empty, Arthur?'

Puffing on his pipe, he was watching Tommy through the plumes of smoke. When his wife jabbed him in the ribs, he jumped. ''Ere, what were that in aid of?'

'Hell's teeth. What's wrong with youse two the night? I were saying, have we supped up?'

'Oh. Aye, aye. Have I to fetch another?' he asked hopefully.

Ivy's eyebrows rose to meet her hairline. 'Nay, you bleedin' well shouldn't! You and Tommy's had your fill by the looks of it. Like talking to the wall, it is. It's your beds youse need, not more ale.'

Dolly grinned. 'Aye, I'm tired; must be all the excitement. I think I'll be away home.'

For the first time, Tommy's face relaxed in a ghost of a smile. 'I'll walk thee.' He'd donned jacket and cap and was at the door before she'd reached for her bonnet.

Sally busied herself with Jonathan. She could feel Tommy's stare but didn't lift her head.

The rest of the day had been as uncomfortable as she'd feared. She'd tried her very best to appear cheerful. She'd swallowed her pain and praised Shaun when he'd shown off his latest carving. She'd managed to laugh along when Ivy told of the preacher discovering they'd lied to him – Ivy had feigned ignorance and he'd huffed and puffed 'like a pair of owd bellows' yet had no choice but to drop the matter.

Worst of all, she'd had to endure Dolly's adoring looks to Tommy and hear about their future, which the pretty bride-to-be had evidently planned long ago.

Throughout, his presence overrode everything. Like a moth to a flame, she was powerless to resist him. When her defiant eyes flicked to him, his grey-blue ones met them every time and she'd looked away, afraid she'd reveal her feelings. His, however, didn't waver.

Now, as evening turned to night, she was at breaking point. He resented her being in his home, had only refrained from speaking out for Ivy's sake. Why else was he unable to take his penetrating gaze off her?

That everyone was avoiding the attack wasn't helping. Whether it was to spare her embarrassment, so as not to upset Ivy, or they were too enraged, she didn't know. It hung over them, clogging the air like smoke.

She couldn't leave without voicing it. Whether the men accepted her apology remained to be seen, but apologise she must. She liked Arthur a great deal. And Tommy . . . However sharp the pain of unrequited love, she'd sooner have him as a friend than nothing.

She tucked the blankets around the baby and stole a look across the room. Misery clenched her stomach to see him still watching her. His anger must be eating away at him and understandably so. But dear God, it *hurt*.

As Dolly trilled goodbyes, Tommy turned the knob and she screeched when the door burst inwards. A black shape threw itself at him, knocking him to the floor.

Shaun collapsed in fits of laughter. Tommy glared at him and his guffaws grew, smothering Sally's gasp.

'Shield! Come away at once!' She rushed forward, face ablaze. 'I'm sorry, I completely forgot about him. He's been outside this whole time and . . . Shield, will you get off!' To her surprise, Tommy chuckled.

'Ay, cabbage breath, how are you? Tha frightened me half to death, then. Come on, let me up.' With a struggle, he pushed the dog off, stood and, for the first time since her arrival, smiled at her. 'Gorra thing for me, ain't he?'

Relief like no other washed through her. That he wasn't angry, was *smiling* at her . . . She laughed softly. 'It seems so.'

Something akin to pain appeared behind his eyes. 'It's been nice seeing thee, Sally.'

Her tone was just as gentle. 'You too, Tommy.'

'Time's running on, lad. Dolly wants to be home.'

Arthur's words shattered the moment and Tommy went a dull pink.

Sally stood rooted to the spot. The way he'd looked at her . . . almost as if . . . No. Her cruel mind was playing with her. He was in love with Dolly, was *marrying* Dolly. Why wouldn't these wicked imaginings leave her?

Head bowed, Tommy exited the cottage but instead of following, Dolly turned. Her expression was blank and when she smiled, it didn't reach her eyes. 'Goodbye, Sally.'

Before she could respond, Dolly was gone. She blinked, dazed. Dolly sensed her feelings for her beloved. She knew. *Dear God, she knew* . . .

Shaun yawned. 'I'm away to bed. Goodnight.'

Along with his mother and father, Sally mumbled goodnight to him. At first, she thought it was her imagination but no – definite tension had filled the kitchen. Ivy and Arthur looked decidedly uncomfortable, eyes flitting anywhere but at her.

Lord above, *they* didn't know, too? Was it so obvious?

The agonising silence grew and in desperation she blurted the first thing to enter her head: 'May Shield sleep inside, tonight, Mrs Morgan? He'll be no trouble.' She almost cringed at the inanity, but it seemed to work.

Ivy smiled her usual smile. 'Aye, he can kip by the fire. Now, I'll brew a fresh pot and make up a plate of bread and butter then we'd best get some shut-eye, or we'll be fit for nowt come the morrow.'

She needed to be alone, to make sense of these whirling emotions. As soon as she could, she'd make her excuses and retire, she vowed. She just hoped she'd escape before Tommy returned. She couldn't see him again tonight, didn't trust herself, for surely he'd sense her longing. He was bound to, if everyone else had. The shame of that really would be too much.

Sipping her tea, her eyes strayed to the door continually, heart banging. The moment her cup was empty, she lifted the basket.

'You off to get some kip, lass?'

'Yes. The travelling has worn me out,' she lied. She bid them goodnight, stroked Shield, then escaped to the familiar room next door.

She undressed and slipped beneath the blanket on the sofa. Today had been a disaster. What did tomorrow hold? Where would she go? Her future was as uncertain as the last time she'd lain beneath this roof. However, at least then she'd had an idea of her intentions. All she faced now was stark emptiness.

Yet again, Tommy crept into her mind and she moaned softly. *Had* Dolly, Ivy and Arthur sensed her burning love? She'd been such a stupid, naive fool . . .

She heard the sound of the cottage door opening. Murmurs followed, intermingled with Ivy banking down the fire. Two sets of feet ascended the stairs, then silence.

Fine hairs on Sally's arms stood to attention. Tommy was still in the kitchen; somehow, she could feel his presence. She listened intently. Footsteps sounded and she waited for his tread on the stairs, but they drew nearer. Through the gap beneath the door, two shadows appeared.

She held her breath, her body, to her shame, tingling. Suddenly, the feet disappeared. Moments later, they mounted the stairs.

Throughout the lonely night, confusion and longing were constant companions. Whys and what-ifs tormented her. Should she have gone to the door, asked what he wanted? What would he have answered?

When sleep did claim her, she woke frequently. Stirring again as dawn broke, she threw back the blanket in defeat, dressed and went to the window. Slivers of silver-white sliced the indigo sky. Distant birdsong had replaced owls' hoots. A wispy mist caressed the hilltops beyond, adding to the ethereal scene, and calmness enveloped her.

She loved it here. Despite the terrible memories, Spring Row would always hold a special place in her heart. She'd give anything to remain, to raise her son amidst the sweeping greenness and clear air. But it was an impossible dream she couldn't fulfil. Shortly, they would leave once more. And they would never return.

Scratching sounded at the door. She opened it a crack and Shield's tongue poked through, making her smile. She led him back through the kitchen, opened the cottage door and watched him trot down the row.

The sky had lightened further and, folding her arms, she gazed about. She took deep breaths of sharp air. She knew wherever she went today would be rife with factories and cotton mills' belching chimneys, and closed her eyes, savouring every lungful.

At first, she didn't sense anything amiss. No sound penetrated the stillness. It was an icy shiver the length of her spine that made her open her eyes.

The shock was so overwhelming, not a muscle moved. Her only reaction was the widening of her eyes.

'Hello, whore.'

The hissed words acted like a hammer blow. Her mouth opened but before the scream reached her lips, Joseph's fist slammed into her face.

She knew a split second of intense pain. Then the world faded.

It had been too good an opportunity to miss.

Joseph caught Sally as her legs buckled. Her weight no encumbrance to his powerful strength, he threw her over his shoulder with ease. At the feel of her, droplets of sweat sprang at his temples and blood pumped furiously through his veins. He sprinted to the hedgerow he and Nancy had spent last night hiding behind.

He couldn't afford to hang around. The consequences would be dire if Arthur and his son discovered him.

He hadn't planned it to be like this, wanted to take his time, get it just right. But seeing her standing there . . . He'd been unable to hold back. He could scarcely believe he had the bitch at last.

Stiffness from hours of crouching, he now forgot; the wait had been worth it. Not once had his narrowed gaze, trained on the Morgans' door, shifted. Despite his dew-drenched clothes, he hadn't noticed the cold; adrenaline, coupled with the flask of whisky he'd brought, kept him warm.

He couldn't say the same for Nancy. She'd done nothing but gripe and he'd used the back of his hand numerous times to shut her up. Eventually, she'd fallen silent and he was able to keep watch in peace.

Shaking in anticipation of catching a glimpse of Sally, he'd waited. His excitement reached fever pitch when, at one point, the door opened. But it turned to deep frustration when the Morgan son and a young woman appeared. Then a massive great dog launched itself at the son, knocking him flying, and Sally's voice had sounded. His mouth had twisted in glee.

Knowing she was definitely there, he found the waiting easier; she had to leave some time and he'd be ready. The son had left with the woman, returned alone and soon afterwards, light at the cottage window went out. Realising he wouldn't see Sally that night, he'd prepared himself for the long hours stretching ahead.

Now, he grinned, thrilled his perseverance had paid off. The sight of her had struck him dumb. The terror in her eyes' blue depths . . . He'd missed that. All those weeks of sleepless nights and drink-sodden stupors her absence induced, his futile meeting with the workhouse master and hours tramping Manchester, and now . . .

He could barely breathe. He had her. And by God, she wouldn't escape again.

He flung her to the damp grass, fell to his knees and gazed in awe.

Nancy, too, gazed at the woman she'd come to loathe. She was even prettier up close, she saw with scorching envy.

The wife. The one legally bound to Joseph. *Her* Joseph. Suddenly, the prick of doubt she felt when overhearing customers' conversations in the shop, of how Sally had suffered at his hands, returned. But as always, she forced it away. Vicious lies, that's all they were. Spread by this bitch.

He wasn't the monster they thought. They didn't know him like her. He loved her and she loved him. They were meant to be together. And once he'd dealt with Sally, they would. Soon, *she'd* bear the name Mrs Goden.

'I've got thee. I've finally got thee,' Joseph murmured, his tone laced with menace. Eyes travelling the length of her, he licked his lips. Her figure was more rounded. She was fuller of breast and hip. Motherhood suited her.

This evoked, for the first time, faint curiosity for the child he'd spawned and he glanced to the Morgans'. Yet as swiftly, it vanished. Children were nothing but a trial. Like bloodthirsty leeches, they drained your soul. They sucked and sucked long after you were bone dry, left you potless, bitter and old before your time. You'd only to look at Alice for proof.

Turning his attention back to his wife, his pulse raced with thoughts of her naked body. Christ, what he'd do to it when he got her alone . . . Feeling Nancy's jealous watch, he tore away his gaze with a frustrated growl. He couldn't risk Nancy flouncing off. The old whore had almost served her purpose. Almost.

He threw Sally over his shoulder again, shot a smirk at the Morgans' and signalled to Nancy to follow. Passing the dog that lay beside a ditch, a pool of blood spreading beneath its head, he smiled proudly. He'd taken care of it before making his move on Sally; after its attack on the stationmaster, he wasn't taking any chances. When it wandered by the hedgerow, he'd smashed its head with a thick branch. It dropped without a sound.

He set off across a tree-lined field. Sally's arms bumped limply against his back and he smiled again, her touch comforting.

'Where we going, love?'

His face melted in a snarl. 'Just get a move on. Folk will be up and about, soon. We'll be all right if we stick to the fields but happen we do pass someone, and they ask what's up with her, I'll do the talking. You say nowt, d'you hear? When we reach the end of the next field, you slip through the fence and cut across O'Brady's farm. It'll bring you out near your house. You stay put today, right?'

Nancy nodded and he strode on, mind on the fun he'd soon have with Sally.

'You have my permission and gladly. I know you'll look after her, make her happy.'

Staring at the ceiling, Tommy let his thoughts run. He didn't have the strength to fight them, had given up trying hours ago.

'She's a good lass and like her mother afore her, will make a fine wife.'

The speech echoed on.

'You're the only fella our Dolly's ever wanted. It does my owd heart good to know you feel the same.'

Knowing what came next, he squeezed his eyes shut.

'You're a sound lad, Tommy, a sound lad.'

Dolly's father couldn't have been more wrong if he'd tried. A sound lad? It was almost laughable. Maybe, once. Not any more.

He swung his legs out of bed, pulled on his trousers and paced the room. Glancing at his sleeping brother, envy churned in his breast. What he wouldn't give to be him, without a worry in the world.

He'd thought the day couldn't get worse. Knelt in proposal to a woman he'd all but ruined and didn't truly love was soul-destroying enough. What occurred next . . . Dear God, he'd never known shock like it, had to stop himself crying out. *Sally. His Sally* . . . A blade of grass could have felled him. In that moment, everything, *everything*, turned on its head.

Remembering what he'd almost done last night, his step faltered. He'd been a hair's breadth from entering her room, declaring his love, insisting the proposal was a mistake. Where he found the strength to desist, he didn't know, but was glad he had. He'd made enough of a fool of himself gawping at her all day – until, to his mortification, she'd avoided eye contact.

And there was Dolly. He must marry Dolly.

Standing before Nat Jenkins, Tommy had almost hoped he'd refuse permission. Of course, he hadn't. He was well aware of Dolly's long-held wish to become Mrs Morgan. But he hadn't consented purely out of love for his daughter. He sincerely believed his future son-in-law a sound man.

That bred within Tommy a tumour of shame that grew still. It was ruined, all of it. He'd made a mess of everything.

Time alone, to gather his thoughts before his family roused, was crucial. Mindful of the creaky spots, he descended the stairs. A bitter breeze met his bare arms and chest midway and his gaze went to the cottage door. He frowned to see it wide open.

He glanced to the fire and, seeing Shield absent, swallowed hard. *Sally was awake.* She must have taken the dog out to relieve itself. Despite his brain telling him to return to his room, avoid her for sanity's sake, his legs refused. Disgusted at his weakness, he made for the door.

Eyes hungry for a glimpse of her swept the row, but it was deserted. Maybe she'd taken a walk with Shield; but to leave the door wide . . . ? A sense that something wasn't right stirred in him and he headed for the front room.

He knocked, heart banging. What if she answered, had merely let Shield out and forgotten to close the door? he thought suddenly. What on earth would he say? But all that greeted him was silence and the sliver of dread returned. He turned the knob.

At first glance, the room appeared empty. Catching sight of the basket, his worry abated. Sally couldn't be far. She wouldn't leave the child unattended for long.

He returned to the cottage door and scanned the row again. Still there was no sign and, despite his reasoning, unease resurfaced. Joseph's snarling face crashed through his mind and fear clutched his heart. Surely to God, no . . .

He slapped the wall in fury and raced upstairs.

Chapter 26

FLASHES OF BLACK came and went, came and went, merging with the grey. Sally blinked drowsily then winced as agony scorched the length of her face. She was aware of a jolting sensation and nausea was rising.

From beneath lids lead-heavy, she glimpsed the shapes again. They appeared then disappeared, appeared and disappeared, blending with the greyness until everything swirled together. Another wave of sickness swooped and she closed her eyes.

A steady drum of noise grew and her fog-filled brain counted: one, two, one, two, one, two. When she opened her eyes, her vision was clearer. The blur receded and she saw the grey was cobblestones. She squinted at the flashes of black – one, two, one, two. The sound was coming from them.

They were feet.

The answer came suddenly. They were the backs of someone's clogs, appearing then disappearing with each step. At once, her mind snapped into shape. Snippets of memory . . . standing at Ivy's door, Joseph, pain . . .

Clarity brought fear so overwhelming, she gagged. Rearing back, she screamed at the top of her lungs. His hold tightened and she thrashed wildly. They reached a door and, realising he was taking her within, she gripped the frame but he prised her fingers away and hauled her, kicking and screaming, inside.

He slammed the door and threw her to the floor, the impact knocking the breath from her. She gasped for air then grimaced when a fetid stench hit the back of her throat. A long ago memory . . . That smell was unmistakable. *Dear God, no!* A familiar cackle sounded; hesitantly, she turned.

Alice sat grinning by the fire. 'Well, look what we have here. And where the divil have you been, you loose young bitch? All go well?' she added to Joseph.

'Aye.'

'Tha weren't seen? How about just now? I heard her screams from here.'

'Nay. Folk will still be kipping off last night's ale. A farmer asked what we were about when I were crossing his field, but I told him she were half-slat from last night.' Crossing his eyes, he made drinking motions with his hand then laughed. 'He swallowed it, said his wife liked a tipple too much herself, gormless shit.'

'Harold left at first light in search of a day's graft – as if the useless swine will find owt – and what children come home last night have gone out. Where's anyone's guess; probably on t' thieve somewhere, bloody wastrels. I'll take meself to Nellie's, leave youse two alone.' She grinned at Sally, donned her shawl and left.

Seeing Alice, bile had risen in Sally's stomach. However, the fear her sister-in-law evoked was nothing compared to the sight of Joseph. Their gazes locked and the room swayed.

His eyes bulged from his stubbled face, as though he couldn't quite believe what he saw. He stepped towards her. 'Well? Ain't you gorra welcome kiss for your husband?'

Her heart banged but hot anger was growing. The faded welts along Ivy's neck flashed into her mind and her fury boiled over. Of its own accord, her chin rose.

'Don't you *dare* come any closer. I'm not afraid of you. The days of my putting up with you are over. Take one more step and I'm warning you, Joseph, I'll—'

'You'll what?' He lunged and grabbed her throat. 'Grown some backbone since you've been away, ain't you?' He leaned in until their noses touched. 'Well, don't fret, my girl, for I'll soon have you back to the snivelling wreck you've allus been.' Shaking his head slowly, he curled his lips in a snarl. 'You're one sneaky, thieving young whore – what are you?

'Think you could hide for ever, did you? Did you?' he roared. 'You've ruined me good and proper, lost me my home, job, my good name, everything. I've nowt left to lose, now. I warned what would happen if you opened that mouth of yourn.' His grip tightened. 'Have a fine ol' time in Manchester, did you?'

Her eyes showed her surprise; he smiled. 'Oh aye, I know where you've been. A rat allus returns to its hole. Well, I hope you enjoyed your jaunt, my girl, for I promise you summat, you'll not escape me a second time. For the rest of your days you'll suffer for what you've done, you little bitch.'

She'd forced her anger down and listened to his rant without resistance. Years of torture had taught her well. She knew how to respond so as to receive the least pain possible.

She'd almost reacted when his hand tightened but willed herself to remain impassive. Incurring his wrath further wasn't an option whilst he squeezed her throat; he'd rendered her unconscious that way more times than she could remember. She needed a clear head, must play this right if she were to escape alive.

Relief that Jonathan was safe at Ivy's flooded through her. Dear Lord, if he'd discovered him . . . The notion was horrifying. He'd do anything to hurt her, and would have no qualms about using their son to do so, she was certain.

Surely, soon, the Morgans would notice her missing and come looking? Please God. She just hoped that until then she'd have the strength to endure the inevitable abuse to come. What further injuries he'd inflict, she dreaded to imagine. Her face was ablaze, her nose likely broken. But she knew better than to show it. He'd only strike it again for the enjoyment of seeing her suffer.

'Undress,' Joseph barked suddenly, unfastening his belt with his free hand.

Trying desperately to remain calm, she shook her head.

'I *said* undress.'

'No.' The word had barely left her when, to her horror, he grabbed her blouse and tore it open.

Her breasts spilled into his waiting hands and, despite her terror, fury charged through her feeling those all-too-familiar fingers on her flesh. She smacked them away fiercely and covered herself with her arms but before she could jump to her feet, a slap sent her sprawling. Her head hit the flags, blurring her vision, and moments later, his hands were on her thighs.

When he threw her skirts over her head and ripped away her undergarments, she kicked out, but he caught and spread her legs. He growled with pleasure and her panic reached fever pitch. His jerking member prodded and a scream tore from her.

Bucking wildly, she lashed out with nails and fists. He caught her wrists in an iron-like grip and wrenched them above her head.

'Go on, whore, fight it. I love it when you scream and struggle, makes it all the more enjoyable,' he panted, forcing her legs wider with his knee and positioning himself between.

'Please, don't do this.' She knew begging was useless but crippling desperation chased away logic. 'Beat me, do whatever you want, but not this. *Please. Not this!*'

Joseph looked deep into her eyes and uttered two words she knew would haunt her the rest of her life:

'Welcome home.'

A scream froze on her lips as he savagely thrust inside her.

Ivy held Jonathan against her chest and, making soothing noises, rocked him. His cries merely grew and her gaze strayed back to the window.

With each minute, her anxiety had mounted. Her husband and sons were out scouring the lanes and with all her heart she hoped they would find the lass safe and well.

Arthur had insisted they would prove her worries unfounded, that Sally had likely taken a walk with Shield and lost track of time. But she knew he was wrong. Sally doted on Jonathan, would never leave him alone.

She returned her attention to him, desperate for distraction. His hungry screams intensified and she began praying again for his mother's safe return. Suddenly, the cottage door burst open and she whipped around.

Arthur and Shaun, faces drawn, entered. Tommy followed, holding a black mass.

'Oh, dear God, is Sally—?'

'We didn't find her,' Arthur cut in. 'We found the dog in a ditch but there's no sign of the lass.'

Tommy laid Shield on the rag rug. 'It's had a nasty blow to the head but it's alive. Goden's done this, I'd stake my life on it. He's been back and Sally . . . I *knew* we should've checked that cottage of his sister's last time. I'll *kill* the evil bastard when I get my hands on him.'

'Dear God, if he's got her . . . if he could do what he did to me, that poor lass . . .' Ivy's words were lost in Jonathan's cries. She swallowed her feelings and turned to Shaun. 'Fetch Mrs Oakes, will you, lad? She'll wet-nurse this poor beggar, I'm sure. Let's pray we'll not need her long. Mother of God, if Sally . . .'

Arthur drew her into his arms. 'We'll find her, wench. We'll fetch her back, don't you fret.'

With increasing anger, Tommy watched his mother gulp down tears. She'd changed since the attack, wasn't the stoic woman they knew and loved. That bastard had knocked out of her a little of the fight they had always admired. Lord, when they found him . . . 'We're wasting time. We need to go,' he said abruptly.

Face as though set in stone, his father nodded. He kissed Ivy and strode to the door.

'Find Sally, fetch her back but please, be careful,' she begged him.

'Don't fret, wench. We'll not swing for him.'

Leading the way, Tommy left the cottage. Reaching the gate, he saw Shaun and Mrs Oakes hurrying up the row. 'Look after the dog while we're gone, lad,' he called. 'If it'll let thee, tend to that gash on its head, see what the damage is.'

'And call on Martha Smith,' added his father, 'ask her to sit with your mam till we return.'

Spurred on by worry and fury – and eager to give Joseph the beating of his life – they made good headway and in no time were nearing Bolton town. When Deansgate came into view, Arthur slowed his pace.

'Wait up, lad. I've summat to say.'

'Can't it wait?'

'Nay, it can't. Last night—'

'I know what you're about to say, but—'

'You couldn't keep your bloody eyes off the lass! How your mam didn't notice, I don't know. And raging as you were when we returned with the dog . . . Folk will start questioning your intentions if you don't keep a rein on that tongue of yourn.'

'We'll talk about this later, we're wasting—'

'You'll hear me out, first,' ordered his father. 'Son, this has to stop. You're betrothed to Dolly, now. She's a nice lass with enough love for the pair of you to make your marriage work. You could be happy with her but you've got to meet her halfway. For God's sake, get whatever designs you have on Sally from that head of yourn and start thinking on your future.'

He sighed helplessly at the raw pain Tommy knew shone from his eyes. 'If we find her, whatever's happened, whatever state she might be in . . . for the love of God, don't let your emotions get the better of thee. Don't go making no declarations nor saying summat you'll regret. Please, for all your sakes. Promise me.'

Heavy silence hung between them.

'I promise,' Tommy murmured without an ounce of self-conviction.

'Right. Come on.'

As they drew level with Deansgate, there came a rumble of wheels in the distance and they saw a cart approaching along a dirt road. His father didn't give it a second glance. But Tommy stopped dead in his tracks. *Surely not . . .*

'What's wrong?' Arthur followed his gaze back to the cart but clearly saw nothing that could have caused his face to pale, as Tommy knew it had. 'Lad?'

His eyes flicked to the female passenger then again rested on the man beside her. 'That fella on t' cart, there, don't half favour . . .' *It couldn't be him. It wasn't. It was merely his mind playing tricks.* 'Never mind.'

Falling back into step, his father frowned. 'Who did he look like?'

'It doesn't matter,' Tommy muttered, and was thankful when Arthur didn't press him.

On reaching Chapel Alley, his father made to hammer on number thirteen, but he shook his head. 'We'll not be knocking this time. Children or no, Sally's life could be at risk. They'll not get chance to cover their tracks this time.'

At his first kick, the rotten frame splintered and the door flew open.

The kitchen proved empty and they rushed to search the other rooms – his father making for the stairs, Tommy the front room. Within seconds, they were back in the kitchen.

'Nowt?'

Tommy shook his head.

'There's no one upstairs, neither.'

'Did you check everywhere? Happen he's hiding or, or he might—'

'The place's empty, lad.'

Kicking over a stool in frustration, he raked his hands through his hair. 'What do we do? The bastard's got her, I know it.'

His father headed for the door. 'We'll ask on the neighbours either side. Happen someone's seen or heard summat.'

'And if not? What then?'

'We keep looking. I gave your mam my word we'd fetch the lass back, and we will.'

Alice watched Joseph as he drank. When he placed his empty tankard on the table and motioned to Nellie for a refill, she shook her head.

'You've gorra problem with the ale, Joseph. You want to mind you don't finish up like our old man.'

He wiped a dribble of ale from his chin. 'Don't start, Alice, for Christ's sake. I'm celebrating, ain't I? Anyroad, you've room to talk. You've never been one to turn your nose up at a drop of gin.'

'Aye, mebbe, but you're supping like there's a shortage. Look, look how your hands are shaking. You've dragged her over here to fill your belly with ale; you should be lying low in case them fellas come looking. Start slowing down, for you'll need your wits about you if you're to keep a grip of that one.' She glanced to the corner. 'Slippery little bitch, she is. Turn your back forra second and she'll be away, you mark my words.'

But Joseph's attention was on the counter. 'Nellie, where's that ale?' he barked. 'Fetch another gin for our Alice while you're about it. Nancy will clear it, later.'

Nellie's serving girl glanced across the inn, frowned at the curled-up figure then lowered her head. Poking her nose into customers' business would earn her a thick ear or, worse, dismissal. Though she hated the position, she needed the brass.

None the less, she couldn't help sneaking another look to the corner. Pity filled her but she knew she couldn't intervene. Dropping her gaze, she continued to the door.

Stepping outside, she emptied a pail of slops on to the cobbles and was about to turn back when two men blocked her path. The elder smiled but the strikingly handsome one remained stiff-faced.

'Can I help thee with summat, mister?'

'I hope so, lass. We're looking forra fella, name of Goden, what's lodging round here with his sister. You don't know of him, d'you, or where he could be? We've asked at the cottages hereabouts but no one knows owt. There'd be some coppers in it for thee.'

She bit her lip for a long moment then through the side of her mouth, whispered, 'Is anyone watching me?'

The elder man looked to the inn door. 'Nay, lass.'

'How about the window? Look in t' window. My mistress ain't watching?'

Again, he looked behind her. 'Oh, aye, I see her. Have no fear, she's busy at the counter. Have you summat to tell us? D'you know Goden?'

She hesitated. But remembering the desperate state of the woman in Joseph and Alice's company, she nodded. 'Aye, I know him. He's in here all the time. In fact, he . . .' Her words trailed off as glancing to the window she saw Nellie staring back, face scarlet with fury. 'Oh Lord, I must go!'

The handsome one caught her arm. 'Wait, what were you about to say? In fact what?'

'Leave go! She'll flay me alive if I don't get back.' She tried tugging free but his grip tightened. 'Please, mister!'

'Tell us, lass, please. Has tha seen him today? Has he . . . ?' His questions died, his hold with them. 'He's here now, ain't he?'

Without waiting for confirmation, he pushed past her and charged into the inn.

'Well, look who's here.' Hot on Tommy's heels, his father stared in distaste at the lone customer. 'Right, where is he? And don't bother lying for the bastard, for it won't wash. Not this time.'

Joseph's sister took a slow sip of her gin, then another. 'Back again? Well, you've had another wasted journey, for I ain't seen nowt of our Joseph since last time you asked. Go on, sling your hook. Or have you a mind to belt me one as you did my husband?'

In all his life, Tommy had never laid his hands on a woman, hadn't come close. At this moment, however, he struggled not to lunge at this sickeningly smug one. 'Liar. Where is he? Where's Sally?'

'How the divil should I know where that whore is? What right have youse interfering in other folks' marriages, anyroad?'

'I'm warning you, woman.'

Her smile deepened. 'Tell them, Nellie. Our Joseph ain't been here for weeks, has he?'

Without hesitation, she shook her head. 'Nay, Alice. I've not seen him forra while.'

Tommy shot her a disgusted look then glanced at the serving girl's bowed head. 'Lass, if tha knows owt, please—'

'She don't, for there's nowt to tell. Is there?' Nellie asked with a dig to her ribs.

The girl's response was barely audible. 'There's nowt to tell. He's not been in for weeks.'

Tommy made to protest but his father stopped him. 'Save your breath, son, they'll not talk.' He jerked his head to a door behind the ale-splattered counter. 'Mind, if they've nowt to hide, they'll not bother about us searching the place.'

Nellie's mouth dropped open. ''Ere, you've no right going through there! Them's my own private quarters.' She tried blocking their path but they shoved her aside. 'Get out of my inn, now, the pair of you.'

'Oh, let them look,' called Alice. 'We know they'll find nowt, but if they've time to waste . . .' She grinned at them. 'Go on, have a good look. You'll not find him.'

As the men's footsteps thundered upstairs, Nellie shook her head at a now-worried Alice. 'Well, they called your bluff! If they find him—'

'Keep your voice down,' she hissed. 'Joseph ain't daft. He'll have found somewhere to hide.'

'If they find him,' Nellie repeated, 'you take yourselfs off, the lot of you, and battle it out elsewhere. I'll not have trouble here, don't want no police sniffing about my inn.'

'Shurrup, they're coming.'

They re-entered, grim-faced and seething.

'See, what did I tell youse?' Relief tinged Alice's gloating smile. 'He's not here, just as I said. Now go on, bugger off and don't come back.'

'We're going nowhere.' Despite their rage, the younger one spoke calmly. 'We'll bed down outside yon cottage the night if we must but I promise thee, we'll not leave till we've found Sally and made that evil bastard pay. One way or t' other, we'll find him.'

When the inn door slammed shut behind them, she hurried to the window. They crossed the road to her door and she shook her head. He'd been true to his word; it didn't look as though they were going anywhere.

'They gone?'

She turned and breathed out slowly. 'Aye. That were a close 'un, eh? How didn't they find thee, Joseph?'

Face void of colour, he peeked about. 'They definitely gone?'

'The sods have made themselfs comfortable outside the cottage. What will you do? There's no chance of leaving without them—' A noise like the cracking of a whip cut her speech. She nodded in satisfaction to see the serving girl in a heap on the floor, one side of her face livid red.

'Don't fret,' said Nellie. 'She'll get more of the same, later, loose-tongued little bitch that she is.'

Amusement creased Joseph's eyes. 'Ta for the warning, Nellie. How did you—?'

'Know they were after thee? I didn't. But by the look of that one, it's clear summat's up.' She jerked her head to Sally's limp form under his arm.

'I owe thee.'

'Aye, tha does. I'll not ask what's afoot, for I don't want to know. Just don't make a habit of what's occurred today, d'you hear?'

He nodded, but even Alice knew that if the time came again, Nellie would help him out. He – well, Nancy – spent a good deal of money here. She wouldn't risk them finding another watering hole.

Alice returned to the window. 'What will you do, our Joseph?' she asked over her shoulder. 'They're not for shifting.'

As though discarding a piece of rubbish, he threw Sally back into the corner and dragged a hand through his hair. 'Keep a lookout while I think. There's gorra be a way.'

Uneasy silence filled the inn. For several minutes, the only sounds were those of the serving girl going about her duties.

'Oh, for Christ's . . . That's all we need.'

He was ready to snatch up Sally in a heartbeat. 'What, Alice? They coming back?'

'Nay, our Lily's just rounded the corner. She knows not to say owt, they all do. Mind, you never know with that one, sneaky bitch that she is.'

His face contorted in utter fury. 'See the trouble you've stirred up, you filthy slut? By God, you'll spend the rest of your days paying for this, you see if you don't.' He delivered savage kicks to Sally. 'I'll not lose thee again, I'll not,' he muttered over and over. 'You'll not escape me a second time. With my bare hands, I'll kill you first.'

After getting in several kicks herself, Alice headed for the door. 'Stay on your toes, lad. I'll be back in a minute.'

The dead cat had been horrible, all bloated belly and gooey eyes. Lily shuddered at the memory.

The twins had cajoled her into seeing it, had made it sound like a smashing trip, something she'd be real daft to miss.

'I bet she screams,' sniggered Sid, rolling his eyes at girls' soft ways.

But she didn't. As she wrinkled her nose at the smelly heap of fur, a small grey lump, then another, had caught her eye. The first was unmarked, looked to be asleep, but the other, squashed and bloody, had had a nail driven through its eye. Her brothers had left their find to poke her offspring but Lily grabbed their sticks.

'Don't, they're only babbies.'

'They're dead, our Lil,' Joey scoffed. 'They can't feel nowt.'

Ignoring his laughter, she'd scooped them up and laid them by their mother's battered head. 'Let's leave them, now, eh?' she'd begged. 'It's a shame, it is.'

'Aye, come on, our Sid. The stink's getting worse.'

Planning their day in whispers, they slunk away. It was then she'd seen it: movement by the mother. A muffled cry followed and a tiny head had appeared between her paws.

Now, heading home with the survivor nestled in her arms, Lily frowned. What should she name it? It must be special, she decided, nodding. It was very lucky to have been spared. One foot in the gutter, she plodded on, lost in thought.

Suddenly, her fingers stilled on the silky fur and she swore under her breath. Her mother was crossing the road towards her and didn't look best pleased. She thought about stuffing the kitten up her frock or behind her back, but it was too late. She stopped in her tracks at the demand to wait and, tears pricking, prayed *she* wouldn't make her get rid of her new friend.

Her mother glanced at the squirming bundle but, to Lily's astonishment, uttered nothing. Instead, she looked beyond her daughter, laughed for a reason Lily couldn't fathom, then motioned her to follow. Frowning, Lily obeyed. When she and her mother reached Nellie's inn, she glanced over her shoulder. Two men leaning against the wall of their cottage in Chapel Alley locked eyes with her and her mouth ran dry.

The blokes who had threatened Father! Had they returned to give him a proper thrashing? She opened her mouth to yell at them to go away and leave him alone, but her mother yanked her inside the inn before she could.

'Sit.'

Filled with confusion, she perched on a stool. 'Why are them fellas back, Mam? They'll not touch Father again, will they?'

Alice had returned to the window but hearing Lily's terrified tone she swivelled around. Nodding slowly, she crouched before her.

'Aye. They're back to finish him.' She forced a sob and hid a smile when the young face crumpled. 'Me and Uncle Joseph, we're that frickened for him. Happen you could persuade the swines to bugger off, our Lil, like last time? Tell them your uncle's not been near. Put the tears on, lass, beg them to go. It might do the trick again.'

'Aye, do as your mam tells thee,' Joseph added from the corner, leaning forward to block her view of Sally. 'Lay it on good and proper, mind, or it'll not work and they'll kill your father. You don't want him to die, d'you?'

'Nay!' Lily cried. 'Nay,' she repeated, shaking her head and sending tears spilling.

Moments later, Alice watched the skinny legs cross the cobbles.

'You reckon it'll work?' Joseph asked.

She shrugged. 'The young sneak can lie through her teeth easy enough when the mood takes her. She'll lay it on thick; she's allus been soft on that wastrel father of hers. Get thinking on what you'll do if it don't, mind. Tha can't stop here for ever, Joseph, and nor can I.'

'A few hours, that's all I need,' he muttered. 'Nancy will do my bidding. She'll get me some brass so I can be away. By the time she realises I'm taking Sally and not her, it'll be too late. We'll be away; away from here, Spring Row and the bastards what live there. A few hours. Just a few more hours.'

Groaning floated from the corner and Alice clicked her tongue. 'That one's rousing. Take her back upstairs afore she starts bleating. I'll shout a warning if owt occurs.'

Tommy and Arthur had their targets in sight. Ahead was the inn, and left and right gave a clear view of Deansgate. Goden *must* be hiding nearby. If he tried scarpering, they would spot him.

The child who defended her father last time emerged from the inn and their eyes narrowed. They had planned to question her earlier but her mother dragged her away. Now, it seemed, they would get their chance; surprisingly, she was heading towards them.

When the scared-looking bundle of rags halted, Tommy crouched to her level and smiled. 'Hello, lass. That's a bonny young thing you've got. What's his name, then?'

She blinked at the kitten then back at him. Despite his manner, he knew she was remembering their treatment of her father. *These two are slippery buggers, all right. I must be careful if I'm to keep him safe*, her stare screamed. She bit her lip until her eyes watered then gazed up, chin quivering expertly.

'Why, mister? Why have you come to kill Father?'

'Nay, lass, nay. Fancy thee thinking that. Last time were a mistake. We'd not touch him again. We're that sorry you and the other little 'uns saw that carry-on. We didn't know children were present, you see.'

His father squatted beside him. 'That's right. It's your uncle we've come for, like last time. Only to talk, mind,' he added with a disarming smile. 'You know where he is, lass?'

It was evident that she didn't believe a word. Face a picture of innocence, she shook her head. 'I don't, mister. He's been gone weeks. Please leave us be. We don't know where he is, honest we don't.'

Anger rose within Tommy. The poor mite was lying and it didn't take much to work out who had put her up to it. Of all the dirty, rotten tricks . . . using an innocent child to save your own skin. What a low and wicked depth to sink to.

She looked at the scrap of life in her arms. When she raised her head, genuine tears lit her blue eyes. Her hold tightened but she murmured, ''Ere, mister.' She held the kitten up. 'Leave us be, go on home, and you can have her. I love her, I do, but I love Father more. That's a fair deal, in't it, mister?'

He half turned and sighed. Her distress was hard to stomach. He placed a large but tender hand on her shoulder.

'Lass, listen to me. I give thee my word; we'll not touch a hair on your father's head. May the Lord strike me down, that's the 'onest truth. Your uncle . . .' He paused, chose his words carefully. 'He's been a bad man, you see. He hurt my mam and will hurt a nice lady if we don't find him. Please, lass, if you know where he is, it's important you tell us. Sally's in real danger.'

Her eyes widened. 'Sally?'

'Aye. Have you seen her? Is she here with your uncle?'

This quandary dizzied Lily. *Was* Sally the kind lady from the market who gave her food and a shilling, smiled, spoke to her softly, told her she was clever? The lady she'd prayed and prayed, every night since, had taken her with her? But why would Uncle Joseph hurt her?

He *had* wanted to find her. He'd gone off in a right old rage that day – with her precious coin, too. Had he now found her? She wasn't in the inn; though he could be hiding her . . . And what of her tiny baby? Was he in danger, too?

She'd processed these thoughts in seconds when another struck. He'd hurt another lady, she remembered. She'd heard her the other week, moaning and groaning and panting like a dog, as though she couldn't breathe. Afterwards, he'd sneaked her from the cottage. He thought no one saw, but she had. She couldn't have stopped him hurting that lady. Perhaps she could with Sally.

If she did, maybe this time she'd take her home with her. She'd try harder, beg on her knees. If she'd give a shilling and grub as nice as she had for help with a rotten old basket and blanket . . . She'd take her to live with her for sure.

But were these two truthful? Mam said . . . mind you, Mam said things aplenty that weren't true, Lily reminded herself. Still, could she risk Father getting a thrashing? Were they *really* only here for her uncle, for Sally?

She chewed her lower lip raw as she agonised over what to do. Suddenly, she ceased gnawing. There *was* a way to be sure, she recalled. Father always said when a man gave his word, he shook on it, that a vow made on a handshake was worth its weight in gold.

'What you said, about Father—'

'It's the truth. We're here for Joseph, nowt else.' Without realising, the younger man secured alliance – he held out a hand. 'You have my word, lass.'

She placed her tiny one into his and nodded solemnly. *What Mam would do when she found out*... Pushing the thought away, she adopted the twins' motto: Mam could eat shit, for all she cared.

Despite her cunning from years of necessity, Lily knew she'd have to use all her wits to pull this off. Her mother was clever.

But as the lady at the market told me, she remembered with a determined smile, *so am I*.

Eager-faced, the men leaned in.

'He's snidy, my uncle. Snidy and slippery as a kipper. You need to be cleverer. I'll show you how but you've gorra listen. You've gorra listen and do everything I say.'

She'd been sick again.

The last acrid dribbles ran down Sally's cheek and neck. Spears of pain faded again and she welcomed impending release with a sigh.

Oblivion was on the cusp of taking her when rough fingers chased her descent away. They lifted one of her eyelids then the other. Then they raised her head from the ground.

The now-familiar scorch worked its way down her throat and on instinct alone, she spluttered and gagged. Senses too debilitated by injury and alcohol to resist, the dreamlike state imprisoned her once more.

She floated beyond reality. Her thoughts felt weighted, impossible to process. Where was she? How long had she been here? A day? Three? A week?

Place and time didn't apply to her any more. She'd wake in fits to the fiery liquid and sporadic blows – or the searing between her legs when he took her at will.

Like now. He was doing it again.

Awareness swirled around her foggy mind. Survival lent her a spurt of life and she pushed at the looming chest. Her feeble effort produced but a guttural laugh from the demon ravaging her.

As the thrusts intensified, she slipped blissfully into the sea of nothingness.

Chapter 27

'WHAT'S HAPPENING, ALICE? Is she laying it on thick enough? Is she bawling, an' that?'

Alice stroked her chin. 'I can't tell; she's got her back to me. Them two look to be lapping up whatever she's saying, anyroad.'

Nellie's face relaxed a fraction. 'I'll not have those two causing further ructions. Folk frequent my place for its reputation of discretion, where they can conduct what business they've a mind to without fear of police lurking. I want to keep it that way.'

'The young 'un's shaking her hand. I don't know how she does it. Reet devious young swine, she is. Hold up, she's coming back. She's been bawling good and proper; her face is redder than a smacked arse,' she affirmed.

'And them two?'

'Oh, they're bloody following her!'

'For the love of Christ, not again,' Nellie snapped as Lily entered, the men right behind. 'Now look here, I'll not tell youse again—'

'We're not stopping.' The father's words brought a surprised smile to Alice. 'The lass here confirmed what you said. No child could lie that well. We'll bother youse no more.' His voice dropped. 'But for our word, there's a condition.'

'Oh aye? What condition's that, then?'

'That you send word to us at Breightmet if that brother of yourn shows up,' said his son.

Knowing it wasn't worth pushing her luck, she bit back a negative retort. 'Aye, deal. Now sod off.'

Without hesitation, they left.

'Well, I'll be buggered. You really reckon they'll not be back?' asked Nellie.

'They'll not,' Lily said quickly. 'Eeh, Mam, tha should've seen me. Laid it on good and thick, I did, just like you told me.'

Her mother's eyes narrowed. 'And they believed we'd not seen him, just like that?'

She grinned. 'Nay. They knew I were lying about that.'

'Eh? But I thought—?'

'They said they must find him because he'd got someone called Sally, the liars, so I played along. I said I'd tell them a secret if they left Father alone. I said Uncle Joseph brought her to ours this morning, got his things together and hotfooted it to Rochdale.

'I told him he's gone to live there with her; bedding down at a friend's cellar, I said they were.' Doubt was leaving her mother's face. She grinned again. 'I gave them the address, said I'd heard Uncle Joseph telling thee.'

Nellie shook her head. 'Bloody hellfire. She's a rum 'un, she is, Alice.'

Her mother, too, was grinning. 'You lying young bleeder. What address?'

'Clover Lane, number five. I begged them not to tell you I'd told, and we shook on it. They've gone straight there. I hope they get blisters apple big looking for that. They deserve it for what they did to Father.'

Nellie roared with laughter, which brought on a coughing fit. 'You rum young beggar,' she spluttered, thumping the counter. 'You'll be a force to be reckoned with when you're grown. By, you will that.'

Her mother's chuckles added to Nellie's. 'Where the bugger did you pull that from?'

'Well, five, that's my age. And Clover, after my new kitten. She's lucky, she is, like four-leaf clovers. She hid under her mam and didn't get killed.' She held her up. 'Can I keep her? Can I?'

But Alice had stopped listening. 'Wait till our Joseph hears this,' she cackled, heading for the stairs. 'He said they were gormless bastards and by God, he weren't far wrong. Pour us a sup of summat for our nerves, will you, Nellie?'

Lily's heart felt set to leap from her chest but she knew she couldn't coward out now. Footsteps sounded and her gaze swivelled up. *Was* the lady from the market up there? Her heart pounded faster. She must finish this before her mother and uncle returned.

'Can I lie my kitten by the hearth, missis? She's shivering.'

Nellie, still chuckling at the gumption of one so young, nodded. 'Give the embers a prod, see if you can't drag some life from them.'

Lily hurried to the fire, laid Clover at her feet and lifted the poker. She glanced over her shoulder. Satisfied no one was watching, she let her free hand roam. Sweat sprang above her top lip as, upping the noise with the poker, she lifted the latch on a window and opened it half an inch.

Sagging with relief, she closed her eyes. Then she took a deep breath and skipped across the room.

Standing on tiptoe, she lifted the tankard of ale and glass of gin from the counter. 'These for Mam and Uncle Joseph, missis? I'll take them to a table, shall I?'

'Aye. Don't spill them, mind.'

Lily placed them on the table directly beneath the window then perched on a stool.

She could do no more. It was up to the men, now.

At the far end of the inn, the serving girl glanced from the child to the window. Turning to resume her duties, a shadow of a smile went with her.

Tommy's jaw muscles worked furiously; his impatience to begin was at fever pitch. His father laid a hand on his shoulder.

'Deep breaths, son. Not long, now.'

He nodded but his insides smouldered with a host of emotions. If that bastard had hurt her . . . What was she going through, at this very moment, while they stood idle, blindly obeying a child's instructions? His guts twisted but he knew they couldn't act yet.

Despite her limited years, the lass had been embarrassingly right. Goden had evaded them more times than they wanted to dwell upon. He had a knack of vanishing into thin air when sniffing danger; all they had got was dizzy from going around in circles trying to find the swine. This plan just might work. For Sally's sake, they had to try.

Hearing a muffled voice, they crouched lower on the crumbling steps behind the inn and cocked their heads to the window above. It grew louder, making it obvious the speaker stood directly opposite. It was also clear who it was. Thanks to the girl's sharp thinking, the voice travelled through the partially open window perfectly.

Goden. He *knew* it. Where the devil he'd hidden earlier was anyone's guess but now, they had him. They would be on him so fast, he wouldn't have time to blink.

'What did I tell thee? That pair couldn't find a tit in a whorehouse betwixt them.'

Tommy and Arthur glanced at each other, eyes burning with fury, as Joseph's scathing quip earned him a round of laughter.

'I mean, who with half a brain goes all out to search for someone and don't bloody search?' Inflated confidence filled his tone. 'I tell youse summat, that young 'un came this close to us. He had his hand on the knob of the bedroom door we were hiding behind, for Christ's sake, and didn't think to pull it back a bit.' He drew out the last words mockingly, following them with a bellow of laughter.

Tommy's hand tightened around the clump of stone he'd prised from the tumbledown steps. Goden was behind the door with her the whole time . . . Colour born of regret and humiliation flooded his face. How had he been so foolish? *Sally, I'm so sorry* . . .

'And to top it off, they finished up outwitted by a gormless slip of a lass,' Alice added. When the laughter died down, her amused voice sounded again. 'I'll be away to the cottage. Tha best get that one back across the road, an' all. And bring some gin to keep her akip. I'm not listening to her yowling all day.'

His eyes widened and his father shook his head. *Not yet, son, not yet*, it silently instructed.

Alice's footsteps faded to the door. The innkeeper's voice, as she barked orders to her serving girl, revealed she'd returned to the counter. And a loud burp told them Joseph was still by the window, finishing his ale.

This was what they were waiting for. For it to work, they needed him alone. The least support he had in the initial seconds was vital.

They needed no words. A simultaneous nod and they were ready.

His father scurried around the side of the building. Tommy's grip tightened on the rock. He eased the fingertips of his free hand through the window and teased it up a fraction more. It obeyed silently and, smiling grimly, he continued until he'd opened it fully. Then he rose.

Joseph stood with his back to him, completely unaware of what was coming. Tommy's lip curled in hatred; his drunkenness promised only to assist the success of the element of surprise.

With Joseph blocking his view, he stooped again to check the other occupants' positions. The serving girl was busy behind the counter, Alice and Nellie talking by the door. Lily stood beside her mother. Her eyes flicked to him and he nodded. All was ready.

He leaned through the window and lifted the rock above his head. But a movement by Joseph's feet threw him. He froze, all their careful plans melting at the sight of the woman he loved beyond reason. Whom he'd die for in a heartbeat. The woman lying half dead, face battered, covered in blood and vomit.

His hand flew to his mouth, trapping a cry. However, he couldn't contain the venomous loathing for her husband as easily. Lightning fast, he threw his arm around Joseph's neck and smashed the stone into his skull.

He crumpled instantly. Tommy lowered him to the ground beside Sally.

It had happened in the blink of an eye and without a sound. Alice was still talking with Nellie, the serving girl measuring out gin into an earthenware jug, each of them unaware of what had transpired feet away. Only Lily knew her uncle now lay in a heap, but she made no noise, busying herself with the kitten.

Tommy stared, transfixed, at the man he'd just bludgeoned. His father had warned him countless times to keep his calm, do nothing but injure him. As usual, his overwhelming love for Sally overtook all logic. He'd struck him much harder than he should, than they'd discussed. Joseph Goden was dead. And Tommy Morgan would swing.

His eyes swivelled to Sally and slowly they hardened. If he was to dance at the end of a rope, so be it. What that monster had done to her, to his mother . . . He deserved this and more. Joseph could rot in hell.

That he himself would soon join Lucifer for his sin, Tommy, at that moment, didn't care. Knowing this bastard would share the scorching pit would be worth the eternal suffering.

'You're free, my love,' he whispered to Sally. 'You, at least, will suffer no more.'

Calmness settled within him. He lifted two fingers to his lips, and blew. This needed finishing. Consequences could wait.

His father burst into the inn. Alice and Nellie, having turned to the window at the shrill whistle, now whipped back around as the door crashed against the wall. Like a pair of trout gasping for want of water, they gawped left to right, dumbfounded.

'What the . . . ?' Alice managed to croak. 'Where's . . . ? Oh, my God!' She made to rush to her lifeless brother, but Arthur grabbed her and Nellie by the scruff of their necks and bundled them behind the counter.

Tommy hadn't in his life heard his father raise his voice to a woman – now, he roared a threat of such ferocity, they flinched:

'Youse two stay there or so help me, you'll regret it. Same goes for thee,' he told the serving girl. 'You stay put, d'you hear?'

Her answer surprised everyone. 'Nay, mister, not me. I want to help.'

Nellie almost choked on a gasp. 'Oh! Why, you sneaky young—!'

'Shut that fat mouth of yourn and listen to me forra change.' A quaver lurked behind her words but she stuck her chin out. 'I need my head seeing to, putting up with you as long as I have. If I never find work for the rest of my days and finish up destitute in t' gutter, I'll be happier than I've ever been slaving for thee.' She waited for a response but Nellie simply gaped. She nodded once. 'How can I help, mister?'

With a thankful smile, Arthur pointed to the door. 'Keep an eye to customers, will you, lass? Say and do what you must but don't let a soul in. Or out,' he added, looking pointedly at Alice and Nellie. He turned to Tommy. 'All right, lad?'

Having climbed through the window, Tommy had crouched beside Sally. As his father approached, he lowered his head.

Arthur halted. He glanced at the crimson-stained rock, then at the gaping wound it had inflicted. He stooped and pressed two fingers to Joseph's wrist. Without a word, he let the limp hand fall to the ground. In his eyes was a look Tommy had never seen before.

'Father . . . I . . .'

Arthur held up a hand, and Tommy closed his mouth. Words couldn't undo what he'd done. They both knew it.

Arthur checked Sally's pulse. Then he spoke softly. 'Lass? Can you hear me? Can you open your eyes?

You're safe, now. Me and Tommy's here, and my Ivy will mend thee, have no fear.' Her eyelids flickered and he nodded. 'Good lass. Goden won't hurt you again, you have my word. Let's get you home.'

Tommy walked blindly to the door. His own arms burned to hold her but he didn't speak out. He was nothing to her, never would be. And soon, he wouldn't be anything to anyone.

Not a son or brother, future husband to Dolly, father to the child she might be carrying – nothing. He'd be hanged and he'd be dead. As dead as the man by the window.

He took a last look at Joseph then opened the door.

The next seconds played out dreamlike. Two sounds opened the act. The first was the serving girl's gasp, the next a horrified Lily slapping a hand to her mouth. Frowning, he followed their stares. What he saw rendered him immobile. He gazed at the large bulk which moments before had lain lifeless on the ale-soaked ground. *And was now standing behind his father.*

In Joseph's hand was the stone he'd introduced to his head – now set to make acquaintance with Arthur's. As he drew back his arm, his lips followed suit in a terrifying grin.

'*Stop!*'

The thunderous command shattered time in its tracks. At that pivotal moment, it seemed to grasp Joseph's arm in an invisible hold. The speaker charged past Tommy, pushed Arthur aside and landed a bone-crunching punch to Joseph's face. As blood and teeth flew one way, he fell the other, crashing to the ground like a sack of rocks.

In the ensuing bedlam, as Alice rushed to her brother screeching garbled curses, Nellie squawked at them all to leave and Lily clung, sobbing, to the serving girl's skirts, Tommy and his father stared at the newcomer in stunned silence.

He flashed a quick smile, demeanour cool as a summer breeze. 'Are the two of ye all right?' he enquired in a soft brogue. Then his eyes fixed on Sally and his composure wavered. 'Sweet Jesus. Is she . . . ?'

'She's alive. Who . . . ? How did you . . . ?'

'Your wife explained everything. I got here as quickly as I could.' At Arthur's confused frown, he patted his shoulder. 'Sure, there's time enough later for explanations. We need to leave. Sally needs tending to, and fast.' He held out his arms. 'Give her to me, friend. I've a cart waiting outside.'

Tommy's senses snapped back instantly. Joseph's resurrection had struck him dumb. He'd stood by, frozen with disbelief, as the bastard prepared to attack his father. The inadequacy was crippling – more so when he knew the identity of Arthur's saviour, whom he'd recognised on that cart. The man he'd come to hate almost as much as Joseph.

Because he was different from the man whose name Sally bore. One was linked to her by a marriage she loathed – the other, looking every inch the hero of the hour . . . He'd laid claim to her heart.

Seeing him hold out his arms, the last vestige of restraint Tommy clung to, snapped. The nightmare, of this man taking Sally from him, had haunted him for weeks. He'd been unable to stop it in his dreams. It wouldn't happen in reality. He clamped a hand on his shoulder.

The Irishman turned. As they stared at each other, he seemed to read the message in Tommy's hard gaze. With the briefest nod, he stepped back.

Tommy felt his father's eyes boring into him as he took Sally, but didn't care. Neither did he care what her new man thought. This was the last time he'd hold her. This precious moment would see him through the endless years stretching ahead with Dolly. No one would deny him it.

He cradled her as though she was made of the most delicate china and everyone in the world melted away.

'What about that devil?' the Irishman asked Arthur, jerking his head to the prone figure Alice was trying to rouse. 'Sure, Sally will never be safe while he breathes. Next time—'

'There'll not be a next time.' Dragging his eyes from his son, rage swamped Arthur. In a movement that belied his years, he lunged. Alice made to claw his face but a swipe sent her sprawling. Grabbing Joseph's jaw, he lifted his bloody face to his.

'You . . . I've a good mind to kill thee here and now, you worthless lump of shit. You don't deserve to draw another breath for what you've done to that lass, to my family . . . *to my wife.* Get up. Fight me. Do to me what tha did to my Ivy. Up!' He tried to drag Joseph to his feet. 'I'll murder you, yer bastard!' All trace of the man everyone knew and respected had vanished and, like a man possessed, he landed blow after frenzied blow.

'Mr Morgan, that's enough.'

The Irishman made to take his arm but Arthur shoved him aside. Undeterred, he tried again, this time managing to prise his hand from Joseph's jaw. As Joseph slumped to the ground, Arthur made to lunge again but the Irishman wrapped his arms around his middle and hauled him to the door.

'No fellow's worth dangling at the end of a rope for, not even him. Come away, now, come away.'

The fight left Arthur and he ceased struggling. With a calmness that robbed her cheeks of colour, he pointed to Alice. 'You keep him away, d'you hear me? If he shows his face again, I swear on all I hold dear, I'll kill him.' And with every fibre of his being, he meant it.

Moments later, they were aboard the cart and the Irishman instructed the driver to get them to Spring Row as fast as he could. After a last, horrified look at the woman whom, he murmured, he'd brought here only yesterday, he gave the reins a sharp flick.

'Mister, wait!'

Two figures emerged from the inn. For the serving girl, it was undoubtedly the last time. Head bowed, she scuttled away. The other was Lily. Bare feet slapping the cobbles, she ran alongside the cart, face wet with tears.

Arthur held out a hand and she gripped it. 'Thank you, lass. We couldn't have done it without thee.'

'She'll be all right, won't she, mister? You'll nurse her well?'

'Aye. Goodbye.'

'Goodbye, mister. Goodbye, Sally,' she whispered.

The cart gained speed and the small fingers slipped from his. When she was out of sight, he glanced left. The adoration pouring from his son as he gazed at the woman in his arms was, for so many reasons, too painful to watch. With a bone-weary sigh, he closed his eyes.

This wasn't going away. He was at his wits' end with the whole bloody business. He'd have to talk to Ivy. He'd carried this burden alone for long enough.

Chapter 28

SHE'D ASKED FOR him.

Heavy clouds scudded, promising more snow. Occasionally, chinks of sunlight penetrated but did little to brighten the row. It remained a colourless canvas, devoid of life and beauty. The temperature had plummeted and a steady wind had taken hold, whistling around the cottages like a living thing, its haunting moan encompassing all it touched.

Hunched against the wall, arms folded, Tommy stared through the window, seeing nothing.

His physical self had separated from his mind. One stood in a small cottage in Spring Row, the other was worlds away, trapped in a darkness he doubted he'd ever break from. He was dimly aware of the hum of voices behind him but they didn't mean a thing. Nothing did. Nothing mattered. Nothing.

She'd asked for him.

Tommy had carried her from the cart, up the stairs. He'd lowered her into his own bed and dropped to his knees. Flitting figures, voices – his mother, the woman on the cart with *him* – swum on the outskirts of his awareness. Like a starving dog eyeing a bone, he'd guarded the precious being from all who surrounded her.

For a long time, Sally had lain prone, eyes closed. Suddenly, taking everyone by surprise, they sprang open. The glassy pools had fixed on a point behind Tommy then her body jolted. Pungent liquid spilled from her mouth, drenching her torn blouse. He'd lifted her head, the flow ceased and she'd continued to retch, dry heaves bending her double.

Finally, her face relaxed and he'd lowered her blindly, tears obliterating his vision. As he blinked them back, his stomach had lurched to see her staring straight at him. Her gaze was steady and when her lips moved he'd had to dip his head to catch her words. What he heard shattered his heart into a thousand pieces.

She'd asked for Con.

The name scorched his soul. His head had jerked in a shake of denial but she'd looked through him and said it again. Then *he* was there. He cupped her face, caressed her cheek with his thumb, murmured her name. Sighing, Sally had closed her eyes.

For hours, Tommy's mind had replayed the scene. Throughout, the cottage was a hive of tears and voices, yet he'd heard but that one word. His was the first face she saw upon wakening. And the Irishman was the one she'd wanted.

Deep down, he'd known the truth. She'd now confirmed it, with her own lips, and crushed his heart to pulp.

'Merciful God, release me from this living hell,' he murmured against the cold pane.

Maggie glanced in turn at the people around the table. Clasping steaming cups of tea, they conversed in subdued voices. Anger, tears, questions and explanations had dwindled. Now, they shared but one concern – Sally's best interests.

'I don't want to leave her,' Maggie said. 'That swine might come back; I'll not risk that happening. Sally speaks highly of thee, Mrs Morgan, and I don't doubt you care for her as much as we, but it's just not safe, here.'

'I've a mind to agree, but what choice is there? It'll take more than a few hours' kip to sleep off all that booze. Then there's her injuries. I dread to think what pain she'll be in when the ale's not there to take off the edge.' Ivy patted Maggie's hand. 'I've known thee only several hours but see why Sally chose you for a friend. You're a good soul, with a kind heart to match. But you can't move her, lass, not today.

'My offer still stands, mind,' she added when Maggie sighed. 'You're all welcome to bed down here the night. If Sally's up to the journey the morrow, youse can set off home in t' morning.'

Martha Smith nodded agreement, followed by Con.

'She's right, so, Maggie. Sally's in no fit state to be moved.' Catching Arthur's eye, his turned icy. 'As for her husband, if he's fool enough to show his face again—'

'Then God help him,' Arthur finished for him.

Having given Jonathan a last feed with promises to return if needed, Mrs Oakes had left shortly before. Sated, he lay in Maggie's arms. She stroked his hand and nodded. 'I'll stop the night, Mrs Morgan. Thank you.' She turned to Mr Lynch. 'Are you . . . ?'

'Nay, I can't stop. My wife would fret herself sick. I'll be back the morrow, lass.'

'Ta, Mr Lynch.'

'Nay, no thanks needed. That lass upstairs is niece to my owdest friend. I'm only happy to help. I'll call on Ed and Grace, tell them what's occurred.'

'Play it down, will thee? There's no point worrying them witless. There'll be time enough for explanations the morrow, once we've got Sally home.'

He nodded. 'Tha stopping, lad?' he asked Con.

'I . . .' Con glanced from the stairs to the window. 'Well, I . . .'

'You go, Con. She's in safe hands,' said Maggie quietly. The concern in his eyes pained her a little and instantly, she felt ashamed. Her dearest friend lay broken and all she could think of was her own wants. She lowered her head in self-disgust yet Con, putting his finger under her chin, raised it again.

'And you, Maggie? You'll be all right?' he murmured.

'Aye.' Stupefied, it was all she could utter. She smiled and he returned it then made for the door with Mr Lynch. They bade all goodbye and were gone.

Arthur looked to the window, gave a small sigh and went to join his younger son by the fire. The lad sat cross-legged, stroking Shield, and he crouched beside him to inspect the dog's progress. It was sleeping, its breathing steady. Hopefully, it would recover. As with its mistress, they could only pray.

Martha poured weary-looking Ivy a fresh cup of tea then motioned to Maggie.

She shook her head absently. Con's image burned behind her eyes and his touch lingered on her skin. Flushing with pleasure and shame, she headed upstairs.

Dawn hadn't yet broken when Sally stirred. A distant smile lingered, half her mind still suspended in a dream.

She was with her mother and Jonathan, Shield trotting alongside. They were walking through an emerald-green field abloom with cowslip and buttercups, the air heady with love. Rose held Jonathan up and he laughed as she planted kisses on his cheek.

When he turned to look at his mother with smiling eyes of the same sapphire blue, Sally's heart swelled with pride for the fine-looking boy he'd become. They sat in the sweet-smelling grass and she lifted her face to the sun with a rush of such happiness, it stole her breath. Rose drew her close and she rested her head on her shoulder.

Her heart skipped as she caught sight of a tall, dark-haired man heading towards them across the field. His face was in shadow but she knew without question that she loved him, and that he loved her. In his muscular arms, he carried a girl with hair the colour of corn. She lifted a tiny hand and Sally waved back . . .

Dull pain and a raging thirst like nothing she'd ever known were pulling her from the beautiful scene. She heard her mother's voice, soft as a whisper on the breeze:

'*All's not over. Be strong, lass. Be strong.*'

The pain came in waves and she drifted further until her loved ones were but a blot in the distance.

'Mam? Mam, I cannot find you. Please, Mam,' she cried, fingers searching the air.

'Sally? 'Ere, lift your head, lass, take some water.'

Water. Yes, she needed water.

The room was too dark to see. Fiery fingers clawed every inch of her. Her head was lifted and she guided the hand to her mouth. Cold metal brushed her lips and for a full minute she drank. She lay back against the pillow. Footsteps sounded and streaky light flared then dipped as a candle was lit.

'How are you feeling? Oh, I've been that worried.'

'Maggie?' Her voice was scratchy and she frowned, hearing it. 'Maggie, I don't . . .'

'Shhh. Everything's going to be all right. You rest.'

Another spasm cut through her and she sucked in air sharply. 'It hurts.'

'I know, lass,' Maggie murmured, a catch behind the words. 'D'you remember . . . owt? Oh, I don't know what to . . . I'm so sorry.'

Sally's breath came in short gasps. 'Tell me . . . Please, tell me the truth. My child. Is he . . . alive?'

'Oh, love. The babby's fine. He weren't with you, remember?'

She released a sob. 'Thank God. Where . . . ?' She wept when her friend placed Jonathan in her arms. Ignoring the pain, she held him close. 'I remember. Joseph, he—' Her head shot up. 'Where is he? What—?'

'Don't you fret about that divil,' cut in Maggie venomously. 'He'll not harm thee again. Mr Morgan and his son – Thomas, is it? – they found you, lass.'

'Tommy . . .'

'Aye. And Con—'

'Con? How . . . ? And *you're* here. Am I at your home? Are we in Manchester?' Her voice rose in distress. 'I, I don't understand what's happening, I—'

'Shh. Easy, now. You're at Mrs Morgan's. Con's returned to Manchester with Mr Lynch but they'll be back today. Try and sleep. I'll explain everything later.'

With a hint of her former strength, she responded firmly. 'No, Maggie, tell me now. I must understand. Please. Tell me.'

For the next hour, they talked and cried in equal measures. Maggie prompted her to begin from the earliest point she remembered and, with supportive hand squeezes, helped her give voice to her ordeal.

Frequently, her memory failed and, if able, Maggie filled in the gaps from Arthur's and Con's versions.

'That's all there is to tell. You were sick summat awful yesterday, but I think you're over the worst.'

Her friend tore her gaze away and Sally's hand strayed to her face. Inside she was on the mend; outside was clearly another matter. 'Is it so bad, Maggie?'

'We . . . Mrs Morgan, Mrs Smith and me, tended your injuries best we could. Mrs Smith set your nose well, and we bathed your bruises with gentle care, lass.'

Looking down, she saw they had replaced her torn blouse with one of Ivy's. 'Oh, Maggie. Con's lovely gift . . .'

'Eeh, don't fret on that. Aye, you look much better than you did when . . . when . . .' Sally took her hand, and her facade crumbled. 'Oh, lass, your poor face and body! It's hard believing you're the same woman we know and love. I could kill that bastard with my bare hands!'

'Don't fret, Maggie, please. They'll heal.'

'Aye, lass,' she agreed determinedly. 'You'll be back to your owd self in no time. Besides the thirst, you slept well through the night. I gave you sips of water when you wakened—' She broke off, cheeks flushing. 'I latched Jonathan on to thee when he were clemmed. I hope you don't mind, only Mrs Oakes had gone—'

'Of course not. I must remember to thank her. And you,' Sally added, lips trembling. 'You, the Morgans, Con, Mr Lynch . . . I owe you all so much.' She fell silent. Words could never portray her gratitude. 'The child, too, who helped Mr Morgan and Tommy; what was her name? Alice and Harold, they . . .' This conjured up her sister-in-law's image and Sally breathed deeply. 'They have quite a few children.'

She cast her mind back. Alice was with child when she and Joseph dwelled with them before moving to

Spring Row. She'd previously borne twins but, if Sally remembered correctly, they were boys. There was also another boy, a year or two older. She trawled her memory for the senior children.

'One was Mary. And another . . . Lizzie? Yes, Lizzie.' She nodded then frowned. 'There were more but I cannot recall their names. Was it either of those, Maggie? Mary, Lizzie?'

'I don't think so. You'll have to ask Mr Morgan.'

Sally was quiet for a moment before asking, 'Is Shield hurt badly? I know I haven't had him long but I don't know what I'd do if he died.'

'Aye,' Maggie answered truthfully. 'As I said, he's gorra terrible cut to his head. But Mrs Morgan's sons kipped down in t' kitchen so we could have their beds, so don't fret, he's not alone.'

Sally shook her head and fresh tears welled up. 'So much damage . . . He's caused so much hurt and pain. He did attack Mrs Morgan; I just knew he had. I loathe him so much I can taste it.' She gripped her friend's hand. 'He forced himself on me, Maggie. Countless times. What if I'm with child? I, I couldn't bear—'

'Oh, Sally. Oh, my poor love. Whatever happens, you're not alone, not while I draw breath.'

Sally began to weep. 'I want my mother. Oh, Maggie, I miss her so much.'

'I know, love, I know. You called for her when you wakened.'

A flash of emerald green, her mother, Jonathan . . . A man, a small child in his arms. It had been a wonderful, bittersweet dream. She sighed longingly and, from far away, heard again her mother's warning from beyond the grave.

'Remember, you'll allus have us,' Maggie was saying now. 'Me, Con, the Morgans and your family. There's no real substitute forra mother, but—'

'He hasn't finished, Maggie. All is not over.'

She spoke in such a chilling, knowing tone that Maggie paled. 'Nay, lass. By the end of the day, we'll be in Manchester—'

'And he'll find me. I'll never be free of him, don't you understand? I'll never be free.'

'Then you must go somewhere else. Get right away from here; out of England, if you must.'

'What? But—'

'However much the thought of never seeing thee again pains me . . . What your husband's capable of is clear to see. If your prediction proves right, he might not spare your life next time.'

'Where would I go? What would I do for money? It's hopeless, Maggie, hopeless.'

'Ah, but it ain't.'

She frowned. 'What do you mean? You and Con – why *are* you here? What's going on?'

'Oh, Sally . . .' Maggie's eyes shone. 'After you left, Saturday, Father Collins came to see you. I shouted but you were too far away to hear. I were beside meself, unsure what to do. Thankfully, Con visited that night and when I told him, he went to ask your aunt's advice. She said to find thee, to get Mrs Morgan's address from Mr Lynch.' She reached for her hands and squeezed. 'Oh, you'll never believe.'

'What, Maggie? What did Father Collins want?'

'You're bloomin' rich, lass. Mrs Sharp's left you money – lots of it, by all accounts. Eeh, I'm that pleased for thee!'

Sally gazed at her.

'Father Collins didn't go into detail. He needs to speak to you; urgent, like, he said.'

'I . . . Why on earth would she leave *me* money?'

'I don't know, but don't you see? This changes everything. You'll have enough brass to see you and Jonathan set for life. You can get away, away from Joseph, for ever. You're free.'

She was still dreaming, had to be. Or Maggie was mistaken.

'I'll make some tea. Will you be all right while I'm gone?'

Sally nodded. When her friend's tread on the stairs faded, she released a long breath. One thought, one tantalising possibility, consumed her.

'I'm free,' she whispered to the empty room. 'Oh, Mrs Sharp . . .'

For the dozenth time that morning, her tears flowed. Only now, they were of hopeful joy.

Having drifted off, Sally jumped awake when Maggie re-entered. Fear and confusion must have shown in her eyes, for her friend hurried over, her own soft with pity.

'It's all right, lass, it's only me.' She placed two cups beside the bed and smoothed the hair from Sally's brow. 'Could you eat? Mrs Morgan's just up and preparing breakfast for the men. Have I to fetch thee summat?'

'No, thank you. Are the men awake?'

'Aye.'

'Would you ask them to come to me? I need to speak with them.'

Maggie frowned. 'Are you sure you're up to it? You should get some rest afore Mr Lynch arrives, build up your strength.'

'I cannot leave without seeing them. I owe them my life. Please, Maggie.'

'All right. I'll fetch them.'

Gritting her teeth against the pain, she pushed herself up in bed. A light knock sounded and Arthur entered.

'Morning, lass.'

Emotion choked her reply. She held out a hand. 'Oh, Mr Morgan . . .' He made to take it but she threw her arms around his neck. He held her gently until her sobs subsided. 'I'm sorry,' she murmured when they drew apart. 'I'm simply . . . Thank you. Thank you.'

'There's no need for thanks, lass.'

'Oh, but there is, I—' She broke off as a figure appeared in the doorway. The sight of him took her breath away. Again, she held out a hand. 'Tommy, I . . . wanted to thank you—'

'As Father said, there's no need.'

He remained by the door and she lowered her hand. 'Nevertheless, thank you.'

He nodded and turned to leave, but Arthur stopped him.

'Son, wait. Wish the lass well and say your goodbyes,' he instructed him quietly. Then he bid her farewell and slipped from the room.

Sally sensed tension between the men, but the object of her attention overrode everything. He hesitated then crossed to the bed.

He perched on the edge and she held out her hand, albeit hesitantly. She thought he'd rebuff her again but he took it in both of his.

Without doubt, this was the last time she'd look upon him. This man, whom she barely knew yet felt she did completely, and he her, inside out. With whom she'd hardly spent any time and yet she felt they had shared a lifetime together already. This man, who invaded her thoughts, filled her with shame, confusion – and a need to be with him so fierce, it pained her physically. How, why, she harboured this love she was at a loss to understand. But she did. Lord, she *did*.

She'd struggled to show restraint, fought herself relentlessly. And as she curled her fingers through his, she ached anew for what might have been, what never could, never would be – and what she'd have given for it to be. Her hold tightened. She'd cherish this moment, always.

'Are you well enough to travel today?'

Fresh longing flowed through her. He'd spoken softly, almost caringly. 'I think so.'

Tommy was silent. His thumb began stroking the back of her hand.

The urge to wrap her arms around him was unbearable. 'I've been meaning to apologise,' she blurted for want of something to say. 'My arrival on Saturday, interrupting as I did . . . I'm sorry. I hope you and Dolly will be very happy together.'

He opened his mouth, then closed it. He gazed at her for an eternity. Then he sighed and lowered his head. 'I'll be late for work.'

She swallowed her pain as he rose. Their fingers were still entwined and when she squeezed, desperate for his touch a second longer, he did likewise.

'Goodbye, Sally.'

His hand slipped from hers. Gripping the bedclothes, she watched him walk from her for ever.

'Goodbye, my love,' she whispered when the door clicked shut. And deep within her breast, part of her died.

Chapter 29

AGAIN, MAGGIE CROSSED to the window. She glanced along the street, clicked her tongue and returned to the table.

Sally was the picture of composure. She sipped her tea, attention on Shield by her feet.

For days, she'd willed him to pull through, praying infection wouldn't take hold. To her blessed relief, it worked. He was more alert today and, despite a shaky start, was walking around again. Love and attention were what he needed and he had them by the shovel load. Whenever she left him to attend to Jonathan, Maggie's twins would sit with him; they, too, were desperate to have their friend back. She was confident that in time, they would.

'How you're so calm, I don't know,' Maggie marvelled, gaze straying back to the window. 'I'm on pins for thee.'

'I see no point in this meeting. I've made my decision.'

'I wish you'd think about this—'

'There's nothing to think about,' Sally cut in mildly. 'That money is tainted, Maggie. It was simply another opportunity to rub her daughter's nose in the dirt. If Mrs Sharp had died from natural means, Miss Sharp would have been virtually penniless. She chose me as beneficiary for the sole purpose of destroying her child's life. I want no part in it. No part at all.'

'And Joseph?' asked Maggie bluntly. 'I get no pleasure mentioning him but you need to think on you and that babby. All that money . . . you'd want for nowt the rest of your days. This could be a fresh beginning, away from him. Can't you put your beliefs to one side, lass? If not for thee, for Jonathan. Do it for him.'

She stared at her son, asleep by the fire. She'd been so hopeful, so happy – so selfish.

It was only afterwards, when the news sank in, that her joy had turned to disgust. Remembering her excitement had her cringing with shame. As Agnes had proved countless times, she thrived on causing Pru misery. This was no different. This parting gift had been intended to crush her daughter a final time. Well, Sally wouldn't give her the satisfaction. Not a single farthing would pass through her hands.

'Even Manchester's not altogether safe,' Maggie pressed, buoyed by her silence. 'He could track you down if he'd a mind to. I feel sick thinking on it. We only want what's best for thee. Don't do owt rash when they arrive, eh? Just think on it a while more. Even your aunt agrees you should take it.'

Despite herself, Sally couldn't contain a smile at the mention of Grace.

She cast her mind back to Monday. On Tommy's departure, her spirits had plummeted to rock bottom. If she lived to be a hundred, she'd never love another man. Not like that, with him. He'd been the first to bear proof that all men were not the same. He'd awakened that something inside her, something she hadn't thought herself capable of, following Joseph's evil.

Con's arrival had eased her inner darkness somewhat. He'd held her, soothed her. He'd admitted he hadn't been able to face saying goodbye in Manchester but was here now, and he and Maggie would take good care of her.

However, her lift in mood was short-lived – she'd sobbed to see her beautiful, gentle giant. Shield had tried to rise for her but his legs buckled and he'd whimpered, as though apologising for his failure to protect her. She'd reassured him, hugged Shaun for tending him. And saying goodbye to Ivy shattered her heart.

Ivy had fussed around the cart tucking blankets about her, asked repeatedly was she up to the journey, was her pain manageable, was she warm enough . . . Then she'd grasped her hand and begged her never to return. Despite the sorrow that agreeing brought, Sally promised.

As she'd made for the town she thought she'd seen the back of, anguish had threatened to consume her. Passing Deansgate, she'd refused to think, feel. She'd eased off her marriage band and dropped it over the side of the cart. She'd felt numb at the thought of Joseph, then, still did.

Initially, she blamed herself for what had happened. Countless obstacles scuppered her return, almost foretelling imminent doom: Peggy's death, Grace's revelation, the Sharps' deaths – like a higher power warning her not to go. Ignoring the signs nearly cost her her life. She should have left after seeing Ivy was safe. She should have *left* after witnessing the proposal – another shadow of warning, to be sure.

Yet gradually, she realised she wasn't at fault, knew that to move on from this she must put it behind her. She was used to his abuse and she'd recover, as she had many times. She refused to be broken.

On reaching Ancoats, a numbness his evil wasn't strong enough to penetrate had wrapped around her. Shoulders back, head high, she'd greeted a horrified

Ellen with dry-eyed calmness. She'd then noticed the kitchen's other occupants.

Grace had caught her in a tight embrace, crying and railing over Joseph. Ed, white with shock and rage, held her next. When he stepped aside, revealing the person behind him, Sally's mouth fell open. She'd stared, elated and terrified, unsure what to do. Stan made the decision for her. Wrapping his arms around her, he'd uttered the most precious words:

'I could've lost thee. Oh, Sally, forgive me . . .'

And those long, torturous hours of rape and abuse seemed worth it. She had her family back. She had her brother.

They had asked her to come home and she'd agreed to, soon. Despite her joy at reconciling, she had to be sure they – or more to the point, Stan – wouldn't have a change of heart. She couldn't bear things going wrong again.

Now, as Maggie returned to the window, Sally sighed. She wouldn't dwell on her future. She'd take each day as it came; it was all she could do. Her friends and family were of one mind: accept the money, build a new life for herself and Jonathan. But she couldn't. If her decision proved disastrous, she'd suffer the consequences. Yet she'd do so with a clear conscience.

'Maggie, please, sit down.'

'He said one o'clock and it's nearly two. Where the divil are they?'

'Haven't you listened to a word I've said? I won't accept it.' She'd spoken more sharply than intended and sighed again. 'I'm sorry. I don't mean to be short with you, it's just—' A knock cut her off. Maggie rose and she grasped her hand. 'Please respect my decision. I won't be dissuaded.'

Sighing herself, Maggie went to answer the door.

Father Collins entered, all smiles and apologies. Catching sight of Sally, they died. He took her hand. 'My child. I was not aware that your injuries were quite so extensive. Mrs Benson said you suffered an accident in Bolton, but . . . Are you quite well enough to receive us?'

'Yes, Father.'

He looked as if he'd ask more but when she looked away, changed his mind. He motioned to a gentleman in the doorway. 'This is Mr Stockton, of Stockton and Coburn Solicitors. Mr Stockton, may I introduce you to Mrs Swann?'

Her eyebrows rose. The short, balding man who stepped forward was no stranger. His wry smile as he removed his hat showed that he clearly remembered her, too.

If her appearance shocked him, he didn't show it. He shook her hand warmly. 'Ah! These young ladies came to my rescue last week,' he informed the priest. 'My papers were headed for the gutter but Mrs Swann and Mrs . . . ?'

'Benson, sir.'

'And Mrs Benson, mercifully averted disaster.'

'Take a seat, Mr Stockton, Father. I'll brew a fresh pot while you discuss . . . matters. Mam's out with the kiddies. You'll not be disturbed.'

Tight-lipped, Sally watched Mr Stockton extract papers from his case. *Agnes's will.* The very sight made her feel ill.

'I trust you are aware of what this meeting is about, Mrs Swann? I believe Father Collins explained to Mrs Benson that the late Mrs Agnes Sharp—'

'I know what this is about.'

His hands stilled on the documents he was sifting through. 'I see—'

'And I want no part in it whatsoever. I want nothing from that woman.'

'Mrs Swann, I don't quite—'

'Do you have children, Mr Stockton?'

'Why, yes. Two girls and a boy.'

She ignored Maggie's soft sigh. 'Tell me, sir. Have you ever caused them unnecessary pain? Do you relish seeing them upset? Would you deem it acceptable to destroy their lives?'

His mouth dropped open. 'Absolutely not!'

'Then you'll understand when I tell you I won't accept what that woman has bequeathed me.'

'Mrs Swann, I'm afraid I haven't the slightest notion what you're talking about.' He shot the priest a puzzled frown. 'Father?'

'The Sharps had . . . a tumultuous relationship, shall we say. I'm afraid at times one could only describe Mrs Sharp's treatment of her daughter as deplorable.' Father Collins looked at Sally kindly. 'I think what Mrs Swann is trying to say is that she believes this money was merely a ploy to hurt Miss Sharp.'

Mr Stockton nodded slowly. 'I see. However, Mrs Swann, you are quite wrong. Mrs Sharp has indeed bequeathed you a rather substantial sum but I'm certain it was not with the intention of hurting her daughter.'

'Then why—?'

'If I may?' He selected a folded sheet sealed with a wax stamp. 'I'm sure once you have seen this, all will become clear.'

'Whatever the contents of that will . . .'

'Will? No, no, Mrs Swann. This is no will.' He pushed it towards her. 'Are you able . . . ?'

'Quite, thank you,' she affirmed with a proud lift of her chin. The daily readings Agnes insisted upon had vastly improved her literacy skills. She broke the seal and unfolded the sheet. 'This is a letter.'

'Indeed. Apparently, it explains everything.'

At Maggie's encouraging smile, she began:

Well, girl. If you are reading this, I can be sure of two things: I am dead and my solicitor has earned his reward for a job well done.

Thus, he is not completely incompetent, despite his revolting habit of housing kipper skin in his teeth. Conversing with him is an altogether unpleasant experience, don't you agree? His cook deserves a stern talking-to for serving such unappetising fare.

Sally glanced at Mr Stockton then back to the letter. Even in death, the old woman's tongue was sharp enough to cut through steel.

I am guessing I have flummoxed you by bestowing such a generous gift. And, knowing you the little I do, I suspect you are considering rejecting this offer. I am right, aren't I? You really ought to climb down from that high horse of yours occasionally.

Indignant colour flooded her cheeks, yet the hint of a smile hovered. Shaking her head, she continued.

In a moment, Mr Stockton will hand you an envelope. Contained within is two hundred pounds. It is yours to do with as you wish. I make no demands as to how you choose to spend it. However, if you do accept, it comes with but one condition.

My request is a lifelong commitment, but one I trust you will not deem undesirable. Prudence is now alone in the world and I want you to rectify that.

You must remain with her as friend and companion. You and your child will reside with her – my room is of an adequate size, I am sure. It is also of paramount importance that you assist my daughter in running the business. The shop is her main source of income; you must ensure that standards do not slip.

This may surprise you, but I care a great deal for my daughter. Her welfare after my death has concerned me a long while. The thought of her as destitute pains me considerably. You must ensure this never happens. Should you let the customers take advantage of her good nature, the business would go under in no time.

I have made some choices in my life of which I'm not proud. This, I am certain, is not one. I see something in you which I admire. You have integrity. You also possess a pure heart. I know you will not let me, or, more importantly, Prudence, down.

I leave you to ponder my terms. A comfortable life for you and your child and more money than you will know what to do with are yours for the taking, so long as you don't allow your pride to rule your judgement. Know this and take my word as truth when I tell you I would not bestow such opportunity upon just anyone.

I did not make your position easy, yet you served me well. Take it, also, as a token of my appreciation. You have earned it, girl, thrice over.

Yours in hope and faith,
Mrs Agnes Elizabeth Sharp

The paper slipped from Sally's fingers and fluttered to the floor.

Chapter 30

FATHER COLLINS FOLDED the letter. At Sally's request, he'd read it aloud, tactfully omitting the reference to the solicitor. Before her lay the unopened envelope. They stared at it in silence.

'What will you do?' asked Maggie. 'This changes everything, surely? Mrs Sharp didn't leave it you to hurt Miss Sharp; she did it to protect her. And as it says at the end, well, she wanted you to have it for serving her well, lass, an' all. Happen it's her way of saying sorry for the way she treated you, for the burden heaped on you at finding out about the goings on betwixt the pair.

'You were a true and loyal friend to Miss Sharp. Happen she were grateful for that, an' all. Who knows what went through that head of hers? But you can be certain of one thing, now,' she added, eyes gentle. 'That money's yours. You need feel no guilt in taking it. With no ill intentions in mind, I believe she wanted thee to have it, regardless. It's there in black and white.'

Sally bit her lip. 'The shop and everything else . . . ?'

'Mrs Sharp's effects – the business, all monies and possessions – she bequeathed to her daughter,' the solicitor confirmed. 'As the beneficiary committed both murder and self-destruction, and without kinsfolk to contest entitlement of ownership, those effects revert to the Crown.' He inclined his head to the envelope. 'I received a letter from Mrs Sharp the week before her death. It was delivered to my home address, not to my office as one would expect.'

Sally closed her eyes. *The letter she'd given to the maid* – Mr Stockton's maid, she realised. She'd never have dreamed it held this.

'Inside was the envelope you see before you and the letter you have read,' he continued. 'There was a second, addressed to myself, containing instructions along with my fee. Our first meeting could have saved a considerable amount of time had I known . . . You see, the reason for my haste that day was that she instructed me to deliver this to you at her funeral. She was certain you would attend.

'Alas, unrelated matters detained me and I was running dreadfully late.' His countenance turned decidedly uncomfortable. 'Mrs Sharp insisted discretion was of the utmost importance. She touched upon your marital difficulties and was adamant that your husband should not find out. Indeed, if she'd bequeathed this in her will, by law, ownership would have passed to him.'

Sally was stunned. 'But how . . . ? I mentioned nothing to her regarding my past.'

Mr Stockton smiled. 'Who knows? Mrs Sharp was extremely astute, Mrs Swann. Maybe she guessed, or perhaps it was a mere suspicion and she decided upon this route for any eventuality.

'In any case, it was a shrewd decision. The sum is yours without record of its existence, bar our letters. Only we in this room bear knowledge of it.' His eyes softened as he studied her injuries, clearly guessing who had inflicted them. 'As for myself, you need harbour no concerns as to my discretion. Once I leave this house, it shall be as though this meeting had never taken place.'

'I second that notion,' murmured Father Collins.

Too overcome with emotion to speak, Sally nodded.

When Mr Stockton took his leave, Maggie made a fresh pot of tea and the three of them discussed the day's discoveries.

Sally prodded the envelope. 'I'm still not entirely comfortable with this. I hardly knew her. I shouldn't lay claim to her money.'

'Whatever her failings, Mrs Sharp was no fool,' Father Collins said quietly. 'Had she not wanted you to have it, that envelope would not be lying there. You may not have known them a great length of time but you clearly made an impression upon both women. Furthermore, as Mrs Benson stated, you were a true friend to Miss Sharp.'

'I could have been a better one, Father. Perhaps if—'

'Alas, hindsight is an unforgiving mistress, my child. No one could have foreseen the outcome. You went above and beyond to help Miss Sharp – in death as well as in life. I am in agreement with Mrs Sharp; I too believe you have earned this money.'

'I cannot fathom it. If she cared for her daughter as she claims, why treat her so abominably? It makes no sense.'

Father Collins steepled his fingers. 'Many years ago, Miss Sharp spoke to me of her troubles. Naturally, priests cannot repeat, to anyone, disclosures made during the sacred act of confession.' He paused. 'However, my and Miss Sharp's conversation took place not in the confessional box, but a pew by the altar.'

'Father?'

'Under Church regulations, confidentiality of disclosures depends upon whether they are made in private or in public. Anything disclosed in settings where others may reasonably overhear, as in this case, could be seen as without intent to confidentiality . . .'

'Do you have something to tell me concerning Miss Sharp?'

'Some would deem it was with confidential intention . . . However . . . in what Miss Sharp revealed, and her reasons for doing so, the intention was simply, I am certain, to rid herself of the burden she'd carried for so long. I am equally certain that, in telling you, I shall not come to regret it.

'It has no bearing on anyone connected; no harmful actions can result from the telling. It may bring you, however, if not comfort then closure. *Not* to tell you would be an unnecessary cruelty.'

Sally touched his arm. 'I give you my word it shall go no further.'

Drumming his fingers together, he met her gaze. 'Are you aware Miss Sharp had a child?'

She knew her expression was answer enough. 'Father, are you certain—?'

'Quite. What I am about to reveal may pain you. Are you sure you wish to hear it?'

She and Maggie glanced at each another then nodded.

'While growing up, Miss Sharp was close to her mother. Her father showed her little interest but it didn't unduly bother her. Love she lacked from him, her mother more than made up for.' He cleared his throat. 'Forgive me for what I am about to say. I would not do so if it were not paramount to the events which followed.'

As he sought the right words, a knot of dread formed in Sally's stomach. This must be what Pru almost confided to her . . . She fumbled for Maggie's hand.

'When Miss Sharp reached adolescence, her father became attentive, affectionate. They would take walks together or, in inclement weather, play cards by the fire. Upon discovering her love of literature, he began inviting her to his study, where they pored over books for hours. The indifferent father was gone and Miss Sharp was delighted.

'Eager to retain this new relationship, she was blind to the fact that time spent with her mother dwindled. And her pure young mind was unaware that this was what he wanted. As she and her mother's closeness decreased, her relationship with her father took on an altogether . . . different nature.' He paused, shook his head. 'Barely a month into her fourteenth year, she was with child.'

Sally screwed her eyes shut, heard Maggie mutter angrily.

'Confused and afraid, Miss Sharp withheld the truth, and Mrs Sharp failed to see who had fathered the child. She discovered, upon informing her husband. She expected him to be as devastated as she – yet instead, he took the news calmly, dismissing her suggestion that their daughter be sent away to give birth and that the infant be adopted.

'He insisted she stay, that they would raise the infant as their own. Mrs Sharp's world shattered, with the terrible realisation. He denied her accusation of incestuous acts and, threatened into silence, so too did Miss Sharp.'

'Eeh, the poor, poor lass,' Maggie murmured.

'Mrs Sharp, too,' added Sally. 'Dear God, what a dreadful thing for a mother to discover.'

'Miss Sharp said her mother was never the same. Half mad with grief, with little choice but to accept his decision, she shut herself away. Despite Miss Sharp's pleas, she refused to see her. Until, that is, her pains came and she was forced to deliver her daughter's infant.'

Sally covered her face with her hands. Her words weeks before . . .

'Never in my life had I prayed as fervently . . . I waited, waited, watching that chest rise and fall. And as the new day dawned, I knew He would not claim her . . .'

She wasn't referring to Pru, at all. She'd prayed not for her daughter's death, but for her release from the ill-gotten child. The secrecy, all those unanswered questions. Everything was falling into place.

'Despite her loathing for her father, Miss Sharp loved her daughter on sight. She was adamant that she would raise her and – perhaps afraid that refusal might loosen her tongue – he agreed. He devised a plan. The family would relocate and Miss Sharp, an early bloomer much older looking than her tender years, would pose as a young widow.

'The very next day, his brother in Ancoats passed away, bequeathing him everything. It was perfect timing; they left Shropshire and took ownership of the pawnbroker's. Weeks later, Mr Sharp suffered a fatal blow to the head. Police surmised he'd likely disturbed a break-in during the night. No one was ever brought to justice. Miss Sharp suspected that a break-in never occurred.'

'You mean . . . ?'

He nodded solemnly. 'She never questioned her mother. They simply erased him from their lives. However, they could not dismiss him completely. Miss Sharp bore no resemblance to her father, but her child did. As she grew, so too did the repulsion Mrs Sharp felt for this constant reminder of the husband she loathed.

'This put heavy strain upon mother and daughter's delicate relationship. The stronger her hatred grew, the more Miss Sharp defended her child. The devastating event which later occurred ensured reconciliation remained a lifelong impossibility.'

'Are you referring to the child's death?'

'Indeed. Shortly before tragedy struck, she'd asked about her father. Mrs Sharp reacted badly to the innocent question and struck her. Miss Sharp warned her mother that if she ever laid a hand to her child again, they would leave and never return. Fearful of being alone, Mrs Sharp vowed to treat her granddaughter better. She was true to her word and the child warmed to her.'

'And just when their relationship was blossoming . . . Oh, how very sad. How did she die, Father?'

'She drowned while out making purchases with Mrs Sharp. Miss Sharp had remained behind to see to the shop. Watching them leave hand-in-hand, she was hopeful, for the first time, about the future. Her dreams soon crumbled. Her mother returned in a dreadful state accompanied by a constable, who revealed the child had fallen into the canal.'

'Dear Lord, how?' Sally whispered.

'Mrs Sharp said it happened in the blink of an eye. She tried her best to save her but the child's heavy skirts sucked her under. Mrs Sharp almost suffered the same fate; the constable heard her shouts and dragged her out just in time. A party of men searched the waters to no avail. The child had vanished.

'It broke Miss Sharp completely. Her mother offered comfort but, eaten up with grief, she rebuffed her. Mrs Sharp ceased trying, became distant, embittered. The strokes, which later left her body useless, further warped her mind. Her behaviour became increasingly volatile. You are aware of the incident involving her previous employee?'

Sally nodded numbly.

'As for Miss Sharp . . . Her father, mother, child – all contributed to her mental decay. I pray she's now at peace.'

For several minutes, Sally struggled to digest the harrowing tale. Did Agnes taunt Pru the day they died? She'd the cruellest tongue when the mood took her. Perhaps she mentioned the child and Pru snapped? Or was it a remark about her father? she wondered, recalling Agnes's scathing comment:

'*What he saw in her, I will never know.*'

Sadness constricted her chest. It was as though, over the years, Agnes convinced herself that the blame lay with her daughter. Pru referred to the secret plaguing her as 'my sin', said that she'd made but one mistake; was it that of trusting her father? Did her mother convince her, too, that the fault was hers? It was such a tragic mess.

Her granddaughter's demise clearly tipped Agnes over the edge of insanity. To witness, yet be powerless to prevent, such a thing would make a lasting impact upon anyone. As for dear, sweet Pru . . . It was a miracle she remained sane as long as she did.

Sally felt an overwhelming urge to be near them, tell them she understood.

'May I walk with you, Father?' she asked when he rose. 'There's something I must do.'

'Of course, my child.'

'Aye, lass, you go,' said Maggie, guessing her intentions. 'I'll mind Jonathan.'

Drawing her shawl low to cover her injuries, she followed him out. A stirring of hope fluttered. God willing, this visit would lay her guilt to rest. Afterwards, she'd light a candle for Pru's daughter, she decided. And she'd say a prayer that all three had found peace. Each deserved nothing less.

She sighed at the thought of the envelope. Agnes's letter had swayed her somewhat, it was true, and yet . . . She was certain of only one thing: if she did accept, fortune's hand wouldn't touch her alone. Used wisely, that money could change her loved ones' lives for the better, too.

By the time she reached the church, her mind was set.

Passing through the gates, she smiled. She'd made the right decision.

Chapter 31

FROM HIS MOTHER'S knee, Jonathan had a clear view of Grace, opposite. When she approached, his podgy legs kicked wildly, bringing chuckles from both women.

At four months old, he'd recently discovered the delights of solid food and would treat them to his hilarious dance each mealtime. His legs opened the show and his arms followed suit, as though performing a lively jig.

'Ready for your pobs, lad?' He answered Grace with a gummy grin and she laughed. 'Pass him here, lass, afore he has a fit.'

Watching her feed him the gloopy white mixture of mashed-up bread soaked in warm milk and sugar, Sally smiled. When she'd first taken on the new venture, she'd worried herself sick whether Grace was ready to care for him again.

Peggy's passing was still raw but the heartbroken mother had been delighted to resume the role, assuring Sally it was what she needed to take her mind off her grief. Grace loved nothing more than parading Jonathan around in his perambulator, proud to show off the bonny child.

'Goodness. He hasn't come up for air, yet!'

Grace smiled knowingly. 'Secret's in t' sugar, lass. Aye, my Peggy loved her pobs, she did, would've ate it until it came out of her ears. Ay, now, don't go starting all that nonsense about me looking after him,' she added when Sally bit her lip. 'I'd go barmy in t' house all day on my own. He's a tonic, he is. Ain't you?' she cooed, chucking him under the chin. Her tone caught Shield's attention. Tail swishing, he nudged her arm and she laughed. 'Lord, you're a jealous beggar, you are. Aye, you're a tonic, an' all,' she said, rolling her eyes.

Mercifully, Shield had made a full recovery and, as she did daily, Sally thanked God. Bar the knobbly scar on the back of his head, no one would guess he'd been attacked. *Another failing on Joseph's part*, she thought in satisfaction then swiftly evicted him from her mind. His evil had no place in her life these days.

The past months had nurtured strength in her she'd never have believed possible. She too had mended, and not just physically. Her nose, though now slightly misshapen, and the multitude of bruises had healed, but so had her mental wounds.

She'd developed a somewhat detached approach to Joseph and all he stood for. She refused to be cowed. And she refused to run away as she'd previously considered. If he discovered her, so be it. As she'd done last time, and countless times before, she'd survive. She was bone-weary of fleeing. She had friends here, family, a life. She wouldn't sacrifice those for anyone.

She'd give anything to live in peace but knew it wasn't possible while he drew breath, so simply took each day at a time, resigned to the fact that he might find her but determined to live life as best she could. If she must get back up and dust herself off a thousand times, she would. She was damned if he'd win.

When her monthly bleed arrived, she'd sobbed and it spurred the healing. Her friends and family were also instrumental to her recovery – as was the bold project she'd undertaken. *Her business, her sanctuary* . . . She could scarcely believe it.

'Eeh, it's lovely we're seeing that bonny smile of yourn more often.'

Sally sighed contentedly. The walk home after making peace with the Sharps had set her on a path of extraordinary adventure. 'I was just thinking . . . I wonder what became of that mother and child, Aunt Grace?'

'They're well, I'm sure, thanks to thee.'

She'd witnessed an exchange outside a lodging house between the housekeeper and a woman clutching a baby who, by a farthing, was short for a bed for the night. Despite the woman begging her to show mercy for the sake of her child, who would surely perish if he spent another freezing night without shelter, the housekeeper refused admission.

Her plight had affected Sally deeply. It could so easily have been her and Jonathan but for the wonderful people in her life. She'd taken the sobbing woman to Maggie's and from the envelope pressed several notes into her hand. Her grateful tears, and certainty they would sleep easy in a warm bed as a body deserved, touched Sally.

In that instant, she'd known what to do with the money. Not only could it benefit her loved ones, but many others, too. And so the germ of an idea formed: she'd open her own lodging house. Hers would be a refuge. She'd never turn anyone from her door.

Now, she squeezed Grace's hand, then – as she did each morning – gazed around the good-sized kitchen; her favourite room.

Pale-blue curtains hung from its two windows, lending it a light and airy feel. In the centre stood a large table and, to the left, were two comfortable chairs either side of the fire.

A scullery and pantry, with shelves for dry foods and marble slab for perishables, led off to the right. By the windows, another door led to a small yard, now home to half a dozen chickens which, as well as eggs, supplied unlimited entertainment for the children.

She'd set to work making her dream a reality immediately and had discovered a run-down, two-storey house on Pollard Street. The possibility of Joseph finding out and claiming ownership had struck fear and fury in her. She'd therefore asked Uncle Ed to bear his name on the deeds. She trusted him implicitly and Joseph would be unable to prove anything; he'd never get his hands on it.

'It's a far cry from what it were, eh, lass?' said Grace, as though reading her thoughts.

She'd secured the nine-roomed property at a good price but it proved a mammoth task. However, she'd relished the challenge.

'Alive with damp and vermin . . . holes in t' roof . . . You'd never believe it were the same house.'

Sally nodded. With enough money left for supplies, the exterior's restoration had reached completion in no time. Work on the interior then began and, during their free time, Con, Ed, Stan and Mr Lynch undertook the heavy duties, replacing the odd floorboard and smashed window and whitewashing the walls.

She, Maggie, Grace and Winnie then took over, while Ellen minded the children, and for days swept and scrubbed every inch of every room until the house gleamed.

'It wouldn't have been possible, Aunt Grace, without the many helping hands. Con's market contacts, too, proved invaluable. The furniture, bedding, curtains, rugs, crockery and the million and one other necessities . . . Thanks to him, costs were minimal.'

''Ere, don't go being modest, lass. You worked harder than anyone; threw yourself into it with gusto, you did.'

A soft smile stroked Sally's lips. 'The second week of the new year, when I opened for business, do you know what I did before affixing the "Beds Vacant" sign in the window?'

'What, love?'

'I drifted from room to room and cried tears of joy.'

'Ay, Sally. You'll have me blubbing in a minute.'

'With unwavering dedication, we did it, together.'

'Aye, we did that,' murmured Grace with a watery smile.

Sally pressed her hand again then wandered from the room. The ground floor boasted three: one at the far end of the passage, one to the immediate right upon entering, and hers and Jonathan's. Humming softly, she climbed the stairs. Each of the four rooms on this floor held three beds – the two larger rooms, on the second floor above, four apiece. This enabled rest and shelter for twenty people at any one time.

She could have squeezed in more but refused to conduct her establishment as many did. She'd heard of lodging houses in appalling states, beds crammed to the rafters, maximum profit the owners' sole concern. Poor souls endured such conditions through sheer desperation; she'd been determined her guests wouldn't share that fate.

Cleaned daily by herself and Maggie, each room had a rag rug covering the bare boards, a picture or two adorning the walls and a washbowl and pitcher, with hot water available upon request. It was no surprise that business was thriving.

'I never dreamed I could be this happy,' she whispered to herself, leaning against a doorway. 'This time last year, life was as bleak as it's possible to be.'

'Aye, now look at thee. And no one deserves it more, lass.'

Sally turned to see Maggie, broom in hand. Smiling, she linked her arm. 'Come. You look fit to drop.' After leading the way to the kitchen, she poured her tea from a pretty green pot and when Maggie flopped into a chair, shook her head. 'I do wish you wouldn't tire yourself so. We're meant to perform the chores equally.'

Her friend blew at a damp curl, which had escaped from the red scarf around her head. 'And you fret too much. This is the best job I've ever had. Besides, I like keeping busy.'

'You're working yourself into the ground and there's really no need.'

Maggie lowered her head. 'I'm sorry. I'm grateful, lass, is all.'

'Oh, Maggie. I'm the one who should say sorry.'

'You? Nay, love, nay—'

'Yes, me. When I returned to Aunt Grace's at the start of the restoration ... Well, during those weeks, this house wasn't the only thing that slowly improved – my relationship with Stan did, too. Preoccupied with the first, magical Christmas with my family, all that was going on ... I neglected you, Maggie.'

'I'd not call assuring me a position for life once business was up and running neglect!'

'But I failed to wonder how you'd manage in the meantime. When you revealed your landlord was threatening eviction ... I was racked with guilt.'

'Oh, lass.'

She'd made to tell Maggie she'd clear the debt but an idea had stopped her. She'd put the proposition forward – that they reside at the lodging house with her and Jonathan – and to her delight, her friend agreed. Sally's joy, when she'd assigned the largest room, between her own and the kitchen, to the family, now returned.

'You've no reason to prove your gratitude. I love having you all here and don't you ever forget it.'

Maggie sniffed, swallowed hard, sniffed again. 'Ta, love.'

They were sipping their tea in companionable silence when Grace asked, 'Where's your mam, lass?'

A grin spread across Maggie's face. 'Gone for a walk.'

'With . . . ?'

She nodded, and Sally and Grace grinned back.

'Eeh, I were horrified in t' beginning with thoughts of you all spending the nights with a houseful of strangers. You could have been robbed, attacked in your own beds, or owt. I thank the Lord that Mr Lynch provided a solution.'

'Aye, so does Mam!' said Maggie, winking, and they all chuckled.

Teddy Lynch Jr, a seaman of some thirty years, had recently left the waves behind. He hankered to settle down and, when his last ship docked, decided not to sign on for another voyage. His return, however, proved problematic. His parents' house was bursting at the seams with children and grandchildren, and he'd found the squeeze tiresome.

Mr Lynch, Uncle Ed's friend, had asked if his son could have a permanent bed at the lodging house until he found a wife, that he'd pay generously for the privilege. Sally readily agreed – having a man about would ease their concerns if trouble did arise with lodgers – and the kindly bear of a man, with a thatch of dark, curly hair and thick beard, took up residence on the first floor.

He and Ellen had hit it off immediately and all agreed wedding bells would be tolling in the not too distant future.

'Are you going to the Roundhouse today, lass?' asked Grace now, and Sally nodded.

Each Sunday, she visited the Sharps' graves. Without them, the help she'd provided to so many wouldn't have been possible. Half an hour of her time one afternoon a week to show her gratitude wasn't asking much. It also gave her the opportunity to tend little Peggy's grave.

Maggie drained her cup, and rose. 'I'll finish the rooms while you're gone – and no arguments,' she added before Sally could object.

Clicking her tongue, Sally donned her shawl. 'I shan't be long. When I return, I'll prepare a lovely dinner – and no arguments!' she said when Maggie, who usually cooked, made to protest.

Grace chuckled. 'What are you like, youse two? Bloomin' stubborn, they are, lad, the pair of them,' she told Jonathan, and Sally and Maggie grinned.

'Aye, go on. I'll do the rooms and you do dinner,' Maggie agreed, shooing her out. 'Just try not to burn the soddin' thing like last time!'

Sally was still smiling when she reached the church. Life at present was rosy. She had her family, friends, the business – what more could she want?

The answer came immediately. If within her power, she'd alter two things: Joseph's existence and the Morgans' absence from her life. Sadly, both were beyond her control and always would be. Joseph would probably live to a hundred just to spite her, and the Morgans could only ever be dear friends from afar.

As for her third, deeply concealed wish . . . That, she knew with certainty, could never be.

Her step faltered. Tommy might well be married by now. Dolly could be with child at this very moment. Her guts lurched, imagining them together, loving one another . . .

'Stop it,' she told herself. 'Be happy for him and move on.'

Immersed in thought, her mind didn't at first register the crouched figure up ahead. Doing a double take, she gasped in surprise.

On all her visits, she'd never seen any indication that someone else had been. Who on earth . . . ? Was Mr Stockton mistaken when he'd said the Sharps were without kin? If so, why didn't they attend the funeral? She was debating whether to make her presence known when suddenly the woman turned.

Sally's mouth dropped open. She knew who this was. There was no one else it could be.

Deep embarrassment replaced the woman's shocked expression. Tugging her shawl over her face, she leapt up and ran for the trees.

'Wait! Please, wait!' Sally picked up her skirts and sprinted after her. 'I mean you no harm. I simply—' To her relief, the woman halted. 'I just want to talk. Please.'

Keeping tight hold of her shawl, the woman half turned. 'Leave me be. I've nowt to say.'

'You needn't fear me, nor should you have fled. You've as much right as I to visit Miss Sharp's grave. I know who you are—'

'And I know thee. Now please, let me go. I must go.'

Despite this, she made no attempt to leave and Sally stepped closer. Tentatively, she touched her shawl. 'Please, let me see,' she said softly. The woman sighed but didn't object, and Sally eased it from her face.

'Take a good look. Take a long, hard look then get down on your knees and thank the Almighty you were spared. It could well have been you bearing this disfigurement.'

Her words sent ice down Sally's spine. Pale-pink patches stood stark against what hair remained. Further down, clumps of puckered scars marred a face that might once have been beautiful. But it was her eyes, pools of melted hazel, lucid with unspeakable sorrow, which tore at Sally. They told of a deeper suffering than her flame-ravished skin ever could.

'Was she the cause of that? Did she wield that poker at thee, an' all?' the woman asked.

Sally's fingers fluttered to her nose. 'No, no. This happened at another's hand. Mrs Sharp never . . . I saw the results of her attacks on her daughter, but she didn't attempt it with me. I loathed that poker with a passion. I once threw it through the window.' She nodded when the woman lifted an eyebrow. 'Oh yes, straight into the street. Of course, she ordered Miss Sharp to retrieve it—'

'And so sealed her own fate. And by God, she deserved nowt less.'

Silence hung between them.

'What happened? Why you? One could say I gave her cause to lash out numerous times, yet she didn't. What happened that dreadful day?'

Hugging herself, the woman's eyes strayed across the churchyard, but instead of answering the question she murmured, 'I weren't surprised when I heard. A body can only take so much, you know? Mam begged me not to come but I had to, had to tell Miss Sharp she weren't bad, that she weren't to blame. I saw you and another wench with Father Collins. I saw what he did for Miss Sharp. Did you . . . ?' At Sally's nod, she smiled faintly. 'Thank you.'

Sally held out a hand. 'I wish you'd approached, but a belated introduction is better than none. I'm Sally.'

She hesitated then shook it. 'Anna.'

'Do you visit often, Anna? I've never seen—'

'Only Miss Sharp. Never *her*. And then only when it's quiet.' She tugged her shawl self-consciously. 'I don't venture out much; the stares, you see. It's allus the stares what bother me most. The jeering and name-calling, aye, they hurt, but the silent stare . . . eyes young and owd filled with disgust . . . They're the worst. Aye, they're the worst.'

'I'm sorry.'

'Don't be. Nowt will cure folk of their ignorance. I manage as best I can. Mam's an angel from heaven; without her . . . I discovered long ago no employer wants a face like mine amongst their workforce. Mam works her fingers to the bone, takes in washing from the big houses up in Salford. A purer heart you'll not find. I pity Miss Sharp that most. She never knew a mother's love.' Her eyes hardened. 'I discovered summat she'd forgot.'

'You . . . ?'

'The day she sent me stumbling into the fire. I'd discovered summat she'd forgot.'

She held her breath. 'What, Anna?'

'A letter. Nay, norra letter as such – a receipt, I suppose you might call it. Miss Sharp had a child, a daughter.'

'Yes. She drowned.'

Anna shook her head. 'No, she didn't. Mrs Sharp had her committed to New Bridge Street Workhouse.'

Sally's mouth fell open but horror chased away a response.

'She paid the master a tidy sum to take her in. I found proof bearing his signature.'

He bought as well as sold . . . Sickness rose within her. 'I . . . don't . . . Why would she *do* such a thing? All those years, to have Miss Sharp believe . . .'

'I dropped a button while darning a nightdress and it rolled beneath the bed. Careful not to make a noise, for she were sleeping, I felt around. That's when I found it, a reticule covered in dust and cobwebs. I were curious. Happen it were wrong . . . I looked inside.'

'And Mrs Sharp—'

'Aye, wakened and caught me reading it. Happen she hadn't trusted the master, wanted in writing that he'd uphold his end of the deal in keeping his silence. She thought she'd destroyed it years afore, begged *my* silence, insisted she'd done it for her granddaughter's own good.

'Her hatred for her grew daily; she were scared she'd harm the girl, said she'd had no choice, that it were for her safety. She'd been certain Miss Sharp would get over the loss.'

'Well, she was wrong! That poor woman suffered until her dying day.'

Anna nodded, eyes steely. 'She fooled everyone, concocted the whole canal tale for her own ends, watched her daughter mourn a child very much alive.'

Sally felt light-headed, had to grasp Anna's arm for support. Had gaining the child's trust been nothing but a ploy? Was she pretending all along, so not to arouse Pru's suspicion once she put her plan into action? Realisation sickened Sally to the core. She'd forgiven Mrs Sharp, excused her behaviour as a result of mental trauma. This sin was too despicable to excuse.

'I cannot believe it. That poor, poor girl. How utterly terrified and confused she must have been.'

'I suppose you're wondering why I didn't tell Miss Sharp what I'd discovered. I wanted to, truly. I told Mrs Sharp I couldn't keep silent about summat that dreadful. She pleaded, said it were pointless, for the past couldn't be changed.

'She said she'd had word from the workhouse years afore that the child died, that revealing all to Miss Sharp would break her heart all over again. I'd not listen and as I made to leave, she turned wild with fury. She said she'd destroy me and all I held dear if I spoke out, said she had the money and means to have me locked away. Then she grabbed the poker.

'When the force of the blow had me stagger into the fire, d'you know what she did? D'you know what I heard as I fell into the flames? Laughter. She laughed, Sally, laughed as I burned. She were more evil than Satan hisself.'

'Mother of God, I cannot . . .' Words failed her.

'Keeping silent haunts me. I heard later she'd told Miss Sharp she caught me stealing and lost her temper, that my fall were an accident. I should've told her the truth.'

'And your mother? Did she advise against it?'

'Aye. She said if the child *were* dead, then I should say nowt. Better Miss Sharp remained ignorant than know the truth of her mother's actions, of her poor daughter's suffering. The pain of it would've sent her mad.'

'Anna, I have a terrible feeling . . .' She ran a shaky hand across her mouth. 'Mrs Sharp was lying, I'm certain of it. If her granddaughter's still languishing in that place . . . Mrs Sharp's money paid for my home and business. If she's alive, she's entitled to it, to everything. I could never keep it, knowing . . . I must find out.'

'Oh, Sally, d'you really think . . . ? Will you meet me here next Sunday, tell me of your findings? Dear God, if she *were* lying . . .'

'I'll be here. Her name, Anna. I must know her name.'

Backing away towards the trees, she nodded. 'Aye, it were on t' receipt. It's Isobella Dickinson.'

For a full minute, Sally stood frozen.

'Dicksy . . . !'

Her cry floated above the cold gravestones as she sank to her knees.

Chapter 32

'CON! CON!'

Two whirlwinds of fair curls and gap-toothed grins hurtled down the passage. Four small arms wrapped around his legs and sweet giggles rang through the house.

'That's a grand welcome, so it is!' Taking a twin in each arm, he swept them into the air.

Maggie smiled from the kitchen doorway. 'Let him over the step afore you pounce on him,' she called over their squeals then blushed when Con winked at her.

'How's yourself, Maggie?'

'Besides these terrors running me ragged, I'm all right.'

He flashed his slow smile. 'Sure, ye don't look a bit ragged. You look grand, so.' Carrying the children upside down, much to their delight, he crossed the passage. 'Is Sally ready?'

Flustered from the compliment, she could only nod. Self-consciously, she brushed a curl from her face and stepped aside to let him pass.

He lowered the twins into a heap at his feet and wiggled his fingers. At the threat of a tickling, they pelted for the kitchen, helpless with laughter.

Watching them go, she smiled softly. 'You're good with them. Since their father passed on, they've missed . . . Well, they enjoy your visits.'

'So do I.'

Their eyes locked. She froze as he reached out and, ever so slowly, brushed his thumb across her cheek.

'Flour.' He showed her, smiled, then stepped past her into the kitchen.

Groaning inwardly, she cursed her thumping heart and returned to her baking.

Sally nodded grimly when Con entered, glad he'd insisted he accompany her. She'd need every ounce of strength and support she could find to see this through.

Despite glimmers of spring, it was bitter out and she wrapped her shawl around herself tightly. Then she kissed Jonathan in Ellen's arms, took a deep breath and headed for the door.

'Good luck, Sally.'

'Aye, good luck, lass.'

The smile she gave Maggie and her mother was of pure gratitude. Since hearing of her meeting with Anna yesterday, both agreed she must find out whether Dicksy was still alive. They also agreed that, if so, the house and remaining money were rightfully hers.

Sally couldn't have been more thankful for their understanding. This could mean homelessness for them all, yet they understood completely her need to discover the truth, and she loved them all the more for it. As for herself, a possible reunion with her dearest friend took her breath away. She'd give anything, *everything*, in a heartbeat to have her back.

That Pru was Dicksy's mother had shocked her senseless, but now she accepted it as though she'd always known. Such gentle dispositions, caring, sweet-natured – they possessed the same qualities entirely.

Though Pru had clearly registered Dicksy's birth under a false surname to uphold the pretence of widowhood, and Dicksy didn't share her looks, she should have made the comparison earlier. On reflection, Pru's company had felt familiar, like stepping back in time.

She and Con were approaching Miller Street when panic began to churn her guts. The streets throbbed with daily life but she saw and heard little, senses gripped by the sinister-looking building ahead. She'd spent years fleeing the memories of that place. Could she really re-enter the darkness within?

'Are you sure about this, acushla?'

She gritted her teeth and nodded. For Dicksy, she'd do anything.

Gripping Con's hand, she set forth for the gates of hell.

Whatever hopes Sally harboured were shattered in less than twenty minutes.

It was true, all of it. For once, Agnes had been telling the truth. Her Dicksy was dead.

She walked blindly from the master's office, down the dreary corridors and into the weak sunshine, pushing aside anyone who was in her path. Gasping with sobs, she picked up her skirts and ran for the gates.

'Sally. Sally, wait. Sally, stop.' Con caught her in a tight embrace and she crumpled.

'It's not true, Con, it's not true! He's lying!'

'Shhh. I know it hurts but it must be; the master confirmed it. Sure, the extra money you offered would have loosened his tongue if nothing else,' he added, tone hardening. 'He wants reporting to the Board of

Governors, so he does, and will be before the week's through if I have anything to do with it.'

She buried her face in his chest. 'I thought she'd gone for ever, that she'd been sent into service. Yet she'd merely been assigned other duties and moved to another ward. All the time, she was but blocks away and I had no idea.' Her grip on his jacket tightened. 'Did she suffer? Does the typhus fever bring painful death? The truth, Con, please.'

'No, acushla. No, she didn't suffer.'

Then why had he breathed a Hail Mary before answering? For her. He'd lied for her. She raised her head to look at him. Then, stretching on tiptoe, she pressed her lips to his.

'Take me home, Con.'

From the workhouse shadows, Joseph watched them leave. When they disappeared through the gates, he snatched up the woman leaning heavily on Nancy and hissed in a voice that trembled with fury:

'Follow them.'

Sally folded her arms against the cold. Evening was drawing in, splintered rays slowly sinking beyond the rooftops.

'Go on in, you're shivering. Try to get some sleep.'

'Con, wait.'

He turned back and she closed the lodging-house door and motioned to an alleyway. He followed wordlessly.

'Thank you for accompanying me. I still cannot believe . . .' Tears thickened her voice. 'Listen, Con . . . that kiss—'

''Tis all right. You were upset.'

'Nevertheless . . .'

Leaning against the wall, he peered down at her. 'Sally, I'll not deny it was nice. And I'll not deny that I love you, because I do. Sure, I love all of you. You're as dear to me as my own family. Do you remember the day *I* kissed *you*?' She flushed and he laughed softly. 'Aye, you do. My feelings for you were like nothing I'd known. But it wasn't love, acushla, I see that now. Lust, desire, call it what you will, but it wasn't love.'

'I did try to tell you, if you recall.'

'Aye, you did. Stubborn as I am, I couldn't see it. I do now and I'm sorry.'

'Sorry?'

'For trying to force you to love me back. Sure, you must have despaired at times but you never gave up on me and for that, I thank ye. I value our friendship, Sally. There's something about you I'm drawn to, have been since the day I saw you on that platform at Bolton. You have a way about you, something within that makes folk want to care for you. And I do, always will—'

'But as a friend,' she finished for him, eyes twinkling.

He smiled. 'As a friend.'

'Con?'

'Aye?'

'Tell me to mind my own business . . . Do you have feelings for Maggie?' His embarrassed laugh brought a wicked grin to her face. 'Mr Malloy, are you blushing?'

'Does she . . . ? Has she said anything?'

'She's mad about you! Surely you've noticed?'

'Mebbe. I wasn't altogether sure.'

'Talk to her, Con,' she urged, a warm glow spreading through her. 'Tell her how you feel before another man beats you to it. She's a good woman. She won't be alone for ever.'

'Ye wouldn't mind?'

'Mind? I'd be delighted! I love you both so very much. I wish you nothing but happiness.' She smiled gently. 'Do you recall that day at the pie shop when you said that us meeting as we did was fate, that it was meant to be? Well, I agree. I believe we *were* meant to meet to enable you and *Maggie* to meet. It's a queer old world, isn't it, Con?'

'And what of you? Will you one day take your own advice?'

'What do you mean?'

'Come on, Sally, you know what I'm talking about. The Morgan fellow you've been in love with since before we met.'

'How . . . ?'

It was his turn to grin. 'Because it's obvious to anyone with eyes in their head, so it is. And what he feels for you . . . That's love, Sally. I knew whatever designs I had on you weren't, when I looked into his eyes; they shone with something I've never seen before in a man, for any woman.

'Sure, that fellow would tear out his beating heart if he thought it would make you happy. Take your own advice, tell him ye feel the same. Aye, you're married still, I know, I know – oh, to hell with it, live in sin!' He grinned when she slapped his arm, chuckling, before finishing earnestly, 'You, above anyone, deserve happiness.'

When they parted, she returned to the lodging house with mixed feelings: hope for her friends' blossoming romance and sadness at Con's blindness. He'd guessed her feelings. Yet he was as wrong as it was possible to be if he believed Tommy reciprocated them. Dolly was proof of that.

The hum of Maggie's and Ellen's voices, intermingled with Jonathan's babbles and the twins' laughter, drifted from the kitchen and she forced a smile. She'd burdened them enough with her tears for one day. She was midway down the passage when a knock came at the front door.

The woman on the step looked vaguely familiar but for the life of her, Sally couldn't think why. 'May I help you?' she asked.

'I hope so, Sally.'

That she knew her name took her aback. 'Do I know you? You do look familiar but I'm afraid . . .'

Her visitor smiled broadly. 'I'm Nancy Skinner, Percy's daughter.'

'Percy?'

'Aye, runs that little shop at Spring Row.'

Her own face creased in smile. 'Percy, yes, of course. Nancy, did you say?'

'That's right.'

'What can I do for you, Nancy? Oh, where are my manners? Please, come in.' She held the door wide but Nancy shook her head.

'Nay, I can't stop. I need thee to come with me.'

'Come with you?'

'Aye. It's Ivy.'

Her knees went weak. 'Mrs Morgan? What's happened? Is she all right?'

'I'll explain on t' way but you must come now and you must come alone.' With that, she turned and scuttled away.

'Wait, I'm coming!'

With nothing in mind but her friend, Sally hurried down the darkening street after Nancy.

Chapter 33

AFTER TEN MINUTES, Sally was still none the wiser as to the reason for Nancy's visit. Despite her pleading, Nancy said there wasn't time to explain, that all would become clear when they arrived. When Sally asked where they were going, she merely told her to hurry.

Following through the maze of tumbledown streets and alleys, mind reeling with worry for Ivy, she was brought up short when Nancy pulled her inside a dilapidated house. An unidentifiable stench burned the back of her throat and she peered around the dimly lit passage in confusion.

Before she could ask what was going on, Nancy flitted through the gloom. Battered doors lined the walls and she made for one at the far end. When Sally reached her, Nancy knocked twice and entered.

A stub of candle atop a wooden box in the centre was the only light. The weak glow quivered across Nancy's face, lending her a ghoulish look.

'Nancy, what . . . ?'

Her face was stony. Then her gaze swivelled behind Sally and she smiled.

'Tha did good, Nancy.'

Sally froze. *Surely not . . . ?* She whirled around, then staggered back in horror.

The change in Joseph was striking. The bulk of pure muscle was gone. In its place stood a withered wreck. He'd lost a considerable amount of weight. His sallow-skinned face was skull-like. Dishevelled clothes hung loose and a pungent odour wafted from him as he swayed drunkenly.

She ran for the door but his iron grip yanked her back; despite his outward frailty, he'd lost none of his strength.

'Get your hands off me!' She pushed him hard, sending him stumbling, but he pulled her along. The stench of him, as he crushed her to him, made her gag and she cried out when his erect member pressed against her. She craned her neck. 'Nancy, help me!'

Nancy arched an eyebrow and, with a curl of her lip, looked her up and down.

Terror gnawed at Sally's every nerve as, with sinking heart, realisation slammed home. Nancy had tricked her. She'd *tricked* her and lured her back to hell. 'Dear God . . . *Why?*'

'Shut your trap and sit.' Joseph pushed her into a sagging chair. Arms folded, he stared down at her, his expression oddly calm.

Nancy sidled up to him. 'You want to know why? I'll tell you why, you bitch. Because I loathe the very sight of thee.'

The hatred pouring from her was tangible. Sally shook her head in shocked confusion then gasped when Joseph struck out at Nancy.

'I warned you to keep quiet,' he snarled, revealing gaps where the teeth Con knocked out once were. 'Get and fetch some ale. And remember,' he added when she'd staggered up, 'breathe a word to anyone and I'll tear your throat out. Hurry up.'

Nursing her cheek, Nancy nodded and slipped out.

He grinned at Sally. 'The dried-up whore has her uses. Her body's norra patch on yours, mind.' Bending, he squeezed her breast then slapped her face when she tried pushing him away. 'Sit!' he roared as she made to lunge from the chair.

All's not over... Her mother's warning from her dream had come true. Dear God, how had she been so foolish? She'd followed Nancy blindly, never suspecting... She and Joseph were clearly lovers: did Nancy see her as a threat, want rid of her to have him to herself?

No one knew she was here. No one would come to her rescue this time. If she were to escape again, she'd have to do so alone.

She must think fast. Once Nancy returned, she wouldn't stand a chance; he'd immobilise her with ale like before.

At the prospect, rational thought vanished. Crippling fear of what he'd made her suffer a few short months ago sucked the breath from her lungs and in desperation she dived again. This time, a clog to her stomach killed her attempt. She doubled over, winded.

'I told you to sit.'

'What do you *want* from me?' she croaked. 'For the love of God, why can't you leave me be and let this hideous marriage die the death it deserves? You have your family, and Nancy. Forget about me, live your life. Let me live mine. Please.'

He stooped so that their faces were level. 'You're forgetting one thing: I own thee, paid for thee fair and square.' Grabbing her chin, he stared deep into her eyes. 'You've ruined me. Look at the mess of me. You've done this, you.'

'Ale has turned you into the wreck that you are, not me.'

He studied her for a moment and laughed. 'The girl I bought's long gone, ain't she? I don't know whether to admire your boldness or knock it from thee with brute force.' He grazed her cheek with his fist. 'How long?' he murmured. 'How long afore you'd be back to the wreck I made you into? Days? A week?'

'Joseph, please—'

'You can't escape me however much you run, d'you not see that by now? I'll hound you till your dying day. I want thee and I mean to have thee, one way or t' other.'

She flinched as he rose suddenly. He paced the room and she glanced to the door.

'Don't even think about it,' he said without looking at her. 'I'll kill you where you stand afore you reach it.'

She forced herself to remain seated. She didn't disbelieve his threat for a second.

'I saw you today at the workhouse.' He smirked when her head jerked up in astonishment. 'Oh aye, I saw it all. I bet that Irish gutter rat can't make you scream in bed as I can.' Eyes narrowing, he rubbed his crotch. 'Don't fret, you can have it soon. Tha must be panting for it, my girl.'

Her flesh crawled in utter disgust but she willed herself to stay calm. 'How did you know I'd be there?' she asked, desperately changing the subject before he pounced. 'The master didn't recognise me and I didn't remind him.'

'You weren't the reason I were there.'

'Then why? What could you possibly want with that place?'

His sunken face stretched in a grin. 'Same as thee. Only I succeeded.'

'Succeeded—?'

'I noticed you and that Irish filth left the way you came. Did you plan on three of youse leaving through them gates?'

Fury and disbelief, not to mention utter confusion, swamped her. How, *how* . . . ? She leapt to her feet. 'You . . . ? You got the master to lie, didn't you? She's not dead, is she?'

His grin vanished. 'She will be, you along with her, if you don't sit.'

'Mother of God—'

'Sit!'

Shaking with a sea of emotions, she obeyed.

'Tha can't beat me in nowt, don't you understand? You asked and went away empty-handed. *I* asked and . . .' He let his words trail off.

'Where is she? If you've hurt her—'

'She's safe – for now,' he growled, words heavy with threat.

Sally crossed the space and stood before him. 'Joseph, please. I'm begging you. Please, don't hurt her. I'll do anything.'

'I thought you might.' He grabbed the knot of hair at her nape and drew her face to his. 'I'll not get you away without a fight, will I, you little bitch? Not without them gullible bastards you've got fawning over you getting in t' way.' He winced suddenly and touched the back of his head. 'Willing to kill for thee, ain't they? Got them wrapped right round your finger, ain't you?

'Well, this time, I'll have the final laugh. If you want her to see another sun, you'll do as I say. D'you hear?'

She nodded without hesitation, Dicksy's safety paramount.

'Put up a fight, try alerting any of them bastards, and she's done for. Understand?'

She nodded again and he flung her across the room.

'Now sit and shut your trap till it's time.'

'Time?'

'I *said* shut it.'

'Where is she? Please, let me see her.'

He raised his fist. 'I'll not tell thee again.'

Swallowing a protest, Sally lowered her gaze. And from far away, a gentle whisper caressed her like an embrace:

'*Be strong, lass. Be strong.*'

Strong porter normally worked when the hammering set in but today it wasn't having the desired effect.

Joseph took another swig as the thumping in his skull, as though someone was trying to break free from the inside out, intensified.

'You all right, love? That pain back?'

Slamming his palm to his forehead, he squeezed his eyes shut. The blows had damaged something, he just knew it. He'd not been right since that lot got a grip of him.

'Is there owt I can do?'

'Aye, shut your trap.'

Nancy bowed her head but it sprang up again when a whimper drifted through the adjoining wall. 'Shall I—?'

'Stay put. I'll go.' Making for the door, he shot Sally a glance and his anger mounted.

He'd had to put up with the whore next door all day for that bitch. She'd done nothing but whinge since they'd fetched her from the workhouse and he was nearing the end of his tether. If he didn't need her so much, he'd have done for her hours ago.

But need her he did. Sally would kick and scream every step of the way without his human bribe. She had to come quietly. Besides anything else, he couldn't chance another beating the way his head was. Another round like the last would finish him.

Recalling Alice's pleas, he sighed inwardly. Apart from himself, she was the only person in the world he held in the slightest regard. He'd miss the fat sow, he realised with surprise.

It had taken weeks to recover from the onslaught at Nellie's but as soon as he'd felt strong enough, his quest for Sally returned with a vengeance. Alice was aghast on hearing his plans:

'I believe in t' sanctity of marriage as well as the next, but this is madness! They'll do for thee next time. Leave it be, Joseph. The whore ain't worth it!'

Of course, he'd ignored her. He'd been in this stinking rat-hole that was Manchester a fortnight, now. By God, he couldn't wait to be gone – would be by morning if Nancy agreed to what he wanted.

For her own sake, she'd be wise to comply. This time, he'd planned everything meticulously. If she thwarted it, he'd show no mercy, would snub her out in a heartbeat. And he'd enjoy it.

Now, despite saying he'd go, he heard Nancy following and forced himself not to thump her back into her seat – then thump her again for not doing as she was told.

He wasn't worried in the slightest about leaving Sally alone. She wouldn't waken from her ale-soaked slumber for a while. Even if she did, she wouldn't take advantage of the empty room to make her escape. She'd never leave without the other workhouse whore.

The stench of stale urine and faeces hit him in the face as he threw open the neighbouring door. Covering his nose, he peered towards the bed. He could just make out the curled figure and his eyes narrowed.

'You'll shut your trap if you know what's good for you. How many times d'you need telling?' She answered with a moan and, clenching his fists, he stalked towards her. '*Shut* it, I said,' he snarled, and she shrank back against the wall.

'She'll quieten down. Come back next door.'

At Nancy's voice, the woman raised her head. 'Sally?' she asked weakly.

With the toe of his clog, Joseph jabbed her in the ribs, grinning when she whimpered. Nancy winced and he snorted. 'She'll have had worse than that over the years. The master rules them with an iron rod.' He stared down coldly. 'Now think on. One more sound and I'll—'

'You *bastard*!'

He whipped around to find Sally in the doorway. 'Get back in there. Tha sees her when I say. Don't make me tell you again, my girl—'

'I'm going nowhere. Get away from her, the pair of you!' She flew to the bed and dropped to her knees. 'It's me. I'm here, I'm here. Oh, I'm so sorry . . .'

'Sally?'

'Yes, yes, it's me. I'm here, I— Oh!' She fell back with a scream. 'God, no!'

Holding out stick-thin arms, Rose Swann smiled. 'My lass. Oh, my lass . . .'

Nancy touched Joseph's sleeve. 'Leave them be; they'll try nowt. The owd 'un can barely stand.'

He glanced at mother and daughter, weeping in each other's arms, and nodded. This needed finishing. 'Leave both doors ajar so we can keep an ear out.'

Nancy followed him next door, sat at a small table and folded her arms.

'What's wrong?'

'Nowt, just...' She rubbed her chin agitatedly. 'What's going on, love? You mean to get shot of Sally; why fetch another into it? That's two you've gorra get rid of, now. I'd rather not know your plans, it's true, but... You do want us to be together, don't you, lad?'

His hands itched to hit her. 'How many times d'you need telling? I've my reasons for fetching her mam, reasons you don't need to know, right? All we have to do is stick it out here the night. At first light, we'll be away.'

'Sally...? She'll be dealt with by morning?'

'Aye.'

'And we can be together? Just you, me and my little 'uns?'

He suppressed a grin. 'Aye. I've got it all worked out, found us somewhere to dwell, an' that. Once I've done for that whore in there, we'll be off.'

She clapped her hands like an excited child. 'Where is it, our new home? Nay, don't tell me, I want it to be a surprise.'

He allowed his smile to surface. 'Oh, you'll be surprised, all right.'

She giggled, then bit her lip.

'What now?' he asked.

'Father. I feel terrible leaving him, love.'

Joseph licked his lips. This was what he'd been waiting for. Slipping his hand into his trouser pocket, he fingered the small package.

'I mean, he'd not know how to peel a tatty, never mind cook hisself a meal. How he'll manage without me, I don't know.'

'He'll not have to.'

'Eh?'

Joseph placed the package on the table.

'What's that?'

'Open it.'

Frowning, Nancy obeyed. The frown deepened when she saw what she'd revealed.

'There's threepence worth there. The apothecary weren't for selling it me, said he had to know a body first, but I got round him in t' end. I gave a false name. Nowt will come back on us once he's gone.'

'Once who's gone?'

'Your father. If we're to be together, it's the only way.'

She jerked back as though he'd slapped her. 'What? Why this to be together?'

'We need money if we're to start afresh elsewhere.'

'But, but surely there's another way—'

'He must be loaded, running that shop all these years. D'you know where he keeps his brass? Well, do you?' he demanded.

'Nay, but—'

'And if he caught thee searching his cottage? Would he stand there and say nowt?'

She gave a small shake of her head.

'Nay,' Joseph went on. 'He'd shout blue murder; half the row would be there in seconds. It's the only way. A meal laced with this – he'd not suspect a thing. Or do you not love me, after all? Has tha spoken nowt but lies, is that it?'

As Nancy gazed at the small measure of arsenic, it was clear from her colour that her dinner of liver and onions, washed down with a copious amount of gin, threatened to make its escape. Her voice was firm. 'I'll not do it. I could never harm him, never.'

Joseph grabbed her hair. 'I – we – need brass, you silly bitch. How far d'you think we'll get otherwise?' Her eyes sparked with a defiance he'd never seen before and his face twisted. 'Don't try that look with me or so help me, I'll tip the contents of that there packet down *your* throat.

'You'll do this, for I tell you now, if I'm called to answer for owt, I'm dragging you down with me. You've abetted me all the way. You're in it up to your neck so just you think on.'

A burst of angry voices drifted from the street.

He darted to the window and peered at a group of men across the road. They staggered off and when their drunken shouts faded, he heaved a sigh. Christ, he must get Sally away. He turned to glare at the only obstacle standing in his way. The hammering, never gone long, struck inside his skull and he gripped his head.

'I'll do it.'

He squinted through the pain to the table. The package had gone. 'Aye?'

Nodding, she patted her pocket then held out her arms. He walked into them and she clung to him.

'You'd best be gone if you're to be back by morning,' he announced, pulling away. 'Fella next door's gorra horse and cart in his backyard; he'll give thee a lift to Bolton on t' promise of being paid well, I'm sure.' He lifted an oil lamp from a shelf. 'Here. Tell him to fetch one, an' all. They'll light your path well enough.'

'Tell me you love me. I want to hear you say it.'

Joseph swallowed an angry retort. He couldn't mess this up, now. 'I love you,' he said flatly.

Calmness filled her eyes. He clutched his head again and she nodded to the table. 'Sup your ale. It'll ease the pain.'

Then she turned and walked out.

*

Pausing at the neighbouring room, Nancy glanced to the women, still wrapped in each other's arms. Sally locked eyes with her over her mother's shoulder and, with a whisper of a smile, Nancy continued on her way.

Outside, she sucked in a lungful of cold air. And as she disappeared into the night, she wore the expression she had when she'd walked away from the man clutching his injured genitals months before.

No one disrespected her and got away with it. No one.

Chapter 34

'BITCH, GET IN here!'

Sally tore another strip from the bedsheet. She found a cracked pitcher holding several inches of murky water and dipped the rags in.

'D'you hear me, whore? In here now!'

With neither fire nor candle to light the room, she wrapped her arm around her mother's waist and guided her to a stool by the window.

'Christ, my guts . . . You bitch, wait 'til I—' Whatever threat Joseph meant to deliver was lost in a string of retches.

She tilted Rose's head and, by the full moon's glow, studied her appearance.

'Oh, oh God . . . Do as you're told, bitch!'

Her mother glanced to the door fearfully and Sally took her hand. 'It's all right, Mam. I'm going to get us out of here very soon, I promise.' Gently, she began cleaning dirt, mucus and dried blood from Rose's face.

'He struck me, lass. I needed to relieve myself and kept asking to go, for I were desperate. He struck me; it ain't half sore.'

She lowered her head. *You bastard, you bastard*, she silently screamed. She'd kill him for this. With her bare hands, she'd kill him.

'I, I'm soiled, Sally. The smell . . . I'm sorry—'

'Oh, Mam.' She dropped the rag and took her in her arms. 'Don't fret so. We'll be home soon and everything will be all right.' Avoiding her gaze for fear of breaking down completely, Sally untied the string from her mother's hair and gathered her grey-blonde locks into a tidy bun.

'I'll wring your *neck* when I get my hands on thee! Come here, I need—'

She frowned slightly when again violent retching cut Joseph's speech. She guided her mother to the bed then crossed the room.

'Nay, lass! Don't go to him!'

'It's all right, Mam. I'll be back in a moment. Rest a while.'

There wasn't an ounce of fear in her; bubbling rage blotted out all else. She thrust open the neighbouring door and charged inside.

The sight momentarily threw her.

'Dear God, don't just . . . stand there. Fetch . . . help. Now, you gormless bitch, I'm in ag—' A stream of vomit erupted from his mouth.

She stared at him coldly. Whatever ailed him, she neither knew nor cared.

Crouched in the foul-smelling fluid, arms around his middle, he squinted up. 'Fetch . . . someone. Need . . . help.'

'All those years. You had me believe my mother was dead *all those years*? I hope you burn for eternity for all you've done, you evil bastard, you.'

Pain contorted his face. He clutched his head then his stomach again. 'For the love of God, help me!'

'Help you? Help *you*?' she murmured incredulously. 'After everything you've done to me, my friends, my mother?' She crossed the small space, halting inches from his bowed head. 'You've made my life a misery for more years than I want to think, and you want me to *help* you?'

He tried lifting his head and failed. 'Please . . .'

'My mother and I are leaving. If you try to stop us, if you *ever* come near me again, I swear to God, Joseph, I'll kill you.'

'You . . . bitch.'

Kicking at his feeble attempt to grab her foot, she spat on the ground and turned.

A hacking cough sounded next door and she paused. She glanced at the tankards on the table. One was empty, the other quarter-full, and this she lifted to take to her mother.

Between retches, Joseph's voice followed her. 'Get back here. Get back . . . here!'

'It was all I could find, Mam.'

Rose held the tankard to her lips then pulled back, grimacing at the strong ale's smell.

'Drink it, it will ease your cough,' Sally encouraged her.

Yet as her mother tilted it to take a sip, Sally frowned when, in the moonlight, she glimpsed something at the bottom.

'Wait. Let me see that.' Turning the tankard this way and that, her frown deepened at the blackish substance. She sniffed the contents then set the tankard on the floor. 'Never mind that. Let's get you home. Here, put your arm around my neck. That's it, take your time.'

Slowly, Sally guided her from the room. Looking left when they entered the passage, she halted. 'I shan't be a moment. There's something I must do before we leave.'

Joseph lay on his side, eyes half closed. His corpse-grey, sweat-slicked face twisted as she approached.

'Whore. Workhouse . . . whore.'

From beneath the folds of her skirt, she extracted coins from a pouch attached to her waist by a ribbon. She selected a shilling, stooped and pressed it into her husband's hand.

'You own me no more, do you hear me?' she whispered. 'You own me no more.'

His eyes widened as she rose. 'No. No, wait. Bitch! *Bitch!*'

Without a flicker of emotion, she turned her back on the devil incarnate and walked away.

Chapter 35

THE MANCHESTER COURIER
Saturday, 25 February 1854

On Tuesday morning last, Mr Rawley, the city coroner, held an inquest on the body of Joseph Goden, aged forty-eight years, who resided until a few weeks prior to his death with his sister at Chapel Alley, Bolton.

The deceased was discovered on Monday night at a lodging house where he had boarded on Lomax Street, Manchester, by Mr Greene, the proprietor. Assistance was obtained but life was quite extinct. The deceased had taken arsenic whilst intoxicated.

Enquiries were made with several apothecaries in the vicinity as to whether the deceased had recently purchased arsenic from their premises but each, upon viewing the body, answered in the negative and could offer no clue to his identity.

However, upon questioning, a fellow lodger gave information that he had witnessed the deceased the previous evening in the Bull's Head Public House, London Road, in the company of the Master of New Bridge Street Workhouse. After viewing the body, the Master identified it as that of Joseph Goden, a resident of Bolton.

Mr Goden's sister revealed he had been much troubled in his mind and had been drinking a good deal of late.

Dr Croft, of this Borough, was present at the inquest and a post-mortem examination of the body having been made, the effects of the deadly drug were plainly visible.

The Jury returned a verdict that the deceased came to his death from poison administered by his own hand whilst in an unsound state of mind.

After reading the article several times, Sally tore the newspaper into tiny pieces and threw them on to the fire. She stared at the grey ashes for an age and closed her eyes.

In the solitude of her kitchen, she sent up a thank-you to the Almighty.

Then she issued another, to Nancy.

Chapter 36
Late May 1856

THROUGHOUT THE AFTERNOON, tension within the Malloys' kitchen had steadily mounted.

Flo and Harry sat cross-legged by the fire, half-heartedly playing with a pile of wooden bricks, and along with the adults would glance up when their mother's cries sounded. They understood what was happening, had watched Maggie's stomach grow over the months with fascination and itched to meet their new sibling.

Con prayed their wait wouldn't be much longer for an altogether different reason. Why, he didn't know, but he couldn't shake the feeling . . . No, he told himself firmly. All will be well. *Merciful Jesus, please* . . .

He glanced at Rose and Teddy Lynch, sipping tea. They'd ceased trying to distract him with conversation long ago. Another wail drifted through and Teddy laid a hand on his shoulder.

'Let me take thee forra jar, lad. There's no use you wearing the floor out. There's no place for men at times like these; best to stop out of the way, leave the wenches to it.'

Con shook his head.

'Teddy's right, love,' added Rose. 'It could be hours yet. Babbies come when they're good and ready and not afore. I'll send for thee when it's over.'

'No. I'll not leave my Maggie till I know all's well. Sure, there'll be time enough later to sup the child's health. I'll stay in case she needs me.'

Jonathan squirmed to get down from his grandmother's lap and when he'd toddled to the twins she lifted the teapot. 'I'll brew a fresh pot then go up, see how things are progressing. I'm sure—'

'Mam, we need you up here,' Sally shouted. 'Quickly, Mam.'

Blood drained from Con's face. He made to follow, but Teddy stopped him.

'Nay, lad. The wenches know what they're about.' His eyes softened when tears filled Con's. 'My Ellen won't let nowt happen to her Maggie or the babby. Tha can be sure of that, lad.'

Ten torturous minutes later, a gusty cry rang through the house. Teddy grinned, and this time nothing stopped Con from rushing to the door.

He almost collided with Sally at the foot of the stairs. 'Maggie, is she . . . ?'

'Mother and baby are fine.'

Closing his eyes, he heaved a sigh. 'Can I see them?'

'Soon. Let us make Maggie and your son presentable then they are all yours.'

A slow smile spread across his face. 'The child's a boy?'

'Yes, and he's huge.' She wrapped her arms around him. 'Congratulations, Con. I'm so very happy for you both.'

He kissed her cheek soundly and with a whoop, punched the air.

Making for the kitchen for hot water, Sally let her smile slip.

The strapping child had become stuck and blind terror had rendered her and Ellen senseless. Without her mother's intervention, events could have taken a devastating turn. Worrying Con now was pointless; glory be to God, Maggie survived. Some were not so fortunate . . .

Forcing a smile, she got on with the task in hand.

Later, the bedroom made a beautiful scene. The proud father, perched beside his wife, gazed adoringly at his son and, exhausted but smiling, Maggie lay listening to the twins' name suggestions. At the foot of the bed, Ellen wiped away happy tears and Teddy, arm around her, looked as proud as Con, his joy at being part of this lovely family evident.

After a last look around at the people she adored, Sally took leave with her mother and Jonathan. They were nearing home when she noticed Rose scrutinising her.

'What's troubling you, lass?'

To her horror, tears welled and she quickly busied herself with Jonathan.

'Sally?'

'I'm just tired. It's been an eventful day.'

'Lass, I've missed out on so much of your life but I'm here now. If owt's troubling thee, owt at all, I'm here to listen, to help.'

Guilt stabbed at Sally but saving her mother worry remained her focus. 'I know. I'm fine, Mam.'

'If you're sure . . . ?'

'I'm sure.'

'Right, well, I'll take a walk to our Grace's. I'll take Jonathan, let you rest awhile.' Rose smiled down. 'Shall we visit Aunty Grace, lad?'

He grinned and prodded his chest. 'I come! I come!'

Sally watched them go, smiling when her son turned to flap a podgy hand. She waved back then turned into Pollard Street.

Inevitably, her thoughts returned to the man never far from them. Had he been as excited as Con the day he became a father? she wondered sadly. She pictured his smiling face, grey-blue eyes alight with anticipation.

That day would have begun as the happiest he'd known. Yet fate's cruel hand turned it into the worst of his life.

Tommy's suffering had tortured her; her very soul had ached to comfort him. She'd worn a brave face for friends and family but at night cried herself to sleep for many months. She'd imagined the scene repeatedly, saw him pacing the floor, anxiously awaiting the first cry. And hearing it, rushing upstairs, giddy with joy, only to discover that his wife of barely a year hadn't survived the birth.

Dwelling upon his plight had almost consumed Sally and for sanity's sake she'd *had* to force him from her mind.

After Maggie's brush with death today, however, he'd returned with a vengeance.

She paused to regain her composure but it was useless. She may have fooled her mother but Anna saw through her immediately.

'What's wrong?' she asked the moment Sally entered the kitchen. 'Maggie, the babby . . . ?'

'We delivered her of a healthy boy. Both are well. Is there tea in the pot?'

'Aye. So what's troubling you? You look like you've lost a sovereign and found a penny.'

Sally's fragile facade crumbled. 'Oh, Anna. I'm so wretchedly ungrateful. I have so much and yet . . .'

'Yet what?'

'It's not enough,' she whispered. 'It's just not enough.'

'Eeh, lass, what's up?'

Sally dropped into a chair and held her head in her hands. 'So much has happened these last years. They have been full of highs and lows but for every negative, a positive occurred to lessen the blow. I discovered Dicksy was dead; I lost her, yet gained a new friend in you. I suffered that final encounter with Joseph, yet from it, got my mother back. Do you see, Anna? Good always follows bad.'

She nodded thoughtfully. 'Aye, I suppose it does. I cursed the day I applied for a position as Mrs Sharp's companion but if I hadn't, I'd never have met thee. Aye, Mrs Sharp's assault upon me were the bad. My appearance stopped me finding employment, yet good followed – you gave me a position. And when my dear mam passed away and I couldn't bear living alone – the bad – you offered me a home – the good.'

'You see? Good does follow bad, for everyone.'

'So what's bothering thee?'

'The balance has shifted.'

Anna frowned. 'How?'

'I've had my mother back over two years and they've been the happiest of my life.'

'That's good, surely?'

'I'm not so sure, Anna. Look.' She counted on her fingers: 'I got my mother back. Joseph died. You moved in and have been a wonderful friend. Then Maggie and Con married; as did Ellen and Teddy the following month.'

'Sally, I don't—'

'Today, I helped bring a beautiful little boy into the world. He's perfect, Anna, in every way. And moments ago, I watched my mother with Jonathan. She walks tall, now. You remember her dreadful state in the beginning. Those dark days were not easy, for any of us.'

'She came through it, though, love. You built her strength, gave her a happy home same as you did me. I cope with my looks, now. The ignorance of some can't hurt now I'm accepted by so many. Tha brought me back to life and same with your mam.'

A small smile stirred. 'Her reconciliation with Aunt Grace aided her recovery.'

'Aye. She's strong and she's happy. When did you last hear her crying in t' night? The nightmares, they've left her.'

'Yes. Yes, they have.' Sally stared into the fire and sighed.

'What's wrong, lass? This ain't like you. What's this ungrateful nonsense? What d'you mean with the balance shifting?'

'It's not enough.'

'What's not? Sally, please, you're fair worrying me—'

'How many items did I list just now? Seven, Anna. *Seven.*'

'Aye. Seven happy events—'

'Precisely. Seven good and only a single bad between.' She lowered her gaze. 'Do you recall Mrs Morgan and Mrs Smith visiting last spring?'

'Aye. Con bumped into Mrs Morgan and gave her your address, didn't he?'

'At the market, yes, when calling on his cousin at his Bolton stall. Oh Anna, it was so very lovely to see my dear friend after so long. I scarcely believed my eyes when I saw her on the step. What I told no one afterwards was, Mrs Morgan imparted something that day. Her son, Tommy . . . His wife had died the previous summer during childbirth. Their daughter survived – one small mercy – but Dolly . . . She was so young, so pretty. Such a dreadful waste of life.'

'Oh, love. Why didn't you say owt?'

After a long moment, Sally met her gaze. 'Because I love him, Anna. I love him with every part of me.' She dipped her head, cheeks burning. 'That's the first time I've said it out loud. I barely held it together while Mrs Morgan was here; I couldn't have spoken of it afterwards without breaking down and revealing my feelings.'

'Eeh, Sally. I don't know what to say.'

'I simply cannot keep this inside any longer, Anna. My God, how I've tried to forget him! I cannot. Con and Maggie today . . . I'm so happy for them, truly I am. To love and be loved . . .' Her eyes misted with longing. 'I'm so very lonely at times. And that's why I'm ungrateful. I've had a clear run of good fortune – happy, happy, happy. I have wonderful friends, family and a beautiful, healthy son. I'm free of Joseph. I have the business, a home, and still . . .'

'It ain't enough.'

'And never will be without Tommy. But he feels nothing for me, Anna, in that way. And the balance between good and bad shall, I believe, ensure he never does. Besides Dolly's tragic passing, the road has been smooth. I fear I'm set for a series of unhappy occurrences to even things. Or perhaps that one torturous truth, that the only man I'll ever love will never be mine, shall mar life instead. Yes. Just that one to even the balance.'

Anna drew her into her arms. 'Oh, Sally. Ain't there a chance? Couldn't you speak to him? Tha can't be certain otherwise. You're free to love again, as is he. The time what's passed would've eased the worst of his grief. Couldn't you visit Bolton, see how matters stand?'

'I ache to see him more than I can express. I've worried myself into terrible states, yearn to know how he's faring. But I cannot see him. Being apart is hurt enough. To be in touching distance yet unable to be with him . . . That really would be too much. I cannot do it.'

Sighing, Anna held her closer.

'It pains me greatly keeping Mrs Morgan at a distance. Joseph's death gave me freedom to see her again but I have just that once – only then because she sought me. I pray things could be different but they cannot.'

'Does anyone else know of your feelings?'

'Con guessed long ago.' She pulled back to look at her. 'You won't speak of this to anyone, will you? Please. I, I couldn't—'

'I'll not breathe a word.'

Sally wrapped her arms around her once more.

'Aye, don't fret, lass,' Anna murmured. 'Don't you fret about a thing.'

The following days brought little change to Sally's mood and by Sunday Anna was in no doubt she'd done the right thing. Seated beside Sally by the lodging house step, she glanced left frequently, awaiting the familiar figure turning the corner.

Clement weather had brought Pollard Street's residents from their dank homes, eager for the sun's touch on their pallid faces. Men lounged on corners, sleeves rolled to their elbows, talking quietly, whilst their womenfolk, having abandoned their chores, sat on stools by their doors, gossiping and drinking tea.

Barefoot children of all ages filled the narrow street, their shouts and laughter ringing across the cobbles.

Boys raced or fought with imaginary swords and girls free to indulge in games collected stones, which they used as coins to play shop or create drawings on the flagstones. Those with harassed mothers played as best they could while lugging baby brothers or sisters in their small arms. Toddlers were left to their own devices to frolic in the gutter.

Whispering and laughing, lads too old for play stole glances at elder girls sitting on windowsills and flagstones who, mindful of their mothers' inevitable clouts for loose behaviour, mostly ignored the attention and instead half-heartedly watched younger siblings for squabbles breaking out.

Sally stroked Jonathan's hair as he played quietly with Shield. She gave Anna's conversation attempts brief responses and occasionally even managed a smile. But it didn't reach her eyes and too soon her morose expression returned.

Preoccupied, watching for Con, Anna jumped when Sally touched her shoulder. 'Sorry, lass. What did you say?'

'Would you mind Jonathan while I brew some tea?'

She nodded and when Sally disappeared inside, returned her attention to the corner.

He appeared and she rose, stomach fluttering in anticipation. 'Well?' she whispered. 'Will he come?'

'He will. Is Sally inside?'

'Aye. When will he be here?'

'Soon. When he appears, I'll make my excuses and ye do the same.'

'It'll work, won't it? Does he . . . ?'

The Irishman winked. 'Oh aye. Head over heels.'

'Who is head over heels?'

Neither had heard their friend emerge. They jumped apart guiltily. Anna opened and closed her mouth but Con recovered quickly.

'Me. I'm head over heels for my Maggie, for life, for the beauty that is God's green earth!'

Sally smiled. 'Is Maggie well? Baby Brendan?'

'Both are grand.' Suddenly, someone caught his eye at the end of the street. 'Well, I'd best be away.'

'But you've just arrived.'

'Sure, 'twas just a quick stop to say hello. Maggie's expecting me.'

Anna avoided Sally's gaze. 'I'll walk with thee, Con, stretch my legs. You want to come, Jonathan?' He nodded and she took his hand. 'We'll not be long, Sally.'

'Oh, Shield and I will come. We could call in at Aunt Grace's. My mother's there; perhaps they would care to join us.'

'Nay, you can't.'

She frowned, surprised. 'Why, Anna?'

'Someone needs to be here for folk wanting beds. You stay, lass. We'll be back soon.'

Disappointment glimmered in Sally's eyes but she smiled and nodded.

When they reached the corner, they glanced back. Sally and Shield were gone, and Con gave a wink to the man across the road.

'Well, we've done all we can, Anna. 'Tis up to them, now.'

'There may be some boiled ham from yesterday. Come, let's see if we can find you some scraps.'

Shield didn't need telling twice and eagerly followed Sally down the passage. Reaching the kitchen, however, he stopped. He looked back to the front door, lifted his nose and sniffed.

'What is it?' she asked when he whined. 'Is the bitch from number twelve waiting for you? Let's find you that ham and you can go back out.'

Shield gave a last, long sniff then obeyed.

After feeding him and pouring herself tea, she stared around and sighed. The house was so quiet these days. Mercifully, her mother and Anna remained but she missed the early days when Maggie, Ellen, the twins and Teddy dwelled here. Then, the house buzzed with life and laughter.

Anna had taken over their room, and Rose, who had shared Sally's since arriving, joined her to give her daughter and grandson more space. Sally's room seemed so empty afterwards and she thanked God she had Jonathan's company. The nights would be unbearably lonely when he grew and required his own.

'Stop these self-pitying thoughts,' she scolded herself now. Her loved ones were happy. That's what mattered.

She saw Maggie and Ellen at least once a week; Aunt Grace, Uncle Ed and Stan frequently. And she had her neighbours, who had accepted her into their community from the start. Their children were company for Jonathan, the women friendly, and there were any number of men to call upon for assistance with troublesome lodgers. She was by no means alone, and had much to be thankful for.

'Yet it's not enough,' she whispered to the emptiness.

The Morgans – one in particular – were the missing piece, their absence a yawning cavern nothing could fill.

'Oh, I must stop this!' she told the dog. 'No wonder Anna didn't want me accompanying them, souring the mood. What's wrong with me, boy? Why can't I free my mind of him, however hard I try?'

Shield peered down the passage. His ears pricked and his tail wagged furiously.

Moments later, there came a knock.

Winter brought lodgers to her step in droves, yet milder months still saw a steady flow. Anna was wise in insisting she stay behind. Customers' needs must come before her own pleasures. After tidying her hair and apron, she fixed a welcoming smile and opened the door.

'Good after—' The greeting caught in her throat.

'By, it's good to see thee, Sally.'

If a feather had blown through, it could have knocked her to the ground, so absolute was her shock.

Mesmerised, she watched Tommy sweep hair from his forehead, shoulder muscles rippling beneath his shirt. When he smiled, her own lips parted and a sigh escaped.

'Can I come in?'

She motioned to the kitchen. He led and her gaze travelled the length of him in wonder. She was dreaming, must be. Fuzziness overtook her. She felt weightless, as though she might flutter away like a leaf on the breeze.

He sat at the table and she drifted to the fire for the kettle. After filling it, she busied herself with cups and saucers. All the while, she felt his stare. Her hands began to shake and, abandoning the crockery, she went to fetch the caddy. As she passed him, he caught her arm.

Her every nerve leapt. She was as powerless to break free as if he had held her vice-like. She gazed at his hand, heart racing.

'Sally, leave the tea. I don't want tea.'

'Then what do you want?'

She held her breath as his hand strayed. His fingers closed around hers and her legs threatened to buckle. This wasn't real. *This wasn't real.*

'You, Sally. I want you. I've only ever wanted you.'

He rose and she saw his mouth move to hers. His lower lip grazed her own with the softest of touches and she closed her eyes. 'Am I dreaming? Are you really here?'

'Could I do this in a dream?' He wrapped his arms around her waist. 'Or this?' he asked, brushing his lips across her throat and jawline. Slowly, slowly, they returned to hers. 'Or this?'

His kiss stole her breath.

'Yes,' she breathed. 'In my dreams, yes.'

'Oh, Sally.' Her body dissolved against his and he sat and lifted her into his lap. 'It's always been you, only you. Lord, how I love thee.'

'But . . . when did you . . . ? How . . . ?'

'Explanations can wait for later, my love.' He removed the pins from her hair. Chestnut locks cascaded over her shoulders and he buried his hands in the silken mass. 'Marry me, Sally. Be my wife and make me the happiest man on earth.'

Gazing into the grey-blue eyes of the man for whom she'd yearned with all she was for years, pain stabbed her.

'You want to marry me? But I . . . I'm spoiled, Tommy. Joseph . . . the things he's done to me . . . I'm, I'm—'

'Perfect, d'you hear? Perfect. That's over with, finished. I swear to thee, Sally, with every piece of my heart, you'll never know a moment's sadness as my wife. All I've ever wanted is to make you happy. I'd deem it an honour to spend the rest of my days doing just that. You have me, mind and soul, allus have. Please say you feel the same.'

'I feel the same and more,' she choked. 'I've never wanted anything more than to be your wife.'

Their lips found each other again and the world faded.

When he carried her to her room, she gave herself completely. He took her tenderly, with understanding, and she loved him all the more for it. Afterwards, as they lay entwined in each other's arms, their soaring hearts beating in perfect rhythm, she wept with sheer joy.

Finally, she knew how it was to be loved. And it felt wonderful.

Upon the others' return, Sally knew not a shred of shame for how she and Tommy had spent the afternoon. What they had shared was the most natural thing in the world and she regretted nothing.

She was no slip of a lass whose head had been turned with passion. She was a widow, mother, a woman who had endured more than most twice her age. She'd harbour no guilt for loving and being loved by the man she adored.

When she'd informed her mother and Anna of Tommy's proposal, and their tears and congratulations died down, she took Jonathan into another room. In terms he'd understand, she explained how the future was to be, that he'd have a new friend – Jenny, Tommy's daughter – and that they would all live together.

He thought for a moment then pointed to Shield, and when she assured him yes, him too, he clapped his little hands excitedly. And she laughed through blissful tears for her beautiful boy. For the first time in his short life, he'd know a father's love.

After the evening meal, her mother drew her aside and said she'd have Jonathan in with her tonight. A hint of embarrassment touched Sally's cheeks, then, but Rose's eyes told of her understanding, her pleasure that she'd finally found what she'd searched so long for. Sally couldn't have been more grateful or loved her more if she tried.

That night, she and Tommy talked and made love until the sun peeped over the grey rooftops.

They spoke of Dolly and Joseph, Con, their children and families. They discussed their future, hopes and wishes. They cried, laughed, kissed, their bond strengthening with each minute, hour, that floated by. And they loved as neither had nor thought possible. They were one. Their unity had made them whole.

After a lingering goodbye the following afternoon, Sally watched him walk away with a peaceful heart. Once he'd seen to business in Bolton, he'd be back. And she'd be counting the seconds.

Chapter 37

MAGGIE EXTRACTED THE poker from the fire. The heat had turned it orange-red and, after blowing off ash, she tilted Sally's head. Tongue peeking from the side of her mouth, she wrapped a length of hair around. When she unwound it, it bounced around Sally's face in a perfect curl.

Sporting new hats and matching smiles, Rose and Grace looked on, shiny-eyed with love and pride. Anna, too, wore a new hat in periwinkle blue and she lifted its short veil to wipe a happy tear.

'Hold still,' Maggie instructed when Sally shifted to glance at the clock, 'else you'll be walking down the aisle stinking of the goose fat we'd have to put on your burns. That would be too much even for Tommy, daft for thee as he is.' The women laughed and Maggie smiled. 'Not long now, lass. A few more and we're done.'

When at last she stood before them, there wasn't a dry eye. Her mother had dressed her hair and beneath the lace veil, delicate as a spider's web and studded with imitation pearls, she'd left several curls to flow. They framed a face alight with anticipation, midnight-blue eyes sparkling and cheeks, which had needed no pinching, delicate pink.

Around her throat lay a string of tiny pearls, a wedding gift from Maggie and Con, which set off the stunning, cream-coloured taffeta gown to perfection. This too had imitation pearls along the seams; she'd fallen in love with it on sight. Though initially she'd baulked at the dressmaker's quote, her mother, aunt and friends had insisted this was the one.

Sally was glad they had. It felt glorious, like a second skin – a far cry from the tattered, earth-coloured one the first time around.

Rose took her hand. 'Oh, lass. I'm so very proud of thee.'

'And me,' choked Grace. 'Eeh, tha look as pretty as a picture.'

Maggie and Anna nodded agreement.

'He's a lucky fella, he is.'

'I'm the lucky one, Aunt Grace.' She squeezed her hand, then turned to Maggie. 'How are you feeling?'

'Aye, all right.' Glancing at the bump beneath her new dress, her friend smiled ruefully. 'Little divil's been jigging all morning. Must be all the excitement.'

Falling pregnant barely a month after Brendan's birth had pleasantly surprised Maggie but was proving a trial. Aches and lethargy had replaced the sickness she'd suffered from dreadfully in the early months, and Sally had promised Con she'd ensure she didn't tire herself today.

'Well, remember, take it easy or Con will have my guts for garters.'

Maggie clicked her tongue but the twinkle in her eye for the husband she adored belied her exasperation. 'Con frets too much. I intend to enjoy myself today. Anyroad, never mind about me; how are you feeling? Tha must be sick with nerves. I know I were – both times.'

The softest smile lifted the corners of Sally's mouth. 'I feel nothing but peace. Tommy's my everything. He completes me.' Four pairs of arms enveloped her. Tears threatened and, laughing, she pulled back. 'Please, you'll have me weeping.'

Her mother caressed her cheek. 'Right, lass, you ready?'

She nodded. She'd never been more so for anything in her life.

That balmy August afternoon held no resemblance to the day of Sally's marriage to Joseph Goden. This day, she glowed with an inner light apparent to all.

Outside, a sea of loved ones hugged and kissed the new Mr and Mrs Morgan. They had filled the church to bursting; their smiles, as Sally glided down the aisle on Ed's arm, brought tears to her eyes.

On one side were seated her mother, Jonathan, Stan, Grace and Winnie; Anna, Maggie, Con and the children; Ellen, Teddy and his father, Mr Lynch. Numerous neighbours also attended. In the opposite pews she saw more dear faces, none more so than Ivy, Arthur, Shaun and little Jenny.

Tommy's elder siblings, their spouses and children, were a happy sight; Sally had met them the previous month and couldn't have been more delighted with her new in-laws. Several pit lads were present, and Martha Smith. George Turner was also there, suspiciously bleary-eyed but smiling.

They couldn't have hoped for a better turnout; even Shield had been in attendance, albeit on the church steps.

After thanking Father Collins for conducting the beautiful service, the party returned to the lodging house, where a lavish wedding tea awaited.

They didn't have to spare a thought for paying lodgers as, for the first time, there were none. Sally had freed the rooms for her Bolton guests, who would travel home the following morning.

When all were assembled in the kitchen with drinks, Tommy called for attention.

'On behalf of myself and my wife, thank you for coming today.' He and Sally raised their glasses. 'A toast, to you all.'

'To the bride and groom!' trilled the grinning guests.

He turned and raised his glass again. 'To my wife. You've made me the happiest man to ever walk the earth. Thank you.'

'And to you, my husband,' she murmured then smiled shyly at the guests' collective 'Aww'. She raised her glass once more. 'Last but by no means least, please join us in raising our glasses to absent friends.'

Two people instantly sprang to mind but she dashed them away. Absent they were, but friends they certainly were not. As far as she was concerned, despite the good that had come from the money, Agnes harmed too much in life to be remembered in death. As for Joseph . . . all she'd ever wish for him was to burn in hell for eternity.

'To Jonathan Swann who, despite everything, was a good father to me. To my dear cousin, Peggy. To my friends, Dicksy and Miss Sharp. And to Dolly,' she added, squeezing Tommy's hand.

'To absent friends,' they chorused, more than one wiping away a tear.

'Now, let's celebrate!' Tommy ordered, then kissed his wife soundly, much to their guests' delight.

And so they enjoyed themselves for all they were worth. Everyone got along brilliantly, mutual love for the bride and groom binding them in friendship. They ate, drank, laughed and sang and, thanks to the carter's accordion skills, danced for hours.

At one point, Ivy took Sally and Tommy aside and held them close. 'I'm so very happy for youse,' she said huskily. 'Me and Arthur guessed of your feelings years ago.' She smiled wryly at their sheepish expressions. 'Aye, we're not bloody blind. It's been a long time coming, has this. Now you've got each other, you hold on tight and don't let go, d'you hear?'

When they nodded, she stroked Tommy's cheek tenderly. 'Don't hold no self-reproach over Dolly. Tha were a good husband to that lass. You put her happiness first and for that, I'm proud of thee. It's time, now, to think of *your* happiness. You have Nat Jenkins's blessing. Make the most of what you've allus wanted, lad.'

He caught her in a hug. 'I love you, Mam.'

'And I you, son.' She turned to Sally and took her hand. 'You've been part of my family from the start; I can't tell thee how glad I am it's official. You've made my young lads happy, changed both their lives. You've an angel's heart. Don't let bad memories of that divil have any part in your new life. You're free of what's gone afore, lass.'

Tears spilling, Sally embraced her. Then George started up a new tune, Tommy took their hands and they laughed and danced, bringing smiles from everyone.

Later, they thanked Anna yet again for intervening, then sought out Con. When he'd shaken Tommy's hand, Sally hugged him tightly.

'Thank you,' she told him for the dozenth time. 'If you hadn't gone to Spring Row and told Tommy how I felt . . .'

'You'd have found each other eventually, regardless. True love will out, so it will. Be happy, acushla,' he added softly.

The twins' giggles rang above the noise and, turning, they saw Maggie and Ellen, helpless with laughter, dancing a lively number while Teddy, holding little Brendan, looked on with a smile.

'Mind you're not for tiring yourself, so, Maggie,' Con called and when she rolled her eyes and beckoned him to join her, grinned. 'Sure, let's show them how it's done.'

Despite her aching feet, Sally allowed the men to lead her. Others vied for a dance with the new bride until, finally escaping the floor, she flopped beside her aunt at the table.

'Look at them two, lass,' Grace murmured, nodding to her son and sister dancing together. 'Things turned out well in t' end, for us all. I can't believe I've got my Rosie back. And to see her with Stan . . . It's more than I deserve but by God, I'm happy.'

Since reuniting, the sisters had cried an ocean between them. They had righted wrongs and at long last buried the past. Rose's years in the workhouse put the precious gift that was life into perspective; she understood more than most that it was far too short to hold grudges.

Sally sighed contentedly then turned with a groan, feeling a hand on her shoulder. 'Oh, Anna, please don't ask me to dance,' she begged, laughing. 'My feet are throbbing.'

'There's no fear of that, lass. I've two left feet; you'd not get me up dancing for owt! Nay, someone's asking for you at the door. I invited her in but she refused, said she needed to talk with thee in private, like.'

'Did she give her name?'

'Nay, lass.'

Frowning, Sally slipped from the kitchen. Everyone she knew and loved were beneath this roof; who could be asking for her, and at this hour? When she reached the door, her mouth fell open.

'If you want me to leave, I'll understand.'

'What do you want?'

'To explain. To say sorry. To say thank you.'

After a long moment's deliberation, Sally stepped outside, shutting the door behind her. 'I haven't got long. I have guests to attend to.'

'Congratulations to youse both.'

Sally nodded and folded her arms. Under her steady gaze, Nancy flushed.

'Knowing you were wedding today, that you'd found happiness at last as you deserve . . . I had to come. I've put this off long enough. I'm so very sorry, Sally. I were weak with infatuation. He were evil and I couldn't see it. I couldn't *see* it.' She glanced left and right then leaned in. 'It were me. I killed him.'

'I know.'

Nancy's mouth stretched into an O.

'Joseph was too selfish to end his life. If he'd had his way, he'd have lived to a ripe age – to spite me, if nothing else.'

'Then why didn't you . . . ?'

'Shout what you did from the rooftops? That you lured me back to a man who had caused me more pain than you could imagine? That you were a murderess? That *you* slipped that lethal dose into his ale?' Sally shuddered, recalling how close her mother had come to drinking the deadly brew. 'I had my reasons.

'I didn't mention your name to anyone and my mother was in too poor a state to remember. I told my loved ones Joseph came here, threatened to hurt my mother if I refused to go with him, but that we escaped. They wanted to hunt him down but I said I couldn't recall the address.'

'Why, Sally?'

'I'd left him in a state of illness but never thought ... or perhaps I did. Perhaps, in the back of my mind, I knew Satan was soon to collect his favourite son.'

'And if you'd told, they might've found him afore he died?'

'Precisely. I believe I wanted to avoid that.'

'But weren't they suspicious upon hearing he'd died?'

'They were simply glad he was gone. If they suspected foul play, they didn't voice it.'

Nancy nodded. Tone soft, she asked, 'Why keep silent about me? Mercifully, the housekeeper at that lodging house made no mention to the police of me or your mam having been there. Whether it slipped his ale-sodden mind or he didn't want the greater scandal of murder tarnishing his place, I don't know. And I told Alice I returned to Bolton the night afore Joseph died, pretended to be as shocked as her.

'I said he'd sometimes spoken of ending it all, never thinking he'd act on it. She didn't suspect a thing. I knew you were the only one with the power to see me swing; it were torture. Yet you kept your silence. Why?'

'You gave me back my freedom,' answered Sally thickly. 'In return, I ensured you kept yours.'

'Thank you.'

'Thank *you*. I hold no ill feeling towards you, Nancy. You were under his control as much as I. Difference is, I didn't have the courage to end his life.'

Nancy's hardness surfaced. She lifted her chin. 'I can't believe I were so blind for so long. I convinced myself he loved me. I let him strike me time and again, telling myself he didn't mean it. I neglected my children to be with him, stole from my father to please him. Everything were for him.

'The thought of losing him filled me with such terror, I were prepared to do owt. Even at the cost of your safety.' She cringed at the admission. 'I've done some terrible things and for the remainder of my days must live with the guilt. But I don't regret removing him from this earth. I don't regret that forra second.'

'What made you see him for what he was?'

'That poison were intended for my father.' Nancy nodded when Sally shook her head in horror. 'Joseph wanted him gone and his hands on his brass. His words were like a pail of icy water in my face. He didn't love me at all. I knew that, then. He never had.'

Sally frowned at the question that had niggled at her for years. 'There's one thing I don't understand. How did he find me? Manchester is vast; just happening to see me at the workhouse is too incredible a coincidence. I'm right, aren't I?' she asked when Nancy looked away.

Her eyes burned with humiliation. 'He ordered me to ask around. I sniffed about the row like a stray mongrel, desperate for scraps, desperate to please *him*. Dishing out Father's dinner one day, I heard him enquire about your health to Martha Smith. She told of the hard time you'd had, said you'd worked for that mother and daughter what were in the newspapers.

'Father never throws nowt out; I searched his owd papers for the article. It said where it occurred, so we had an idea of the area you lived. We trawled Ancoats for days and one afternoon saw two little 'uns playing with yon dog.

'We waited forra sighting of thee but the dog must've remembered Joseph's scent. It began barking, forcing us to scarper, but we knew then we had the right street. Then Joseph said we were collecting your mam. I were flummoxed but he said not to ask questions. You see, he . . . he . . .'

'He what?'

'He said he'd get shot of thee so we could be together. I didn't know his plan but God forgive me, I went along with it. I'm so sorry . . . that I'd stoop to such wickedness . . . Leaving the workhouse, we spotted you. We couldn't believe it. He had me follow to see where you dwelled, while he . . .' Sighing, she closed her eyes.

'Dragged my mother to that stinking lodging house?'

'Oh, Sally. You'll likely not believe that your mam's state and how he treated her hurt me, but it's true. How's she . . . faring?'

'She's as happy as a body could wish.'

'Lord, tha must loathe me. *I* loathe me. All I were focused on were us skipping off into the sunset, foolish bitch that I am. I realise now he collected your mam to bribe you back. If we'd not seen you at the workhouse, he'd have lain in wait in this here street till he spotted you. He'd have let me murder Father then used the money to scarper with thee.'

Sally released a long sigh. 'Put it behind you, Nancy, as I have. Forget him, live your life. Concentrate on your children, your father. Don't let his ghost consume you. Don't let him win.'

'By, you're a fine woman. I wish I had an ounce of your goodness.' Nancy shook her head in wonder then drew up her shawl. 'Goodbye, lass.'

'Goodbye, Nancy.'

Having laid to rest another demon from her past, Sally walked into Tommy's arms with a lighter heart. She could now put to him the secret wish she'd carried for so long. Only thoughts of seeing Nancy had deterred her; now, nothing stood in her way.

He wrapped his arms around her waist, saying 'I love you.'

'And I love you.' She glanced about, then took a deep breath. 'Tommy, there's something I've been meaning to speak with you about. How would you feel—' There was tugging at her skirt. Glancing down, she saw Jonathan and Jenny smiling up.

'How would I feel about what, my love?'

'Oh, it will keep.'

She took the children's hands and Tommy did likewise. And as they danced, Shield bounding between, they heard more than one guest remark that they made the most handsome family they had ever seen.

Evening turned to night and the exhausted children were put to bed. The adults continued the jollifications and it wasn't until much later that Sally and Tommy snatched a moment alone. He found her by the window, pink-cheeked but still smiling.

'Finally, I've got thee to myself,' he whispered, nuzzling her neck.

'Tommy, people are looking!'

'Let them.'

She giggled then stared at him earnestly. 'What I said earlier . . . that I wanted to speak with you . . .'

'Aye. What is it?'

'I want to return to Spring Row.'

He pulled back to gaze at her.

'Years ago, I promised myself if I had the chance, I'd leave the smoke of Manchester behind and raise Jonathan amongst Breightmet's green hills. I miss it, Tommy. I miss the freshness, the meadows, the tranquillity. I miss the people, the cottages; the row itself. Manchester holds a place in my heart and always will, but it's not home. Spring Row . . . It's like a yearning inside. Can you understand?'

'I can, but Sally . . .' He ran a hand through his hair. 'The memories, everything you've been through—'

'Cannot hurt me any more. Not now I have you.'

'But your family, friends, this place. You'd leave all this behind?'

'I'd still see them. Bolton is but a train journey away; one I'm sure I could brave with you beside me. As for this place . . . I'll explain later.' She caressed his cheek. 'You were willing to leave behind all you hold dear for me. But I know that, in your heart, you share the same love for Breightmet as I. And there's Jenny. Dolly's parents deserve to see their grandchild grow. She's all they have of their daughter. I couldn't take that from them.'

Tommy's eyes could have shone with no purer love. He kissed her tenderly. 'Dear God, I love you. More than you'll ever know.'

'I simply pray . . .'

He followed her gaze to Rose, who was chatting with Grace. 'Will she agree?'

'I do hope so. I cannot be without her, not again. Yet the thought of taking her from Aunt Grace pains me, Tommy.'

'As you said yourself, Bolton's but a train away.'

'Still . . .'

'You'll not know until you ask, love.'

Sally's heart was thumping as she took her mother aside, but she needn't have worried. Rose shared her sentiments entirely: where her daughter went, she went. Grace shed a tear upon hearing, but once Sally reassured her they would visit often, agreed she must do what made her happy.

'It's what youse both want?' asked Ivy excitedly.

Tommy nodded. 'Mind, we might have to live on here a good while,' he told Sally. 'Cottages don't come empty often.'

Ivy bit her lip. 'Nay, they don't, but . . .'

'But what, Mrs Morgan?'

'There's a young Irish couple moved in last year. The lass were telling me only yesterday they'll soon be moving on.'

Sally laughed delightedly. 'Oh, what marvellous good fortune!' Bewilderment replaced her joy, when she saw Tommy's expression. 'My love?'

He stared helplessly at Ivy, and it was she who mumbled, 'The cottage they dwell in . . . It's your owd 'un, lass.'

Sally was silent. When finally she turned to her husband, her voice was calm. 'How would you feel living there? If you're fine with it, I am.'

'But . . . the hell. The horrors you went through . . . I don't want you reliving that past every day. Surely you'd never know peace beneath that roof? I vowed today, besides the rest, to protect you. That means all of you, body *and* mind. I'll not have memories of that divil clinging to our marriage, our family, our *home* like a cancer.'

'That could only happen if we allowed it to.' She rested her palm against his chest. 'Would living there be so very difficult for *you*, my love?'

Tommy answered without hesitation: 'Truthfully? Nay. Nay, it wouldn't. My past doesn't dwell within those walls. I hold no nightmares of the place. It's not myself I'm thinking about, but you. And it's forgetting all that's been that I want to help you to do.'

'But I don't want to forget, Tommy.'

'You . . . don't—?'

'Hear the lass out, lad,' murmured Ivy, nodding slowly, and Sally knew the older woman understood.

'To forget is to pretend it didn't happen. It did. And in a way, I'm almost glad. I don't expect you to understand,' Sally told him when he frowned. 'I realise it must sound madness to you. But you see, I view life as I never would had I not encountered Joseph. I'm grateful for each day, every breath. Enduring what I did makes what I have now all the sweeter. I cherish this, with you, more than you'll ever know, *because* of him. No, I don't ever want to forget, I know that now. What I want is to accept. Accept that it happened, put it behind me, finally, and live happily. Whether in that cottage or the other side of the world makes no difference to me. None whatsoever. It truly wouldn't to you, too?'

'What you went through there, it pains me, imagining . . . I'll not deny it. But if you can face it, I can, if it's really what you want . . . ?'

'It is.'

'You're certain?'

'As long as I'm there with you then yes, I'm certain. It will be different this time. We'll make it a happy home, we six, together.' She held out a hand and smiled. 'And now, Mr Morgan, would you care to dance?'

As had Nancy, he shook his head in awe. 'Mrs Morgan, you *incredible* woman, I'd be honoured.'

Chapter 38

'SIT YOUR ARSE by the fire, you big bugger, afore you knock me south.' Ivy jerked her head across her kitchen, expression stern, but couldn't contain a smile as Shield sloped off. 'He's like a bucking hare, ain't sat still since you arrived.'

'He's excited to be back, I suspect,' said Sally, then chuckled, seeing her mother grinning at Ivy's no-nonsense way.

Ivy sat with a groan. 'Eeh, my bleedin' back. Rotten owd age, I could swing for it.'

Rose could hold back no longer and laughed. 'Oh, Ivy, you're a tonic. I sympathise, mind. My knees ain't what they were; creak like an owd barn door, they do.'

'Aye. They don't know when they're well off, these young 'uns, Rose.' She nodded to Sally. 'You wait till you're owd and grey. There'll come a day when your crumbling bones struggle to shift thee.'

'I shan't mind. I'll have my husband to carry me in his arms.'

Ivy hooted with laughter. 'Soppy bugger, yer. By, but it's good seeing you sat there, lass. Have you really no regrets? Don't you miss yon lodging house, not even a bit?'

'No,' she answered truthfully. 'It shall remain what I intended, with or without me. That's what matters. Oh, Anna's face when I handed her the keys and deeds. The woman whose money bought that house, all she suffered at her hands . . . Anna deserves it far more than I ever did.' She peered around the cosy kitchen she'd so missed. 'Oh, it's good to be back.

'Truly, it is,' she insisted when Ivy shot Rose a look. 'I feel nothing but hope, Mrs Morgan; that won't change upon Tommy's return. Do you remember my taking the carrier's cart all those moons ago?' she asked quietly.

'I do.'

'As we passed through the row, I admit, I vowed never to set foot inside there again. But it wasn't the cottage I loathed and feared, I know that now. From today, it will be what it never could under Joseph's rule. It will be a home.'

Ivy's eyes were suspiciously bright. 'Drink your tea, lass, afore it grows cowd.'

Sally and her mother shared a tender smile for this woman. Having her for a neighbour was a delight; a friend, more so. To call her family was a blessing from heaven. Their futures were all the brighter for having her.

Voices sounded beyond the door. The children burst inside, holding hands.

'Go see, Mama, go see!' said Jonathan excitedly.

'See, see!' mimicked Jenny.

Sally chucked the toddler under the chin then ruffled her son's hair. He had no idea she was no stranger to the cottage soon to be his home. And she hoped he never would. She glanced to Tommy in the doorway. He held up a key and winked, and she smiled.

'Let your mam and father look round by theirselfs,' said Ivy. 'We'll stop here, eh, and have some fruit cake.'

With her mother's encouraging hug, Sally took her husband's hand. His love lent her strength and as they passed up the familiar path, her step didn't falter.

Inside, he hung back and she was grateful for his understanding. As she'd secretly feared, past demons lingered and she knew if she was to be happy here, she alone must banish them. No one could do it for her.

She wandered through the rooms, long-ago memories flitting then disappearing. At last, she returned to Tommy, pale but calm.

'Can you face it, Sally?'

'Yes.' Though she spoke truthfully, she knew pain flickered behind her eyes.

He wrapped his arms around her. Then he took her face and kissed her.

Taking her hand, he led her to the next room. Again, he held her then kissed her softly. This, he repeated in each. They spoke no words and needed none. After holding her in the last room, his kiss was more tender still. When they drew apart, Sally knew he saw a different look: one of peace and hope.

She stared around through fresh eyes. With each embrace, each kiss, the badness had seeped away. This wasn't a house any more but a home. They had blessed it with their love.

'Happy?'

'Happy,' she answered on a sigh of serenity.

They left hand in hand. At the gate, she motioned to Ivy's. 'You go in. I'll follow in a moment.'

Alone, she gazed at her new home and smiled for the future. She envisioned family life: eating dinner together at the table, the children's laughter as they played with Shield, sipping tea with her mother by the fire on wintry nights, she and Tommy making love beneath the eaves . . .

'Hello, missis.'

Sally turned in surprise.

The child, a fluffy cat in her arms, was taller, cleaner, less pinch-faced. None the less, there was no mistaking her. 'Lily? It *is* you! Oh, how lovely to see you!'

'Please don't be angry with me.'

It was then that Sally noticed the dread in the blue eyes, the nervous biting of her lip. 'Lily, what's wrong? Why on earth would I be angry with you? I'm delighted to see you after all these years.'

'Aye?'

'Of course.' She tapped the tip of her nose. 'Why would I ever be angry with you, lass?'

'Because of Uncle Joseph.'

'Your . . . Uncle . . . ? Dear God, it was *you*? Tommy said the child who helped them was named Lily, but I never . . . never imagined . . .'

'I'm sorry, missis. I never knew you were his wife and when I saw you in fat Nellie's, and what he'd done to you, and I knew it were you from the market, I cried, and I'm sorry, and, and—'

'Shhh, Lily, it's all right. It's all right.' Sally drew her, sobbing, into her arms.

'He were wicked, he were, wicked. I thought you'd not want to be my friend if you knew he were my uncle. I thought you'd be angry, that you'd tell me to bugger off.'

'Oh, Lily. You're as innocent as a lamb. You helped the Morgans rescue me. You saved my life. You've been only brave, clever and good. I could never be angry with you, never.'

Lily wiped her nose on her sleeve. 'You mean it, missis?'

'Of course.'

The cat struggled for release. Setting it down, Lily pulled a face. 'Bleedin' heavy, that thing. I've carried her all the way. Never go nowhere without Clover, I don't.'

A slow frown creased Sally's brow. 'How did you know I was here?'

'I were at the market, earlier, saw thee and another lady and Mr Morgan's son boarding a cart. I thought my eyes were having me on.'

'The lady's my mother. And Mr Morgan's son, Tommy, he and I are married now, Lily. We left Manchester this morning.' She pointed to her cottage. 'There's our new home.'

Lily smiled. 'I saw that babby of yourn, an' all. Grown, ain't he?'

It suddenly struck her that Lily and her son were cousins. Lord, but it was a small world. 'You can come say hello to him if you like.'

'Can I, missis?'

Sally nodded, wondering how this lovely girl had come from the womb of such a terrible woman. And with thoughts of Alice, her smile melted.

'Does your mother know you're here?'

'Nay. Long gone, she is.'

'Gone?'

'Aye. Father had enough and slung her out. She's been gone this past year, thanks be to God. He'll not mind me seeing thee, for he knows you never did wrong. He couldn't stand Uncle Joseph, neither.'

'Well, I don't know what to say. And your mother's never returned?'

'Nay and I'm glad. She worsened after *he* died, began drinking more and thumping us about. She said you drove him to do away with hisself with your wicked ways. We knew she were wrong; he were the wicked 'un, not thee. Home's better, now. Father's not sad and he's gorra job. And our Lizzie's returned with her babby.'

Their conversation at the market, of Lily's sister allowing her master's son in Manchester to have his way, came back to Sally. Little had she known it was Alice's Lizzie the child was referring to. 'I'm so very glad you're happy, Lily.'

'Ta, missis.'

She held out a hand and asked, 'Shall I take you to see your cousin?'

Lily clasped it with a nod and a grin. 'Stay there, you,' she told Clover. 'The missis here's gorra dog the size of a horse. Gobble you up in one, he would.'

'If we hurry, there may be some cake left,' Sally said as they headed for Ivy's. 'Are you hungry?'

The child smiled at what she clearly still deemed a daft question. 'Do fishes have a fondness for water?'

Epilogue

BIRDSONG BROUGHT A smile to Sally. Gazing at larks swooping and gliding through the azure sky, she sighed contentedly.

She was with her mother and Jonathan, Shield trotting alongside. They were walking through an emerald-green field abloom with cowslip and buttercups, the air heady with love. Rose held Jonathan up and he laughed as she planted kisses on his cheek.

When he turned to look at his mother with smiling eyes of the same sapphire-blue, Sally's heart swelled with pride for the fine-looking boy he'd become. They sat in the sweet-smelling grass and she lifted her face to the sun with a rush of such happiness, it stole her breath. Rose drew her close and she rested her head on her shoulder.

Her heart skipped as she caught sight of a tall, dark-haired man heading towards them across the field. His face was in shadow but she knew without question that she loved him, and that he loved her. In his muscular arms, he carried a girl with hair the colour of corn. She lifted a tiny hand and Sally waved back . . .

This time, there was no pain. The beautiful scene didn't blur. As Tommy drew nearer, a long-ago whisper echoed on the breeze. And Sally smiled.

Indeed, all was not over. It was just the beginning.

Acknowledgements

To my agent, Judith Murdoch, for everything, and my editor, Francesca Best, for her sound advice and understanding. Thanks to you both.

A MOTHER'S DILEMMA

For my readers – thanks to you all. Without you, it's simply words on a page. And my ABC, always x

About the experienced masters in the craft, there is the quiet canniness of the devil.

*Benjamin Waugh, founder of the
NSPCC, on baby farmers*

Author's Note

It was whilst researching for something else that I first stumbled upon the subject of baby farming. Both horrified and fascinated, I was driven to find out more and the idea for this book was born.

Baby farming was a scourge of the Victorian era. The term referred to the act of accepting custody of an infant, usually illegitimate, in exchange for money. Social conditions of the time forced desperate mothers to use such services in their droves. However, though most baby farmers were paid with the understanding that care would be provided, not all were as trustworthy as they seemed. Once the fee had disappeared, the child quickly followed suit.

The heinous practice was widespread and vast numbers of children were disposed of by so-called 'angel makers'. Rising numbers of convictions for murder and neglect finally forced Parliament to confront the epidemic, and proper fostering and adoption regulations were introduced. The last baby farmer to be hanged was in 1907.

Research for *A Mother's Dilemma* made for grim reading, but immersing myself in a subject matter is vital to bring the reader an authentic portrayal. Bygone times were hard for the people that lived them and I always strive to weave the fact into my stories. I do hope you enjoy Jewel's journey.

Emma Hornby

Chapter 1
1856

THE BABY'S GUSTY yell filled the kitchen again and Minnie Maddox chuckled. A healthy pair of lungs on the tiniest scraps of life always brought warm happiness to her. It was the quiet ones you had to keep an eye to, for Death's cold claws never hovered too far away. Were it to catch you unawares, the shadowed fiend would spirit a body away in half a heartbeat. She should know. Hadn't she borne witness to such, time and again?

Abandoning her baking and wiping her floury hands on her apron, she then lifted the lid of a small saucepan. Before dipping a fingertip inside and wiggling it around to check the temperature, she glanced to the damp-stained wall to her left. Muffled shouts could be heard from next door and, though Minnie wasn't one to eavesdrop on other folks' business, how could you close your ears to such goings-on when the dividing bricks were as thin as theirs were and the voices so loud with the passion of their disagreement?

'Please. Oh, won't tha reconsider?'

'I'll not waste another breath on this, woman.'

'But Fred, we could make it work, aye, if only you'd give it half a chance—'

A thud, sounding like a fist meeting a tabletop in

angry frustration, smothered the pleas. 'Nay, I said! That's an end to it.'

Minnie lowered her stare with a small, sorry sigh. As she knew it would, seconds later, her good friend and neighbour Flora Nightingale's harsh weeping pushed next through the crumbling plaster: 'Husband, please, please . . .'

'I'll not – cannot – fetch up another fella's babby.' Fred's words had lost a little of their hardness but still, his tone was firm. 'It's a child of our own or none at all.'

'I'm fifty-one years of age, Fred. There's been norra glimpse of a monthly bleed from me this past year or more – it's over for me that way, can't you see? Yet there's babbies aplenty needing homes still and always shall be; we could give such a thing to one. A poor mite without a mam or father to call their own could be ours, if only you'd—'

'It's not to be for us and that's that. The Lord has made His decision loud and clear and it's not for us to question His design.' He paused. Then he took a loud, shuddering breath that relayed locked up inside himself a mountain of disappointment and pain. 'Now, we'll speak on this no more. That's an order, Flora.'

Gulping sobs were the only sound as his wife struggled to stem her heartache in compliance, then silence fell. Minnie wiped away a tear for the couple next door and returned her attention to her task.

When the child yelled out once more, this time, it brought no laughter to Minnie. Instead, she bit her lip, for if she heard as easily as she did business from the Nightingales' dwelling, so they must hear well enough the noises in here, and how much worse must Flora's emptiness stab to hear what she craved more than anything else in the world? Minnie was heartsore for her – for the pair of them.

She craned her neck to glance to the staircase, calling, 'Eliza, lass? Cradle the new mite, will thee, whilst I prepare its grub? Poor divil shall waken the rest, else, and that's the last thing we need.'

A girl around ten years of age, a floral-patterned scarf tied around her head, emerged at the top step. Her face, hands and apron were grubby with coal dirt and her equally dark brows drew together as she clattered down to the kitchen. 'Thought tha told me to see to the fire up yonder?' She flicked her eyes in the direction from which she'd just come. 'I can't be in two places at once, you know. If we're to make the bedroom presentable for the next what calls with a full belly, you can't keep yelling for me to aid you in this and t' other—'

'Shurrup blathering and see to him, will thee?' Minnie cut in mildly. 'He just wants a cuddle. Reassuring, like. He's likely fretting for his mam.'

With an exaggerated sigh and a roll of her eyes, the girl crossed to the sagging bed wedged into the alcove by the fire. Arranged in a neat line the length of it and wrapped in an assortment of clean but ragged coverings were half a dozen bundles – babies of varying ages. Eliza reached for the smallest one snuggled between two others and held him against her chest, making clucking sounds of comfort.

The mixture in the pan Minnie was occupied with, which had been warming by the fire for most of the day, still held some heat; she nodded, satisfied. She poured the pap – a creamy concoction made up of water, flour and animal milk, sweetened sufficiently – into a glass nursing bottle. Checking that the fine twine that attached the sparkling white calf's teat to the bottle's neck was secure, she too now crossed to the bed. Before relieving Eliza of her burden, she drew a little of the food through to warm the teat, thus heightening the chance of the baby not rejecting it. Some children required gentle manipulation for them to believe it was what nature intended and not the artificial but adequate thing it was. She prayed this child would be easy to hoodwink.

'There, now. That's right. Ay, you're not fussy, are thee? Good lad,' Minnie cooed with approval as the scrawny fingers clamped around the feeding vessel, drawing it closer. Grasping the teat between his lips, he drank heartily, eyes too large for his monkey-like face at once growing drowsy with satisfaction.

Her own misted at the sight. Poor young devil – and oh, his poor young mother, too. Hadn't she wept something awful this morning when she'd deposited him here? She'd loved him, that much was plain. But what was an unfortunate of this city, with nothing in life, to do? She couldn't very well have kept him with her in the one room she shared with two other women of her trade, could she? Customers wouldn't much like that, nay, and besides, it was no life for a child, his mother had insisted, and Minnie had agreed. Best he was given half a chance, eh, at this struggle most called life?

As she had then, filled with pity watching the streetwalker count out the necessary coins, Minnie silently swore again she'd do her best for him. And she would. She did, for them all. Every child who entered her home would only leave it for one better than anything its mam could have dreamed to offer it. That was her mission. As far as she knew, she'd failed none yet.

'Min?' Eliza's whisper sounded behind her, pulling her from her musings.

'Aye, lass?'

'This one's dead.'

She swallowed in cold dread. 'What?'

'This one's dead,' the girl repeated.

Slowly, Minnie forced herself to turn. In the crook of Eliza's arm, the grey-white face and colourless lips outlined with their ring of blue confirmed it. Minnie deposited the feeding child into the girl's free arm and lifted the still-warm body of the other, larger child. But for his bloodless features, he appeared to be resting. Just sleeping the deep slumber of the innocent, not dead, gone ... Her voice was hollow. 'All right, poor angel. Aunt Min is here.'

'Seems to have slipped away, quiet like, whilst you were about your baking. He'd not have suffered none, Min,' the girl offered gently as reassurance.

Though Minnie knew her words to be right, still the truth did little to dampen the hurt, the guilt. *One baby departs this earth, another arrives to take its place in the world* ... She released a pain-filled sigh.

'Don't be for blaming yourself,' continued Eliza, as though reading her thoughts. 'He weren't for settling from the off, was he?'

She shook her head. 'Mind, it's not only that he were sickly in health and strength, nay. He's pined away, that's what. Watched him wither before my eyes, I have, these past weeks. What was there for me to do? Feed, bathe, clothe – love even, aye – I can do that. Mend a broken heart, I can't. That's what's finished him off. Being parted from his mam proved too much for the poor soul, I reckon.' She looked to Eliza for confirmation and, receiving it in way of a nod, breathed deeply again in an attempt to pull herself together. She couldn't afford the luxury of a good weep; besides, what good would that do? She had the scant burial to plan, the others to care for, her home, her baking to see to. Babies came and babies went. One way or another.

Throughout the following hours, necessary arrangements were conducted and life in general behind the door of number six Kirby Street continued, as it must. Now, the departed soul, washed and wrapped in a white blanket, lay in a tiny, rough wood coffin, which the undertaker's boy had carried upstairs shortly before to the bedroom Minnie and Eliza shared. The remaining infants, as though sensing his departure and the heaviness in air wrought by the loss, had been quieter than usual – Minnie was thankful for it. She couldn't wait to get into bed later and allow herself that cry. Aye, that's what she needed: a cup of tea and a good bawl. The latter would have to wait a few more hours, but the former, she could do.

Eliza, one eye on the bed and the sleeping babies within, the other on the ancient blanket she was darning, glanced up as Minnie passed her fireside chair en route to the teapot. 'All right?'

'Aye. I'll grab some air forra minute, lass. Just yell should one of the babbies stir, I'll hear thee.'

The early June sun barely touched the dying afternoon. Sitting like a dull white disc in the smoke-choked sky, it acknowledged the inhabitants of this grey industrial city with little more than a passing glance. The daily struggle of its rays to pierce the sulphurous fog from an army of cotton-mill, factory and domestic chimneys, whose numbers had astronomically increased throughout the century, had left its mark – it had given up the fight long ago. Even in the height of summer, the haphazard maze of cobbled streets, lanes and narrow courts remained imprisoned in impenetrable gloom. Unsurprisingly, it mirrored the mood of an already suffering populace entirely.

Glancing to her left, Minnie eyed the mass of sooty

red bricks that was the Manchester Flint Glass Works. The main works building of the ever-expanding premises, nestled at the south side of Kirby Street and adjoining Canal Street, loomed like a guard overseeing its workforce. Indeed, a large fraction of those who laboured hard beyond its doors resided in the surrounding streets. Situated strategically along the bank of the head of the Islington Branch Canal, which fed into the main line of nearby Ashton Canal, it transported its raw materials and finished products through the short body of water continually. Canals fostered the growth of industry with their ability to carry bulky goods long distances cheaply and efficiently – like many other businesses, the glass works took full advantage of the fact.

Aye well, thought Minnie with a bitter shake of her head. So long as the labour was completed in as short a space of time as possible and the profits were healthy, the masters were happy. Mind, much of their workforce were not afforded the luxury of those descriptions – healthy, happy – were they?

Her long-departed husband had been employed there most of his life – today, along with hundreds more men, women and children, Fred Nightingale next door still was. He and her Walter had been firm friends since they were kiddies and, when Fred secured the neighbouring house shortly after his marriage, she and new bride Flora had instantly grown just as close. A grand couple, they were, and a great comfort to her when Walter succumbed to the harsh conditions of his trade.

The life of a glass blower was not for the meek of heart. The majority died young. The long, irregular hours were hardship enough. Yet it was the great heat that proved the crux for many. Temperatures reached such hellish heights that it was not unheard of for the very boards on which the workers stood to catch fire beneath their feet.

Besides the obvious susceptibility to burns, as well as violent bouts of nausea and rheumatic disorders, their sight and lungs were also affected – her beloved's red eyes and rattling wheeze were what she remembered most about him now. The chest affliction that carried him off had taken a piece of her, too. But for the now-grown children born from her womb and those she cared for today with as much attentiveness and affection – none more than Eliza – she'd have followed him to the soil many a long year before this one, she was sure.

And what had she to show for an early widowhood and the torment that came with it? Her gaze flicked behind her indoors, to linger on the sideboard against the back wall. Winking atop it in the fire's glow stood an eight-inch-tall, thick glass candlestick of cut prisms, presented to her after Walter's death as a token of acknowledgement for services rendered. Quite exquisite; a fine example of industrial art. However, a poor comparison to a blood-and-bone companion.

Yet despite it all, he'd had work, and that wasn't something to sniff at. Brass to pay the rent, keep the cold from their marrow and hunger from their bellies. The unemployed of this city would give their right arm and leg, as well as eventually their life, she'd bet, for the chance to earn an honest crust. It was how it was. Aye, she'd known loss, but who hadn't?

Again, Minnie's eyes travelled inside, only this time towards the stairs and the chilled body of the poor dead babe now free of this life of want. Fresh tears stung. She hugged herself.

'Hello, Minnie.'

Lost in thought, she jumped at the quiet greeting

and fingers squeezing her shoulder. 'Flora, love. All right?'

The slightly built woman rested her back against the bricks by her own front door. 'Catching some air, Minnie.'

'Aye, and me.' She stole a sidelong look at her friend. 'And how's Fred?' she asked carefully, not wanting to give away that she'd heard their ruckus earlier and embarrass the woman.

Her response was barely above a whisper. 'Abed. He's on night work the night.'

Minnie turned now and eyed Flora properly. She looked terrible, all pale cheeks and purple-rimmed eyes. 'You sure you're well, wench?'

'Nay, if I'm honest. That pain's nagging me again. Feel queasy summat awful, an' all.'

Minnie frowned worriedly. For many months now, her friend had been blighted by internal complaints and sickness. She also seemed to have a permanent headache – stress, Flora reckoned, but coupled with her other symptoms, Minnie wasn't so sure. She'd attempted several times to coax her into getting the doctor out, but Flora wouldn't hear of it. His services cost money they could ill afford; she'd be right as rain soon, she'd insist, yet her ailments showed no signs of abating. She looked to be getting worse, if anything.

'Fred said nay again.' Flora shrugged miserably. 'I don't know why I keep going on about it. Does no good at all. He'll not consider another fella's offspring.'

Minnie's voice was soft. 'Some men can be funny about things like that, that's all. He's not denying thee to hurt thee, wench.'

'I know. He's a good husband to me. I just can't understand . . . It matters norra single bit to me. I just want . . . any would do, any.'

'Eeh, love.'

Tears had thickened Flora's words, but she cleared her throat and a wistful smile appeared. 'Remember when me and my Fred were wed, Minnie, and came to live here?'

'I do. I were just thinking on that a minute since, as it happens.'

'Ay, we had all our lives before us. So hopeful, we were, for the future. Never did we think that the Almighty would turn His back on us and deny us the one thing we both yearned for more than owt else.'

Minnie had heard such lamentations hundreds of times over the years and now, as always, she simply listened. It was what Flora needed: a frequent, open ear to which she could unburden her heartache. Minnie, unable to imagine what a motherless existence must be like, offered it always, willingly.

'Fred says it's His will we weren't blessed,' Flora continued. 'I don't know. It just don't seem fair to me. I'd have made a good mam, Minnie.'

''Ere, course tha would.' She reached across and squeezed her hand. 'By, the best, I reckon. I'd not let these babbies I care for go to just anyone, now would I? And ain't I allus said, you and Fred could have had any one of the poor blighters what's come to me. For I know you'd provide the love and care they deserve, no doubt about that, nay. But Flora, lovey . . .' Minnie broke off to sigh.

As much as it would pain her, and likely the woman beside her, to say this, it needed voicing. It was doing her friend's health – not to mention her marriage – no good. No good at all. 'I think it might be time to . . . you know. Accept things as they are, like. Fred'll not be swayed and, well, husbands are the ones what have the final say.

I'm that sorry, oh I am, to be saying this. But for your own wellness of mind and heart . . . you need to accept how it must be, wench. It'll make you iller still, else.'

Flora didn't respond, simply heaved a long, slow breath that seemed to come from her very soul. 'Can I come in and see them, the babbies? Give them a bit of a cuddle, like?'

'Course you can.' Minnie nodded, smiling. 'You do most days, don't you? Have I ever turned you away afore now?'

'I'll not be in your road? You're not busy?'

'Nay, nay.'

Eliza had dozed off and, likewise, in the bed facing her chair, the line of babies slept on peacefully. Flora's eyes shone as she approached them, and Minnie had to swallow down her pity. Her words to Flora about putting aside her wish of becoming a mother herself had fallen on deaf ears. Flora wouldn't – couldn't – ever accept it, it was obvious.

'Ah, the new angel. A tiny thing, he is.' Flora brushed a finger across the cheek of the child Minnie had fed earlier. Suddenly, she turned, eyebrows knotted. 'Where's t' other one?'

'Upstairs.' Immediately, her eyes were wet, and she had to gulp her next words out. 'The precious thing passed away, Flora love, earlier on.'

Despite her own upset at the news, Flora came to put her arm around her friend's shoulders. 'You're not to blame yourself.'

'I do all the same. Babbies come and babbies go, I know it, but it never gets easier.'

It was the other woman's turn to offer some sage advice. 'You did your best for the poor mite, I'm sure.' She motioned to the girl by the fire. 'Look at the lass akip, there. And where would she be, I'd like to know, but for your kindness? You kept her on with you when no one wanted the sorry, half-lame soul. Fed, clothed and kept a roof over her head, you have, when many a body would've left it to the workhouse to provide.'

'Aye, well. I weren't aware of Eliza's bad legs at the time. She were but a few hours old the day her mam dropped her off here – it weren't 'til later, after her mam had long scarpered, that I noticed her affliction. And well, when couple after couple turned their noses up at adopting her because of it, what were I to do?'

Flora inclined her head again, this time to the rag rug and the animals snoring softly there before the leaping flames. The ancient one-eyed dog lifted its head, yawned and returned to its dreams. The contented three-legged cat with only half a tail, however, didn't stir. 'And them two – not to mention countless other strays you've took in afore them?'

Minnie shrugged. 'Couldn't very well leave the buggers to starve or freeze to death on the streets, now could I?'

'Nay, and shall I tell thee why? For you're the keeper of the waifs and unwanted of this city, and honest as the day is long. For you've a golden heart, allus have had. But your ways, you play them down. Truth is, you love that girl there as if she were one of your own. The animals, an' all. As for the babbies you find new lives for, well, just what would they do without you? Be at the mercy of others pretending to ply a similar trade to yours, that's what. Now, admit it.'

'I do, aye. I grow to love every one of them, be it beast or child, what passes over yon threshold, however long I have them for,' Minnie admitted, smiling.

'Don't ever doubt your goodness. Promise me.'

'Aye, wench.'

'And you'll cease blaming yourself over that poor dead babby up yonder?'

Minnie held Flora close. 'I will.'

'Good. Good.'

'There's some tea not long since brewed if you're for wanting a sup?' Minnie asked softly, filled with love for this small woman she didn't know what she'd do without. However, her friend didn't answer and, when Minnie pulled back to look at her, her lips bunched together. Flora was ashen and was gritting her teeth in obvious discomfort. 'Flora? What is it, what's to do?'

'That pain, it's back again.' She pressed her palm to her ribs. 'Don't fret none, it'll pass in a minute,' she gasped out.

'For the love of God, wench, will you see the doctor? Please, for me? This has gone on long enough, you can't keep putting it off and—'

'I'll be off home, now, Minnie,' Flora cut in quietly.

'Wench—'

'I'll be seeing thee, love.'

Insides churning with frustration and worry, Minnie could only watch as her friend slunk away. The front door shut and she lowered herself into the chair facing Eliza's. However, her gaze remained on the door and, despite the passing minutes, her anxiety refused to leave her. Possible causes affecting her friend's health flitted through her mind, each more fearsome than the last. What if it was this illness, that disease . . .

'Stop it,' she told herself firmly, though it did no good. Her friend needed medical attention, there were no two ways about it.

Suddenly, another thought struck and the worry lines faded from her brow. Flora wouldn't listen to her, that much was clear. Fred, on the other hand, was another matter.

Her eyes strayed to the clock and she quickly calculated the time yet to pass until the night shift began at the glass works. Mind made up, she folded her arms with a determined nod.

*

Eliza's frightened yell, swiftly followed by the fretful cries of several of the babies, hauled Minnie from her dreams in a heartbeat. A crick in her neck jarred as she bolted up; wincing, she rubbed the spot and blinked around the room, senses muggy with sleep.

The fire had burned low and she had to squint through the gathering gloom at the girl. 'What's all this? What's to do with you? Set the babbies off, you have, with your noise—'

'Never mind my noise,' Eliza cut in, jabbing a finger to the street outside. 'Some mad swine hammered hell out of yon door; frickened me half to death, it did— Eeh!' she added when, sure enough, on cue, another heavy thump sounded. 'Ay, Min, what's afoot? I'm scared.'

'Now then, no need for all that.' She tried to sound more nonchalant than she felt. Moments like this, when it could be anyone out there in this impoverished, crime-riddled city trying to gain entry, made her wish all the more that she still had a man about the place. But she didn't. She must be the protector, always. Squaring her shoulders, she headed for the door.

The knocking struck up again as she reached it, more insistent than before. When she opened it wide, an admonishment ready on her tongue for whoever was causing the disturbance, she found herself almost barged to the ground as the visitor rushed inside. Gazing up, her anger instantly gave way to dread. He wore no shirt and his dark red hair stood up in all directions, as though he'd rushed straight from his bed to here. Though his eyes sparked with emotion, the rest of him was expressionless, as if frozen in panic.

'Fred? Lad, speak to me.'

His mouth flapped open and closed but no words emerged. He shook his head.

'Flora . . .' The name trembled from Minnie's lips and in the next moment she'd pushed past Fred and was running outside, through the Nightingales' open door and into the kitchen. She stopped dead in her tracks.

'Mi— Minnie. Mother of God, the pain . . .'

'Wench!' She hurried towards the table and her friend beside it in a heap on the hard floor. Next to her, a chair lay on its side – likely its falling over the sound which had awoken Fred. 'What happened?'

Having followed Minnie home, Fred answered for his wife. 'I heard a crash and her cry out like a beast in pain. When I ran downstairs she were lying there like this. She couldn't speak, then, with the shock, like. I came straight to yours, didn't know what to do.' He crouched beside her to stroke his wife's head. 'Flora? You well now, lass?'

'Course she ain't ruddy well.' Minnie spoke more harshly than she'd intended, worry and not a little anger bursting out before she could stop it. 'The poor love's been unwell for months and months – why didn't you notice, Fred? Why didn't you drag that doctor round here to attend to her? And now see what's happened, look at the state she's in—'

'It's not . . . not Fred's fault. I've hid it from him, Minnie. He knew nowt . . . nowt about it.'

Fred's face creased with hurt. 'Why, Flora?'

'I didn't want you fretting is all. I thought it'd . . . pass soon enough.'

'Eeh, lass, you should have told me!'

'I know, I'm sorry, I—' A wail ripped from Flora's throat, killing her speech. 'Merciful God, my insides . . . the pain . . . !'

As though absorbing all he'd heard, Fred released a low gasp. His face had turned corpse grey and he grasped Minnie's arm with such force she winced. 'Fred?'

'Flora's father, and her grandfather afore him . . .'

'What? What?'

'They both died from the stomach cancer. God above, it can't be. My Flora can't . . . She can't . . .'

Minnie tried desperately to swallow down the shock and horror clogging her throat, but it was useless; she burst into tears. Her friend had stated only a few short hours ago her belief that God had turned His back on them. For reasons she'd never fathom, it really did seem He had. She fumbled for Fred's hand and squeezed. By now, Flora was slipping in and out of consciousness. Minnie shook her by the shoulders to rouse her. 'Love, stay awake. Please. You're going to be just fine, you'll see. Fred's off to fetch the doctor.' To him, she added, 'Quickly, lad. Go now.'

'Why didn't I give consent to taking on one of them babbies of yourn?' he murmured, eyes fixed on his wife's face, as though he hadn't heard Minnie. 'It's all she ever wanted. All she wanted her life through. Had I, she'd have told me she were ill sooner. A child would have given her summat to want to go on for.' Gruff sobs bent him double. 'I could have fixed her broken heart and never did, were too hung up on my own feelings to think of hers and all. Lord forgive me!'

'You mustn't think like that. Now, the doctor, Fred,' Minnie told him, more firmly this time. 'Fetch him, go on.'

When he'd stumbled off she placed her palm on

Flora's stomach and, gently, felt about. The woman didn't stir and nothing, as far as Minnie could ascertain, seemed out of the ordinary. Then she shifted it around to Flora's side and immediately her fingers brushed a large, hard lump behind her ribs. Her mouth ran dry. Hand trembling, she retraced the area. She pressed it lightly. To her astonishment, the mass pushed back – she felt it clearly against her skin. She snatched her arm away with a cry.

It had almost felt for a moment there that something, some living thing . . . Minnie's lips parted and her mouth fell open. Her eyes followed suit; wide with incredulity, they studied the prone woman, now, in a fresh light. The months and months of sickness and lack of bleeds, the clear swell of Flora's normally flat breasts . . . 'Good God, it cannot be,' she murmured to the empty room. Her banging heart threatened to spring from her chest in euphoric realisation. Given her years of experience, the countless expectant mothers whose babies she'd helped bring into the world . . . How had she not noticed? She hadn't suspected a thing, never considered for a single moment . . . 'Wench? Wake up, please, wake up. Does tha hear me?'

'Mm?'

'Oh, Flora, love.' Minnie could barely give life to her words and her vision was blurry with tears. 'I think . . . Mother of God, I do actually believe— Eeh!' she exclaimed on broken laughter when, suddenly, like a river bursting its banks, water gushed from between Flora's legs.

'Minnie?' With a small frown, the woman blinked up at her drowsily. 'What's occurring? I'm . . . wet. Wet and . . . Why are you laughing? Where's my Fred? Where is he?'

'Oh, wench.' Tears of joy streamed down Minnie's cheeks unchecked. 'By, you daft bloody bugger, yer.' She reached for Flora's hand and kissed it soundly. 'Fancy you frightening the livers out of us like that and all the time . . . Flora, you're with ruddy child!' She bobbed her head in confirmation when her friend simply gazed at her. 'And said child is set to make its appearance – right now!'

Flora hadn't the chance to respond; her face contorted and she let out an agonised scream. 'Down below, it feels . . . I want to push!'

'Then you do it.' Gathering back control from sheer instinct, Minnie rolled up her sleeves with a firm nod. 'Listen to your body, wench. Do as it's telling thee and you'll not go far wrong. Now don't you fret none, for I'm here. I'll not let nowt happen to thee, you have my word on that.' Positioning herself between Flora's legs, she lifted her friend's skirts, whipped down her undergarments and examined her, murmuring soothingly all the while. From what she could tell, this miracle child would be here in a matter of minutes, if not sooner. Swallowing down her excitement, she instructed quietly but firmly, 'At the next pain, I want you to bear down with all your might. You understand, wench? Nice deep breaths and a strong, steady push.'

'I can't . . . don't know what's happening . . . A cruel trick, that's what this is! There's no baby, there's not, it's a mistake—!'

Minnie cut off her high-pitched shouts with a chuckle. 'No mistake, Flora, oh nay. Now, remember what I said. At the next pain—'

'Oh Lord, oh, it's coming back.' Flora writhed to her hands and knees, grunting and groaning. 'God above, the pain's too much, I can't, can't . . .'

'Tha can and tha shall. Deep breaths, wench.' Minnie crouched behind her and now, taking another look between her legs, she gasped. The child's head was crowning. She was overcome with emotion at the sight – quickly, she swiped an arm across her eyes. There would be time for all that later. Right now, her friend needed her to remain composed and aid her through this. 'Harder!' she urged, when Flora, panting on all fours, began to push. 'More, wench, that's it, go on, a last big strong 'un . . . ! Ah! Good girl, you've done it!' she cried, catching the slippery body in her firm grasp as it emerged into the world. 'Eeh, Flora! Oh, wench. Would you look at that – oh, beautiful!'

Flora sank to the floor, sobbing loudly. 'How can this be?' she repeated, over and over, dumb with shock. However, when Minnie placed her child into her arms, the words melted on her lips and she gazed, awestruck, her breaths coming in short bursts.

'It's a girl, love.'

'Minnie, I never knew. I thought I were long past my time for it to ever be possible. I thought I had the cancer, were dying. How could I not know?' She burst into tears again, only now her weeping held snatches of wild, ecstatic laughter. 'I've gorra babby. I'm a mam!'

Minnie giggled through her own tears. 'Aye, you are. Babby must have been lying more towards your back behind your ribs; that's why you've not showed none at the front. It ain't uncommon – I've heard of such happening over the years. Hiding from your mam and father, were you, eh?' she added tenderly to the child. She shook her head. 'Eeh, I just can't . . . I'm lost for words, I am, really.'

'Fred! Lad, can you believe . . . ?'

Her husband, who had entered breathlessly, the doctor in tow – he bumped nose-first into Fred's back as he juddered to a halt – gawped at the incredible scene. Flora repeated herself but still he stood mutely, as though set in stone.

Rubbing his nose, the young medical man stepped around him. He nodded down at mother and babe and smiled. 'Well. This is a grand sight to behold. From Mr Nightingale's explanation, I was prepared for something else entirely.'

'It's a certain miracle, Doctor!'

'Indeed.' He grinned at Flora then turned his attention to Minnie. 'The child was delivered by your capable hands, Mrs Maddox?'

'Aye, Doctor.'

'No complications?'

'Nay, none.'

Relief passed over his face. He rolled up his sleeves. 'Excellent. I'll take it from here, Mrs Maddox. I'm sure your girl . . . Eliza, is it?'

'That's right.'

'Her legs are well?'

'Well as they can be. We've not been in need of you of late, as you'll have noticed, anyroad. They don't bother her so much as she gets older, glory be to God.'

'Good. Well, I'm sure she will agree you've earned a cup of tea for your work here today. Instruct her to put in a drop of brandy for your nerves.'

It was her turn to grin. 'I shall, Doctor. And aye, aye – it give me quite the shock!'

'And me, though I'll not hold it against her. My precious jewel.' Flora lifted her head and her eyes were bright with tears. 'Jewel . . . Suits her that, I reckon. My Jewel. Aye.'

'A bonny name for a bonny lass,' Minnie wholeheartedly agreed. 'I'll be away, now, let you grab some rest. Eeh, wench.' She caressed her friend's cheek then the baby's. 'I'm that happy for thee.'

'Ta, love, ta for everything. Minnie?' she added as her friend rose to her feet.

'Aye?'

'I'm complete.'

The two words, spoken with such raw simplicity, such truth, brought a lump to her throat. 'Bye for now, wench.'

Patting Fred's shoulder with a chuckle as she passed him, Minnie stepped into the cobbled street. And as she closed the Nightingales' door behind her, she was just in time to hear the new father rouse from his shock and his tearful laughter and heavy clogged steps as he rushed to his family's side.

*

'Eeh, lass.' Having filled Eliza in on the incredible occurrence, Minnie dropped into a chair at the table. 'I'm in need of a strong sup after that, I am. Nay, bugger the tea, just fetch the brandy.'

The girl obeyed, bringing down from a shelf the ready supply kept for rubbing on to the swollen gums of teething babies. She pulled out the stopper and pushed the bottle across. 'A rum do is that. I ain't never heard the like. Aw, bet the pair are fair daft with joy.'

'They are that.'

'Lord bless them.'

Minnie took a draught of the fiery drink and her eyes flickered towards the stairs. What a day. One soul departs this mortal realm, another enters it. Such was the world over, every second of the day. It was a queer old doing, this thing called life.

Her gaze moved to where Eliza limped around the fire, dragging her twisted leg behind her, busy at a fat-bellied cooking pot – preparing their evening meal of mutton broth by the smell of it. On impulse, she crossed the room and hugged the girl close. Eliza didn't question it, simply returned the embrace. And Minnie breathed a slow sigh.

It might have come late but those good people next door had got their happy ending. Not many did, that was for sure.

This day, right now, all was well with the world.

If she could have held on to the moment, kept it safe in her bunched fist and never let it go, she would have. Because for reasons she couldn't fathom, a quiet panic had settled in her breast and she was powerless to shake it.

Chapter 2

'MADDOX, IS IT?'

Minnie opened the door wider. The surly-faced woman before her whose harsh knocking had pulled her from her chores offered not a glimmer of a smile, and her next words were as hard as the first:

'Well? Are you deaf or summat, or do I have the wrong dwelling?'

'I'm Mrs Maddox, aye.' And who the devil was this? she wondered. Certainly not the sweet young lass she'd been expecting, had the room upstairs all ready for, that was for sure. She eyed the shabby, squirming bundle in her visitor's arms. 'And what can I do for thee?'

'What d'you think?' Without waiting to be invited, she brushed past Minnie into the house. Here, in the kitchen's glow, her features were more visible – Minnie saw instantly that she'd been crying, though she was doing her utmost to appear stony, unfeeling. Minnie felt herself soften towards her.

She'd seen this stance a hundred times over. Some women wailed and wept the moment they entered and were still doing so upon leaving. Some ranted and railed, puce with rage, against life in general, while some were meek or as silent as the grave. Others adopted this one here's approach, believed that in quelling the emotions the stab in their hearts at what was to come would be less and the wrench easier to bear. One did what one must, what suited each best, was right for them. Minnie neither assumed nor judged. But she felt, oh she did, for all of them, every last one. And their babes, too. Poor devils.

'How much?'

Minnie paused in her task of checking the teapot's contents to glance over her shoulder. Hopping restlessly from one foot to the other, the woman was biting her lip. Minnie gave her a soft smile. 'Sit thee down, lass, and take a sup. Let's discuss matters proper, like.'

'Nay, I ain't got time for all that bother.' Despite her thick, dun-coloured shawl and the room's good fire, the woman shivered. 'Just name your sum, then I can be away from here.'

Minnie sat anyway and, before lifting her cup to her lips, enquired, 'How did you come by my name?'

'Friend of mine. You took her burden off her hands a fortnight past.'

The slight but robust, monkey-featured mite who had taken so well to the bottle . . . Realisation brought a nod from Minnie. Only this morning she'd waved him on his way to a new life with a well-to-do childless couple from neighbouring Salford. If she remembered rightly, his birth mam had been an unfortunate of this city – one of many lost souls who plied what was between their legs on these mean streets. Was this acquaintance of the same trade? she wondered fleetingly, then cast her musings aside. It mattered not, at least to her. The well-being of the children was her concern, not how their mothers chose to survive this life. Her place was not to judge but to help. As usual, she would ask no questions. Not part of the deal, not her concern. Only the welfare of the child.

'Look 'ere, I've places to be. Now will you take this in or won't yer—?'

'All right, all right, calm thee down,' Minnie interrupted the outburst. 'If you've not the time for tea, you've surely some to spare to hear my terms.'

The woman's face relaxed a fraction. 'You mean you'll have it?'

Her choice of the term 'it' brought a disapproving frown to Minnie's brow. Nonetheless, she held her tongue and nodded. 'Aye. Now, let's iron out the details.' She motioned to a chair and, this time, the woman accepted, perching on the very edge as though prepared for flight at the earliest opportunity.

'I will start by saying I don't normally, as a rule, deal with folk turning up at yon door as you yourself have the day. I solicit infants through proper and above-board means: adoption advertisements in newspapers, through nurses, midwives, keepers of lying-in houses, that sort of thing.'

Though she had a single room upstairs, Minnie didn't class hers as a lying-in establishment. Such places – private houses where poor, unwed women could pay to give birth and arrange for the transfer of their infants to women such as herself – were generally a saviour to those in need of them. She'd only take in a woman with whom she'd some connection: a family member of a friend, that sort of thing. Her main business was in finding new homes, new lives, for children. And she was proud of that fact.

'I'm a respectable procurer,' she continued. 'Don't turn no babby over to anyone else, unlike some of my trade I could mention. Pocket the initial fee, some do, then if they can't find parents or are too impatient to look, dump the young angels on anyone with the promise of a cut of the brass – they've earned money for nowt, then, you see, and to hell with the child. Aye, it's to them a quick and easy way to make a few bob. And the one what took it off their hands . . . Well, once their sum has run out . . .'

She paused and lifted her shoulders in a small shrug. Raising a child cost money. Disposing of the millstone round their neck, in whatever way their conscience saw fit, was soon to follow. She shuddered to dwell on the evil of humans. 'Nay. Babbies comes to me from their mams and they stops with me until such a time as they are found new – permanent – homes with fresh parents. Good parents, to boot, aye. The best.'

'How much?'

The cold tone of the woman before her brought Minnie's brows together again in a frown. It was as though she hadn't heard a word she'd said. Such utter indifference, and at such a thing – on one so young, too – was unnerving. She'd be glad to rescue the infant from her, she admitted to herself, hoping God would forgive her for thinking such a thing. Mothers being separated from their babies . . . well, it wasn't the natural way of things, was it? Yet with this one . . .

'Well? Are you for bleedin' telling me or have I to take the thing elsewhere?'

Minnie was struggling to cling on to the last shred of her patience. If this unfeeling piece referred to the mite just once more in the way she kept doing, she'd be powerless to stop herself giving her a whipping from her tongue. 'Depends,' she forced out through gritted teeth.

'On what?'

'Whether it's weekly or monthly fostering you're after, or a permanent adoption. I'll require two shillings a week, or eight shillings per month – and at least with these options the child would stop with me and you'd maintain contact, get to visit, like, when you dropped off payment—'

'Nay, none of that. I want shot. Permanently.'

'The cost will be greater, you understand?'

'Aye, and worth every copper coin. The sooner I'm rid, and for good, the better.'

Minnie nodded. 'Then adoption it'll be. I'll find someone decent, no need to fret on that. A respectable couple what can give the precious mite a sound future.'

For the first time a flicker of something flashed across the woman's face, softening her features. She blinked twice, cleared her throat. Then the stony look returned and she nodded stiffly. 'How much?' she barked again.

'Four pounds.'

Eliza had been hovering nearby, and the woman thrust the child into her arms and extracted a cloth pouch from the folds of her skirts. She counted out the relevant coins and placed them on the table. Then without another word or glance to anyone, including her offspring, she swung on her heel for the door.

'Wait.'

Though she paused at the threshold, she didn't turn.

Shaking her head – Minnie had never encountered anything quite like this, like her, in all her days – she crossed the space towards her. 'I'd like some details: your name – the child's, too, and age,' she added. 'And Lord in heaven, besides owt else, won't you be wanting to say your farewells, like?'

'Nay.'

'Lass, listen to me. Don't come to regret your haste. Once new parents have been found, you'll not—'

'No goodbyes.' Still she had her back to her, and Minnie could gauge nothing from her tone. 'My name's Webster. Miss Webster, if you'd not already guessed.'

'My place is not to judge—'

'Huh! You'd be the first, then, let me tell thee.'

Pity stirred within her. Whatever the woman's attitude – and to all intents and purposes, it could very well be a front to hide how she really felt; though, by God, if so, she was a fine pretender – she didn't know her story, did she? Neither did she know what had driven her to this point in her life, this day, here. Nor who was to blame. After all, unless she was the reincarnate of the Holy Mother, women didn't get a bellyful of baby by themselves. 'And the child?' she asked quietly.

'I gave birth three weeks ago.'

'A name?'

She shook her head.

'But . . . surely you've been calling the mite by summat these past—'

The slamming of the door at the woman's sharp exit was the only answer. Minnie and Eliza shared a shocked and saddened look.

'A queer 'un, she were, and no mistake.' Eliza moved to the window to pull aside the length of faded curtain. She flicked her gaze left and right along the street. 'She's gone.'

'Aye well. Pass the child to me, lass. Let's take a look at what we've got here.'

'Reet cold, weren't she?' the girl continued as she handed the grubby bundle over. 'Nowt beating in that breast of hers at all, I'd say.'

However, Minnie wasn't so sure. Why, if she cared nought for the infant, take the trouble to seek her – a respectable, trustworthy minder – out? Her friend had clearly told her that Minnie was clean-living, God-fearing, honest, and the woman just now had sought her out on the strength of that reassurance to offload her child. And paid a small fortune to do so.

There were a hundred and one other avenues she could have chosen to dispose of the child if she'd a mind to; plenty that wouldn't have cost her a penny. Countless others did, in the most heinous of ways. And if you hadn't the nerve or stomach to do it yourself, this city and beyond were teeming with unscrupulous characters who would willingly take the task on for a lot less than four pounds. The canal, not an arrow's flight away, which she'd likely passed on her way here, was another example. Lord only knew how many people, desperate or otherwise, had taken advantage of its dark, watery belly to rid themselves of unwanted life.

Yet she hadn't. And though still it told nothing of her decision, her choice to come here instead said it all. Spoke a thousand words, it did, aye.

'Now then. Who've we got here? Oh, would you look at that.' Having laid the child in the centre of the table and drawn aside the swaddling, Minnie stood back to fully assess her latest charge. Eliza shuffled to her side and Minnie smiled down at her. 'What d'you reckon?'

'Bonny as the day is long, Min.'

'I'll say.'

The child was a picture of health, despite its somewhat grubby appearance. The nose and eyes were clear of discharge and crust free – good signs that illness wasn't present – and the cheeks held a soft bloom. Breathing sounded steady, no rattling in the chest indicating bad lungs. Minnie counted the little fingers and toes – all present and correct.

She nodded, satisfied. 'A fair size, an' all. Looks to have entered the world near full term. Good, good.'

''Ere, is it a lass or a lad? I don't recall the mam saying, do you?'

Minnie blinked, surprised to realise she'd allowed the

oversight and that Eliza was right. She peeled back the child's clothing. 'We have a girl. Mind you ...' She motioned downwards and Eliza nodded understanding.

The tender flesh was raised in shiny red pimpled patches, and caked powder in the creases of her thighs and groin had hardened, causing further irritation. However, it wasn't the worst case of napkin rash she'd seen. The skin wasn't broken; there was no spotting of blood on the sopping material. This could be put down more to lack of parental experience than neglect. The infant was well fed and free of injury. All in all, the waspish woman from before had provided adequate care, despite her stance that she worried not for her daughter's welfare.

'Poor love. Looks sore, that does,' stated Eliza.

'Aye. Sour smelling, an' all, she is, but we'll soon remedy that.' Minnie rolled up her sleeves before filling a large, chipped ceramic bowl with water still warm from the kettle. 'Go on, lass,' she told Eliza, 'give her a good soaking whilst I sort her with a fresh rig-out. Gentle, mind, as I've shown thee. And be mindful of supporting her head.'

As the girl softly splashed water over the baby's body with a clean rag, cooing and smiling, Minnie lowered herself to her knees and opened the deep bottom drawer of the dresser. This was filled to capacity with woollen clothing in various sizes, each piece knitted by her own hands and which had served countless nurslings to have passed through her care. After selecting what she needed and leaving them by the fire to warm, she went to fetch the bottle of olive oil for use on the angry rash. Then she went to stand beside Eliza.

The baby, rosebud mouth pursed in mild interest at the proceedings, offered no resistance. Her violet eyes flicked about, taking in everything. In turn, Minnie watched her keenly. She seemed to possess an intelligent, almost wise air; Minnie was charmed.

'Look see at this.'

'What, lass?'

Eliza tilted the child with a jerk of her head. 'The shoulder, there.'

Minnie stooped to finger what she'd indicated – a neat, coffee-coloured stain the size of a farthing coin. She smiled. 'Only a simple birthmark, nothing to fret about. I think it's fair becoming, actually. It has the uncanny shape of a sycamore leaf, you see?'

Eliza nodded, though no doubt she couldn't rightly say she'd ever seen one, never mind the trees whence they sprung. Industry had swallowed up their city's green spaces long ago.

'Right, let's be having her. You clear away her old clothes and her blanket – oh, and put that soiled napkin in the pail of cold water ready for washing and boiling at the day's end. Good lass.' She wrapped the wet body Eliza held up in a scrap of towel and, sitting in a fireside chair, dried the baby before the heat of the flames. All the while, that cut-glass gaze remained locked to her face, beautiful and bright with implicit trust. Minnie softened towards her further.

She'd find this one an extra-special home, she determined. Not that she let her charges go anywhere but the best she could find. She always made sure she'd selected the right parents before setting a child loose from her fold. However, this one deserved that extra bit more care, she reckoned.

Returning to the table, Minnie dried the infant's sore skin thoroughly and applied olive oil to the affected area. She'd just folded around her a clean napkin and was securing it in place with a pin when a knock came at the door. 'That'll be the lass we're expecting, come to make use of yon room upstairs,' she said, indicating for Eliza to admit the visitor. 'She's a bit late, mind— Oh, it's thee, hello wench,' she added, face spreading into a smile, when instead Flora entered the room.

'Hello, Minnie, love. Glorious day, in't it?'

Her smile spread into a grin to see that, though Flora's greeting had been meant for her, she'd directed it instead to baby Jewel, cradled tenderly in her arms – her friend had eyes only for her daughter these days. The change in the new mother was nothing short of a miracle. Minnie knew she wasn't exaggerating – her friend looked to have shed at least two decades in appearance; every worry line, every grey hair seemed to have faded, the dark circles gone from beneath her eyes just as sure as the pain of want within them had. Radiant, that's what she was – there was no other word to describe it. She shone from the inside out with happy light. It was lovely to see.

Minnie left the new baby to Eliza to dress and crossed to the fire, saying over her shoulder, 'Sit yourself down whilst I brew a fresh pot, wench.'

'Oh, no tea for me, ta, Minnie. I can't stop. I've my purchases to make if I'm to have summat on the table for Fred's evening meal. I just nipped in to say hello, like, on the way.'

And show off the precious being in her arms, no doubt, thought Minnie with warm amusement. Flora did so any opportunity she got and Minnie neither blamed nor begrudged her it one bit, bonny babby that she was. 'Now don't talk daft – sure, you've time for a quick sup,' she told her on a chuckle. 'Take the weight off, go on, and I'll see to the kettle.'

'Aye. All right, love. Ta, Minnie.'

They had their teas in their hands and had been conversing for all of half a minute when a gust of rain assaulted the draughty window, sending the thin glass rattling in the frame. They turned as one, Flora's face falling at the sight of the rapid droplets bouncing off the panes. 'Bugger.'

'I'll go and fetch your foodstuffs, Flora,' offered Eliza. 'Save you and the babby trudging out in that foulness.'

'Ay, good thinking, good lass.' Minnie nodded in agreement. 'You'd both be soaked to the bone in moments, Flora, wench, else. That'll not do, nay it'll not, Jewel as young as she is.'

'I were for calling in at my mam's, though, on t' way. She ain't been too well these few days past, as you know.' Flora gnawed her lip. 'Mind, I'd not want the babby here to develop a chill . . .'

'Course you don't. 'Ere, you leave Jewel with myself and Eliza, how about that? That way, you can check in on your mam still.'

'Oh, I don't know, Minnie . . .'

'Now come on, wench. Now you know she'll be in safe hands with me. God above, the number of babbies that have been in my care—!'

'I know, I know, love,' Flora cut in quickly. 'Eeh, there's norra soul more experienced than thee where infants are concerned in all the land, I'm certain. She couldn't be in safer hands, nay. It's just . . .' She swivelled her gaze to drink in her daughter's delicate features. 'Well, happen the weather will brighten in a minute, eh? Mebbe we should wait it out.'

'Aye, and yon shops will be closed and bolted by then, an' all. And what will your Fred say to that, coming home famished after a day's graft to an empty table? He'd be for taking his belt to you, missis, and you'd not blame him for it.'

Eyes still on the child in her arms, Flora chewed her lip again. 'Eeh, I don't know . . .'

'Wench, she'll be fine. I'll not take my eyes off her bonny face forra second, you have my word. Anyroad, I reckon the break will do you good. Not been from her side since birthing her, you've not, and it ain't healthy. You need space to breathe, an' all.'

'She's precious to me is all.'

'Well, of course she is. By, you waited for her long enough. But it's me what will be minding her, remember? Besides, you'll not be away long, eh? Tha can be there and back again in less than ten and twenty minutes.'

Flora nodded, albeit reluctantly. 'Aye, all right then. Ta-ra, you,' she told her child, planting a tender kiss on her brow. 'I'll see thee soon and ay, you be good, now, for your Aunt Minnie.'

'Course she will.' Minnie lifted the girl and waved her friend off. 'No need to rush back, neither, wench. Take a sup of tea with your poorly mam and be sure to send her my love whilst you're about it.'

The woman dithered by the door. Minnie flicked her hand, shooing her on her way, and, chuckling, Flora drew her shawl over her head against the elements and left the house.

'Eeh, I don't know,' said Eliza, crossing to the bed to lay the new, freshly bathed and clothed baby with the others. 'Protective ain't in it.'

'And who can blame her?' Minnie motioned to Jewel, asleep in the crook of her arm. 'Waited half a lifetime for this angel, she did.'

'Suppose so. Oh!' Eliza looked to the door as knocking came and, at Minnie's nod, went to answer it.

Their visitor was the pregnant young woman they had been expecting; Minnie waved aside her apologies for her lateness and ushered her inside. 'Bedroom's all made up ready for thee, lass. Eliza here will show you up and get you settled in whilst I brew us a fresh pot.'

'Ta thanks, Mrs Maddox.'

'Plain owd Minnie will do, lass. Go on now, go and get yourself out of them wet things and we'll speak in a minute over a sup of tea.'

They disappeared upstairs and Minnie released a small, sad sigh. Worried witless, the poor thing had looked. A full belly, no ring on her finger, and with the same old sorry tale to tell. The fellow she believed loved her had had his way with her then reneged on his promise of marriage, denying any involvement in her predicament into the bargain. At her horrified parents' insistence, here she was, sent before her belly began to grow so as not to arouse their neighbours' suspicions – gone away working or nursing some sick relative or other, they would no doubt be told in explanation of her absence.

When the time came, Minnie would deliver the child and see to its adoption whilst the lass returned home, taking no baby and therefore no shame on to the family with her. Likely a gaping hole in her heart that would never be filled, too.

Aye well. Hers wasn't to question the rights and wrongs, was it? she reminded herself, placing Jewel on the bed and heading off to refill the kettle. She'd just begun pouring out tea into three cups when Eliza's thin figure appeared at the top of the stairs:

'Min?'

'Aye, lass?'

The girl's voice dropped further. 'Come up, will thee? She's overcome with upset up here; I don't know what to do.'

Minnie gave a sad nod. 'Poor thing; it's likely just hit

her what being here means. Hang about, I'm coming.' She abandoned the teapot and, flashing the babies a look to check they were all right and wouldn't miss her, made for the bedroom.

Ten minutes later, after much tears and talk, the woman was undressed and in bed. Quieter now she'd finally unburdened her worries to someone, and that Minnie had put her mind at ease as to her child's future, she settled down for a well-needed sleep.

'You rest easy, child,' Minnie told her softly. 'The lass, here, shall stay with you awhile whilst I get back to my duties.'

Holding Eliza's hand, eyes drooping, the woman murmured a thank-you, and Minnie headed back downstairs.

What alerted her to the fact that something was wrong she couldn't say. She felt it the instant she entered the kitchen. She scanned the space, frowning – all appeared as it should be. Then her eyes settled on the bed and, for reasons she couldn't fathom, her heart tripped a few beats in quick succession. She swallowed hard and made her way across.

One by one, she peered at the slumbering babies. All the while, she knew, she just knew . . .

She touched a trembling hand to the last infant's cheek. Still warm. So perfect, peaceful . . . She fixed her gaze on the tiny chest anyway, watched intently for its rise and fall. It never came.

As though observing the scene from afar, Minnie watched herself cover the purple-tinged mouth. Then, with the tip of a finger, she compressed one nostril; into the other she blew steady puffs of air, inflating the lungs, all the while praying silently, fervently, the words falling over each other in her mind. And yet she knew – knew – her pleas were landing on deaf ears.

Again, as if witnessing everything from outside of her body, her hands loosened the clothing then turned the child's body on to its right side. She saw herself reach for the brandy, dip her fingers inside the bottle. Starting at the head, she quickly, sharply, rubbed the spirit the length of the spine to evoke heat in it – a tried-and-tested method that had worked more than once over the years. But not now. Not this time. Once more, her lamentations filled her brain. Still, she knew she'd hear no gasp, no cry – faint or otherwise.

Nothing could alter the truth that Jewel Nightingale was dead.

A sudden clap of thunder broke through the rain, momentarily dazzling the room with light – and Minnie stilled. Like herself, many believed thunder following a death to be a sign that the recently departed had entered into heaven. She didn't much go for the idea that children who passed from this life before they had a chance to be baptised were set to languish in some form of infant limbo for eternity. What God would allow such an awful thing? No. The Lord she knew and worshipped received every lost soul into His arms, she was certain.

Gently, Minnie laid the girl down and on limbs that felt attached to someone else's body crossed to the window. The chimney-stack sky held its usual factory tint – a red sheen that cast the city in a haunting light. A numbness had seized her brain in its grasp and she could neither feel nor think. A strand of sound tapped at the mind fog. She heard in her memories the decades of bitter tears telling of Flora's painful yearning. And she heard the joyous cries as she'd held her so-longed-for child in her arms. Then she imagined the unearthly ones to come at her friend's return to discover she'd had the priceless title of motherhood snatched away from her.

Flora would die, too. There wasn't a single doubt of that. She would follow her daughter into the black ground, would make sure of it, for she could never function, never exist, now, without her.

As with the child Eliza had found in this very bed, deceased for no apparent reason, who had lain cold in his box in Minnie's bedroom until she'd watched him be buried only last week, the dreaded cradle death was commonplace. Small babies were spirited away in their sleep sometimes, everyone knew it; though why was another matter.

Neither rhyme nor reason could explain either case, here. The children in her care had suffered no injury, their little faces hadn't been accidentally covered by the bedclothes, nothing like that. It was just something that happened, with no explanation or means of prevention. It didn't make it any less heart-rending. Nor did it make the truth easier to accept. And Flora wouldn't, not at all. She'd do whatever it took to be with her daughter, whether that meant in life or death. She'd do it, all right.

Minnie's breaths came in short gasps. She glanced up and down the street then behind her towards the stairs. Then she hurried to the bed.

Her gaze went not to Jewel but the female child with the violet eyes who had been thrust into her care not half an hour ago. She was virtually the same size and stature as the dead girl. They shared the same colouring, the same button nose and rosebud mouth, both no more than a dusting of downy hair. They even had the same features, as far as she could see. The passage of time hadn't yet begun to define their individuality – babies at the beginning of life did, by and large, look the same. Aye, they did . . .

Tongues would wag for certain, questions would be raised. The demise of two of her charges in as many weeks – whom she'd received money for, no less? The possibility of her coming under suspicion by the authorities was a very real one. Her good name, her spotless character, would be tarnished. She'd be ruined. And she didn't care. Flora mattered more to her. Much more.

Now, Minnie was in full control of her actions. Swiftly, deftly, she stripped the new girl of her clothing. Then she did the same with Jewel.

The beautiful garments Flora had lovingly knitted, she now dressed the new girl in. Seconds later Jewel was wearing the items from the dresser's bottom drawer. After switching their blankets and wrapping both children up, Minnie stepped back and surveyed them through eyes blurry with tears. She swallowed at the panic threatening to choke her.

They really did look one and the same. To her, at least. But what of a mother? Would Flora . . . ? God above, what was she doing?

'I don't know.' Minnie answered her own thought in a small whimper. 'Don't know what I were . . . were thinking . . .' With a cry, she rushed forward to right the madness of her actions. She'd begun removing the babies' blankets when the sound of rainfall filling the room as the door was opened, then Flora's cheery welcome, halted her in her tracks. On jerky legs, she turned.

'Eeh, it's foul out there!' Flora jiggled on the spot, shaking the outside from her wet shawl. 'Ta ever so, Minnie, love, for minding my angel. How's she been?' Her hungry gaze looked beyond her to the bed, seeking out her child. 'Not fretting over me, were she?'

Minnie couldn't breathe. Speaking was an impossibility. She shook her head.

'Oh, I am glad. Been worried summat sick, I have.' Flora flashed a sheepish grin. 'What am I like, eh? I knew she'd be gradely, course I did. I'm a daft beggar, that's what.' When Minnie didn't answer, she cocked her head. 'You all right, love?'

'Aye.' Her voice sounded off to her own ears. Short, high-pitched. Guilty. She tried to smile but failed. She watched Flora's own smile slip from her lips, watched unable to do anything, wide-eyed and frozen, as her friend crossed the space towards her. Towards the bed. Towards the children. Again, that sensation of being out of her body had returned and, like the rest of her, her tongue acted without her say-so: 'The lass . . . The new lass entrusted to me earlier has passed away, wench, in her sleep.' She waited. Nothing. Flora was staring intently at the sleeping infant adorned in her daughter's clothes. 'Love? Love, I—'

'I'll be off home, now, Minnie.'

Minnie's brow creased in a frown. She exhaled slowly. Flora was still stooped over the children and her eyes swivelled continually from one girl to the other. Her expression was unreadable. After a last, lingering look at her dead daughter, she lifted the other girl and turned for the door. Close to tears, Minnie stumbled after her.

'Ta again, love, for minding my Jewel. I'll be seeing thee.'

Before she could say or do anything – grasp at Flora's arm, pour out her guilt, cry, beg her forgiveness – her neighbour was gone. The door clicked shut and Minnie sagged against the wall.

She knew. Minnie had heard it in her flat tone when she'd bid her goodbye, had seen it in her eyes before she'd turned dazedly for home. She knew. She knew and had done nothing. God in heaven above. Horror and panic swamped her – she gripped the mantel for support as her legs threatened to buckle. She knew.

But did she really? Surely any mother would have said something – anything. Surely she would have? And yet . . . Minnie shook her head. She felt dizzy and sickness was swooping through her guts in waves.

It was only then that she remembered the birthmark.

Like that of little Jewel lying feet away, her own heart ceased its beating. Stare fixed on the fire's hypnotic flames, she felt behind her blindly until her fingers brushed the shelf and the brandy atop. *One baby departs this earth, another arrives to take its place in the world . . .*

With tears coursing down her lined face, Minnie lifted the bottle to her lips.

Chapter 3

'BY GUM! WHAT a sight. I ain't never seen the like.'

Esther Powell shoved her niece aside with an ample hip. Resting her arms on the windowsill, she squinted through the driving rain to the square below. 'Well, what do you expect?' she asked in her usual withering tone. 'It's Bolton's first royal visit. A bit of bad weather weren't about to put the townspeople off catching a glimpse of the Prince and Princess of Wales, now, were it?'

Biting down on her tongue to stem a retort, as she was frequently forced to in the prickly woman's presence – Esther had a knack of making a body feel as thick as a brick with her caustic remarks – Jewel returned her attention to the heaving crowds. As well as a strong police presence, there had to be thousands of people down there, she reckoned. By, but it was a gradely sight to behold.

'Anyroad, lady.' Her aunt speaking again scattered the smile from her face. 'Why you up here, like? You finished your duties downstairs? Nay, I'll bet. Skiving as per usual. Take yourself away and get back to it. That shop floor won't scrub itself, you know.'

Jewel felt her cheeks flame with indignant colour that matched that of her hair – a sure sign her temper was about to show itself, whether she wanted it to or not. Fortunately, her uncle intervened:

'Let her be, Esther. Sure, the cleaning ain't going nowhere. The day's an important one, after all, and should be marked as such; by everyone, aye. Besides, don't it also happen to be the lass's birthday an' all, to boot? A few hours away from the grind won't hurt none.'

Jewel flashed him a grateful look and he gave a discreet nod back. Esther merely sniffed. What she'd do without Bernard Powell on her side, Jewel dreaded to think. She wouldn't stay, that much she knew. She'd turn stark staring mad without him here to buffer her from the worst of his wife's nastiness, she was certain. Or finish up in a prison cell for bashing Esther's podgy face to a pulp, which most of the time she'd really like to do.

That last wicked thought – oh, if only her aunt could hear them! – brought a bubble of laughter, and she chewed her bottom lip to stop it escaping.

The electrifying atmosphere outside carried through once more and her smile returned. Despite the inclement weather, the scene was mesmerising. The Market Square, or the Town Hall Square, as most now called it – a proper market hadn't been held here for years since the nearby constructions of the impressive Market Hall and Fish Market – had been transformed. So, too, had the carriageways and streets forming the route of the procession, which had been barricaded since ten o'clock that morning and would remain so until after the event. People and horses alike, scrubbed and groomed, stood proudly in their best, waiting patiently. Building fronts and gas lamps were garlanded with large, swaying flags, banners and bunting, which reflected in the glistening-wet cobbled setts, adding splashes of welcome colour.

To the north side of the square, where the Powells' umbrella shop stood, a battlemented archway as tall and wide as the abutting buildings had been erected. Through this, the royal carriage would emerge from Oxford Street, containing their long-awaited visitors. Nose almost touching the pane, Jewel craned her neck left towards the decorated wooden structure, checking for their imminent arrival, but there was no sign yet. Instead, she trained her gaze on the centrepiece facing and the purpose of this auspicious occasion: the new Town Hall, towering over the town.

Neoclassical in style, the vast sandstone edifice was majestically designed. On both sides ran a high basement storey, above which sat two floors dotted with arched and rectangular windows and broad columns. At the centre was a six-columned portico and pediment adorned with sculptures. Bolton's elephant-and-castle emblem, human and lion heads and figures by the doors holding date stones into which were carved this year, 1873, were included in the embellishments.

The entrance itself was reached by a bold flight of over two dozen wide steps. Either side of these near to the top stood a pedestal, intended to hold a large stone lion. Alas, the beasts had not been completed in time for today's grand opening and so potted shrubs were positioned in their place.

The finishing touch was the tower, boasting four clock faces and stretching two hundred feet into the sky. The overall impact was, in a word, magnificent.

Inside consisted of a large meeting hall, council chamber and committee rooms, mayor's parlour, reception and banqueting rooms as well as numerous offices. Little Bolton town hall, the modest building that held the county sessions court, constabulary station and lock-up and was situated at the nearby junction of St George's Street and All Saints' Street, which had served them until now, paled dramatically in comparison.

Bernard had followed Jewel's gaze. He puffed out his chest, face holding pride; smiling, she did likewise. Everybody in the town was inordinately proud of their new structure, which had taken seven years to construct, and deservedly so.

'Not long to wait, now,' her uncle announced, glancing from the clocktower to his pocket watch then adjusting the latter to run at 'town hall time', as did Bolton's inhabitants and industries alike. 'It's a pity Wigan town had His Royal Highness before us – I read in the paper he's just opened the new infirmary there. But no matter, no matter. Better late than never, eh?'

Jewel nodded in agreement. Then she, too, glanced at the hour, and frowned. Her mother should have been here by now. She'd hate for her to miss something as momentous as this.

Here, from the Powells' private quarters above their shop, they had the best view possible. For weeks, they and the owners of surrounding premises had been inundated with offers from people desperate for a clear vantage point to rent out their rooms – some even prepared to brave the rooftops – and willing to pay handsomely for the privilege. Fortunately, her aunt and uncle, not wanting to miss the proceedings themselves, had flatly refused.

She'd just told herself she'd give her mother another five minutes then go and collect her when she heard the door opening. She turned expectantly but, to her dismay, it wasn't Flora but a pimply, overweight youth who entered the room – her cousin, Benji. He smiled at her and she forced one back.

'All right, my lad?' Esther's tone was sickly sweet. 'Come on over here next to your mam. I've saved the best spot for thee.'

Benji crossed the space. As he normally did any opportunity he got, he stood as close to Jewel as he could, their hips touching, his arm pressed against hers. His hot breath fanned her bare neck and, after making sure her aunt wasn't watching, she shoved him away with a narrow-eyed look. Mild hurt flitted across his face then the corners of his mouth lifted. He resumed his position and she swallowed a sigh of irritation.

His unwelcome attentions had begun out of the blue several months ago. They had never really been close – even as children, they did nothing but bicker – but lately, he wouldn't leave her alone. Of course, her aunt wouldn't believe a word of it, so what was the point in complaining? Whether her uncle would, she couldn't say. Not that it would matter either way. His wife would turn his thinking, had the final say with their lad, always did. Her precious son could do no wrong in her eyes – sunbeams shone from his earholes, as far as she was concerned, aye. She'd defend him to the death, no matter the issue. Besides, Jewel was no tell-tale. She could handle this – him. She'd show him if he dared push his advances. If he went too far with her, he'd bloody well regret it.

'I don't know where Mam could be,' she announced now, catching sight of the time again. 'I'd best run home and fetch her; she'll miss the royal pair, else.'

'I'll walk with thee, shall I?' offered Benji.

Jewel shook her head. 'There's no need. It'll not take long.'

'You reckon?' He jerked his head at the crowds outside. 'You'll have a job getting through that lot. I'm bigger than you; I'll get us past the mob in half the time.'

As he'd spoken his arm had moved without her noticing; discreetly, he fondled her buttock. Incensed, she dug her nails into the back of his hand then gave it a thump for good measure. She stalked to the door, saying over her shoulder, 'I'll manage, I'm sure.' And when her aunt mumbled something about her being an ungrateful piece for turning down her son's generous offer, Jewel quickened her step before her temper boiled over.

Outside the room, she paused to take some deep breaths. Swine! She'd give him a tongue-lashing later, all right. He was growing up, she understood this – most lads were beginning to get certain urges, such as he clearly was, at his age – but still, he had no right to mess with her like that. She frowned as a sudden thought occurred: was he in love with her? Was it possible that he knew what love was at fifteen? Even she didn't, today at seventeen. Did she? She was very fond of Jem Wicks, a handsome lad who dwelled in the next street whom she'd been courting for several months, it was true – but love? She honestly couldn't say.

Smoothing her long, red plait, as thick as a man's wrist, over one shoulder, she donned her shawl and left the shop. The very air buzzed with feverish anticipation; all thoughts of Benji and lads in general melted from her mind as, once more, the atmosphere of the day swept her up and made her giddy with excitement. With smiles and apologies, she fought her way through the throng. Then, reaching the edge of the square, she picked up her skirts and ran, past the mouth of Exchange Street and the Grapes Hotel pub on the corner and on down the narrow, cobbled road adjoining it.

Her clogged footsteps rebounded off the buildings' sooty bricks as she continued at a sprint for the two rooms she and her mother occupied in a tumbledown dwelling at Back Cheapside. When she burst inside, breathless and laughing, her mother whipped around with a gasp from where she stood by the fire.

Jewel grinned. 'Sorry to make you jump, but we must hurry. The time . . .' Her words petered out as, on closer inspection, she saw that Flora's face was wet with tears. 'Mam? Mam, what is it, what's to do?'

The older woman quickly scrubbed at her eyes with her sleeve. 'Ah, nowt to fret over, my lass. Smoke from yon fire is all it were. Sets my eyes astreaming, it does.' She flashed a bright smile. 'Now, what is it that had you tearing in here and frickening me half to death?'

'Lord, Mam, surely you ain't forgot? The royal visit!'

'Oh, that. Course I've not forgot. I were just about to join youse at the shop when you came careering in.'

It hadn't looked that way – she'd seemed in a world all of her own, Jewel thought, but nodded nonetheless. Then her mother moved to fetch her shawl from the nail in the wall by the door, and that's when Jewel saw it: a small, cream-coloured heap on the hearth. Mam must have dropped it when she'd startled her. She went to retrieve it and discovered it was a baby's woollen vest. Frowning, she held it up. 'Mam?'

'I'll take that.' Hurrying over, Flora almost snatched it from her grasp. She folded it carefully and placed it in a cupboard against the far wall. 'Right then, let's get going afore we miss the event altogether,' she said, heading for the door.

'Mam.' Jewel's voice had softened; she took her mother's hands in hers and squeezed. 'That were my vest from when I were a babby. You were looking at it, reminiscing, afore I came in, weren't you? Is it because it's my birthday? Eeh, Mam.' She chuckled, then kissed the lined brow. 'Whatever my age, I'll allus need thee. You know that, don't yer?'

'My baby. My daughter.' A single tear accompanied Flora's whisper and splashed to her cheek. Then, blinking, she reached out to stroke her hair with a loving touch. 'My precious Jewel.'

'And you're my precious mam. And there ain't none better in the land than thee. And now we must hurry – come on!' she finished on a laugh, shooing a now-smiling Flora into the street.

The crowd's furore had intensified further still – the air crackled with expectancy. Glancing at the clock-tower, Jewel gasped. It was just a few minutes to the appointed hour. 'Quick, Mam!'

Pulling Flora behind her, she shoved and elbowed her way through the mass of bodies to finally fall, puffing for breath, through the shop door. With no time to waste on catching their composure, they rushed upstairs.

'Well, youse are cutting it fine! Come on, they'll be here any moment.' Esther shuffled closer to Bernard and Benji, Jewel and her mother squeezed in close, and they waited in charged silence.

When the clock chimed, releasing three long bongs into the grey afternoon, they and every other spectator craned their neck towards the man-made arch. Then there it was. Flanked by an entourage of dragoons and territorial volunteers, the royal carriage glided into the square. The crowd broke into warm cheers, waving hats and handkerchiefs, beaming from ear to ear, and the family following the proceedings from the umbrella-shop window matched their vigour entirely.

What made Jewel look past the regal scene, she

couldn't say. Some fifty years earlier, when the square was created, a striking ornate gas lamp had been donated to mark the occasion – and there, leaning against the circular water trough surrounding its base, stood Jem Wicks. However, her usual smile of delight upon seeing him didn't appear now. For by his side was a lass she vaguely knew from their cluster of streets – a loose piece, to boot, if rumours were correct. Of all the . . . !

Anger rose up in her and she swallowed hard. She saw him laugh at something the girl had said and slip an arm around her waist. To her utter shock, they then kissed, right there in public – on the lips!

Before she knew what she was doing Jewel was leaning out of the window: 'Jem!' But he was too far away to hear her – though several others certainly did, and had turned to gawp up at her. 'Jeremiah Wicks, you rotten dog, yer! I'll tear you limb from limb, just you see if I don't!' she yelled across the square, her burning fury overriding thought and reason, until:

'Mother of God. Oh, the shame of it!'

Her aunt's horrified squawk brought her back to the present. Following the quivering finger as Esther pointed outside, Jewel slapped a hand to her mouth.

Whilst her attention had been on the cavorting couple, the carriage had pulled up by the broad town hall steps and the royal pair had alighted. And it was evident that the prince had heard – he was looking over his shoulder towards the shop! A terrible thought occurred: what if His Highness had caught only part of her outburst, believed her insult and threat were meant for him? Her aunt was right: Lord, the shame!

With a squeak, she ducked out of sight, face ablaze. She'd never been so embarrassed in her whole life.

Damn and blast Jem Wicks – and so, too, this infernal tongue of hers!

As if Jewel didn't feel bad enough, Esther shook her roughly, hissing, 'Why, you devil-tempered article – look what you've done! Sullied our name and reputation to royalty, you have. God above, future monarch King Edward VII at that! Oh, I'll never forgive you for this, never!'

'All right, woman, don't fret so.' Bernard spoke placatingly, though definite laughter danced behind his eyes. He motioned to the square. 'See, look. The Prince and Princess have forgot the incident already.'

Jewel braved a peek over the lip of the window ledge – sure enough, the pair had ascended the steps, their attention once more on the task in hand. 'Terrible sorry, truly,' she murmured. 'D'you think the Prince can forgive me?'

'Now, lass, enough of that.' Flora didn't try to mask her amusement; she chuckled quietly, much to her sister-in-law's annoyance. 'What's done is done; and it's that young bugger Jem's loss, aye. Come on, ruddy hiding down there, up you get.'

Jewel allowed her mother to help her stand. She tried her best to enjoy the proceedings but, for her, the day was ruined. Esther's sly, angry glances didn't help none. Jem Wicks, the low-down dog – she'd believed him to be fond of her. She'd been a fool. He'd bloody pay for this!

The grand opening of the new civic building, constructed for the needs of present and future generations, had brought out high and distinguished guests. The town's leading gentry and political and industrial dignitaries joined, amongst other important people, the town clerk, councillors and Mayor. Even the building's talented architects were in attendance, on the steps. Men, impeccably dressed in dark frock coats and top hats, predominated but several ladies, in colourful bustled dresses heavily adorned in pleats and ruffles and wearing magnificent hats, were included in the smiling party circling the royal couple.

Jewel couldn't help stealing a glance at her own clean but heavily patched skirts in comparison. Though the dream of owning clothing like these ladies flitted into her thoughts, it quickly vanished again – a reality such as that would never be. She accepted this without a flicker of resentment. Your station in life was determined at birth and no one got a say in it, to choose. It was how it was.

After being welcomed by the Recorder of Bolton, who read an address on behalf of the Mayor, the Prince offered his and his wife's gratitude for their visit to the town today. He touched upon its importance as a manufacturing centre and announced it gave him and the Princess very great pleasure to be present on such an important occasion as the opening of the new town hall of Bolton. Jewel tried to listen but ignoring her embarrassment was difficult. And at one point, when thanking everyone for the beautiful appearance of the streets – and the order that was kept – she was certain the Prince looked her way. She ducked out of sight amidst her family's laughter – all but Esther's, in any case.

Nevertheless, the Prince couldn't fail to lift her spirits – his effusiveness held the inhabitants in the palm of his hand – and she was soon smiling, along with the rest. When he praised the townsfolk's declaration to the throne and his high gratification with the very sunny, gladsome reception he'd received, she cheered with everyone else – which reached a crescendo when he stated that he wouldn't fail to inform the Queen of the truly loyal manner in which they had been welcomed. He finished by saying he would not very easily forget his visit to Bolton – this time, there could be no denying his twinkling glance in the shop's direction – but now, though her cheeks again flamed brick-red, Jewel couldn't contain a giggle. His affable nature was a treasure and she loved him for it.

The crowd erupted in rapturous applause – even her aunt managed to crack a smile. The vicar of Bolton then opened with prayers and, when he'd concluded, there came the moment they had all been waiting for: stepping forward, the Mayor presented a silver key and asked the Prince if he would be kind enough to accept it. The spectators held a collective breath as he unlocked the door. When he turned to the assembly and formally declared the town hall open for public services, every man, woman and child cheered for all they were worth.

The double doors were thrown wide open and the Prince and Princess were escorted inside to the Great Hall for the banquet. Not quite sure what to do with themselves now, and unwilling to bring an end to the event, the townsfolk milled around the square in their soggy boots.

Tomorrow, the newspapers would be singing with details of the bill of fare those dignitaries had enjoyed – most of the foodstuffs listed, the poor of this smoggy little town wouldn't ever have heard of, never mind be able to imagine how they tasted – and all the while, most folk found it a daily struggle to keep body and soul together. And yet the lower orders flocked to events such as this, marvelled at the evident wealth of their betters, their clothing and carriages, acknowledged their lofty demeanour and superior station with easy acceptance. It was as normal to them as breathing, this strict hierarchy. Such was life, and most never thought to question it at all.

Jewel and Flora went to make a pot of tea whilst Esther, still carrying a definite air of annoyance, took herself downstairs to the shop. Bernard, with a slight roll of his eyes to his sister and niece, who smiled, followed his wife to attempt to calm the waters.

'Jeremiah Wicks don't deserve thee. Tha knows that, aye?'

Her mother's words, calm but warm with love, brought tears to Jewel's eyes. She blinked them back. 'Aye.'

'Young swine. He'll think so when our paths next cross.'

'It's all right, Mam. He ain't worth the aggravation.' She didn't want Flora involved. She'd be the one to dole out the tongue-lashing he had due to him.

'Aye well. He'll rue his folly the day. You're worth a dozen of him.'

Benji had been hovering nearby; at this from the older woman, he nodded, saying, 'Aunt Flora's right. By, he wants his brain looking at snubbing thee.' *I'd not*, his gaze added, boring into Jewel's. Frowning, she looked away.

'You off soon to continue the festivities at Bolton Park, lad?' Flora asked him, oblivious to the tension between the two. She smiled when he confirmed he was. 'Take our Jewel along with thee, eh? She could do with cheering up – and her that's had this rotten fortune on her birthday, to boot! What says thee?'

'I say it's a gradely idea, Aunt Flora.' He beamed. 'Jewel?'

She shrugged. She may as well go. Better that than moping around here for the rest of the day with Esther's acid presence.

'Right, well, you leave them cups, lass, and fetch your shawl. Youse take a slow walk there, enjoy the air. I'll see thee later.'

Many were still present in the square, whilst others, hoping for a last glimpse of the Prince and Princess, had walked the short distance to Trinity Street Station, where, soon, the royal train would depart for London, bringing an end to the brief visit. Others of a similar mind to Jewel and Benji were heading in the direction of the park situated on the west side of town by Chorley New Road; at a leisurely pace, they joined the throng.

Created from meadow and pastureland following the Bolton Improvement Act of 1864 and officially opened two years later, the beautiful pleasure grounds were a favourite amongst the townsfolk. Some fifty acres, surrounded by lakes and woodland, it featured grassy slopes and curving paths generously planted with shrubbery, trees and immaculate flowerbeds. By the time the cousins reached the pavilion in the centre of the park, thousands of spectators were already gathered in readiness. By five o'clock, the heaving mass of bodies, swelling in number by the minute, spread as far as the eye could see.

Jewel began to wonder if she'd made a mistake in venturing here. Jem's betrayal still stung and the beginnings of a headache throbbed dully behind her eyes. However, at least the weather had brightened and Benji's roving hands were behaving themselves. Best she tried to enjoy the evening here than be alone with her thoughts at home.

A band had struck up a song to please the townsfolk whilst the entertainment prepared to get under way and there was much jollity from young and old alike. Then the huge balloons, one of which had been named Alexandra in honour of the Princess, began their ascent into the white-grey clouds amidst the crowd's collective 'Ooh!' and 'Ahh!' – Jewel herself was entranced. The daring fliers grew smaller and smaller until the balloons' baskets were nothing more than brown smudges in the sky. The impressed audience cheered and stamped their feet with gusto.

'I'll fetch us both a penny pie and a pot of ale, shall I?' Benji shouted above the medley, inclining his head towards a gathering of hawkers beyond the park's enclosure.

She nodded. 'Aye, all right.'

'I'll not be long.' Elbows at the ready, he set off to fight his way through the crush.

Jigging couples bumped Jewel this way and that with grins and breathless apologies; laughing, she looked about. A group of children playing catch in a less crowded spot nearby drew her attention, and she watched them with a smile. Seemingly out of nowhere, a toddler with tight blond curls suddenly appeared amongst them, screeching in delight, and attempted to join in the fun in a wobbling run. The children fell over themselves, giggling, and Jewel chuckled along. Then a tall, well-dressed man with dancing brown eyes was striding towards them. He wagged a finger at the toddler, who was clearly his daughter – grinning, she attempted to dash off again, but he gathered her up in his arms and smothered her in kisses.

As he made to carry her off, as though sensing he was being watched, he glanced in Jewel's direction. She smiled. With a slight incline of his head, he returned the smile. Moments later, he and the child were gone, lost amongst the crowd.

Longing stirred in Jewel's breast; she turned away with a small sigh. She'd have loved to have known her own father. Fred Nightingale, from what her mother had told her, sounded like a very nice man, fair and hard-working. He'd passed away before she was old enough to retain any solid memories of him and, for that, she felt cheated. This day seventeen years ago was the happiest of his life, Mam told her often. If only he could be here now to share it with her, wrap his arms around her as that man had just done with the girl, tell her he loved her . . .

''Ere, grab yours. Eeh, that's good.' Dragging Jewel from her musings, Benji dumped her meat pie and ale into her hands before taking another long draught of his own drink. 'Eeh,' he said again, wiping his mouth on his sleeve. Then he nodded down. 'Eat up then afore it grows cowd.'

Before she did, she scanned the area where the children had been playing but, again, the father and daughter were nowhere to be seen. Swallowing another sigh, she turned her attention to her food.

'What's to do with thee?' asked Benji after some time. 'Still wasting your thoughts on Wicks?'

'Am I hell. He can rot there, an' all, for me.'

Benji smiled, pleased at this, and inched closer to her. Jewel hadn't the energy to scold him. At least he was keeping his hands to himself.

'Well, you're quieter than normal,' he continued after some moments. 'Summat's up.'

Once more, the toddler and the man with the dancing eyes crept into her mind. She shrugged. 'Bit tired is all. Anyroad, will tha pack it in with the questions? You're getting on my nerves.'

He did, and she was free to forget her thoughts in the entertainment. The festivities continued for hours and, by the time they set off back to town, her mind was more at ease. Entering the square, she smiled. Gas illuminations had been lit throughout in celebration; the scene was dazzling.

'Don't know why you couldn't of stayed with me longer at the park – at least 'til the fireworks,' Benji grumbled, thrusting his hands into his pockets as they reached his parents' shop door. 'Your mam's not expecting you yet, so what? I thought you were enjoying yerself.'

'I were.' She meant it. The day hadn't been a complete nightmare, on the whole. 'I'm ready for my bed, though, now.'

'Aye well. Do what tha likes, then. I ain't mithered.'

His pouting face made him look like a three-year-old who couldn't get his own way rather than the overgrown young man that he was. 'You could of stayed, didn't have to miss the fun,' she told him. 'I'm big enough and ugly enough to see myself home.'

'You're ugly all right.'

She rolled her eyes. 'Grow up, Benji. 'Ere, anyroad,' she added in a hiss, anger sparking, 'I can't be that foul-looking, going by your behaviour – you're bloody fortunate I agreed to accompany you at all after your antics earlier at the window up yonder. And I'll tell you this for nowt: should them hands of yourn stray in my direction again, I'll chop them off – and summat else, an' all, if you're not careful. You hear?'

He released a snort of laughter then opened the door. 'If tha says so.'

'I bleedin' do.'

'Night night, Jewel.'

'Sod off, Benji!' she shouted after him as, still chortling, he disappeared, slamming the door in her face. 'Bloody lads, I've had a bellyful for one day,' she told the darkening sky. Just who did they think they were, anyway? They thought they could treat lasses as they liked and to hell with their feelings. Swines. They could go and rot for all she cared, every last one! Turning on her heel, she headed for home.

She'd almost passed the town hall when she saw him. Leaning against the corner premises on Newport Street, Jem stepped forward as their eyes locked. He held out his hands. 'Jewel . . . I can explain . . .'

'I'll bet tha can.' Surprisingly – she'd thought she would struggle to stop herself clawing the flesh from his face when their paths next crossed – she felt little anger.

'I called in at your dwelling earlier but your mam said as how you'd gone to Bolton Park with your cousin.'

'That's right.' Jewel's glance swivelled towards the umbrella shop. Benji was watching them in the distance from his upstairs window. 'Had a gradely time, we did, an' all. What?' she asked when Jem's face fell. 'Did tha think I'd be wallowing at home instead? You think too much of yourself, Jeremiah Wicks. That loose piece you were slobbering over is welcome to thee. Now, if you don't mind . . .' She made to step around him but he caught her wrist. She stared at his hand for a moment then brought her gaze, now burning with fury, to his. He had the sense to release her. 'Now shift out of my way,' she growled.

'Jewel, please. I made a mistake, a terrible one, and . . . We weren't that serious, me and thee – least I didn't think so – but now . . . I want us to make a go of things, proper like. We'll . . . we'll . . .' His eyes narrowed as he searched around inside his head for something to win her around. Suddenly, he clicked his fingers. 'We'll get wed. Aye, yeah.' He nodded, smiling. 'What d'you reckon?'

She could only stare at him with incredulousness.

'We're meant to be, you know it. Remember, I'm the gem to your jewel—'

Seeing his hand reaching for her again, her temper reached its peak – throwing out her own, she delivered a slap to his cheek. 'You're no gem – a mucky lump of coal, more like!' To her chagrin, tears were threatening; she blinked them back furiously. 'I'll take the head from your neck for you if yer don't get lost, I mean it—'

'You heard her.'

Spinning around, she saw Benji standing behind her, arms folded. Despite herself, she was touched by his support. When Jem, admitting defeat, sloped off with a shrug, she cast the lad a wry smile. 'Ta. Though you know there were no need for you to involve yourself. I can fight my own battles, thank you very much.' Her tone softened. 'I'll tell you what, how's about we have a walk back to the park? We might still be in time to catch the fireworks?'

His face lit up. 'Aye?'

'Yeah, sod it. Come on.'

The display was already under way when they arrived. Clutching pots of ale, they grinned and cheered with everyone else as one firework followed the next, bursts of light whizzing through the night sky like a shower of golden rain.

'May Bolton prosper!' The cousins added their voices

to the thousands ringing out across the park. 'Long live the Prince!'

'I'll fetch us another ale,' Benji shouted above the high-spirited noise some time later, but Jewel only half heard him. Her attention was on the faces to her right – she could have sworn she'd just spotted a familiar one: the toddler's father from earlier. However, if she had, he wasn't there now; shrugging, she continued with the merriment.

When less than ten minutes later Benji made to go and replenish their drinks yet again, she shook her head. 'Nay, no more, lad. Your mam will have a blue fit were you to roll home skenning drunk.'

'A few pots ain't doing no harm. Well, d'you want one or don't yer?' He wiggled his eyebrows and she chuckled.

'Well, I suppose it is a celebration . . .'

'Your birthday, to boot.'

'Aye. Aye, all right. Last one, mind.'

Watching him walk off, she sighed happily. It felt good to throw caution to the wind for once. Work and want were forgotten for the moment; this day had turned into the best she'd known for many a long year. Picking up her skirts, she danced along to the fiddler's lively song with the rest of the townspeople.

By the time Benji rejoined her she was helpless with laughter and having the time of her life. Through smiling eyes, he watched her as he drank. The ditties were thirsty work; before she knew it, her pot was empty yet again and, this time, when her cousin held out a hand, she gave it to him without protest. What did it matter so long as they were enjoying themselves? A day like this didn't happen often – royalty, in their town! And how handsome the Prince of Wales had been! By, it had been a grand experience and one none of them would ever forget.

'You all right?' Benji asked her some time later, grinning. 'Happen you should take a sit down forra while.'

'Aye. Aye, yeah.' Squinting through one eye, Jewel allowed him to guide her through the throng. She felt queer; her head felt light yet heavy as lead at the same time. 'Oh 'eck, lad. How much have I supped?'

'A fair bit. Come on.' Taking her elbow, he led her to a more secluded spot. 'Here, rest yourself on the steps here. You'll feel reet in a handful of minutes.'

Jewel plopped down on to the edge of the cool stone. Her surroundings had started to spin – she rested her head in her hands. 'Benji?'

'Aye?'

'I think I'm going to be . . .' Slapping a hand to her mouth as the contents of her stomach rose, she jumped to her feet. Fancy her getting herself into this state. In public, too. Lord, the shame . . .

'Over here.' Supporting her, he headed for a cluster of trees nearby. Whether accidental – though she very much doubted it, given his previous conduct – the hand of his right arm, draped over her shoulder, brushed against her breast with each step. However, she hadn't the sense nor the strength to scold. Sickness, rising by the second, was washing over her in dizzying waves.

When they reached the seclusion of the canopy of thick-leaved branches, she leaned her hip against a trunk and bent forward. 'God, I feel awful.'

Benji didn't respond. He moved her long plait away from her face and rubbed her back.

'Mam'll give me a dressing-down good and proper to see me like this.'

'Nay.' His voice was a murmur and his hand moved

up, down, up, down, in firm but steady strokes. 'We'll stop here 'til you feel well enough. She need never know. That's it, now sit down here,' he told her when her retching subsided. He helped her to the damp grass.

Lying back and closing her eyes, she instantly regretted it as nausea swooped again. Groaning, she tried to haul herself up.

'You're all right. It'll pass in a minute.' Ignoring her meek protests, Benji pressed her back. 'You're all right,' he repeated. 'Close your eyes, rest.'

'What . . . ?' Was he? she asked herself, the thought jumbled. He was. He was touching her thigh. She knew a moment of confused panic but her lids were weighty and her eyes wouldn't open properly. 'What are you doing?' she croaked.

His only answer was his heavy breathing. He lifted her hand and closed her fingers around something warm and hard. She tried to pull away but his hold tightened around hers; he moved her hand up and down in rapid jerks. What was . . . ? What was he . . . ?

His other hand had risen to the sheltered place between her legs. Feeling his fingertips play at the down there lent her a burst of fight – eyes widening in horror, she opened her mouth to scream. Lightning fast, he clamped a hand over it before the scream could escape.

Her heart was beating so fast she could barely feel it. Peering up, her bleary gaze picked out parts of his face. Dappled moonlight filtering through the leaves distorted his shimmering features. She could only stare, mind and body locked in hazy fog as he exposed her breasts. His breathing grew to heavy pants as he fumbled at them with his hands and mouth, and still she was powerless to do a thing, too numb with confusion and shock and terror to even squeak. Neither did she cry out when once more her skirts lifted and now, his fingers probed roughly. Her screams remained deep within; not for anything could she push them past her lips.

The last thing she was aware of before blackness claimed her was the hot breath on her face and the crushing weight as her cousin climbed on top of her.

Chapter 4

'jewel? customer! wake up, for the love of God.'

'Oh. Aye. Sorry.'

Esther threw her a look of disdain. 'You need a firework up your backside this morning, lady.'

Fireworks.

Dancing, ale. Trees. Wet grass, *pain* . . .

She swallowed hard; once, twice.

'I knew – didn't I tell Bernard it were a mistake having thee out front?' Esther continued, through the side of her mouth so the man perusing canes across the shop couldn't hear. As well as their staple of umbrellas, items such as walking sticks, cigars and pipes could also be purchased at Powell & Son's. 'Useless, you are, that's what.'

'And didn't I tell him I'd be just that: no use? I'd much rather have stopped out of the way out back or upstairs with my scrubbing. It were him what wouldn't take nay for an answer.'

A meeting at the bank had pulled her uncle from his duties and, though her mother helped out with the serving of customers in such an event, Flora was at this minute tucked up in bed with a chest cold caught from yesterday's damp weather. Esther, of course, wouldn't dream of soiling her hands in the shop. Besides, it was

Friday: the day she regularly partook of refreshments and gossip with several other traders' wives in the front parlour of the bonnet-makers' shop across town. As for Benji, where he'd disappeared to was anyone's guess.

Disgust, fast becoming a familiar foe, slithered through her guts at the thought of her cousin. Disgust at him. Disgust at herself . . .

'Look lively.' Esther's hiss, accompanied by a swift elbow jab to Jewel's ribs, sliced through her thoughts. 'Good morning, sir,' she continued, tone now sickly sweet, face bright in smile, to the gentleman customer who had approached the counter. 'I'm afraid I've been called away on an important engagement but my very competent niece, here, will see to your needs. Have a pleasant day.' She straightened her bonnet, flashed another smile then crossed to the door – but not before shooting Jewel a warning look over her shoulder. Then she was gone, leaving a faint scent of musky perfume and the unspoken threat of what would befall her niece should she put a foot wrong in her wake.

Resisting the urge to sigh deeply, Jewel turned her attention to the customer's purchases. When, minutes later, the bell above the door tinkled, signalling his exit, she leaned her arms on the countertop and, dipping her head, closed her eyes.

She had to confront him.

Waking earlier in her own bed at Back Cheapside with an ache in her head that felt like a dozen cantering horses had taken up residence there, she'd been at a loss to remember the tail end of the previous night. She'd had to ask her mam when she'd come to rouse her with a cup of tea and slice of bread and pork dripping. Benji had brought her back, Flora had told her, with a tut-tut of disapproval at her inebriated state on their arrival.

Good lad, he was, seeing her right home – anything could have occurred in her condition. And what would Esther say should she hear, and her good enough to give her time off yesterday to enjoy the festivities? Best that she get up and swill with cold water, dash the drink pallor from her face, and quick sharp before she made matters worse by rolling into work late. The last thing they needed was her – or the pair of them – losing their positions, for coal and rent and grub didn't fall freely from the sky, did they? Then where would they be? Rapping at the workhouse doors, that's what. And on . . .

But Flora's words had stopped meaning anything. Slivers of memories had begun to trickle through the fog. Yet wispy as a spider's web, they broke just as easily when she dug into them too much, leaving nothing but cold blankness.

Something had happened, she knew instinctively. Squeezing her eyes shut hard in concentration, she'd tried again to remember . . . something, anything. Slowly, Benji's face had appeared through the mugginess. If the jumble of emotions she was experiencing, a mixture of confused shame and simmering panic, couldn't shed light on events then the tenderness between her legs told her all she needed to know.

She'd risen, dressed and broken her fast with numb calmness, though her remembrance of this was now hazy. She couldn't even recall arriving at the shop. Yet here she was, as though nothing had occurred, nothing was out of the ordinary. In reality, the world as she knew it had shattered to dust. Half her mind was vaguely aware of this, but the rest, including her body, didn't seem to have caught up, was suspended in some frozen, unfeeling state that she neither understood nor could attempt to understand. She'd turned in on herself, closed down, this she knew. And here she'd prefer to remain. For the alternative, the truth . . .

'Jewel.' Now, Benji paused on the threshold, blinked twice, then closed the shop door. 'All right? Has Mam already left?'

Outside, rain pelted the windows, its steady drum filling the silence. Her head moved of its own accord in a nod.

'Bad again out there.' He shook the water from his cap and tucked it under his arm. 'All right?' he asked again.

'Last night.' Once more, her actions were not her own – she felt her lips move but hadn't commanded them to. 'At the park.'

'Aye?'

'You . . .'

He broke their stare. 'We did, aye.'

We . . . ?

'Does tha regret it?' he added quietly.

We. Him and her. The two of them? But . . . This couldn't, couldn't be . . .

'I don't,' he continued. 'It were gradely. Christ, the feel of thee . . .' He cleared his throat. 'I'll not tell no one.'

She'd consented. She'd allowed him? Never, she'd never . . . And yet doubt pierced like hot knives inside her chest. She felt breathless, light-headed. She had to say it: 'I lay with you willingly?'

Again, his gaze flicked away. He looked at his feet. 'So tha does regret it.'

God in heaven above . . . 'I need . . . need some air.' She stumbled past him and out of the shop.

Jewel's feet took her in the direction of Deansgate. Grinding to a halt at the corner, she viewed the bustling street through a film of tears.

She'd consented to relations with her cousin – he but a boy at that. Though unable to grasp why, she knew she would bear his child, could almost feel his seed inside her.

And if she should, would he deny all involvement? The Powells would take his word; would Mam? Would she blame her for allowing herself to get drunk, letting it happen? And if Benji did hold his hands up, what of it? The lad was fifteen years old, for God's sake. They *couldn't* wed – not that his parents, particularly Esther, would consent in a month of Sundays to such a notion anyway.

Covering her face with her hands, Jewel gave the bitter sobs life. There was no way out of this. Everything was ruined, everything. She'd be shunned by all she knew and loved, cast out with nothing, no one. Her life was in tatters, over . . .

The scrape of iron-rimmed wheels caught her attention and she paused. Peering through her fingers at an approaching cart, a thought entered her mind. What if she was to step into the road? The horse's large hooves would have power enough to trample her skull to pieces, and then she'd be dead and all this would be over with. Swept away by her emotions, her heartbeat quickened in relief at the prospect.

Putting out a foot, she took a step. Her other foot followed.

She moved forwards again. By now, the sound of the clomping hooves was deafening. The toes of her clogs brushed the road's edge – this was it. She took a deep breath, closed her eyes and stepped out.

Hot air from the beast's frightened snort fanned her face. Coming up against solid muscle, intense pain shot through her right hip and the cobblestones swept away from beneath her feet. Muffled yells faded to nothing.

'Lass?'

Splintered light filtered through her lids. Grey figures hovered above her.

'God in heaven above . . . Help me get her up, will thee, Mr Birch?'

'Yes, of course.'

Jewel felt hands go underneath her. Her cheek rested against a firm chest and she wanted to take her fists to it, beat it with all her might, for she was alive. No, no! Why couldn't they have left her be, to die in the gutter as she'd planned, as she deserved? Bastards! But it was useless – she seemed to have left her strength by the roadside and could do nothing but lie mutely in these unfamiliar arms, though inside she was screaming.

When the shop bell rang above her head, followed by Benji's shocked enquiry as to what had happened, her heart sank further and, now, she was glad of the sanctuary afforded by the man carrying her – she hid her face in his chest. He smelled of soap and fine cigars. She breathed the scent of him in, finding it pleasant despite herself. Anything to distract her mind from the lad speaking. The lad she'd . . . Fat, silent tears dripped down her cheeks and soaked into his crisp white shirt.

'Lay her down there, Mr Birch. That's it.'

'Uncle?' Jewel croaked as she was lowered on to a bed, brows knotting to realise it was Bernard speaking, had been from the start. He'd instructed this Mr Birch to aid him in getting her up. He'd found her in the road. Had he seen what she'd done? Lord, what must he be thinking? How would she explain this away?

'Don't try to talk,' Bernard murmured, covering her with a blanket and tucking it beneath her chin. 'You rest. Doctor's on his way. Fetch Flora, lad,' he added, to, she assumed, Benji – she still couldn't open her eyes, let alone move. Every ounce of energy seemed to have deserted her. She just wanted to sleep. Sleep and never, ever wake up . . .

'I'm afraid I must get back to the bank, Mr Powell. Unless you still need my assistance . . . ?'

'Nay, nay, you go. My thanks to you, Mr Birch, for your help. I – my niece here, too, I'm sure – appreciate it, sir.'

Jewel felt pressure on her fingers as they were squeezed lightly, then Mr Birch spoke again: 'I wish you a speedy recovery, Miss . . .'

'Nightingale,' said Bernard.

'Miss Nightingale. Indeed. Yes, well, I'll be on my way. Do not hesitate to send word should you need me for anything further, Mr Powell. Good day.'

'Ta, thank you, sir. Good day to thee.'

His footsteps died away then all was still. Though Bernard didn't make a sound, Jewel felt his presence beside her; it was comforting, safe. Sighing, she slipped into a heavy slumber.

*

What could only have been minutes later Flora was chafing her hands with soothing words. Now, when Jewel tried to open her eyes, they obeyed without resistance. Surprisingly, she felt alert, refreshed, as though she'd rested the day away. 'Mam. Oh, Mam.' The worry in the older woman's eyes tore at her. 'I'm sorry, I—'

'Hush now. Don't fret so. You're going to be just fine.' There was a break in Flora's voice. 'Doctor, here, shall fix you up, lass.'

A large, frowning man loomed above her and began prodding her stomach and examining her head with clipped instructions to say so if an area hurt. She winced once or twice – more from his harsh handling than possible harm inflicted by the cart – but otherwise, she felt fine.

God above, why? she raged inwardly, bunching her hands into fists until her nails bit into her palms. Why couldn't I have died and taken my problems with me to the grave, then no one need ever have known . . .

'Remarkably, you don't appear to have sustained any obvious injuries,' the medical man announced finally. He turned to Bernard. 'I shall return to check on her tomorrow in case of delayed damage. For now, see she gets plenty of rest. If her condition should change, send for me immediately.'

'Aye, Doctor. Ta, we will.'

Her uncle left to show him out; alone with her mother, Jewel avoided her gaze, certain she would see the truth burning in her own, that this wasn't an accident, as they all seemed to be assuming, that she'd . . . Her hands clenched tighter. That she'd wanted to die and did still.

'What happened, lovey? Weren't tha watching where tha were going? Or happen it were the driver's fault? Is that it?'

Outside, rain was pattering steadily once more. Jewel closed her eyes and listened for a while. Then: 'It were my fault. I stepped out without thinking, judged yon cart to be further away than it were. That I've worried thee so . . . I never meant to . . . Eeh, I'm that sorry, Mam.' And she was. For this, at least. Not that she'd done it, though. Not that. Yet how utterly selfish she'd been; she hadn't given a thought to Flora, to how she would have borne the loss, had her actions had the desired effect. She was a terrible daughter, she was. A terrible, foul rotten person . . .

'I don't know what I'd ever do without thee, you

know?' Her mother gripped her hand tightly and her usually tired eyes burned with no purer love. 'Never leave me, my lass. You must promise me.'

In that moment Jewel knew there was no escaping this. She couldn't flee from her problems, from what was to follow. She'd been foolish to think she could. She must face this, however difficult, whatever the outcome, the loss. 'I promise,' she whispered thickly.

'What's all this Bernard's just informed me of? What am I hearing, lady?' Esther's heavy tread on the stairs accompanied the questions – mother and daughter shared simultaneous sighs. As if matters were not bad enough, *she* was home.

'Here we go,' muttered Jewel.

'Well!' Her bulk filled the doorway as she paused, hands on hips, and took in the scene. 'What on earth has occurred here the day in my absence? Answer me.'

'Jewel took a tumble at the road's edge and was knocked down by a horse.' Flora spoke for her. Rising from the chair by the bed, she added, 'A terrible shock, she's had, and it's rest she needs now.' She moved towards the door but, clearly, her sister-in-law was deaf to the hint of leaving Jewel be.

'Well, of all the dim-witted, brainless . . .' Esther shook her bonneted head with a snort of disdain. 'And what, pray, were you doing, taking leisurely strolls around the town when you were meant to be working?'

'I . . . felt bad of a sudden, needed some air.'

Her aunt's eyes narrowed. 'You sickening for summat? That Wicks boy on your mind, was he, instead of your duties? Pining for him, were thee?' she finished spitefully, mouth lifting at the corners, as though thoughts of Jewel heartsore brought her pleasure.

'I care naught for Jem Wicks.'

'Hm. And what of the shop? Did you leave the place unattended, lady?'

'Course not. Benji were here.'

'Thanks be to God for that. Poor lad, burdened with the running of the business all afternoon and at his age.'

A simmering rage was building in Jewel – with effort, loath to make matters worse, she bit her tongue. *Poor lad?* Huh! This blinkered fool didn't know her precious son as well as she believed; nay, not a bit. And anyway, what about her? There was no thought of poor Jewel, who had toiled in this rotten shop since she was knee high. No poor Jewel, with the chapped and mottled hands since the age of seven from daily scrubbing this family's living quarters for a pittance. She'd broken her back in this shop almost her whole life to ease the financial burden on her mother's shoulders, and had done so without ever a word of complaint. Poor lad, my left eye . . .

'You'll work the doctor's fee off, lady, let me tell you that as well. Oh yes. Why must we be expected to fork out for your stupidity? Then there's your poor mam, here. Tearing her from her sickbed and frickening her half to death, I'll bet. By, I just don't know what's the matter with you at times, I don't, really—'

'That's enough, Esther.' Flora's tone was firm. 'The lass has suffered enough for one day.'

'Oh, Flora.' Esther addressed her with exaggerated patience, as though talking to a child. 'When will tha stop making allowances for her daftness?'

'When I'm snug in my grave beneath the clay, that's when! Jewel's sorry, so why don't you just leave her be and—?'

'Now then, wenches.' Bernard had appeared behind his wife and, as always, his quiet tone had the desired effect; they fell silent and he nodded. 'Flora, would you brew a pot of tea?' To his wife, he said, 'Come, let our niece rest up. Sleep is what she needs, aye.'

He led the women from the room and, before disappearing, turned to give Jewel a soft wink. She smiled gratefully. The door clicked shut and she trained her gaze on the ceiling.

How could life as she knew it change so rapidly in so short a space of time? The question swirled around her mind for a moment as though searching every nook for the answer. Of course, it wouldn't find it; there was no explanation, no sense or reason. What she wouldn't give to turn back the hands of time, be the carefree girl from a day ago, before the park and Benji, before the town hall, the Prince, Jem. For that's the point at which things had started to spiral into trouble, she understood this now.

'*That Wicks boy on your mind, was he, instead of your duties?*' Esther's assumption, so far removed from the truth of things, came back to Jewel and she almost laughed. If only that was what troubled her! Jem, the past months, their misguided feelings for one another, seemed embarrassingly childlike now. So, too, did his scratching at an excuse when he realised he'd been caught out, his wild suggestion that they wed . . .

Her brow cleared. She sat up in bed. Somewhere deep within her, a spark of hope smouldered and spread. She swallowed hard, her heart beginning to bang.

'Aye,' she whispered to the empty room. Beneath the bedclothes, her hand travelled to her flat stomach. 'Aye, yes.'

Chapter 5

LOOKING BACK, JEWEL couldn't say how she bore the following days.

Flora had been reluctant to see her go back to work, suggesting that returning the very next day following her 'accident' was too soon, that she must have time to recuperate. Jewel had dismissed her worries with quiet resolution. Not only was remaining at home impractical – the rent was due and they required her wages to supplement it – she also desperately needed the distraction. She'd lose her mind entirely were she to waste away the hours fretting in bed.

Besides, what impression would it give to Benji if she stopped away? He'd believe she was avoiding the place – him. She wouldn't give him the satisfaction of that. Never one to wallow for long, she'd always had a steady outlook, refused to let life knock her down for too long. She wasn't about to change now.

Lifting a figurine from a side table in the Powells' parlour, she ran the duster over it in swift, efficient flicks. She'd definitely made the right decision in coming back to work. For the very first time she was glad of Esther's slave-driver ways – the hours marched steadily by when she was engrossed in her duties and she was thankful of it. Fortunately, too, it looked like Benji was giving her a wide berth. Now, if only matters could stay the same until the end of the week . . . If she could just get through these next few days drama free . . .

Pausing in her task, she sneaked a hand to her midriff. Brows knitting in a frown, she stroked it slowly. Would her monthly bleed come? she asked herself, though she knew almost with certainty that it wouldn't. And yet . . . yet . . . The prospect of what that meant no longer filled her with all-consuming terror. Not since the solution had presented itself.

In odd moments of reflection – she did her best to quell memories of the incident with the cart, though, sometimes, they stole to her mind unsummoned – she still marvelled that she'd escaped unscathed. It truly was a miracle she hadn't been at all hurt; even the doctor said as much during his final obligatory visit the following day. It was as if it was somehow . . . meant to be . . .

Instantly, her hand sprang from her stomach to retrieve the duster and she resumed her cleaning with gusto. Don't harbour such thoughts, remember? she told herself firmly, mouth set. What shall be shall be – in no way, though, is this a positive thing. Stepping in front of that oncoming beast as she had – well, her mind hadn't been her own, had it? It was a flash of madness, she knew this now. Yet though she was grateful she was still here to ponder on such things, that her life had been spared, the fact that her stomach hadn't received at least a hard knock from the cart or cobbles, or a kick from a hoof, was something to be regretted.

Although, would it have made a difference so soon after . . . the deed, with Benji? Surely the child to come couldn't yet be removed from her body, by brute force or otherwise? Surely it needed to grow some for that to be possible? Oh, she'd been so foolish to think . . . to risk everything . . . If only she could speak to her mother. Of course, that was a cavernous impossibility. Flora knowing – God above, the thought made her want to be sick. She could never discover that her own daughter had lifted her skirts for a lad willingly. The shame would surely kill her.

No. She'd remedy this mess. She'd got herself into it; she and she alone would drag herself out of it, somehow, God willing. And there was but one person who could make that possible.

She'd put off seeking him out long enough – time she spoke to him, saw how matters stood, for this wasn't going away. The sooner she put her plan into action, the better.

Even as Jewel made these resolutions, she knew it was wrong. Desperate she might be, but this cruel streak she saw emerging in herself was new to her – could she really go through with this? Jem Wicks had hurt her, yes, it was true, but he didn't deserve this, did he? Hers would be a whole other level of betrayal.

'But do I have a choice?' she whispered to the empty room. Tears welled. She gulped them back and with an angry flick of her wrist flung the duster into her cleaning box. This she then returned to the cupboard on the landing before heading downstairs.

Bernard glanced around as she entered the shop. 'Finished for the day, lass?'

'Aye. I'll be away home now, Uncle Bernard, unless there's owt else . . . ?'

'Nay, nowt.' He flapped a hand. 'You go, I'll see thee the morrow.'

'Ta, thanks.' Jewel retrieved her shawl, draped it around her shoulders and left the shop. Outside, her gaze went in the direction of Jem's home and she took some deep breaths. She felt sick with nerves. Guilt, too, but she wouldn't dwell on that – couldn't. Sucking in a last lungful of air, she headed across the square.

After knocking at his door and being told by his mother that he wasn't yet back from work, Jewel went to wait for him at the corner. The passing minutes felt like hours and with each one that crawled by her nervousness steadily grew. Eventually, hooters from the surrounding cluster of mills and factories sounded and the town began to tremble quietly with the thud of clogs. They grew louder by the second and workers appeared, trudging through the grey streets like living corpses. Some chatted amongst themselves but, mostly, the exhausted crowd passed along mutely, minds on hearth and home and, if they were lucky, a meal of sorts awaiting them on the table.

By the time she saw him appear, empty bait tin swinging in one hand and flat cap in the other, his dark hair and clothes flecked with cotton spores, her heart threatened to smash through her chest. She stepped forward as he neared the ginnel's entrance and he slowed, his face showing his surprise.

'Jewel.'

'Hello, Jem.'

They stared at one another for some seconds until, his brow creased slightly, he asked cautiously, 'All right?'

She nodded. 'Aye, you?'

'Aye.'

Again, silence fell between them. In the past, he'd told her a little of his work as a mule spinner, that cotton pieces clung to the air in the mills like thick snow – it had made her glad she was employed in clean and respectable shop work. Now, a white wisp bobbed on his eyelashes as he blinked; without thinking, she reached out and brushed it away with her fingertip.

He smiled. 'Was tha waiting here for me?'

Again, she moved her head up and down. Stabbing guilt returned, twisting her guts into knots, when his mouth spread further in pleasure. 'Can I talk with thee?' she forced herself to ask.

He led her through the cobbled entry to the familiar nook between two houses. Here, until not too long ago, they had shared innocent clandestine kisses. She was glad of the bad lighting that helped to conceal her flush at the memories and regret at what must come. 'Jem, I—'

'Please, let me say summat first.' He stared at his feet. 'I've been daft, Jewel. I miss thee, you know?'

'I know,' she murmured. And she knew he told the truth. It was clear in his tone. She couldn't, however, return the sentiment in either feeling or speech. If she was true to herself, she hadn't missed him, had she? Once the initial sting of betrayal had worn off, she'd found herself over him relatively quickly – proof their relationship hadn't meant that much, really. Nor would she now say she had. The lies to come, the ones she must force herself to see through, would be enough. She wouldn't add to them if she could help it and so she remained silent.

'She, she meant – means – nowt to me.'

'Happen I were hasty in ending things. Between us, like.'

Jem's eyes widened. 'Tha means that?'

'Aye, I do.' The words tasted bitter on her tongue and she had to swallow several times before continuing. 'Mebbe we . . . well, we could begin afresh. What d'you say?'

'I say aye, Jewel. Eeh, lass, you'll not regret it.' He took her hand in his. 'I'll do nowt to hurt thee again, you have my word on it.'

She blinked rapidly, nodded twice. 'Right then. That's sorted. I'd best get on home afore Mam gets worried.'

Jem walked with her. At the turning to her street he planted a loud kiss on her cheek. 'Ay, I'm that happy.'

'Aye,' was all she could muster.

'Bye for now, then.' Whistling a cheery tune, he turned and sauntered back towards his house.

She watched him go through a film of tears. That was that, then. And how easy it had been. He hadn't a single inkling of what she was about, the scheme she'd hatched, of just what he'd let himself in for.

She'd hoodwinked him without any effort at all.

She was the most despicable being in the world.

With effort, she suppressed her emotions. Where did feelings ever get you, anyway? she told herself bitterly. She squared her shoulders, lifted her chin and continued home.

*

Focusing on the here and now worked best for Jewel, she found. Were she to let her mind wander even a day into the future, she'd begin to shake all over and her brow and palms broke out in a cold sweat.

How her mother didn't guess that something was amiss with her, she struggled to think. Of course, Bernard was too busy to notice. Esther wouldn't have cared even if she had. As for Benji, she barely set eyes on him. Life was seemingly continuing just the same as it ever had for him. He made no other mention of what had taken place between them. She could have almost imagined the whole thing had never occurred – if the reality wasn't embedded like a cancer in her mind, that was.

Then came the day that she'd been awaiting with a

mixture of frantic hope and heavy dread. It brought with it sickening, world-shattering truth, and she knew life as she'd known it would never be the same, for any of them, again.

Despite her having already accepted it from the start, still she found herself slipping out to the privy hourly. There, she would offer up a silent prayer before checking her underwear. Every time, the longed-for crimson staining was absent. And she just knew – knew – that what she'd feared all along had happened. Mother of God, how would she bear this?

She'd told herself that should, by some miracle, her bleed arrive, she'd make her excuses and call the whole thing off with Jem Wicks. After all, she'd have no use for him then, would she, and everything could return to some semblance of normality. How could she be so utterly deceitful? She avoided asking herself that, for her terror and self-loathing that it had come to this, that she had sunk to such a low, was like a physical pain.

But survival, self-preservation, were much stronger forces. Desperate folk did desperate things. Now, she had no option but to see her plan through. None.

She wouldn't – couldn't – bear the world knowing the real circumstances. Judged, disowned, loathed . . . The stigma of bastard clinging not only to herself but to the child, for ever more . . . She really would sooner die than that.

And no one did need to know, did they? If she played this right . . .

'I'll be a fair wife to you, Jem, I promise. I'll devote my life to making it up to you, making you happy, I swear it,' she whispered now through trembling lips to the cloud-filled sky, arms wrapped tightly around herself. 'Forgive me. I'm sorry but I must do this.'

'Lass, are you all right? Your grub's growing cowd, here.'

'Coming, Mam.' Scrubbing at her wet cheeks with the back of her hand, she pushed herself away from the outside privy wall she'd been sagged against and dragged herself back indoors.

'Good potato pie, that is, and you've barely touched it.' Flora pointed at Jewel's plate with her fork. 'You sickening for summat? You've been back and fro to that privy the whole day long.'

Jewel forced down a morsel of pastry. 'I reckon I'm sick, aye, Mam. My guts are off, must be summat I've ate.'

'Coming out of both ends, is it?' asked her mother sympathetically, adding, 'Well, you get yourself an early night the night. There's nowt cures a body better than sleep.'

Jewel nodded, though she had no intention of upholding the agreement. Tonight, the deed with Jem must be done – the sooner the better. Her entire future depended on it.

The following hours crawled by agonisingly slowly. Sitting at opposite sides of the fire, she and her mother darned in companionable silence. Finally, through the flames' cosy rose-gold light, she spied her mother's eyelids drooping. Jewel's heart gave a few heavy thumps in response. Not long now. Almost time . . .

'Ready for bed, lass?' Dropping her sewing into the wicker basket on the table, Flora rose and stretched. 'Go on up, my love. I'll join thee in a minute once I've banked down the fire.'

'I'll do that, Mam.'

Her mother made to protest but tiredness won through: 'You sure?'

'Aye, go on. I'll not be long.'

'A good lass, that's what you are,' her mother said as she climbed the stairs, and Jewel could have cried.

Oh, Mam. Good I ain't. Nay, not now. It's foul and wicked I've become and there's worse still to come. I'm sorry . . .

'You asleep?' she asked minutes later as she entered the tiny bedroom. It was clear Flora was; her steady, rhythmic snores proved it but still she pressed closer to the bed they shared, had to be certain: 'Mam?'

Nothing. Watching her sleep, Jewel's eyes filled with shameful tears. She reached out a hand to stroke her mother's hair then, fearful of waking her and her plan being ruined, let it fall back to her side. She straightened and tiptoed from the room.

Avoiding the stairs she knew creaked, she reached the kitchen again with barely a sound. The ill-fitting door refused to cooperate and released a low groan as she opened it – cursing it under her breath, she squeezed her head through the gap and peered through the cool, indigo night. A full moon threw its cream-coloured beam along the cobbled expanse and after some moments she picked out a familiar figure through the shadows. A sigh of relief escaped her that he'd received word and had showed. She'd paid an urchin boy to call on Jem with the message earlier, but they couldn't always be trusted to deliver; sometimes, they would simply scarper with the brass, never to be seen again. She beckoned Jem across with a flap of her hand.

'All right, Jewel—?'

'Sshhh.'

'Sorry,' he whispered back.

'Come on in. Hurry, in case we're seen.' She pulled him inside and closed the door.

'So.' He removed his cap and placed it on the back of a chair. 'Tha wanted to see me? All's well, ain't it?'

'Aye, aye.'

'Then what . . . ?'

'I just wanted to see thee is all. Here, sit down.'

Looking pleased – which tore at Jewel – Jem did as she said. He smiled in surprise when, instead of taking the seat opposite, she perched on the arm of his. He took her hand in his. 'By, I've missed thee.'

She motioned to the ceiling and held a finger to her lips. 'Quiet, lad. We don't want to waken Mam.'

He nodded agreement. But something behind his eyes told her he wasn't altogether comfortable with this – Jewel was quick to reassure him.

'Don't fret, it's all right, really. She's a fair heavy sleeper.'

'I just don't . . . Why did you ask me here at this hour, lass? You ain't ever afore now.'

He was on to her, knew she was up to something. Paranoia stole through her, bringing heat to her cheeks. Her behaviour had made him suspicious – he was right, she'd never initiated anything like this in all the time she'd known him. She must take this slow or else all her carefully made plans would be ruined . . . 'Like I said, I just wanted to see thee. I wanted to be alone with thee. Proper, like. We never really have time to ourselves. Do we?'

'I . . . suppose not, nay.' Understanding had finally filled his eyes. His licked his lips in a nervous yet excited motion. 'Jewel?'

'Aye, Jem?'

He wetted his lips once more. 'When you say "time to ourselves", do you mean like . . . well, you know?'

What if I do the deed with Jem and my bleed comes after all? The thought crashed through her brain. What if I'm wrong, if I'm not carrying Benji's child? I'd have given myself – chained myself – to this lad here for nothing. Yet didn't it arrive right on time every month? When had she ever been even a day late before? Never, that's when – she could usually set the clock by it. Besides, hadn't she just known that this would be the outcome of her shameful behaviour with her cousin? Instinctively, she'd felt the truth of it from the very start.

There was no mistaking it, however much she wanted to. She was with child. The sooner she had Jem's seed inside her, the better for all concerned. For once he discovered her condition – which he would believe to be his doing – he'd wed her just as he'd suggested when hoping to win her back, she was certain of it. He'd be none the wiser to the real truth of things, she'd do her utmost to create a happy marriage and home for him in return and her reputation would remain unblemished. More importantly, the child would be spared the stigma of illegitimacy. After all, when all was said and done, none of this was the poor blighter's fault, was it?

She was confident that Benji hadn't the sense to put two and two together. He was too young, too immature, to understand the female body and its workings, surely? He couldn't yet have any real knowledge of bleeds and dates and suchlike. Even if he was to suggest anything, she'd deny it to the hilt. He'd have no choice but to take her word as truth. It wasn't as if he'd ever be able to prove otherwise.

Nothing stood in her way but her conscience. Could she really see this through? Did she have it in her to trick this lad like this, in the worst way possible?

'Why don't you come and sit here?' Jem mumbled, hauling her mind back to the present. His cheeks had taken on a cherry hue – it was clear, despite his behaviour with that other girl, that he'd never before gone further with a female than kissing. He was as awkward as a young boy. 'That's if you want to, I mean,' he hastened to add, flushing further. 'If you'd rather not, if you're comfy enough where you are, then ... well, I just thought ...'

Jewel snaked an arm around his neck. Then avoiding his gaze, she slid into his lap. Immediately, she felt his arousal straining through the coarse material of his trousers. Panic swamped her; she shifted instinctively but the motion proved only to stoke the flames to an inferno – he grew harder, groaning low in his throat.

'Jewel ... Oh, love.' Wrapping his arms around her, he covered her mouth with his.

She matched his passion but, inside, her every sinew screamed at her to leap up and run as fast and as far away from him as she could. For his touch had awakened memories she'd thought the drink had killed for ever. She remembered. Benji's podgy fingers probing painfully where they shouldn't ... His hot palms on her thighs, drawing them wide ... Lord, no, don't make me live it, not again ...

Jem broke their kiss to fumble at his belt buckle and it took everything she had not to shriek and cry and slap his face again and again and again ... She must allow him, must see this through. Jesus, give me strength.

'Are you certain about this?' Jem whispered through his panting.

Jewel doubted he'd be able to contain himself much longer but the fact that he'd even asked ... Tears sprang to her throat and her guilt reached fever pitch. The enormity of what her answer would be was crushing her like a ten-ton weight.

'We don't have to, Jewel. Not if you ain't ready.'

Oh Jem, Jem . . . Her heart was hammering so fast she thought she was going to pass out. Then, 'I can't. I'm sorry.' She disentangled herself and scrambled to her feet. 'I'm sorry, Jem.'

He closed his eyes and nodded. 'No bother.'

'You . . . don't mind?'

'Nay, course not. Just . . . give me a minute to cool down.' He flashed a self-conscious grin then closed his eyes once more as he strove to steady his breathing.

She'd worked him up to such a level and yet . . . At least now she knew some males could control their urges if they wanted to. His understanding tore at her heart. How had she considered manipulating this decent lad for her own selfish gains? God, she was rotten through and through . . .

He deserved better. Oh, he did that. And she deserved everything she had coming to her, and more. She'd never forgive herself for what she'd almost done tonight. 'Happen you should leave,' she murmured.

He turned to look at her and frowned. 'Aye. If you're sure?'

'I'm sure.'

'Jewel, are we all right?' Putting on his cap, he took her hand.

For the briefest moment, she squeezed back. Then, biting back tears, she slid out her fingers from his hold. He made to reach for her again but she stepped away, shaking her head.

'You seeking me out the other day; was you acting through spite all along? Was tonight, all of it, about revenge for what I did to thee?'

Nay. Oh, nay. God above, she couldn't bear this . . .

'Jewel?'

'Goodbye, Jem.'

He stared at her for a long moment. His shoulders slumped and, sighing, he turned and left the house.

'It's for your own good, lad,' Jewel mouthed to the closed door. 'You'll see that one day.'

Pressing a fist to her mouth, she crumpled, sobbing, into the chair.

Chapter 6

THE FLASH OF colour from the mass of bedding plants on the sloped bank captured hints of the sun's gold. Sat on a set of steps at the south end of the park, Jewel hugged her knees and watched the delicate petals bobbing in the breeze.

Oddly, being here aroused no feelings of fear or disgust within her – in fact, she found that the park still evoked the same emotions it always had: calm and quiet enjoyment. For this, she was more grateful than she could express. Her drunken wickedness hadn't tainted at least this one aspect of her life.

She heaved a sigh. She was due in work in half an hour and each passing second felt like a step closer to the gallows. She might as well find a rope and put it around her neck herself now, save her family the trouble.

Cotton manufacturing being the staple trade of the borough, a body could never escape the fact, whichever direction in the town they took – in the distance, mills and chimneys hovered on the skyline like silver-black bricked ghosts. Up and beyond, rising stately, proud, stood the tower of the new town hall. The sight made her want to weep. She could scarcely believe how different things were since that opening day. Had it really been but a few short weeks ago?

'Sod them, all of them,' she whispered fiercely. 'To hell with their judgement. I'm past caring.'

Nonetheless, prickly heat flooded her face at the unavoidable confession to come. All was lost with Jem. Hiding her condition for long was impossible. There was nothing else for it – she had to come clean.

In desperation, she focused her concentration on the flowers once more; following tradition since the park opened, they formed the name of Bolton's current mayor. But her distracted stare refused to linger on the letters for too long and, all too soon, her mind strayed to thoughts of the abhorrent words she must soon speak. That terrible, existence-shattering truth . . .

'Hello. Miss Nightingale, isn't it?'

The easy tone from close by had her whipping her head around as though the speaker had yelled the greeting into her ear.

'Forgive me. I didn't mean to startle you.'

Jewel squinted up in surprise. She glanced to the man's side but the mischievous toddler she'd first seen him with in this park was absent.

'How are you?'

'I . . . I'm well, ta.' She nodded in confusion when he indicated if he could sit. He lowered himself on to the step beside her and her brow creased. 'You called me Miss Nightingale. How do you know my name?'

'You don't remember?'

Her frown deepened. 'Remember . . . ? But we've never passed words.'

'Yes, indeed, that much is true.'

'Sorry, I don't under—'

'No need to apologise; after all, you'd had quite the shock that day, when you . . .' He paused to clear his throat.

Realisation brought embarrassment to her eyes and

heat to her cheeks. She recognised his voice now all right. 'The day I walked in front of a passing cart?' she finished for him quietly.

'Yes, well.' He shrugged matter-of-factly. 'We all make mistakes.'

Was that a hint of amusement pulling at the corners of his mouth? she asked herself. Anger rose within her. He was mocking her? Just who the hell did he believe himself to be to even think of taking such a liberty with someone he barely knew? As far as she could see, it was no bloody laughing matter. Sod him, too. Sod them all! She rose abruptly.

'Oh. I do hope you're not leaving on my account?' he asked, almost disappointedly.

She released a soft snort. This one didn't half think a lot of himself. 'I'm due in work.'

'You're employed at Mr Powell's premises in the square, is that so?'

'That's right.' She rearranged her shawl, nodded a stiff farewell and set off across the grounds.

However, after only a few steps, Jewel found herself reluctantly turning back towards him. He was her uncle's acquaintance – and a gentleman, to boot. Bernard wouldn't be best pleased to learn she'd acted rudely towards him. And when all was said and done, he *had* come to her aid that day, had carried her back to the umbrella shop. 'I . . . well, your assistance after my accident . . . Thank you.'

The man stared at her for a moment. Then, smiling, he held out a hand. 'Maxwell Birch.'

She felt her hand slip into his. 'Jewel.'

'What an interesting name.'

'So I'm told.' Surprising herself further, she resumed her seat beside him.

'You have some time to spare after all?'

'Aye, mebbe. Well, a little.' Colour touched her cheeks again. She shot a sidelong glance to see him smiling wryly and, this time, her own lips twitched in response.

She would have guessed him to be in his middle fifties. A slight dusting of grey at his temples correlated with her assumption, although this only added agreeably to his looks. His broad upper arms and shoulders and firm-looking thighs showed her he took care of his physical fitness – no doubt chasing around after his live-wire daughter helped with that. Besides the laughter creases around his deep brown eyes, his open face was unlined. Perhaps his nose was a little too large and his lips a little too thin but, nonetheless, he cut an attractive figure.

Bringing her gaze back to the flowerbed before he noticed her staring, she said, 'Sorry, Mr Birch, for being short with thee earlier. It's just—'

'You believed I was poking fun at you,' he observed mildly. 'I wasn't, you know. It was simply my attempt to lighten the mood but, evidently, it failed miserably.' His smile broadened. 'You see? We *do* all make mistakes from time to time.'

'Aye.' *But God above, me more than most*, she added in her mind.

'Your uncle is most fond of you.'

A stirring of pleasure chased away Jewel's misery. She smiled. 'He told you that?'

'He didn't have to. It was clear to see upon him realising that the girl lying by the roadside was his niece.' Maxwell turned fully to look at her now and all traces of laughter had left his face. 'I'm senior clerk at the Bank of Bolton, and it was during my meeting with Mr Powell that the incident occurred.'

She nodded. Puzzlement had brought her brows together at the sudden seriousness of his tone. 'It was fortunate that he was close by, that he spotted me, aye.'

'Miss Nightingale . . .' He paused to run a hand through his thick hair.

'Yes?'

'It was I who alerted your uncle. I saw it happen from the window.' His voice dropped. 'I saw it *all*.'

'You did?' She swallowed hard when he nodded. Further words deserted her. She could only stare at him dumbly. Then was he aware it had been no accident, that she'd intended for that horse to hit her . . . ?

'Why did you do it?'

Oh, he was aware all right. His quiet question hung between them. She closed her eyes.

'Miss Nightingale?'

'Yes?' she whispered.

'What on earth prompts a young woman such as yourself, with her whole life ahead of her, to attempt . . . Why?' he repeated.

'I don't know.'

'You don't know?'

'Nay.'

'However, you don't deny it?'

Jewel opened her eyes. They were blurry with tears. 'I did intend it, you're right. It were a mistake, mind; I see it now and I regret it. It were nowt but a second of madness.' What was she doing? Why in the world was she admitting this to him? He had a way of putting you at your ease, making you comfortable in his presence . . . Sudden panic gripped her. She turned wide eyes to him. 'You'll not tell anyone – not the police?' Suicide was, after all, a criminal offence. 'Surely not my uncle? Please, I . . . I were wrong, I know it now. I'll never do it again, nay, never.'

'I rather think you should be the one to tell—'

'Nay. I can't!'

'Miss Nightingale.' Maxwell's voice was low, gentle. 'Your family would be only too willing to help with whatever it is that troubles you, I'm certain.'

'Please . . .'

'You must understand my predicament. If you were to attempt something similar and the results next time proved disastrous, I would never forgive myself for keeping my silence—'

'I shan't. Mr Birch, I told thee, it were but a daft, brainless mistake.'

'Be honest with them. I'm sure—'

'I'll be going now.' On shaky legs, she rose and backed off towards the park gates. Scalding tears clogging her throat threatened to choke her. To think she'd believed that things couldn't get any worse. Here was just another of her sins set to be exposed. Her mother would die from the shame of it all, she would, without doubt.

Maxwell called her name but, shaking her head, she turned and hurried away.

He thought her insane. Of course he did, and who could blame him? Perhaps she was. She didn't even know herself any more.

Troubles ran on in her mind, unrelenting as she trudged through the dank-coloured streets. The gentleman she'd just fled from believed her capable of attempting self-murder again, at any given time, and was worried that he was privy to the fact. That she'd dragged yet another innocent being into this putrid mess! Just how many decent people's lives would she taint or ruin completely before all this was over?

Right now, she didn't class Benji as being half to blame. She'd been the one to agree to lie with him, after all. She was the elder, supposedly had more common sense. Hadn't he been after her for months? She'd been well aware of it; his hungry eyes and hands when he was around her made it impossible not to be. She should never have let herself get into the inebriated state she had, shouldn't have let herself – let the two of them – get into the situation they had.

Without question, fault lay with her. However much people would hate her once the truth got out, it wouldn't even begin to touch the level of black loathing she carried for herself.

*

Benji was lounging behind the counter looking bored when Jewel entered. She glanced around. 'You here alone?'

'Aye. I ain't sure when Mam and Father will be back – they've gone calling on a sick friend or summat – but Aunt Flora should be here shortly, thank God.' He released a theatrical sigh. 'It ain't half dull in here.'

He looked like a spoilt youngster who had been told he couldn't go out to play. God above, to think she was to have a child with him ... He was nowhere near mature enough for this – well, obviously he wasn't, he was fif-bloody-teen! she reminded herself, angry tears threatening. Just what the *hell* was she going to *do*?

'Make a fresh sup, eh, Jewel?'

Nodding distractedly, she made for the door that led to the Powells' living quarters. As she collected cups and spooned tea from the caddy into the small teapot, she rehearsed in a whisper the conversation she must have with her cousin: 'Benji, listen, our night together ...' She paused to close her eyes, grimacing. Just uttering those words made her feel sick.

However, she must. There was no putting this off any

longer. Best she made him aware of the circumstances before the rest of the family heard it. At least then, she'd be a little better prepared, would know his feelings on the matter. He might even come up with some sort of solution . . . She dismissed the last notion immediately. What in God's name *could* he think up? There *was* nothing that would remedy this, was there?

The spoon clattered noisily as she threw it inside the cup with a cry of frustration. Splaying her hands on the table, she closed her eyes again, her breathing ragged. Hearing footsteps behind her, she forced herself to regain her composure, though her chest burned with unshed anguish. She rescued the spoon and reached for the caddy once more, saying over her shoulder, 'Benji, you shouldn't leave the shop; I'll fetch the tea down.'

'Well, when? I'm parched.'

'When it's bloody ready,' she snapped, turning towards him, hands on hips. 'You'll think so, should your mam and father return and catch you leaving the business unattended. Go on, get back down, will thee?'

'Customers are slow this time of day.'

'Even so—'

'We'll be all right for a few minutes.'

She'd returned her attention to the teapot – now, at his last quiet statement, she swivelled around again. 'What's that meant to mean?' She frowned when he didn't answer. 'Well?'

Benji moved so quickly that Jewel didn't have time to process what was happening until it was too late. His chubby hand groped clumsily at her breast and, after initial shock, blistering fury gushed through her veins. She staggered back against the table. Then she struck out with all her might, landing a deafening backhander across his stunned face. She moved in for a second time, sending his head swinging in the opposite direction as she slapped his other cheek, the sound like the cracking of a whip.

'Listen to me, you foul little divil,' she hissed through gritted teeth, shaking him by the front of his jacket as he whimpered and twisted, trying to break free. 'Touch me one more time and I'll cut them sweaty hands of yourn clean off. You understand?'

'But I thought . . . after last time . . .'

'Don't speak of that, just you don't! You thought wrong, by God you did.' She flung him from her, then to her horror promptly burst into tears.

Benji stood scowling before asking after some moments, 'What you upset for? It's me should be bawling.' He reached up to touch his tender face. 'Bitch. I've a good mind to tell Mam you put your hands on me.'

'Is that so?' Though tears still streamed down Jewel's cheeks, her voice was now void of emotion. 'Not before I do, lad. Aye, it's me what's to do the telling – about *you* putting your hands on *me*.' She nodded when his face paled. 'Consensual it might have been, God help and forgive me, but it's gone beyond a drunken fumble now. I'm with child. Do you hear me? I'm growing your bloody babby. There's no getting out of this – not even for thee. We're done for, lad.'

Whatever response she'd expected, it certainly wasn't what she received – her cousin folded his arms, expression calm. 'Happen it's Jem Wicks tha should be spouting this to, not me.'

'You what?'

'You heard. Word has it you offered yourself to him, an' all, not a week since. Not for the first time, I'll bet.'

She couldn't breathe. Though she tried to brazen it

out, she knew the guilt in her voice gave her away: 'I don't know what you're talking about, Benjamin Powell.'

'Aye, you do. Sneaking him in your rooms, eh, whilst your mam were abed above youse . . . ?' Shaking his head, he clicked his tongue several times.

'Nay. Nay, that's not . . . not right, I . . . !'

'Aye, it is. Jem's told all the lads at the mill. I overheard a few laughing and discussing it in t' square.'

Jem . . . Lord, how could you? Jewel thought her heart would break in two. Could things get any worse than this?

'I'm surprised Aunt Flora's not got wind of it yet . . .'

'Don't you dare try to threaten me,' she choked out, disgusted at the smug look Benji now wore. 'You've no idea what you're saying. Despite what you've heard, me and Jem Wicks have never . . . *You're* the only one I've ever . . . I'm telling our family the truth of things, whether you like it or not. Them believing me is another matter, but I have to—'

'I'll deny it, Jewel. Just so you know.' Unnervingly, there was no malice in his words, only certainty. 'And once you've finished with the telling, I'll be the one informing them of a thing or two – that Jem Wicks is the father of the child you reckon you're carrying.'

Helpless rage made her hands, hanging loosely by her sides, shake. She bunched them into tight fists. What she wouldn't give to thump the pockmarked face before her to dust. She'd underestimated him, thought him but a simple kid, when all along . . . He'd likely planned this from the off.

Yet surely there was a way around it? she thought desperately. Jem would confirm what she was saying was the truth: they hadn't lain together, had they? But how could she trust him now? She'd hurt him – humiliated him, even – it was true. Still, she'd have never believed him capable of such cruelty, never. Thanks to him, her name was dirt enough before the reality of her condition had even emerged. Could she rely on him to back her up? Did she even know him at all? It certainly didn't feel like it now. Though Jem wouldn't want folk assuming he'd fathered her child, that didn't mean to say he'd help her expose Benji as the culprit. Jem might very well put it about that she'd had other lovers besides, or some other such fabrication – who knew what? As far as she could see, the lad she thought she knew was a stranger capable of saying anything.

Benji had outwitted her. They both knew it. Taking in his self-assured expression, a familiar emotion washed through her and she shivered: she really did want to die. Anything was preferable at the minute to this hell called her life.

'What will you do, then?'

'I'm telling them the truth, have to,' she whispered.

'You're daft, that's what. Everyone else will think it, too, for I'll deny everything. Not that it'll take much effort, mind – I mean, come on, who will believe at all that we . . . you know?'

Incredulous, she shook her head. 'Why are you doing this?' He didn't answer and her voice broke as she added, 'You'll ruin me.'

'Well . . .'

'Well, what?'

Burying his hands in his pockets, Benji shrugged. 'Say you were attacked by some unknown man. Tell folk you don't know who it were and that, afterwards, you were too frickened and ashamed to speak up.' He lifted then dropped his shoulders again. 'Most won't hold you to blame for bearing a bastard child in that way, will they? Not if you have them think it were no fault of yours.'

Despite her anguish and fury, she knew a trickle of relief at his suggestion. Why hadn't she thought of something like that? Could it work? Some in the town would doubt her, it was guaranteed. Nevertheless . . . However, a thought struck her and her building hope dimmed. 'And if the child should look like you? What then?'

Silence thickened the air between them. Benji broke their stare to look at the floor.

'Hello? *Hello?*' Flora's puzzled voice drifted upstairs from the shop, slicing through the charged atmosphere like a hot knife through butter. 'What the divil . . . ? Where is everyone?'

'What then?' Jewel repeated in a whisper to her cousin.

Finally, he lifted his eyes. Neither fear nor worry, arrogance nor anger were reflected in their grey depths – there was nothing. They bore blankly into hers like those of a dead kipper.

'Well?' Jewel hissed.

As though he hadn't heard her, he turned his head slightly towards the door. 'Coming, Aunt Flora!' he called downstairs. He continued staring at his cousin for some moments before walking from the room.

Jewel dropped into a chair at the table. She had to call on all the restraint she could muster to stop herself from grabbing the teapot and hurling it at the wall in a pique of anguish. Bernard's newspaper, neatly folded, lay by her elbow and, instead, she gripped this in her two hands, squeezing with all her might, teeth gritted, which eased her bubbling temper a little.

She had a good mind to storm the shop and reveal all to her mother this instant. Yet where might that get her? It would cause a holy hell of trouble; should Mam believe her, she would understandably kick up war with Esther and Bernard – maybe even give Benji a well-deserved clout in the process. The family would be ripped apart and no one would suffer more than Flora as a consequence.

They were the poor relations, always had been; they relied on the Powells' support significantly. Not only would the truth mean inevitable unemployment for the pair of them – if Esther didn't throw them out on their ears, then Flora would certainly insist they were finished with the shop – it would also mean losing the only kin they had left. Jewel couldn't deny that her uncle and aunt had been there for her mother both financially and emotionally throughout the years since Fred Nightingale's death. This would fracture beyond repair a relationship that her mam not only held dear but depended upon.

Concocting a tale of a mystery attacker was becoming more appealing by the second. Could she pull it off convincingly? Would her family believe her? Could her tongue really allow her to see her cousin walk away scot-free from this mess he'd helped create?

Crushing powerlessness swamped her and her shoulders sagged. She took some deep breaths to steady her frayed nerves. She must get up and see to her chores, couldn't let her mother see her like this, had to go on as normal without arousing suspicion until she had a concrete version of events devised in her head. She couldn't afford to slip up, had to get this right if she was to do it at all.

She rose from the table, then, catching sight of the scrunched pages of Bernard's newspaper, clicked her tongue in contrition. With care, she smoothed it out as best she could and placed it back where she'd found it. She was about to make for the fire when her eyes, straying to a particular piece of smudged text, picked out a few words. She paused.

Thanks to her uncle's patient teachings, Jewel had learned to read sufficiently well alongside her cousin at a young age. Though she hadn't revelled in it quite as much as Benji did, she had still grasped enough to be able to read at an adequate level. Now, lifting the paper once more, she scanned the short advertisement:

> *NURSE CHILD WANTED, OR TO ADOPT.*
> *Widow with moderate allowance would be glad to accept the charge of a child. Age no object. If sickly, would receive a parent's care. Terms 15 shilling a month or would adopt entirely for small sum of £10.*

Jewel re-read the words a half-dozen times or more. Her heartbeat had quickened and her hands felt clammy. This sort of thing really happened? There were folk out there willing to take a child off your hands, no questions asked? For what purpose? A married couple unable to bear a baby of their own, she could understand, but a widow? *Dear God, what did the ins and outs matter?* her mind yelled. This could be the answer to her prayers . . .

Just as quickly as it had risen, the rush of hope drained away and disappointment replaced it – ten whole *pounds*? How in heaven could she ever dream of having such an amount at her disposal? Even the monthly fee this widow was asking was beyond her means. Jewel handed over her wages to her mother each week, and the little that Flora gave back for her to treat herself with didn't amount to anywhere close.

Looking down, she was surprised to see that her hand had travelled to her midriff. It had done so of its own free will, almost as if to shield the life lying within from the article, from its mother's contemplations . . .

'Shut up,' she told herself firmly. 'Daft imaginings like that will get you nowhere but the asylum, for you'll bring on the madness with such thoughts.' And yet . . .

Her gaze once more swivelled to the paper. But again, the impossibility of it was undeniable. She shrugged, sighed and gave the advertisement underneath it a cursory glance. Again, the word 'Wanted' leapt out at her, only this one was followed by something else – something that brought heat to her veins and excitement to her breast more than the first had done.

Bringing the newspaper closer to her face, she read on quickly:

WANTED, IMMEDIATELY, GENERAL SERVANT. A gentleman's family seeks respectable girl to attend a young child as well as regular household duties. Good wages. Character reference required. Apply to Mrs Kirkwood after 6 p.m. at the following residence . . .

Scanning the address, Jewel's face lit up to see it was no distance from her own home. Then surely this instead was the answer, albeit a temporary one, to her prayers: escape.

Anything could happen over the course of the next few months: she could lose the child naturally – it happened to women all too often, she knew. Should that occur, she'd be all right, could continue with her life afresh. And if the child didn't break from her before its time . . . well, then she'd just have to try to hide her condition from these potential new employers for as long as she could.

It would be a while yet before her belly began to grow.

Time in which, mercifully, she wouldn't have to be in Benji's presence, wouldn't have to look at the hard-faced swine, nor be forced to resist smacking him in the teeth . . . Also, being so close to home, this family might just be persuaded to let her stay on at Back Cheapside with Mam.

She was aware that general servants – a glorified title for maids-of-all-work – normally lived in, but there was no harm in asking, was there?

But the ad stated that her duties would involve caring for a child. She had no experience of such a thing. However, how hard could it be? If the family asked, she'd say she'd cared for little 'uns before – surely this would arouse no suspicion and she'd learn as she went along? Besides, if it came to it, it would be much-needed practice for when her own baby came along, God help her.

She nodded to herself, her enthusiasm mounting. Her mother and, undoubtedly, Esther would want to know why she'd decided to leave the shop but, for now, explanations could wait. At this moment, she could think of nothing but doing all in her power to secure this position. The fact that the prospect evoked this level of pleasure proved to her she was doing the right thing.

It could be said she was approaching such a career relatively late. Most girls began at thirteen, often younger – how they coped with such responsibility at that tender age, Jewel didn't know. Not only was it a solitary situation but a gruelling one. Arising with the lark and to bed barely shy of midnight, general servitude was not for the faint of heart. A maid-of-all-work was just that: a sole servant with an endless list of tasks that were seemingly never done. Housemaid, kitchen maid, cook, washerwoman, seamstress – and at this residence, nursemaid, too – rolled into one.

To make matters worse, vast numbers of girls received rough treatment from their employers and endured a miserable existence with next to no thanks. She just prayed the gentleman and his family were kindly and didn't use her too hard.

After memorising the house number and returning the newspaper with a determined nod, Jewel set to her chores with gusto. The hours flew by, and before she knew it Flora appeared in the doorway informing her it was time to come home. She smiled, nodded and went to collect her shawl, then she and her mother set off on the short distance across the square.

Jewel had spoken to her mam at odd intervals throughout the day but to her cousin she'd uttered nothing more. Likewise, Benji hadn't spoken to her – what, after all, was there left to say to each other? He'd made his feelings known and she, unable to see a way forward in that respect, had kept the truth locked within.

She wouldn't, as she'd sworn she must, tell their family anything just yet. One matter at a time – securing the servant's job should take priority. When she did eventually break the monumental news, a faceless attacker being the culprit, as Benji had suggested, would be the explanation she'd go with. This she'd decided during her work, and the more she'd mulled it over the more sensible the idea had become. Though she was loath to let that swine off the hook like this, she could see no other option for a quiet life. He'd get his comeuppance some day, somehow, she was certain. Past wrongs had a funny way of catching up with you like that and she looked forward to the time Benji was called to answer for his. Oh, she did.

'More bread, lass?'

Reasoning that she might as well learn the outcome of

her interview before revealing to her mother her decision to leave the shop, Jewel had done her best to act naturally whilst helping Flora prepare their evening meal. Inside was another matter; anxiety coupled with hopeful anticipation had churned her stomach throughout – she'd struggled to get the food down. Now, as Flora lifted the knife to the stale loaf, Jewel shook her head quickly.

'Not for me, ta, Mam.'

'You sure? Another sup of tea, then?'

She shook her head once more. Avoiding her mother's gaze and forcing herself not to gawp at the cheap tin clock yet again – she'd barely taken her eyes from it since they arrived home – she pushed back her chair. 'D'you know, I fancy a walk.'

'Now?' Frowning, Flora glanced to the window and the pale grey sky beyond. 'It favours we're due rain.'

'Nay, it's brightened up a bit, I reckon,' she responded mildly; inside, however, her heart was thumping like a drum. 'Anyroad, I'll not roam far and I've got my shawl.'

'Aye, all right. Thinking on it, the air will do thee good after being holed up in that stuffy shop the day through. Mind, you never bemoan it. You're a good lass, aye.'

The soft pride in her mother's tone brought a sting of guilt. They had never kept secrets from each other and she hated the fact that she'd started now. Before leaving, Jewel bent over her and pressed her cheek to hers. She closed her eyes. 'I love thee,' she murmured against the warm, lined skin.

Flora stroked her daughter's long plait which lay between them. 'I know, lass. And I thee. Now, go on, enjoy your walk. I'm for putting my trotters up awhile by the fire.'

The town hall clock struck five thirty as Jewel stepped outside, and excitement stirred in her. Positioning her shawl to drape loosely around her shoulders against the midsummer breeze, she turned her clogged feet towards the square.

She'd take a wander around, after all, until the appointed time; hopefully, it would help to calm her racing heart and mind.

Chapter 7

HERE, MERE YARDS from the slum dwelling Jewel had always called home, was like stepping into another district altogether. Lined with fine, mainly three-storey late-Georgian town houses and institutional buildings, Mawdsley Street was an attractive spot.

Naturally, the very best places to be were the villas in areas away from the belching chimneys of industry; by Bolton Park, for example. That was where the wealthiest and most important – the cotton merchants and their ilk – made their homes. They wouldn't dream of polluting their own lungs with the noxious smoke their businesses created. They left that to their workers, who could afford rent only on the crumbling rooms clustered around their mills and factories. Money didn't just talk here, it bellowed for the world to hear. Such was life.

Nevertheless, despite its central location, Mawdsley Street was certainly not to be sniffed at. You could quite easily forget the truth that its residents lived cheek by jowl with the less fortunate packed into the tight grid of lanes surrounding it once you turned the corner into this straight and narrow, well-kempt road.

Jewel paused outside the address and looked about. Some of the mixed stone and brick edifices were more elaborate and imposing than others, but each seemed like a royal palace compared to what she and everyone she knew was used to. And to think she might shortly be living amongst this, too, she thought excitedly, eyes drinking in the clean and quiet surroundings.

The private residence before her boasted a pedimented entrance and a tall, shiny dark-wood door with a brass knob and knocker – these, she spied, were dull and in need of a good polish. In fact, looking more closely, she saw that one or two other things showed subtle signs of neglect. The sash window panes appeared a little dirty and the front step looked as if it hadn't seen a scrubbing brush in months. She frowned. Then the corners of her mouth lifted and she nodded. It seemed she'd come at just the right time.

After quickly tidying her hair and smoothing down her skirts and shawl, she took a deep breath and knocked. The door opened almost immediately and she stepped back in surprise. 'Oh. He–hello.'

'Yes?'

'My name's Jewel Nightingale. I'm here about the general servant's position advertised in the *Bolton Evening News.*'

A tall, well-dressed woman with greying brown hair secured in a neat bun who she assumed was the mistress, Mrs Kirkwood, lifted an eyebrow with evident interest. 'I see. Follow me, please.'

She led the way to a good-sized drawing room in dusky blue. Like the curtains, the sofa was a shade darker and complemented the space beautifully – to this, the lady motioned and, tentatively, Jewel sat.

'It is not quite six yet. The advertisement did stipulate that all applicants were to apply here after that time.'

'I'm sorry . . . Should I come back later?' Jewel had

half risen as she spoke, but the lady brushed her suggestion aside.

'No need, you're here now. You're able to wait?'

'Aye, yes, Mrs Kirkwood.'

'Good. He's normally home a few minutes after six, then we can get down to business.'

Jewel smiled and nodded instead of letting her frown show. He? Husbands never usually involved themselves in such matters – the taking on of staff was left to the mistress of the house to deal with. Something else didn't quite add up: the terms mentioned she'd have to care for a young child, yet Mrs Kirkwood appeared a little long in the tooth to have recently borne one. She was fifty if she was a day. It *was* possible at such an age, it was true – Mam was proof of that – but still . . .

'Have you experience of domestic servitude, Miss Nightingale?'

Snapping out of her reverie, Jewel chose her answer carefully. Though she'd cleaned at the umbrella shop and helped with the cooking for her and her mother for just as long, she hadn't ever actually held the title of servant . . . 'I can scrub and cook with the best of them, Mrs Kirkwood,' she announced with what she hoped was confidence.

'Good, good. And children?'

Again, Jewel thought her response through. 'I have a younger cousin.' That Benji was barely two years her junior, she didn't mention. To her relief, the lady took from this what Jewel had hoped she would – Mrs Kirkwood nodded, satisfied.

'Well, so far so good.'

The ticking of the clock on the ornate mantel filled the silence for a minute or two until, finally, there was the sound of the front door opening and closing.

Mrs Kirkwood disappeared into the hall and Jewel

took the time alone to prepare herself for the interview proper, checking again that her hair and clothing were neat and taking some slow, deep breaths. She'd just fixed a small, polite smile to her lips when the drawing-room door opened and the couple stepped inside.

'Oh.'

'*Oh.*' Jewel echoed the man's surprised greeting. Blinking in confusion, she could lay her tongue to nothing more: what on earth was going on?

'The two of you have already made one another's acquaintance?'

Maxwell Birch nodded to the equally puzzled-looking lady. 'You could say that.' A definite smile lingered behind his eyes. 'Her uncle is a client of mine at the bank.' To Jewel, he added, 'Miss Nightingale, may I introduce Mrs Kirkwood, my sister.'

Sister? But she'd assumed . . . God above, how could this be? Her shoulders drooped and disappointment pained her chest. That was her dream of employment here dashed right away. Given what he knew of her, that he believed her to be of unsound mind, there was no chance he'd want her beneath his roof, and especially tending to his child . . .

'Shall we begin?' Maxwell removed his dark jacket, which his sister took from him and left the room to hang up, then loosened his stiff collar. Then he motioned to the sofa and when Jewel, after a long hesitation, resumed her seat, he sat in a chair facing her. Resting his elbows on his knees, he steepled his fingers and stared at her.

She dropped her eyes to her feet. 'Mr Birch—'

'How are you?'

Their encounter at the park that morning played in her mind and her cheeks grew redder. 'I'm well, ta. Look, Mr Birch, I shouldn't have come—'

'You've changed your mind about the position?' he interrupted again. 'So soon?'

'You mean . . . ?' She lifted her gaze to his. 'You don't want me to leave your house? You're prepared to interview me, sir?'

A quiet smile appeared at Maxwell's mouth. 'Why ever would I not be? Is there a reason why you deem yourself as undeserving of a fair trial, same as everyone else?'

'You know there is.' She spoke in a dull whisper. 'You believe me to be mad. To be honest, I don't blame thee. Often question it myself of late.'

For a full minute, he was silent, then: 'I think you are unhappy, and deeply so. Something troubles you which you feel unable to disclose, even to those nearest to you. However, I don't think you are mad. Not at all, Miss Nightingale.'

Jewel's eyes filled with tears at the sincerity of his tone. To hell with the job – she just needed someone to talk to. She opened her mouth, fully intending to spill her secret, for that's how this man affected you. He made you feel . . . *safe* was the only word she could summon to mind. Aye, secure in the knowledge that he would listen without judgement. That he'd understand, maybe even offer a solution. That it was just you and him, here in this moment, in the whole world . . . Until, the door opened and Mrs Kirkwood breezed back in, snapping Jewel back to her senses.

God above, what was she playing at? That she'd almost . . . had actually considered . . . To *him*?

Her mind was racing; she needed to leave, must get away from this house and Maxwell Birch. She watched in dismay as, before she had a chance to make her escape, the lady took a seat in the chair facing her brother as though to continue the interview.

'So, Miss Nightingale.' Mrs Kirkwood raised her brows encouragingly. 'You were saying earlier about your experience in tending to children?'

'I . . . Well, I . . .' Jewel's face burned brighter still. She licked her lips. 'Aye, yes. Well, what I, I mean, is—'

'Blast, there is the door,' Mrs Kirkwood cut in as a knock sounded. Flashing an apologetic smile, she rose and disappeared from the room once more, unaware that Jewel was secretly thanking God for the diversion.

Now is your chance – think of an excuse, quickly! her mind yelled. She jumped a little too suddenly to her feet, as if she'd been bitten on the backside or some such; her embarrassment heightened yet further at Maxwell's surprised frown. *Damn it, I have to get out of here!* 'Mr Birch, I'm afraid I must go.'

'Oh?'

She nodded. 'Aye, I've just remembered there's summat I need to . . . there's somewhere I have to be, like, so I'll take my leave of thee now and—'

'Brother.' Yet again, Mrs Kirkwood had re-entered to shatter Jewel's train of thought.

She cursed under her breath, forgetting what it was she'd been saying; *please, just let me leave* . . .

'There is another girl arrived interested in the servant's job,' continued the lady. 'I've left her waiting in the hall.'

Maxwell nodded, though his stare was still on Jewel, who was now standing uncertainly in the centre of the room. He released a long, quiet breath. Then he turned his head towards his sister. 'Please inform the newcomer that the position has been filled.'

'Oh, you mean . . . ?' Mrs Kirkwood inclined her head to Jewel. At her brother's nod, she smiled brightly. 'Wonderful. Miss Nightingale appears a clean, tolerable, respectable young woman.'

Jewel almost baulked at the last description. *Respectable.* If they only knew . . . She dropped her gaze quickly lest her sin gave her away.

'Indeed, a sound choice,' added the lady, blind to Jewel's shame. 'I'll tell the other girl right away.'

'Thank you,' Maxwell responded, his eyes now back on Jewel.

Before leaving, Mrs Kirkwood placed a friendly hand on her shoulder. 'Welcome to the family, Miss Nightingale. You're just what my brother has been searching for, I'm sure.'

The drawing-room door shut behind her and Jewel and Maxwell Birch were alone once more. She simply gazed at him, lost for words. What the hell had he gone and said that for? She didn't want the wretched job any more, did she? She just wanted to leave this house and never have to see it or its master again. Well, she'd tell him so, she would—!

'You're angry?'

Queerly, him bringing light to the fact in that calming voice of his caused her temper to rapidly diminish. 'What makes you think that?' she asked quietly.

'Your eyes, they give you away. Right now, they're spitting steel. You don't desire to work here? Is that it?'

Despite herself, she shook her head, found it impossible to lie. 'Nay, that's not it, sir. Toiling here would be gradely, I'm sure.'

'Then . . . ?'

'Are you certain it's me tha wants?' He didn't answer. Sighing, she continued. 'I haven't even fetched a character reference—'

'Don't worry about that. It shan't be necessary, given that I know your uncle.'

'That's not all. I must be honest with thee, I bent the

truth to Mrs Kirkwood. I've no experience of minding youngsters—'

'But you can clean?'

'Aye, but—'

'And cook?'

She nodded. 'Aye, I can, but Mr Birch, sir—'

'Then that is all that matters. The rest will come naturally to you, I'm sure. Constance is a happy child; albeit a little mischievous, perhaps, as you saw some weeks ago at the park . . .'

At this, a smile lifted Jewel's mouth. The lively toddler with the golden curls who had excitedly stormed the children's games, wanting to play, flashed into her mind. Then a sudden thought struck her and she frowned. She glanced at the door. Why was Mrs Kirkwood presiding over this household and not the mistress? Where was the infant's mother, Mrs Birch?

'Mary, my wife, passed away last September,' Maxwell murmured, as though seeing into her thoughts. 'She was always one to flout convention, insisted upon us not having servants, was a very involved wife and mother.' A wistful look, tinged with pain, appeared in his eyes. 'She was certainly one of a kind. Alas, the cancer cares not about such things, nor who it strikes.'

'Eeh, I'm sorry, sir.'

He nodded. 'My sister has proven to me that guardian angels do exist. What Constance and I – Roland, too – would have done without her these past months, I shudder to imagine.'

'Roland, sir?'

'My son from my first marriage. I shall introduce you to him later.'

Then this was really happening. She was here to stay. The reality quickened Jewel's heartbeat but, oddly, the feeling of trepidation had left her now and only a pleasing sense of readiness remained.

'My sister and I have both agreed that the time for her to return to her own family permanently has come. It has taken some persuading, however; she has been loath to leave me—' He broke off, then smiled. 'Mary's passing was very difficult for me to accept. But, by the grace of God, each day gets a little easier. And, of course, having a piece of her in Constance helps.'

Jewel didn't know what to say. His plight had touched her deeply. His daughter's, too; motherless at such a tender age. Life could be so cruel at times.

'Yes, indeed, my brother-in-law will certainly be glad to have my sister home,' Maxwell added. 'Her dividing her time between him and me cannot have been easy for him; his patience throughout has been nothing short of remarkable. Now you're here, she will return with an easy mind, I'm sure.'

Now you're here . . . Jewel's shoulders involuntarily straightened. She lifted her chin, the sense of responsibility leaving a warmness inside that both surprised her yet felt natural, almost comforting.

'There is just one thing I feel I must ask.'

Dread trickled back, for she knew what he was about to say. He wanted to know her secret, what troubled her to the point she'd attempted self-murder. *Dear Lord, he'd know soon enough once her belly expanded, but she couldn't tell him here, not now.* 'Aye?' she finally forced herself to respond.

'Your uncle and aunt won't miss you?'

Releasing her breath slowly, she swallowed her relief. 'Nay, sir.'

'You didn't leave on bad terms, I trust?'

Only now did she remember that she was yet to inform

them of her decision to terminate her employment. Esther would probably have a blue fit, rail at her for what she'd deem her ungratefulness, which would likely upset her mother into the bargain ... She drew in a deep breath of determination. That, she would worry about later. Whatever resulted, she wouldn't be swayed, *couldn't* remain in that shop another day with that cousin of hers.

'Nay, sir,' she repeated. 'I fancy a change of work is all.'

His face spread in a slow smile. 'Well, I'm glad you happened upon here.'

'As am I, sir. Ta ever so for taking me on.'

After a long moment, Maxwell shook his head. 'No, Miss Nightingale. Thank *you*.'

*

The kitchen, which Mrs Kirkwood led Jewel to minutes later, was reached by a set of narrow stone steps that were in need of a scrubbing – Jewel discreetly pulled a face.

Maxwell's sister might well have done a good job of looking after her brother and his children's immediate needs over the months, but it was plain that she wasn't used to the more menial aspects of running a home. Likely she had maids in her own residence so hadn't the experience of keeping house. How nice it must be to not have the need to sully your own hands!

They emerged into a fair-sized room, though what a contrast to the scrumptious house proper above. The space was stark, serviceable, fit entirely for purpose. The design of homes such as this was no accident – the sole purpose was to keep 'uppers' and 'lowers' apart. Down here, in these lonely holes in the ground, the work was completed out of sight by unseen hands, thus not impinging in any way upon the lives of the genteel whom they served. Sights, sounds and smells were contained, as the families desired them to be. Their needs were pandered to without attention being drawn to this, such were the rules of this complex world.

Houses, particularly larger establishments, wouldn't have been able to function without an army of staff to see to their smooth running. However, a vast number of the underclass would likewise be lost without the call for domestic positions. Masters and the staff they employed needed each other, perhaps equally. So long as respect was shown on both sides, thus avoiding the inevitable ripples of contention, relationships between the two glided without a hitch.

If lucky to find a decent household, domestics were happy to devote their whole lives to service. A true testimony to their loyalty. Many even grew to love the families they served, regarding them almost as their own kin. In turn, it wasn't unknown for their rulers to grow fond of these people they paid to see to their every whim. Proof that, if done right, and with continued effort from each party, these agreements could and did work well.

Pay and treatment differed widely from residence to residence but, nonetheless, the career was a respectable one. That servants were fed, housed and in most cases provided with uniform, all without costing them a copper coin, was a desirable proposition and highly sought after.

Though the choice wasn't hers to make – once the baby made an appearance, even before then, she'd be forced to leave here – Jewel couldn't see this as *her* life for ever. She wanted to marry one day, aye. She didn't want to be a spinster, toiling for someone else's family for all her days – a family of her own was what she desired.

Huh! And what make of man will take you on, now? a small voice inside her head mocked.

The stinging truth crushed her heart. Blinking back tears, she forced her attention back to the kitchen.

A cooking range, shiny pots and pans hanging from long hooks either side, dominated the left-hand wall. A large cupboard stood beneath the high, thin strip of window facing her and in the centre of the room a scrubbed, light-wood table and one chair took up most of the floor. There was a scullery-like area to the opposite side of her for washing dishes and vegetables, and this concluded the furnishings. Or so she thought. Turning, she spied in a dim far corner behind her a small, iron-framed bed. Neatly made with thin pillow and plain sheet and counterpane, it looked neither warm nor comfortable. *Well, hopefully, she wouldn't be in need of that . . .*

To think that most girls would barely leave their kitchens – day, week, month, year following year – was a depressing notion. They had no cause to, after all; everything they needed was right there in their one stuffy, solitary little room.

'Mrs Kirkwood, I wanted to ask.' Jewel pointed to the sleeping area. 'Could I please be permitted to stop on at home rather than dwell here? Mine and Mam's house is but a stone's throw away in Back Cheapside—'

'I'm afraid that would not be practical, Miss Nightingale,' cut in the lady, though not unkindly. 'Has it been just yourself and your mother?' she asked when Jewel's face fell.

'Aye, Mrs Kirkwood.'

'This will be your first time away from home?'

'Aye,' Jewel murmured again, with a terrible feeling of regret. She should never have come here, had naively assumed she'd be permitted to stay on at home. How could she leave her mam all on her own? How would *she* cope without Flora?

'You would have to be here to light the fires and so forth for when my brother and his children awaken. It really wouldn't do if you had to knock them up of a morning to admit you into the house, now would it?'

She shook her head; she hadn't thought of that. 'Nay. I suppose not.'

The lady stepped back and surveyed the space. 'It isn't awfully inviting in here,' she admitted. 'However, once you've made it your own, I'm sure it will feel more like home. Yes, yes,' she added thoughtfully. 'A few pictures, perhaps, to brighten the walls . . . Leave it with me, I'll see what I can do,' she finished with a nod.

'Eeh, you don't have to trouble yourself with that, Mrs Kirkwood.' Though surprised and not a little grateful for the offer, Jewel didn't want to appear to be taking liberties. However, the woman brushed her worries aside and Jewel thanked her warmly for her kindness.

'Now. You will rise each morning at six o'clock. My brother breakfasts early, you see; this should give you ample time to complete your early duties before seeing to his meal.'

Jewel nodded then listened intently as the lady proceeded to rhyme off the complete list of chores that would be required of her, not wanting to miss anything, for she was eager to make a good job of this. Maxwell Birch had been generous enough to take her on, despite everything; the least she could do in return was serve his household with the respect and efficiency it deserved. Its smooth running was vital.

'The doors are locked and bolted at ten o'clock each night – a duty my brother undertakes himself – and you are then free to retire to your bed,' the lady finished.

'Aye, Mrs Kirkwood.'

'Is there anything you would like me to go over with you again?'

'Nay, I think I've got it all, ta.'

'Sunday afternoons are yours to spend as you wish – resting in preparation for the week ahead would be wise.'

The lady had a point. Such multifarious occupations could easily become overwhelming. 'I'm sure if I divide my time successfully, I'll not wear myself thin and make myself ill, Mrs Kirkwood. I'm sure to be fatigued at the day's end, aye, but not completely fagged, so long as I plan accordingly. A thorough clean of different rooms on different days, with regular duties in between, of course, would work well, I reckon.'

'Oh?'

'Like, say, I tackled the drawing room on a Monday, the dining room and hall on Tuesday, stairs and nursery on Wednesday, the master's bedroom on Thursday and his son's on Friday. Saves running myself ragged trying to see to it all in one day at the week's end. This will leave me with Saturday to scour and scrub the kitchen and get everything in nice neat order.'

She appeared impressed with this, maybe even somewhat regretful that she hadn't come up with the scheme during her stay here. 'A sensible approach. You will receive twelve pounds per annum, although this may be increased later on, should you prove satisfactory. Which I'm sure you will,' she added, smiling. 'I can see you're an industrious girl.'

'Aye, Mrs Kirkwood. Hard and honest toil is in my blood,' Jewel stated proudly.

'Yes, I can see that. Well, I think that's everything,' she added, crossing to the stairs. Before ascending, she looked at Jewel over her shoulder. 'Leaving this family in the morning shall be a wrench, indeed. However, I'm most reassured knowing they are in your capable hands.'

'I'll do my very best, Mrs Kirkwood.' And she meant it.

Midway upstairs, the lady paused again. Her tone was thick as she murmured, 'You will look after him, Miss Nightingale?'

Jewel's response held just as much sincerity as before. 'I will. You have my word.'

*

'Leave the shop? Why?'

The hour was approaching nine. A curve of the frigid moon, visible through the ill-fitting curtains, lent its light to the small kitchen Jewel had called home for as long as she could remember. Her mother had slowly lowered her darning into her lap at her announcement and was gazing at her in shocked puzzlement.

Doing her best to appear nonchalant, she shrugged. 'I fancy a change is all, Mam.' The false explanation she'd given to Maxwell Birch tasted acrid on her tongue when she used it with her mother.

'Nowt's occurred? That Esther ain't done you wrong, has she?'

'Nay, nay.' Jewel gave her an easy smile. 'It ain't so big a deal really, Mam. I'll be no great distance away, eh? Besides, I'll have Sunday afternoons off, which we can spend together. *And* the brass is better.'

'But . . .' Flora plucked at her lip. 'I'll miss thee, lass.'

Christ, she was going to cry. Hell's damnation to that swine Benji and all he'd helped create! She wished to God he'd never been born, wished they were not related so they never would have met. And all the while, he'd slithered his way out of blame completely, leaving her to deal with the muck storm alone.

'We've not spent a single sun without each other since the day tha arrived to brighten my world. Norra one. But ay, I'm being selfish. You must do what you want to do, never mind my ramblings. You're a sound worker, lass, and don't often get what credit for it you deserve. Anyroad, I'll have to let you go some day, won't I, for you'll soon have scores of lads queueing at yon door, vying to wed thee.' She flashed a wobbly smile. 'Aye. Now's as good a time as any. You've my support and more. I only ever want thee to be happy.'

Jewel was speechless with emotion. *Oh, Mam. My hand has been forced in this, and I ache to tell you why, tell you everything, but I can't. As for getting wed . . . Never that. Not now.*

'Go on, lass,' Flora added. 'You take yourself up and get a healthy sleep for the morn. Start as you mean to go on, bright-eyed and bushy-tailed. I'll follow shortly. 'Ere, and don't go fretting over that wife of our Bernard's, neither. I'll inform her of you leaving when next I see her.'

'Aye?'

Her mother nodded. 'She'll like it or lump it, an' all, and I'll tell her so.'

Again, Jewel was overcome with a host of painful emotions. 'Ta, Mam,' she managed to croak before quickly escaping upstairs.

Savouring the room, its feel, its smell, she was afforded some comfort, but still her breast throbbed with the devastation of it all. For the last time, she snuggled beneath the coverings. Sleep wouldn't come, Jewel knew that, but simply being here, beside her mother shortly, was enough. She'd wait until Mam dropped off to sleep then hold her plump body so tightly, more than she ever had before, and she'd tell her in her mind how much she regretted that things had come to this and how sorry she was to have to leave her. She'd tell her how much she loved her, more than any other single being on this earth. And she'd vow to her that she'd never forgive herself for it all.

When muffled weeping seeped through to her from downstairs, Jewel's heart finally broke. That she'd brought about such suffering to the selfless woman undoubtedly now feeling adrift, dreading the loss of her and fearful of being alone, was simply too much to bear; she curled in on herself like pummelled wax.

An image of her mother huddled in her fireside chair, face wreathed in sorrow, burned itself in her mind. Jewel just knew she'd be holding to her breast the glass candlestick, as she was wont to in times of woe. It had been a last token of love from her father – all, besides her memories, that she had of him now. But Jewel couldn't trust herself to go to her. She'd end up blurting the truth, she would, then all would be completely lost.

This night, another plane of hatred was born.

Foul and black towards Benjamin Powell.

More so for herself.

Chapter 8

'HM. IT'S RATHER a large fit.'

Stretching out the full, ankle-length apron then letting the voluptuous material fall back to her sides, Jewel chuckled. 'Mrs Kirkwood did her best at such short notice, sir, I'm sure.' She gave the matching white cap, which had slipped over one eye, a shove to the back of her head. 'This, too, shall be right as rain once I've secured it well with some pins,' she assured him.

Maxwell covered his twitching lips with his fingers. 'You're certain?'

'I am. Now, sir, you pass the little lady to me and take yourself off to the bank afore you're late. She'll be just fine. Won't you, Miss Constance?' she added smilingly to the flaxen-haired beauty, holding out her arms.

'Lizzie will be here at eleven,' he told Jewel yet again, almost apologetically – though she couldn't think why. Hadn't the position advertised in the newspaper stated clearly that part of her work would include tending to his daughter?

The lass Lizzie he referred to was Constance's nursemaid but, with an ailing mother, she'd had to cut her starting hour to when her married sister was free to call to share the daughterly duty of care. Jewel was certain she'd manage the child well enough until Lizzie arrived.

So long as she kept her occupied she should be free to get most of her chores done as planned.

The morning had been an emotional one – and, she suspected, not just for herself. Despite her best efforts, her mother had been unable to hold back her tears when kissing her goodbye. And afterwards, clutching her small bundle of possessions, Jewel had stood for an age outside her house, desperately wishing she didn't have to leave it or the woman within. Finally, biting back heartache of her own, she'd turned her clogged feet in the direction of the new place she would from now on call her home.

What would Esther say later – Benji, too – when Mam revealed this new development? she'd asked herself repeatedly. Flora had assured her she'd give it to them straight and they could deal with it, and not to fret, but Jewel couldn't help it. What if her aunt grew suspicious of her motives? Yet how could she? she would remind herself. She was being paranoid, that's all. There wasn't a chance in a hundred lifetimes that Esther could ever guess the real reason behind her sudden move. As for her cousin, well, he wasn't about to reveal anything, was he? He'd likely be glad to have her out of the way now, given what he knew. Rotten young swine that he was . . .

When she'd arrived at Mawdsley Street, Maxwell had answered her knock with a definite look of strain on his face. His sister had left shortly before, he'd informed her quietly; that the parting had been a wrench, for all involved, had been clear to see. Jewel had felt the urge to offer him comfort but couldn't think of anything to say or do that wouldn't seem like she was overstepping her station.

Instead, she'd followed him down to the kitchen in silence, where he'd shown her where to put her things and pointed out the neatly folded pile of material on her bed – her uniform, which Mrs Kirkwood had procured for her before her departure. That wasn't all. True to her word, she had indeed found her several cheap pictures, and the calming woodland scenes broke up the blank expanse of wall beautifully. That lady was a kind and thoughtful soul, and no mistake.

Now, as Maxwell headed off for work and when his footsteps had died away on the stairs, Jewel glanced down again at the apron and allowed herself a relieved smile. Thank the Lord he hadn't insisted she had the thing altered. With any luck, it would conceal her sin once her belly began to swell for a little longer than she'd anticipated. God, but she hated all this deception. He, not to mention Mam, didn't deserve this. *She* didn't deserve their trust and kindness.

'Down! Down!'

Bringing her mind back to the kitchen and the child now doing her utmost to wriggle from her hold, Jewel nodded with quiet resolution. Time to stop these destructive thoughts. She must simply make the best of a bad situation – it was all she could do for now – and suffer the consequences of her wickedness later.

'*Down!*' the youngster demanded again; chuckling, Jewel lowered her to the flagged floor.

'You're not one for doing nowt, are thee, lass? Like a cat on hot bricks, you are. Oh, 'ere, missy, don't do that!' she added on a gasp as, lightning fast, Constance, having dragged up the rag rug from in front of the fire, made to toss it on to the leaping flames. 'Eeh, young imp!' Jewel gathered her back up into her arms, much to the toddler's disgust. 'I can see I'm to have my hands full with thee.'

'No! Down!'

'Now then, less of that. Come on, let's find you summat to do. I've my chores to see to.' Had she bitten off more than she could chew here? Jewel was beginning to think so. She'd no experience with children, had she, and it was starting to show. Would she be able to manage? Time would soon tell. She'd give it her best, in any case.

She stuffed a few rags and a tin of polish from the shelf by the fire into her apron pocket. Then, collecting her brushes box from the large cupboard and the broom propped in the corner on the way, she took the child upstairs to the main part of the house.

Upon reaching the hall, she sat her on the black-and-white, diamond-shaped tiles and opened out the box. Constance's eyes lit up at the array of items she'd never seen before, and Jewel smiled. That should keep her busy for a few minutes whilst she swept the floor.

Working deftly, figuring it was worth leaving the patch that the child occupied so as to get the rest cleaned, she had the space done in no time. Nodding in satisfaction, she now turned her attention to the mats and gave them a vigorous shake outside.

She glanced to the child, still happily playing with the brushes, and smiled. Maybe she wasn't all that bad with children as she'd feared. Now, if she could just get through the next few hours until Lizzie arrived . . .

Minutes later, Jewel's arms ached terribly, but the results of her efforts had been worth it – she'd polished the brass knocker and door handle to within an inch of their lives and they dazzled like stars in a midnight sky.

By this time, Constance had grown bored of the playthings; not trusting her to be left alone, Jewel lifted her up and carried her down to the kitchen. The large pan of water she'd left heating on the fire was bubbling nicely – after filling a pail, she lugged it and the girl back to the hall. Now, already, her back hurt as well as her arms. Lucky for her she was no stranger to hard toil and had grown accustomed over the years to pushing through the fatigue. No wonder the house had slowly fallen into disarray under kind but privileged Mrs Kirkwood's watch. It required a dogged worker unafraid to get their hands dirty to keep a place ship-shape.

After carrying the pail outside, Jewel took Constance's small podgy hand and helped her into the street. She handed her the smallest brush from her box. 'Watch me, lass. Like this.' She dipped her own brush into the water and nodded when the child copied her. 'That's it. Eeh, you are clever.'

'Clever?' Constance beamed.

'Oh aye. Now, give the stone here a good scrub. Look, I'll show thee.' Kneeling on the flagstones, Jewel moved her brush in circular motions across the surface of the doorstep. 'That's it,' she encouraged at the child's attempt to imitate her. 'Good girl.'

'By gum, did you ever see the like!' The statement rang out across the street and was followed by a hearty guffaw. 'You're a bolder one than me, lass. That you are!'

Jewel looked over her shoulder towards the source of the voice and was surprised to see that the young woman who had spoken was addressing her. 'Sorry, what?'

Similarly dressed in apron and white cap, knelt with pail and brush outside her own door, the woman bobbed her dark head towards Constance. 'I were saying, you've got pluck, setting the young miss to such a task – in full public view, an' all, by all accounts. Who ever heard of a servant turning their master's daughter into a skivvy? Not I, nay.'

Jewel glanced down at Constance. As the woman's words sank in, her cheeks reddened in horror. She hadn't thought about her actions at all, had merely been trying to keep the toddler occupied. Lord, but the servant was right. What on earth would Maxwell say to see such a thing? He'd likely be furious, maybe even throw her out on her ear, and who could blame him? This would be seen not so much as overstepping her station but leaping over it headlong.

Quickly, she took the brush from the child and shot the woman across the road a grateful look. 'Ta ever so. I don't know what I were thinking.'

'Ay, don't fret on it, lass. This your first day?' At Jewel's nod, she tossed her own scrubbing brush into her pail and sauntered across the street. She had a pleasing face with what Mam would describe as 'eyes in love with each other' – a heavy squint that gave the impression she was staring at the tip of her nose. Smiling down, she held out a hand. 'Maria. Pleased to meet thee, I'm sure.'

Jewel shook it warmly. 'Aye, you too. I'm Jewel.'

'Bonny name.'

'Ta, thanks. Yours, too. So, you're employed at that residence there?' she asked, motioning to the attractive house opposite.

Maria snorted. 'Oh no, I were just passing and spotted their step were a bit on t' grubby side, thought I'd do them a favour . . . Course I'm bloomin' employed there!' she burst out good-naturedly. 'By, you're a bit daft, ain't yer?'

Jewel couldn't help grinning. 'Suppose it were a silly question. Well, I'd best get on. Nice talking to thee, Maria.'

But the woman had stopped listening, was peering past Jewel along the street. 'Eeh, you are a lucky divil to have the excuse of being under the same roof as him, lass,' she whispered out of the side of her mouth. 'Tending to his wants . . . well, that's summat I *would* willingly do for nowt, aye.'

Frowning, Jewel followed Maria's gaze. Thirty-something, tall and broad-shouldered with wavy brown hair and smoke-grey eyes, she could see why the gentleman approaching them had Maria in such a tizzy. But what had she meant about her being lucky to be under the same roof . . . ?

Roland. It had to be. Maxwell had said the previous evening that he'd introduce her to his son, but he hadn't returned home in time. Neither had she caught sight of him this morning. Mind you, judging by his rather crumpled clothing and fresh stubble, it was little wonder – he'd clearly spent the night elsewhere. What were his father's feelings on such behaviour? Didn't Roland have a job to go to?

'And how are you on this fine morning, Maria?'

The young woman blushed to the roots of her hair. She smothered a giggle with her hand. 'Gradely, sir, ta for asking. And yourself?'

'Oh, all the better for seeing you.' He flashed a dazzling smile then turned to enter his house – and almost toppled on to Jewel, still knelt by the step. 'God alive! I didn't see you there!'

She scrambled to her feet and attempted a clumsy curtsey. 'I'm Jewel Nightingale, sir, Mr Birch's new maid.'

Roland lifted his eyebrows. 'Ah, I see. Yes, I recall my aunt mentioning she was to put an advertisement in the *Bolton Evening News*. Well, welcome to our abode, little nightingale. Seems my father has been most astute in his selection.' His let his stare linger over her for a moment before touching his hat and brushing past her into the house.

'You've snared his eye all right,' Maria announced with not a little envy. 'Eeh, you are lucky.'

Jewel pulled a face. She had to admit, he'd seemed

pleasant enough and she'd take that any day over the poor treatment some domestics faced. Nevertheless, just let him try anything with her and he'd know about it. It was common knowledge that many young men of privileged households saw their female staff as fair game – it was almost like a rite of passage to bed the family's maids. God help him if he was of the same mind. She'd had a bellyful – literally – of the male species, enough to last her a lifetime already.

There was no denying Roland Birch was devilishly handsome, but boy did he know it. His easy-charm talk with Maria was proof he enjoyed flirting with anything in skirts. Though, unlike the swooning maid, such an attitude did nothing for her. She much preferred his father's subtle confidence and maturity.

The observation halted in its tracks, stopping further musing. Why on earth had that entered her mind? What a thing to be thinking – about her master, to boot. She just hoped her blush didn't show.

'I'd best get back to that ruddy step. My mistress would have a blue fit were she to spot me gossiping here with thee. Not that she's likely to, mind, what with her hard at work whiling her day away on the pianoforte, eating cakes and drinking tea . . .' Maria gave Jewel a wry grin. 'I'll be seeing thee, lass. Bye for now.'

She watched her go with a smile. Maria was a rum 'un all right. Hopefully, they would become friends. The woman was nice in a mildly brash sort of way. Besides, right now, Jewel needed every ally she could find.

*

By the time Lizzie arrived to take over Constance's care Jewel was mentally exhausted. Who knew caring for a child could be so fatiguing? Keeping the boisterous girl from becoming bored, and therefore wreaking havoc in the kitchen, had taken every ounce of energy her brain possessed. No sooner had she invented some game or other to occupy her than Constance was up and toddling off in search of mischief again.

No wonder Maxwell had appeared apologetic earlier over Lizzie's changed hours. Could she really cope with this particular duty? Jewel asked herself as she lay, spreadeagled on the bed, eyes closed, savouring a few precious minutes of peace. *More to the point, how would she manage her own child when it arrived – not only full time but alone?*

The prospect made her feel ill. There would be no palming the life growing inside her on to a nursemaid when she needed a break, would there? No time to spare lounging on the bed with a child to care for as well as money to earn to support them both. Christ, how would she manage? Just what the hell was she going to do?

'Nay,' she whispered to herself fiercely, swinging her legs off the bed and dragging herself up as panic threatened to swamp her. 'Don't dwell on it, any of it. It'll do thee no good.'

Expelling her worries temporarily on a deep sigh – aye, for she knew they'd be back soon enough, were always lurking close by – Jewel crossed to the fire to heat some water, tackling the mucky upstairs windows she'd spied yesterday, now at the forefront of her mind. *Anything* so long as it offered a much-needed distraction.

*

'Will that be all, sir?'

Placing his newspaper on the table, Maxwell nodded. 'Yes, thank you.'

Before leaving him to his meal, Jewel watched him

lift the serviette she'd spent ages shaping into a fan and shake it out without seeming to notice.

In fact, she pondered upon reaching the kitchen, he'd seemed somewhat distracted since this morning. Clearly, his sister returning home had affected him more deeply than she'd realised. Her heart contracted a little for him and she vowed to do her utmost to see he overcame the loss in whatever way she could. After all, hadn't she given Mrs Kirkwood her word that she'd look after him?

As she washed up the dirty pots and pans, she smiled, pleased with herself that she'd chosen lamb stew as her first meal to cook for him. It was one of her specialities and her mam's favourite. She hoped Maxwell liked it as much. It was important to her that she made a good impression. Though whether his son would enjoy it, dried up as it would be by the time he got to it, remained to be seen.

She hadn't seen Roland again following their meeting with Maria outside. He must have taken himself up to his room, though she hadn't heard a thing from inside when crossing the landing on occasion. Likely he'd gone to bed to catch up on sleep he'd missed last night elsewhere. Neither was he present in the dining room just now. Maxwell hadn't seemed too concerned at this, had asked her to leave his son's meal to warm by the fire.

Her thoughts switched to her mother, who, for the first time, would also be eating alone at this moment. Guilt pierced her and she closed her eyes. She was missing her terribly and she knew Flora would be feeling the same. Jewel just prayed her venomous aunt hadn't kicked up much of a fuss about her leaving and taken it out on Mam. That poor woman would be suffering enough.

Flora was still on Jewel's mind later when she climbed

the stairs to draw the curtains and extinguish the lights before retiring to bed. She'd been up earlier to clear the dining room – like his son, Maxwell was nowhere to be seen – and she'd finished up her chores with a heavy heart. Already she had begun to see that life as a general servant was indeed a lonely one.

Reaching the drawing-room window, Jewel's gaze immediately went left up the street. Again, she pictured her mother at Back Cheapside, this time alone in their bed, the pillow soaked with her tears . . . As she struggled to swallow the lump in her throat, a movement across the street caught her eye. There, looking back at her from her own residence as she carried out the same late-night task as herself, stood Maria, flapping her hand wildly. The friendly sight was like a balm.

Smiling, Jewel waved back. And as she returned to the kitchen, she did so a little lighter of heart.

Chapter 9

TONGUE PEEKING OUT in concentration, Jewel raked out the dead ashes as quietly as she could manage. The early-dawn lighting of the bedroom fires without waking the family was a real skill that all maids had to master – thankfully, she seemed to have got the hang of it quickly, hadn't disturbed any of the Birch members up to now.

In the four-poster bed behind her, Maxwell lay on his back, one arm resting above his head on the pillow. The new sun trickling through the gaps in the curtains, which lent Jewel the only light whilst she went about her task, fell in straight, silver rays along the bedclothes and up across his bare chest, picking out the thatch of dark curls there. But it was his face when she glanced over her shoulder to check his sleeping, worried she was creating too much noise, that caught her attention and kept it there.

Turning fully to face him, she sat back on her haunches. He wore a look deep in forlornness. His brows were together in a slight frown, the corners of his mouth down. He put her in mind of a youngster having a bad dream, and this she would have believed and given it no more thought had she not glimpsed now and then since arriving, when he let his gladsome mask slip, him wearing the same expression in his waking hours, too.

Did his sister's absence trouble him still? After all, he hadn't been his usual self since – Jewel had noticed his withdrawal. However, she sensed something more now, that he couldn't conceal fully in this state of unconsciousness: raw grief. She recognised it unquestioningly; she'd seen her mam wear it often enough.

Lowering her gaze, guilty to be secretly intruding on his inner feelings, she returned her attention to her work. She'd just finished black-leading the fire and was wiping her soiled hands on a scrap of rag when, again, her attention was drawn to the man. She hesitated then crossed to the bedside. His frown was still in place and now his lips were moving – tilting her head, she listened but no words emerged. Only a moan, low with sorrow, escaped on his breath. His pain was tangible.

Jewel's heart contracted for him. What made her do it, she couldn't say – perhaps it was the promise she'd made to Mrs Kirkwood – as ever so gently, she laid her palm on his slick forehead. Instantly, the skin-on-skin contact seemed to comfort him; his brow smoothed out on a soft sigh.

She removed her hand but continued watching him for some seconds. Satisfied he was calmer, she gathered up her box of cleaning brushes and slipped from the room.

Later, Maxwell entered the dining room wearing the easy smile Jewel hadn't seen since their earlier meetings. He seemed fresher, brighter somehow, and she was glad of it.

'Good morning, Jewel.'

'Morning, sir.' She stole another look at him as he sat. 'You're . . . well today, Mr Birch?'

He appeared to consider his answer. His smile returned. He nodded. 'Yes. Yes, I think I am.'

With a happy smile of her own, she finished setting the table then left him reading his paper to collect breakfast from the kitchen.

Today was her first Sunday off. Thoughts of spending the whole afternoon with her mother brought excited flutters to her stomach and she quickened her pace. However, midway down the stairs, cooking smells reached her nostrils and a sudden bout of nausea whacked her full across the face. Her guts changed direction, somersaulting worryingly, and she bolted down the remaining steps. She reached the kitchen just in time to heave up what felt like her soul into the stone sink.

Sweating and shaking, she took some deep breaths – realising too late her error when the broiled mackerel gripped her insides again as though with invisible hands. She swallowed quickly, this time managing to stem the sickness, but was still forced to drop into a seat for a minute to regain her composure.

Slowly, clarity reached her – her eyes swivelled to her midriff. She could have cried, for this had made her terrible predicament all the more real. The seed inside her was growing by the minute into a real person; it was as if her body had realised and had decided to begin reminding her of the fact. As if she could forget. It was with her every waking moment. *God, help me.*

With great effort, she forced herself back to her duties. Holding her breath, she dished out the meal and hurried as fast as the tray would allow her back to the house. The sooner she had delivered this disgusting fare upstairs, the faster she could escape from here for a few hours.

When she re-entered the dining room, she saw that Roland had joined his father in her absence. Lounging in a chair at the table, he watched her approach with lazy interest. She placed his breakfast in front of him and he cocked his head for a better view of her face.

'Are you feeling well, little nightingale?'

Embarrassment brought heat to her cheeks. Stemming her anxiety, she nodded. 'Aye, Mr Roland.'

'You're rather pale. I hope my father isn't working you too hard,' he added with mock-sternness to the older man.

'Nay, sir.'

Maxwell had lowered his paper, was regarding her with something akin to concern. Her face flushed a deeper red; cursing it, she averted her head, saying, 'Will that be all, sir? Mr Roland? Only I planned to visit Mam . . .'

'Of course.' Maxwell looked as if he'd say more but, after glancing towards his son, changed his mind. 'Off you go, enjoy your afternoon.'

'Ta, thanks. I will, sir.'

In less than a minute, she'd donned her shawl and was stepping into the street with a thankful heart. High clouds framed a pleasant sky and a slight breeze took the edge off the humid air. Drawing in a long, slow breath, she turned her back on the house and set off for Back Cheapside.

'Mam?' Jewel burst through the door at a half-run, giddy with anticipation, but her happiness was soon dashed. She halted and took in the scene before her. Two figures were seated by the fire drinking tea and eating slices of bread and dripping. Her mother turned with a joyful cry at her entrance – the other simply stared and didn't utter a word.

'Eeh, lass. By, but it's good to see thee.' Flora fussed around her daughter, removing her shawl and stroking her hair, before pulling her close in a quick hug. 'Sit yourself down, I'll pour thee a sup,' she told her, unable to keep the smile from her face as she crossed to the table.

All the while, Jewel's gaze never strayed from her cousin's. Just what the hell was *he* doing here? What she wouldn't give to dash across and slap *his* face daft for him until the flagged floor ran red. Was there no escaping him at all? Hadn't she a constant reminder burrowed in her womb without this? Today of all days – but, of course, he'd have known she had the afternoon off from work, must have planned this. All she'd wanted was to enjoy a few precious hours in her mam's company, but he'd spoiled it, like he had everything else. Lord, how she loathed him.

'Does tha want a refill, Benji, love?' asked her mother, busy with the teapot, her back to them. 'Ay, lass, he's been an angel hisself this past week,' she informed her daughter. 'Reet looked after me, he has, running errands and the like. He's just this minute finished fixing that sideboard door we've had trouble with for ages. Shuts perfect now, it does, thanks to him. Well, lad? Will tha stop for another sup?' she asked him again.

He broke Jewel's stare to glance inside his cup. When he brought his eyes back to hers, she sent him a look that held both pleading and warning. *Don't you bloody dare accept, just you get gone from here*, she silently screamed at him.

Benji's gaze swivelled to her breasts, much to Jewel's disgust, then he trained it towards his aunt. 'Ta. I will, aye. 'Ere and after, I'll take a look at that shelf up there; seems a bit lopsided to me.'

Anger shook Jewel's very bones. By God, he'd pay for this.

Groping behind her to where her mother had hung up her shawl, she plucked it down and dragged it across her shoulders.

'Lass? What—?'

'I meant to explain right away but hadn't the chance . . .' Wincing at the confusion in Flora's wide eyes, Jewel busied herself with securing the garment. 'Mr Birch asked me to work this afternoon, you see. I said aye, for he's stuck without a nurse for the child, and . . . He needs me, so I'll have to go. He said I could dash home to inform thee but I've to be right back. Sorry, Mam.'

Flora was crushed. 'Oh, lass . . . Well, if you must, then you must. Eeh, but I were so looking forward to having thee by yon hearth forra few hours.'

'Sorry, Mam,' Jewel repeated, before rushing from the house, sure she'd explode into violent sobs – or blurt out the truth behind her need to make a speedy exit – were she to remain here a second longer.

Her tears flowed freely as she pelted, shawl flapping behind her and her long, swinging plait whipping her back, towards the park. There was nowhere else to go. She certainly couldn't return to Mawdsley Street so soon; what would the Birch men make of that? Questions would be asked as to why she wasn't using her free afternoon as it was intended, and she really hadn't the energy to spin off a convincing untruth. Besides, she must look a state. They wouldn't fail to notice something was amiss. One show of kindness or concern and her resolve would crumble. She couldn't risk that.

Today, the serene grounds did little to ease her worries. She walked aimlessly, mind going over the scene, her anger slowly building into the familiar rage now with the passing seconds. Her mam, praising *him* . . . But, of course, she wasn't to know. None of this was her fault. He was at wrong here. He was up to something, must be. He'd never shown much interest in his aunt or her home before now. And the way he'd looked at her with that lustful glint in his eye she'd come to loathe. Did he honestly think she'd let him . . . a *second* time? Perhaps having claimed her once, he now believed he could have her whenever he chose.

Her mouth moved of its own accord into a grimace. God above, just let those foul hands of his come anywhere near her again! She'd kill him. She would.

A familiar giggle drifted through the swaying branches of a cluster of trees to her left. Now, her spirits did lift somewhat and she stepped closer to peek through the shiny leaves. Maxwell was sat cross-legged by a flowerbed in the distance. His sleeves were rolled to his elbows, his dark coat and hat lying in an untidy heap beside him where he'd tossed them on to the grass. He pretended to pounce and his daughter let out another squeal of laughter, her small, chubby legs tripping over themselves in escape.

Despite her earlier concerns regarding him seeing her and guessing all wasn't well, Jewel's feet itched to go to them. Mind made up, she quickly tidied her hair and rearranged her shawl – then turned sharply as, again, a voice she recognised rang out in the opposite direction, this time calling her name:

'Over here, lass! Jewel, it's me!'

Maria's grinning face came into view and Jewel forced down her disappointment. 'Hello.'

'What you standing there for on your ruddy own?' The maid beckoned her across. 'Come on, take a walk with me, lass.'

Maria would think her stark, staring mad were she to turn down her offer to instead spend her free time with the master and miss. Didn't Jewel see enough of them the rest of the week? she was sure to ask. And what answer she'd give Maria, she didn't know, couldn't explain the desire to be with them even to herself.

'Well? Is tha coming or no?'

Glancing back through the foliage, Jewel swallowed a sigh then ran to catch her up.

'So.' Maria linked her arm through Jewel's. 'What *were* you about just now, hiding in yon trees?'

'I weren't hiding, just resting is all.'

'Don't you have a home to go to?'

'Don't you?' shot back Jewel, her irritation rising. However, at Maria's grin, she couldn't help chuckling. 'You're annoying, you, d'you know that?'

'Aye, I do know.' The servant shrugged good-naturedly. 'It's just my way. We all have our crosses to bear.' She spread her hands wide. 'I'm annoying, you're a moody cow. You see?'

Again, Jewel laughed. Despite her disappointment when the woman had appeared, she was now glad she had. Maria was a tonic for the soul, there was no denying it.

'Mam died when I were little but I've a father and two sisters, if you must know. Called in on them earlier, I did, but father was skenning drunk, as per usual. His nastiness had driven the others from the house afore I arrived; I didn't see the point in sticking around myself. He'd have only started on me had I stayed. Sod. I only drag myself there of a Sunday for the lasses' sakes.'

'Sorry to hear that.'

Again, Maria shrugged. 'It's all right.'

Turning right, they wandered along the grassy expanse in companionable silence. Overhead, a flock of small birds glided and swooped. Bees hovered around the colourful flowers dotted about and their hum mingled with that of conversation from others out taking advantage of the weather and pleasant surroundings. Jewel felt she could have remained here for ever.

'What's your story, then, lass?'

'I've a mam. I called in earlier but . . . Well, I didn't want to stay. It's nowt, really,' she continued carefully when her friend frowned curiously. 'My cousin were there and I don't much like his company.'

'Tries messing with thee, does he?'

Jewel was too shocked to respond to the accurate assumption spoken so matter-of-factly. She simply gazed straight ahead, wide-eyed. Her silence spoke volumes; Maria nodded.

'Aye, thought so. My brother were the same afore I got my position. Always trying to get at me, he was, touching and what not where he shouldn't. I were glad when he wed and buggered off out of it.'

'Maria, that's terrible.' Jewel was wholly sorry for her. 'Didn't your father do anything?'

'I never told him. Doubt he'd have done much anyroad if I had.'

'But why? You should have gone to him, lass.'

The servant cocked an eyebrow. 'Like you, yer mean? I take it your mam's not aware of your cousin's antics, eh?'

Maria was right. How could she, in her position, stand here and spout hypocritical advice? She nodded, shamefaced. 'I'm sorry. I just can't tell her, Maria. The trouble it would create . . . Aye well. Least I'm away from him now, at any rate. Mind, he'd best not be hanging around

Mam's next Sunday, let me tell thee. He'll bloody know about it if he is. No way will he stop me and Mam seeing each other. Never.'

'What will you do?'

But Jewel hadn't an answer. Talk was cheap; reality was an entirely different matter. She banished Benji from her thoughts and the women continued on their walk.

*

'Here, sir, let me.'

'Ah! Thank you, Jewel.'

Abandoning her chore of dusting the mantel, she held out her arms to the weary father with a smile. Constance, grisly with tiredness, wriggled to be set loose again but Jewel hushed her soothingly. 'All right. Let's take you forra little lie-down, eh? You'll feel the better for it, aye.'

'Thank you,' Maxwell said again when she re-entered the drawing room to resume her duties, the child now napping peacefully upstairs. 'You're good with her, you know.'

'Aye?' Surprised pleasure brought a pink glow to Jewel's cheeks. She'd doubted herself constantly since arriving here because of her inexperience with caring for youngsters and fretted herself sick over how she'd cope with her own. To hear this from him was a precious boost to her confidence.

'I mean it. She's taxing, I understand, but you manage her admirably.'

Though he spoke the truth – the girl in the nursery was an exhausting whirlwind of energy – still, she felt the urge to defend her. 'She's but a babby, sir. The world and everything in it is so much more interesting and exciting to her; she can't help but want to explore it. She'll settle down, no doubt, as she grows.'

Maxwell nodded slowly. 'Do you know, I've never thought of it that way. Of course, everything is new to her young senses. Here am I accusing her of making mischief. I feel ashamed.'

'Oh, don't. You're a wonderful father. It can't be easy for you, raising her by yourself—' She broke off and cleared her throat, regretting her bold overfamiliarity. It wasn't proper to put voice to her observations. It wasn't a servant's place. 'What I mean is,' she added quietly, 'well . . . you're doing just gradely, sir.'

Maxwell's eyes creased. When he spoke, his words held a deeper meaning: 'As are you, Jewel.'

Thanks to thee. In a way, you've saved me, Maxwell Birch. Saved me from myself. And you don't even know it. The response swirled safely inside her mind. Though she could never voice it out loud, it didn't make it any less true.

For a long moment, they stared at one another silently, gratitude in their eyes.

'I'd best get on with my work, sir,' Jewel said finally. 'You put your feet up awhile, enjoy the peace afore the evening meal.' She smiled, turned and made back towards the fire. She heard the door click shut behind her, telling her that Maxwell had heeded her advice and had taken himself to his room. With another small smile, she got on with her dusting.

As she worked, her mind switched to her afternoon with Maria. She was seeing a different side to her new friend and felt guilty that she'd judged her as brash on their first encounter. She wasn't at all, no, just lively of spirit. Despite her harsh beginnings, she was generous and caring and fun. She was also desperate to be liked, it was clear to see.

Well, Jewel *did* like her, a lot. A connection had been formed when they had revealed their shared experiences with rotten family members of the opposite sex. For the first time, she felt she had an ally, and it brought her comfort. They understood in a world where it seemed no one else did. Perhaps they could be there for one another now, when either needed it, with a listening ear and a hand to hold. Hope made her heart warm.

The front door opening and closing heralded Roland's return and, again, Jewel's musings went back to the domestic across the street. Maria had revealed that he worked at the bank with his father. A few weeks before Jewel had begun her position here, Roland's intended had broken off their betrothal after discovering he'd been romantically liaising with another woman. Servants talked – Maria was friendly with a maid who knew a maid employed by the betrayed fiancée.

'Mr Roland'll never be tethered down, I don't reckon,' Maria had told Jewel. 'Likes the lasses too much, aye. And they like him, though I can't say I blame them. Handsome divil, he is. He's allus off gallivanting with Lord only knows who and coming home at all hours; not until the following day, oftentimes. Mind, his father must be weary of covering for him at the bank – he's away from his work more than he's in. Whether he's tried curtailing his son's antics or no, I can't say. In any case, it don't appear that Mr Roland is for changing his ways any time soon.'

Jewel wasn't overly shocked at hearing any of this. Hadn't she witnessed with her two eyes his flirtatious manner with Maria, and suspected that was his way with women in general? And she herself had seen him slinking home early morning from a night spent goodness knew where. Nor did Maxwell tolerating such behaviour surprise her. He was a kind and decent man, and clearly a dedicated parent. No doubt he disagreed with Roland's antics and hoped he'd soon curb them. However, he'd never cast him out or turn his back on him – Jewel knew this instinctively. She'd never met a father quite like him; he seemed to live and breathe for his children.

Despite what she knew, she couldn't dislike the wayward Birch. She could see it to be a weak and immature trait he possessed rather than intentional badness. It appeared he couldn't help himself where the fairer sex was concerned. Some men were like that, God only knew. Thankfully, he hadn't turned his attentions in her direction. Besides the occasional lingering look and his overfamiliar habit of calling her 'little nightingale', he'd so far left her be. He'd do well to make sure it stayed that way, too.

After supper, when Jewel had tidied and swept the dining room, she closed the door with a thankful sigh. It had been a long and emotive day. She couldn't wait to drop on to the lumpy mattress and rest her body and mind.

Crossing the hall towards the kitchen stairs, she caught sight of Maxwell at the opposite end, busy battening down the hatches for the night. He'd already extinguished the lights, bar the single gas lamp left burning whilst he completed his task, and his tall figure cast its shadow, like a pool of shimmering smoke, across the tiled floor. She watched through the amber glow him reach up to fix the bolt in place then, changing his mind, open the front door wide. His head swung left and right along the street; then, sighing, he stepped back inside and secured the lock in place.

He must have been checking if his son was on his way home, Jewel thought; she'd seen Roland exit the house shortly after the evening meal. She'd been right, then, in her assumption that his lifestyle wasn't something his father bore without disapproval.

Anger that his selfishness was causing unnecessary concern for the older man sparked inside her. It was no doubt one more worry Maxwell could do without.

Not wishing to startle him, she cleared her throat softly – nevertheless, he turned sharply and she flashed an apologetic smile. 'Goodnight, God bless, sir.'

'Goodnight.'

Jewel had reached the top of the stairs when she heard him call her name. She glanced back over her shoulder. 'Aye, sir?'

'What you said earlier about Constance ... and myself ... my abilities as a father ...'

'I meant it. She's fortunate to have thee. As is Roland,' she hastened to add.

Maxwell's voice was barely above a whisper. 'Thank you.'

'I never really knew my own father. He died afore I'd time to store any real or lasting memories.' She spoke just as quietly, surprised at herself that she was revealing this to him and not knowing why, other than having the strongest urge to reassure him that, as a new widower, he was handling life, his family, just fine. Also, she knew, it was this man's way again, making you want to open up, that sense of trust he exuded. 'But sir,' she added, tone dropping further still, 'if I had known him ... I'd have wanted him to be just like thee.'

Leaving the admission hanging between them, she smiled, turned and continued on her way to the kitchen.

Snuggled beneath the bedclothes minutes later, Jewel

was on the cusp of unconsciousness when Maxwell's image flitted on the outskirts of her mind. She watched him draw closer, saw herself move forward to meet him. What she pictured next caused a frown to accompany her on her sleep's final journey. For despite what she'd told her employer in the hall, the kiss he gave her – and that she returned with full fervour – was anything but that from a father figure.

Chapter 10

JEWEL HAD CALCULATED that the child would be due in early March. By November, she'd never felt so thankful for anything as she was for the oversized apron.

She'd been steadily loosening her corset for weeks and, only yesterday, the laces had reached their maximum length – she'd known panic at the realisation. She couldn't hide her condition for much longer, and then what would she do? The neat globe was certain to expand significantly over the coming months and no amount of apron material would conceal that. Folk were bound to start noticing any day now. She was done for.

What would happen when the child actually made an appearance, she'd steadfastly refused to dwell upon. Terror of the unknown had seen her bury her head, for it was easier that way. Would she go along with Benji's suggestion that she was attacked by a stranger, hadn't revealed her condition through fear and shame? Would people believe any of it? And if they didn't? If Mam chose to disown her, what then?

She couldn't stay on at the Birch household, that much was clear. What would she do should she find herself destitute? How would she and the child survive with no dwelling, brass or support from a living soul? It would be the workhouse for the both of them, for sure.

And she'd rather be gone from this world, once and for all, than that. Imprisonment in those harsh and heartless institutions was a fate worse than death and she'd make sure she didn't mess up the second attempt.

The time was approaching noon. Though several more hours of daylight remained, already winter's fingers were stroking the light grey sky, and the diluted sun seemed to shiver with the rest of them.

Soon, the frost would come and the town's poorer inhabitants would struggle still more than usual. With little or no money for coal and a daily hot meal, droves wouldn't last through to spring. The sick and weak were particularly susceptible. Friends and neighbours, though having next to nothing themselves, would make it their mission to keep a caring eye to the more vulnerable, sharing what they could, when they could. It was the same year in, year out. The lower class, above all others, looked after their own – an unwritten rule that most adhered to with unshakeable belief.

Ignoring her aching back, Jewel bent again to rinse out her cloth in the pail of water by the front door. She had just reached up on tiptoe to get at the window's corners when hands on her shoulders from behind had her jumping out of her skin – she turned with a squeak.

Maria could barely get her greeting out through her snorts of laughter. 'By, your phizog! I only nipped across to say hello. Did I fricken thee so bad?'

Jewel forced down her annoyance. Building worry and lethargy had of late brought brooding black moods she found increasingly difficult to shake. She gave her friend a rueful smile. 'Aye, you swine. I didn't hear your approach; tha near caused me a mishap there.'

'So I see.' Maria nodded down to Jewel's apron, where

soapy water had splashed when she'd squeezed her wet cloth in her fright. 'Come here, daft ha'porth.'

'Nay! Don't!' Seeing the maid's hand going to her midriff to wipe at the suds, panic filled Jewel and, without thought, she smacked it away fiercely. In the ensuing seconds, as Maria rubbed her stinging fingers, they gazed at one another in shocked silence. Jewel recovered sooner. Swinging her head slowly in horror, she stammered, 'Maria . . . I, I'm sorry—'

'No harm done.' But the maid's tone held a stiff note. 'Well. I'd best get back to my own duties.'

'Please, wait.' Jewel caught her sleeve as she made to leave. 'Eeh, Maria. What am I to do?'

'Do? 'Ere, what's the matter?' she added with concern, seeing that Jewel's eyes had pooled with tears. 'Lass?'

After glancing around, Jewel smoothed her apron against herself, revealing the outline of her bump. 'What am I to *do*?' she repeated in a fearful whisper.

'Mother of God . . .' The words fell from Maria's lips on a sorry sigh. 'You bloody idiot, Jewel. How've you found yourself like that?'

'How d'you think?'

Again, Maria sighed. She scratched her head then her chin. 'Is it Roland Birch's doing?'

Jewel was aghast. 'Nay, nay. It . . . you don't know him. A mistake occurred and . . . I'd rather not talk of it. I need your help,' she finished, a lone tear escaping to splash to her cheek. 'I'm that frightened, Maria.'

'That cousin of yours, him you've spoken on afore. This is his doing, in't it?'

'Aye,' Jewel whispered after some moments, feeling the weight of the crippling secret ease somewhat from her shoulders at the admission.

'Bastard.'

Dropping her gaze, Jewel shook her head. 'Nay, not that. May God forgive me, I consented. I – we – were full of ale. Nonetheless, why I allowed him . . . I'll never know. To top it all, he's denying all involvement.'

'They allus do. Eeh, lass. Does anyone else know about this?'

'Nay. Norra soul.'

'When's it due?'

'Around March. What am I to do?' she beseeched yet again.

Maria's eyes softened. She reached for her friend's hand and Jewel gripped it. 'That depends on thee, lass.'

'What d'you mean?'

'Is tha for keeping the child?'

'What choice have I?'

The maid lowered her voice. 'There's allus a choice, lass.'

For the first time in many months, Jewel knew a stirring of hope. 'There is?'

'Not here. Meet me the morrow at the park. We'll talk on it more then. And Jewel?'

'Aye?'

'You're not to fret no more, you hear? I'm here for thee now. All will be well, you'll see, lass.'

She could barely speak past the lump of relieved emotion in her throat. 'Thank you.'

Maria gave her hand a last supportive squeeze then hurried back to her own residence across the road.

For the remainder of the day, Jewel could think of nothing but their conversation. Had she done the right thing in confessing? she agonised continually. By, but it had felt good to share the burden. What suggestions would her friend come up with tomorrow? Was there really a way out of this hell? Maria had seemed quite convinced there was.

Following that first Sunday off, her afternoons had been incident free. Mercifully, Benji appeared to have got the message – she'd encountered him no more when visiting her mother. It was lovely to spend time with Flora again, just like the old days – albeit for a few short hours and always, at the back of Jewel's mind, with the fear her mother would notice her growing stomach, though she did her utmost to casually conceal it with her shawl. Hopefully, her cousin would continue to steer clear of her; for this, she prayed daily.

What excuse she'd give Mam for missing tomorrow's visit, she hadn't the strength to think on right now, would cross that bridge when she came to it. She must meet Maria, had to hear her apparent solution. Her future – her whole *life* – depended on it.

That night, she took her time completing the last of her duties; anything to prolong the inevitable sleepless hours tossing in bed with worry that she knew were to come.

Maxwell had already locked and bolted the doors, and he and his son had retired to their beds some half an hour before. The house was still, the dying kitchen fire bathing the room in cosy pink light. Forcing her mind on the present – were she to allow it to stray to thoughts of the next day, her heartbeat would quicken painfully – she softly hummed a childhood song.

From its bed of clouds, the arch of silver moon peering through the narrow kitchen window followed her as she pottered about wiping and tidying the already clean and neat space. Though her newly swollen ankles ached, she ignored them – just one more result of her pregnancy that she'd now become adept at pretending wasn't occurring. Gritting her teeth, she trained the cloth on the sink and gave it a thorough wiping. She'd just rinsed it and laid it over the sink's stone rim to dry when she sensed she was being watched. Frowning, she turned towards the stairs leading to the house – and let out a loud gasp to find Maxwell standing staring down at her.

'Jewel—'

'God in heaven above! Sir, tha startled me.' She crossed towards him. 'Is everything all right?'

'Yes, I . . . Forgive me for the lateness of the hour. You must be tired. Would it be too much trouble to ask for a last pot of tea?'

She blinked, surprised. 'Nay, sir. Course not. I'll brew a fresh sup now.'

To her confusion, he didn't instruct her to fetch the beverage to the drawing room or some such then return upstairs. Instead, he remained exactly where he was, saying nothing, whilst she moved around the room seeing to the kettle and fetching a cup and saucer.

Should she enquire after his health? she asked herself, glancing furtively at him once or twice. His behaviour was out of character – never had he sought her out in the kitchen late at night before. He appeared . . . She couldn't put her finger on it. Not ill, in any case. And not so much troubled, more distracted. As though in a world all his own. Before she had the chance to decide, he broke the silence:

'You visit your mother every Sunday afternoon?'

Jewel looked up from the table slowly. His face was unreadable in the dim light and guilt whizzed through her, making her dizzy. Why ask such a thing? What concern was it of his how she chose to spend her days off? Unless . . . Her eyes widened. She swallowed hard. Surely he didn't know, hadn't somehow heard . . . ? Was he aware of her planned meeting with Maria tomorrow instead? And the reason for it? But *how*? Her friend wouldn't have breathed a word to anyone. Would she?

How well did she know the girl across the street? The sudden thought brought panic to her veins. She'd spilled to her her innermost secrets, blindly trusted her in the hope she'd help, when all the time . . . *Dear God!* She'd *kill* her for this! She would, she'd—!

'Jewel?'

'Hm?' She licked her dry lips. 'Sorry . . . Aye, I do. Mostly, aye. Why . . . why d'you ask, sir?' she forced herself to say, her cheeks growing hot with dread.

Maxwell was quiet for a moment, then: 'Tomorrow would have been my wife's birthday.'

'Oh.' *What's that got to do with anything?* she stopped herself from adding just in time, confusion still holding her in its grasp. 'Oh,' she repeated, this time with more feeling, glimpsing the hollow sadness in his eyes. 'You must miss her terribly, sir.'

'Yes.'

Again, silence fell between them. Quickly, she finished making the tea and went to collect a tray. So this was the reason behind his nocturnal wanderings, she realised. Memories of his poor wife were keeping him from his sleep. On significant dates, her absence must, after all, sting especially so. She swallowed a sorry sigh for him and his suffering, couldn't imagine his hurt. Yet why his question as to her habits in her free time? What *had* that to do with his wife?

'Thank you.' Maxwell took the tray she held out to him.

Jewel waited with bated breath but, when no more from him was forthcoming, she murmured, 'Sir?'

'Yes?'

She had to know. 'Why did you ask about my visits to Mam?'

'Ah. Yes. Well.' He cleared his throat. 'It's silly, really. Please forget that I asked.' He flashed a half-smile. 'Well. Goodnight.'

He was walking away. But . . . Wait! She had to know.

'Has Maria said summat?' she blurted to his retreating back. 'Is that it, sir?'

'Maria?' He was staring at her in puzzlement over his shoulder. 'Maria?' he repeated.

'The . . . maid, from across the street. I . . . thought . . .' She rummaged around inside her head for something to fill the agonising silence. To think she'd believed her friend capable of revealing her secret; her paranoia was skewing her judgement. Oh, she was wicked-minded, didn't deserve Maria's kindness. 'I – Maria and me, that is – have planned to meet the morrow, sir, forra walk in the park is what I meant. I'm for giving a visit to Mam's a miss this week.'

'Ah, I see.' Maxwell's face relaxed in understanding, then his brows drew together and, again, he cleared his throat. 'As a matter of fact, the park was the reason I enquired about your plans, I . . . Well . . .'

'Aye, sir?'

He smiled self-consciously and looked away. 'I was going to ask whether you would like to accompany Constance and me tomorrow.'

'To the park?'

'Yes.'

'Me, sir? Really?'

'Yes,' he said again, quieter this time, and Jewel felt a queer warmness flow through her. 'Several hours away from this house and the memories it holds will be beneficial to my daughter and me, I believe,' Maxwell added.

'However, please don't give it another thought – like I said, it's silly, really—'

'I'd love to.'

He raised his brows slowly. 'You would? But your plans—?'

'Maria won't mind,' she cut in again, at the same time asking herself what the hell she was playing at. She *had* to see the maid, didn't she? Her friend had vowed to help her, and Lord did she need it. Yet here she was instead, speaking these words to this man, without a clue as to why. What she did know instinctively was that it wasn't out of pity for him that she'd accepted his invitation. Nor was it from a sense of duty.

Then what? her mind asked. The answer that whispered on the outskirts of her mind had her glancing to her feet, for the truth of it she couldn't deny. She wanted to spend time with him. Constance, too. Everything else, even her own trials, paled in comparison. The realisation left her bewildered.

'Well, if you're certain . . . ?'

'I am, sir.'

'Excellent.' A genuine smile spread across Maxwell's face. 'Constance will be pleased. She'll enjoy the excursion infinitely more with you in attendance, I'm sure. You have a knack of keeping her entertained.'

She knew a sensation akin to her guts falling from a height and struggled to keep the disappointment from her face. That was why he'd asked her along: for his daughter's sake. He wanted her there as a nursemaid, to keep an eye to the child. And why should it be anything more? she insisted to herself. *Stupid, stupid.*

'Right, I shall leave you in peace.' He motioned to the tea things in his hands. 'Thank you.'

'No thanks needed, sir.'

'Goodnight.'

'Goodnight.'

She watched him until he disappeared from sight then crossed to the bed. She perched on the edge. Her mind really wasn't her own of late; being with child was warping her common sense, she was certain. The thoughts she found creeping in sometimes shocked and filled her with shame in equal measure. For since her dream, of she and Mr Birch together, their *kiss* . . . Cringing, Jewel heaved another long breath. Was she developing madness on top of everything else? It really wouldn't surprise her, the way her luck was going at present!

Cancelling her plans with Maria was proof that she was losing her grip on reality, surely? Just what was she thinking? What was she going to do now? Would her friend be upset with her for choosing to spend time with the Birches instead? After all, she couldn't very well go back on her agreement with Maxwell now. Would Maria still be willing to help her?

Busy with her thoughts, Jewel at first took the faint flutters and taps in her stomach to be but nervous tension. When another more forceful blow struck beneath her ribs, she glanced down with a mixture of horror and awe.

Over the next few minutes, as the life growing within her made for the first time its presence known, a clogging ball of conflicting emotion built to a ton weight in her breast.

She looked to the heavens through a blur of tears then closed her eyes in despair.

*

Jewel awoke the following morning with a scratchy throat and a head that felt home to a dozen drummers;

wincing, she flopped back against the pillows. Illness must have dragged her back to sleep, for the next thing she was aware of was full daylight filtering through the high window – her early starts were in pitch-darkness during winter months – and she dragged herself up with a gasp. Pain speared inside her temples at the movement and nausea rose. 'God above, I feel terrible,' she croaked to what she thought was the empty room.

'Indeed, you look it. No offence.'

Opening one eye, she squinted up in surprise. 'Sir.'

'Forgive my intrusion, but I felt I ought to check in on you, given your absence.'

'I'm sorry, I—'

'You'll do no such thing,' Maxwell instructed her as she attempted to rise. 'You must rest.'

'But sir, the fires haven't been lit.' No doubt it was this which had caused him to seek her out. 'Your breakfast. The house, my duties . . .'

'Your only task today is to remain in your bed. That is an order.' Though he spoke firmly, a hint of concern showed in his eyes.

He was likely worried she'd pass whatever ailed her on to his family, Jewel thought, and who could blame him? Young Constance especially was of an age where severe colds could easily develop into something more serious. Nonetheless: 'But . . . the park, sir,' she couldn't stop herself from saying, unable to hide her disappointment. 'You said yourself, Miss Constance will want me there . . .'

'As do I. Alas, these things cannot be helped. Now, try to get some sleep. It's the body's natural healer and will do you the world of good. I'll check in on you again upon our return.'

'Ta, thanks.' Already, her lead-heavy eyelids were drooping. 'Sorry, sir.'

'Shh. Sleep.'

Maxwell's whisper floated on the edges of her consciousness. Then what felt like a hand gently brushing damp hair from her brow seeped through to her and she knew she was sicker than she'd realised. Delirium had her in its grasp, was causing her to imagine things. Groaning, she turned over and fell into a heavy sleep.

She awoke some time later to light tapping coming from above her. Her wooziness was worse than before and the hammering inside her head had spread; it was like a physical thing gnawing on her skull. Assuming she was hallucinating again, she closed her mind to the noise.

'Psst. Lass, it's me. Is tha all right?'

Frowning, Jewel peered up at the window. Beyond it, kneeling on the flagstones in the street, was Maria. Hands cupped around her eyes, she was staring through the pane. Jewel gave her a weak wave then held a hand to her forehead and imitated a cough to show she was unwell. Her frown grew when, catching her meaning, her friend stood and walked away without another word. But Jewel felt too rotten to dwell on it; she closed her eyes once more.

''Ere, lass. Sup up.'

Again, the world came into focus. To Jewel's astonishment, she saw her friend perched on the bottom of her bed. She glanced around the room – yes, this was definitely her kitchen. She hadn't wandered off in her confused state; nor did the smiling woman seem to be an apparition. Then how on earth . . . ? 'Maria? Is it really thee?'

'Aye. I let myself in. Don't fret,' she added when Jewel's eyes widened in horror. 'No one will know – I'll be away afore Mr Birch returns. Lift your head, that's it. Mind now, it's hot.' She supported Jewel as she took sips of the sweetened brew. 'Better?'

'Nay. I feel bloody awful.'

Maria resumed her seat on the bed. 'I spotted your Mr Birch exit with the little 'un earlier. Looked back at the house several times whilst walking away, he did, as though reluctant to leave. I figured summat were afoot.'

'He did?' At Maria's nod, something came back to Jewel that she'd been too poorly earlier to register properly. 'As do I.' That's what Maxwell had said when she'd mentioned that Constance would miss her presence at the park. *As do I*. She allowed herself a small smile.

'And well,' continued Maria, 'when you didn't show at the park . . .' She spread her arms wide. 'I thought it best to check in on thee, guessed you'd been taken ill.'

'Ta, thanks. For the tea, too. Eeh, but Maria, fancy you letting yourself in here.' Despite herself, she couldn't help chuckling when her friend grinned. 'You're a mad bugger, you are.'

'I told thee, don't fret. I'll say I spied you through yon window and that you looked reet bad, that I were afraid you were close to death or some such. No one could punish me for that, now could they?' When their laughter died down, Maria added, quieter now, 'How are . . . things?' She inclined her head to Jewel's stomach. 'All right?'

Jewel nodded. 'I felt it kick for the first time last night.'

'Eeh, lass. Jewel, listen, is there really no way . . . ?'

'Nay. I can't keep it, I can't.'

'Happen you were to speak with your mam, tell her what that cow-son cousin of yourn did. Surely she'd understand—'

'I can't *do* it, Maria. Don't you see? It would stir up a

world of trouble. Benji will deny everything and I'd have no means of proving it, now would I? It would tear my family to tatters, and for what? The truth won't change nowt, will it? I'd still be left holding the baby – a bastard at that – alone for ever more. For let's face it, no one would want me, would they? What fella wants to shackle himself to a lass what's been deflowered by another? Who would want to wed a whore?'

'Ay now, don't speak of yourself so—'

'Why not? It's true!' By now, tears were coursing down Jewel's face. 'I lay with the lad, Maria. Willingly.'

Silence hung between them. What else was there to say? She spoke sense and they both knew it.

'Besides, who says I *want* to keep it?' Jewel murmured after some moments.

'Do you?'

She answered with a sigh. The thumping in her head increased and she closed her eyes. Now, however, Jewel accepted the pain almost with gladness. For wasn't this a sign? Was it not strange that she'd been struck down with a head cold today of all days, had been forced to cancel Maxwell's invitation? She was meant to see Maria instead, it was obvious now. Fate had intervened, and had done so for a reason. She must give up the child. 'Will you help me still?' she asked with feeling.

'Happen you're a bit too far along now for gin and hot baths, or to seek out someone handy with a knitting needle.'

Jewel shuddered at the thought of that particular practice. Complications resulting in death at the hands of untold numbers of backstreet butchers were all too common. 'Nay, not that. I couldn't.'

'Aye. Besides, it'd mean a lengthy stretch in prison were you to be found out. Tha can't risk that.'

'Then what, Maria?'

'Well, there's allus adoption. There's wenches aplenty take in unwanteds and find them new guardians; desperate couples what can't produce their own, like. Make a handsome living from it, an' all, I'll bet.'

The article she'd spotted in her uncle's newspaper months before came back to her. She nodded slowly. Hadn't she given this avenue consideration back then? Again, she nodded. Then she was reminded of the reason she'd initially dismissed the idea and her shoulders slumped. 'The prices they ask, though, for taking the child off your hands is sky high. I could never scrape together such an amount.'

The maid stroked her chin. 'Aye, you're right enough there. Unless . . . ?'

'What?'

'You could try blackmailing your cousin into coughing up the brass, threaten to expose him to your family if he don't. You never know, it might work.' She shrugged. 'It's worth a shot, eh?'

'Benji's but a lad; he hasn't that sort of brass neither.'

'Nay, but his parents do.'

'You mean . . . ?' Jewel bit her lip at Maria's solemn nod. 'I couldn't force him into stealing it from the shop. It'd be Uncle Bernard that he'd be taking from – he doesn't deserve to suffer for this.'

'Jewel, lass. You need to turn a deaf ear to that heart of yourn and instead start listening to your head. The situation you're in . . . You need to switch your thinking, aye, begin planning a way to get yourself out of this, for there's no one else to do it for thee. Sod 'em, the lot. Put you and that babby first forra change. You're a good lass, deserve a second chance. As for the mite inside thee . . . Just think, a loving family what'll cherish it all of its days. Don't you at least owe the poor bugger that? It's not to blame, is it, after all? Seek out that cousin. Needs must, lass. To hell with the rest.'

'Eeh, Maria.' She covered her face with her hands. 'How have I let myself get into this mess?'

'Mistakes happen, lass.'

The straightforward answer, spoken without hesitation in that easy tone, brought tears to her eyes. Jewel doubted her friend had a single judgemental bone in her body. Maria was a true treasure and no mistake. She dreaded to imagine life without her now. Still, could she do what the maid had suggested and bribe Benji? Would it even work?

'You could hunker down at a lying-in house until you've given birth. That way, no one you know will be aware of a thing. You hand over the child afore leaving and return home alone; norra soul will be any the wiser.' Suddenly, Maria rose and hurried for the stairs. 'I'll be but a minute; wait here.'

'Where are you . . . ?' But her friend had already disappeared into the house proper and Jewel awaited her return with a frown. 'Eeh, Maria,' she said when the maid reappeared and clattered back down the stairs, a newspaper under her arm. 'That's Mr Birch's—'

'Aye, well, he's not in need of it at this moment, is he? I'll return it to the drawing room exactly as I found it in a minute, don't fret. Sooner we get looking, the better for thee.' She resumed her seat and began flicking through the pages, eyes narrowed, tongue poking out in concentration; it was plain she wasn't a strong reader. ''Ere, look. That there word says "wanted", don't it?' she announced after a time.

Jewel eyed the thick black text Maria was prodding. She nodded. 'Let me see.' Scanning the advertisement, her brows lifted in recognition. It appeared to be the same one she'd spotted months before; the request was identical word for word.

'What's it say, lass?'

'A widow reckons she'd be glad to accept the charge of a child, any age.'

'Aye? How much is she asking for to adopt?'

'Eight pounds.' This, Jewel noticed, was the only change – if she remembered rightly, the price had initially been ten.

'Blooming 'eck.' Maria puffed out air slowly. 'That's a lot of brass.'

That it was, even with the reduction. Benji would never be able to get his mitts on such a sum. Would he?

'Does it state whether hers is a lying-in house as well?'

'Nay. But that's what I'll need, Maria. I can't hide my condition much longer. And if by some miracle I managed to conceal it throughout, what about when my time comes? What will I do? Give birth to it here in the kitchen alone?' The notion terrified her. 'Besides, the household would hear my labour cries for certain.'

Maria nodded agreement. 'One what will only take the child when it's born is no good. Tha must have a lying-in house. If this widow *don't* offer such a service, happen a bit extra would change her mind? Another pound, say.'

'Aye, more likely than not.' But Jewel's glimmer of hope was dashed as a sudden thought occurred. She closed her eyes. 'What am I thinking? It's impossible, Maria, impossible!'

'What is, lass?'

She'd been so caught up in her desperation, her need for somewhere to place the child, that one crucial aspect had escaped her attention entirely. 'How on earth am I to explain away my absence to Mr Birch, to Mam?'

Chewing on her thumbnail, Maria thought for a moment. Then her face brightened. 'You could tell your mam that Mr Birch's sister . . . what's her name?'

'Mrs Kirkwood?'

'Aye, that Mrs Kirkwood's sick and you've offered to go and nurse her, and that Mr Birch has agreed.'

'And the man hisself? What tale will I spin him?'

'The same, only that you've been called away to nurse a sick relative at your mam's request.'

'But Maria, disappearing for . . . ?' She did a quick calculation on her fingers. 'Three whole *months*? Mebbe more? That's a hell of a long time to be away. Nay, it's no good. It'd never wash with them.'

'What choice have thee but to try?'

None. She had *none*. She screwed her eyes shut once more.

'I've a sister currently out of work what would willingly take over your position here 'til you return, so Mr Birch can't grumble about a lack of a maid. And surely your mam won't question your story, will she? What reason would she have to?'

Jewel had to admit her friend spoke sense. 'I suppose you're right . . .'

'Mr Birch and your mam ain't likely to seek one another out to ask about thee, are they?'

'Nay, probably not.' At least she prayed so.

'Right, well. That just leaves the babby's father to deal with.'

Maria talked as though this was the easy part. In truth, the prospect made Jewel feel physically sick. Just how would this work out?

Chapter 11

WITH PLANS NOW in place, Maria gave Jewel a supportive hug and left her to get some rest. Going above and beyond further still, she'd offered to call in on Flora to explain her daughter's absence; Jewel was more than a little grateful and had told her so.

Maxwell and Constance returned from their outing not long afterwards and, true to his word, Jewel soon heard his tread on the stairs as he came to check on her.

His footsteps halted before they reached the kitchen and, for a long moment, there was silence. Though Jewel had her eyes closed, she felt his gaze from above but didn't react. She was too wrought with grief from recent developments to endure company, even his, and craved to be left alone. To her relief, feigning sleep worked; seemingly reluctant to disturb her, Maxwell left her be.

The door clicked shut behind him and Jewel opened her eyes to stare unseeing at the ceiling. Body and mind felt weighed down yet empty at the same time. A detachedness had settled within her. She felt lifeless, hollowed out. And things were only set to get worse from here on in.

She could have remained here for ever, cocooned in her misery beneath the sheets, but Maxwell's return late afternoon put paid to it. This time, he came right into the kitchen and, leaning over the bed, spoke to her:

'Jewel? How are you feeling?'

'Better, sir, I think,' she lied. She felt sicker than ever.

'Hm. You have a look of the fever about you still.' Frowning, he studied her more closely. 'Perhaps it would be wise to send for the doctor—'

'Nay. Sir, really, there's no need.' *God above, not that.* The last thing she wanted was the medical man prodding and poking about her person, for he'd be quick to discover she was carrying more than a simple chill. 'See, sir, I'm almost recovered,' she added, ignoring her aching joints and head as, reluctantly, she covered herself with her shawl and dragged herself from her bed.

'If you're sure . . . ?'

'Course I am. Now, you take yourself to the drawing room and put your feet up and I'll fetch you up a sup of tea. I'll bring milk and biscuits for Constance, an' all, shall I, sir?' she asked, doing her best to remain upright and not sag against the wall, as she wanted to. Her limbs seemed void of strength; she felt as weak as a kitten.

'Thank you, we'd welcome that.' He gave a grin. 'She's worn herself out with her games at the park – me, too, for that matter!'

Again, Jewel felt a pang of sadness that she'd missed the outing. 'Sounds like youse had a gradely time, sir. Sorry I missed it.'

'There's always next time.'

Warm pleasure filled her. Before she could respond, Maxwell flashed another smile and was gone. She stood for a moment, a smile of her own touching her lips. It stayed with her as she saw to her duties. In more ways than one, she didn't feel so bad any more.

That night, as the Birch household slept, she suppressed her own need for rest and instead reached for her shawl. After padding up the stairs and along the hall, she let herself out of the house, closing the front door quietly behind her.

The chill night was black and eerily still. Glancing about her, it seemed she was the only soul left in the world. At the south end of Mawdsley Street, the darkened spire of St Patrick's Church loomed sharply through the shifting shadows. Mist obscuring the view in the opposite direction slowly closed in on her, swirling about her feet and legs like smoky breath, and she shivered, wishing she was tucked up in her small bed. However, this meeting needed addressing, and the sooner the better. If she left it a day, she just knew her resolve would crumble and it would turn into two, then a week, until eventually she'd talk herself out of it entirely and all the carefully thought out plans would be ruined. Shawl pulled low, head down, she stole through the emptiness towards the square.

By now, the potted shrubs used to adorn the pedestals either side of the town hall steps during the opening ceremony were gone. The long awaited lions had taken their rightful place. Poised gracefully atop their sandstone stages, they guarded their domain with military attention.

Jewel kept a watchful eye on them as she passed. They were but statues, hadn't the power to pounce and wreak havoc, she reminded herself. Nevertheless, she involuntarily quickened her pace.

Only last year, a lion tamer was mauled to death in this very place. The travelling menagerie he belonged to had been in Bolton almost a week when, during a farewell performance before heading to nearby Bury, the unthinkable happened. The tamer, though somewhat the worse for drink, was successfully conducting his show in the den when his five male lions set upon him in a frenzied and prolonged attack. It had taken some moments for the audience to realise this wasn't part of the act, and for applause to give way to screams. Fearing he'd be ripped to pieces, panic ensued.

Like the hundreds of other spectators that fateful evening, Jewel still recalled vividly the smell of blood and gunpowder as, despite his obvious agony, he'd kept his cool and fought back gallantly with his revolver and sword; though the blank cartridges and blunted blade had little impact on the manic animals. Likewise, the sound of crunching bone as a black-maned cat seized the showman's only arm – his other had been but a stump, having been lost in a previous lion attack during an exhibition in Liverpool years earlier – was something she'd never forget.

By the time the townsmen had managed to beat the beasts off with pitchforks and hot pokers through the bars of the cage, and drag the tamer to safety, it was too late. Scalped, gouged and gashed, his costume and the flesh beneath it torn to shreds, he was past all aid.

Benji had clung to Jewel, sobbing, as the man's shattered frame was carried to the nearby infirmary, where he'd died from his horrific injuries on arrival, and she'd comforted him like a big sister might.

When – *why?* – had the lad changed towards her? she asked herself again now with heavy regret. Just how had this night come to this?

Witness to such a dreadful demise, it was little wonder then that folk were wary of the town hall's lifelike additions. Rumour had it that once twilight fell they might come to life and strike down without mercy anyone fool enough to keep such ungodly hours.

'Huh. Silly talk,' Jewel told herself, at the same time breaking into a trot just to be on the safe side.

Oxford Street and the umbrella shop on the corner drew closer and she took a few juddering breaths. As she'd surmised, the premises were in darkness. After searching the ground for a stone, she aimed at Benji's bedroom pane. She knew the noise might alert instead Bernard, or worse, Esther, but was past caring. One way or another, she just wanted this whole thing to be over.

'Down here,' she hissed when the window was lifted and her cousin's tousled head appeared.

'Jewel?'

'Aye, it's me. Come down.'

He disappeared and she moved to the entrance to wait for him. Seconds later, there came the scrape of the bolts being drawn back. The door creaked open several inches. 'Jewel?' he asked again, as if to convince himself he wasn't imagining her. 'What the divil are you—?'

'I need to talk to thee.'

'Aye?' His voice held a note of surprised pleasure. 'You want to come in?'

She struggled to suppress a grimace. What was that smile of his for? Did he honestly think she was here, at this time of night, to boot, for friendly reasons? Lord, he really was deluded. Or blinded by arrogance; one of the two. She shook her head. 'I'll not if it's all the same to you. Look, Benji, I need thee to do summat for me. Well, for *us*, really. You see—?'

'You sure you'll not come in?' he cut in quietly. 'Mam and Father are abed. We'll not be disturbed.'

So *that's* what he's a mind for, Jewel realised, watching his small, dark eyes rake over her breasts. God above, the gall of the foul whelp!

Bubbling rage coursed through her. Grabbing a handful of his shirt front in her fist, she pulled his face close, lip curling in disgust. 'Now you listen to me, yer vicious young swine,' she whispered, voice like ice. 'I'm not here the night on a pleasure visit – Christ, I'd rather be any other place on God's green earth than here with thee.'

'You what?' He tried twisting from her hold, but she held on tighter. 'What the hell's wrong with thee? Why the nastiness? What have I done, like?'

'What have you . . . ? What have you *done*?' She shook her head in disbelief. '*Every*-bleedin'-thing, that's what! But nowt neither, aye. Not yet at least.' He stared back in confusion and she took a deep breath. Her thumping heart felt fit to burst and tears were threatening. 'I need brass. Aye, that's the top and bottom of it. And you're going to help me find it.'

'Brass?'

'That's what I said, in't it?'

'Brass for what?'

With her free hand, she grabbed one of his and placed it on her stomach. His fingers stiffened but he didn't attempt to sever the contact. 'For this. For your bloody child. I'm for getting rid and that don't come cheap.' The words tasted acrid on her tongue; a sob of self-loathing shuddered from her. She sounded like a monster. An evil, unfeeling, heartless devil. And yet it was the truth, all of it. *What had she become?* 'There's people . . . wenches what'll take a babby in forra price. They find them new parents, ones who want and will love them, and you've never to worry about it again. I – we – *must* do it. There's no other way.'

'Aye well, like I've said already, tha don't know it's owt to do with me. It could be anyone's—'

Jewel ended Benji's speech with a back-handed slap across his mouth. Temper had her trembling from head to toe. Nostrils flared, eyes blazing, she shook him until his head wobbled on his neck. '*Bastard*, you're nowt else! Tha knows fair well you've planted this life in me, have from the start. I'm done keeping my trap shut to save blowing up a storm. *Done!* It's time you took a share of responsibility for your part in this, this . . . *hell* on bleedin' earth *I've* been living for months. Nine pounds – find it and fast. For I'm warning you, lad, you'll wish you had once I'm done with thee. If I'm to go down, I'm hauling you every step of the way along with me. Right?'

'How much?' The youth was panic-stricken. 'But Jewel, where . . . ? How . . . ?'

'Beg, borrow or steal. I don't care a fig how you find it. Just do.'

'But *Jewel*—'

'You see them?' She jabbed a finger towards the town hall steps. 'I'll climb to the very top, right here and now, and scream our guilt to the bloody stars unless you agree. I'll waken every man, woman and child – including Uncle Bernard and Aunt Esther – and they'll all hear about it, everyone. You want that, d'you?'

The quaver in his response belied the nonchalant lift of his chin. 'You'd not.'

'Aye? Try me. Take a long look at me – I've nowt left to lose, lad. So just you think on that.'

After a charged silence, Benji's shoulders sagged. He dragged a hand through his hair. 'Right, all bloody right. If you keep quiet 'til April, I'll ask permission to wed thee. I'll be sixteen, then, won't I? Mind, I'm not promising nowt; we'll have to see what Mam makes of it.' He folded his arms with a petulant pout. 'That do thee? Happy now, you spiteful cow, yer?'

Utter incredulousness chased away a response. For a full minute, Jewel could only gaze at him in dumb silence. He was truly demented, had to be. She'd heard it whispered over the years that a well-to-do cousin of his mother's – Caroline, was it? – had been committed to an asylum. Clearly, madness ran through Esther's bloodline and she'd passed it on to her son. Benji *couldn't* be right in the head if he thought for a single moment she desired to wed him. It was almost as if he believed she'd planned this from the off to snare him. Mother of God, surely not? Surely she'd misheard?

'Is it a deal, then?'

'You're serious, ain't yer? I don't want to wed thee. Not now, not ever!'

'Why not?' His voice had risen to a child-like whine. 'And what's up with me, then?'

Feeling her anger resurfacing, she forced her hands to her sides before she lost control and smacked the snivelling sod's face black and blue. In clear, concise terms she hoped he'd understand, she repeated slowly, 'Nine pounds, Benji. Find it, fast, else I'll do for you.' And she meant it, too.

Leaving her threat to sink in, she turned and darted through the darkness back to Mawdsley Street.

Would he comply?

Pray be to God, time would soon tell.

*

To Jewel's great surprise, tell it did – the very next morning, in fact.

'There you are.'

Busy making Roland's bed whilst keeping an eye to Constance playing quietly at her feet, she hadn't heard the knock at the front door, nor Maxwell entering his son's room to deliver the message. She jumped then held a hand to her heart, smiling. However, her employer didn't return the smile. 'Is there a problem, sir?'

'There's a young fellow outside asking to see you.'

He was surveying her with a less than pleased expression and she blushed scarlet. This was totally improper; what must he think? Who on earth . . . ? 'A fella, sir?' she asked.

'He gave his name as Benji.'

The colour drained from her face then rushed back again at a dizzying speed, leaving her light-headed. She nodded. 'Do I have permission to speak with him? Just forra minute or two? Benji's my cousin, sir.'

'Oh. I see.' Maxwell's expression slowly changed. His brow cleared and his mouth softened. He cleared his throat. 'Of course. Take as long as you need.'

'Ta, thanks.' Though relieved he now saw the visit as innocent – he and Bernard were but acquaintances, after all; there was no reason why he should know Benji's identity – still her colour crept up further with shame. *If only you knew.* Avoiding his eye, she slipped from the bedroom and hurried down the stairs.

Benji greeted her with a scowl but, before he could speak, she held a finger to her lips. 'Not here. Come on.' She led him to the end of the street, where, satisfied they wouldn't be overheard, she turned to face him. 'I must say, I didn't expect to see thee so soon. D'you have it? The brass?'

'Nay.'

'But . . .' She frowned in confusion. 'We had a deal—'

'I agreed to nowt. You thought yer could bully me last night but you were wrong. I've told Mam and Father everything, about all your lies – and the rest.' He jerked his head to her stomach. 'You're for it now, our Jewel.'

A whooshing sound filled her ears; she couldn't

think, breathe. She swung her head in horror-filled disbelief. 'Nay . . .'

'Aye. So, you see, this ends here. Just you leave me alone, you hear?'

As she watched him – it was all she could do; her voice had deserted her – she noticed a flicker of something behind his eyes and her every nerve sparked with overwhelming relief. The uncertainty in their dark depths was undeniable. He was lying. *Thank you, Lord* . . . 'Nice try. You're too much of a spineless dog to tell.' She was gratified to see his face fall in disappointment and, again, she thanked God she'd been right. 'This is just your lame attempt to slither out of trouble. Trouble you helped create, remember?'

'It's not. I, I *did* tell—'

'Liar.'

'Bitch!' he shot back, looking as though he might cry and reminding Jewel again how young and immature he was.

'This ain't going away, Benji. Find that bloody brass or so help me . . .' Shaking her head, she let her tone drop to a growl. 'Just find it. Else your mam and yer father *shall* know what's what, all right. Only it'll be me what does the telling – aye, and for real.'

When he'd stormed off, she took some deep breaths to regain her composure then returned to the house. Inside, she found Maxwell waiting for her in the hall with his daughter. Her blush returned instantly – surely he could sense her guilt? – and though it was a struggle, she brought a smile to her face. 'I'll get back to my duties now, sir—'

'He wasn't bearing bad tidings, I hope? Your family are well?'

'Oh, nay. All's fine.' She smiled again whilst in her mind praying he wouldn't probe further.

'That's good.' He nodded then asked, 'You and your cousin are quite close?'

'Nay, we ain't.' She cursed herself inwardly, had fired back her response sharper than she'd intended. 'What I mean is . . . Well, not really, sir.'

'It's just that I recall you being in good spirits the last time I saw you both together. I simply assumed . . .'

What?

'Of course,' continued Maxwell, 'I should have recognised him when I opened the door as being the lad in your company at the park – although I didn't realise he was your cousin. Alas, my memory isn't what it was. Cursed old age.'

This time, the word was given life: 'What?' she murmured, cutting off Maxwell's chuckle.

'My age—'

'Not that. What was it you said about the park?'

'The day of the town hall opening. I saw you dancing together at the park.' A small frown creased his brow. 'Jewel, are you all right? Your recent bout of illness hasn't returned?'

She shook her head. It was true. Besides a little muscle achiness and a sore throat, she was back to her normal self. It was another ailment altogether that held her in its grip now: she felt stomach-churningly sick with dread. She thought she'd seen Maxwell there that fateful night – he'd seen them, too? Just how much? *What* exactly had he witnessed? 'Sir, I . . .'

'Yes?'

'I . . .' Her breathing was heavy.

'I think I know what's bothering you, Jewel.' Maxwell's voice, much to her bewilderment, held a hint of laughter. 'Please, don't be embarrassed. It was a special occasion, after all. To be honest, I myself partook of more than I should have that night. The drink,' he explained with a conspicuous wink when she frowned in puzzlement. 'You were somewhat merry.'

She stared hard at her feet. 'Aye. Benji and me . . . We both were.'

'You more so by the night's end, I suspect.'

Jewel's frown returned. She glanced back up questioningly.

'I spotted your cousin discreetly pour his drink on to the grass.' Again, Maxwell winked. 'I believe he probably began to feel the effects before you did and wanted to save face. After all, not many lads would be willing to admit otherwise – particularly when up against a member of the fairer sex – would they?'

The universe seemed to hold its breath. Thoughts crashed and exploded through Jewel's brain. Then: 'Aye. You're likely right there. Daft lad.' She smiled with a roll of her eyes. Then, holding out her arms, she took Constance from him and moved towards the stairs. 'Well, I'd best get on with my work, sir.'

'Yes, of course. I, too, must get going to the bank.'

'I'll see thee this evening, sir.' A last smile at him over her shoulder and she was free to flee.

As with her easy response to her employer's shattering revelation, it took every ounce of will and self-control she possessed to make it back to Roland's room without breaking down. Her legs shook, her chest throbbed, and she wanted nothing more than to howl her throat raw. Instead, she returned the toddler to her games and curled into a ball on the floor beside her.

He poured away the majority all night, I just know it. He wasn't inebriated as he claims. His thinking wasn't muddled by drink like mine at all. He plied me with ale after ale whilst all the time remaining fully conscious himself. He planned it.

He lured me to those trees, knowing exactly what was to come. He knew I was past refusing. He had me believe it was consensual. He didn't care. He raped me. He raped me. He raped me . . .

'Benji raped me.'

Once the words were forced through her lips, the screams inside her head halted.

'Benji raped me,' she said again to the blue carpet.

Trickling from her scorching brain to her toes, an arctic calm encased her. She sat up, folded her hands in her lap.

Dry-eyed, she watched the clock's journey to the eleventh hour and the nursemaid's arrival to take over Constance's care.

Chapter 12

'BY, LASS, I'M pleased to see thee. You're looking well.'

Jewel stared at her uncle without seeing him. Her being was focused on but one thing: 'Where's Benji?'

'He's upstairs. 'Ere, how's your new position going?' added Bernard, smiling. 'Mr Birch and his lot treating thee well, I hope?'

She nodded. Then fixing her gaze on the door behind the counter that led to the Powells' living quarters, she crossed the shop floor.

'Aye, go on. You nip up and see the lad, then. I'd be grateful to thee if you'd brew a pot whilst you're up there, lass. We'll have a sup, eh, afore you leave?'

This time, Jewel didn't respond. Pace and countenance controlled, she ascended the narrow stairs.

At her entrance, Benji looked up from the table. Surprise, swiftly followed by suspicion, passed over his face. He returned the hunk of cake he'd been eating to his plate and swept away crumbs from his chin with his sleeve. Folding his arms, he glared at her. 'What you doing here?'

Jewel closed the door quietly and made her way towards him.

'Well?' Though he tried to mask it with a scowl, worry now shadowed the youth's florid face at her unsettling silence. 'Oi, you deaf or summat?'

She paused in front of him and flattened her palms on the tabletop. Tilting her head, she surveyed him, letting her eyes travel down, down, until they settled on his crotch. Pure disgust rolled through her guts but she kept her tone mild: 'Give it to me, Benji.'

'Eh?'

'Give it to me,' she repeated, reaching down to cup the private area and swallowing bile when he began to harden instantly. 'Let me see.'

He laughed in shock and embarrassment. 'Jewel, what—?'

'Shh.'

'But . . .' A low moan chased away his half-hearted protest as she undid his trousers and extracted his member.

She pulled at it lightly, indicating he should stand, and he obeyed without question. Nor did he say a word when she motioned for him to lie on the rug by the fire. Passive as a lamb, he did as she bid and she straddled him, her hold still fixed on him.

When his hands moved behind her to fondle her buttocks, she avoided eye contact lest he saw the choking loathing she was struggling to contain. Slipping her free hand inside her apron pocket, she closed her fingers around the metal handles and slowly took out the pair of large scissors she'd brought along from the house. Face void of emotion, she held them aloft.

Benji stared at the instrument but his expression didn't change. Dumb with confusion, he stared from them to her and back again in silence.

In one swift movement, Jewel positioned his penis between the scissors' cold blades and tightened just enough that he couldn't move. Finally, she lifted her hate-filled gaze to his. 'You forced yourself on me that night, didn't you?' she asked in a murmur.

The colour had drained from his face. He tried to shift his body but her weight on his legs prevented him. Then she closed the scissors' handles slightly, letting the blades bite into his soft flesh, and he went rigid.

'You have to pay. You understand that, right?'

'Jewel.' His breathing came in short gasps. 'I don't know what you're talking ab—'

'Aye, tha does.'

'I didn't know what I were doing. I were drunk is all—'

'You weren't, though, were yer?' She tightened her hold a little more. 'You lied. You got me skenning on purpose, planned it from the off. You violated me. You *raped* me.'

'Nay—'

'You've ruined my life. Now, I'm going to ruin yours by ensuring you never get to hurt another lass with this thing again.'

Petrified tears were coursing down his face. 'Please, don't. I'm sorry.'

'So.' Her lips drew back in a snarl. 'You admit it?'

On a noisy sob, he nodded. 'I'm sorry,' he blubbered again.

Could she really do it? Her eyes flicked to his imprisoned genital. She'd intended to on the walk here, there was no denying it. Never in her life had her temper been up as much, or her mind filled with such murder as it had been then. However, now, finally vindicated, she didn't know what to feel. Rather than stoke the flames of fury, his admission had quelled them instead and she hadn't a clue what to do, hadn't expected this at all.

'I've got the brass, just like you asked. It's here, in my jacket. Feel.'

Frowning, she patted his pocket. Sure enough, the jingle of coins greeted her.

'I were going to fetch it round to thee later. I were, 'onest.'

'It don't make everything all right, though, does it?' she spat, leaning in close. 'It won't change what you've done, what you've put me through . . .'

'I'll tell you a secret if you let me go.'

The unexpected announcement momentarily threw her. She cocked her head, eyes narrowed.

Seeing he had her attention, Benji's eyes widened with hope. He licked his lips with an eager nod. 'Promise you'll let me be?'

Though aware he was clutching at straws, was desperate to distract her attention from the matter in hand, from his guilt, she could tell he did have knowledge of something she didn't. But what?

'You can't tell a soul I've told you, mind. You must keep it to yourself.'

Curiosity got the better of her. She nodded.

'Your mam ain't your mam.'

'What are you talking about?'

'It's the truth. I've heard whispers of it over the years.'

'Whose whispers?' He didn't answer and she shook her head. He really was grasping at anything to wriggle free from this. But what an absurd thing to make up. How did his warped mind work at all? 'Fool,' she said, releasing him and returning the scissors to her apron before shifting off him and rising to her feet.

Benji clutched his groin protectively. His relief was tangible. He closed his eyes, his breathing heavy.

'The brass.' Jewel held out a hand and her cousin quickly fumbled for the gold sovereigns and dropped them into her palm. She placed them with the scissors and headed for the door, knowing not whence he'd acquired them and caring less. He owed her – more so after today. It was a small price to pay for all he'd done, as well as walking from this with all his body parts intact.

'Jewel?'

She glanced over her shoulder.

'I am sorry, you know.'

'Sorry tha got found out.'

With that, she left the room and made her way back down to the shop. To her relief, her uncle was busy tending to a customer and she was able to slip away without further conversation.

Oddly, she felt lighter of mind on the walk back to Mawdsley Street. It was as if the truth of that horrid night had set her free, though she was incapable of understanding why. Surely the new-found knowledge should have made her feel worse, and yet it didn't. Perhaps it was having proof that she wasn't a loose piece, as she'd grown to view herself over the months, that explained her feelings. She'd berated herself continually, and now that could stop, couldn't it? She was blameless, had been from the start. The relief this carried was like a balm to her soul. She wasn't foul or wicked or wrong. She'd *been* wronged. The realisation was comforting.

Drawing level with Maria's residence, Jewel saw her friend cleaning the inside of the windows and slowed her pace, hoping to catch her attention. She did, and lifting her hand made the money sign by rubbing her index and middle finger against her thumb, then patted her apron pocket. Catching her meaning, Maria gave her a thumbs-up.

Fortunately, her short absence had gone undetected and, slipping inside and back to her kitchen, Jewel busied herself with work. All the while, she rehearsed in her mind the conversation she must have later with her employer regarding her planned departure. Would he be disappointed, angry? Would he agree to Maria's sister taking over her duties until she returned? Would she even have a position to return to afterwards? As for breaking the news to her mother . . . Well. She'd tackle that aspect when the time came.

'Sir? I'd like to speak with thee, if you can spare a minute or two of your time?'

Seated at his desk in the firelit drawing room, Maxwell looked up from his papers. 'Jewel.' A genuine smile touched his mouth. 'Of course. Come in.'

The family had finished the evening meal some time ago. Constance had been put to bed and Roland had gone out; Jewel had been awaiting his departure as her cue to seek out his father. She closed the door and stood facing him, fingers plucking nervously at each other.

'To be honest with you, your presence is a welcome distraction.' Maxwell motioned to the desktop then rubbed his tired eyes. 'Cooped up in a stuffy office all day drawing figures, the last thing I desire of an evening is to do the same at home. Alas, someone has to. As senior bank clerk, that must naturally fall to me.'

Tasked with overseeing the clerks below him, dealing with rich and important clients, the vast sums of money entrusted to his keeping . . . Jewel eyed him with more than a little awe. She couldn't have imagined anything worse, was useless when it came to numbers. What a responsibility he had – and what challenging work that entailed. She bit her lip guiltily, regretting having disturbed him.

'What I have to say can wait, sir, if you're busy—'

Lifting his hand, he cut her off. 'Not at all.'

'Well, it's like this. Mam sent word earlier that an owd aunt of hers has taken ill. She wants me to go to her, nurse her a while.'

'I see. When?'

'Tomorrow, sir.'

'*Tomorrow?*'

She nodded. After all, she didn't see the point of drawing this out. The sooner the matter was dealt with, the better.

'Is this what your cousin came to see you about this morning?'

Benji assaulted her mind. The sickening feel of him, the scissors, his eyes wide with terror . . . Swallowing hard, she quickly pushed the images away. 'Aye. Aye, that's right. It didn't seem the right time to tell thee earlier, what with you on your way to work.' She lifted her eyes to gauge his reaction in his, but he'd lowered his gaze, was staring at his steepled hands. 'I'll not leave thee in the lurch, sir. A friend of mine says her sister will take on my duties in my absence – if you're in agreement, of course. She's a respectable lass; trustworthy, hardworking—'

'How long will you be gone?' His words were quiet, flat.

'A few months is likely.'

'A few . . . ? There's no one else?'

'Nay, sir. We're all the wench has. And Mam hasn't the strength for it she once had, would wear herself out and become ill herself should she take on the task.'

'Then of course you must.'

'Aye?'

Maxwell nodded. 'I insist.'

'And my job, sir . . . ?'

'Will be here waiting for you.'

His goodness cut her to the quick. Her wretched deceit seared further. Sudden tears filled her eyes. Turning, she made for the door.

'Jewel?'

'Aye, sir?'

'You *will* return . . . won't you?' He'd risen from his chair. Hands hanging loosely by his sides, his stare was full of expectancy.

An overwhelming urge to run to him, to throw her arms about his neck and never let go, filled her. 'Just as soon as I'm able,' she said earnestly. 'You have my word.'

In the ensuing silence, Maxwell took a step towards her. As though by some unspoken instruction, she did likewise.

'I – that is, *we* . . . shall miss you.'

'And I you, sir.'

And she meant it, with every whisper of her heart.

Chapter 13

VOICE CRACKING, MARIA clung to Jewel. 'You send word should you need me, d'you hear?'

'I hear.'

'And don't you fret. That sister of mine shall take sound care of your Mr Birch and his kin.'

'You'll remember to call in on Mam when you can, won't you, Maria? Check she's well?'

'Course, aye.'

Again, the friends embraced tightly.

'Ta, thanks. For everything,' Jewel told her as they drew apart, her own cheeks wet with tears.

'Eeh, lass.' Despite the maid's efforts to keep a brave face, it creased. 'Take care.'

'Oh, Maria, I am frightened,' she admitted, her own resolve wavering in turn. 'What if summat should go wrong—?'

'Now you mustn't think like that.' Reverting to her brusque self, Maria wagged a finger. 'Nowt shall, nay. You'll see. You'll be back home where you belong in no time at all.'

And if I'm not? If something *should* go awry? she wanted to press, fighting the urge to grasp Maria and shake the answers from her. Things could and did. Any number of women the world over died daily from childbearing. Why should she be different?

Suppose the widow from the newspaper, whose acquaintance she was soon to make, wasn't as capable as they assumed; what, then? On nothing but blind trust, she was putting her life in the hands of a complete stranger. God above, how had it come to this? Could she really go through with it?

I have no choice. The response tapped at her mind in an instant. *I must.*

Lifting her chin bravely, she bid Maria farewell. Forcing herself not to look back at the house she'd come to regard as home, she set off on the fifteen-minute walk to Lum Street where, God willing, she was to hunker down to see this nightmare period through. That it was in quite close proximity didn't unduly worry her. Once settled, she'd be sure not to leave the house under any circumstances so wasn't at risk of encountering anyone she knew.

She'd purposely turned right, taking the side streets to avoid Back Cheapside and Town Hall Square – and further heartache. Reaching Crown Street, she breathed a little more easily. She didn't trust herself not to break down if she had to suffer another goodbye with her mother. Last night's had been difficult enough.

The memory of Flora's sad eyes flashed in her mind afresh and Jewel sighed. After giving his permission, Maxwell had sent her to inform her mother – and so the next round of lies had been spun. She'd put to Jewel the same questions he had: 'When will you go and for how long? Several *months*? Oh, lass, as much as that?' Jewel had done her utmost to play the length of time down, telling her it would pass before they knew it, though it had done little to ease her mother's upset.

'Can't someone else do it? It's nice and all that Mr

Birch, insisting he wants someone he knows and trusts to nurse his sister back to health, thought of thee . . . but still . . . Is there really no one else?' Jewel had shaken her head and her mother had done likewise, with dull acceptance. 'Their lot click their fingers and we beneath them jump, aye. I know, lass, I get it – owt forra quiet life. By, but I'll miss thee.'

'And I'll miss you,' Jewel whispered to herself now as she dragged her feet, head down. 'More than you could ever know.'

When Benji flitted into her thoughts she instantly pushed him away. She didn't want to dwell on him; not now, not ever again. With her uncle, she did likewise, though for widely differing reasons. It was clearly his money paying for this – the knowledge fed her guilt by the hour. Bernard was a good man, didn't deserve to suffer any of this.

The next image, on the other hand, refused to leave her. And her attempt to scatter this one was feeble at best.

Maxwell had left for work this morning without saying goodbye. Though he'd wished her well last night before retiring to bed, it wasn't the same and she couldn't help but feel upset. She thought he would have at least sent her on her way with a kind word or two – though his presence alone, just one last look at him, would have been enough, something she could have taken with her to look back on over the coming months. Then again, why would he? How could he know what was in her head? She didn't even understand these feelings of hers herself.

She'd consoled herself instead with a hug from Constance, whom she knew she would miss just as much. Even Roland, who *had* offered a warm farewell, she felt a pang at leaving. She really had taken the Birches to her heart, had come to regard them almost as a second family. Whether that was sensible, however, remained to be seen. What was she to them, after all, but a paid skivvy? And now, not even that.

As Jewel emerged from Bow Street and on to Folds Road, her emotions were once more in disarray – though, now, fear overrode all else. She paused to gather her nerves. Beyond Mill Hill's two mills in the distance lay the sprawling moors and meadows of Tonge and Breightmet, and she was tempted to continue past approaching Lum Street and all that went with it. Yet what could other districts offer her? Where would she go, and to whom? She'd just left all she knew and loved behind her. There was no one else. She forced herself onward.

A light drizzle had started up, dulling further an early sky already shrouded in grey from the multitude of surrounding factories' spewing chimneys. She drew her shawl closer around her. Minutes later, heart hammering, she turned the corner of what would hopefully be her temporary home.

Here, she halted again and glanced along the grim-coloured street, scanning the stretch of beer houses, shops and dwellings for one number in particular. When she spotted it, the corners of her mouth lifted slightly. It appeared half-decent; more so, in fact. The step was scrubbed, the windows and curtains beyond them clean. A tidy-looking abode by all accounts – certainly better than she'd dared hope.

Jewel checked inside the rough canvas bag she carried. Nestled amongst the few items of clothing was a cloth pouch which held the precious coins. She nodded. Everything was set. All that was left to do now was to knock . . .

After building up courage with a few shuddering breaths, she did just that.

'What can I do you for?'

Tall and thin, dark hair pulled back into a tight bun and darker eyes narrowed questioningly, the woman who answered the door folded her arms. Like her home, she, too, was neat and clean. Though the greeting wasn't unfriendly, she possessed an assured, somewhat formidable air. Jewel's anxiety heightened further.

'You left an advertisement in the *Bolton Evening News*,' she stammered. 'I, I'm in need of your services, like.'

'Oh aye?'

Fumbling inside her bag then holding out the pouch, her tone was desperate. 'Will you help me, missis? Please?'

The widow gave her and the pouch a long look. Then her stare fell to Jewel's stomach. 'That the one you want shot of, then? But it ain't even ready. I only normally take in babes in arms—'

'Normally?' Jewel's heart had dropped to her clogged feet but, with that one word, a little hope had returned.

'Eh?'

'You said "normally". That means you *do* sometimes offer lying-in?'

'Well . . . I might consider it, aye. If the price is right, of course.' She plucked the cloth from Jewel's hand and tipped out the contents into her own palm.

'There's a pound extra,' Jewel told her as she counted the sovereigns. 'Would that be enough for me to stay until after the birth?'

The woman flicked her eyes up and down the street. 'I don't discuss business on t' doorstep. Too many nosey divils around. Come inside.'

Hope fluttered once more. Surely if she was unwilling, she'd have turned her away by now? Inviting her in was a good sign, wasn't it? Quick on her heels, Jewel followed her into the house.

Like outside, in here it shone like a new pin. The walls were freshly whitewashed and the scrubbed flagged floor gleamed. Every piece of furniture – some good pieces there were, too, nothing battered or worn – was polished, and the blackleaded fireplace shone in the flames' glow. Jewel allowed herself a pleased smile. This was better than anything she'd imagined. Of course, she'd have given anything not to have to be here. But she did, and it was proving more than adequate.

'Sit down, then.'

'Thanks, Mrs . . . ?'

'Just call me Mater. That'll do.'

Considering this to be a rather queer request, Jewel hid a frown. It was only then that she noticed the silence. She glanced around the space again but saw no signs of there being children beneath this roof. No tiny items of clothing, feeding vessels or the like. 'You're not nursing any babies at present?'

'Aye. I've five under my care at the moment. They stop upstairs.'

'Oh.' She was both surprised and saddened. So many. And her child was soon to add to the number of the unwanted. Just another throwaway. *Forgive me* . . .

'I've a girl lying in already, an' all. She's further along than you look to be, is due any day. You'll have to share with her if you're for staying. I've only the one bed spare, you see. Take it or leave it.'

'I'll take it,' Jewel responded without hesitation. What choice had she? It was a small price to pay. She just hoped this girl was an agreeable sort, that they would get along. The last thing she wanted was grief, had had enough lately to last her two lifetimes. To burrow herself away in peace was all she craved.

'Right, then. Hang up your shawl and set the kettle to

boil. Tea caddy and cups are in the cupboard – there.' She jerked her head towards an alcove then sat back in her chair, arms folded.

Though thinking a 'please' wouldn't have gone amiss, Jewel smiled and nodded nonetheless and got to her feet.

'I'll have a sup if there's one going begging,' piped a voice from the stairs.

Jewel turned to see that it belonged to what must be the other expectant mother she'd be sharing a bed with. The widow wasn't wrong when stating the girl was due any day; she was as round as a penny.

'You finished up there?' asked Mater when the girl had seated herself at the table.

'Aye.'

'I'll be checking to make sure, an' all.'

The girl rolled her eyes to Jewel, who responded with a puzzled half-smile. Finished what? she wondered. Perhaps she'd been seeing to the children? Would she herself be expected to perform such duties whilst dwelling here? She really hoped not. The last thing her fragile emotions needed right now was for her to be caring for other babies. The very thought was abhorrent to her, given that she planned to do no such thing with her own. Tend to others throughout the coming weeks then abandon hers upon its entering the world? No. She couldn't do it. She just couldn't, and would tell the widow so.

Tea made, the three of them drank in silence. When a sleepy-sounding cry drifted down, Jewel held her breath and prayed she wouldn't be asked to see to it. But though the widow sighed, she didn't turn to her or the girl; instead, she herself rose and disappeared upstairs.

Alone with Jewel, the girl's lacklustre demeanour changed. She sat forward and flashed a pouty smile. 'All right?'

'Aye. Well, you know . . . ?' Jewel motioned to her stomach. 'As well as I can be, at any rate.' Her voice thickened. 'Coming here . . . I had no choice.'

'Do we ever? Never the fellas left to suffer the result of their fun, though, is it?'

Jewel shook her head, whispered, 'Were you forced, too?'

'Me?' The girl's mouth stretched in a slow grin. 'Oh nay. I were willing, all right.'

'Oh. Oh, I . . .' Colour had washed across her face. She eyed the girl with a mixture of disapproval and curiosity. Not knowing how to respond to the shameless declaration, she lifted her cup and sipped at her tea.

'He reckoned he wanted to wed me. Silly bitch that I am, I fell for it. It wasn't 'til I'd been caught with this,' she added, jabbing at her huge bump none too gently, 'that I discovered he were already married to another. Promised me the world, he did. Instead, he were planning on putting me up in a few rooms, where I was expected to dutifully wait for his visits if and when he felt like it. No, thank you. Rent and everything else paid for or no, I'd sooner go it alone than live like that. That's no life, not really. I wanted all of him or nowt at all.' She shrugged. 'It is how it is. His wife's welcome to him, poor cow.'

'The swine, that's awful. Does he know you're here and what you're intending?'

Again, the girl grinned. 'Where d'you think the brass came from to pay the fee? I didn't just have all them pounds lying around doing nowt, you know. Aye well, sod him. Once I've rid my body of this thing, I'm off out of this shit-tip town; to hell with the pair of them.'

Jewel was lost for words once more. This girl's hardness, her apparent sheer dispassionateness, was difficult to fathom. She hadn't spoken with anger or bitterness or even regret, not at all. She was simply matter-of-fact about the whole business, almost unfazed.

'So what's your story?'

'My cousin decided to take what weren't his.' It was Jewel's turn to shrug. 'I couldn't let on to Mam, the family. It'd be harder still now; it's gone too far for that, I reckon. Hopefully, once all this is over with, I can carry on like afore and no one will be any the wiser. The trouble it would cause, the shame . . . I can't do it to Mam, I can't.'

The girl took a swig of her tea. 'Louise.'

'Eh? Oh,' she added, smiling, when the girl pointed to herself. 'I'm Jewel.'

'Has that one upstairs told you yet that you're to call her Mater?'

Louise's words had been tinged with amusement. With a curl of her lip and a roll of her eyes, Jewel nodded, and they both chuckled. 'What's the deal with that, then, you reckon?'

'Likes her privacy, don't she? The less we know of her, the better – who can blame her in her line of work?'

Jewel frowned. 'But why the secrecy? She's providing a social service is all.'

'Ho! That's one way of putting it.'

Her confusion grew. As far as she could see, this was beneficial for all concerned. Without such procurers, mothers lacking the support of a husband, family or friends found it nigh on impossible to keep themselves and their child out of the workhouse. Few private charities extended help to fallen women, less so their offspring – English society placed little value on illegitimates. To do so would, they believed, promote bastardy and encourage immoral behaviour. Regardless of circumstances, it was deemed that fault lay with the female.

This blinkered ideology only compounded matters for an already shunned and struggling minority.

In addition, women like the widow, in need of income, got by on the premiums they charged, procuring in return adoptive parents willing and able to offer infants a brighter future. Therefore, surely this route, which provided all with a lifeline, was for the good? Furthermore, it was simple, quick and legal, with few questions asked.

Alternatives were limited. Abandonment was a criminal offence – as, too, was abortion, which commonly resulted in severe haemorrhaging or even death. If the woman survived and was found out, imprisonment awaited her instead.

'Where would I – both of us – be at this minute but for folk like her?' asked Jewel. 'I can't see the bad in it at all. Besides, what they do don't go against the rules of the law, does it?'

'Oh, come on.' As though debating whether Jewel was having her on, Louise ran a hand through hair the colour of spun silk, eyes creased. 'Surely you ain't so green?'

'What d'you mean by that, like?'

'Surely you know . . . ?' Realising she didn't, Louise shook her head slowly. '*Mater* is a baby farmer.'

Jewel stared back blankly. A what?

'Or as I like to think of them,' added the girl, 'an angel maker.'

'I don't . . . What—?'

'Shush,' Louise whispered, cutting off her questions as approaching footsteps from above sounded. As though not a word had passed between them, she picked up her cup and resumed drinking her tea.

Jewel was more mystified than ever. What was going on? What had she meant? What on earth was a baby farmer? She had to know, though now wasn't the time to probe further; the girl clearly didn't want to speak on it in front of the older woman. She'd get it out of Louise later, she determined.

Even so: *baby farmer*. The term swam around her brain as she, too, sipped her drink. *Baby . . . farmer?*

The widow, a brown blanket-wrapped bundle under her arm, descended the stairs then disappeared without a glance at either of them. Moments later, shifting and banging noises drifted up to them from the cellar – peering at the ground, Jewel frowned. 'What's she up to, I wonder?'

Though her gaze had dropped, too, Louise offered no suggestion. Placing her cup on the table, she scraped back her chair. 'I'm going forra lie-down.'

Jewel watched her lumber off up to the bedroom. She looked to the floor again when silence fell then fixed her eyes on the door – however, the widow failed to reappear. Taking her frown with her, she busied herself washing up her and Louise's cups and saucers.

Eventually, still clutching the bundle, Mater emerged from the cellar. Now, she gave Jewel a long look before disappearing once more, this time to the back yard. Dogs' barks sounded then died away. When she re-entered the house, she was empty-handed. Without a word, she resumed her seat at the table, picked up the teapot and refilled her cup.

After putting away the tea things, Jewel, too, made to return to the table. Then, changing her mind, she crossed to a fireside chair. Watching the dancing flames without seeing them, she tried to make sense of what had transpired since her arrival. Louise's words; the widow and her bundle; the queer, unsettling feel of the place . . . But she could fathom none of it.

Have I made a mistake in coming here? she wondered for the first time. And without understanding why, her hand drifted unconsciously to her stomach.

Chapter 14

AS IT TURNED out, Mater didn't expect her lying-in guests to lend a hand in tending to the children in her care at all. In fact, she positively insisted they steered clear of the back bedroom altogether.

Though thankful when Louise revealed this to her, Jewel couldn't shake her curiosity over the unseen scraps of life. Despite this now being her third day here, she'd seen nothing of them at all. A faint cry would ring out now and then but, once the widow had been in to see to them, they wouldn't hear a thing more for hours.

'I'll not be asked to tend to the babbies, will I, Louise?' Jewel had asked her that first night when she'd joined her in bed. The girl had told then how Mater preferred them not to interfere with her charges. The rest of the house, however, was another matter – that's what Louise had been doing when Jewel first arrived: scrubbing her bedroom floor, not seeing to the children, as she'd assumed.

'I may as well tell thee afore she does – we're to pull our weight,' Louise had continued. 'The cleaning, sweeping, washing, cooking . . . that's our job beneath this roof. I'll be glad of the help now you're here, to be honest. I've never toiled so hard as I have these past weeks since I myself happened upon her doorstep. But what can you do, eh? If she says we must see to the chores, then we do it. That or likely get slung on to the street. Aye well, it'll not be for much longer; for me, at least. God above, I can hardly wait to be rid of the child and away from here.'

Looking at the mountainous stomach beneath the bedclothes, Jewel had been shocked. Fancy Louise having to see to the entire household duties this far along in her carrying. How had she coped, particularly given the widow's very high standards? It was a wonder Louise hadn't collapsed through exhaustion. She'd be sure to take on the donkey's share from now on, save the girl from making herself ill, Jewel had resolved. It was only right. She herself wasn't so big yet; she'd manage things much easier.

Though Louise had no qualms about relaying the rules of their stay, when Jewel had brought up their earlier conversation and asked again just what on earth a baby farmer was the girl had immediately clammed up. She'd feigned tiredness and attempted to turn away, but Jewel had been insistent: 'You must tell me, for I can't make head nor tail of its meaning. What is she? What, a farmer of babies? But what does that mean? It don't make no sense.'

'Bloody hell's fire, shurrup about it, will thee?' Louise had eventually groaned, pulling the blankets above her head to drown out the questions. 'I meant nowt by what I told thee. It's nowt, just another name for nurses is all.'

'And what you said about how *you* see them? Angel makers, was it? Aye, that were it. What did that mean, then?'

'Oh, I don't know. Just that, in a way, they *do* make angels out of the devils that sinners like us have created.

Aye, little cherubs what unlike us will go on to live wholesome, holy soddin' lives. All right? Happy? Will you let me get some rotten kip, now?' But though Jewel nodded, Louise had made no attempt to rest. Instead, she'd stared at her for a long moment then added, voice almost kind, 'Look, Jewel. All this business . . . It's the best thing all round. You'll see. Once you're shot of the child, you can begin life over again. That's what you want, in't it?' At her nod, she'd continued. 'And the babby; you don't want it, right?'

'It's impossible.'

'Nor do you want to ever see it again, d'you? Run the risk of it tracking you down one day? Everyone you know and love knowing, judging, turning against thee?'

'It's impossible,' she'd murmured again.

'Well, then, here's the thing. Birth it, walk from this house and put it from your mind for ever. It's the only way.'

Jewel knew she was right. Still, it hadn't stopped her from crying herself to sleep.

Now, the hour was approaching nine. Shortly before, breakfast had been eaten and the dishes washed and put away. Louise had taken herself back to bed, and Mater was tending to her charges. Seated at the scrubbed table, Jewel itched for something to do. Having swept and scoured the place to within an inch of its life yesterday, there was nothing to occupy her now for a few hours until lunch needed preparing. She really wasn't used to this inactivity. The boredom was sending her mad.

Generally, it wasn't so bad during the day. The household chores she was instructed to complete kept both body and mind busy but, as night fell, restlessness would creep up on her and she'd yearn to leave the house, go for a walk, anything to kill the stale monotony.

Of course, venturing beyond the door was an impossibility. What if someone she knew saw her? Or, as she'd begun to fear, what if she was unable to stop herself from seeking them out? For the pain of separation was like a physical thing. Though, obviously, she missed Mam, it wasn't the gut-churning pining she'd felt when she'd first left their home. Time at Mawdsley Street had already dulled that particular loss to a manageable ache; she'd grown used to not seeing her daily. Maria and the Birches were another matter.

The maid had become dear to her over the months and she'd have given anything right now for one of her cheeky grins or warm hugs. Though Louise was similar in age to them both, she wasn't the kind of person you could naturally befriend. Whereas Maria harnessed her worldly-wiseness into helping and advising others, Louise's had had the opposite effect on her personality. Her experiences looked to have not so much hardened but developed in her an apathetic passiveness that was difficult to penetrate. Jewel missed the rapport, the banter, the support; the big sister she'd never had.

Little Constance, even Roland, she also wished to see. Was the child missing her? Were the family's needs being met and the household running as smoothly as it should under the new servant? She fretted about them frequently. As for *him* . . .

Sighing, she rose from the table and made her way to the back yard for some air – and much-needed distraction. The man with chocolate-brown hair and eyes to match lingered on the outskirts of her mind constantly. The longing to see *him* was a gnawing in her guts and her chest – her very bones – that wouldn't leave her, though she prayed the pain would dim with time. Whether he missed her or not, she refused to ponder upon. For the answer she suspected stung more acutely still. Why would he? If her temporary replacement was doing her job well, he probably hadn't noticed she'd even gone.

The widow's two large dogs, tied up with rope, lay snoozing on some old sacks. They lifted their heads from their paws and wagged their tails, and she stroked them in turn. As the minutes ticked by, the stillness soothed her racing thoughts a little. Hugging herself, she closed her eyes.

'Go on in afore you catch your death of cold.'

Mind still elsewhere, Jewel hadn't heard the widow's approach; she almost jumped from her skin. 'Eeh, my heart,' she said on a chuckle.

The woman's expression, however, remained impassive. Holding the door wide, she repeated, 'Go on in.'

As Jewel passed her to return to the house, she caught a whiff of gin on her breath. Not only did this surprise her, given the earliness of the hour, but she hadn't realised the woman was fond of a sup. Should she really be at the bottle with young 'uns to care for? The thought made her frown. It grew when she also noticed that, again, tucked beneath the woman's arm, was a wrapped blanket. Eyeing it, she couldn't hide her curiosity.

Seeing this, the widow was quick to explain. She held it up. 'Grub for t' dogs.'

Indeed, her hounds had leapt to their feet, were panting in hungry anticipation.

Jewel smiled a little, nodded, then headed back indoors. Reaching the kitchen, she saw a thin trail of dark droplets across the flagstone floor – blood. It must have seeped through the bundle without Mater noticing.

No wonder the dogs had been excited; the meat inside it must be as fresh as it came, she thought as she went to fetch hot water and a scrubbing brush. Fancy giving the animals good grub like that when folk around here could only dream of affording such luxury. It was blind broth, named so as it consisted almost entirely of vegetables with next to no meat, for some most days. That woman must have more money than sense.

When a knock sounded at the front door, she abandoned the cleaning and, wiping her hands on her apron, went to answer it. The widow had mentioned last night that a new baby would be arriving today; this must be them.

Before opening it, she fixed in place a small smile of understanding for the mother's benefit, guessing all too well what she must be feeling at this moment. Yet it quickly melted when the visitors were revealed.

'Mrs Bickerstaff?'

Jewel gazed at the tall and grim-faced policemen in turn. 'Who?'

'We're here to speak with Ada Bickerstaff.' The burlier of the two stepped closer. 'Is she present?'

They had to be referring to Mater. What was all this about, then? What had she done? 'I'll just fetch her, sir.'

'No need, I'm here.' The widow had entered the room. She bestowed on the men a sickly smile – the first of any sort Jewel had seen her crack since she'd been here. 'Good morning, constables. What can I do youse for?'

From the corner of her eye, Jewel noticed that Louise had appeared at the top of the stairs. Her normally pink cheeks were ashen. Did she have some inkling as to why the law was here? Curiosity mounting, Jewel focused her attention back on the trio.

'We've received reports of suspicious activity being carried out at this property, Mrs Bickerstaff.'

'Oh?'

'Namely that children regularly appear to be deposited here. A mother arrives, babe in arms, only to leave shortly afterwards alone. Inasmuch, we have sufficient reason to believe you're operating a baby-farming business. Is this indeed the case?'

After some seconds, the widow responded calmly. 'I run a foster service, sir. All proper and above board, I assure thee—'

'That's not quite correct, Mrs Bickerstaff, is it?' He raised an eyebrow. 'Under the Infant Life Protection Act, passed last year to regulate and monitor such practices for the safeguarding of children, all persons boarding more than one infant in return for monetary payment are bound to register their houses with their local authority. According to our recent checks, there is no such record held of either you or your home.'

'Oh, ain't there?' the widow asked. She pulled an apologetic face. 'I could've sworn I put my address down . . .'

'I'm afraid not, Mrs Bickerstaff.'

'Oh, I am sorry. I'll be sure to do that first thing in t' morning.' Smiling, she moved to the door to see them out. 'I hope you'll accept my apologies, constables, for taking up your time.'

But they made no attempt to exit. By now, Louise had joined them – the policeman who had spoken before took in her and Jewel's conditions. 'You provide lying-in, too, I see.'

Though the widow's tone remained light, her throat bobbed in a visible gulp. 'Not as a rule, sir. Hardly ever, in fact. These two, well, they . . . they just happened to need some place to stop on and . . . and well, I—'

'Perhaps this is on a larger scale than we first thought,' he cut in to murmur to his colleague, who nodded. He turned back to the widow, whose unruffled stance was rapidly waning. 'How many children are currently under your care, Mrs Bickerstaff?'

'Three, sir.'

'But—' The word escaped Jewel's mouth before she could stop it. Throughout the discourse, she'd barely grasped what was being said, knew nothing of acts and regulations and legal talk. This last answer from the woman, however, she'd understood loud and clear. Understood, that is, that it was a lie. For hadn't she herself queried that very thing on her arrival, to be told the number was five? And as far as she was aware, no baby had left this house since – and especially not two. Nevertheless, all eyes were now on her and she clamped her lips shut, cursing her tongue and wishing she'd stayed well out of it.

'But . . . ? But what?' asked the constable.

'Nowt, sir. Nothing at all.'

His stare remained on Jewel for a long moment. Then he swung it back around to fix on the widow. 'Mrs Bickerstaff. May we take a look around?'

'A look . . . ? For what?' She tried an easy laugh but failed. Her voice rose. 'But . . . I'm a professional, re*spectable*, procurer, sir!'

'If you could just lead us to your charges, Mrs—'

'But . . . ! There really is no need for this, none at all—!'

The constable's clipped interjection brooked no argument: 'Your charges, Mrs Bickerstaff.'

Slowly, the widow's shoulders sagged. Eyes like huge black smudges in her pasty face, she turned as though in a daze and crossed to the stairs. The men followed close behind. The moment they disappeared on to the landing, Louise grabbed a fistful of Jewel's blouse.

'Run.'

'Eh?'

'*Run.*'

Before Jewel knew what was happening, the girl had ripped wide the front door and dragged her into the street. Too dumbstruck to resist, she allowed her waddling captor to lead her in a half-stumble, half-run.

Crouching out of sight in the shadows of the gasworks, the looming gasometer beyond, they fought to catch their breath.

'Louise, what the *hell* is going—?'

''Tain't safe yet. Come on.'

Again, Jewel found herself hauled along the road. They turned bend after bend, skittering through the maze of grey streets, until eventually emerging into Churchgate. Here, Louise ground to a halt, purple in the face and puffing fit to collapse.

'Are you all right?' Jewel gasped out between pants, touching the girl's shoulder in concern. She herself had struggled with her bump's extra weight – goodness knew how cumbersome Louise, due literally any moment, fared.

'I will be.'

As her breath returned, so too did her senses and Jewel suddenly realised where she was. Bare-headed, with nothing to conceal her face, having left her shawl as well as her other possessions behind at Lum Street in the mad dash, she glanced around with a bite of her lip. Mam's dwelling, her place of work, were worryingly close for comfort. How could this be? What was she even doing here? What the *hell* had just happened back there?

'Right, I'm off. Bye, then.'

'What? Oi, hang bloody on!' Momentarily too shocked to move, Jewel had to run to catch her up. 'Where you going?'

'Home.'

'And where's that?'

'Manchester.'

'*Manchester?* But . . . Well, where am *I* going?' Louise stared back blankly and anger washed through Jewel. 'What the divil is the meaning of all this? You've plucked me from the only place I had left to turn and dumped me but an arrow's flight from where I fled – for what? What did we just witness? Why the police? Mrs Bickerstaff, as we now know her to be, what has she done?'

Louise heaved an exaggerated sigh. 'Does it matter?'

'Course it does! Just tell me, will you?'

'Look, I know nowt, all right? Only it seems she's been up to summat, don't it, the way she were acting? And from the look on their phizogs, those constables thought the same. I weren't for taking no chances; whatever's afoot, they might have thought me privy to it and carted me off to prison along with her. I reckoned it were best to get out whilst the going was good.'

'And dragging me along with thee – you're saying you were doing me a favour?'

'Huh. If you're going to be like this about it, I wish I hadn't bothered.'

'*I* wish you hadn't, an' all! I can't believe I let you do this.' Tears of rage and desperation stung. 'And what if you're wrong? What if the widow's committed no crime and it's all just a misunderstanding? *Where* am I meant to go *now*?'

'Erm . . .' Puffing out air, Louise lifted her arms and let them fall back to her sides.

'Well, that's just bleedin' gradely, that is. Thank you very much for nowt!' Biting back her emotion, Jewel peered in the direction they had come. 'I'll have to return, find out what's occurred, whether it were all a mistake. Happen she'll take me back in—'

'She'll not.'

'She'll have to. I've no place else. Besides, I paid her for my stay fair and square.'

'She'll not,' Louise repeated quietly. 'She can't, for she'll not be there. She'll be on her way to the cells as we speak. Trust me. I just have a feeling about this.'

Sheer hopelessness overcame Jewel. Her legs threatened to give way and she leaned against a butcher's shop wall with a low cry. 'I'm done for.'

'Well . . .' Louise shrugged when Jewel lifted her head slowly to look at her. 'You could come along with me?'

'With you? To Manchester?'

'Aye, why not?'

She opened her mouth but no excuse was forthcoming. Besides, what other option was there? 'You really mean it?'

'I'd not have said, would I?'

A flicker of a smile touched her lips. She wiped her eyes on her sleeve. 'Ta ever so. Truly. I'll not forget this.'

'Come on, then.' With a jerk of her head, the girl set off towards Trinity Street Station.

'Oh, no.' Jewel had fallen into step but paused suddenly as a thought occurred. 'I've no brass for the fare.'

'None?'

Heart dipping, she shook her head. 'Norra single copper coin.'

'Well, that makes two of us.'

'What? Then how . . . ?'

'Fret not. I'll sort it.' Eyes narrowed, Louise scanned their surroundings. Something caught her attention by the Man and Scythe, an ancient hostelry, and her face cleared. 'Wait here. I'll not be long.'

Though Jewel had followed her gaze, she could see nothing in particular that could help with their situation. She watched in puzzlement as Louise walked away. The girl approached an elderly man weaving his way down the street, clearly the worse for drink, and said something. They smiled at one another, a few more words were exchanged, and Louise linked her arm through his. They turned and headed towards a narrow alleyway.

When they disappeared, Jewel scratched her head and frowned. Then realisation dawned and, swearing under her breath, she closed her eyes. Louise was going to rob him. God in heaven, what was she thinking? In her condition, too – anything could happen. She'd clearly targeted him because of his inebriated state, but what if he still had enough wits about him to realise her game? He'd be mad with rage, could turn violent, and what would she do then? How could she be so foolish – not to mention cruel?

Mind you, I'm no better, am I? Didn't I force Benji's hand to steal from his father?

Her chin dropped in remorse. Uncle Bernard hadn't deserved that either, yet she'd had no choice. Desperation had driven her to it – just as Louise felt now. Rightly or wrongly, when it came down to survival, needs must. Turning a deaf ear to her guilt, she awaited Louise's return.

Minutes passed without a sign of them and her anxiety was mounting. Jewel was about to go in search of the girl when suddenly she appeared, thankfully looking none the worse for her escapade. No bloody nose or fat lip, no drunkard close behind yelling out her crime – it would seem she'd been successful in lightening his pockets without detection. Jewel rushed to meet her.

'All right?'

Louise nodded.

'Did you . . . ?'

'Aye.'

Sensing from the girl's set mouth and her stare fixed straight ahead that she didn't wish to discuss the matter further – perhaps she did possess a conscience, after all – Jewel kept her quiet.

Once more, they set off to catch the train.

Chapter 15

THEIR TRAVELS PROVED a quiet affair. Throughout the ten-mile journey, Louise mostly snoozed. When she did rouse for brief periods, she barely uttered a word. The moment the train choked and juddered to a halt, however, and they alighted on to her home ground, she suddenly came alive.

Emerging from Victoria Station, the girl tipped back her head and took a long sniff of the sulphurous air. 'Eeh, am I glad to be back.'

As far as Jewel could tell, this was no different from the town they had left behind; albeit here was larger, louder and much, much busier.

As in Bolton, over the past century the Industrial Revolution had swallowed much of Manchester's green and pleasant land. Now, pewter was the uniform of the north. The pace of change was staggering and on still it swept, gobbling up every pocket of empty space it found.

Those desperate for employment clambered upon the towns and cities in their droves, toiling in deplorable conditions in order to survive – and help their masters' purses grow plumper. The social gap between rich and poor had never been wider, though only the one side suffering the effects of this seemed to notice or care.

Hastily built, poor-quality workers' houses, some

crumbling with age, a great deal damp and verminous, almost all bursting at the seams with as many folk as could be squeezed into them, squatted around the multitude of mills and factories. These vast buildings and disease-ridden slums alike, clogging the skyline with their spewing smokestacks, had changed the face of the landscape and its people for ever.

And yet... it was home. Despite the inequality, despite the hopelessness and the dankness, the filth, the stench, troubled times brought the struggling masses together. Kinships were formed and nurtured through shared hardship, *cherished*, in ways the more privileged could never begin to understand nor be fortunate enough to belong to. When one fell, they all did. It was the fact they helped each other back to their feet that made the difference.

'Have you allus lived here?' Jewel asked Louise now as they passed down a broad street thronged with carts and people.

'That's right. Eeh,' she repeated fondly, drinking in her surroundings, which brought to Jewel a pang of loss for her own town. 'Come on, this way.'

Gradually, they left the centre of the city behind. Streets of densely packed houses grew narrower, branching off every which way into dark lanes, courtyards and alleyways. When Louise stopped before a door in the heart of the squalid maze, Jewel's heart dropped to her toes.

Rotting refuse, mixed with human waste spilling from the nearby privies, sullied the cobbles and she struggled to hide a grimace. Unconcerned, filthy and ragged children played barefoot, their screeches ringing off the smoke-blackened bricks. Across the road, scowling men lounged against their houses, flat caps pulled low, and women in grubby aprons sat on doorsteps gossiping. The misery and poverty were the stuff of nightmares.

Not wanting to offend the now-grinning girl, Jewel smiled back, though dread was coiling her guts.

Please, she prayed. *Please let inside be better.*

It wasn't.

In fact, as she followed Louise into the fetid hall and up a flight of stairs, she wished she'd stayed outside.

The girl made for a room with several fist-sized holes in the door, and Jewel's mood slumped further. When Louise threw it open, this time Jewel couldn't mask her disgust and had to press her nose into her shoulder to block out the stale smell.

Furnished with an unmade bed and two sagging sofas, there was barely space for anything else bar a small, wobbly-looking table in the centre. On this were two quart bottles of dark brandy, one full and one empty, and an uncovered pot of beef dripping, a fat black fly walking along its rim. A grubby sheet had been nailed to the window and no fire burned in the grate; the poor light added to the dinginess.

In short, it was a hovel. What a contrast to the sparkling house she'd just left, where she'd hoped to have her child.

Lowering herself on to the bed, Louise sprawled out with a contented sigh, obviously pleased to be home – though, for the life of her, Jewel couldn't imagine why. 'Come in, then. Sit down.' She motioned to a sofa and, when Jewel was seated, raised herself on an elbow. 'The others must be out. No matter. They'll be back soon, no doubt.'

'How many do you dwell with?' asked Jewel, astonished she hadn't thought to query this until now.

'Only the four of us.'

Only? Four – five now she was to join them – in this one small room? *Dear God* . . .

'You'll have to make yourself up a bed of sorts in front of the fire. We'll figure blankets out later; I'm sure we'll find one or two to spare thee.'

Forcing her gaze not to swivel to the mucky flagstones, Jewel nodded. 'I don't suppose there's a sup of owt going begging, is there?' she asked, her thirst winning through her unwillingness to partake of anything prepared in this room.

'Erm . . .' Looking around, Louise's eye fell on the strong spirit atop the table. She pointed at it, but Jewel shook her head and she shrugged. 'Please yourself. Happen there's some tea lying about somewhere . . . I don't know. You'll have to look.'

A furtive glance around showed Jewel that her search would be pointless. 'It's all right, it don't matter.'

'Please yourself,' the girl said again. Then she yawned loudly, turned over in the bed and promptly fell asleep.

For the next half an hour or so, not knowing what else to do, Jewel attempted to pass the time with rest, too. She turned and shifted on the sofa but the lumps and scratchy horsehair poking through the numerous holes in the material made it impossible to get comfortable. Finally admitting defeat, she rose and went to seek out a teapot; her thirst was worse than ever. Not only that, she was now hungry, too. Just how did these people survive? How could they live like this at all?

'*Well.* See what we have here.'

Nose deep in a broken cupboard in the corner, which the dim light had failed to pick out upon her arrival, Jewel sprang around. In the doorway stood three women. Though each gave her a fleeting glance, none spoke to her, instead turning their attention back to the girl snoring in the bed.

The eldest-looking of the trio spoke again: 'She's back, look. By, the size of her.'

'Aye,' a female a year or two older than Louise piped. She reached up to remove her hat, a gaudy-coloured item overly decorated with imitation flowers and stuffed birds, and tossed it on to the table. 'Like a sow, she is,' she added, her disdainful gaze running over Louise once more.

The third woman said nothing. Though her attire was plainer than the tawdry finery of her companions, her cheeks were rouged just the same, and the too-low bustline of her dress showed more than was decent. She crossed to the table and picked up the brandy bottle. Clearly from long practice, she glugged the fiery liquid without wincing. Wiping her mouth on her hand, she took a seat on a sofa.

'Lou?' The elder woman had crossed to the bed. She slapped the sleeping girl's thigh a few times, though without much force. 'Oi, come on, waken.'

'Hm? Oh.' Rubbing her eyes, Louise stretched like a lazy cat. 'Hello, Mam.'

Mam? Jewel's brows rose in surprise. Somehow, she hadn't imagined that Louise lived with her parents. Given her unconcerned attitude at returning home and what reception she'd receive regarding her keeping a lover and the resulting child, she'd assumed she dwelled alone or with friends.

'Hello,' the woman responded cordially, sitting on the edge of the bed. 'All right?'

'Aye. Mind, I'll be glad when this makes its appearance.'

Looking down at her daughter's stomach, she nodded, saying matter-of-factly, 'Can't be much longer, I'd say.'

Jewel had slipped to the other sofa and she viewed the scene with increasing puzzlement. She could see where Louise got her temperament. This woman's lack of any emotion was queer, to say the least. Despite their months of separation, they appeared not to have missed one another in the slightest; no hugs or affection at all, as if they were mere acquaintances who had bumped into one another in the street. That this indifference, from both, still carried when speaking of the baby was the most unnerving aspect of all. Thinking of her own mother, her lovingness and attentiveness, *their* meaningful relationship, Jewel just couldn't fathom these people.

'Didn't take thee long to come scuttling back home, did it, sis? What's up? Your fella grow bored of you, did he?'

Louise looked down at the grinning younger woman now sprawled across the foot of the bed. Like it was all some big lark, her own lips stretched in a chirpy smile. 'Shut it, you. If you must know, I got shot of him.'

'Huh!'

'I did, I tell you. The dirty dog were already wed.'

At the revelation, her sister doubled over, screeching with laughter, whilst their mother rolled her eyes with a chuckle. Even the third woman, still clutching the brandy bottle, shook her head and smiled.

'Hawked him right off, I did. It's all or nowt with me; I ain't being anyone's mistress, no thank you.'

'Ho! Don't knock it, love. All the perks and none of the drudgery? It suits me just fine.'

This, from Louise's sister, had Jewel's mouth falling open in shock. Not that anyone else seemed bothered by the shameless statement.

'Fancy him lying like that, though, eh? Carting me off to Bolton town as he did and for what? Nowt but lies and false promises. Swine.'

'Ay well, you weren't to know,' her mother told her with a shrug. 'He even had us fooled. You're home now, anyroad, so no harm done.'

No *harm* done? Was she really witnessing this or was it all some strange dream? Jewel genuinely began to wonder. No harm? A member of their family, barely an adult herself, was due to give birth to a married man's bastard. Could it *get* much worse than that?

'And who is that?' As though she'd just remembered she was there, the mother jabbed a finger towards Jewel.

'Oh, her.' Louise let her shoulders rise and fall. 'She had nowhere else to go.'

All eyes were on Jewel; she turned her attention to the mother, saying, 'I'll leave if you'd rather?' and almost wished that she would.

'Nay, you're all right.'

'Ta, thanks.'

'You're welcome, aye.' She eyed Jewel keenly for a few moments then, nudging Louise, added, ''Ere, she's a bonny 'un, your friend.'

'Lovely hair,' agreed her sister, stretching across to stroke Jewel's plait.

The attention brought pinkness to her cheeks. She smiled and lowered her head, and the three women shared a quiet laugh.

'You got any brass?'

'Not much after train fares.' Louise brought out a few coins and handed them to her mother. 'That's it.'

'Well, you'll have to come out later and earn some more. Us three have barely made a farthing betwixt us today – mind you, work's allus slow mid-week, eh? Happen you'll have more luck with that – get more takers, like.' She prodded her daughter's bump. 'Some have a taste for all sorts, after all.'

Releasing a tired sigh, Louise nodded nonetheless. 'Aye, all right.'

'Good. In t' meantime ...' Her mother quickly counted the money then held it out to the brandy drinker. 'Nip down to the inn, Sarah, and get us each a penny pie. Pick us up a sup, an' all, whilst you're there.'

Putting down the bottle with some reluctance, the woman did as she was bid.

'Move up, our Lou.' Budging her across, her sister snuggled beside her beneath the covers. 'I hope Aunt Sarah ain't gone long; I want to grab some kip after my grub, ready for tonight,' she told them on a loud yawn. 'I'm fagged.'

Louise nodded agreement. 'I'd best do the same. That run earlier has left me spent.'

'What run?'

'Eeh, Julia, it were a close call,' she told her sister. 'Two bobbies, bloody hulking they were. I'd not have stood a chance of fighting them off in my condition.'

'Why, what occurred?'

'I decided I had to be shot of the child upon discovering what it's good-for-nowt father were about. But the baby farmer I sought out got her collar felt, that's what. I weren't for returning to Manchester 'til I'd got shot of the babby but, well ... Today put paid to that, so here I am. Lucky we got away when we did, an' all, for we'd be languishing in a cell along with her, if you get my meaning.'

'Aye, you *were* fortunate, then. As for the child ... Not to fret. We'll sort summat out when the time comes.'

Their mother nodded in agreement with Julia then added something to the conversation, but Jewel had already ceased listening. Her head felt muggy and her every muscle was rigid with horror-filled shock. '*Some have a taste for all sorts, after all ...*'

My God. Oh, dear Lord in heaven . . . How had she not realised before?

The memory of Louise escorting that man down the ginnel in Bolton now held devastating clarity. She hadn't picked his pockets at all. He'd handed over his money willingly. And in return she'd . . . Jewel closed her eyes to the truth. *I suspected nothing, hadn't the slightest inkling . . .* Her face burned with foolishness.

These women were streetwalkers, and this their den of vice. She'd been so blind. Just what was she going to do? Leave? Where would she go? She knew nowhere, no one, here. She also hadn't a half-penny to her name, couldn't return to Bolton if she'd wanted – which of course she didn't, because what was there for her either? Oh, it was all such a *mess*!

'All right, Jewel?'

Jolting from her whirring thoughts, she brought her gaze to Louise. 'What? Aye. Aye, yes.'

'Happen you're short of a rest, too. I'll find you them blankets I promised once we've had our pies.'

The sheer hopelessness of her situation brought a choking sob and, before she could stem them, gushing tears broke from her to cascade down her face.

'Eeh. What's to do?' The girls' mother moved to her side and placed an arm across her shoulders, but Jewel couldn't help shrinking from the touch. It was neither cosseting nor comforting; never had she ached for her own mother more than she did now.

'Leave her be, Mam. It's been a fraught day is all. It's nowt a good kip won't remedy, I'll be bound.'

'Louise is right.' Forcing her pain down, Jewel flashed a watery smile – anything to reassure the older woman enough for her to remove her arm. 'I'm just tired, honest.'

'Here. Go on, take it.' Having picked up the bottle

from the table, she waved it under her nose. 'It'll calm your nerves.'

Past caring, Jewel took it from her and took a long draught. She heaved and spluttered, much to the others' amusement, but by the third swig her body got used to it and she closed her eyes, sipping at it now, welcoming the fuzzy warmth it brought.

*

When bone-numbing coldness dragged her from her stupor some time later, she at first hadn't a clue where she was.

Squinting through the darkness, she rose unsteadily from the sofa. The room was empty. She stood for a moment, unsure what to do, then crossed to the door.

Voices and laughter drifted from the adjoining rooms but of Louise and her family there was no sign. Jewel retraced her steps and dropped back on to the sofa, wincing as hammers of pain shot through her temples.

She put her head in her hand. Fancy getting herself into this state; what had she been thinking? How much of that brandy had she consumed? Enough, that's what. Lord, she felt rotten. Guilt added to the mix at movement inside her stomach. Sighing, she sent down a silent apology.

After several more minutes of waiting for the women's return to no avail, she swung her legs up and lay down. Nausea swooped then abated and she fell back into a fitful sleep.

'Nay, not Maxwell, lass. Mick's what I go by.'

Jewel's lips moved again and a frown accompanied the name when a hand stroked her hair.

'All right, then, call me what tha likes. I ain't much mithered, not really. Now, let's see these fresh young titties you've got for me.'

The gruff words slowly pulled Jewel back to the present. The clammy hand that sneaked inside her clothing and lifted out one of her breasts had her bolting upright as if she'd been scorched. Rigid with shock and horror and confusion, she could only gaze at the stranger's red, stubbled face.

'I'll not hurt thee. I'll suck them nice like Maxwell does—'

'Get your foul hands off me, you bastard!' Panting with fury, she lashed out with her fist but he caught her wrist before it could reach its mark. 'I said, leave *go* of me!'

'A regular viper, you are. Mebbe you like it rough instead, that it? Well, Mick don't mind that – prefers it, in fact.'

Before she had time to blink, the thickset man was on her, clawing at her chest, rubbery lips and ale-sodden breath on her neck. For a moment, overwhelming terror engulfed her. Then Benji's face, the feel of him on her body, the jumble of devastating emotions she'd suffered since and still did burst from her in a scream of such a pitch that the man jerked up to look at her in surprise. Jewel took her chance. Raising her knee, she struck with all her might.

Like a frozen corpse, he rolled from her, stiff face locked in shock, and crashed to the bare flags. Gasping and crying, she leapt away from him and bolted for the door. It opened as she reached out to grasp the knob and she let out another scream as she collided with Louise's mother. The woman grasped her arm to stop her from falling then, eyes wide, took in the scene before her.

'He . . . he . . . That filthy owd swine there tried . . . he tried to—'

'Sweet baby Jesus – look!' She cut off Jewel's hysterical

accusations to squawk to her daughters behind her. Pointing at the prostrate man, she doubled over, laughing, and the others followed suit. 'Bloody daft sod got his stick slapped!'

'Wha—?' Jewel was aghast as they stumbled past her and flopped down on the sofas, tears of mirth running down their faces. 'Did youse hear what I said? He tried—'

'All right, screechy. Bloody hell.' Bleary-eyed, Julia frowned across at her. 'You could waken the dead in their graves with that gob.'

'You gave him what for for his troubles, didn't yer, so no harm done,' added her mother.

Even Louise's voice carried a gin slur: 'Aye, no harm done,' she repeated.

Jewel was lost for words. Still gripped in the throes of shock and fear, she was trembling from head to toe, and now fresh tears of injustice and frustration burned her eyes. She shook her head slowly. 'What is *wrong* with you people?'

'"You people"?' Louise's head jerked up. 'Oh, like that, is it?'

'And what's that meant to mean?'

The girl pushed herself from the sofa and placed her hands on her hips. 'Don't you look down your nose on me and my family, Jewel. Don't you bloody dare. But for us, you'd be sleeping in the gutter the night with the sky pissing on your head!'

Jewel opened her mouth but the retort never came. She pursed her lips and breathed deeply. For as much as she hated to admit it, Louise was right. They *had* come to her rescue, hadn't they? They had taken her in when she'd had nowhere else to go. God help her, she was beholden to them. The truth deflated her. She dropped her gaze to the floor.

'You calmed down now?' asked Louise after some seconds.

She nodded. 'I'm sorry.'

'Forget it. Come on, come and sit down.'

Jewel crossed the space, avoiding looking at the still-prone man as she passed, and took a seat on the sofa furthest from him.

'He weren't meant for thee.' Louise prodded him in the ribs with the toe of her clog. 'He were told to wait up here for our return – bloody landlord pounced on us in the hall demanding late rent, you see. We didn't want this one growing bored and leaving, so sent him up in front. He must have spotted you and thought you were fair game, an' all.'

Jewel hid a shiver. 'Don't the landlord mind, then?'

'Nay, so long as he gets a cut of what we earn on top of the rent.'

'Oh.' It was all she could find in way of response. God above, were there any morally sound people in Manchester? she wondered. Not from what she'd seen so far.

'Right, then.' Louise heaved a sigh then nudged her mother. 'Rouse him, Mam, will thee? Let's get him seen to and on his way, then we can all get some shut-eye.'

'Aye, all right.'

The sisters watched in amusement as the older woman shook him awake. After much groaning and cursing, she'd managed to get him sitting up propped against the sofa. 'What were his name again?' she asked the girls, who both thought for a moment then shrugged.

'Nay, not Maxwell, lass. Mick's what I go by.' His words came back to haunt Jewel and she shuddered. However, she also knew a flush of shame, for how had he known the name special only to her unless he'd heard it from her lips? Had she spoken it in her sleep? Must have.

She'd clearly been dreaming about him again, though for the life of her she couldn't recall it. She was almost saddened by this. What she wouldn't give right now to see his face . . .

'Were it Rick?' proffered Julia.

'Mick,' Jewel murmured. 'His name's Mick.'

'Aye, that's the one.' Louise's mother nodded then shook his shoulder. 'Come on, Mick, my darling. Up tha gets.'

'Huh, where am I?' Seemingly unaffected by his topple to the hard floor – and, to Jewel's relief, holding no memory of it – he lifted his cap and scratched his head.

'Canal Street, of course.'

Squinting, he tried to focus on her face. 'Eh?'

'It's us, remember? We were supping with thee in t' Colliers Arms on t' corner?'

Slowly, his face cleared. He flashed a slack smile. 'Aye, that's right. 'Ere, the other one . . . Louise, her name were. Where's she, then?'

'I'm here, lovey.' Holding out her hands, she helped him to his feet. 'Let's get thee on t' bed, shall we? It's a sight comfier than this rotten floor.'

'Ay, aye.' A lustful growl escaped him as he pulled her closer. 'I fancy that, lass.'

'You sure you can manage it?' Julia called across with a grin.

Bobbing his head, the man puffed out his chest. 'You'd better believe it. Why, you up for joining us, like?'

Jewel had to swallow down her disgust – and it grew when the sisters turned to each other and shrugged.

'Cost thee double, mind,' piped their mother, eyes coming alive with the prospect of more money, and Jewel turned her face away with a grimace. Her very being was void of even the most basic of maternal instincts, had to be. *Lord, she really was deplorable.*

'There you are.' The man tossed several shillings on to the table. Swaying on the spot, he nodded once at her, and she nodded back. Then he held out his hands to her daughters.

Giggling, they led him to the bed.

After laying him down, Louise pulled across a length of curtain to afford them a modicum of privacy and, before she disappeared, she glanced across the room and her eyes met Jewel's. The ghost of a smile, one of reassurance tinged with dull acceptance, touched the girl's mouth. She broke the stare and returned to her customer.

The sounds that were soon reaching them from beyond the makeshift screen were unendurable – for Jewel, at any rate. Her utter mortification was absolute. In contrast, the older woman appeared totally unfazed.

Unable to bear it a second more, she rose, face ablaze, and took herself off to the landing. Shutting the door on the depravity, she closed her eyes and heaved a long, shuddering sigh.

'How was your pie?'

Jewel turned in surprise at the quiet words to find Louise's aunt sitting on the top stair. 'Sorry, what?'

'Your pie what I fetched thee. You fell asleep. Have you had it yet?'

'Nay, I . . . Nay.'

Sarah surveyed her in silence for a moment as she drank from the bottle she held. Then she asked, almost hesitantly, 'All right?'

'I'm not, as it happens.' Jewel could feel her temper rising to the fore. 'The goings-on in that there room, right now, as we speak . . . I, I just can't . . . !'

'Aye.'

'Do you have children, Sarah?'

The woman took another long swallow of brandy. 'Nay.'

'Would you ... could *you* condone ... encourage what your sister in there—?'

'Nay.'

Catching the spark of passion in her tone, Jewel felt a stirring of alliance. Studying the woman properly, she decided she was quite attractive. Unlike her sibling, her figure was slim, her hair free from grey and her skin of blemishes. Her eyes, however, could have belonged to someone twice her age. Dull green, as though life had faded from them long ago, they were strife-worn, deep with untold disappointments.

Jewel moved closer and motioned to the space beside her. 'Mind if I join thee?'

Sarah shook her head. When Jewel was seated, she glanced across at her stomach. 'You should eat, you know. For t' babby.'

'Aye. I am clemmed, if I'm honest. And by, what I wouldn't give forra sup of tea.'

'We've nowt to make a brew inside.'

'Nay.'

'Mind you, it'd not be much use if we did – we ain't got a teapot.'

Jewel couldn't help but chuckle. 'Bloody hell.'

They looked at one another and smiled.

Pushing the stopper in the top of her bottle, Sarah rose to her feet. 'Hang about, I'll not be a minute.'

She headed downstairs and Jewel heard her knock at someone's door. Muffled voices followed, then the door was shut and Sarah made her way back to the landing. In her hand, she carried a steaming mug.

Jewel was touched. 'For me?' she asked when Sarah held it out to her.

'Aye. Wench down there's a kind sort. Go on, sup up.'

Savouring every precious sip as though it were liquid gold, Jewel now watched the woman head for her own room. She emerged seconds later with a grease-stained parcel. Sitting back down, she handed it over.

The meat pie inside was hard and cold, the jelly congealed. In her ravenous state, Jewel had never tasted anything as delicious.

'Better?' asked Sarah when she'd finished the feast.

Jewel nodded. On impulse, she reached across and pressed the woman's hand. 'Thanks, Sarah.'

And somehow, Manchester and this whole situation didn't seem so terrible any more.

Chapter 16

LATER, AS A weak dawn was breaking above the city, Louise's pains began.

Woken by her groans, Jewel rose from the rag rug in front of the fire and padded to the bed. 'Louise? Have I to rouse your mam?'

'Nay . . . Aunt Sarah. Fetch Aunt Sarah.'

Over the next few hours, the two of them worked together. Whilst Sarah saw to the physical side of things, Jewel hovered by the head of the bed, dabbing Louise's hot and sweaty face and neck with a wet rag and offering words of comfort and encouragement.

Astonishingly, her mother and sister hadn't stirred – likely owing to their gin comas. They snored on, oblivious to it all.

Finally, on a long, beast-like grunt, Louise gave a last push. A grey-white object slithered from her body and into Sarah's hands. Heavy silence filled the room. The three women glanced at each other.

'Is it . . . ?' whispered Jewel.

Sarah placed her hand on the tiny child's chest. Then, frowning, she put her ear close to its nose. Slowly, her face cleared. She lifted her head and nodded to her niece. 'It breathes, but only just.'

Releasing a relieved sigh, Jewel squeezed Louise's hand. 'Thank God—'

'Pass it to me.' The new mother's interjection was toneless, flat.

Sarah looked from her to the child several times, eyes creased. 'Lass . . .'

'Pass it to me,' Louise repeated, firmer now. She held out her arms.

Lifting the almost pulseless piece of life gently, Sarah gazed down on it then, with a pained expression, turned her face away. Before handing it across, she nodded dully to Louise, and her niece returned it.

Jewel thought the girl would attempt to clear the child's mouth and nostrils, help bring life to its airways. However, Louise simply stared down into the perfectly formed, unmoving face, and tears sprang to Jewel's eyes. Louise believed it useless, that hope was gone, it was clear to see. Jewel's heart contracted for her, for though she hadn't intended on keeping it, Louise had wanted it to have a future, hadn't she? A bright one, aye, with people who would love it – why else had she been at the house in Lum Street? She waited for Louise to hold the child against her chest, soothe its passing as only a mother could but, again, she was wrong – Louise didn't do this either.

Instead, she laid the child on the bed in front of her. Then, looking with dead eyes straight ahead, she placed a hand over the baby's nose and mouth and pressed down.

It took a few seconds for Jewel to understand what was happening. With a cry, she grasped Louise's arm and tried to pull it away, but her hold was iron-strong. '*Louise*, please!'

'Come away, lass.' Taking Jewel by the shoulders,

Sarah tried to guide her from the bed, but she shook her off.

'Nay, I can't! I won't just stand here whilst she . . . whilst she—!'

'It's for the best,' Sarah told her, taking hold of her again, and there was a catch in her voice.

'But . . . Nay. *Stop*, Louise, *please*.' However, it was as if Jewel's words didn't have the power to touch her. Still staring in front at nothing, Louise remained unresponsive.

The child had put up no resistance. A small, thin leg twitched twice then was still. Louise removed her hand and closed her eyes.

'This is the kindest thing all round – lass, wait!' called Sarah as Jewel pushed her off savagely and ran for the door.

'Nay. Nay! It could have been adopted still, given a better life. She never even gave it a chance!' she shot over her shoulder before bolting from the room.

Blinded by tears, Jewel rushed down the stairs and out of the front door. Her legs took her up the street and around the corner until, overcome with sobs, she crumpled to the step in an inn doorway.

That poor child! How *could* Louise? As for Sarah condoning her actions . . . They were all as bad as one another: wicked to the core. She had to get away from here. She wouldn't dwell amongst such evil. She *must* leave today, now. Go somewhere, *any*where!

'Jewel.'

She didn't lift her head from her hands. 'Leave me alone, Sarah.'

'You have to understand. That poor mite . . .'

'You shouldn't have followed me. Just go on back, let me be—'

'Will you tell?'

'What?'

'What you've witnessed the day ...' Sarah's voice dropped. 'Will you alert the authorities?'

Jewel's hands dropped slowly into her lap. She gazed up at the woman incredulously. 'That's all you're mithered about, in't it? God above!'

Sighing, Sarah perched on the step beside her. 'Think about it. What else was Louise meant to do?'

'She could have had it adopted out to a kind and caring—'

'Could she hell. You saw it: it were frail, lass. Likely wouldn't have survived the day.'

'So you're saying that smothering your own offspring is for the good, aye?'

'Aye, mebbe,' the woman murmured after a pause. 'For some, aye. I reckon she did that poor mite a kindness.' She sniffed then nodded. 'It were a girl, you know? The child were a girl. If, against all the odds ... where d'you reckon it could well have finished up, eleven or twelve years from now? You've only to look at Louise and Julia to know.'

'You mean ... ?' At Sarah's nod, Jewel lowered her head. 'Mother of God.'

'It could have followed the same path as them, its grandmother, *me*. That's no life, lass. No life at all.'

Jewel swivelled her gaze to look at her. Fresh lines scarred the woman's brow and a sea of misery shone from her eyes' depths. 'Why do you do it, Sarah?'

'To eat. To survive.'

'But there's other means of supporting yourself.'

'Not for the likes of me. No respectable employer wants an ale-soaked mess amongst their workforce.'

'Do you ... enjoy it?'

Sarah released a soft and bitter snort. 'I endure it. That's all we can do.'

'Happen you could knock the bottle on the head, go straight, *find* yourself decent work—'

'And be alone with my demons? Oh nay. Nay, lass. The drink dulls what's in here.' She tapped her temple. 'And in here,' she added, repeating the action at her breast. 'Without it . . . Well. I'd not be on this earth for long, and that's the truth.'

Though tempted to ask what from her past plagued her so much she'd rather die than face the memories raw, Jewel didn't. Sarah would have revealed them if she'd wanted to and, besides, she had enough problems of her own at present to cope with anyone else's. Unsummoned, Louise's face flitted into her thoughts – and now, she saw the emotion behind the empty façade, the pain in the outwardly dead eyes. Jewel realised that everything Sarah had just said, Louise knew it, too. In the girl's mind, she hadn't murdered her child. She'd saved her. She wasn't heartless but hardened, and this life had made her so. Poverty brutalised folk. The sufferings for many of this cruel and unforgiving existence . . . it was just so unfair.

'I'll not tell,' Jewel heard herself say.

Sarah smiled softly with her eyes. 'Will you come back with me or are you for moving on?'

To where? Besides, she felt she owed it to Louise to stick around – for now, at least. She rose. Without another word, the two of them headed back to the house.

When they arrived, the child was gone.

Upon entering the room, Jewel's gaze had gone immediately to the bed but, in her absence, all trace of the birth had been removed. Someone had stripped the soiled sheets – clearly, they were the only ones they possessed, and Louise lay now beneath a few ragged shawls. Julia and their mother, pale faced on the sofa, sat smoking in silence.

Jewel made for the girl staring blankly at the mould-spotted ceiling. 'Louise?' she whispered, and as she'd expected received no response. 'I'm sorry. For everything.'

Slowly, Louise turned her back on Jewel and the room and curled into a ball.

'Leave her be,' said Sarah quietly. She patted the space beside her and, with a heavy heart, Jewel went to sit beside her on the other sofa.

*

That night, the women went out to work as usual.

Louise hadn't stirred once throughout the strained hours and now, alone with her, Jewel attempted to strike up conversation, hoping the girl might open up without the others' presence. She didn't. Though her eyes were closed, Jewel knew she wasn't asleep, and was eventually forced to give up. Nevertheless, she knew, sooner or later, Louise would have to face up to this. Keeping it all locked within would do her no good at all.

Later, as she lay in her hearth bed watching the flames of the low fire lick hypnotically over the coals, Jewel couldn't get the dead child's face from her mind. What had become of it? She'd managed earlier to pull Sarah aside and ask in a whisper of its whereabouts, but the woman had told her not to dwell on that, for it wouldn't change anything nor fetch it back.

Neither, Jewel knew, would there be any repercussions. In an age of high infant mortality, the death of a small child attracted little attention. Even when a baby's body *was* discovered and the circumstances were suspicious, it was often impossible to trace the mother.

Whatever the mite's resting place, Jewel just hoped it had found the peace it deserved.

Before sleep claimed her, something else Louise's aunt had mentioned came back to her, and she nodded in grim determination. If *her* child was to have any fighting chance, she must do all in her power to free it of this hopeless existence and have it placed with decent adoptive parents. To achieve that, but one thing stood in her way:

She would have to find the brass for it all over again, and fast.

Chapter 17

'WHAT, NOW? TODAY?'

'Aye, why not? Lust and loaves wait for no man.'

'But Louise, Christmas Day?'

Putting the finishing touches to her painted cheeks, the girl snorted. 'Oh, what? You reckon Jesus will be upset with me, is that it?'

'Don't talk daft. It's just . . . well, I thought we could spend the night together, relax and have a laugh, like. Wench downstairs lent me the borrow of some cards. There's only two missing from the pack; we could still enjoy a game. Besides, it's bitter out there. Why not stop in, eh? Stay warm by the fire?'

Louise's face softened slightly. She secured her hat in place with a sigh. 'We need the brass. Look, I'll try and be back a bit earlier, all right? 'Ere, and if I make enough, I'll fetch us back some hot chitterlings from the inn to eat whilst we play. That do thee?'

Knowing she would have to be satisfied with the compromise, Jewel nodded.

The festive day had been a long and lonely affair. Since awakening, her mother had dominated Jewel's thoughts, and with the hours the physical pain in her heart had only grown. Was Flora missing her just as much? she'd agonised, wishing so but hating herself for it, too. That she was causing her upset like this killed her inside a little more each day. Mam didn't deserve a daughter like her but one so much better.

The one small consolation was knowing that at least Flora wouldn't have been alone. Each year, her aunt and uncle insisted they spend the special day with them at the shop. And thankfully, she would also have eaten well. The Powells always went all out with the Christmas fare.

Now, at the thought of food, Jewel's stomach growled. The meagre spread of calf's-head broth and half-rotten vegetables that she and the women had had to look forward to this afternoon was barely sufficient to fill a bird. But, she reminded herself, at least she'd had *something* to tuck into, unlike many poor souls out there.

When the women had gone, she busied herself with tidying the frankly unimprovable room – anything to pass the time and distract her mind from those back home in Bolton. Since she'd begun lodging here, the cleaning had become her role – not that she minded. After all, with no income, she was living here rent free; the least she could do was keep the place decent whilst the others went out to work. However, there was only so much that water and a scrubbing brush could achieve.

The discoloured walls and the floor's cracked flags she couldn't improve the appearance of, however hard she worked. But at least now, her dogged determination was keeping the creeping, air-polluting mould at bay. Left unchecked even for a day or two and in it stole, leaving every corner and crevice damp and stinking. And the owner of the house, and millions like him, had the audacity to actually charge desperate folk – some, extortionate amounts, too – for living here in such health-destroying conditions. The despicableness of such blatant exploitation made Jewel's blood boil.

Having wiped down the mantel, she then swished her rag at a cobweb above with care, mindful of the crumbling plaster and fearful of an avalanche. One end of the silken thread stretched to the corner of the only picture to adorn the walls: a scuffed depiction of a vase of geraniums. Again, she flicked the duster – then swore quietly when the action dislodged the painting from its nail, sending it clattering to the floor.

Jewel retrieved it, relieved to see no further damage had befallen it. Yet as she made to fix it back into place, she paused. In the lighter-coloured rectangle of wall behind where it had hung was a ball of material, stuffed into a hole in the brickwork. She fingered it in confusion then, after glancing towards the door to check no one would return, she eased it out.

Measuring its weight in her hand, she frowned when its contents released a metallic jingle. Carefully, she pulled back the folds and peered inside.

In the following seconds, her eyes grew rounder and rounder as she counted the pile of coins. *Almost twenty-eight pounds.* What the devil . . . ? She'd never seen such an amount in her life. She staggered to a sofa and sat down heavily, mind spinning.

Again, she prodded in awe at the fortune – and her burning curiosity as to whom this astonishing find could belong was salved. Beneath the money was a small gold band holding a ruby stone. *Julia.*

This morning after breakfast, Louise's sister had donned her best hat and sauntered out for a brief clandestine meeting with her lover at the nearby inn. Her eyes had glowed like stars upon her return and, with a flourish, she'd waved her hand beneath their noses to show off her Christmas gift from the married man – the beautiful ring now sitting in Jewel's palm.

However, that didn't explain the money. Had she stolen it, saved it? Or was this also spoils acquired through being a mistress? Come to think of it, she *had* mentioned the role's perks once before, when Louise spoke derogatorily of the lifestyle . . . Bloody hell. And she'd been keeping it secret from everyone this whole time!

Jewel knew this to be true without question. Given her mother's clear hunger for money, no way would this hoard exist had she been aware of it. Only a few hours ago, after eyeing her daughter's ring for most of the day, she'd hinted at the pretty penny it would fetch at the pawnshop – no doubt why Julia had hidden this, too, behind the picture.

Well! Jewel couldn't help but smile in admiration. The woman had worked for it, she supposed. Though just what she had planned for it was another matter – and one which was really no concern of hers.

'In all sincerity, I wish thee the best of luck,' she murmured, securing everything back inside the material and heading to the wall. Then a sudden, heart-shattering thought crashed through her and she gasped.

Could a portion of this wealth have paid to find adoptive parents and save her niece's life? Happen if Julia had told of this money, given Louise a chink of hope, she wouldn't have felt driven to commit her desperate deed . . . ? But hadn't the child been sickly? And yet . . . Devastatingly, they would never know.

Nevertheless, to Jewel the money now felt tainted and she hurried to return it to its hiding place. The very touch of it against her palm made her flesh crawl with the what-ifs. After poking the bundle back between the bricks, she re-hung the painting and wandered back to her seat.

One thing she knew for certain: she couldn't mention it to Louise. After weeks of silent, inner grieving, she'd finally emerged from the darkness. Discovering something like this could set her progress back and cause her unnecessary further suffering – and besides, what would any of it achieve in the long run? The past couldn't be changed, and circumstances would remain just the same. Best all round she told no one of her find.

Falling and stumbling into the room hours later, laughing raucously, the women were not alone. Though Jewel wasn't surprised, her stomach dropped all the same. What she wouldn't give to climb into bed at a decent time and enjoy a sound and uninterrupted night's sleep for once, she thought, dragging herself into a sitting position on the rag rug.

Often, the streetwalkers would simply slip into the nearest dark ginnel with customers then return to the inns; back and to, back and to, throughout the night. Yet other times, such as now, they would fetch their work home with them, and Jewel was forced to wait out their lascivious exploits on the landing. She was almost always exhausted and was bone-weary of being part of this lifestyle. Something had to give, and soon.

'See, I didn't forget.' Louise wiggled her brows and smiled, waving a paper-wrapped package under her nose. 'Chitterlings. Get them down thee.'

Forcing a smile in return, Jewel took them from her, although she no longer had an appetite. She'd have much preferred the girl's company earlier instead, had felt more alone than usual today, given the occasion. However, she didn't voice her feelings. As much as she disagreed with the way her room fellows made their living, she was, after all, here on their charity – though being kept like this didn't sit well with her and she vowed to herself daily she'd repay their kindness somehow, one day.

'No need to run off, is there?' Louise's mother clamped a hand on Jewel's shoulder as she made to head out to the landing. Like her daughters and sister, her speech was slurred and her sight squinting. 'Stay awhile with us, enjoy the party.'

Eyeing the knot of men in the centre of the room, all in a similar state to the women, Jewel shook her head. 'No, ta.'

'Ay, come on. Oh no you don't,' the older woman added on a guffaw as Jewel tried to swerve past her. 'Now I'll not take no for an answer. Sit down here, aye. Well, go on, then!'

Having drawn the attention of the others – all except Sarah, who had slipped away with one of the males to the curtained-off bed – she encouraged them to help her in persuading Jewel, which they did with gusto. Outnumbered and not wishing to appear churlish, Jewel was forced to accept. Suppressing a sigh, she went to sit on a sofa.

Almost immediately, a young man with smouldering good looks and arrogance to match sauntered over and took the space beside her. She returned his slow grin with a tight smile then fixed her attention across the room in the hope he'd get the message and not attempt conversation. No such luck.

He leaned in and nudged her playfully with his shoulder. 'All right?'

Nodding, she discreetly inched away.

'Them smell good.'

She glanced to the food she still held and had forgotten about. 'Here. Have them.' At least if he was busy eating, he wouldn't be talking to her.

'Aye?'

'Yes, go on.'

'Ta very much. You'll have some, mind, won't thee?'

'Nay, I'm not—'

'But you must. I'd not enjoy it else. I can't swipe a lass's supper from her and scran the lot myself, now can I?'

Biting back an irritated retort, she shrugged in defeat. *God above, anything for a quiet life.*

On the next sofa, Julia and her mother sat straddling two men in their middle years. Julia's customer had exposed her breasts and was trying to coax her mother to kiss them – both women were helpless with laughter. Swallowing down her disgust, Jewel scanned the room for Louise. She spotted her and a grey-haired man slouched in the corner, backs against the wall, kissing passionately. When the bedsprings began their rapid squeaking, intermingled with the gruff moans of Sarah's customer, Jewel had had enough. She rose abruptly.

'Where you going?' asked the man beside her. He attempted to catch her hand but she pulled it from his reach.

'I'll not be long,' she lied. She had no intention whatsoever of returning until, lusts spent, the males had all buggered off home where they belonged.

'Scuttling off so soon?' Louise's mother yelled across. 'By, I thought you were enjoying yerself?'

Jewel didn't answer. Head down, she hurried her step. However, the moment she opened the door the man she'd been sat next to pressed it shut again from behind with the flat of his hand. She hadn't heard him follow her and, frowning, she turned to face him. 'What—?'

'Stay awhile,' he said thickly, cutting her off.

'I told thee, I'll not be long.' She pulled at the door

knob but it didn't budge; his hand was still there, preventing her from escaping. 'Shift,' she said as calmly as she could, though, inside, panicked anger was rising.

'Sit back down forra bit first,' he wheedled, moving in close to nuzzle her neck.

The slap she delivered to the side of his head had Louise's mother roaring with laughter. It turned into a coughing fit and, gasping for breath, she flapped a hand at Jewel. 'Here, that's it, aye – he's partial to a good spanking.'

Ignoring her, Jewel brought furious eyes back to the unfazed man, who was rubbing the spot she'd struck, smiling. Her words came through gritted teeth: 'Let me go.'

'No.'

'What d'you mean, no? You bleedin' well will or else—' The rest of her speech was smothered in his kiss. Rearing back, she pushed hard against his chest. In the next moment, her feet swept out from under her as he lifted her bodily from the ground and, whistling like this was some big joke, carried her back to the sofa. 'Get *off* me! Nay, leave me be!'

'Calm down, for God's sake,' he said on a chuckle, dropping her down on the seat and climbing on top of her. 'Whores like you should be grateful for a fella like me.'

'Leave go of her.'

Gasping in sheer relief at the sound of Sarah's command, Jewel pleaded with her as she struggled beneath him: 'Oh, Sarah, help me. Please!'

'Keep your snout out, you,' Louise's mother piped up. 'It's fair time that one began paying her way around here, I reckon.'

'Aye, too true,' threw in Julia.

Good God, they had set this up? Jewel felt sick with betrayal.

'Nay.' Sarah's voice was firm. 'She ain't rotten like us. And that's how it's staying.'

'Is that so? And what's that, then, growing in her belly? The next Lord and Saviour?'

Ignoring her sister's remark, Sarah turned back to the man. 'Off her. Now!'

Finally, mumbling profanities, he shifted his weight. Jewel could barely breathe with relief as she wriggled out from under him and ran into Sarah's arms. She clung to her, shaking uncontrollably.

'Come on.' Sarah guided her to the door and, now, no one tried to prevent Jewel's exit.

Julia had returned her attention to her customer. Though her mother and the thwarted man shot daggers at Jewel, neither said anything further. As for Louise, in her drunken stupor beneath the man now ravishing her body, she was oblivious to it all.

'Where will I go?'

They had paused on the landing. Sarah gnawed her lip for a moment in thought. Then she nodded. 'Wench downstairs will take thee in the night, don't fret.'

'And the morrow?' Jewel's throat was thick with tears. 'Sarah, what the hell am I going to do?'

'Shh. Come. Things won't seem so bad in t' morning, they never do.'

*

To Jewel's surprise, Sarah's prophecy bore fruit. She awoke in the strange dwelling the next day to find Louise standing over her.

'You all right?'

'Aye.'

'Mam were wrong fetching that fella back for thee.'

'Mebbe, but . . .' Jewel shrugged. 'She's right, though, in't she? I should be paying my way.'

'Well, they ain't out of pocket none, are they? I'm the one tipping up extra brass for thee.'

'All right, well, it ain't right *you* keeping me, then.'

'What you saying?'

Jewel held out a hand and, when Louise had helped her to her feet, she nodded determinedly. 'I'm for finding myself employment. I'll pay youse back somehow.'

'Don't be daft. Who'll take you on in your condition?'

'I ain't an invalid, Louise. There's plenty I can manage. Besides, I ain't so big yet, am I?' Looking down at the neat globe of her stomach, she pursed her lips. 'Happen I could still conceal it for now . . .'

'Where will you ask, like?'

Again, Jewel shrugged. 'The inns or shops, see if any require a skivvy. It's worth a try. 'Ere,' she added suddenly, face brightening. 'Happen you could enquire along with me.'

'Me?' The girl was genuinely surprised at the suggestion. 'But I know nowt.'

'You could learn. What have you got to lose? Surely to God, Louise, you can't enjoy what you're doing now.'

A defensive look crossed her face then slowly melted into one of despondency. 'Course I don't. I mean, sometimes it ain't so bad with the sound sorts. It's the others, the dirty buggers with a fancy for filth, who spoil it. Relations with *them* I can't stand.'

'Well, then. I know it's Boxing Day, but there's bound to be a few places open.' The Bank Holidays Act, passed two years before, was designed to ease the pressure on workers. However, some family-run businesses, unwilling to lose a day's earnings, chose to ignore it. 'So?' she pressed. 'You'll come out looking with me?'

There was a long hesitation, then: 'Aye, if you like.'

Jewel smiled, filled with hope. She'd failed to convince Sarah there was another way, but now, just maybe . . . Oh, if only she could help Louise free herself of this life her feckless mother had normalised for her, she'd feel her time here had meant something after all.

'We've got bacon going on t' fire. You coming up?'

With thoughts of facing the others, Jewel's mood dipped. 'What about your mother, Julia?'

'It's all right; there's enough bacon for us all.'

'I weren't talking about the grub, and you know it.'

Louise flashed a grin. 'Forget about all that, now, eh? Mam has.'

How very noble of her – she's the one in the wrong, not I! thought Jewel, bristling. But she kept quiet. Louise was trying to be peacemaker and she wouldn't throw it back in her face. However, if Louise's mam ever pulled another trick like the one last night, Jewel knew she wouldn't be responsible for her actions. No one got to mistreat her like that twice and get away with it.

'Come on, then. I'm clemmed.'

After thanking Sarah's friend for her kindness in putting her up, Jewel followed Louise upstairs. When they entered, neither Julia nor her mother, who were huddled around the fire nursing thick heads from last night's gin, looked up. Nor did they make mention of Jewel's assault, and she was inclined to follow suit, preferring not to converse with them now, anyway, unless necessary.

'All right?' Sarah mouthed across to her as she sat down, then winked softly when Jewel nodded.

'Where you off to, then?' Louise's mother asked her a little after breakfast when she and Jewel donned their shawls – Jewel's being an old one of the girls' given to replace her own left behind in Bolton; she was grateful for it as the weather grew more bitter with the shortened days – and headed for the door.

Louise hesitated before answering. 'Forra walk.'

'A walk?' sniggered Julia. 'Since when did you go for walks?'

'Since now, all right, so shut tha trap,' Louise snapped, and Jewel saw her confidence about their job search begin to wane.

'Come on, then,' she urged before Louise could change her mind. 'Fresh air will do us good.' She waited until they had reached the street before asking, 'Why didn't you tell them the truth about where we're going?'

'I don't know. Happen in case they laughed?'

A wave of sadness for this girl and the horrid lifestyle she had only ever known washed through Jewel. She brought her to a stop and took both her hands in hers. 'You deserve more than this. You're *better* than this – better than the pair of them back there, an' all – and don't you forget it.'

Louise blinked with an expression of slight puzzlement, as though Jewel had spoken another language she hadn't understood. Though Jewel knew she was likely at a loss how to respond. Evidently, she'd severely lacked any form of support or encouragement throughout her life.

'Shall we try there first?' Jewel pointed to a boot mender's up ahead. 'What d'you reckon?'

'Do I look presentable?'

'Aye,' she was able to answer truthfully; Louise spared the rouge and ostentatious headwear during the day. 'You'll be fine,' she encouraged, sensing the girl's nervousness. 'Just be polite. Oh, and don't forget to smile.'

Despite their best efforts, they were no closer to finding employment two hours later. Thirsty and tired, their teeth clacking from the cold, they eventually drew to a halt with simultaneous sighs.

'We could allus try again the morrow,' suggested Jewel, though her words held little enthusiasm.

'Aye, come on. I'm frozzen.'

Each place they had tried either already employed a scrubbing girl or they took one look at Jewel's full stomach and empty ring finger – though she did her best to hide both – and quickly sent them on their way.

'I'm for thinking, Louise, happen you'd be best going out by yourself next time. I'm just hindering your chances with my condition. You'd fare better at finding summat were I not with thee.'

'Nay, I—' But the girl didn't get to finish her sentence, for a voice behind them stole their attention:

'Miss Nightingale?'

Halting in cold shock, Jewel turned slowly.

'Why, it *is* you, Miss Nightingale! Hello!'

Good God in heaven. No . . .

'I believed at first that my eyes were deceiving me, but no. What are you doing here?'

'Well, I . . .' Trying desperately to hide her bump beneath the folds of her shawl, Jewel cleared her throat. 'I didn't know you hailed from Manchester, Mrs Kirkwood.'

'Yes, yes.' She held up the wicker basket she carried, filled to the brim with provisions. 'I'm out delivering alms to the needy. So many poor wretches of this city without even a crust of bread most days . . .' Voice soft with compassion, she shook her head. 'A travesty, oh indeed.'

'That's kind of thee, Mrs Kirkwood.' And Jewel meant it. Not many from the privileged classes gave such consideration to their less fortunate counterparts. Mind you, this lady had shown herself to be sound-hearted since the day they had met, hadn't she? She was certainly a rare breed. 'Oh, I wanted the opportunity to say,' Jewel added suddenly as the thought occurred, 'ta ever so for them pictures you got me back in Mawdsley Street. Reet bonny, they are, and brighten the kitchen walls up no end.'

'Oh, you're most welcome. We must spread happiness where we can.' She motioned to the basket to reiterate her beliefs and smiled. Then: 'So, Miss Nightingale?' she pressed. 'What *are* you doing here?'

'I . . . I'm in Manchester caring for a sick aunt. Aye. Mr Birch, he kindly gave me leave. But he's gorra new lass to tend to his household until I return,' she was quick to reassure her.

'I see. Well, I do hope your aunt regains good health soon,' the lady offered sincerely. Her eyes then flickered to Louise with interest.

'This is . . . my cousin, Mrs Kirkwood. She's seeking new employment and, as my aunt was comfortable and sleeping, I offered to accompany Louise in her search.' Jewel's heart was beating so fast she could barely feel it. The lies were tripping from her tongue and she knew that, unless she cut this astonishing meeting short, and soon, she'd slip up and all would be lost. *Take your leave of us, Mrs Kirkwood. Please, please . . .*

'Do you have experience of being in service?' Mrs Kirkwood had turned her smiling face to Louise. 'It just so happens that friends of mine, who reside not too far from here, are currently an under-housemaid short. I could put you in touch with them if you'd like?'

'Ay, ma'am. You'd do that for me?' The girl's face was alight with amazement.

'Why, of course.'

'Oh. But . . .'

'Yes?'

'I've never done maid work afore. Happen they'll want someone what don't require training.'

'Hm, perhaps. But there is no harm in trying. Would you like the address? You may, of course, mention that I recommend you for the position.'

Louise glanced to Jewel, who nodded encouragingly. 'Can I ask, ma'am, d'you know what the wages will be?'

Jewel shot the girl a warning look, but she ignored her. *Fancy asking summat like that of the lady!*

'Oh, I . . . I'm afraid I couldn't say. That would, naturally, be at your employer's discretion—'

'But if you had to hazard a guess?' the girl persisted. 'What's the going rate, like?'

'Louise.' Jewel tried to communicate again with her eyes. 'Mebbe don't put these questions to Mrs Kirk—'

'I need to know is all.'

'I suppose, initially,' intervened the lady, though it was evident she found the topic somewhat unorthodox, 'I would place the figure at around ten pounds per annum.'

Louise did a quick calculation on her fingers. She lifted her head slowly. 'But that's not even a pound a month. Me, toil morning noon and night for less than five shillings a week? Huh! Sorry, but no thank you!'

The ensuing silence was deafening. Mrs Kirkwood had blushed a soft pink. Jewel, on the other hand, was scarlet with mortification. Hand on hip, Louise looked from one to the other with an incredulous arch of her eyebrow.

The ungracious, thankless young . . . ! 'Lou*ise*,' Jewel hissed through the side of her mouth. 'God above—'

'Oh, I meant nowt by it – honest, I'm grateful to thee for wanting to help,' she added to Mrs Kirkwood. 'It's just, well, at the moment, I can earn that in a single shift on a good day.'

Mother of God. Jewel's hand crept up to cover her burning face. *You foolish bloody idiot! Why would you say that? Now she knows . . . she knows . . . !*

'Is that so?' Mrs Kirkwood's lips had stiffened slightly in understanding. 'Then I don't think there is anything further to discuss.' To Jewel, she continued with a small frown, 'Well, I must get on with my house calls. Good day, Miss Nightingale.'

'Goodbye, Mrs . . .' But the lady was already striding up Great Ancoats Street. Cringing, Jewel buried her face in her shawl. 'My *God.*'

'What's the matter with thee?'

'What's the *matter*? That was the sister of my employer back in Bolton. What d'you think she'll say when she sees him next? How d'you think *he'll* react to hear of the company I've been keeping in my absence? He'll dismiss me for this, for certain.'

'I don't see how. I didn't make mention of how exactly I make my living—'

'Oh, wake up, Louise!' Hands bunched into fists, Jewel trembled with anger. 'Someone of your standing – *our* standing – fetching home such a sum as five shillings a day? How else would that be possible?'

The girl thought for a moment then shrugged. 'Aye, all right. Happen I shouldn't have said it.'

'Nay, that's correct, you shouldn't. And your rudeness, to boot! She went out of her way to help you, and what did yer do? You threw it back in her face. I'm so bloody disappointed in thee. I thought you wanted to change things, improve your life?'

'Aye well. Not for a pittance, I don't.'

Jewel closed her mouth. What was the use? However

much she could argue the point, it would make no difference. Her advice was falling on deaf ears and she hadn't the energy for it any more. Sod her. Let her live a life of debauchery for ever more. She was done.

'Domestic service, mill work, scrubbing shop bleedin' floors . . . it might pay poorly to your standards, aye. But d'you know what, Louise?' Her voice shook with quiet passion. 'You can't put a price on respectability.'

Louise said nothing.

After a last look in the direction Maxwell's sister had disappeared in, Jewel sighed and headed back towards Canal Street.

Chapter 18

FEBRUARY WINDS BLOWING in across the River Irwell throttled the house, breathed its dull howl down the chimney and rattled the windows in their rotten frames. On her bed of rags before the long-dead fire, Jewel gritted her teeth against another spasm.

Over the past hour, the dragging ache in her lower back had spread around the front and now, spears of fire were attacking her stomach at regular intervals. Running a hand over the taut mound, she swallowed hard. Then, once more, she began to pray.

'Jewel?'

She blinked through the thick darkness. It couldn't be. Her senses were skewed; she'd imagined it. It *couldn't* be.

'Lass, are you awake?'

'Mam?' The name fluttered through Jewel's lips like a mist on the breeze.

Footfalls sounded, drew nearer, grew still close by. 'Has it started?'

'Mam . . .'

'It's Sarah, lass. Hang about, now, whilst I fetch a candle.'

An amber flash split the air. Squeezing shut her eyes, Jewel turned her face from its luridness.

'You're as pale as tripe. Why didn't you alert one of us? Is the pain bad?'

'I want my mam.'

The woman sighed. Placing on to the table the tin plate holding the candle, to allow the guttering light to illuminate a wider area, she said soothingly, 'You'll have to make do with me, but I'll see you through this, fret not. I'll not stray from your side.'

'It's not . . . time.'

'How early are thee?'

Another pain ripped through Jewel. She panted through it before answering. 'A month. Mebbe six weeks.'

'Well, the babby's not looking like it's for stopping put, so we'll have to make the best of it. Now, I'm just going to lift your skirts and see what's occurring. All right?'

'Aye.'

Kneeling before her, Sarah threw the folds of material back and removed her underclothes. She reached for the candle and brought it near – then let out a short, sharp gasp. 'Oh, hell's teeth!'

'What? What is it?'

The woman rose slowly. The candlelight fell across her face and Jewel saw it was now white with worry.

'Sarah?' she pressed.

'It's like this, lass. The child's coming out in an unnatural position. I just . . . I ain't never seen the like afore, I . . .'

'Unnatural?' Prickles of fear journeyed down Jewel's spine. 'How?'

'An arm, it . . . it's out. There's an arm. I can see it.'

Too stunned to speak, unable to process the statement, Jewel simply stared at her open-mouthed. Then another blade of agony tore through her insides, making her scream, and this seemed to jolt Sarah's senses.

'Right.' She nodded wildly. 'All right, erm . . . Oh God, what to *do* . . . ? Nay, mustn't panic. Ah, I know. I know!'

She leaned in close and, breathing heavily with anxiety, stroked Jewel's hair. 'I'm going to have to leave thee just forra short while—'

'Nay! Sarah, please—!'

'Lass, I *must*. Look see, the others shall keep watch whilst I'm away,' she added, glancing around the room to where the women were sitting up, roused by the ruckus. 'I'll be as quick as I can, I swear it.'

'But where are you going?' whimpered Jewel before yet another contraction gripped her: 'Oh, Mother of *God*, it hurts so much!'

'I know, my lovey. Eeh, I must go!' Scrambling to her feet, Sarah tore towards the door and was gone.

The intensity of the pain was stealing Jewel's faculties. Pins of light popped behind her eyes and all sound faded. She was vaguely aware of Louise and her sister and mother crowding around her but she couldn't talk or move at all. Then an aged face appeared through the dim light. The mouth smiled, and something within the eyes' grey depths brought a whisper of comfort. They spoke of wiseness, life experience and of trust. And somehow, she knew she was in safe hands.

'There were only one person whose professional services I could call upon,' said Sarah, dropping to her knees again by Jewel's side. 'This here's Minnie Maddox, and she's going to help thee through this, God willing. If anyone can, it's her.'

'Lass?' The voice was soft but assured. 'How are you feeling?'

'Please . . . Help me, Mrs Maddox.'

'No hysterics. They'll do no one any good. Deep breaths. Now tell me, how do you feel? Are the pains strong and frequent?'

'Aye.'

'And what's the pain like?'

'Knives,' Jewel forced out through her teeth.

'Where?'

'My back and stomach.'

'Between your legs also? Is there much pressure?'

'I don't think so. Nay.'

Minnie nodded. Rolling up her sleeves, she turned to Sarah. 'Pass me my bag, lass. The rest of youse,' she told the other women, 'move back, now. Give the girl some air.'

'Will I die?' whispered Jewel as the wizened woman returned her attention to her.

'I'll do my best for you. You have my word.'

Inexplicable terror gripped Jewel in its jaws. 'And the child?'

'We'll see.'

For the next few minutes, Minnie worked in silence. She examined between Jewel's legs then felt her bump, pressing firmly all over. Finally, she reached inside her bag and brought out a spool of thick twine.

'What's to be done, Minnie?' asked Sarah.

'What we have here is an obstructed labour. As you've seen, the left hand, arm and shoulder are presenting. They need pushing back up, then we rotate the child so as it can be delivered breech. Risky, I grant you, but it's the only way. Left much longer, the shoulder will get lower and the chest will become wedged in the pelvic cavity. If that occurs, the baby will suffocate, and the lass could suffer a rupture.'

'Will tha turn the child by massaging the lass's stomach, then?'

'Nay. It must be an internal rotation.'

Every woman emitted a collective breath, though, in her semi-delirious state, Jewel failed to understand why, couldn't make sense of anything much.

'Oh 'eck,' Sarah murmured shakily. 'Have you performed this afore, Minnie?'

'Not me, but I've witnessed it.'

'And . . . was it successful?'

The woman was silent for a moment. 'Nay.'

'Oh 'eck,' Sarah repeated.

'But, as I vowed to the lass here, I'll do my best. Mind, if the child does pull through, the trauma will likely leave it with abnormalities.'

'I don't care a fig about that.' The words left Jewel's lips of their own accord. 'Just save it. Please save my baby.'

Minnie's eyes creased. Then, squaring her shoulders, she nodded once. 'You feel to be dilated enough, so . . . let's get to work.'

'What can I do to help, Minnie?' Sarah asked.

'Fetch some lard.'

Sarah hurried off to borrow from the wench downstairs what Minnie had requested. Meanwhile, Minnie busied herself making a slip noose with the twine from her bag.

Sarah returned triumphant, and Minnie liberally slathered her left arm in the greasy white substance. Then she grasped the baby's limb and slowly, carefully, passed it back inside Jewel. This done, she took the noose and once more inserted her hand. Pursing her lips, she pushed up inside the uterus to the elbow, and Jewel's terrible screams rebounded off the walls.

'Be still as you can, lass,' Minnie murmured, face wreathed in concentration. 'Almost got it . . . There. It's done.' When finally she extracted her arm, she still held in her hand a length of the twine. Only, now, the noose end was inside and had been passed around the baby's foot and secured around the ankle.

'What's next?' panted Jewel, doing her utmost to

remain brave, though she was convinced she was dying. She had to be; it wasn't humanly possible to experience this level of pain and survive, surely?

'Now comes the internal rotation, lass. You're doing reet well, but I'll need to use two hands for this so brace yourself.'

As Minnie lubricated her other arm, Jewel scrunched her eyes tight shut. In her mind, she prayed to God, and to her earthly father, Fred, to keep and protect her. All the while, she wished with all that she was that her mam was here. She'd have given anything for it to be so. *Anything*.

After taking a long deep breath, Minnie now inserted her right hand. Further, further she continued to push, manoeuvring the child up and around. Then she inserted her left hand still holding the twine again, and tugged the foot downwards.

If Jewel had thought the agony couldn't get worse, she was mistaken. It increased in violence by the second and, though her voice screamed on, she felt herself slipping away. This must be what disembowelment was like. It truly felt as if her viscera were being hacked from her with hot blades. She couldn't keep her lids open, was leaving this place, dying . . .

'Thanks be to God, the other foot has followed.' Minnie's words scratched on the outskirts of Jewel's brain. 'Right, lass. Lass? I know you're exhausted but come, you must wake up.'

Jewel blinked up into her worried face. 'I can't. I'm . . . finished.'

'Nay, you ain't. Now listen. The child is in the breech position. The feet are out already and, when your next pain comes, I want you to push for me. All right?'

'Can't . . .'

'Yes, you *can*. We're nearly there.'

The familiar scorch built and tore through her body. Lifting her knees, Jewel thrashed her head from side to side.

'Push! Push!'

Bearing down with all her might, she released a high-pitched shriek to the ceiling. A gush of warm liquid spilled from her, then the child forced its way out. Crying and laughing in sheer relief, she grasped at the air with hungry hands. 'Give it to me. Give me my baby.'

'It's a girl.' Grinning from ear to ear, Minnie placed the slippery, squawking infant on her chest.

Jewel gazed in open-mouthed infatuation at the miracle in front of her. 'Is she . . . ? Is there anything . . . ?'

'There don't appear to be any damage to the child,' Minnie told her. 'Mind, I'll check her over in a minute. You enjoy her awhile first.'

'Eeh, lass.' Sarah put her cheek, damp with tears, against Jewel's.

'My daughter, Sarah. I have a daughter.'

'Aye, you do.'

Memories reached her of the birth that had taken place in this very room not so long ago, and she glanced around in search of Louise. Their eyes met, and the girl smiled without a hint of bitterness for her own lost child. Jewel returned it then gazed up at the elderly woman to whom she owed so very much.

'Mrs Maddox, I don't know what to say, don't know how I'll ever be able to thank thee—'

'There's none needed. I'm glad I could help, aye.' She motioned to the baby. 'Shall I have a look at her, then, see that she's well?'

Nodding, Jewel handed her over. Though she knew that no matter if something – anything – did ail her, physically or mentally, she couldn't love her less. And love her she did, more than she'd ever dared believe. Benji and all that went with it meant not a thing any more. *Her child, and hers alone . . .*

'Norra thing wrong with her, as far as I can see,' Minnie eventually announced with some amazement. 'You, lass, could do with tending to, mind. Glory be to God, you didn't bleed too heavily; though you tore quite a bit, aye. You'll be tender forra good few weeks, I'm betting.'

'I'll patch her up, Minnie,' said Sarah.

'You sure?'

'Aye, I know what to do. You go on home and get some rest and take my true and honest thanks along with yer. I don't know what we'd have done without thee.'

After seeing the woman out, Sarah reached beneath her skirts into the cloth pouch attached to a length of string around her waist and extracted some coins. She handed them to her sister. 'Here. Youse three go and get a bite and a sup at the inn whilst I clean the girl up, like.'

The women didn't need telling twice and after donning their hats took their leave – though Louise did give Jewel a last small smile before following the others out.

With the help of a little brandy to take the edge off, Jewel bore the stitching. When Sarah was done and had helped her into the bed, Jewel held out her arms eagerly. The child was placed into them and she breathed easier.

'She's a bonny 'un, all right,' murmured Sarah, gazing down at her. 'Do you have a name yet?'

'Nay.' Jewel's tone was quiet but firm. 'Nor will I bestow one. That's summat for her new parents to decide.'

'Oh, I see. That's what you're intending, then?'

'It is. What can I give her? Love just ain't enough, Sarah. It ain't.' Tears thickened her throat. 'She deserves a home, regular food in her belly, decent clothes on her back. A proper family, with a mother *and* a father. She'll not get them from me. What Louise felt she had to do . . . this is me doing the same. Sparing the suffering. Putting my child first.'

'For what it's worth, I agree.'

A little of Jewel's guilt subsided. 'You do?'

'Aye. It's the one, most selfless gift a parent in our position can give. Trust me, you're doing the right thing.'

The love that this life had awakened in Jewel was like nothing she'd known before or would ever have thought possible. Now, she was more determined than ever that her daughter would have the very best future she could deliver. And she'd do everything in her power to see that it happened. Whatever it took.

Her eyes flicked to the painting of the geraniums. She lifted her chin with resolution. *Whatever it took.*

'Sarah? Do you know of anyone who can help?'

'With getting the child adopted?'

'Aye.'

'But where in the world would you find the brass?'

Jewel glanced away as she sought to think up something feasible. But, of course, she couldn't. All the women knew she hadn't two farthings to rub together. The child arriving early had only complicated matters further. She'd still been holding on to the hope that she'd find some mode of employment before it made an appearance, and that she'd be able to put money aside for this very eventuality. Anything would have been better than nothing; she'd have begged the procurers on her knees to consider dropping their fee, to take instead what she would have had to offer. She couldn't do that now, could she? You couldn't barter a deal with nothing.

'I don't know,' she was finally forced to respond. 'But say I did have the means? *Is* there anyone you know of?'

'Aye.'

'Eeh, that's great. Who?'

'Minnie.'

'Mrs Maddox, really?'

'Really,' Sarah murmured.

A sob caught in Jewel's throat. For the first time in a long time, she saw a ray of happiness on the horizon. 'I can think of no one else I'd rather go to. After what that woman did for us the day . . . I know she'd do me – do the baby, here – right.'

Sarah's words were softer still. 'Aye, she would.'

Left alone soon afterwards to get some rest, Jewel allowed herself to dream of the tantalising possibilities not too far from her reach. She envisioned a handsome lady tenderly cradling the child, whilst her husband looked on with an adoring smile. She saw her daughter through the years, shiny-haired and pink-cheeked with health, watched her slip from infant to youth into womanhood without a moment's want or strife. A future worth the living, as she deserved. And yet . . .

Jewel tried her best to dispel another image that had crept in amongst the rest, but it refused to leave her. It was of herself falling to her knees, hand outstretched in desperation to the retreating backs of the couple carrying her baby away. No matter how hard or how long she screamed, they didn't seem to hear and continued on, taking their precious cargo out of her life for ever . . .

Throat thick, chest heavy, eyes burning with the

searing pain of it all, she shook her head. 'Nay,' she told the room on a shaky growl. Then louder: '*Nay*.'

She wouldn't ruin this for the child. She refused to allow her own selfish yearnings to win through, to dominate her decision, affect her daughter's destiny.

That truly would be a cruelty she'd never recover from.

Chapter 19

AS THE PASSING days slipped into weeks, life in the small, cramped room in Canal Street became intolerable.

Though Jewel hadn't expected the women to cease their drunken, nocturnal antics upon the baby's arrival, she had hoped they would curtail them somewhat. But if anything, things seemed to have grown worse.

At least if they had limited their work to the backstreet adjoining the inn, things wouldn't have been so bad. But no. Still almost nightly, once the beer houses had kicked out, they fetched back any number of men, and their 'parties' could go on right into the following morning.

The noise was like a torture device from which she couldn't escape. Laughter, singing, shouting, arguing – they seemed to roll on a continual wheel. Then there were the other sounds, the ones that came with their trade, relentless, day and night. The child was constantly being woken and Jewel barely ever managed to drop off to sleep at all. The stress of it all was beginning to affect her well-being and the end of her tether was growing ever nearer. She *had* to get out of here.

Despite her desperation, Jewel had recognised that she wasn't yet strong enough to be up and about. She'd suffered severely from the extraordinary birth. She was weak, grew fatigued easily. Unable to rest properly in comfort and peace was only delaying her progress.

It was midday on a Saturday towards the end of the month when matters eventually came to a head. Louise and her mother had been sniping at each other since rolling from their beds, and the rowing had intensified as the day wore on. Glad of the curtain around the bed that shut her off from the room, Jewel lay with gritted teeth to wait it out.

Julia hadn't been home for two days and the women blamed each other for her absence. Where had they last seen her, and with whom? This wasn't like her at all, to fail to come home. Their line of work brought them into close contact with all manner of people, some worse than others. Anything could have happened to her and they wouldn't even know until a body turned up, as those of streetwalkers did all too often. And on, and on.

'You should have kept an eye to her,' Louise's mother snapped, sounding more disgruntled than worried about her missing child's welfare. 'Don't I allus say you must stick together on t' nights?'

'You're her mam, not me. Why didn't *you* keep a check on her movements?' shot back the girl.

'Aye well, it's all the harder you'll work, let me tell thee. Until she returns, we're an income down. Mine and Sarah's owd cunnies don't attract the fellas like they used to. It's young ones like yours they prefer – and you'll give it to them, an' all, at double the rate from now on.'

Jewel shook her head. Money. That's all it ever boiled down to with the so-called mother of these girls. She possessed not a single ounce of real love for either of them. She truly was the most grotesque person she'd ever had the misfortune of meeting. No wonder Julia had gone. Chances were she wasn't in any danger but had seen the light at long last.

And yet . . . She saw in her mind's eye the picture – and the money nestled behind it. She'd checked only last night, fearing the worst – her daughter's whole future depended on it, after all – but no, it was still there. If Julia *had* deserted, she'd have surely taken her treasure trove with her.

'There's no way I'm toiling extra hours to keep thee in gin. It ain't happening.'

'You'll do as I bleedin' well *say*.'

'Aye? Watch me!' retorted Louise.

There followed next the sound of scuffling. Then the curtain collapsed inwards as both women fell, clawing and tearing at each other's hair, on to the bed, missing the sleeping baby by inches.

With a scream of horror, Jewel snatched up her child and, caring naught for her stitches, jumped from the bed. Burning fury rapidly replaced her shock and she jabbed a finger in their direction. 'You pair of gutter dog bitches, yer!' But lost in their battle, they didn't hear, and she turned instead to Sarah, who was trying to split the women up. 'Take me to Mrs Maddox's.'

'What, now? But Jewel, your confinement's not over—'

'I'm well enough,' she barked, snatching up her shawl and wrapping it around the baby tightly. 'If I stay here any longer, they'll finish up doing my child a serious mischief – or, God help them, *I'll* end up going at the pair of *them*. Just get us out of here, Sarah. Please.'

A woman with dark hair and small, quick eyes opened the door to Minnie's house minutes later. 'Hello, Sarah.'

'All right, Eliza? Is Minnie home?'

'Aye, come on in.'

Following behind, Jewel took stock of the kitchen

they entered. Like the procurer's house in Lum Street, this, too, was clean and tidy. Only here there was a marked difference: it was cosy and welcoming and oozing warmth. A sudden lump came to her throat and she swallowed hard. It was almost like stepping into Mam's house. Yet another difference here was the bed by the fire, upon which lay a row of contented-looking babies sleeping peacefully, not holed away in the back bedroom in the way Mater had operated.

'Hello, Sarah love,' called Minnie from her fireside chair. Then her gaze shifted to Jewel and a wide smile spread across her lined face. 'Lass! By, I see you're progressing well. And is that the young angel you've got with thee? Ay, give us her here, let me have a cuddle of her.'

Smiling back, Jewel placed the baby into her arms. 'It's nice to see thee, Mrs Maddox.'

'And youse, all three.'

'Take the weight off,' Eliza told them, nodding to the table before limping to the fire. 'I'll brew a fresh pot.'

'So,' asked Minnie, pausing in her cooing at the child, when they were seated. 'To what do I owe this fine pleasure?'

'I want the child adopted, Mrs Maddox,' Jewel blurted out before she could stop herself. 'Please, will tha help me?'

Surprised silence filled the room for a moment. Minnie glanced to Sarah then back to Jewel.

'Can I ask why, lass?'

'I can't give her the life she deserves. That's the top and bottom of it.'

The old woman nodded. 'It seems to me this ain't a fresh decision. You've given this matter thought forra good while?'

'I've known I couldn't keep the child since the day I discovered I were carrying it.'

A shadow of understanding crossed Minnie's face, and Jewel knew she sensed Benji's crime. Given her experience, she'd likely witnessed this scenario many times over.

'So will you help me, Mrs Maddox?' she continued on a note of pleading. 'Can you find my daughter a better life?'

'There's no going back, lass, once the deed is done.'

'I understand that. Please, you're my last hope. I did find another baby farmer who promised to help, but she—'

Minnie and Eliza cut her off with a collective gasp.

'What is it?' Jewel glanced from one to the other in puzzlement. 'What did I say?'

'How dare you.' Eliza's voice shook with offence. 'Min here is no bloody baby farmer!'

'Oh. But I thought—'

'You thought wrong, lass.' Folding her arms, Minnie's face was grave. 'I have no part, nor have I ever, in that scandalous practice. If it's *that* you're here seeking, you've come to the wrong place – and shame on you!'

'But . . .' Jewel was miffed. 'Baby farmers are a godsend to women like me. They offer a solution, a haven—'

'*What?*' Eliza gazed at her as if she were mad. 'Them beasts are one of the great plagues of society. How can you condone – *accept* – the slaughtering of innocents? Commercial infanticide, that's what it is!'

Jewel's mouth fell open. 'What the divil are you talking about?'

'Lass,' interrupted Sarah quietly. 'Baby farmers are a whole other breed of procurers – and Minnie ain't one of them. She's decent and respectable. Honest, not callous. To put your little one out to nurse, and to *farm* them out, are two different things.'

Minnie and Eliza nodded their agreement. Still, Jewel was no closer to understanding. She shook her head, and Sarah continued:

'The term "baby farmer" is used as an insult and implies improper treatment. No respectable wench would call herself so. Baby farming is an accusation, not a profession.'

'That's right,' followed up Minnie. 'I care for the mites I'm paid to rear or rehome, I don't abuse and neglect them.'

Jewel's mind spun in her struggle to digest what she was hearing. Then Minnie spoke again, and all the blood drained from her face:

'Take that Bickerstaff piece from Bolton town. A regular hell-dweller, and no mistake.'

'Did you say Bickerstaff? *Ada* Bickerstaff?'

'That's the one.'

'What about her?'

'Do you know the divil?'

'Aye. She's the procurer I went to first, months ago, but the arrangement didn't work out.'

'Then, by God,' breathed Eliza, shaking her head, 'yon babby here must have a guardian angel looking out for her to escape them clutches.'

The police storming Lum Street, the children hidden away upstairs . . . Jewel's breathing quickened. She was almost too afraid to ask. 'How do *youse* know of her?'

The old woman wrinkled her nose as though smelling something unpleasant. 'Her name's been in every newspaper in the land – strikes horror still into the hearts of all good and decent folk it does, an' all. I mean, there's been a few sensational cases regarding this in t' press over the years, but nowt on this scale.'

'What's she done?' Jewel whispered.

'Murdered an untold number of babbies, that's what.'

No...

'She opened the door one day last November to who she thought would be a customer she were waiting on, only to find two constables standing there.'

Oh, dear God in heaven, it was true...

'Top and bottom of it is,' continued Minnie, 'they did a search of the property. That's when the gruesome discoveries were made: body parts wrapped in blankets in the cellar. She'd been dismembering tiny babbies down there, then feeding them to her dogs to get rid of the evidence.'

'*What?*' She was going to be sick.

'Aye, beggars belief. Three infants were found alive still in a back bedroom, all in a pitiable state and weighing half what they should. They were removed to the workhouse but never recovered from her neglect and died soon after.'

She'd been there. She'd lived, ate and slept beneath that roof, when all the time, right above her head, in the next room... She'd suspected nothing. *Nothing.* This couldn't be happening. She was stuck in some nightmare, had to be, and would waken soon, surely?

'Them angels were simply left to wilt away and die,' Eliza was saying now, though Jewel barely heard her, with the blood crashing through her ears. 'She deliberately forewent even the most basic of care. They were neither fed, bathed nor shown the slightest attention. It were all about the brass she got from taking them on. That's all she wanted and, once she had it in her sweaty palm, the children were nowt but an inconvenience, for their upkeep would have only ate away at her profits. But a mistreated babby is a noisy babby, so she dosed them with "quietness" – narcotic potions and deadly syrups such as laudanum and Godfrey's Cordial – to render them docile. The little loves didn't stand a chance.'

That's why she'd hardly heard the poor souls' cries. When she had on occasion, they were but sleepy-sounding mews. *I'm so sorry, so sorry . . .*

'Seems likely she'd been carrying on her evil trade for ten years or more, could have murdered hundreds of children in all.'

Jewel swallowed down bile. This just got worse and worse . . . 'Mother of God. How was this allowed to happen?'

'Well, the registration of births, live or dead, ain't compulsory, is it? If the authorities ain't aware of a babby's existence, it can be got rid of without anyone knowing the difference. Besides, she moved on regular to avoid detection, changing addresses and aliases as she went. I just thank the good Lord she's been stopped at last and can do no more poor innocents harm.'

'She admitted to everything?'

'Well, she didn't have much choice, did she? The evidence were there for all to see. She made a full confession whilst in prison. She swore she never murdered them with her two hands, by strangulation, say, couldn't bring herself to. But well, leaving them to slowly rot as she did instead is worse in my eyes. It would have took weeks for them to die. What they must have suffered . . .' Minnie paused to wipe away a tear. 'She were charged with five counts of wilful murder – all they could pin on her with the evidence they had, though she were guilty of many more, I'll be bound – and sentenced to death.

'Her defence tried claiming insanity and she were examined. They found she were sane, all right, just bleedin' wicked to the marrow. She claimed whilst holed in the condemned cell that she'd performed but acts of charity. That the children were unwanted and she'd just sent them on to God to be looked after by Him. Bloody warped bitch. I hope she died with a struggle, an' all, knew then how it felt. I *pray* that noose didn't afford her a quick release.'

With a shuddering sigh, Jewel dropped her head in her hands. 'I had no idea. Truly. She practised so openly, were advertising in the paper. That's why I believed it to be above board.'

'Aye well. Reformers are fighting tooth and nail to stamp it out completely. Hopefully, they one day will.'

'I just can't . . . I suspected *nowt*, believed her to be reputable, that she were doing lasses a kindness, that's all. I didn't realise that to be a baby farmer was a bad thing.'

Louise. She'd been the one to tell her that Ada Bickerstaff was one such. Was she, too, unaware of the meaning behind the title? Had to be. She must see the girl, inform her of what she'd discovered, what an incredibly lucky escape they – their children – had had.

'I must go.' She rose shakily, and Minnie handed her child across. Gazing down at the pure and harmless being in her arms, Jewel wanted to cry. *I've wronged you so many times, little one, but I'll make good in the end. I promise you.* 'Mrs Maddox, Eliza, ta ever so for telling me all you have the day. It's made me see even more that this child here must have summat better than this, than me. Please, will you help with getting her adopted? I'll do anything, *please*.'

Minnie was silent as she looked from mother to baby with sadness. Finally, she patted Jewel's hand and nodded. 'All right, lass, aye. I will.'

'Oh. Oh, thank you, *thank* you, so very much.' *All I need now is the money. And by God, I'll get it*, she thought, determination washing through her. 'I'll be back the morrow, Mrs Maddox. You really . . .' She had to clear the tears from her throat before continuing. 'You really don't know what this means to me, my child. Thank you once again, from the bottom of my heart.'

The old woman rose to see them out and, as Jewel followed her to the door, something on the sideboard against the back wall made her do a double-take. She stepped towards it and her eyebrows lifted.

'My mother has this candlestick.'

'Oh?'

'Aye. Very precious to her, it is. But how . . . ?' She glanced over her shoulder to the old woman in amazement. 'Mam's allus said that hers were a last gift from Father afore he passed away. She said it were 'specially made, that there's none other like it in the whole world.' Turning it this way and that in her hands, Jewel's bemusement grew. Some eight inches tall, with exquisitely cut prisms . . . it could have passed itself off as her mother's without a doubt. 'It's exactly the same. How queer.'

Minnie's brows had reacted, too, only hers did the opposite, dropping into a frown. 'Aye well,' she said. 'Happen the designer made more than one after all.'

'Aye, mebbe.'

After the old woman had waved them off, she and Sarah lowered their heads against the cold and set off back to Canal Street. They were almost at the door when Jewel realised how quiet the other woman was and had been throughout the meeting. When she asked her if she was all right, and received but a nod from Sarah in response, she put it down to the recent shocking revelation concerning that wicked piece Bickerstaff, and left her be. She knew exactly how she felt, could barely wrap her brain around it all herself.

Inside, the fight had ceased at least, and mother and daughter were nowhere to be found.

'Probably taken themselves off to the inn to continue their spat there,' Sarah surmised with a roll of her eyes. 'The state they've left the place in, though.'

After laying the baby on a sofa, Jewel took proper stock of the wrecked space and nodded. It seemed they had thrown in anger, or knocked into during their scuffle, every item in their path. Bottles and dishes littered the floor. The table lay on its side and the makeshift curtains had been torn from the window. Then a sudden wave of dread assaulted her and she turned slowly, almost not daring to check. Yet to her sheer relief, the picture remained where it always had, appeared to be the only item to have evaded the onslaught. *Thank God.*

'Youse are back, then?'

Jewel and Sarah turned to find Louise's mother swaying in the doorway. She, too, glanced around at the carnage and, pulling a face, shrugged. 'And where's that hell cat, then? Slunk off to lick her wounds, has she?'

'Place were empty when we returned,' Sarah told her. 'We thought Louise were with thee.'

'Huh, not likely. Vicious young bitch. She'd do well to keep out of my road forra while if she knows what's good for her.'

'Is there no word as to Julia's whereabouts yet?'

'Nay. Ah, to buggery with the pair of them. Bleedin' ingrates. Anyroad, sod it, I'm going to get some kip,' the woman grumbled, shoving past them and stumbling over the debris-strewn floor towards the bed. She fell across it – shawl, clogs and all – and promptly fell fast asleep.

Jewel and Sarah exchanged a weary look. Without a

word, they rolled up their sleeves and set to tackling the mess.

*

Nightfall rolled around and still there was no sign of either of the sisters. Their mother snored on, oblivious to everything, but Jewel and Sarah had begun to get concerned.

'I'm off to search our usual haunts, see if there's been a sighting,' said Sarah, reaching for her shawl. 'Julia's been gone way longer than what's normal; I'm going to report her missing at the police station the morrow if she still ain't back. Not that the bobbies will offer much help,' she added with a note of bitterness. 'Girls in our trade vanish all the time. What's one more missing slum whore to them? But for Louise to disappear . . . The lass ain't as hardened as her sister, nay. And what with how her mind's been of late since the babby . . .' Biting her lip, she set off to scour the inns.

Alone, Jewel's eyes immediately strayed to the picture. Ashamed, she tore them away, but they soon returned, and her feet itched to go to it. For though she, too, was worried about Louise, and even about the spiky Julia, another thought overrode all else: the future happiness of her child. To her, nothing was more important than that. Unable to fight the urge any longer, she hurried to the wall.

After a quick glance towards the bed and the woman within still lost in her drunken stupor, she nodded, satisfied. Then she lifted the picture from the nail and propped it quietly against the sofa.

For a full minute, she could do nothing but stare at the empty cavity between the bricks as the world slowly shattered around her. The cloth purse and the small fortune it contained were gone.

Breaths coming in short spurts, she swung her head. 'Nay. *Nay!*'

The picture had clearly been disturbed after all. Louise must have spotted the secret hoard after her mother had taken herself off to the gin palace following their fight. She'd snatched away the lot, ruby ring and all, and had it away on her toes. Jewel was doubtful anyone would see the girl again. And despite her devastation, she blamed her not one bit. Who wouldn't do the same in her situation; the family, the life, she'd been cursed with? Jewel knew, had it been her, she'd have certainly taken the opportunity of a fresh start far from here.

But God above, where did this leave her child? Just how would she pay Minnie Maddox?

Her last hope now dashed to the wind, the fight within her followed suit. With a moan, she sank to her knees on the cold, flagged floor.

Chapter 20

AS SARAH HAD predicted, the desk sergeant at Kirby Street Station had barely batted an eyelid when she went to report her niece missing.

Despite the previous day's search, she'd had no luck – no one in the inns, including their regular customers, had seen hide nor hair of the sisters. And so, as she'd vowed, Sarah had braced herself to go and ask the police for help. No small task for the majority of their class, to whom the law was rarely a friend.

Jewel had felt it only right to tell her about the money, and her subsequent suspicions regarding Louise's disappearance. Sarah had been in agreement therefore that the younger girl had gone off of her own free will, so there was little point mentioning her absence at the station. Yet it also reinstated the likelihood that Julia, given she'd left all that behind, almost certainly hadn't gone by choice.

'Three days? That's no great length of time, now, is it?' the bewhiskered officer had insisted, waving away her concerns.

'Well, nay, I suppose not. But Julia, she's never afore—'

'She'll turn up, you'll see.' *Like the proverbial bad penny; your kind usually do*, his eyes had seemed to add.

'And if she don't, sir? What then?'

'Has it occurred to you that she might not want to be found?'

'Well . . . nay, but I don't think—'

'Something to consider then. Look,' he'd relented when Sarah showed no signs of budging, 'we have her description and will keep an eye out for her. I'm afraid there's nothing more we can do.'

And that had been that. Many cared little for people, particularly women, who slipped below the line of moral respectability. It was simple in their eyes: choose to live a sinful existence, accept whatever fate befell you. Sarah was certain that whether Julia's bloated corpse washed up in the river, was found broken and beaten in some ginnel, or she turned up healthy and well, it was all the same to him and his ilk.

She'd relayed the brief meeting to Jewel shortly before with a touch of bitterness but no surprise. As she'd pointed out, in their line of work, assault and even murder was an occupational hazard. That the worst could occur with every customer, they acknowledged with grim acceptance.

'Not that me and the girls are particularly close,' Sarah admitted. 'It just felt like the right thing to do, lass, you know? Someone had to at least try summat, for their mam wouldn't get around to it.' Sighing, she shrugged. 'If they return, they return. If not . . . Well, I can but pray that they're safe and wish them both well.'

Despite the earliness of the hour, the girls' mother was already out, propping up the inn's counter, drowning her self-pity in funds she'd begged from Sarah. Jewel's patience with the selfish article was wearing thin, though Sarah, God alone knew why, seemed to take in her stride everything her sister threw at her.

'You still for taking the little 'un to Minnie's today?'

asked Sarah now, and tears immediately sprang to Jewel's eyes. 'Ay, it's all right, lass, if you've changed your mind.'

'It's not that. Oh, Sarah, it's all ruined.'

'Julia's brass? Is that it?'

Jewel raised her head and her face flushed pink. 'I didn't want to steal it, you understand? It was for the child, to buy her a brighter future.'

'You were desperate. I get it, lass, don't fret. You do what you must for your kiddies. That's a mother's job.'

'But what will I do now? Louise has taken the lot. I'm out of work, haven't a penny to my name, will *never* find enough to pay Mrs Maddox's fee—'

'Come on, dry your eyes.'

'But Sarah, it's hopeless. *How* will I—?'

'I'll pay.'

'What?'

'Rather than give Minnie a lump sum, we'll see if she'll allow me to pay weekly for the child's upkeep until new parents are found. I were for putting the self-same notion to Louise but, well, given how frail the poor divil she birthed turned out to be . . .'

'Aye.' Sarah was right, Jewel saw it now. Neither hers nor Julia's money could have made a difference to *that* poor soul.

'Please,' Sarah continued. 'Let me do it for thee.' She extracted some coins and pressed them into Jewel's palm. 'Here. Give her that to be getting along with.'

Jewel was almost too choked to speak. 'You'd do that for me?'

Sarah nodded.

'But why?'

'Because you're a good lass with a golden heart. For despite the pain that's eating away at thee at the thought of parting with your daughter, you're willing to suffer it to put her first. I'd say you're one of the bravest lasses I know.'

Now, when Jewel burst into silent sobs, Sarah let her cry. She put her arms around her and hugged her close, and Jewel clung to her.

'It's *killing* me.'

'Eeh, lass. I know.'

'Will I die from it, this agony?'

'Nay.' Sarah's voice was husky with emotion. 'You'll bear it, somehow.'

'She will be all right, won't she? Mrs Maddox will honour her promise?'

'Fret not over that at least,' answered Sarah without hesitation. 'Minnie shall find her nowt but the very best people.'

'And she'll care for her well until then?'

'That you could even wonder at it. Some, aye, are wholly unqualified for the task of hand-rearing babies – not Minnie. What she don't know ain't worth knowing.'

Ada Bickerstaff entered Jewel's thoughts and she shuddered. 'I almost gave her up to an infant killer, Sarah. She insisted no one but her was to enter their room so as not to disturb them – *how* could I be so blind? Louise told me what she were. *Baby farmer.* But I'd never heard the term afore, and when I questioned her, she insisted—' She broke off suddenly as the memory of their conversation flooded back. She lifted her head to look at Sarah. 'Did Louise know what Bickerstaff was about?' she whispered. Then with dread: 'Please tell me Louise didn't know.'

'I'll not lie to thee, lass, she likely did. Though some mothers, victims like yourself, pay baby farmers believing care will be provided, others know the truth. There's an understanding of sorts that the child's chances of survival will be slim.'

Angel makers. That's how the girl had referred to them. Of course, it was all making sense now.

'Whether her child had been born in Bolton or Manchester, weak or robust ... she didn't want it,' Sarah continued. 'Adopted out or snuffed out, so long as it were off her hands one way or another, it didn't matter. Mind, she didn't expect the end result to fall to her; that's why she sought out a baby farmer in the first place. To her, it were less personal, like. Luckily for her conscience – and mine, for I were witness to it, weren't I? – the child arrived as it did: at death's door through sheer fate alone. Had Louise not intervened, it still wouldn't have lived. I'm certain of that.'

'How can you speak of it so calmly? You don't agree with it, surely?'

'Course I don't. But what could I have done? She's a grown lass; aye, with a callous streak beneath, to boot, like her mother. Nowt I could have said would have changed her mind.'

'She would have let me send my child to the slaughter, though, too. What say if I'd changed my mind soon after handing her over, gone back to reclaim her, only to find ...'

'Aye, you're right. And it happens, lass, too: some never hear from their child again. Most are too ashamed or frickened to probe, or take their worries to the police, and so it goes on, with baby farmers continuing their trade undetected.'

'How could Louise risk that? How could she be so wicked?'

'You mebbe deciding you'd made a mistake ... perhaps she didn't think that far ahead.'

'She still should have *told* me, Sarah.'

'What would you have done had you discovered the truth?'

'Left! Immediately!'

'And gone where?'

Jewel opened her mouth but, to this, she didn't have an answer.

'Happen in her mind, shielding thee from this foulness was her way of doing you a kindness. She knew you couldn't keep your child and mebbe thought you'd be stuck getting rid of it, if not with the Bickerstaff one. Who knows? But she saw thee as a friend, I reckon. She fetched thee here with her, didn't she? Whether she did or not, I think the intention to help thee was there.'

Reluctantly, Jewel knew she couldn't deny that. In her own way, Louise had been there for her. She hadn't had to take her under her wing, had she? And the girl hadn't wanted anything in return, can't have done, for she'd had nothing to give. Louise had done it because she wanted to.

'Now, why don't you go and put my proposal to Minnie?' A sad smile touched Sarah's lips when Jewel's arms tightened instinctively around her daughter. 'If it's what you want, of course.'

'It is. It has to be.'

'Then I think it's time, lass. Prolonging things will only make it harder on the pair of youse.'

Jewel's voice faltered. 'You'll be here when I get back?'

'I'll be here,' Sarah whispered. 'Good luck to thee. Be strong.'

*

If Jewel hadn't willed herself on with every step, she would never have got to Kirby Street.

Her every instinct was telling her to turn tail and run, but she silenced it with the mantra she'd adopted months ago: *I must. There's no other way. I must.*

Eliza welcomed her inside then discreetly took herself

off to make tea to give her and Minnie some privacy. Taking a deep breath, Jewel looked to the older woman, sitting smiling softly by the hearth.

'Hello, lass. Come on in, proper like, and sit yourself down.'

She took the chair opposite. 'Ta, thanks.'

Minnie's voice was gentle. 'You all right?'

'Aye. Nay. I hate myself for this, all of it. How have I got here, Mrs Maddox? *How* did things get to *this*?'

'Don't bottle it up, lass,' insisted Minnie when Jewel attempted to gulp down the tears that hadn't been too far away all morning. 'Let it out and gain some relief. There's no shame in showing emotion.'

For the next few minutes, she did just that. Holding her daughter close, her bitter weeping mingled with the sound of the crackling fire. Finally, she wiped her eyes and nodded. 'You were right. I can breathe a little easier now.'

'I'm glad. Now, drink your tea, there's a good lass.'

Eliza had placed it on a side table by her elbow and, between sips, Jewel explained to Minnie the situation and Sarah's generous offer.

'She's a kind soul. Course I'm in agreement to that, aye.'

'Really?' She closed her eyes in relief. 'Eeh, Mrs Maddox, thank you.'

'And lass?'

'Aye?'

'I'll find the very best parents for the little angel there that I can. Never fret on that. You have my word.'

Tears returned to Jewel's throat, making it impossible to respond. Instead, she conveyed her overwhelming gratitude with her eyes.

'Now, there's just a few things I need to ask of thee, if that's all right?'

'Aye.'

'Has the babby developed any health problems since the birth? The labour, it's not had no effect on her?'

'Nay, none.'

Minnie nodded, satisfied. 'And does she have a name?'

'I thought it best not to. You know?'

'I do, lass. Some prefer it that way.'

'Is there owt else you need to know, Mrs Maddox?'

'Aye, just one more thing.' A small smile deepened the lines around her mouth. 'What's *your* ruddy name? By gum, d'you know, I don't even know?'

'It's Jewel, Mrs Maddox.'

The sharp gasp from Minnie, and the clanking of Eliza's cup as she dropped it on to the table to cover her mouth with her hand, rent the air. Jewel stared at them in puzzlement.

'What is it? What's wrong?'

'Who . . . ?' Minnie was gazing at her open-mouthed. '*Who* did you say?'

'Why Jewel, for that's my name.'

The old woman rose from her chair. 'It can't be, it can't.'

'It's uncommon, I know. Folk allus react in surprise when I introduce myself,' she said, frowning in confusion as Minnie began pacing the floor. 'But Lord, never to this extent . . . Is tha all right?'

Receiving no response, Jewel looked instead to Eliza for help but, like the other woman, she, too, had paled and was wringing her hands. *What was going on?*

'Mrs Maddox?' Jewel crossed the room and touched her shoulder, bringing her to a juddering halt. 'Mrs Maddox, you're not well. Come, sit down.'

'Sorry. I . . . I'm sorry.'

'What made you react so?' she asked when she'd guided her back to her chair. 'Eliza, too. What is it?'

Minnie cleared her throat. She stared at her for a long moment then cleared her throat again. 'The night you went into labour, when Sarah called here asking for my services ... she just said that her niece's friend needed help, never mentioned your name. And then again yesterday, I never thought to ask, I ... I never ... could *never* have guessed ...'

'Guessed what? *What*, Mrs Maddox?'

'I once knew someone with the self-same name as yours. But it's *impossible*,' she added, almost to herself. Then she looked past Jewel slowly to stare into space, and her lips mouthed the name of another: *Sarah*. 'Oh my God,' she choked.

Jewel's bafflement had reached fever pitch. 'Sarah? What about her? Will someone please tell me what the divil's going on?'

Eliza settled on her haunches in front of Jewel and took her hand in hers. Her expression was one of fearful expectancy and deep pity. 'Lass?'

'What? What is it?'

'Are you Flora's girl?'

Now, it was Jewel's turn to ask: 'Who did you say?'

'Is your mam Flora Nightingale?'

She glanced away from her to Minnie, who was sitting on the edge of her seat wide-eyed, awaiting her answer. 'Aye. But how ... ?'

'Mother of God, I don't believe it,' Eliza whispered, whilst the older woman promptly burst into tears.

'Who are youse? How do you know my mam?'

'She were my neighbour; oh, the best friend a body could ask for,' sobbed Minnie, holding tight to Eliza, who had hurried to comfort her.

'That can't be. She ain't ever stepped foot in Manchester in her life; least not that I know of.'

'It's the truth. She dwelled right there, beyond yon bricks.' Minnie pointed across to the adjoining wall. 'She moved after Fred's death, when you were but a babby, to be nearer to her brother in Bolton town.'

Jewel's mouth formed an O. Why hadn't Mam ever told her they had lived here in this city? She'd assumed that the town she'd grown up in had always been her home. But if this *was* correct, and this woman and her mam had been such firm friends, why hadn't they stayed in touch? It didn't make sense.

'How is she, lass, Flora?' Tears still streamed down Minnie's lined cheeks. 'She's well?'

'Aye, yes. But, I don't, don't understand what's . . . You clearly felt a lot for her, Mrs Maddox, so what occurred? Why did youse lose contact?'

'I forgot about it, you see.' Moaning softly, Minnie rocked back and fro. 'I dressed thee and watched Flora carry thee home, but I'd forgot.'

'Min, think about this you're saying,' Eliza told her, tone deep with warning.

'I have thought, oh, have I! Long and hard, and round and round, for the past seventeen years. I vowed if I ever got the chance to put this to bed, to confess what I did, I would. They need to know.'

'But Min—'

'Nay, Eliza. I'll speak it. I must.'

Eliza made to protest further; then her shoulders sagged and she nodded. She and the old woman turned to Jewel with what could only be described as pure dread.

Throughout the women's war of wills, she'd simply gazed on in confusion, understanding nothing. Now, fingers of apprehension snaked down her spine. She lifted her brows hesitantly. 'What is it tha must confess?'

'I forgot about it,' repeated Minnie. 'I for*got* about the birthmark on your shoulder.'

Jewel's hand strayed up involuntarily to the distinctive marking stamped there beneath her clothing. 'What d'you mean?'

'Flora entrusted me to mind her child. And I did, barely took my eyes from her, but it were no good. She died anyway. No rhyme nor reason for it, as sometimes happens in life. So peaceful, she looked. So bonny, like a true angel. And I knew it, knew without question that Flora would wither and follow her to the grave with the grief. I believed it were for the best, that I were preventing a cruelty. I removed that dead babe's clothing and I put it . . . I put it . . . on thee. And she looked at you, Flora, upon her return. She looked at you forra long minute and she took you home.

'A child bearing a birthmark that shouldn't have been there. A child she never questioned me about, not once. That she poured into all that love she had and more. Never a murmur from either of us. Just like it hadn't happened. But it did. It did. And in t' end, it came betwixt us, that deed. She left here needing to start afresh. Needed to flee the memories, the truth. Me. What I'd set in motion.

'But I'm making it right; now I am. God's sent you here. He saw, and He knows you must hear it. And now you have. I'm so sorry, so sorry, for everything.'

'I'll tell you a secret if you let me go.'

Jewel's head swayed in denial. 'Nay.'

'You can't tell a soul I've told you, mind. You must keep it to yourself.'

The memory of Benji's lies, which she hadn't given a single thought to since he first spewed them, were like knives in her brain. 'You're wrong.'

'*Your mam ain't your mam.*'

Yes, she was. She was. 'She is!'

'*It's the truth. I've heard whispers of it over the years.*'

Everyone knew. All of them. All except her. 'Mam. Mam. Mam!'

'Where you going? Eeh, lass, wait. Please, just let Minnie finish the telling—'

With a swipe of her arm, Jewel sent Eliza stumbling into the wall. Eyes glazed, step unsteady, she laid her daughter with the other babies on the bed and crossed the room.

'But you must know, Jewel. Please. Sarah, she—'

The slam of the door at her back extinguished Minnie's voice. Jewel ground to a halt in the centre of the road, closed her eyes and drew in a long, slow breath. Then she turned and made off at a sprint for Victoria Station.

Chapter 21

JEWEL'S FEET GUIDED her from the train, the fare for which she'd paid with Sarah's money, along the platform and out of the station into Trinity Street. For a full minute, she stood stock-still and, as Louise had done the day they arrived in Manchester, breathed in her own town's smoggy air.

The sky of late afternoon had dulled to sludgy mink and off-white clouds cloaked the mill chimneys in the distance. Once more, her feet set off, and she saw they were taking her towards Town Hall Square.

When next she paused, she was at her mother's front door. Again, she stood unmoving, staring at the paint-chipped wood, mind void of thought. Her hand raised itself to the handle but stopped before it could reach it. Her arm fell back to her side. She turned on her heel and walked away.

Bolton Park seemed to offer a whispered greeting as she passed through it, and dim awareness sparked within her. Then, as quickly, it dissipated, leaving now-familiar emptiness. She sat on a hilly rise, tucked her skirts around her and folded her hands in her lap.

Maria saw the procurer's address in the article I answered – has she yet learned of Bickerstaff's heinous crimes? Was the maid worried sick, been forced to tell someone? And what of

Mrs Kirkwood: has she mentioned our meeting in Manchester to her brother? Has he passed on the information to Mam? Have my lies been exposed? Does everyone know my secret? These worries, amongst the rest, had tormented Jewel incessantly over the weeks. Now, she gave not one of them a single care. Nothing mattered. How could it now, given what she knew? How could anything mean a damn thing ever again?

'Who am I?' she asked of a tree's swaying branches nearby. But, like herself, it didn't have the answer.

A moan broke from her and she tore up fistfuls of damp grass. Her whole life a lie? All of it? Who was her real mam, then? What of her father? Who was he? Did anyone know? Flora? Had Fred before he died? What about her uncle and aunt? They clearly knew she wasn't of Flora's flesh – how else had Benji discovered it otherwise? He had to have overheard it from them. Everyone she'd thought she knew, whispering about her throughout the years, discussing and judging and tittering at her sordid mess of a life. And not one – not *one* – with enough decency to tell her the truth. Apart from Benji. Him, of all people. The irony would be almost laughable if it wasn't lacerating her heart to ribbons.

So why was she here, instead of in Flora's kitchen, demanding an explanation? She hadn't an answer to this either. Nothing at all made the slightest bit of sense.

Some time later – how long, Jewel couldn't say, wasn't aware of anything any more – a burst of giggles caught her attention. She turned her gaze to a cluster of bushes; beyond them, Maria and what must be her sister, given their likeness, walked arm in arm.

Of course, it was Sunday. It should have occurred to her that the maid might be enjoying her day off here. Though her eyes creased to see her friend, she didn't call out or go to her. It was like all life had been sucked from her; she could do nothing and felt even less.

'Jewel? Nay, it can't be her . . .' Spotting her moments later, Maria stared wide-eyed. 'Well, bugger me, it is. Jewel, lass! Over here!'

She tried to lift her hand in greeting but failed. Sighing, she watched the females hurry towards her.

'Eeh, lass. What are you doing *here*? When did yer get back?'

'I don't recall.' Jewel's voice sounded queer to her own ears.

'Are you all right?' Studying her more closely and realising she wasn't, the maid turned to her sister: 'Lass, go on and wait for me by the gate. Look at me,' she added quietly to Jewel when they were alone. She put a finger under her friend's chin and brought her head around to face her. 'Speak, lass. What's occurred? The babby . . . ?'

'I gave birth to a girl.' Jewel's chest tightened in searing loss.

'Was she born well, like?'

'Aye. Perfect.'

''Ere!' Maria exclaimed suddenly, grasping Jewel's wrist, 'I heard about that Bickerstaff one you went to. God above, who'd have thought it? What happened?'

'I weren't aware of owt whilst under her roof. Police came and I left with another lass. She put me up 'til I had the child.'

The maid nodded. 'I figured you would have found another procurer. But by hell . . .' She shook her head. 'I ain't half been worried about thee, lass. I'll be frank, I've been on t' brink of calling to your mam's for weeks and confessing what I knew, just didn't know what to do upon hearing of Bickerstaff's arrest. I didn't, mind,' she added quickly when Jewel turned to look at her.

'Don't fret, no one's aware of owt. I figured I'd give thee a bit longer, see if you showed, and if not then it were time to come clean. Thanks be to God you're here and you're well.'

Jewel looked away. 'Ta for not telling,' she offered, though, underneath, she really couldn't have cared less. Not now. Not any more.

'You found another procurer well enough, then, aye?'

She swallowed hard at the memory of her meeting with Mrs Maddox earlier and all that had gone with it. 'Aye.'

'Eeh, lass.' Maria covered her hand with hers. 'Was it so hard, saying goodbye? To the babby, I mean.'

'Aye,' she whispered.

'I am sorry, Jewel.'

'So am I.'

They were silent for a while until the maid asked, 'Did your mam believe your tale, then? She weren't suspicious at all?'

A ball of something hard and clogging settled in Jewel's guts. She shook her head. 'I ain't seen her yet.'

'What? Why? Did you go straight to Mr Birch's?'

'Nay. I came straight here. I ain't seen none of them.'

'Right, what's afoot?' Though Maria spoke with concern, her tone was firm. 'Come on, out with it. Summat's to do here; you're not yourself at all—'

'My mam's not my mam.'

'Eh? What does that mean?'

'I don't know. I were told ... told summat, and, well ... Oh, Maria.' She burst into tears and hugged her knees. 'I don't know what the hell is happening!'

'Ay, come here. All right, now. Shh.' The maid rocked her in her arms as one would a child. 'Tell me, what's all this you've heard?'

With stops and starts, intermingled with gasping sobs, Jewel relayed Minnie's confession. 'I mean, what am I meant to do with this, Maria, you tell me that? My head, inside . . . It's like it belongs to another. I don't know who I am, don't know what to think, to feel, to *do*—'

'Shh. Eeh, Jewel love.' But that's all Maria had, not that Jewel blamed her – what on earth else *could* she say? That she was stunned by the revelation was clear to see. 'I just, just don't know what to say, like, I . . .'

'Aye, me neither.'

'Can't you go and see your mam, ask her yourself?'

'I don't . . . I can't. For what if she admits it and makes it real? She's my own mam! Except what if she ain't?'

'Right, well.' Maria thought for a moment then nodded. 'If it were me, I'd do nowt.'

'Aye?'

Maria shrugged. 'For the time being, at least. After all, what if this Maddox wench is lying? Lord knows why someone would about summat so awful, but well . . . You never know, do you? Takes all sorts to make a world – bleedin' mad buggers as well as the rest of us.'

'Nay. She knew too much, about me, Mam . . . Besides, what would she gain from it? It just don't make sense.'

And yet the more she thought about her friend's advice, the better it sounded. She was dimly aware that she was being a coward not confronting this, but she couldn't. *God, give me strength, I just can't bear it.*

'Happen I could sleep on it? What d'you reckon, Maria? Should I wait and see how my mind sits the morrow?'

'If you think that's best, then aye. Will you return to Mawdsley Street?'

'If Mr Birch still wants me.' Jewel bit her lip with thoughts of what he might know, had Mrs Kirkwood

745

decided to get a message to him. 'Has your sister mentioned . . . anything to thee, Maria?' she asked cautiously. She couldn't bear to admit even to her friend where she'd been and with whom. The depravity she'd lived with these past months, the things she'd witnessed . . . The shame of it was crippling. God above, if Maxwell should be aware . . .

'Nay, she ain't said nowt. Mind, he promised your position would be waiting for thee, didn't he? My sister's served the family well, lass, but I'm sure yon master shall be glad to have thee back.'

'I ain't half missed— erm, little Constance,' Jewel corrected herself in time, her breathing quickening at what she'd almost blurted out. Though it was true in part: she did long to see the young miss. 'Well, them all, really. I'll be happy to be back, aye.'

'Shall we walk back? Or d'you need more time to gather your thoughts? Just say the word, lass. I'm here whatever you decide.'

'What did I do to deserve a friend like thee, eh?' Though Jewel nudged her playfully, her lip wobbled and grateful tears glistened on her lashes. 'Thank you,' she whispered.

'Eeh, lass.'

'Come on.' Jewel rose and held out her hands, and when Maria placed hers into them helped her to her feet. 'Let's go.'

And yet the nearer the three of them got to their destination, the worse Jewel's pain grew. Being in such close proximity to Back Cheapside and her mother after so long apart was heart-wrenching. Not wanting to see her for fear of what she might learn was all that kept her from running the short distance at full pelt, though her longing to see the woman she loved with every part of her was nigh on impossible to suppress. By the time they reached Mawdsley Street, she was shaking and once more on the brink of tears. Before approaching the Birches' door, she paused to suck in some deep breaths.

'You certain you're all right, Jewel?' asked Maria gently.

She nodded. 'I'm a big girl with broad shoulders; I'll be fine.' She had to be, didn't she?

'Well, I'd best get back in, else my mistress will be having kittens.'

'You go,' Jewel told her. 'And Maria? Eeh, I've missed thee.'

The maid winked, flashed a grin then scuttled to her own residence across the road.

Looking down at the girl beside her, Jewel pulled an apologetic face. 'Thanks for covering my position whilst I've been . . . away. I am sorry to be leaving thee out of a job, lass.'

'Don't be daft, nay.' Just like her sister in personality, it would seem, as well as looks, she gave a warm smile. 'I knew the score afore you left, didn't I, knew you'd be back, that it were but temporary?'

Jewel smiled then peered towards the house. 'Are the family home, do you know?'

'Mr Roland were out when I left, but the young miss and their father should be present. 'Ere, I reckon Mr Birch shall be happy to see thee. He made mention of you regular in your absence.'

Something fluttered in Jewel's breast. 'He did?'

'Aye. Said as how he'd been sad to see thee go. That you're a fine servant – the best.'

'Oh. Aye, yeah. Well, that were nice of him,' she insisted, whilst inside, the small flare dimmed and died. With a soft sigh, she knocked at the door.

'Hello.' Clearly taken aback to see her, it was a few seconds before Maxwell spoke.

'Hello, Mr Birch.'

'You're returned? Your relative has regained good health?'

'Aye.' She felt herself redden a little, and not just at the deception. Those eyes of his . . . She'd almost forgotten how arresting they were. 'Aye, I'm back.'

Still, he continued to stare at her, his lips slightly parted. Finally, he ran a hand through his dark hair and laughed quietly. 'My apologies, Jewel. Please, come in.'

'Hello there, Miss Constance. By, how you've grown!'

The giggling youngster, who had come toddling down the hall to greet her, held out her arms. Picking her up and holding her close, tears pricked Jewel's eyes. Oh, but it felt good to be back.

'I'll just collect my things, Mr Birch,' announced Maria's sister, smiling, as she headed for the kitchen. 'And I just want to say thanks to thee for being a fair and pleasant master. I've enjoyed working here, really I have.'

As Maxwell offered kind farewells to the girl, Jewel looked on with a smile, though inside, as much as she felt mean about it, she was willing her to make haste and leave. She just wanted things to go back to how they were, to be alone with the family, as she used to be. Normality was what she craved right now more than anything else.

Some time later when her friend's sister had gone and Constance had been taken to the nursery for a nap, Jewel headed downstairs to her haven. The familiar surroundings were like balm for the soul. She ran and threw herself on to the bed. Hugging the bedclothes, she closed her eyes, and for the first time allowed herself to think about her daughter. Crushing emotion slammed home. Her arms ached for the touch of her tiny, warm body, and her milk-heavy breasts, bound tightly as she'd seen Louise do to dry them up more quickly, throbbed with their need to sustain, to nurture.

She hadn't even said goodbye. So consumed had she been with the unfathomable news, she'd simply left the child and fled. Though if she thought about it, perhaps that had been for the best. For had she been forced to speak to her, to look into her baby's perfect little face and tell her she was leaving her, she'd have faltered for certain, wouldn't have been able to see it through. Then what would they have done? She'd have spoiled everything for the child.

'I couldn't keep thee,' Jewel whispered into the sheets. 'But know that I love thee, oh, I do, and that I'll think of thee always, every minute. I don't care how you were begot. That matters not a bit any more. You were perfect, lass, a true angel. Please, forgive me—'

'May I speak with you, Jewel?'

'Oh, sir!'

Maxwell came down the remaining stairs with his hands held high, but his sheepish smile and apology for startling her died to see her tear-streaked face. He lowered his arms slowly, brows knotting in a frown. 'Jewel? You've been crying. What's wrong?'

'Nowt, sir, honest. Really, I'm fine,' she assured him, scrubbing at her eyes and cheeks with her sleeve. 'I'm happy to be back is all.'

'May I?' He motioned to the bed and, when she nodded, sat on the edge. Head lowered, he glanced up at her then looked away again quickly. 'I'd . . . like to ask you something, Jewel.'

'Aye, owt. What is it?'

'Are you . . . ?' He shifted uncomfortably. 'What I mean is, do you . . . ?'

'Aye, sir?'

'Forgive me. I'm loath to embarrass or upset you further. However, I must ask.' He dropped his tone. 'Are you in the black place, like before?'

'The black place?' She shook her head. 'Sorry, sir, I don't know what—'

'Do you have the urge again to do yourself harm? Only you don't seem yourself at all. The moment you returned, I detected a sadness about you and I thought—'

'Well, tha thought wrong.' Anger and shame and sorrow and suffocating grief were swirling inside her like a bowl of ingredients taking a thrashing from a wooden spoon. She dug her nails into her palms, terrified she would explode.

'I understand, you know.'

His gentle tone did nothing to quell the flames. 'How could *you* possibly understand?' she murmured with bitter incredulousness.

'I know my sister asked you to look after me.'

A little of her frown melted. She blinked in confusion. 'Did she, or did she not?'

'Aye, but—'

'I attempted self-murder a number of times following my wife's death.'

His confession knocked the wind from her sails. She gasped. 'Sir?'

'I never anticipated finding love again after Roland's mother. Therefore, when Mary was taken from me . . . I could think of no way to continue living without her. It was like a darkened shroud had wrapped itself around me, obscuring the light. Nothing and no one could penetrate it for many months, during which I ...' Maxwell paused to look at her. 'Well. Let's just say I was unsuccessful, and that I thank God on my knees each night for sparing me. So you see, Jewel,' he added, hesitantly reaching out and cupping her face, 'I *do* understand.'

Silent tears were coursing down her face. 'I'm sorry.'

'Talk to me,' he whispered. 'A problem shared is a problem halved.'

'I ... can't, sir. Though please know I've no intention of doing owt daft to myself. I promise thee, I haven't, I just ...' She heaved a shuddering breath. 'Please don't fret over me. I'll be all right.'

He was staring at her intently. Though he didn't speak, slowly his thumb moved to caress her cheek.

Jewel's heart tripped over itself in two or three hammering beats. Their heads were no great distance apart and, as she locked eyes with him, she sensed him move closer just a fraction.

'If ever you need to speak to someone, Jewel ...'

'I know,' she murmured. 'That offer also holds for thee.'

'I'm glad you're back.'

Though the words of Maria's sister from earlier whispered in her mind of him merely having missed her servanting skills, the corners of her mouth lifted nonetheless. 'And me. I ... missed you, Mr Birch.'

His eyes darkened with feeling. He opened his mouth to speak, but instead it was Roland's voice that broke the silence:

'Father? Are you down there?'

They sprang apart as if they had been scorched.

Maxwell stood quickly and cleared his throat, and there was a definite flush to his neck and jaw. 'Yes, son. I'll be with you in one moment.'

She felt shaky with confusion, embarrassment, *euphoria*; though all emotion seeped from her, leaving her dead cold inside, at Maxwell's next words. Turning to her, it was as though he had to force his eyes to meet hers:

'I'm so sorry, Jewel. I don't know what I was . . . I must go.'

'Sir, wait.' She reached out to touch his sleeve, but he sidestepped her.

'I'm sorry,' he murmured again. 'I can't, I . . . I'm utterly mortified.' With that, he almost sprinted up the stairs.

Jewel stood gazing at the door above for an age. Prickles of heat spread across her body; she thought she would die from the shame. What had just happened? She'd felt something then, between them. And she'd liked it, she had. He was mortified? Humiliation burned. He'd remembered her lowly station too late, was that it? He was angry with himself – with her – that the boundary had been crossed? But she . . . Oh, she really did . . . *I like thee, sir*, she said in her mind. *I care for thee.*

'I . . . love thee,' she said out loud to the emptiness.

God help her, she did.

*

'Your mother must be glad to have you home?' Roland smiled at Jewel across the dining table.

'Aye, sir,' she lied quietly, whilst praying he wouldn't ask her more regarding Flora. Fortunately, he didn't:

'As are we, little nightingale,' he continued instead. 'Isn't that so, Father?'

She glanced up tentatively from the tray she carried when silence greeted them. Maxwell's full attention was on his food, though he hadn't touched a morsel.

'Father?' Roland laughed.

'Hm?'

'Are you with us this evening?'

'Yes, of course. Sorry, I – I'm rather tired.'

Jewel willed him to look at her but his eyes remained firmly on his plate. Biting back hurt, she dragged her feet back downstairs.

Since the incident in the kitchen a few hours ago, she'd mulled over every detail, again and again, until the last of the day's light had scattered from the sky and her head ached. Still, it made little sense to her. What had it meant? The way they had looked at each other. The way it made her feel.

She was no stranger to what she perceived as love. Jem Wicks had awakened the first flush of attraction in her, and she recognised the signs once more now. But this was different, she saw it instinctively. The intensity was crushing, the yearning of her body for Maxwell's like hot gushes through her veins that left her almost mad for the touch of him, his kiss. And her heart, it, too, was experiencing something altogether new, for the depth of her feelings went beyond mere carnal urges.

She cared for him fiercely, wanted only the best for him, his happiness. What he'd revealed to her about his own dangerous melancholy had struck inside her chest like a blade. The thought of him hurt or sad made her want to cry, and she longed to protect him, shield him from the bad things that life had a habit of throwing in your path, never wanted him to know a moment's sorrow ever again. And that's how she knew: it was love. Genuine, pure, cut-glass-clear love. She wanted no one else, either today or any other. It was all him.

Yet he'd been mortified at the slightest prospect, and that was that. Her fantastical thinking was hers alone, and would remain so; must, for both their sakes.

Busying her physical form with her chores did nothing to distract her obsessive brain – and she knew it would only worsen once she retired to bed. The quiet darkness had a way of suspending a troubled soul in relentless, regurgitated thought, broken only by either sleep or the rising of a new sun – she knew which it would be for her tonight – and she was dreading it.

Would she ever know peace of mind again? she wondered fleetingly as she climbed the stairs to the house, to ask of the family if they required anything else for today. Could she cope with these ever-occurring difficulties, and the heartache with which they went hand in hand, for a whole lifetime? The answer came to her immediately. No, she couldn't. She'd already endured enough for anyone – thrice over.

Upon entering the hall, she encountered Roland on his way to bed. Her surprise that he was forgoing his usual late-night rendezvous must have shown, for his handsome face spread in a grin.

'It's old and boring I've become, little nightingale. Ah-ha, but for very good reason. Yes, indeed.'

'Oh?' she allowed herself to enquire, her curiosity winning through.

'It just so happens that, whilst you were away, I met a pretty young filly for whom I've fallen hook, line and sinker.' His delight grew. 'We're engaged to be married.'

'Eeh, Mr Roland, sir. I'm that pleased for thee.' And she meant it. Perhaps now, the strain of his wanton behaviour on his father would lift, and not before time.

Roland continued on his way, whistling merrily, and Jewel was still smiling as she went to knock at the drawing-room door. Receiving no answer and assuming Maxwell had already retired for the night, she entered with the thought of tidying the space before heading back to her kitchen. However, she quickly saw that he wasn't in bed at all but fast asleep at his desk. She paused for a moment. Then, biting her lip, she crossed the floor towards him.

The sleeves of his crisp white shirt were rolled to the elbow, his collar loose. Head on his arms on the desk, he was dead to the world. Jewel's eyes softened.

'You work too hard,' she whispered with a light stroke of his hair. She turned and padded back out.

After undressing and climbing into bed, she lay staring at the ceiling. She pictured Maxwell up there, oblivious to everything, to her and her feelings, and ached to return to him. Of course, she resisted. But his image stayed stubbornly at the forefront of her mind.

Tomorrow, she would go to see her mother. Her guts churned at the prospect. What would she hear? *Was* Minnie Maddox somehow mistaken, as Maria had suggested? She clung to the possibility like her life depended on it, which it did, then quickly evicted the matter from her head.

A porcelain face with rosebud mouth and light blue eyes soon swam in to take her thoughts' place, and she closed her eyes on the sear of pain. 'My own babby,' she told her over the miles. 'Please be well and happy.' *I beg of thee, merciful God, love and keep her in my place, always.*

The last words Sarah had uttered to her before leaving for Minnie's called to her from somewhere far away, and Jewel's lids fluttered open. *'Be strong.'* She smiled sadly. The woman had been a tower of strength over the last few months. Jewel missed her calm, unassuming presence already. Her failure to say goodbye to her at least, she knew she'd always regret.

To Jewel's surprised relief, tiredness descended on her. Before it consumed her completely, the vague memory of Minnie making mention of Sarah before she fled the house came back to her, to linger unclear on her mind's outskirts. A frown accompanied her to sleep.

Chapter 22

'YOU BE GOOD for Lizzie. I'll see thee soon, there's a good lass.' Jewel handed Constance over to her nursemaid then donned her shawl. 'I shan't be long,' she told the domestic, 'I just have an errand to run.'

Assuming she was off to purchase foodstuff for the family's meal later, Lizzie nodded and waved her on her way, and Jewel reluctantly set out to visit her mother.

Terror-induced sickness washed over her every step of the way and she was forced to stop several times to regain her composure. By the time she reached the house, her nerves were shot to pieces. As she'd done yesterday, she paused outside, unable to knock. And yet at the same time, she longed to see the woman beyond the door. She'd missed her something awful, had yearned for her during those difficult months – none more so than when in the throes of her agonising labour. And now here she was, actively prolonging the separation because of what after all might be one old woman's incorrect rambling. This hope Jewel clung to out of sheer desperation. Though, deep down, she knew the truth of it.

Then, suddenly, another notion occurred to her and her eyes narrowed in thoughtful interest. What if she said nothing? The idea sounded ludicrous at first, but the more she mused on it, the more its appeal grew. Say she simply pretended nothing had happened, erased from her mind all she'd discovered – what then? Everything would stay exactly the same, wouldn't it? Life could return to normal and no one would be any the wiser.

Could she do it? Jewel gnawed her lip in contemplation. Bury down inside the secret she was now privy to and just carry on as before? Was it possible? Would it eat away at her until she spoke out, or could she really try to forget about it? More to the point, did she want to?

'Aye,' she heard herself say. 'I do.'

To live a lie seemed, in her mind at this minute, the lesser of two evils. The reality of what exposing her knowledge of her parentage would mean filled her with such horror it left her gasping for breath. She could lose her mother. It would rip an irreparable hole in their relationship that could never be mended. How *could* something of that magnitude ever be repaired? It was impossible, surely?

'Just say nothing, then?' Jewel asked herself. 'Let the whole thing go?' *For all our sakes*, her inner voice added, and a little of the torment lifted.

She nodded once, twice. Then she grasped the handle and opened the door.

'Lass?'

'Hello, Mam.'

'Oh, my bonny girl, come here!'

Jewel walked into her mother's waiting arms. As she'd feared, a sense of awkwardness marred the overdue embrace; she stiffened slightly at the woman's touch, though she did her best to ignore it.

Flora kissed her brow then motioned to a chair. 'Sit thee down, lass. By, it's blessed I am the day. How've you been?'

'Well and good, ta. You?'

'Not too shabby, aye. Mind, I'm all the better for seeing thee. We must never be parted again, you hear?' she scolded with mock-sternness. Then, smiling, she passed Jewel a cup of tea and sat down facing her. Her soft gaze lingered about her face. 'You sure you're all right?' she asked, and a slight frown appeared. 'You seem . . . different somehow. I don't know, can't put my finger on it. All the bloom's gone from your cheeks. You sickening for summat?'

'Nay, nay.' Jewel cursed inwardly as heat crept up her neck. 'Mebbe I'm tired is all. You not in work the day?' she added quickly to change the subject.

'This afternoon, aye. 'Ere, why not slip across with me – if you've the time to spare, that is? Your uncle and aunt and young Benji would be pleased to see thee, I bet.'

'Aye, we'll see.' This was a lie. She'd make some excuse later, had no intention of showing her face in that shop again if she could help it. Though she had to ask: 'How is Uncle Bernard?' After all, he was the only member of that family she held any real feeling towards.

'Ah, the usual. Hen-pecked to buggery and none the worse for it, you know?'

Jewel chuckled. 'Aye. He must love her a lot, you know – Aunt Esther.'

'Oh aye. Eeh, but rather him than me. That gob on her . . . talk about bleeding earholes.'

Nodding, Jewel laughed quietly again. A thaw was setting in and she welcomed it wholeheartedly. She'd missed this: her and her mam's easy chatter, putting the world to rights.

Mam.

The warmness dimmed somewhat in remembrance

and she beat the thoughts back with a feeling of panic. *Forget it, forget it. It matters not. It doesn't* . . .

'What's to do, lass?'

Flora's words came to her as though from a distance. She couldn't move, speak. For her eyes had strayed to the mantel top and the sight of the familiar piece had seized her in a hypnotic trap.

Following Jewel's gaze to the candlestick, Flora's voice was light with amused puzzlement: 'Lass? You gone daft?'

She couldn't uphold this pretence, had been foolish to think she could. It wouldn't leave her, not for a second, was killing her inside . . . She brought her stare back to her mother, and the name fell from her lips: 'Minnie Maddox.'

'Eh?'

'Minnie Maddox,' Jewel repeated, louder now.

Time seemed to halt in its tracks. Flora's cup slipped slowly from her hand and smashed on the hard, flagged floor. Eyes huge, she shook her head.

'She told me everything,' Jewel murmured. 'I know you're not my mam.'

'Lies. It's all, all lies—!'

'Nay. It ain't. Why didn't you *tell* me?'

The woman released a pent-up sigh. Her shoulders drooped and the corners of her quivering mouth followed. When finally she spoke, her tone was hollow. 'I've allus loved thee.'

'So it is true?'

'You're *my lass*!'

'No, no, no, no, *no*!' Panting with dumbfoundedness, Jewel swung her head. 'I've prayed 'til I ran out of words, convinced myself it were a mistake. But I knew. Deep down, I did. Your child, Flora and Fred Nightingale's long-awaited miracle . . . she died. Mrs Maddox passed me off as her, and you knew. You knew and said nothing.'

Hanging her head, Flora burst into tears.

'Who was I? One of Mrs Maddox's waifs? An unwanted she could do with as she liked, for there was no one to question my true whereabouts, miss me, care? Is that it?'

'I've allus loved thee,' repeated Flora brokenly, then winced when Jewel thumped the tabletop in fury.

'I was second best. I *am* second best. The one whose place I stole, she's from your flesh, the one you wanted. She's your daughter, not I—'

'Stop! I'll not hear that, for it's false, it is!'

'I don't believe you.' Jewel's devastation had reached manic proportions. 'I weren't nowt special. You were just desperate forra child. *Any* child would have done.'

'*You* . . .' Flora's eyes burned with passion. '*You* are Jewel Nightingale. Do you hear me? Well, do yer? You are my child. I am *your mother*. Not you, nor Minnie, nor any swine else can claim different. *Never*. You're my own precious jewel, same as you've allus been. Then, now, always. Right?' She grasped Jewel by her upper arms and shook her hard in desperation. '*Right?*'

'Mam.' She exhaled the word on a tortured breath. 'Oh, Mam!'

'Oh, my lass!'

Sobbing, they hugged tightly. For the next few minutes, neither spoke, simply poured out their grief and pain and love, feeding each other's souls with proof – *truth* – of their unbreakable bond.

'Who am I, Mam? Who am I really?' She felt Flora shake her head against her. 'Please. I have to know.'

'I don't know, and that's the truth.'

Crushing uncertainty left her desolate. She wept anew.

'You poor, poor lass.'

'Oh, Mam.'

'I'm so sorry, Jewel. I'd take this hurt off you in a heartbeat if I could. Eeh, dearest daughter.'

'"Dearest daughter",' she repeated in a whisper. In that moment, she thought the pain would kill her. 'Mam, there's summat I've not told thee.'

She must. How could she continue to keep her secret after all she'd just said to Flora? She was a hypocrite of the highest order, wasn't she? Blasting this woman for concealing the truth, when all the time . . . If there was one thing she'd learned this day, it was the importance of trust. Without it, what was the point in anything?

In broken snatches, Jewel told her mother everything. The ale, the trees. Benji. The shame, terror. Her plan to seduce Jem Wicks. The horse and cart and what she'd intended. The bribery and the scissors, the taking of Bernard's money. Bickerstaff. Canal Street and its occupants, the horrific birth. And her precious offspring. Her agony at the parting, and how much she missed her. She left out nothing.

'There's summat else – tha might as well hear it all,' Jewel continued when Flora had stumbled to her chair and was sitting, staring into space. 'I think I'm in love with my master, Mr Birch. He's thrice my age and a gentleman, to boot, and I've fallen for him.' Shrugging, she laughed mirthlessly. 'My life is a shambles. *I'm* a sodding shambles. So there you have it. I bet now you're wishing Mrs Maddox had given you another babby instead of me, ain't yer?'

For an age, Flora seemed incapable of speech. Then, voice flat: 'Come to me, lass.'

Jewel flew to her. Falling to her knees by her feet, she rested her head in her mother's lap. Flora stroked her hair and she closed her eyes. 'I've made a mess of everything.'

'Not thee. He's to blame for this, that foul young dog across the way.'

'What am I going to do, Mam?'

'We, my lass. You ain't alone with this burden any longer.'

'Eeh, Mam. I wish I'd come to thee sooner. I were just ... so ashamed and ... I just couldn't find the words—'

'I know, I know.'

'I've been that scared.'

Flora breathed slowly and her next words came through gritted teeth. 'Don't tha fear a thing, not no more.'

'What will happen now, with Benji?'

'Shh. That'll come later.'

'And ... what I said about Mr Birch?'

To this, Flora made no comment. Instead, she nodded decisively. 'First things first ...'

'Aye?'

'First things first,' the woman said again, straightening her shoulders. 'We fetch your babby home.'

Jewel's head snapped back to gape at her. 'Mam?'

'Is it what tha wants?'

'Yes! Oh, yes, more than owt, but ... ? What will folk say?'

'I care naught for that, and nor should thee. You've nowt to be ashamed for.'

'How would I manage, what with work and money; husbandless into the bargain—'

'*We*. Remember?'

Eyes swimming, Jewel crushed a hand to her mouth. 'You really mean it, Mam? *Thank* you. I love thee, I do.

Eeh, Mam, wait 'til you see her. She's an angel from heaven, really. When can we . . . ?'

'There's no time like the present.' Rising, Flora inclined her head across the room. 'Fetch me my shawl, lass.'

Jewel's joy was almost too much. How had she ever doubted this woman her pure and selfless heart? Why hadn't she confessed all to her sooner? She'd been such a coward, *such a fool*. But, God above, was this happening? She was to keep her daughter? The child was coming home? Jewel couldn't believe it, wouldn't until she was safely in her arms again. *Please don't let this all be a dream, sweet Lord.*

'Now I don't want thee fretting but I must say this, so take heed,' announced Flora, pausing by the door.

'What is it?'

'Yon babby might not still be where tha left her. Minnie could have found new parents for her already.'

The terrible prospect turned the blood in her veins to ice. With all the strength she could muster, she nodded bravely. 'I understand, Mam. But we must try.'

'That we must, and the sooner the better. Make haste, lass, come on.'

*

'Mam?'

'I'm all right. Just the memories, Jewel, you know?'

'Nay, I don't,' she answered truthfully – what did she know of anything any more? – and Flora winced.

'Course, aye. Sorry, my lass.' She nodded to the imposing building that she'd halted by. 'This here glassworks was where my Fred toiled many moons ago, along with Minnie's husband. The candlestick back home, it were presented when he passed away for his service to the company. All employees received one. I never mentioned that – Manchester, nor the rest – lest you probed further and my lies tripped me up,' she admitted.

Jewel nodded slowly in understanding. That explained then why Mrs Maddox owned the same one. The old woman, clearly sensing that the facts had been bent regarding how her mother came by hers, had withheld the truth, likely hadn't wanted to involve herself in the matter. All this information only now coming to light . . . What else had she yet to discover?

'Eeh, but I miss him.'

'Mam, did Father know . . . about me?'

'Nay. I think it were for the best, an' all. Now then,' she continued, fixing her stare on Minnie's dwelling. 'Let's do what we came here to.'

'You'll not be angry with her, will you? Mrs Maddox, I mean? She did the right thing in telling me; I did have a right to know. Besides, we'd not be here now, come to take my daughter home, if not for her confessing. I'd likely not ever have plucked up courage to tell thee had we not argued about my beginnings.'

'I'm not angry, lass. Truth be told, I've missed the wench deeply. I just couldn't . . . thought it best to put that part of my life behind me upon arriving in Bolton, didn't want to risk you finding out . . . Aye well. It came out in t' wash in t' end, eh, as things allus do.'

Mother and daughter trained their gazes back on the house. They took a simultaneous breath and crossed the street to Minnie's door.

'Hello, Eliza, love.'

'Flora? By!' Her amazement slipped. 'Will tha come in?' she asked hesitantly.

Flora nodded, and Jewel eagerly followed her inside, eyes darting straight to the bed, desperate for a glimpse of her daughter.

Minnie rose slowly from her chair, her dread-filled gaze locking with Flora's. 'Wench . . . Wench, I—'

'Hello, Minnie.' Flora held out her arms. After a long and confused hesitation, a stunned Minnie ambled into them.

'Oh. Eeh, love, I've missed thee. I had to tell Jewel, lass. I had to, for the act has ate away at me each day since. I believed it the right thing to do, I did, I—'

'It's all right, wench. I allus knew it would come out some day. You're right. Jewel deserved the truth. I were just too much of a coward to reveal it myself.'

'Mrs Maddox?' Scanning the infants for a third time, Jewel was becoming frantic. 'Where's my child? She ain't here. Where *is* she?'

Minnie and Eliza exchanged puzzled looks. 'You know where,' remarked the latter. 'You gave your consent, after all.'

Jewel couldn't breathe. 'She's gone?'

'Aye.'

She was too late. *No, no.* 'You've found new parents for her already?'

Minnie was frowning deeply. 'Sit down, lass.'

'Nay! Nay, I have to know where she is, I . . . I want her back. Mam knows everything, has vowed to support me . . . I want my daughter!'

'Sit down,' repeated the old woman. Her expression was serious. She nodded forcefully to a chair at the table. 'Seems I've been hoodwinked, and we need to figure out why . . . Please, Jewel.'

Jewel sat. She grasped one of Flora's hands and the two of them awaited Minnie's explanation with wide-eyed dread.

'Hoodwinked?' asked Flora.

'By who?' Jewel added.

'Sarah's sister came and collected your babby last night.'

'What?'

'She said as how you'd agreed, that Sarah was to raise her as her own—'

'That's lies!' Jewel leapt to her feet. 'Why would you believe that drunken mess? What the hell is her game? How could you hand my child over to her, the *state* of her. I must go there. I'll *kill* her!'

'Wait.'

Something in Minnie's tone made Jewel halt by the door. She turned questioningly.

'I'll tell thee why I let that woman take off with the child. It's because I assumed that Sarah, having discovered . . . I thought she wanted to make things right this time. She has a tie there, after all—'

'Tie? Discovered what? Tell me!'

'When your mother—' Minnie paused and shot Flora an apologetic look. 'When your *birth* mother brought you here that day, lass, she were just like you were – hurting. Difference being, she wore an icy mask that never slipped. It's a common front that a lot of women adopt; self-protection, like, to cover up their true feelings and keep at bay the pain of giving up their child. Anyroad, a few short months after Flora moved with thee to Bolton, your birth mother showed up at my door wanting you back.' She nodded sadly. 'I told her you'd gone to a new family already, that it were too late and nowt could be done, that she must believe you'd gone to a good home and to put thee from her mind.

'She bleated in my arms like a newborn lamb but accepted you would be happy and well cared for, and that this was for the best. It brought her some comfort, you know? Well, from that day, she became a regular visitor, and it grew into a friendship, aye. I were keen to keep an eye on her welfare; she liked the bottle too much, and her family were a no-good lot, with the reputation of it, to boot. I felt sorry for her – and guilty, aye. I couldn't have her tracking down Flora and demanding thee back, for that would have benefited no one. But by, she never forgot thee, lass. You allus – *allus* – held a piece of her heart.'

'Oh, wench.' Flora had her face in her hand, her sorrow tangible. 'That poor woman.'

Minnie nodded. 'As much as my own heart hurt for her, I knew Jewel was better off with thee. What was done was done. Uprooting the lass, wrenching her from you, who she saw as her mam, shattering your life in the process . . . It wouldn't have been right, nay. It wouldn't.'

Jewel had flopped back into her chair. Wordless, head bowed, she tried to process this fresh information. One thing, however, needed no extra thought: Mrs Maddox had done the right thing in leaving her in Flora's care. Had her birth mother showed up in Bolton, taken her away from Mam . . . It would have killed Flora, she was certain. Besides, from the little Minnie had just revealed, it was doubtful she'd have fared well in the other woman's care.

Having been raised by Flora had been a blessing, she realised. Although knowing that her real mother had come back for her, had wanted her after all, hadn't simply abandoned her without another thought, did make her feel ever so slightly better. She wasn't the unwanted she'd come to believe she was, not entirely. Oh, but the whole situation was such a sorry bloody *mess*.

'What has all this got to do with Sarah's sister taking

my daughter?' she asked, though, deep down, she already knew the answer.

That Minnie had wanted to tell her something about Sarah the last time she was here . . . How comfortable she herself had felt from the beginning in Sarah's presence, like she somehow knew her, though she couldn't understand why . . . It all made sense. As if, somehow, fate had finally brought them back together.

All this Jewel processed as though through a sheet of thick glass. Reality was muffled, emotions numbed. The truth was the truth, but it couldn't penetrate the clogging shock she was shrouded in.

'Sarah's your birth mother, lass,' confirmed Minnie, and Jewel accepted it with a nod. 'She came here looking for thee that evening after you fled. She'd been expecting thee back, were worried. I revealed who you were – had to – for Sarah deserved the truth, too, once you knew it. She left here promising to find thee, said that she'd put things right. So, when her sister came later for the child, I believed you'd returned to Canal Street, that you and Sarah had talked – though I see now you're only just hearing of her true identity. I thought Sarah had offered to raise her grandchild for thee, that you were in agreement.'

'Nay,' Jewel murmured flatly. 'I left Manchester without saying goodbye to her, haven't seen her since.' She lifted her eyes to Minnie's. 'How did she take the news that I'm her daughter?'

'As you might expect, lass.' A tear dripped to the old woman's cheek. 'She were beside herself.'

'She told me she didn't have children. I asked her once and she said nay.' Jewel shrugged. 'Well, she didn't, did she? She gave up the title of mother the day she left me here with thee.' She wrapped her arms around herself. 'Do I deserve *my* daughter back? Didn't *I* forgo all rights, too, when I walked from this house without mine?'

'Be that as it may – in your mind, at any rate,' said Flora, squeezing her hand, 'but the fact remains, lass: these wenches lied. They took your babby without permission. That, they had no right to do. Just 'cause she gave her own child away, and whatever the reasons for it might have been, it don't give her leave to steal yours. Now I say we go around there and get the mite back.'

Minnie nodded. 'I'll come along with thee, see if I can't talk some sense into her—'

'Nay.' Jewel looked to them both. 'Please. This is summat I must do alone.'

That it wasn't just her getting the child back that she was referring to, both women seemed to understand. They nodded. Jewel gave them each a sad smile in return, then left the house.

When she reached the familiar dwelling in Canal Street, the front door was swinging wide. She entered, closing it quietly behind her, and climbed the stairs to the sisters' room. As she neared, she heard the distant sound of a child's cry – *my baby*. She cleared the landing in a heartbeat and burst inside.

'Well, looky here.'

Jewel took in the scene slowly. On a sofa, the griping child clutched protectively in her arms, was Sarah. Standing before the dead fire was her sister and, as Jewel's gaze settled on the knife in her hand, she swallowed hard.

'Looky here,' the woman repeated, stepping forward. Her lip curled. 'Shut the door. Now.'

Jewel did as she bade. All the while, it took all her strength not to run and snatch up her baby; the crazed look in the slattern's drunken eye deterred her. She moved gingerly into the room.

'Stop there,' the woman snarled, jabbing the blade through the air between them.

'What's all this?' Jewel asked, heart thumping. 'Sarah?'

'Shut it. You talk to me, all right, not her!' Swaying slightly, the woman swished the weapon again. 'So. You've returned, eh? And, by God, you best have fetched along with thee what belongs to me.'

'I have nowt belonging to you—'

'Liar!'

Jewel glanced once more to Sarah, who stared back desperately, tears coursing down her face. 'What does she mean?'

'I had two visitors at yon door on Sunday, not long after you left,' shot Sarah's sister before she could speak. Nodding, she took a swig from a bottle of strong spirits then fixed her murderous glare back on Jewel. 'First 'un were a bobby to say they'd found my Julia. Seems she fell foul to a bad make of customer. Dragged her from the canal, the police did; naked, beaten and lifeless.'

'Mother of God . . .' Jewel covered her mouth with her hand. 'Eeh, I'm sorry.'

To this, the woman didn't respond. Again, she took a long draught of alcohol. 'D'you know who the second visitor were? Go on, guess.'

'I don't . . .' Frowning, Jewel shook her head.

'Mr bleedin' Brown.'

'Who?'

'Julia's lover.' The woman's tone was high, mocking. 'Remember, him what bought her that pretty ring at Christmas?'

'Him who she were mistress to?'

'Aye, that's the one – you catch on quick, don't yer?'

she sneered with a roll of her eyes. 'Word soon spread to the inns and alehouses that the police had been here and why, and our Mr Brown heard. Hotfooted it here, he did, broken-hearted. 'Ere, and guess what he told me?'

Clueless still, Jewel shook her head once more.

'Turns out that snidy bitch daughter of mine were saving. Fancy that, eh? She'd told him months afore, reckoned she fancied herself a nest egg, summat forra rainy day. He thought it only right to make mention of it, reckoned it might aid with the cost of the funeral. And yet . . .' Rushing to the painting hanging nearby, she swiped it from the wall, sending it crashing to the ground. 'What do I find? Nowt. Empty. Gone!' Nostrils flared, she crept closer to Jewel, the knife's tip pointed straight at her. 'You had it away, didn't yer? You thieving young *bitch*, yer!'

Jewel's face was void of blood. 'Nay. I didn't.'

'Aye, you did. And you'll give it back, or so help me that brat of yourn will cover the costs for the rest of her life.'

'You what?' Hands beginning to shake with white-hot rage, Jewel stepped closer. 'That was your plan, was it? Snatching her from Mrs Maddox 'cause you think *I* stole that rotten brass?' She looked to Sarah. 'You – *you're* in on this? Mother of God, how could you, given what you've learned—'

'Lass, nay. I've played no part in this, I've not. She collected the child without my knowledge—!'

'What you've learned?' The woman turned narrowed eyes to her sister. 'What's she on about?'

'I wanted to go and find thee in Bolton, had to explain . . . *She* wouldn't let me leave, threatened to harm the child if I tried. Besides, I knew you don't need nor want someone like me, I know, I just . . . I just had to see your face one more time. Oh, lass. Oh, I love thee, have *allus* loved thee.'

Jewel stared back through a film of tears. 'Sarah . . .'

'I couldn't give thee what tha needed, had no choice—'

'What's going on?' demanded her sister. 'Well?'

'Jewel, she . . . She's the child I gave up all those years ago.'

'Ay. Fancy that. So, you're one of us, are yer?'

Jewel lifted her chin. 'You're nowt but a disgusting hussy. I'm nothing like thee, and neither is my daughter.'

'Is that so?'

'Nor, for that matter, is Sarah.'

'Huh! That dried up owd slut? She's had more pricks than a second-hand pincushion.'

Seeing shame colour Sarah's face, anger and an odd sense of protectiveness brought blood rushing back to Jewel's own. 'She's got one thing you ain't, though: a heart. You . . . What I've witnessed with my two eyes . . . To sell the bodies of your own offspring like you did all those years without a shred of conscience? You're the devil's own daughter, you are.'

The woman was nonplussed. 'Aye, well. *They've* gone, the pair, now, ain't they?'

'Not afore time.'

'But you . . . you're here, ain't yer?' Wiggling her eyebrows, she nodded. 'And here you'll stay – the infant along with you – until I get my money back.'

'I've told thee, I didn't take the—'

'You'll stop on here whether I have to tie the pair of youse to that bloody bed, and you'll work your debt.' Her eyes moved to the child. 'Oh, yes. There's fellas aplenty what will pay handsomely to be the first to take her innocence. Likes them young, some do, aye.'

'You foul-tongued *bitch*!' Springing forward, Jewel

lunged at the woman – stopping short when metal flashed by her cheek. Gasping, her furious gaze flicked from the blade to the smirking face. In the next moment, her plait was grabbed and her head wrenched back. The cold point dug into her jaw and she closed her eyes.

'You leave Jewel be!' screamed Sarah.

'Where's my brass?'

Beads of perspiration had sprung at Jewel's top lip, and her heart threatened to leap from her chest. After sending out a silent apology to the absconder – and a plea that the girl never returned, if this was what awaited her once the truth was out – she murmured, 'Louise. She took it.'

'Nay. She wouldn't. It's you—'

'Didn't I tell thee? You'd not believe me, would you, but look, *see* the honesty in her eyes. She speaks the truth. Louise has gone, and for good.' Holding the child away from her sister, Sarah rose. Her voice was firm. 'Now let Jewel go.'

'The girl wouldn't do that, not to me.'

'Aye, 'cause you're worthy of her loyalty, ain't yer?'

The venom in Sarah's tone had her sister glancing her way in surprise. It was clear she'd never known her to stand up to her; she was at a loss how to react.

'All these years, I let you convince me I'd not survive without you. I needed you, yer said, for who else did I have? You've ruined me, aye, you have. But d'you know the worst of it? May the Lord forgive me, I've sat back like a bleedin' coward and watched thee destroy them girls of yourn. But listen here. You'll not do the same with these girls – *my* girls. I'll tear your head from your neck for you if you so much as think to. By God, I will. Now, for the last time, let Jewel go.'

As though in a daze, the woman obeyed, and Jewel rushed to Sarah's side.

'Come on.' Eyes never leaving her sister, Sarah guided Jewel to the door.

'Please. I can't be alone. I can't!'

Sarah paused on the landing. 'It's what you deserve and more,' she murmured over her shoulder. Then she put an arm around Jewel and they walked from the house without a backward glance.

Outside, Sarah looked down at the child in her arms. 'This cherub, my granddaughter ... And you,' she added, lifting shining eyes to Jewel. 'Always know I love you.'

Jewel could barely speak past the lump in her throat. 'Sarah ... I—'

'Shh. It's all right, lass. I understand. I'll be all right.' She handed the baby over, gave them each a last, lingering look and walked away.

Watching her retreating back, tears splashed to Jewel's cheeks. She pictured Sarah doing this same thing seventeen years ago, appreciating only too well the strength it had taken. Now, however, must surely sear far more. To meet again the one for whom you never stopped caring, thinking about, yearning for with every fibre of your being, only to face the parting a second time? How did she bear it? Once more, she was putting her own wants, her own pain, aside for what she believed was the good of her child. Here, without doubt, was living proof that a mother's love knows no bounds. Jewel knew that if she'd inherited just an ounce of Sarah's fortitude she wouldn't go far wrong.

The figure up ahead grew smaller. Deep in Jewel's breast, the ache intensified.

Wait.

At the corner, Sarah paused. She made a movement with her head, as if to look back. Then, as though thinking better of it, she picked up her feet and continued on her way.

Wait, please.

When she'd disappeared from sight, Jewel released a soft breath. Then she was running, running, to catch her up:

'Sarah! Sarah! Come back!'

Chapter 23

SHE UTTERED NOTHING when Jewel halted, panting from the exertion, in front of her. Nor did she have to; her eyes said it all.

'I don't want thee to go.'

A solitary tear rolled down Sarah's cheek. She laughed brokenly.

'Flora, the woman who raised me, will allus be my mam. But . . .'

'But?' whispered Sarah.

'I'd like you in my life, an' all. We both would, me and your granddaughter. If you'll have us?'

'Eeh, love. Oh, you don't know what this means, my precious one,' Sarah murmured into Jewel's hair as she enveloped them both in a hug. 'How much and for how long I've dreamed of this moment. I can scarcely believe it's here.'

Jewel smiled softly. 'You'll come to Mrs Maddox's? Meet Mam?'

Her joy visibly waned. 'Happen she won't want me around, though? Not that I could blame her, mind. As you said, she's your mother, lass. Whilst I . . .' Her eyes creased in shame. 'Why would she – why would *you* – want someone such as me in your life? By God, the things you've witnessed in that room back there.' Moaning, she dropped her chin to her chest. 'I'm foul, I am. To have thee see . . . Oh, I can't *bear* it.'

'Sarah.' Jewel took her elbow as she turned to flee. 'I care naught for what's gone afore. It's now and all our tomorrows that matter. Please. Please come.'

Another long embrace and more tears later, they headed arm in arm for Kirby Street.

Flora needed no introductions; she seemed to sense instinctively who the woman with her daughter was. She glanced from one to the other in the doorway, and Jewel felt the foreboding emitting from her. Was Mam worried she'd lose her now Sarah was on the scene? *Oh, Mam. Never, never.*

'All well?' asked Minnie cautiously.

Jewel and Sarah looked at one another then smiled and nodded.

'Eeh, well. Thanks be to God for it.' Eliza patted Minnie's shoulder in shared relief then beckoned them over. 'Sit down, take a sup.'

Flicking her gaze to Flora, Sarah seemed hesitant. Jewel gave her a look of encouragement and, catching it, she perched on a chair. Holding the baby up with tears of pride shining from her eyes, Jewel then crossed to her mother.

'Ay, lass.' Taking her granddaughter into her arms, Flora was entranced. 'By, would you look at her, the little angel. She's your image at that age, Jewel, she is, really.'

'Aye, she is,' agreed Sarah, and lowered her head quickly when Flora glanced up. 'Sorry. I didn't mean . . . What I meant were, it's just—'

'It's all right, Sarah.' Flora's voice was soft. 'All this . . . it's hard for me, an' all. But the fact remains: Jewel were your lass afore she came to me. You've memories of her same as I have. Don't be ashamed or think yourself unworthy of holding them. What happened happened, and it ain't for me nor no one else to judge thee on it. You've a right to know this lass, here, as much as me. You do, aye.'

It was like the sun had come out behind Sarah's eyes; she exhaled what seemed like a lifetime of strife. 'Mrs Nightingale, I—'

'Call me Flora, lass.'

'Flora. Eeh, I were dreading meeting thee. D'you know, I've wondered all these years what the woman who got my daughter might be like, and now . . .' She paused to swallow back a sob. 'Now I see you're all I hoped for. You, Mrs Nightingale – Flora. You're a proper mam, just as the lass needed – *deserved*. I don't know how I'll ever be able to . . .' Taking Flora's hand, she pressed it to her lips and closed her eyes. 'Thank you for being her mother and for raising her with love. Thank you for everything.'

There wasn't a dry eye in the room. In silence, Jewel and the others looked on with sad smiles.

'And thank you, lass.' Flora's voice was just as thick. 'Thanks for the years you gave me with Jewel. There's no ill feelings on my side, nay, and I'm heartened that tha feels the same with myself. Time to put the past behind us, now, eh? Whatever our lass decides is good enough for me.'

The two of them looked to Jewel for an answer, and she breathed deeply. For only now was the full enormity of all that had occurred over the last few days hitting her. Both of these women had a claim to her. Flora would, as she'd stated, always be her mam. Yet a firm bond had already formed with Sarah. Since the night on the top stair of the house in Canal Street, when she'd sat enjoying the cold pie and tea that the closed-off, kind-eyed stranger had given her, she'd felt it. Something. Some tie she hadn't been able to fathom then.

But had Flora really spoken the truth? Would it honestly not pain her to have Sarah in their lives? To share her only child with a woman who, in effect, possessed a stronger link – that of blood – with her? Jewel wouldn't have Mam upset, not for the world. Neither did she wish to hurt Sarah. What was she to do?

'Look into your heart, lass.'

Minnie's wisdom reached out to her across the table, as though she sensed her dilemma, and Jewel looked to her in grateful desperation.

'The decision must be yours alone. These women here want only what you want, for your happiness is their happiness. You see?'

She did. She smiled and squeezed Flora's and Sarah's hands in turn. 'I think . . . I need you both. I *want* you both in my life. If that's all right?'

'Ay, of course it is, love,' Flora told her.

'Oh, lass,' cried Sarah softly.

Looking down at her own child, Jewel was struck with such overwhelming love it took her breath away. A feeling of completeness warmed her soul and she sent it out to encompass the others.

For the first time in a long time the future looked promising. And it felt wonderful.

*

On the train journey home, Jewel and her mother discussed what was to be done about Benji. Though Flora spoke in a hushed voice so that the other passengers wouldn't overhear, her eyes couldn't conceal her simmering rage.

'I'll break his face for him. And just let that mother of his try and deny it and, by, I'll rip her limb from limb, an' all.'

Jewel suppressed a sigh. Though understanding absolutely Mam's feelings, this was exactly what she'd wanted to avoid: the family at war. But the truth was, the confrontation to come was not only unavoidable but necessary. The Powells had to know what had occurred – particularly now there was a visible child involved. Besides, Benji deserved punishment. Nevertheless, the knotting in her stomach only intensified with each passing mile that took them closer to Bolton, and the holy storm of upset she just knew awaited her.

Then there was the other issue that was slowly killing her inside.

Maxwell's face struck in her mind and she winced at what it brought to her heart. Whatever brainless designs she'd had were unquestionably dashed for ever. When he discovered . . . and of course he *must* . . . He'd want nothing more to do with her.

Suddenly, her chin lifted. To hell with it. It had been daft dreamings and nothing more anyway. Besides, she had nothing to feel ashamed about. She'd begot this child here through no fault of her own. What's more, she regretted nothing. Not now; how could she? Her daughter – her gift – was *wanted*. Never would she feel otherwise, never, and if others – the man she loved included – saw it differently, that was their problem. And by God, she'd tell them so, too.

'When we arrive, you take yourself home and get the babby settled,' Flora was saying now. '*I'll* confront that lot at the shop.'

'You didn't mention Uncle Bernard.' Jewel turned to face her. 'You said as how Aunt Esther shall likely deny her son of wrongdoing, but not him. He'll not doubt my word, then, you reckon?'

Flora's eyes narrowed. 'Just you leave it all to me.'

They lapsed into silence. The train hissed to a stop at Trinity Street Station and they set off on the short distance home, and still neither spoke. What was there to say, after all? Words aplenty would follow soon, all right, though none good. This day was to change everything. Once the Powells heard what Flora had to say, life as they knew it would never be the same, for any of them.

At their door, Jewel paused. 'Happen I should come with thee, Mam—'

'Nay. You and the child go on inside. I'll sort it.'

Though ashamed at herself at not pressing her further, Jewel felt relief. Truth be told, the last thing she wanted was to be present when the details emerged. It would be like reliving it all again and besides, Esther's insistence that it didn't happen – for it was inevitable, wasn't it? – she'd rather not see. The anger and pain of it would be too much. More so should Bernard, too, choose to deny it.

She watched her mother stride away across the cobbles. Then she closed the door quietly behind her. Entering the kitchen, a little of her misery faded. She peered around the familiar space with a quiet smile.

'I can hardly believe you're here, precious one,' she whispered to her daughter, brushing her cheek against hers. 'You're home, my lass.'

Sarah, sitting contentedly by Minnie's hearth, entered her imagination and, again, she smiled. Upon hearing that she'd finally broken free of her sister's clutches, the old woman had insisted Sarah stop on with her and Eliza. Warmth, safety and true companionship were hers now, and not before time. Her demons, along with the drink, she could banish. Sarah deserved nothing less, and Jewel couldn't have been more pleased for her. They had agreed earlier to regular visits, and both knew that nothing would stand in the way. They had been parted for too long but had a lifetime to make up for it.

After taking the baby upstairs to the bedroom, Jewel returned to the kitchen and made for the fire to brew some tea, desperate for the distraction. Despite her best efforts, her thoughts had switched to the drama surely playing out right now in the shop, and dread of the inevitable result returned to torment her. Wringing her hands as she waited for the kettle to boil, she almost leapt out of her skin when a knock came at the door.

She stared at it for a moment, picturing her aunt and uncle's livid faces just waiting beyond, the smug Benji with them, and tried to muster up the strength to hold her nerve at the onslaught to come. A second rap sounded. She sucked in a deep breath and forced herself forward to answer it.

'Jewel. Here you are.'

She stared dumbly at her visitor. This was the very last person she'd expected. 'Sir.'

'May I come in?'

'Aye, yes.' She held the door wide and, when Maxwell stepped inside, pointed to a chair. 'Please, sit.'

'Thank you.'

'Sir, about me abandoning my duties this morning without a by-your-leave—'

'I understand.'

Her speech dying, she frowned. 'Tha does?'

'Jewel . . .' Stare fixed on his hands on the tabletop, Maxwell sighed. 'I can only apologise for my behaviour yesterday. I assure you it will not happen again. Won't you please consider coming back?'

He thought she'd abandoned her position because of the moment they had shared in the kitchen at Mawdsley Street. Oh, if only that were it . . .

'Sir, you misunderstand.' She nodded when he lifted his head in surprise. 'The reason I left ain't because of . . . what you think.'

'But . . . I embarrassed you—'

'Nay, sir, you didn't,' she cut in quietly.

'I didn't make matters between us so awkward that you felt you had no option but to leave?'

'Nay.' *A thousand times, nay.*

'Then what?'

Slipping into the chair opposite his, she gave a brittle laugh. 'What, you ask? Lord, where to start?'

'I find the beginning is usually the best place.'

Despite her heartache, she couldn't help but smile when he winked. 'Oh, sir.'

'Tell me. Please.'

'I . . . have a child.' What easier way was there of saying it? There wasn't. Nor was there any point in dressing the facts up. It was what it was.

'Pardon?'

'Aye. A daughter. I'd planned to have her adopted out but changed my mind. That's where I went to the day: Manchester, fetching her home. It were wrong of me to just take off without your permission, but time was not on our side.'

'But . . .' Eyes dazed, he ran a hand through his hair. 'When? *How?*'

'She were born several weeks past. I lied, sir – there were no ailing aunt. That were an excuse to allow me to go away to have her in secret.'

It was evident that he found the calmness in which she was delivering her responses just as baffling as the revelations themselves; his gaze had narrowed suspiciously. 'All this . . . Jewel, is it some elaborate joke?'

She shook her head. 'That it ain't. As to how . . . My

cousin forced himself upon me the night of the town hall opening. You remember mentioning you'd seen him at the park, pouring away his own drink? He got me skenning and took my innocence.' She swallowed a few times before continuing. 'That day he arrived at your house and you opened the door to him? D'you remember, sir?'

'Yes,' Maxwell whispered.

'It were to speak to me about brass I'd told him he must find to pay the adoption fee.'

He rose and crossed to the fire. Grasping the corner of the mantel, he bowed his head. 'Why didn't you tell me?'

'How could I? I couldn't reveal it to a soul. Mam only discovered the truth this morning. She's round there right now, having it out with him and his parents.'

'I've a good mind to join her this instant and—' He broke off and breathed deeply. 'Your child?'

'Upstairs soundly sleeping.'

He was silent for a long moment. Then he turned to face her. 'The incident with the cart.'

'Aye.'

'This is the reason you wanted to end your life.'

She nodded. 'I could see no other option at the time.'

On another breath, he closed his eyes. 'Oh, Jewel.'

'Yesterday, in the kitchen of your house, when you walked in on me crying . . .' Colour pinched her cheeks at the mention of it. 'I were missing the babby.'

He visibly cringed. 'Oh, Jewel,' he murmured again.

'But, sir?' She rose and made towards him when he continued looking at the floor. 'Sir. Look at me, please.'

'Jewel . . .'

'You helped ease the pain a little. Your kindness, warmth . . . It meant an awful lot.'

'No.'

She frowned. 'Sir?'

'No, Jewel. It wasn't . . . *I shouldn't . . .*'

'What—?'

'I wanted to kiss you.' The words tumbled from him. 'You were upset and I . . . I took advantage of you, I'm sorry.'

Her breath came in short bursts. 'Sir . . .'

'I don't know, cannot explain . . . I was drawn to you, Jewel, from the very start. Your vulnerability . . . I saw something in you I recognised. My feelings, they have deepened for you further this past . . .'

Where Jewel found the courage, she couldn't think – she pressed her lips to his, smothering his rant. After a few stunned moments, Maxwell enveloped her in his arms and kissed her back hungrily.

Dizzying sensations touched every part of her; the only thing that was missing was fear. Her attempted seduction of Jem Wicks and her encounters with the Manchester men had brought back the ordeal like a hammer blow, but not now. This time, with this man, no harrowing memories of Benji's assault crept in to mar it. Even when she felt Maxwell grow hard against her, she didn't blanch. Only peace and light – and the fierce need to explore him further – consumed her, and she matched his furore completely.

'Jewel . . .'

'Please, don't stop,' she begged, drawing his mouth back to hers.

A low growl escaped him as, grasping her buttocks, he drew her body closer. Then, with an obvious struggle, he pulled back once more. 'Wait, Jewel, we—'

Passion blazed through every inch of her. 'What? What?'

'God help me.' His breathing was ragged. 'This is taking every ounce of strength I possess, but we must . . . we must stop. We can't. Not here, not like this.'

Though she knew he spoke sense, frustration had her swinging away from him with a frown.

'Jewel—'

'Sorry. You're right. I just . . .' Feeling tears close by, she blinked desperately. 'I wanted to enjoy this moment, even for just a few seconds longer, before . . . before it all ends. For it has to. This – us – it must stop here, I know it.'

'That is what you want?'

'Nay, never. It's what *must* be.'

'Why, Jewel?'

Her emotions got the better of her and she crumpled. 'Because of all I have told thee, of course. Everything that has happened. My *daughter*, remember? It would have been difficult enough without this; who we are . . . you being you, and me being who I'm not. Now, it's impossible.'

'Says who?'

She lifted wet eyes to his. Something in his expression caused her heart to thump in hopeful disbelief.

'You think I care a jot for convention? Jewel, you disappoint me; I thought you knew me better than that by now.'

Her voice was barely above a whisper. 'What are you saying?'

'Isn't it obvious? I love you. I need you. I want you, body and mind. Us, our children, a marriage, home. To spend together what days we have left on this earth side by side, hand in hand, heart to heart. That's what I'm saying. I want it all. I only have to know that you do too.' He took her hands and lifted them to his chest. 'Say it. I must hear it from your lips.'

Her shoulders heaved with elated sobs. 'I want it,' she mouthed.

'Again.'

'I want it!' Now, it was a raw cry. Laughing, they threw themselves into each other's arms.

'Come with me, back to Mawdsley Street,' said Maxwell when they drew apart.

'This minute?'

'Why not? Collect the child and let's just go, start our life together this *second*. What's stopping us?'

Jewel accepted his kisses with a grin. 'My love . . .'

'Is that a yes?'

'The morrow. I promise,' she added when disappointment creased his eyes. 'Tonight, I must be with Mam. We have much to discuss. I have to tell her about us. And I have to hear what's occurred with the Powells. I need her to be all right with it all. You understand?'

He held her closer. 'I do.'

'I love thee.'

After a lingering goodbye, Jewel closed the door behind him and leaned against it, gazing at the ceiling, a smile caressing her lips. She wanted to bask in this fuzzy haze for ever. It was really *happening*! Maxwell Birch loved her back and, right now, here in this moment, all was magnificent with the world.

She'd have given anything for it to remain so but, all too soon, footsteps outside reached her, heralding her mother's return. Masking her regret, she opened the door to let her in.

'How did it go, Mam?'

'A sup of tea, lass.'

Flora's flat tone said it all. Dread rolling through her stomach, Jewel went to fulfil her request.

'Mam?' she pressed quietly when Flora was on her second cup. 'Speak to me.'

'Benji will be gone from here at first light.'

Her eyebrows rose to meet her hairline. 'Gone where?'

'He's to be packed off to Esther's parents', and that's where he's to stay. Mother of God, Bernard's rage ... He's just whipped that boy with his belt to within an inch of his life. But for me – I intervened for my brother's sake, aye, not that swine's – I reckon he'd have done for him. Even Esther didn't try and stop him.'

Jewel derived no satisfaction from hearing this. She felt nothing, was numbed to the whole thing. 'You mean they believe me, the two of them? Benji, he admitted it?'

'Aye, on both counts.'

'And ... the child? Will Uncle Bernard and Aunt Esther accept her?'

Glancing to the stairs, Flora patted her hand. 'They've had a holy shock and a lot to take in. Give them time, love.'

Months of tension rose from her. She released a long, slow sigh.

'It's to the future we must look, now, my lass.'

'Aye, Mam.'

'We'll see this through, me and thee.'

'Mam?'

'Aye?'

'Mr Birch called whilst you were away. He wants to wed me, and I said yes.'

Flora lowered her cup slowly. 'The child ... ?'

'He knows. He still wants me – wants us both. Oh, I'm that happy, Mam! I love him so very much.'

'You do, aye, I see it.' She stood and stroked her daughter's hair. 'I'm away to my bed.'

Jewel was more than a little miffed. That's all she had to say on the matter? 'You're all right, Mam?'

'Aye. Tired, lass. It's been a hell of a day, after all. I'll line a drawer from the chest with a blanket to lay the babby in for tonight.'

Watching the woman walk wearily to the stairs, overpowering love coursed through her. 'Mam?'

Flora turned to look at her.

'You could never lose me, you know. Not to Sarah, nor Maxwell, nor anyone else. You're my number one, allus shall be.'

'Eeh, love.'

'I feel better, you know, Mam. Now the truth of it all is out. Free of mind, aye. No more secrets, eh? No more lies. We must both promise never to keep owt from one another ever again.'

Flora looked as if she'd say something. Then instead she nodded, smiled and continued on her way to bed.

Curling into the familiar chair by the fire, Jewel wrapped her arms around herself with a sense of completeness. She felt whole, at last. The badness appeared to have got bored with her, and good had returned to take its place.

Right now, nothing could touch her. She doubted that anything could go wrong ever again.

Chapter 24

'JUST LOOK AT you.'

Blushing pink, Jewel smiled up at Maxwell shyly.

He drew the bustline of her dress lower still, took her breasts in his slightly shaking hands and pressed his lips to hers.

The nursemaid Lizzie had offered to take Jewel's daughter along with her and Constance on their daily walk. The young miss's perambulator, which she'd recently outgrown, had been brought down and fresh, warm blankets placed inside. The moment Jewel and Maxwell had waved Lizzie and the happy children off and closed the door, they had fallen into each other's arms, right there in the hall. She'd given no protest when Maxwell had swept her up into his arms and carried her to the sofa in the drawing room.

His mouth moved to cover her nipple and the last of her self-consciousness melted. She moaned in rapture. Head back, eyes closed, she ran her hands over his broad, bare shoulders.

The desire he evoked in her amazed her still; she hadn't thought it possible to know such exquisite sensations. The ravenous fire in her veins was building, and she knew that, if not for the fact she wasn't yet healed completely from the birth, she'd have given herself to him in a heartbeat.

As it was, they had to make do for now with caresses and kisses. And though she knew not a scrap of shame for it – nothing had ever felt so right – their union, they had both agreed, they would save for their wedding night. The strength to desist, however, was certain to prove a challenge. It was as though they had been searching for one another their whole lives and, now, their bodies knew instinctively that they had found the missing piece. She let her touch travel . . .

Later, entwined in each other's arms and in between kisses now slow and soft, they were discussing dates for their wedding when the front door rattled open. Like scorched cats, they dived apart and hurriedly corrected their clothing. Maxwell had just finished fastening the last button on his shirt when in breezed Roland.

'Son. Hello.'

Glancing from his father to Jewel, his eyes creased in curiosity. 'Is everything all right?'

'Yes. Fine. All's fine.'

'All's fine,' chipped in Jewel. Her eyes met Maxwell's briefly and, catching the amusement dancing in his, she bit her lip to quell a giggle.

Roland's brow smoothed out and the corner of his mouth twitched knowingly. 'Ah. I see. Well, there's something I need to be getting on with, so if you'll excuse me . . .'

When they were alone once more, Jewel covered her face with a groan. Chuckling, Maxwell removed her hands and kissed her soundly on the lips, and she couldn't contain a laugh. 'Oh, Lord. The shame!'

'That was a close call, hm?' He winked and she laughed again. 'I think the time has come to make it official. We'll announce our union properly, later, over dinner.'

'He will be happy for us, won't he?'

'Oh, I'm certain. Roland's an easy-minded lad. He'll offer his blessing, you'll see.'

'Mam knows; I told her last night.'

'How did she take it?'

Jewel frowned slightly in remembrance. 'Surprisingly well. What I mean is, she didn't really say anything.'

'Could it be she's displeased?'

'Nay, nay. I know Mam; she'd have said outright were she not consenting.'

'Then you must invite her to dine with us tonight. Hopefully, I can make her see that my feelings for you are true and that my only mission in life from this day is to make her daughter happy.'

Jewel's breast swelled with love. Then the problem that had nagged her since last night gnawed at her conscience and she lowered her head.

'Jewel? What is it?'

'There's summat you should know, summat I've recently discovered . . .' Would the telling change things? Would he see her differently when it came to light his future wife was born out of wedlock? She took a shaky breath. 'Flora Nightingale ain't my mam. My real mother weren't capable of caring for me and gave me up. Flora raised me instead, as her own.'

'My darling . . .' Maxwell shook his head. 'I don't know what to say. I'm so sorry this has happened to you.'

'I'm illegitimate.'

'Jewel, Jewel. I care naught for that.'

'You don't?'

'No. None of it is your fault.'

Relief washed through her. 'I – I thought you'd view me differently.'

'Dearest love.' He took her in his arms. 'Your father, do you know . . . ?'

'Nay.' Her voice dropped. 'A resident, someone passing through . . . he could have been anyone. Sarah has no way of knowing. She . . . was a prostitute.'

Maxwell nodded slowly in understanding.

'But she's vowed to change, she has, and I believe she can. She's free from the foul influences of before and has the support of good friends. So long as she steers clear of her old haunts around Canal Street, she'll do just fine, I know it.'

'Canal Street?'

'That's where she lived. It's in Manchester.'

'Yes, I thought it sounded familiar. I've seen the street name in passing when visiting my sister.' He pulled a guilty face. 'Truth be told, I ought to call on her more often. But what with work and Constance . . . Roland, however, journeys regularly. They are quite close. She's been a great support to him, as well as to me, over the years. His mother's death affected him deeply and he often stayed with his aunt thereafter. The change of scene did him the world of good.'

'When was this?' A terrible, terrible feeling had struck her and, as she awaited his answer, she held her breath, hoping, *praying* . . .

'It shall be twenty years next summer that Roland's mother passed.'

Her heart had begun to thump. 'And how long did his stays with Mrs Kirkwood go on for?'

'Jewel?'

'Please. Tell me.'

'Several years; but I don't see what any of this—'

Dragging a hand across her mouth, she rose to her feet. 'So, say . . . eighteen, nineteen, years ago, he would have been there, in Manchester, around that particular area when . . . when . . .'

'When what?'

'When I was conceived,' she whispered.

Maxwell's puzzled frown melted. His mouth fell open. 'Surely you're not suggesting what I think you are. That Roland . . . and this Sarah you mentioned . . . ? No. No, you're wrong, you are—'

'You know what your son's like where women are concerned. He's a thirst for skirt that can't be quenched – no doubt it's been that way most of his life. He'd have been – what? – around my age now at the time that Sarah got caught with me? A young man filled with urges – ones that streetwalkers aplenty would have been only too willing to satisfy . . . ?'

'No. This is madness, it is, it—'

'Ask him. Find out if he ever used the services of the women of Canal Street.' She rushed to Maxwell and clutched his hands when he shook his head. 'I beg of thee. *Please*. Ask him, to be sure.'

'Jewel, I can't just—'

'Please,' she pressed. 'For should there be the slightest possibility, then you know what that means, don't you? Mother of God, you could be . . . *We* . . .'

Sheer horror passed across his face. He sucked in air sharply.

'Seek him out. Go now, Maxwell!'

He made a dash for the door.

The next few torturous minutes seemed like hours. Then the door opened and she lifted her eyes in dread.

The man she loved stood frozen in the doorway. His ashen face confirmed her fears for him.

No . . .

'Roland said yes. He said yes, Jewel.'

*

'Tell Lizzie when she returns to fetch the child to Mam's.'

'Wait.'

'I must leave!'

'*Wait*,' Maxwell insisted when Jewel attempted to flee the room. 'Christ's sake, we can't leave things like this. We have to discuss it, sort out what the hell we're to do!'

'What we're to do?' she asked incredulously. Tears streamed down her face. 'I think we've done enough, don't you!' Her arms folded instinctively across her chest and she shuddered. 'My God, what we've done together the day . . . I feel sick!'

'We don't know, can't be *certain*—'

'Aye, but there's the tiniest chance, in't there?'

Maxwell lowered his gaze then dropped his head into his hand.

'And that's enough. It is.'

'I know. I *know*.'

Her voice matched his in devastation completely. 'We've kissed.'

'Jewel—'

'You've known my breasts with your hands, your mouth . . .'

'Jewel, please—'

'I *took* you in my palm. You . . . You—'

'Stop! Stop it!' Grasping her by the shoulders, he shook her sobbing form. 'Listen to me. We'll drive ourselves mad dwelling on . . . things like that. Roland confirmed he used to visit those women, yes, but can't recall them or their names, nor whether one had been called Sarah. Now, I know there's perhaps the slightest possibility, but Jewel . . .' He shook her again in desperation. 'It mightn't be so. It isn't – can't be – surely. I *love* you, God dammit!'

'Don't. Don't utter those words. Not now.'

'But I do. *We* do. We love each other.'

She raised tortured eyes to his. Despite it all, her feelings for him, still as absolute, crashed in and she let out an agonised cry. She threw herself against his chest and he held her fiercely.

'I can't give you up, Jewel. God help me, I'd die without you.'

Her head sprang up. Knowing what they shared in their pasts, what, like her, Maxwell had attempted when at his lowest ebb – what he might be capable of again – terror filled her. 'Don't say that. Please.'

'Jewel . . .'

She watched his face draw closer. Though her mind begged her to resist, her breaking heart spoke louder and she knew logic couldn't win, not against something this strong. His lips brushed hers in the softest of kisses.

'I love you,' he breathed, and it reached to her very core. 'Say you still feel the same for me.'

There was no hesitation. 'I do. I allus will. But . . .'

He nodded. 'I know.'

This time, when she headed for the door, he didn't stop her.

She glanced back at him over her shoulder. Simultaneous tears made their lonely way down their cheeks. Dropping her head, she walked from the house.

Chapter 25

'YOU'VE SCARCELY TOUCHED your grub again. What's to do with thee, at all?'

Pushing away her plate, Jewel shrugged. 'I've told thee, nowt.'

'Well, it don't favour it to me. Now come on, out with it,' Flora said when her daughter's bottom lip shook. 'I'll not take no for an answer this time, neither. I'm fair worried about thee, lass; you ain't yourself.'

'Oh, Mam.'

'Speak to me. What is it?'

The last few days had been true hell upon earth. Being separated from Maxwell – and the reason behind it – haunted and sickened her equally. Her thoughts were in disarray, totally at odds with each other. One moment, she was filled with horror at the prospect of their being related. The next, half mad with yearning, she was telling herself it didn't matter and could be their secret, that no one need know, that they must be together. Then shame and self-disgust would return tenfold. And on, and on . . .

Overriding everything was the crippling sense of loss, and there were times she genuinely believed she would die from the pain. She should have known it was too good to be true. Her, be happy? Huh! How often did that occur of late? That someone such as he had actually looked her way in the first place was too incredible to be real; she'd known it from the start. Why should this latest development have shocked her? Did she honestly think they – or, more to the point, she – would get a joyous ending?

'Is it your Mr Birch? Has summat occurred betwixt the two of you?'

'He's not my Mr Birch.'

Flora nodded as though she'd solved the mystery. 'Youse crossed swords, then? Eeh, what are you like? All couples have their bickers, lass, especially in t' beginning. You can't let it spoil things, nay. You'll learn as you go that to swallow your pride now and then will make forra quieter life, oh aye. Just so much as he thinks he's in charge, you know?' She chuckled knowingly. 'Some men can be funny about that, like to think their womenfolk are the meeker half. In reality, mind, we know the truth!'

'What are you *talking* about?'

'Lass?'

Scraping back her chair, Jewel stood and shook her head. The tears never far away fell unchecked down her face. 'It ain't some daft bloody spat, Mam. Nor can it be rectified, not ever. It's finished with; done afore it even began. And that's that.'

Flora's frown melted. 'Eeh, you're a dramatic bugger. What, pray tell, can be so bad that you'd chuck aside a fine fella such as he? By, you were mad with love for him not a week past, and now this? Well? What is it, then, that's gone and changed your mind?'

'You really want to know, do you?' Jewel's breathing was ragged. 'Have I to tell thee, aye?'

'Go on, spit it out!'

'His son might have had relations with Sarah. Aye,' she choked when Flora's mouth fell open. 'The man I love, the man I had planned to wed, could just be my grandfather. That's what, Mam.'

The silence was deafening. Bar her wide eyes, Flora's expression was blank. The seconds ticked by and, after a full minute, she still hadn't spoken. Finally, Jewel threw her arms in the air:

'Well, say summat. *Owt.*'

'Lass . . .'

'Now d'you see?' Weeping softly, she dropped back into her seat. 'Mam, what am I to do? How will I bear this? Lord knows I love that man with every part of me. And it's wrong – *foul* – it is, I know, but . . . I want him!'

'Lass. I don't know . . . I . . .'

'Nay, me neither. What *is* there to say, after all?' Her tone softened at Flora's clear distress. 'I just feel I can't let this be it, Mam. I can't just let him go, not until I know for certain.'

The other woman raised her gaze to hers slowly. 'But how will you . . . ?'

'I'll fetch Sarah here. I'll take her to Mawdsley Street, and I'll make Roland see her, and I'll demand they try to remember. Surely one of them will – well, just *know*, when they come together?'

Face corpse grey, her mother squeezed her eyes shut. 'Oh, love.'

'You see why I must find out, Mam, don't you?'

'I do,' she mouthed.

'I simply cannot give Maxwell up like this. Not without a fight. Being parted from him . . . I've never known agony like it.' A heart-wrenching whimper escaped her. 'Why can't I be allowed to be happy, Mam, like others?

Ain't I worthy of it? What's wrong with me? What did I do that was so bad that I'm to suffer like this? Tell me, Mam, please. Make me understand. Why does the Almighty hate me so?'

'Don't think those things. You, you're the kindest most beautiful girl the sun ever shone on. What you've been dealt with, all of it . . . By, you don't deserve this on top. Eeh, nay.' Suddenly, Flora's face cleared. It held a look Jewel had never seen before, something akin to defeat mixed with dull acceptance. 'I must.' She nodded. 'I must.' Dreamlike, she rose and headed for the door.

'Where you going? Mam? *Mam*—' But she took no heed; before Jewel had time to follow, her mother was gone.

Jewel wandered to the drawer by the fire within which her daughter lay sleeping peacefully. Kneeling beside it, she gently traced a finger down the silken cheek.

'Just you and me, lass,' she murmured. 'I thought I'd found thee a father, a proper one like you deserve, but it's all ruined. I keep failing you, don't I?' A sob caught in her throat. 'I vowed when I got you back to be better, that *I'd* give you a good life, that I *could* do it. Turns out it were daft talk, for everything's worse now than I'd have believed it possible. I'm so sorry I keep getting it wrong. I just don't know what to do, love.'

Oblivious to its mother's anguish, the child slept on, and Jewel kissed her brow tenderly. Then she resumed her seat at the table to await Flora's return.

Where was she? Jewel wondered with increasing concern as the minutes wore on. Had she merely gone for a walk to help her process what she'd learned? *Dear God, please don't have gone to see Maxwell*, she prayed fervently. The last thing she could cope with right now was him turning up here. For she knew she'd be unable to send him away. It would be impossible. One word, one look from him, and she'd fall right into his arms, she was in no doubt. And she couldn't do that, couldn't let her heart overrule her head, not in this.

The slight possibility of who he was would be there always, and nothing could change that. Sarah must have had uncountable men over the years, and Roland was little better when it came to his exploits – no way would either be able to recall if the other was one of their experiences. Her plan to get them together and hopefully learn the truth had been a desperate, *brainless* notion. It was all she'd had, but it would never work. She simply had to face facts: the truth of her parentage wouldn't ever be proven. She and Maxwell were no more.

Another glance to the clock showed that twenty minutes had now elapsed. Jewel wiped her tears and went to the window. Still, there was no sign of her mother, and her worry intensified. She plucked down her shawl from the nail and threw it on. Then she crossed back to the fire to get the baby.

Jewel was stooping over her, ready to pick her up, when the door opened behind her. 'Mam,' she said in relief, turning, 'I were just about to come and look for thee – Oh. Hello.'

The man in her mother's company inclined his head. 'Hello, lass.'

Jewel hadn't expected this; she lowered her gaze uncomfortably. Like Esther, Uncle Bernard hadn't been near since the revelation of his son's attack on her. Now, though Flora had insisted he and his wife took her word as truth, she didn't know how to react.

What was he even doing here? she asked herself. Why

would Mam involve her brother in this? What at all good would this do?

Flora heaved a sigh. 'Jewel, love, sit down.'

'But what—?'

'Please,' added Bernard. 'Please just do as your mam asks.'

Frowning, she obeyed. They joined her at the table.

'How to say this . . .'

'Mam?' Jewel reached for her hand. 'You're trembling. What is it?'

Rather than answer her, Flora turned instead to Bernard. 'I can't do it, lad. I can't.'

For a moment, he looked panic-stricken. Then his shoulders sagged and he nodded. 'I should be the one to do the telling, anyroad.'

'What's going on?' Jewel glanced from one to the other with creeping dread. 'What telling? What must I know?'

Bernard swallowed hard. Then, avoiding her eye, he began to undo his waistcoat.

'What's this, Uncle Bernard? Mam, what's he doing?' she asked of them both. Neither offered an answer. She watched on in increasing confusion as he loosened his collar then unbuttoned his shirt. Finally, he raised his gaze to hers. To her great surprise, tears had filled his eyes. 'What?' she asked again. 'Please, tell me!'

Turning sideways in his seat, Bernard looked to Flora, who nodded. Then, slowly, he moved aside the material from his right shoulder.

Jewel's mouth fell agape at what he'd revealed. There, stamped in the same place as her own, was a coffee-coloured birthmark. It was like looking in a mirror. The shape and size were one and the same.

'You see what this means, lass?' murmured Flora.

'Nay,' was her honest reply; her mind was a whirl of shock.

'There's some say they ain't hereditary, aye, but I've heard talk of it afore, of a parent passing such marks on to their offspring . . . What you believe about Mr Birch is wrong. Bernard here is your father.'

'But he can't be. He's my uncle, he . . . *How?*' she rasped.

'It were after a ruckus one night with Esther. They hadn't been wed long, were dwelling in Manchester close to me and Fred. Bernard stormed from home and got blind drunk in a nearby inn. There, he finished up finding comfort in the arms of a streetwalker, but thought no more of it the following day after making up with your aunt. They moved here to Bolton town not long after, and that were that. Or so he thought.'

Shooting her brother a weary look, she continued. 'I'd spotted the mark on *your* shoulder, lass, shortly after fetching thee home from Minnie's, knew she'd switched my child with another and figured why. I also recognised it as being just like the one Bernard bore. When next I saw him, I pointed it out and told him of the facts concerning how you'd come to be at Minnie's in the first place. He confessed to me his adultery, and the pair of us guessed what had happened. The woman he'd briefly known intimately, and the mam who had left you at Minnie's, were the same person.'

Jewel felt as though she was set in stone, could neither move nor speak, even if she'd wanted to.

'Now you know the truth.' Her mother took her limp hand and chafed it. 'You, above all others, deserve some happiness. I couldn't see thee lose the chance of having it through mistaken identity. Mr Birch's son and you ain't linked, nay. You're free to be with the fella you love.'

'We said no more secrets,' Jewel whispered. 'You swore to me there were nowt left to tell.'

'I did. But, lass, I believed I were doing the right thing, never dreamed all this would come to light, that you'd get hurt . . . I didn't *want* thee hurt! The time for full truths is now. I'm glad I've finally brought this whole sorry mess to light. Even if it means you hating me, disowning me for good . . . you had to know.'

'Is Aunt Esther aware of who I am?'

For the first time, Bernard spoke. 'I confessed all to her when I realised who you were, lass.'

'That's why she's allus been cold with me, in't it? It's all making sense. She's never liked me, has she?' Who could blame Esther for that? To have this – *her* – always there, tainting their marriage . . . Jewel couldn't help but feel sorry for her now. 'She resents I were ever born.'

'But you were.' He spoke quietly. 'And I, for one, am glad of it. To watch thee grow over the years . . . It's warmed my heart more than I can put words to, it has. I'm so proud of the fine woman you've become.'

'Oh God. Oh *nay*!' she exclaimed suddenly as another realisation slammed home. 'Benji. What he did . . . And he's . . . ?'

'Now you understand why I were more reluctant still to tell thee?' croaked her mother.

'Your lack of a proper response that night when I told you of Maxwell's proposal . . . I know why, now. Your mind were too taken up with this nightmare to think of owt else properly, weren't it?'

'I'm so sorry.'

'I've borne my brother's child.'

'Lass, lass . . .'

Jewel shook her head as Flora and Bernard made to comfort her. 'I need some air.'

Outside, it was cold and raining, but she paid no heed. She wandered towards the square. Sitting on the town hall's wide steps, she folded her arms around herself.

She felt no anger. A dull throb of betrayal, perhaps, but nothing more. Nor was she surprised at this. For she understood. All these hidden secrets – and, to be fair, she herself had added enough of her own to the mix – were primarily to protect those they loved. That fact made it all a little easier to bear. Done with malicious intentions would have been unforgivable, but this was far off the mark. In each of their minds, they had thought they were doing what was best. That, she knew, she could live with. Were their birthmarks sheer coincidence? Was mere wishful thinking at play here? Surely not.

Still, the shock had yet to abate, she realised this. Yet, in some way, the latest revelation was less shattering than others that had come before it. Though she would always hold Fred Nightingale dear, she couldn't deny that Bernard being her father held some appeal. She had no recollection of the man who would have brought her up had he lived, no warm memories to help ease the feeling of having missed out. Perhaps, after today, she'd get to experience something akin to a father's love. If truth be told, *hadn't* she always loved Bernard as a father anyway?

Jewel's next thought, however, had her biting her lip: would she feel differently towards her daughter, knowing the lad who had helped create her was a much closer relative than she'd thought? But then again, she reminded herself, that was no blame of the child's. If she'd learned anything lately, it was that a body was blameless of its beginnings. Those were wrought by the actions of others; the matter was entirely out of your control.

Despite everything, a small smile touched her lips. A few short months ago, she'd have been bunching her fists and spitting curses, ready to vent her fury over these changes on all and sundry. What had happened to her? *You've grown up, girl, that's what*, her mind whispered, almost fondly. *You're able to see the world now and those in it for what it is – flawed, just like yourself. That doesn't mean they, like you, deserve to suffer their mistakes for ever.*

She wasn't perfect. She could be hot-headed at times, selfish even, for she was only human, after all. She was a mother now, had matured. Mostly, she was bone weary of all the upset.

The decision was hers. Would she let the past go and look ahead to the bright future that was hers for the taking? Or would she cling on to grievances that wouldn't change things or do anyone any good? Repudiate or forgive?

She knew the answer immediately. She rose and headed back the way she had come.

Instead of continuing for Back Cheapside, she found herself taking the few extra turnings to Mawdsley Street. The lightness in her breast remained all the way and, when she knocked at Maxwell's door, a serene smile had joined it.

'Jewel?'

Her feelings for him, unquestionable and unrestrained, shone in her gaze. She held out her arms and he ran into them. He crushed her to him in a long-awaited embrace.

'Oh, my darling . . .'

'My love,' she whispered, resting her cheek against his chest.

In the fading light they stood as one, never needing again to be anywhere else. And all was well with the world.

Chapter 26

'ANOTHER LEMON CAKE, my lass? Go on, then.'

Grinning and clapping her hands, Constance then helped herself from a check blanket spread on the jade-coloured grass.

Flora smiled as she toddled off. Then her mouth fell open and she pointed, chuckling, to where the youngster had stopped by a cluster of waiting birds. 'Well, now! I worried the child were for making herself sick with all them sweet treats, but nay; that's where my ruddy baking's going!'

Sarah threw her head back and laughed. After dropping a kiss on to her granddaughter's head, she passed her across to the older woman. ''Ere, Flora love, you take little Minerva. Come here, you imp!' she added to Constance, rushing towards her, fingers wiggling with the threat of a tickle, much to the child's delight.

Watching the two at play, the group shared a warm smile.

'You wouldn't think she were the same person, Mam, would you?' murmured Jewel, filled with pride.

'And that's all down to thee.' Flora nodded. 'And the little cherub, here, of course. Her girls gave her summat to start afresh for.'

Jewel blinked back tears, then grinned when Maxwell

nuzzled her neck. She turned to him and their lips met in a feathery kiss.

'Eeh, aye. We picked a fine day for it, anyroad,' announced Maria, squinting up at the cloudless sky. 'Ta for holding this on my day off, lass,' she told Jewel as she helped herself to a beef-and-pickle sandwich. 'Reet thoughtful of thee, that were.'

'As if I'd have it any other way. It wouldn't have been the same without thee.'

It wasn't Jewel's birthday for another five days, but they had chosen to hold the celebration the Sunday before to allow the maid to attend. Well, the date which Jewel had always *recognised* as her birthday, at any rate. Truth be told, from what Sarah had said, she'd actually turned eighteen yesterday.

A confusing but happy mess! she thought with a crooked smile, determined now to see the positives where she could. Not many – bar British monarchs, at least – could lay claim to two birthdays, could they? A lucky circumstance, she'd say!

The delicious picnic, prepared by Flora and Sarah this morning, was a sight to behold. Beneath the leafy canopy of a large tree, and amidst much joviality, cold meats, cakes, fruits, custards and pies – washed down with gooseberry wine, Roland and his fiancée's contribution – had been enjoyed by all. The day, so far, had been one of the best of Jewel's life. She really didn't want it to end.

Now, gazing around at the merry faces of the people she loved, she sighed contentedly. What a contrast to life just a few months ago. So much had happened in this one short year, it was difficult to comprehend. And changes wrought were seen nowhere else more than in some of the folk here today.

Again, her eyes sought out Sarah, sober and healthy and glowing with life, and her heart swelled.

Her thoughts drifted to Roland: calmer, matured and besotted with the pretty young woman he was soon to wed. Though not in attendance, the couple had wished the day well, much to Jewel's gratitude. This had strengthened her hopes that despite his initial surprise that she was to join his family, Roland was gradually coming around to the idea. And to think that someone she'd once supposed might be her father would soon be her stepson. She chuckled inwardly. As she'd just mused, definitely a confusing but happy mess! Nor would she have wanted it any other way.

Maxwell's laughter as he watched Sarah sweep his daughter, overcome with giggles, into the air, brought Jewel back to the present. She motioned for him to join them and, after planting another kiss on her, he headed off across the park.

''Ere, I spoke with that Jem Wicks one yesterday,' Flora told her when Maxwell had gone.

Jewel's smiled slowly slipped. 'Oh?'

'We passed in the square and he said as how he'd heard you were to be wed. He asked if I'd give thee his warmest best wishes. He's norra bad lad, really, eh?'

'Nay,' she murmured, her happiness returning as another bad episode in her past was put to bed. There had been wrongs on both sides; if he was prepared to forgive, then she was more than willing as well. Yet another stepping stone towards her fresh start, she knew. 'Nay, he's not.'

Later, out of puff and pink-cheeked, Sarah fell grinning on to the blanket beside her. 'By, I'm fagged! She's a bundle of energy, that young angel Constance and no mistake.'

'And you enjoy every second of it,' Flora told her.

'I do, aye. I look forward to Minerva growing and being able to join in the fun. Eeh, it's in heaven I am,' she finished on a whisper almost to herself. 'Bloody heaven.'

Jewel reached for her hand and squeezed. 'I'm pleased you came today, Sarah.'

'As if I'd of missed it, lass!'

'What time you off back to Manchester?'

'Stop at mine the night if you'd like,' offered Flora, and was rewarded with a huge smile.

'Aye?' Sarah asked.

Flora nodded. 'That way, you'll not have to fret about missing the last train home, can spend more time with Jewel and the kiddies.'

Jewel smiled. That these two had hit it off to the degree they had warmed her heart something lovely. Their relationship may have formed through a shared desire to do what was best for their daughter but had since developed into a solid friendship. She loved the very bones of them both.

'Minnie's well, lass, is she?' Flora was asking now. 'Eliza, too?'

'Oh aye. 'Ere,' Sarah continued, turning to Jewel, 'they were over the moon when I told them what you'd named the child. Minnie cried buckets.'

Taking her baby into her arms, she stroked her cheek. 'Choosing Minerva in homage to Mrs Maddox felt the right thing to do, me and Maxwell both agreed. She did what she did with good in her heart. Without her and the decision she made all those years ago, none of us would be here together today. I see that, and I thank her for it daily. She's enriched all our lives.'

Bright-eyed, the women nodded their agreement.

'I've never been happier than I am now, living with the two of them,' said Sarah. Then her face dimmed a little and she sighed. 'I only wish I could find employment. I've searched and searched, but . . .' She shrugged. 'I hate dwelling on their charity.'

'If it's a position you're after, I reckon Maxwell's sister Mrs Kirkwood would be only too happy to help you, Sarah,' offered Jewel.

'Aye?'

Recalling Mrs Kirkwood's enthusiasm to help Louise last year, she nodded. 'That lady is golden-hearted; it's what her philanthropic soul lives for, I'm sure. I'll introduce you to her, shall I, at the wedding next month?'

'Eeh, aye. Oh, ta, lass,' she cried, beaming.

As the group lapsed into companionable silence, Jewel's thoughts returned to Louise. She'd told Maxwell's sister during their chance meeting that day that the girl was her cousin, little knowing the truth in the statement. Still, there had been no word from her and, in a way, Jewel was glad of this, for hopefully it meant she was settled wherever she'd chosen to go. She was confident that Louise was doing well, had finally found the decent start she deserved. Sadly, it wasn't to be for Julia. A victim of her upbringing, she'd stood little chance. However, Jewel was sure that her sister was making the most of her life, doubly so, for the pair of them.

As for the woman who gave birth to them . . . She shuddered at the memory of her. Sarah hadn't seen hide nor hair of her since, and for that they must all be truly thankful.

'Here's Bernard, look.'

Following her mother's gaze across the park, Jewel

smiled at the man making his way towards them. She knew a throb of disappointment that Esther wasn't with him, but refused to dwell on it. The woman was hurting, in more ways than one. Benji, when all was said and done, and despite his faults, was her only child. She must miss him terribly. Moreover, with Sarah now on the scene, her heart was surely sorer still.

Would they ever be able to get past this, as a family? Jewel certainly hoped so. The past, after all, was where it belonged. Peace, for everyone, and love and togetherness were what she desired more than anything else.

'I'm glad you came,' she told Bernard when he stooped to kiss her cheek. 'Thank you.'

He nodded, smiled. Then, dropping his gaze, he shifted from foot to foot.

'What is it?' Jewel asked.

'Esther.'

'She's here?' She strained her eyes towards the park's entrance. 'Where?'

'By the gates.' His tone held both guilt and hope. 'She told me to go on in front, needed a minute to compose herself, like. But ay, she agreed to coming, eh? That's a good sign, lass, in't it?'

Jewel gave him a small smile of reassurance then, catching sight of her aunt in the distance making her way towards them, she rose from the blanket. Holding Minerva close, she set off to meet her.

'Afternoon,' Esther said quietly with an awkward nod of greeting when she reached her. 'Bernard said it were all right that I came . . .'

'Course, aye. I'm glad you're here.'

Her face showed surprise. 'Aye?'

'Aunt Esther, all that's occurred, what we've learned . . .

I just want to be happy, that's all,' she said earnestly. 'It's all one bloody big mess, I know, but well . . . Can't we try to get past it, together? As a family? Please?'

The woman's stare misted. She looked down at her granddaughter and a ghost of a smile appeared at her mouth. She brought her gaze back to Jewel and took a deep breath. 'I hope youse have saved a bit of grub for me, lass, I'm fair clemmed.'

Tears of quiet relief pricked her eyes. She beckoned for Esther to follow, and the two of them made off to the party.

When her aunt was seated between Flora and Bernard, and Maria's sister – who had reprised her role as Maxwell's maid – had handed her a glass of gooseberry wine, Jewel left her to settle in and went in search of Maxwell. She spotted him at the steps by the colourful flowerbeds. Constance on his knee, he was pointing out the different blooms to the enraptured child.

Pausing for a moment unnoticed, Jewel drank in the scene with a full heart. To think that they were her life now, her family. She surely was the luckiest lass in the world.

'Come here, you two.' Spotting her and Minerva, Maxwell held out a hand. 'What are you thinking?' he asked Jewel, putting his arm around her when she snuggled beside him.

'How things could so easily have been very different,' she murmured. 'I never believed I could feel like this, my love, thought happiness weren't meant for me.' A smile crept across her lips. 'I were convinced you only noticed me for my domestic skills.'

He grinned. 'That's what I liked to have you and others believe, never dreamed you'd think to look twice at an old fogey like me. When you left for all those months . . . God, it near killed me. You were with me in mind constantly.'

'And me. Is that why you didn't say goodbye?' she asked suddenly. 'I've allus wondered.'

He nodded. 'I couldn't trust myself not to beg at your feet for you not to go.'

'What are we like, eh? And ay, don't call yourself that again,' she scolded softly.

'What?'

'Old. For you're not.'

'No?'

She shook her head. 'You're mature, experienced. I like that.'

'So I've noticed,' he whispered with a wink, then laughed when she swatted his arm, blushing. He looked towards the picnic and the wicked gleam in his eye deepened. 'What say we run away to some far-off place where no one will ever find us? We'll do nothing but drink champagne in the sun and make love in the moonlight for the rest of our lives. Are you game?'

Playing along, she arched an eyebrow. 'And where would we find the brass to fund this tempting lifestyle?'

'I'll rob the bank.'

'And when you're caught and prosecuted for embezzlement?'

'Oh, but it would have been worth it!' he growled, pulling her close and kissing her neck.

Laughing, she lifted his chin with her finger. Lips soft and warm found hers and she closed her eyes.

'We had better get back to our guests,' he whispered against her.

She pulled him closer. 'In a minute.'

'I don't have to leave, nay,' she told him when, finally,

they walked arm in arm back to the others. 'I have everything I need right here.'

Things were not perfect yet between them all, it was true, but they were good enough. Besides, the future could only get better. For she had family, friends. She had love.

And, really, what was life without it?

ABOUT THE AUTHOR

Emma Hornby lives on a tight-knit working-class estate in Bolton and has read sagas all her life. Before pursuing her career as a novelist, she had a variety of jobs, from care assistant for the elderly, to working in a Blackpool rock factory. She was inspired to write after researching her family history; like the characters in her books, many generations of her family eked out life amidst the squalor and poverty of Lancashire's slums.

You can follow her on
X @EmmaHornbyBooks and on
Facebook at www.facebook.com/
emmahornbyauthor

DON'T MISS EMMA'S GRIPPING NEW NOVEL COMING IN SPRING 2026

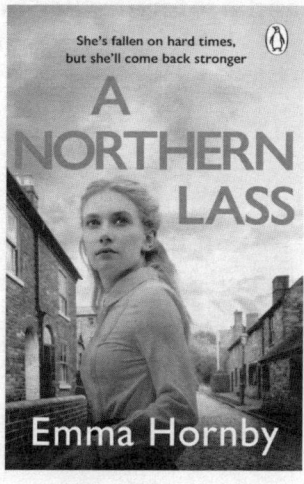

She's fallen on hard times but she'll come back stronger . . .

Slung out from her home and onto the slum streets of Manchester at the tender age of twelve, Perdita Barratt has fallen on hard times. Each day she must toil to earn a penny to secure a bed at a lodging house. Each day is a struggle to survive.

But after a chance encounter with Silas Winkworth, a widowed cart driver who is in search of someone to look after his household, things start to look less bleak . . . And as Perdy settles into the domestic routine of her new life as a daily, Winkworth Cottage becomes her safe haven.

Yet this soon falls to the wayside when Honora, Silas's estranged granddaughter, appears on their doorstep. Unbeknownst to Silas, who has welcomed Honora into his home with open arms, Perdy must steel herself to rise above her incessant snide remarks and wicked taunts . . .

But is there a darker motive than greed behind Honora's return to Collyhurst, and how far will Perdy go to uncover the truth?

How will she choose between following her dreams and protecting her brother?

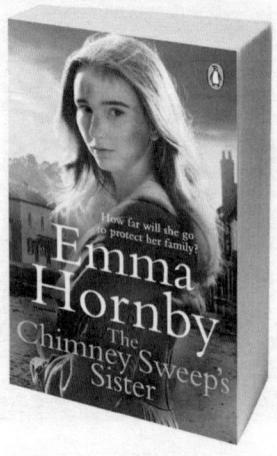

Jenny and her little brother Noah are orphans, living hand to mouth in a cellar dwelling in the heart of the Manchester slums.

At the tender age of nine, Noah is a chimney sweep's boy: a dangerous job, where he's wickedly mistreated. But they survive on his earnings, for which his older sister Jenny feels terrible guilt. It's only her fiery temper that's prevented her keeping down a job herself. With her brother's safety – his life – on the line, Jenny resolves to try and control herself, and put her talent for singing to good use. Can she earn a crust by entertaining the punters at the taverns and inns around town?

It seems like a dream come true when she catches the attention of a music hall manager and is offered a spot on a bigger stage, along with an enviable wage. But there's a darker bargain to be struck in return for their new riches . . .

How far will Jenny go to protect her brother, and will they ever find the security they crave?

AVAILABLE NOW

With all the odds stacked against her, can Phoebe find the strength to overcome her past . . . ?

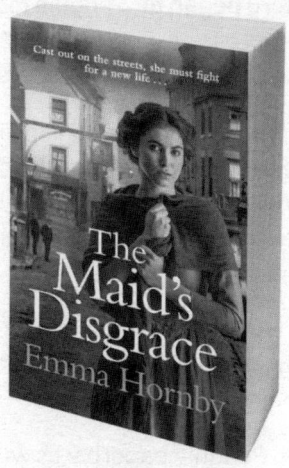

Phoebe Parsons is a liar . . . a shameless harlot with unscrupulous morals . . .

Phoebe Parsons is destitute, disgraced, and alone. After her mistress tragically dies, Phoebe is forced back on to the poverty-ridden streets of Manchester by her unforgiving new master. Desperately searching for work as a domestic maid, Phoebe soon discovers her reputation is in ruins.

Fearing for her future and haunted by the harshness of her abandonment, Phoebe finds herself living with thieves and drunks in the smog and squalor – until she meets Victor Hayes. An officer removed from his duty and shamed by a cruel lie, Mr Hayes is a kind face among the uncertain threats of living in the alleyways. But Phoebe soon realises the sacrifices she must make to rebuild from the ground up . . .

As their two worlds collide, can they make a new life from the wreckage? Or will the judgement of their peers make a pauper of Phoebe?

AVAILABLE NOW

On a station platform, with nothing to read,
and a four-hour train journey stretching ahead of him...

That's where the story began for Penguin founder Allen Lane.
With only 'shabby reprints of shoddy novels' on offer,
he resolved to make better books for readers everywhere.

By the time his train pulled into London, the idea was formed.
He would bring the best writing, in stylish and affordable
formats, to everyone. His books would be sold in bookstores,
stationers and tobacconists, for no more than the price
of a ten-pack of cigarettes.

And on every book would be a Penguin, a bird with a certain
'dignified flippancy', and a friendly invitation to anyone who
wished to spend their time reading.

In 1935, the first ten Penguin paperbacks were published.
Just a year later, three million Penguins had made their
way onto our shelves.

Reading was changed forever.

—

A lot has changed since 1935, including Penguin, but in the
most important ways we're still the same. We still believe that
books and reading are for everyone. And we still believe that
whether you're seeking an afternoon's escape, a vigorous debate
or a soothing bedtime story, all possibilities open with a book.

Whoever you are, whatever you're looking for,
you can find it with Penguin.